MORTAL COILS

OTHER BOOKS BY ERIC NYLUND

Pawn's Dream
A Game of Universe
Dry Water
Signal to Noise
A Signal Shattered

Halo® Novels
Halo®: Fall of Reach
Halo®: First Strike
Halo®: Ghosts of Onyx

MORTAL COILS

ERIC NYLUND

TOR®

A TOM DOHERTY ASSOCIATES BOOK
NEW YORK

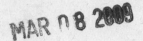

This is a work of fiction. All of the characters, organizations, and events portrayed in this novel are either products of the author's imagination or are used fictitiously.

MORTAL COILS

A Tor Book
Published by Tom Doherty Associates, LLC
175 Fifth Avenue
New York, NY 10010

www.tor-forge.com

Tor® is a registered trademark of Tom Doherty Associates, LLC.

Library of Congress Cataloging-in-Publication Data

Nylund, Eric S.
    Mortal coils / Eric Nylund.—1st ed.
        p.   cm.
    "A Tom Doherty Associates book."
    ISBN-13: 978-0-7653-1797-1 (trade pbk.)
    ISBN-10: 0-7653-1797-4 (trade pbk.)
    1. Twins—Fiction.   2. Teenagers—Fiction.   3. California, Northern—Fiction.
I. Title.
    PS3564.Y55M67 2009
    813'.54—dc22

                                                            2008038363

First Edition: February 2009

Printed in the United States of America

0   9   8   7   6   5   4   3   2   1

For everyone with family . . .
by blood, marriage, or circumstance

ACKNOWLEDGMENTS

Syne, writers can be hermits, bears in caves that growl at all outsiders. Who but another writer to draw me out and keep me sane and civilized with your love? One could not ask for a better soul mate.

Kai, my marvelous son, you were three and four years old when I wrote this, and you helped breathe life into fictional son and father. Daddy promises he's not the Prince of Darkness.

My sister, my mother and father . . . and so many more whom I call "family," you have all been inspirational and close to my heart at all times.

Thanks to my early readers, Elisabeth Devos and Jenny Gaynor, who helped me refocus my attention on the twins.

For my final readers, John Sutherland and Alexis Ortega, a debt of gratitude for your kind words and enthusiasm.

To Tom Doherty and Richard Curtis, my appreciation for your patience, guidance, and support.

Special thanks to Eric Raab. Your editorial acumen and friendship have made all the difference.

And to all my readers, a huge "thank you," especially those that have dropped me a note or e-mail over the years.

EDITOR'S NOTE

Due to the controversial nature of all Post Family stories, and recent revelations that some popular "nonfiction" titles are slightly less than accurate, the editorial board at TOR Books has at this time decided to classify *Mortal Coils* as "fiction." We have no interest in entering the debate over the authenticity of Post Family stories in the popular press.

Footnotes to pertinent resources have, however, been added throughout, so enthusiasts and scholars of modern mythology may follow up with their own research and draw their own conclusions to what is the most exciting contemporary legend of our time.

ERIC RAAB
Editor, TOR Books
New York

When we have shuffled off this mortal coil,
Must give us pause. There's the respect
That makes calamity of so long life,
For who would bear the whips and scorns of time,
The oppressor's wrong, the proud man's contumely,
The pangs of despis'd love. . . .

WILLIAM SHAKESPEARE
Hamlet ACT 3, SCENE 1

SECTION

I

BIRTHDAY

1

TWO LITTLE NOBODIES

Eliot Post and his sister, Fiona, would be fifteen tomorrow and nothing interesting had ever happened to them. They lived with their grandmother and great-grandmother, who, with their iron-fist-in-velvet-glove ways, held them captive from anything exciting.

Eliot slid a plastic milk crate to his dresser and stepped up to see into the mirror. He frowned at his mop of unruly black hair; the bowl cut had grown shaggy. At least it covered his ears, which stuck out. He looked like a dork.

He smoothed his fingers through the mess and it fell into place . . . then the cowlicks sprang up.

If only he had some hair gel. There was, however, a rule banning brand-name shampoo, soap, and other "luxury" items. His great-grandmother concocted homemade versions instead. They cleaned (occasionally stripping off the first layer of skin) but left something to be desired in the fashion department.

Eliot glanced at the pages taped to the back of his bedroom door: Grandmother's 106 rules that governed every breath he took. The lack of hair gel was covered by RULE 89.

> **RULE 89:** No extravagant household products—including, but not limited to, store-bought soaps, shampoos, paper towels, and other unnecessary disposable goods.

Fortunately this did not include toilet paper.

The clock on his dresser made a rusty "ping." It was ten o'clock. The lunch shift started at Ringo's All American Pizza Palace in forty minutes. He suppressed a shudder, already tasting the sweet dough and pepperoni grease that would permeate his skin.

Eliot grabbed his homework off his desk. He flexed his hand, working free the stiffness from writing all night. It'd been worth it. He was proud of his report on the War of 1812. Grandmother would have to give him an A.

His thoughts of the Chesapeake campaign and "The Star-Spangled Banner" vanished as a car drove past outside. Three stories on the street below, its radio thumped and bumped into Eliot's room.

The music washed through him, swept aside all thoughts of homework, pizza, rules, and for one moment he was somewhere else: a hero on the high seas, cannons blasting, and wind screaming through the sails.

The car passed and the music faded.

Eliot would have done anything for a radio of his own. "Music is a distraction," Grandmother had told him over and over. There was, naturally, a rule for it, too.

> **RULE 34:** No music, including the playing of any instruments (actual or improvised), singing, humming, electronically or by any means producing or reproducing a rhythmic melodic form.

It sucked. All of Grandmother's rules did. He never got to do anything he wanted . . . except, of course, read.

Three entire walls of his room were not walls at all, but floor-to-ceiling bookshelves installed sometime in the Precambrian era by Great-Grandmother.

Two thousand fifty-nine volumes lined his tiny bedroom: red spines, gray cloth covers, faded paper jackets, and gleaming gold letters, all exuding a scent of moldering paper and well-worn leather, the entirety a solid mass of age and authority.[1]

Eliot ran a hand over their vertebrae—Jane Austen . . . Plato . . . Walt Whitman. He loved his books. How many times had he escaped to differ-

---

1. Excavation of what experts believe was the Oakwood Apartments building (the alleged Post Family residence) revealed the remains of more than one hundred thousand books on all floors: leather bindings, partial pages, literally tons of parchment ash, and a handful of intact volumes. These fueled the intense blaze that eventually caused the entire town of Del Sombra to burn to the ground. *Gods of the First and Twenty-first Century, Volume 11: The Post Family Mythology,* 8th ed. (Zypheron Press Ltd.).

ent countries, centuries long past, with colorful characters as his companions?

He just wished *his* life could be as interesting.

Eliot went to open his bedroom door, but halted before the pages of Grandmother's rules. He glared at them, knowing the biggest rule of all was unwritten. RULE 0: *No escaping the rules.*

He sighed, twisted the doorknob, and pushed open his door.

Light spilled into the darkened corridor. At the same instant a second rectangle of light appeared as his sister's door opened. Fiona wore a green gingham dress, a tattered suede belt, and sandals that laced up her calves.

People said they looked alike, but she was five foot five inches, while Eliot was still only five foot three inches. For being his *twin* sister, she didn't really look anything like him. Her posture was wet-noodle limp, hair in her eyes except when it wasn't pulled into a tail of frizz, and she chewed on her nails.

She stepped into the hallway at the exact same second as Eliot. She was always pretending this synchronicity thing to annoy him. The myth was that twins always thought the same thing, mirrored each other's motions— were practically the same person.

She must have been waiting at her door, listening for his to open. Well, he wasn't buying it.

"You look sick," Fiona said, her voice dripping with mock sympathy. *"Naegleria fowleri?"*

"Haven't been swimming," he replied. "So maybe you're the one with brain-eating amoebas."

He'd read *Rare Incurable Parasites*, volume 3, as well.

This was their favorite game: vocabulary insult.

"Lochsmere," he said, and eyed her contemptuously.

Her brow scrunched in concentration.

That was a tough one—a character from the thirteenth-century *Twixtbury Chronicles* by Vanden Du Bur. Lochsmere was a plague-ridden dwarf, evil and puppy-drowning vile.

The *Twixtbury* text lay on the top shelf of the hallway bookcase, covered in a layer of dust. No way she had read it.

Fiona caught his look, followed it, and smiled.

"You have me confused for noble G'meetello," she said, "master of Lochsmere . . . who is obviously you."

So she had read it. Okay. The score was still nothing to nothing.

Fiona half-closed her eyes and murmured, "Sometimes, little brother, I think your wit so tantalizing it would be better for everyone if you were at Tristan da Cunha."

Tristan da Cunha? He didn't know that one.

"No fair using foreign words."

Fiona had a talent for languages, while he did not. They had a pact, though: no foreign words from her and no made-up words from him in their games of vocabulary insult. Eliot had a particular talent for finding colorful but nonsensical terms that had no place in *any* dictionary.

"It's not foreign," she said, beaming with satisfaction.

He believed her. They never lied in vocabulary insult.

Eliot tried to puzzle it out. Tristan . . . like the knight of legend? Maybe a castle? Fiona was forever reading travel journals. That had to be it.

"Yes," he said, adopting his best fake ironic air. "Behind its walls I might be safe from seeing your face."

Fiona blinked. "A good guess, but absolutely wrong. Tristan da Cunha is an island in the South Atlantic, thirteen hundred miles from the nearest inhabited land. Population two hundred eighty. I believe their official currency is the potato."

Eliot deflated. "Great, you win," he muttered. "No big deal. I let you. Happy early birthday."

"You've never let anyone win anything." She gave a short laugh. "Happy birthday to you, too."

"Come on." Eliot brushed past her.

She caught up to him and squeezed by. Thousands more volumes crowded the hallway on either side, from hardwood floors to water-stained plaster ceiling.

They emerged in the dining room and squinted as their eyes adjusted to the light. A picture window showed the brick building across the street and a faint band of sky bisected by high-tension power wires, only partially obscured by the overflowing bookcases on all sides.

Great-Grandma Cecilia sat at the dining table writing letters to her many cousins. Her paper-thin skin was a web of wrinkles. She wore a brown dress that buttoned all the way up her throat and looked as if she could have stepped out of a tin daguerreotype.

Cecilia beckoned to them and hugged Fiona, then Eliot, adding a dry kiss for good measure.

He returned her trembling embrace, but oh so gingerly, because he was afraid he'd break her. A hundred and four years old was nothing to fool with.

Eliot loved his great-grandmother. She always had time to listen to him, no matter what she was doing. She never gave him advice or orders. She was just *there* for him.

"Good morning, my darlings," she whispered. Her voice was the rustle of autumn leaves.

"Morning Cee," Eliot and Fiona said together.

Eliot shot his sister a look. She was doing it again: that synchronicity thing. Just to get to him.

Cecilia patted his hand. "Yesterday's homework." She nodded to the papers on the edge of the table.

Fiona was a little closer and grabbed them before Eliot. She frowned, peeling off the top sheets, and passed them to him. "Yours," she murmured, then focused on the rest of the pages.

Eliot took them, annoyed that she had looked at his grade before he could.

A large C+ had been scratched at the top of last week's essay on the Thomas Jefferson Memorial. Next to it was *Fine thesis. Flawed execution. Writing closer to aboriginal than English.*

Eliot winced. He had tried *so* hard. He had all the ideas in his head, but when he put them onto paper, everything got tangled.

He glanced at Fiona; her olive complexion had paled. He stepped closer and spotted the large C– on her page.

"My ideas were 'amateurish,'" she whispered.

"It's okay," Eliot said. "We'll help each other rewrite them tonight."

Fiona nodded. She took bad grades harder than Eliot, as if she had something to prove to Grandmother. Eliot had given up trying to live up to her expectations. Nothing was ever good enough. Sometimes he just wished that she'd leave them alone.

"Alone or together," said Grandmother, "I expect those rewritten tonight along with your new assignment."

Eliot jumped and turned.

Grandmother stood behind them in the hallway, arms folded over her chest, one hand holding two crisply typed pages.

"Good morning, Grandmother," Eliot said.

It was *Grandmother* always. It was never *Audrey* or *Gram,* or any other pet name like they used with Cecilia. Not that it was forbidden, but *Grandmother* was the only thing they ever thought to call her. It was the only title that carried the authority her presence demanded.

Grandmother's thin body stood with perfect posture and towered over them at an even six feet. Her silver hair was shorn with military precision, and her olive complexion had not a single wrinkle, even though she was sixty-two years old. She wore a plaid flannel shirt buttoned all the way to the top, jeans, and steel-toed boots. Her expression, as usual, was one of ironic inscrutability.

She handed them the pages: tonight's homework, which consisted of seven geometric proofs and a new essay on Isaac Newton's personal life.

Eliot flexed his hand and wondered how short he could make this new essay and still get a passing grade. A passing grade according to Grandmother was an A–. She always told them that "excellence is the least that is expected of you" and made them rewrite subpar papers until they were good enough.

"They've had breakfast?" Grandmother asked Cecilia.

"At eight thirty." Cecilia gathered her letters and envelopes into a neat stack. "Oatmeal, juice, one hard-boiled egg."

Boiling water was the upper limit of Cecilia's cooking ability. Eliot always offered to help, but she never let him.

Grandmother plucked up their turned-in homework, and her gray eyes scanned the first lines noncommittally. "They should go," she said. "Being late for work will not do."

"Couldn't . . ." Cecilia's weathered hand curled around her throat. "I mean, tomorrow are their birthdays. Must they do homework the night before—"

Grandmother shot Cecilia a look that guillotined her words midsentence.

Cecilia looked down at her letters. "No, of course not," she whispered. "Silly of me."

Not even Cecilia could get Grandmother to bend a rule. Eliot loved her for trying, though.

Grandmother turned to Eliot and Fiona and tapped her wristwatch. "Ticktock," she said, and leaned closer.

Fiona gave her a polite kiss on her cheek. Eliot did, too, but it was just a formality, part of the morning's scheduled activities.

Grandmother gave him the slightest hug.

Eliot knew she loved him—at least, that's what Cecilia always said. He wished her "love" would be something other than rules and restrictions, though. Just once he wished she'd cancel homework and take them all out for a movie. Wasn't that "love," too?

"Lunch is on the table by the door," Cecilia told them. "Oh, I didn't get to the store yesterday. . . ."

Eliot and Fiona glanced at one another, understanding.

Fiona bolted for the front door first and Eliot followed—but too late. She grabbed the larger paper bag off the table, the one Cecilia had slipped the last apple into, and ran out the door.

Eliot reluctantly grabbed the remaining bag, knowing it only contained a dry tuna-fish sandwich on rye.

"Have a good day, my darlings," Cecilia called after them, smiled, and waved.

Grandmother wordlessly turned away.

"Thanks, Cee," Eliot whispered.

He ran after Fiona, down the hall, past the elevator, and to the stairs. She was always trying to outrace him—everything was a competition with Fiona.

Eliot wasn't about to let her win without a fight. By the time he hit the upper landing, though, Fiona was half a floor ahead of him, her longer legs carrying her farther, faster.

He chased her down the three flights, round and round, Eliot now only a few feet behind—until they burst through the steel security door onto the street.

It was a sunny day in Del Sombra, and they rested a moment in the narrowing shadow of the brick façade of their apartment building.

On Midway Avenue peach trees sat in planters. Their branches swayed in the warm breeze and dropped not-quite-ripe fruit on the road to be spattered by the tourists racing to Sonoma County.

"I won," Fiona said, breathing heavily. "Twice. In one day." She shook her paper-bag lunch. "Extra apple, too. You need to be faster, *Bradypus*."

Bradypus was the genus name for the three-toed sloth, one of the slowest mammals in the world.

Eliot's mood darkened, but he didn't let her bait him into another round of vocabulary insult; instead he just shot her a glare.

He unclenched his paper-bag lunch, still in a tight grip from their sprint. A metallic clink came from inside. Eliot unrolled and then peered into the bag. At the bottom were two quarters. That was Cee, trying to make things even between him and his sister.

Eliot plucked them out and held them up to the sunlight. They gleamed like liquid mercury.

Fiona grabbed for them—but this time he was quicker.

"Ha!" he said, snapping them securely into his fist.

He'd use them to buy carrot juice from the health-food store on his break. Better than the flat soda or tap water they got at Ringo's. He dropped them back into the bag.

Fiona shrugged as if those quarters didn't mean anything to her, and she briskly started to walk down the sidewalk.

Eliot knew her; it mattered.

He caught up to her. "You think anything's going to happen tomorrow?"

"Like what?" Fiona asked. "New rules?"

His stride faltered. It was a distinct possibility. Grandmother's list of rules grew longer every year. The latest entry was just five weeks ago.

> **RULE 106:** No dating—single, double, dutch, chaperoned or not, or otherwise.

As if *that* were going to happen in his lifetime. Maybe it was for Fiona. The guys at work sometimes talked to her.

"I just thought . . . ," Eliot said, running to catch up to his sister. "I don't know. Like school—maybe we'll go to a real school. With other kids. Wouldn't that be better than Grandmother's assignments every night?"

Fiona said nothing, her silence voicing her opinion.

Other kids were sometimes a problem for him and his sister. While Eliot knew the capital of Angola (Luanda), the number of genes in the earthworm, *Caenorhabditis elegans* (about nineteen thousand), ask him to make small talk with a girl and his IQ dropped thirty points.

"Yeah," he said, "maybe not such a great idea."

But something new *had* to happen. Almost fifteen years old. You couldn't live your entire life just doing the same thing every day: Ringo's, homework, reading, chores, sleeping.

Was this what it was going to be like until he was eighteen? Would Grandmother keep them home until twenty-one? Forty? Until they were as old as Cee?

Fiona brushed back her hair, hooking it over her ear. "I want to travel," she said in a faraway voice. "Go to Athens or Tibet . . . actually see at least one of the places we've read about."

His sister had the right idea. He turned the same fantasy over in his head every day: running far away. Where would they go? And more important, how could they ever defy Grandmother?

He and Fiona might as well have been corked inside a bottle, sailing nowhere on a tiny balsa-wood ship.

"Could be worse." Fiona nodded ahead at the entrance to an alley. "We could be like your friend there."

From the shadows in the alley, a pair of worn sneakers missing their laces protruded onto the sidewalk. Holes in their soles revealed bare feet inside.

"He's not my friend," Eliot muttered. "He's just some guy."

Fiona increased her pace as they neared the shoes.

The sneakers were attached to tattered jeans and a tangle of gray rags that might once have been a trench coat.

They saw this old man every day on their way to work. Sometimes he huddled on different corners or like today sat in the shadows. And while his location changed . . . his smell never did: a combination of sardines, body odor, and burnt matches.

Eliot slowed to a halt.

The old man's face squinted up at him, his leathery skin contorting into a mass of deep laugh lines and white scars. His lips parted into a greasy smile; he leaned forward and held out an Angels' baseball cap. A piece of cardboard jammed into the brim had the word VET printed on it.

Eliot held up his hand. "Sorry I don't . . ."

His words trailed off as he saw a kidney-shaped object tucked behind the man. A violin.

Eliot could almost feel the waves of sound resonating off it, almost taste the notes, sweet and wavering, oscillating through his skull. He wanted to touch it—even though he'd never played any instrument before.

The old man followed Eliot's stare, and his smile brightened, revealing yellowed teeth thick with saliva.

He pulled the violin into his lap and ran his thumb over the chipped fingerboard . . . for all the good it would do. All the strings were missing.

The music in Eliot's head screeched to a halt.

He would have given anything to hear him play.

The man's smile vanished and he set his cap over the violin.

Eliot bit his upper lip, unrolled his lunch bag, and fished out the two quarters.

Fiona stopped, watching him. She set her hands on her hips and shook her head.

Eliot didn't care what his sister thought; the money was his to spend any way he wanted.

"You should buy a few strings," Eliot whispered to the old man. "I bet you could make more money if you played a little." He dropped the quarters into the cap.

The man grasped the coins, rubbed them together, gazed lovingly at the violin . . . and then back up to Eliot. He said nothing, but his dull blue eyes brimmed with tears.

2

CHOCOLATE HEART

Fiona couldn't believe her brother. She watched him drop his quarters in the bum's baseball cap. Only ten minutes older than Eliot, she sometimes felt it might as well be ten years. How could he be such a little boy?

She stalked back to extricate him, before he gave his lunch away, too.

The old man looked from Eliot to her and his gaze hardened.

He glanced her over. It wasn't the way boys sometimes looked at her. "Elevator eyes" she had heard other girls call it. This was more as if he could see past her skin, right down to her bones.

She could smell him now, too: sardines, a month of curdled body odor, and smoke.

The stench aside, there was a magnetic repulsion, too. She just wanted to get as far away from the old man as she could. He gave her the creeps.

She grabbed Eliot's hand, which was uncharacteristically ice-cold.

"Come on," she whispered. "We're going to be late." She jerked him toward her.

"Yeah," he said, still looking back at the old man.

They fell into their hurry-up stride.

"You might as well have tossed your money down the storm drain," she said. "That guy can't even play. Probably found that violin in the trash."

"Sure he can play," Eliot muttered, and rubbed his hand. "I bet he's good, too."

Eliot was too nice sometimes, and people like that bum took advantage of him. For a moment she considered turning around and getting his money back. But maybe it would be better if Eliot learned that not everyone operated by Grandmother's 106 rules. At fifty cents, it would be a lesson learned cheaply.

He had that dopey look on his face whenever he talked about music. Fiona knew better than to lecture Eliot about RULE 34—you might as well talk to a trash can about aesthetics, or a brick wall about aerodynamics.

She wondered what life would be like without having to look after him. Eliot was always trying to find ways around the rules, and getting them *both* into trouble.

Like it or not, though, he was her brother—like a third, mutated arm growing from the middle of her chest—he was annoying, but she couldn't quite bring herself to cut him off.

"Cee told me you were adopted," she told him. "I saw the birth certificate. It said, 'Eliot Post. *Sarcoptes scabiei.*'"

This was a microscopic mite that caused scabies, whose symptoms included pimplelike irritations and intense itching.

Eliot scratched his head. "Got to get your nose out of the medical books. I've read them all, too. Are you losing your touch? A dose maybe of *Mycobacterium leprae?*"

That was the strain of bacteria, also called Hansen's bacillus, that caused leprosy. Nice double entendre.

They rounded the corner of Midway and Vine. Across the street was Sol Granda Florists, perfumed by a hundred dozen roses and bushels of lavender. Fiona wished someone would send her roses once in her life. Just once. Anyone.

Kitty-corner from this was The Pink Rabbit, a health-food co-op and juice bar. A plywood rabbit sat upright on the corner drinking from a plastic cup full of frothy green liquid. Eliot loved to hang out there. Thursday afternoons was open mic, where he pretended never to listen to the folksingers.

Opposite the Rabbit squatted the Colonial columns of Ringo's All American Pizza Palace. It was supposed to look like a miniature version of the White House in Washington, D.C. . . . only one of the wings was bare cinder block—a recent addition that would one day house four lanes of bowling. Next to the double-glass-door entrance was a mural of Uncle Sam with a red, white, and blue bowling ball in one hand, and in the other a wedge of gooey pizza.

At this junction, the smells from the three buildings collided: rose, laven-

der, freshly pulped carrots and oranges, clove cigarettes, yeast, and pepperoni.

The nexus of all these things that didn't belong together, of course, was
Ringo's. Pizza originally came from Naples, Italy. Bowling came from Ger-
many or possibly ancient Egypt. And the Colonial architecture drew much of
its influence from Renaissance style. This logically made it "All American."

They hesitated at the double glass doors.

Fiona didn't want to go in. More was wrong with Ringo's than clashing
styles, busing tables, and washing dishes.

Behind them, however, was the invisible hand of Grandmother pushing
them onward. *Work is the cornerstone of character,* she was always telling
them.

They had worked at Oakwood Apartments for Grandmother since Fiona
could remember, sweeping and polishing the miles of wood flooring. As
soon as they turned thirteen, Grandmother obtained work permits for them
(Fiona suspected they were forged) and found them jobs.

Fiona made the first move, grabbing the handle and pulling it open for
Eliot.

"Come on," she said. "It's only a four-hour shift. We can do it."

"Yeah." Eliot's face screwed into a mask of worry. "It'll be easy."

He moved through the doorway and Fiona stepped through with him.
The air-conditioning hit her like an arctic gale. It was always too cold in
here. She should have worn her sweater over this dress.

The day manager, Mike, stood at the host's podium, arms crossed over
his chest.

"Five minutes late," he announced. "I'm going to dock an hour's pay."

Eliot started to step forward, but she bumped him—a warning to keep
his mouth shut.

They weren't late . . . even stopping for that bum, they had had fifteen
minutes to get here. The less said to Mike, however, the better. He'd start
docking them for other things they didn't do.

Mike Poole was back in Del Sombra for the summer. He was a sopho-
more at Berkeley. He might have been handsome with a shock of silky red
hair, and freckled forearms, but his eyes held all the intelligence of a
bovine's and a glimmer of cruelty.

He slipped a slender book under the podium's calendar, but not before
Fiona saw it was Cliff's Notes on *Macbeth.*

She'd read her version of the play a dozen times.[2]

Fiona could probably recite *Macbeth* to Mike if she had to and help him sound out the big words.

"So . . . Fiona." Mike stepped around the podium. "Think over the hostess thing? I could train you. It'd be easy." He smiled and that evil-cow gaze dropped and then traced up her length with elevator eyes. "You'd be great."

Fiona looked away, her shoulders hunched, and she felt her face heat. "Not so good with people," she whispered. "No. Thanks."

"That's part of the training," Mike cooed.

Next to her, Eliot balled his hands into fists.

Fiona stepped in front of her brother. "It's okay," she said. "Busing is fine. It's great."

"Suit yourself." Mike snorted. "Someone on the night shift got sick, and they left the party room for you." Mike finally noticed Eliot and said, "Trash cans need rinsing today, kid. Get to it before dishes. Make sure you use bleach."

"No problem," Fiona said.

She moved past Mike, and Eliot followed her into the dining room. In the back was the separate party room, and to their left was the swinging door that led to the kitchen.

She felt Mike's eyes locked on her backside and revised her estimation of them: They weren't cow eyes. That was unfair to bovines. He had the eyes of a rat.

Sunlight flooded the dining room through picture windows. Five of the fifteen tables already had lunchtime customers, people wearing the uniforms of wine-country tourists: men in khaki slacks and loose silk shirts; the women in designer jeans, sweaters, and sixteen pounds of gold jewelry.

The place would be packed by eleven thirty, and Eliot and Fiona would be running to get everything clean for the real crowds at noon.

Ringo's may have been a conglomeration of unlikely styles and questionable taste, but situated on the most picturesque country artery between San

2. One artifact found intact at the Oakwood Apartments site was a *Complete Works of William Shakespeare*, published in the eighteenth century (ref catalog: 49931-D). It is intriguing as every mythological reference had been stricken with an indelible marker. For example, passages mentioning Hecate, and the entire scene with the three witches, had been redacted from *Macbeth*. *Gods of the First and Twenty-first Century, Volume 11: The Post Family Mythology*, 8th ed. (Zypheron Press Ltd.).

Francisco and the heart of California's wine country; its location was perfect to siphon money from tourists.

Eliot walked straight into Fiona as if she weren't there.

She turned and saw why. His eyes had been glued to Linda, who waited tables today. Linda had that effect on guys.

Fiona grabbed Eliot by the shoulders and pointed him toward the swinging kitchen door. "Better get busy before Mike comes looking," she murmured.

He blinked. "Right."

"Keep your head above water." This was a not-so-veiled reference to his height, his poor swimming ability, and the gigantic sink where he'd be spending the next four hours.

Eliot glowered, then brightened as he thought of his own insult: "Keep it clean."

This was a reference to the messy reality of Fiona's job: busing tables at Ringo's meant getting up close and personal with spattered marinara sauce, spilled olive oil, cornmeal crumbs . . . all of which got in her dress and her hair no matter how careful she was. And although she showered every night, the scents lingered.

Eliot pushed through the kitchen door, and Fiona grabbed the busing cart by the wall, maneuvering it back toward the party room.

She observed Linda as she chatted with the customers about the road and the weather. Customers always laughed at Linda's jokes, and when she suggested the pasta special, they usually ordered it. Maybe it was her looks. She could have been a model with her perfect makeup, spiky blond hair, and the way her skirt, pink shirt, and long, curved nails seemed to color coordinate.

Linda even deflected Mike's come-ons, somehow smiling all the time as he stood too close and stared at her. She always had an excuse not to go out with him, yet he never got angry with her.

She spotted Fiona, gave her a nod and a smile, which instantly faded.

Just like Mike, Linda managed to appear friendly to Fiona without ever really *being* friendly.

Fiona waved awkwardly and looked away. She straightened her dress, although no matter what she did, it still looked wrinkled. She wished she had the nerve to tell Cee she hated the clothes she made them, but that would have broken the old woman's heart.

She snuck another glance at Linda, laughing with her customers. They left her great tips. It wasn't just her looks. Linda knew how to talk to people. Fiona would have given anything to be as confident. Every time she had to talk to strangers, her heart pounded so hard she could barely hear her own mouse voice as it tried to squeak out something clever. She couldn't look someone in the eyes to save her life, and she spent most of the day staring at her feet.

If shyness were a disease, Fiona would have been rushed to intensive care and put on a social respirator.

She sighed and halted at the party room doors.

Something was wrong; they were shut.

The party room was always left open during the day so customers could see the large table that sat two dozen, the wet bar and the television, and be tempted to book it for sports events or birthday parties. Forty dollars and it was yours for the evening.

Then the smell hit her: vanilla and pesto and an acrid scent that wasn't food . . . anymore.

She stiffened and pulled the sliding doors apart.

It was instantly apparent what had happened last night: twenty sugar-crazed spider monkeys had been locked in this room under the pretense of a six-year-old's birthday party. Scattered on the walls, floor, and only by the sheerest of coincidences the table, were pasta, pizza crusts, globs of congealed cheese, baby-blue frosting, and pools of melted ice cream. And over everything was a sprinkling of confetti.

In the corner was a chunky orange spatter, and Fiona then understood that when Mike had told her someone on the night shift had gotten sick, he didn't mean one of the staff.

Fiona pushed the cart in and closed the doors behind her. No need to expose the paying customers to this.

She pulled a hairnet over her head, then tied a bandanna over this. Next came a chin-to-knee, white linen apron, and finally she snapped on thick rubber gloves. This was her armor.

She swept up the confetti, food, and bits of wrapping paper (which had tiny robots on it). She then used the dustpan to scrape off slimier things.

Fiona wondered what it would be like to have a real birthday party. She and Eliot had a brief ceremony on the morning of their birthdays. Cee tried to make something special for breakfast, and they pretended to enjoy it. There were presents: books usually, pen sets, or blank journals. But never wrapped in colored paper. And certainly not paper with robots printed on it.

Of course to have a real birthday party you needed friends and balloons and games. Fiona could never see that happening in Grandmother's apartment.

She halted in the middle of sponging up a puddle of olive oil, suddenly angry at Grandmother and her 106 rules.

Could Fiona be like Linda without those rules? Able to speak to people? Smile? Keep her eyes off her shoes? She wouldn't have a job. She'd have spent her summers at her friends' houses, slumber parties, and midnight movies . . . mythological occurrences that seemed far less real to her than the dusty histories on the shelves of her room.

Fiona felt drained. She would just lie down and they could find her here at the end of the shift.

A flash caught her eye. A fleck of red foil, partially hidden under a paper plate, glimmered. She moved the plate and spied a piece of unwrapped candy. Printed on it were the words ULTRA DARK SPECIAL.

Her heart quickened and she stepped closer.

It was chocolate.

While not specifically forbidden by Grandmother's rules, it was as rare in her life as a day without homework. Cee had it in the kitchen, semi-sweet chips, cocoa powder, or sometimes a brick of bitter baking chocolate . . . which she then transformed into cookies, mole, and Christmas fudge—that were only by a loosest definition "eatable." Fiona had snuck a taste once, a few chips before Cee had rapped her knuckles with a wooden spoon. It had been worth it.

She gingerly removed one glove and picked up the morsel. It was heart-shaped and was at first cold, but then quickly warmed to her touch.

Should she save it for after work? No. A million things could happen between now and then to the tiny sweet—dunked in water, smashed, stolen—best to eat it now.

What about Eliot? She should share it with him, shouldn't she?

It was so small, though. *Maybe* two bites.

She removed her other glove and carefully peeled back the red foil. Inside was a dark lozenge of black with swirls of midnight and eddies of the deepest brown. She inhaled a rich scent of something inexplicable: it was secrets and love and whispers.

She took the tiniest bite.

The chocolate was smooth and yielded to her teeth. She closed her eyes and let it dissolve on her tongue, spreading like velvet. Warmth coursed through her blood into her chest and stomach and thighs. The melting confection was sweet and bitter, smoky and electrically wonderful, and it slid over her palate.

She swallowed and her pulse thundered. She inhaled and held her breath a long moment, then let it all out with a sigh.

It was *so* good.

And then it was gone.

Was that what it would be like to kiss a boy? Like falling? Prickly heat and chills at the same time?

She looked at the half morsel still in her hand, one side scalloped from her bite. Her mouth watered.

As much as she wanted it, she steeled herself, then with great and deliberate care wrapped it back within the red foil.

That was for Eliot. He deserved a little goodness on his birthday, too.

She folded the chocolate in a clean paper towel and slid the precious package into her dress pocket.

Fiona pulled her gloves back on.

She felt better now. Full of energy.

Fiona finished cleaning the room faster than she ever imagined she could. The wooden floor and the Formica table gleamed. The only scent left in the place was a faint whiff of pine cleaner . . . although if she tried, Fiona could still remember the way the chocolate smelled.

She touched her pocket to make sure it was still there.

Fiona then opened the doors and pushed the now laden cart back to the kitchen.

As she wheeled through the swinging door, a blast of steamy air washed over her, along with the smells of strong soap and bleach. The day-shift cook gave her a quick wave. Each of Johnny's massive hands could toss a whirling cake of dough into the air at the same time. He returned his attention to the ovens. He had five pizzas in there, all bubbling with molten cheese.

Eliot was in the back of the kitchen, by the deep fryer. He stood hunched over the sink, which was as large as a bathtub. On either side towered stacks of sauce-spattered dishes, pans, and pots, all apparently left from last night.

Mike was always doing this to her and her brother: coming in the night before and telling the late shift to leave their mess for them.

Did he pick on Eliot because of his homemade clothes? Because he was smaller? Or did Fiona's refusing his offers have something to do with it?

She would never understand Mike Poole, and she didn't particularly want to, either.

"Need help?" she asked.

Eliot continued to scrub under the dingy water. "I'm fine." He tried to wipe the suds off his forehead, but his hand was just as soapy and left a new trail of scum there.

Fiona took the edge of her apron and wiped his face.

"Thanks," he whispered.

Fiona then removed the paper towel containing the chocolate from her pocket. She set it on a high shelf far away from the sink.

"No one's going to notice if I'm gone for a few minutes," she told him. "I'm helping."

Eliot nodded, unable to say "thank you" twice to his sister in the same day. She understood; it was apparently against the brother-sister code of never being *too* nice to one another.

Fiona stepped up to a stack of dishes. Cheese, sauces, and pasta had hardened to iron-hard consistency overnight.

Eliot scraped off the worst of the gunk with a steel spatula, then did a pre-rinse in scalding water before he handed the offending plate to her for final wash and rinse.

In ten minutes working together they moved half of one stack to the drying racks.

Fiona's hair was plastered to her forehead, and her apron was soaked through.

The kitchen door swung open a crack. Linda poked her head inside. "There you are," she said to Fiona. "Stuff's piling up out here." She flashed a not-so-friendly smile, then vanished back to the dining room.

Fiona undid her sopping apron, and underneath her dress was soaked and clinging to her skin. She shivered.

The kitchen door slammed open and Mike walked in, fuming. "Fiona, what—"

The urgency in his face drained away as he looked her over. His eyes bore into her.

"I'm going," she said, and her gaze dropped to the floor. She instinctively hunched over and folded her arms over her chest. Gooseflesh rippled over her body. "I just finished the back room."

"There's no rush." Mike's voice was calm, almost sweet now. He sidled closer. "I *really* want you to think again about the hostess position. The hours are better. Pay's better, too."

Fiona's cheeks burned and the hair on the back of her neck prickled.

"She said she wasn't interested," Eliot said, and stepped in front of her. "How many times does she have to say it?"

Fiona saw he held the steel spatula, the sharp edge angled at Mike's face.

Mike's smooth features rippled with emotion—amazement, anger—then settled into a serious glare.

"Back off, squirt. I'm talking to your sister."

"Don't," Fiona whispered so softly she barely heard herself.

Eliot knuckles whitened around the spatula handle. He took a deep breath, then took one step closer to Mike, who towered a foot over him.

"No," Eliot said. "*You're* done talking."

They stared at each other for a long time, then Fiona couldn't take it anymore. She stood tall, moved next to her brother, and, although it took every ounce of her nerve, locked gazes with Mike.

"I said no once already," Fiona said. "I meant it."

Mike took a step back. For a split second, it seemed he was almost scared . . . of them both. He snorted. "Okay, whatever. Just get out there and get the tables clean. We've got customers waiting."

He turned and stormed through the swinging kitchen door.

"Thanks," Fiona whispered to her brother.

Eliot, trembling, said nothing and went back to the dishes.

Fiona noticed her hands were balled into fists and she relaxed. She felt like throwing up. She'd never stood up to anyone like that before. Neither of them had. Maybe fifteen was going to be a more interesting year than she had thought.

3

BROKEN TEACUP

Eliot, Fiona, and Great-Grandmother Cecilia sat at the dining room table. They all pretended that nothing was happening . . . even though something most certainly was.

The sun was low in the sky and amber light filtered through lace curtains. The polished wood of the table gleamed, and the white porcelain tea set was orange in the twilight.

Fiona had changed into her gray sweats after work and had her nose buried in Isaac Newton's *Philosophiae naturalis principia mathematica*, working on tonight's essay.

Cee squinted through her thick glasses as she wrote a letter to her cousin in Bavaria, scratching out the words with a fountain pen.

Eliot couldn't focus. He kept replaying the confrontation with Mike in his head, and adrenaline shot through his body as he imagined himself punching that creep in the face.

Mike, though, wasn't the only factor that made work impossible tonight. There were two other things.

Encyclopedias lay opened before Eliot. He had been researching Newton's mental breakdown in 1675, but much of the text had been crossed out with a black marker. Eliot inferred these redacted passages dealt with Newton's interest in alchemy.[3]

---

3. To what extent Newton pursued alchemy is unknown as his notes on the subject were destroyed in a laboratory fire. Although occult scholars claim he made breakthroughs in this area that led to later discoveries in mathematics, no evidence substantiates this nor any of the more fanciful legends of his Faust-like bargains with higher powers.

Sometimes seeing the zebra-striped pages made him so mad he wanted to throw the sullied books across the room.

That was Grandmother's RULE 55 in action.

> **RULE 55:** No books, comics, films, or other media of the science fiction, fantasy, or horror genres—especially, but not limited to, the occult or pseudosciences (alchemy, spirituality, numerology, etc.) or any ancient or urban mythology.

Eliot called this the "nothing made up" rule.

Grandmother called the stuff "brain-rotting candy for simple minds."

Honestly, with all the juicy bits blacked out, how was he supposed to write a good essay? At least she could have just drawn a line through the offending text, so he could see what it was all about.

RULE 55 and Mike's bullying, however, were part of the *ordinary* weirdness that was his life. But the thing really bothering all of them tonight was not.

Grandmother walked into the dining room from the kitchen. Her face was a mask of concentration, and her gray eyes looked as if they were staring at something miles away.

Her usual graceful stride was tense, as if she were waiting for something to spring from the shadows. But that was silly. Nothing ever scared Grandmother.

Still, her mood was infectious, and Eliot felt the skin along his spine crawl.

Grandmother stopped and cocked her head as if listening. She then smoothed both hands through her short silver hair and said, "I'm going to check the basement and side doors."

This was her evening security check of the building. It was part of her duties as manager and perfectly normal. Telling them she was doing it, though, like a warning, was *not* normal.

"Of course," Cee said. Her smile fluttered to life; she set her pen down and laid her trembling hands together. "I was just going to pour the tea. Should we wait for you?"

Chemical analysis of Newton's remains shows high levels of mercury, which may have been caused by his alchemy experiments and may account for his aberrant behavior in 1675. *Gods of the First and Twenty-first Century, Volume 3: The Pseudo Sciences,* 8th ed. (Zypheron Press Ltd.).

Grandmother marched to the front door, her boots clipping over the hardwood.

"No," she called back. She opened the door, paused, and said, "Eliot, eyes back on those books."

Eliot looked down immediately.

He heard the door close and the dead bolt lock.

Nothing scared Grandmother. Nothing. And the only other thing that ever put a dent in her totally-in-control armor was when Eliot and Fiona asked about Mom and Dad.

Eliot never thought of himself as an "orphan." Orphans were kids like David Copperfield who lived in state-run gulags. He and Fiona had family, a home, and neither of them even remembered their mom or dad.

But every time they asked, Grandmother would patiently explain that there had been a terrible accident at sea. That it happened when Eliot and Fiona were babies. Grandmother and Cecilia were the only close family, so naturally they took them in. No, there were no pictures. Everything had been aboard the ship that sank.

Whenever Grandmother told them this story, her smooth features scrunched together and lines wrinkled her forehead—not so much in pain, but as if it were physically exhausting for her to form the words.

But that paled with whatever was getting to her tonight. The look Eliot had seen in her eyes, well, the only word he could think of was *sharp*.

Fiona looked up from her books at the same time as Eliot, and they glanced at each other. She was thinking the same thing: something was wrong.

Eliot shrugged. Fiona bit her lower lip.

Cecilia took a jar from the tea set and measured out four spoonfuls—her own special mixture of chamomile, stevia, and green tea—into a strainer. She set this over the open teapot and poured steaming water through. The teapot had a spiderweb etched into its white glaze.[4]

"Did anything *different* happen today?" Cee asked nonchalantly. She handed Eliot his cup.

---

4. "Baba Jaga poured fouled river water, boiling hot, until it spilt from her teapot. The stone pot was coarse and covered with web lace and venomous spiders. 'What are you making?' the lost little girl asked, her eyes wide. 'Tea, babushka.' Baba Jaga smiled showing the points of her teeth. 'Sweet tea for my sweet morsel.'" Father Sildas Pious, *Mythica Improbiba* (translated version), c. thirteenth century.

"What makes you ask?" he said. Grandmother's 106 rules had meticulously been engineered to eradicate anything interesting, and therefore different, from their lives.

Cee's smile vanished for a moment, but immediately came back. "No reason, darling." She handed Fiona a steaming cup. "Making conversation, that's all."

Every night Cee asked, "How was work?" Or once in a great while, "Did you have a nice day?" *That* was just making conversation. This wasn't.

And yet, something different *had* happened: the old man with his violin, then Fiona and him actually standing up to Mike.

"Just another day," Fiona replied as she examined the leaves swirling in her cup.

Cee nodded, accepting this, and drank her tea, one gulp, two, three, and it was gone. That was the way she did it. The hotter the beverage, the faster she seemed to drink.

Fiona didn't want to tell Cee, and Eliot felt the same way. Talking about their bully boss would just upset her.

But there was more to it than that. That moment when Eliot and Fiona had stood up for themselves, they were a lot more than nearly fifteen-year-old geeks. They'd been strong. And if they told anyone about it, maybe the magic of that instant would vanish in a puff of smoke.

Eliot took a sip of his tea. It was sweet. Bits of green-tea leaf whirled around like stars in a galaxy.

Fiona set her hand on his arm and nodded at Cecilia.

Their great-grandmother sat transfixed staring into her empty teacup. Her hand trembled violently and the cup slipped.

It fell to the hardwood floor, bounced, and hit again—shattering.

"Oh, dear," Cee said, blinking. She rose from her chair. "What a butterfin—"

The front door opened with such force that it slammed against the wall and shook a cloud of dust off the nearby bookshelf.

Grandmother stood silhouetted in the doorway, her long, slender arms hanging loosely at her sides, hands open.

"Do not move," she said.

She stepped into the light. Her face was cool and collected, but her gray eyes darted back and forth surveying the room. "There are fragments everywhere. I will get them."

She moved to the table and knelt, plucking up the largest shards. Bits of tea leaves clung to the inner curves of the broken cup.

Oddly Grandmother wasn't just picking them up; in her left hand she cradled them, assembling the base and part of the sides until she held a razor-sharp ceramic lotus.

Grandmother stared into the partially reconstructed cup with the same look Eliot had seen before . . . sharp. As if you had asked her what she was doing and she looked up—the intensity of her gaze would have cut the question out of your throat.

Eliot's hand involuntarily rose to his neck.

Outside the sun set and the clouds blazed orange and scarlet. The light in the dining room tinged red. The white shards in Grandmother's hand looked as if they were dipped in blood.

She drew in a long breath and let it out in a sigh. Grandmother then closed her hand over the broken cup. She stood and looked at Cee, then Fiona and Eliot. Her eyes were their normal iron gray.

"Drink your tea," she murmured.

Eliot and Fiona obeyed.

"Cecilia, clean the rest of this up."

"Of course." Cee hurried into the kitchen for a broom and dustpan.

"I can help," Fiona offered.

"No." Grandmother's face warmed a bit, and a slight smile struggled to life on her lips. "You two get ready for bed."

"We need to finish our homework," Eliot protested. "There's the Newton essay and the rewrite of the 1812 paper."

"Homework is canceled tonight," Grandmother said. ". . . For your birthdays."

Eliot looked to his sister, and she looked to him.

He wasn't going to argue, but homework had never before been canceled. Rain, snow, sickness, or exhaustion, you always turned it in.

Grandmother gave Fiona a hug and kiss, then knelt and beckoned to Eliot.

He embraced her. She barely touched him, though, as if she were afraid she might hurt him if she squeezed too hard. He kissed her cheek, and she his.

Eliot and Fiona marched down the hallway.

"Even," Fiona whispered.

"Fine," he whispered back.

She said, "One, two, three . . ."

They simultaneously blurted out numbers. Eliot's was seven. Fiona had three. Add them together and you got ten, an even number.

She smiled and tromped into the bathroom.

Somehow she always won that game. Eliot hadn't figured out her trick yet, but there had to be one.

He waited in the hallway as it filled with shadows. He snuck a sideways glance into the dining room. Grandmother had her back to him, but he could make out Cecilia as Grandmother spoke to her in murmurs. Cee nodded vigorously, and her hands had stopped their usual shaking. The old woman looked pale.

He caught a few hushed words in their conversation—in hard German consonants. Fiona was good at languages; he wished she were out here.

He made out one word: *versteckt.*

Maybe all the mystery was about their birthdays tomorrow. Maybe they were planning something different. A surprise.

The bathroom door opened and light spilled into the hall.

"All yours, stinky," Fiona said, and marched into her bedroom.

Eliot entered the bathroom and closed the door. It smelled of Cecilia's strong homemade soap. The stuff left his skin tingling, part cleaned, part caustic burn.

His attention riveted to a spot of red in the sink: a circle of reflective crumpled crimson foil.

He carefully picked it up and saw it was a wrapped chocolate. He glanced at the mirror over the sink. There were smudges. He leaned closer and breathed on the glass.

Words appeared in Fiona's looping cursive:

Eat it quick! Happy B-Day.

He peeled back the foil. Inside was half a chocolate morsel with bite marks on one side. Eliot smiled—popped it into his mouth and munched.

It was good . . . but before he could even taste it, it was gone.

He wasn't sure where Fiona had gotten it, but chocolate was a rare treat—especially chocolate that Cecilia hadn't ruined with her cooking. He loved the old woman, but honestly, one day she was going to poison them all.

He carefully wiped the mirror with his towel.

Eliot then wadded the foil, wrapped it inside toilet paper, and flushed it away.

There was no rule about chocolate, but that didn't mean there couldn't be a new one created if Grandmother started finding wrappers.

He searched for more surprises, but found none, so he got out the tooth powder and brushed his teeth.

From the heater vent in the floor he heard, "Psst."

Eliot rinsed and crouched by the vent. "Hey—thanks."

"It was nothing," Fiona whispered back.

This was how they talked after lights out. The vent in the bathroom was best, but they could listen to each other from their bedroom vents, too, if they put their heads to them and covered themselves with a blanket to muffle the noise.

"What do you think is going on tonight?" Fiona asked. "I get chills when I think about how Grandmother's acting."

"Yeah . . ." Eliot remembered the intensity of her eyes, and gooseflesh crawled up his arms. "I heard them talking in German. What's *versteckt* mean?"

"Um . . . to hide. Or hidden, concealed."

"Maybe they're talking about birthday presents?"

"Maybe." Eliot could tell from her flat tone that she didn't think so, either.

They were both quiet a moment, then Fiona finally said, "At work to-day . . . I appreciate what you did."

"It's okay. I think it's going to be better at Ringo's from now on."

". . . Sure. We better go before they hear us."

"Hey, one more thing."

"What?"

Eliot wanted to say a lot of things. Such as, if he had to get saddled with a creepy sister, he was glad it was her. That none of his homework would be half as good if not for her help. That—it even hurt to think about this— he kind of somehow almost liked her.

But instead he just said, "Happy tomorrow birthday."

"You, too."

The other side of the vent suddenly felt empty.

Eliot stood and washed his face, then glanced at the mirror. He still looked like a species of *dorkus maximus*. Maybe that would all change to-morrow. Fifteen.

He sighed and turned off the light.

4

DRIVER'S EDUCATION

Robert Farmington watched his boss, Marcus Welmann, pick the lock on the frosted-glass door.

Technically this was illegal, but it was a lawyer's office, and those guys mutilated the law all the time anyway.

Robert worked for Welmann and Associates Investigations, though there were no "associates," and neither he nor Welmann were licensed investigators. Tonight they were here to find some confidential files on a missing old lady. No big deal.

He glanced down the deserted hallway, then out the window to the street two floors below. This burb was a graveyard at three in the morning. Del Sombra it was called. "Of the shadows" in Spanish. Weird name for a town.

He looked back at Welmann as the man levered the tiny lock with his massive arms.

Marcus Welmann wore baggy camo pants, a black T-shirt, and running sneakers with the reflective stripes ripped off. Not exactly a male model. He was sixty years old and two hundred and fifty pounds of grizzled muscle. His large hands would be the envy of any NBA forward. Great for clobbering. Not so good for delicate work.

Robert inched closer and whispered, "You want me to pop it? I can do it in ten seconds flat."

Welmann turned to Robert. His eyes narrowed—a warning that his protégé better shut his trap or he'd be waiting outside in the car.

Welmann hated saying more than a dozen words a day; it was part of his

Neanderthal act. He had a Harvard MBA and had been a navy med tech, but he always played it dumb, which made people underestimate him.

Robert crossed his arms and did his best James Dean back at Welmann—not a stretch because Robert wore the black leather jacket, jeans, and biker boots that was the uniform of any teenage rebel.

Welmann returned to the stubborn lock and ran one finger over the scratched keyhole.

His face brightened. He grabbed the knob, twisted, and it turned.

"Already opened," Welmann muttered.

Within the office a beam of light bisected the shadows. Someone was inside . . . and from Robert's experience it was rarely the janitor.

Welmann let go of the knob and slid to the side of the door so whoever was inside wouldn't see his silhouette out here.

Robert flattened himself against the outer hall wall, as well.

Welmann waved to get Robert's attention and pointed back the way they had come, indicating that he hightail it.

Robert wasn't going anywhere. Eight months of training, he could handle this.

Welmann reached for the holster in the small of his back and drew a weighty revolver of polished steel, his Colt Python Elite .357 Magnum.

Robert pointed at Welmann's sneaker and made a "give me" gesture.

Welmann unthinkingly grabbed for the Taurus PT-145 in his ankle holster, a tiny polymer gun with a barrel no longer than its slight grip . . . but he stopped, pointed emphatically back at Robert, then jabbed at the floor, indicating that he stay put.

Robert nodded. With one meaty fist Welmann could easily make him stay put.

Welmann gripped the doorknob and burst into the office.

Robert peeked inside, spotting the source of the light: a penlight on a desk. It rolled over empty file folders.

Welmann snatched up the flashlight and crossed it over his opposite wrist, sweeping his aim over the office. The place was the size of a two-car garage, but it was crammed with six desks, a wall of filing cabinets, and posters of mountains and white-water rafters with the titles PERSISTENCE and INTEGRITY. Light from the sodium-vapor streetlamps outside filtered through the windows and tinged it all unnatural orange.

Welmann checked behind every desk. "No one here," he whispered. "Damned weird."

Robert eased inside and double-checked behind the door. Just shadows there. So who had used that flashlight?

Welmann saw Robert and glared, chewing over words that didn't make it out of his mouth. What could he say? The place was deserted.

Robert was about to tell Welmann where he could stuff his "I'm trying to teach you something" shtick—when something appeared behind Robert . . . a creeping presence, big and breathing. It cleared its throat.

Robert wheeled around.

The shadows behind the door parted like a curtain. A glowing cigarette ember revealed a smile that would have made the Cheshire cat blush.

From this slight shadow resolved a Samoan man in a black suit, dark gray shirt, and a black tie with a tiny emerald skull tie tack.

Robert thought it was funny that he noticed that little detail—because this guy was seven foot, easy, and there had to be four hundred pounds of him poured into that Armani.

"Damned weird?" the man said in a rumble of a baritone voice. "An interesting choice of words."

Robert wanted to panic, that's what his hammering heart urged him to do. But Welmann had trained him: made him read a hundred *Vault of Horror* comics and watch every D-grade Italian slasher flick. Robert, at least in theory, was ready for the unexplained and unexpected . . . and a guy that could flatten a professional NFL linebacker stepping out of nowhere certainly qualified.

There was no way they could fight this guy. Nowhere to run. That left two options: shoot him or bluff.

Robert swallowed; his throat was sandpaper. "Hey, how's it going?"

The smiling Samoan puffed on his cigarette. "I am fine, young man." He nodded to Welmann. "Set the pistol down. What are you looking for?"

Robert realized he was in Welmann's line of fire. Rookie mistake. He moved two steps to his left.

Welmann glared at the guy and gripped his Colt tighter.

"I detest *unnecessary* violence," the man said.

A chill ran up Robert's spine as he got the impression this guy probably considered most violence "necessary."

"If you will allow me?" The man reached into his coat.

"Careful, buddy," Welmann growled. "Two fingers."

The man nodded. He plucked out a business card and held it out to Robert.

Big guys like this weren't usually fast. So why did Robert imagine one of those massive hands grabbing him lightning quick and snapping his neck like Styrofoam?

Robert snatched the card.

On one side there were letters so black they didn't look like ink, but darkness coalesced. It took Robert a second to focus on them.

Mr. Uri Crumble

On the reverse side was a holographic logo. The ink was red-black and didn't look quite dry. Robert smelled blood, thick like a slaughterhouse. This odor stuck to the back of his throat and he gagged. He couldn't focus on the design: lines and tiny symbols that stretched into the air and deeper into the card.

Welmann hissed so loud that Robert swore he felt it on the back of his head.

Robert backed across the room and handed the card to him.

Welmann took one look at the thing and muttered, "Oh, hell." He lowered his aim a notch and carefully looked over Mr. Crumble.

"Indeed." Crumble puffed on his cigarette.

Welmann rubbed his face with his free hand. His ruddy cheeks drained of color as he holstered his gun.

Robert had never seen Welmann look scared and never seen him lower his gun. He was a gladiator—kill or be killed—it was genetically hardwired into him. Now suddenly Welmann looked like a little boy with his hand slapped.

And this Crumble, what was his deal? Sure he was the size of a bull ox, but nobody, not even someone that size, stared down the muzzle of a .357 Magnum without so much as a blink.

It was as if all the fundamentals that Robert had learned were being rewritten.

"What are *you* people doing here?" Welmann asked.

Crumble flashed a set of blindingly white teeth. "Looking for someone. Same as you, Driver."

Welmann opened his mouth to say something, then shut it with a click. No one was supposed to know who they were . . . or *what* Welmann was.

"Your so-called car," Crumble explained, "parked in the alley. Such a vehicle with its modifications, here, tonight, could only belong to an errand boy."

He meant Welmann's 2005 Mercedes Maybach Exelero, the thing he prized more than his immortal soul. The one-of-a-kind four-door version had been handcrafted and purred with a twin-turbocharged V-12 that cranked out seven hundred horses. The Exelero was armored and fitted with bulletproof glass. The interior was butter-soft leather and koa wood. Outside she was sculpted mirror-chrome steel and black enamel so deep she made midnight jealous.

"You said you were looking for someone?" Welmann asked.

Mr. Uri Crumble nodded toward the filing cabinets on the far wall. One had its lock popped. "What was your interest in them? I wonder."

Robert made a mental note of "them." His and Welmann's current mission was to dig up information on *one* missing little old lady: Audrey Post. There was no "them."

Robert glanced at Welmann. He had on his poker face, but he'd bet Welmann was thinking the same thing.

Robert looked back to Crumble and noticed his cigarette wasn't burning. Well, it was; it smoldered and smoke curled from the tip . . . but there was no ash and it was the same length as when he'd first stepped from the shadows.

Crumble pulled a long drag from the curious never-and-ever-burning cigarette and caught Robert's stare. He exhaled, saying, "Perhaps we should share what we know and learn more."

Welmann frowned and adopted his best stupid, noir-detective act. "Buddy, you're speaking Greek, and I barely understand English."

Crumble grunted smoke. "Very well." He moved to the door, brushing aside a large steel desk as easily as Robert might have moved an empty cardboard box. Crumble paused and said, "After you report your failure tonight, your employers will not be pleased." He chuckled, the sound a subsonic ripple. "Keep my card. Give us a call. Our organization always has a use for qualified people."

"That'll be the day," Welmann replied.

"Yes . . . it will." Crumble turned sideways to fit through the office doorway and left.

Robert noticed he was holding his breath, so he exhaled. What did he mean by "report your failure"? This guy didn't even know whom they were looking for.

Welmann muttered a string of obscenities and looked down the hallway. "Gone," he said, and closed the door. He moved quickly to the filing cabinets.

Robert saw the one with the popped lock was labeled PA–PO.

"That's who we're looking for, right? Post? Probably the same old lady."

Welmann ignored the question and reached for the handle. He recoiled. "Stand back.".

Robert moved closer to get a better look.

Welmann grabbed a handkerchief from his pocket and pulled the drawer. Smoke and plumes of sparks flew into the air. The files inside had been reduced to a pile of smoldering ash.

He slammed it shut.

Welmann glared about the office and nodded at the computers. "Get to work, kid."

Robert understood that now was not the time to ask questions. He moved from desk to desk, feeling the aluminum cases of the desktop units. "Got a warm one," he told Welmann. He sat and booted the machine.

Welmann hovered over Robert's shoulder, as if he didn't trust him to turn on a computer.

A blue screen flashed on the monitor.

"BIOS setup," Welmann muttered. "The drive has been wiped."

"So let's pull it, take it back, and scan it."

"Don't bother. When those guys erase something, it stays erased . . . permanently."

Robert repressed a shudder. He got the feeling that hard drives weren't the only things Crumble "erased."

"Who was that guy?"

"Works for another side," Welmann replied.

"What *other* side?" Robert turned around. "I thought our boss and the others didn't have sides."

Welmann scrunched his lips into a single white line. "I don't got all the answers, kid, but there *are* others. There's a truce between his people and ours. No one sticks their noses into each other's business. *Capisce?*"

"So this Crumble guy wasn't exactly what he appeared to be?"

Welmann shrugged, which meant yes, and said, "We got to be careful not to get caught between some big wheels. Might get ground to a pulp." His gaze moved from desk to desk. He got up and felt under the top of one. With a rip he pulled free a CD case taped there.

He handed it to Robert. "Lawyers always keep backups."

Robert wheeled his chair to a nearby computer and snapped it on. He spotted a sticky note on the monitor with the password and typed it in. He then inserted the disk, and scrolled through the list of folders that flashed on-screen.

"'Post,'" Robert said. "There's a file on her . . . no, wait. For 'Post, F and E.'" He looked back through the folders. "No *Audrey* Post, boss. Sorry."

"Open the file," Welmann suggested, and pulled up a chair next to Robert's.

Robert did as he was told and legal gobbledygook crawled over the monitor. After skimming a few pages he got the gist of it. "Trust-fund stuff. Some rich kids getting money from their great-grandmother. Blind accounts in the Caymans, Geneva—all over the world. Lucky brats. Not who we're looking for, though."

Welmann squinted at the document, too. His practiced Neanderthal scowl melted as he donned wire-rimmed reading glasses. He hit the PAGE DOWN key a few times.

"No," Welmann muttered. "Crumble said 'them' . . . that he was looking for 'them.' What else do you have on"—he tapped the PAGE UP key thrice— "Fiona and Eliot Post?"

Robert tabbed back to the file folders. "Got a missing-kid kit. One of those jobs you can fill out and give to the police if little Johnny and Jane here ever get lost in the woods."

"Let's see it."

On screen two photos appeared: one of a teenage boy, the other a girl. The pictures were head-and-shoulder shots with strong light and a dappled background. The subjects had forced smiles snapped at the precise wrong moment.

The boy was a few years younger than Robert, with black hair cut short and combed to either side. The kid had a deer-in-the-headlights expression, and the only word that came to mind was *geek*.

The girl looked as clueless as the boy; she had dark hair tied back in a ratty ponytail, no makeup, and a pimple on her chin. Her eyes had the same naïve gleam, and Robert thought of another word: *prissy*.

Robert checked their data sheets. Twin brother and sister, Fiona and Eliot. Robert memorized their address. Their birthdays, he noted, were tomorrow . . . actually today as it was three in the morning.

Welmann folded his glasses and put them away. He stared into the distance. "More than fifteen years," he whispered. "That how long our little old lady has been missing." He looked back at the pictures and squinted. "Has got to be the most cocked-up . . ."

Welmann's face turned ash white.

"What is it?" Robert asked.

"You got their address?"

Robert tapped the side of his head.

Welmann opened the computer's disk drive, grabbed the CD, and snapped it in half.

"Hey! What gives?"

Welmann turned to Robert, and his face set in a cast-iron mask of no-crap-listen-to-me-kid seriousness.

"I want you to get back to the boss and report everything: Crumble, these kids, give him their address. Do it in person. No phones." Welmann stood. "We got trouble two steps behind us. You drive and don't stop. You got to eat, drink, or piss—you suck it up and keep going."

"Okay." Robert wasn't sure what had just set Welmann off, but he wasn't about to question orders when they had gone to DEFCON 2. "What are you going to do?"

"I've got to get to those kids . . . before they do."

"You mean Crumble. This other side, right?"

Annoyance flickered over Welmann's wide face and he got out Mr. Uri Crumble's business card.

"Yeah." Welmann turned his head and blinked as if it hurt to look at the card so closely. He fished out his lighter, struck a flame, and touched it to the paper.

The flame caught. Welmann dropped the card.

Fire licked up the lines, flickered around the angular writing, and covered the logo on the back; white blackened to char, edges curled and glowed with embers; the pattern wriggled in the heat as if it were alive.

Five seconds it burned. Then ten seconds, and it continued to burn. The lines looked like heated metal and glowed brighter, and Robert found himself wanting to touch it . . . let it sear into his skin.

Welmann stomped it flat, and ash plumed over the floor.

Nothing remained except a sneaker imprint of pulverized cinders. Try as he might, Robert couldn't remember the curious design, even though he had just seen it.

"Freaky," Robert whispered.

Welmann reached into his pocket and got his car keys, hesitated, then handed them over.

Robert stared at them. No way was Welmann handing *him* the keys to the Maybach.

"Go on," Welmann said.

He didn't have to say it twice. Robert snatched them up. "You want *me* to drive?"

Welmann looked slightly nauseated, but nodded.

Robert's elation faded. Welmann wouldn't let him drive unless it had really hit the fan, as in, Welmann didn't expect to be able to drive the thing again—ever.

"Take me with you," Robert whispered. "You'll need backup."

Welmann nodded. "I bet I will. But you're not coming." He exhaled and looked Robert square in the eyes. "You got twice the balls that I had when I was sixteen. You're going to make a great Driver." He set a hand on Robert's shoulder and squeezed. "But if you don't do as I told you, I'm going to kick your ass."

Robert wanted to say a lot of things: how Welmann was a son of a bitch, that he never liked him . . . and that the last thing he wanted was to leave him the way he had the string of replacement dads since he was a kid.

He fought to keep his eyes from watering. He was going to cry? Like a baby? In front of Welmann? He fought back the tears and nodded.

Robert moved to the door and paused.

Welmann flashed him a crooked smile and gave him a little wave that turned into a "shooing-away" motion.

Robert wondered when he'd see the guy who'd been the closest thing he'd had to a father . . . or even *if* he'd see him again. He sprinted down the hallway to the stairwell and didn't look back. He had a feeling they were both on their own.

5

BIRTHDAY SURPRISES

Eliot reviewed his escape plan: When he got paid today, he'd head to the bus station instead of home. He'd get to Santa Rosa and hitchhike the rest of the way to San Francisco, where he'd arrange to work on a freighter to Shanghai . . . and from there maybe find his way to Tibet.

He glanced at the clock on his dresser: almost nine thirty. Time for the real world.

There was no escape plan. Eliot didn't have the nerve to hitchhike or con his way onto a freighter. He wished he did, though.

He got angry. Jeez, if he couldn't even escape in his daydreams, what was the point of anything?

He marched over to the milk crate by his dresser, stood on it, and looked in the mirror. He winced. Today he had to wear his "special" clothes. The ones Cecilia had spent considerable time and energy sewing for his birthday. As with her cooking, Cecilia's heart was in the right place, but the results could almost kill you.

Eliot's shirt was a collection of stripes that had once been in style, come back, then forever died the fashion death they richly deserved. Avocado, almond, and burnt orange had been put on this planet specifically to clash. He wouldn't have minded so much, but the alignment was off, so they off-set midway on his chest. The pants were no better. Cecilia had decided pleats were "in," and these permanent creases bunched together around the zipper so it looked as if he wore a diaper.

He sighed, closed his eyes, and hoped he'd be invisible at work today . . . or that Mike would be too busy to harass him.

His daydream of escape returned, and for a moment he tasted salt air on the Indian Ocean—the start of a great adventure.

The clock on his dresser pinged.

He hopped off the milk crate and went to grab his homework, halting at his desk. There was no homework.

It felt good, but somehow wrong, not to have fallen asleep at his desk last night. Grandmother always meant exactly what she said, though, and last night she had said "no homework." Yet, everything about last night seemed wrong: Cecilia acting jumpy; him and Fiona sent to bed early; that broken teacup.

Maybe the change was because of their birthdays. Grandmother had to realize that they'd soon be too old for homeschooling. What was she going to do when they went to college? Grandmother and Cee would be left alone to rattle around in this book-lined tomb of an apartment. He felt sorry for them.

Eliot moved to his door.

The List was taped there, 106 rules that might as well have been 106 feet of chain-link fencing and concertina wire. Every bit of the sympathy he had just felt for Grandmother evaporated.

He wanted to tear the List down, rip it into confetti . . . but the rules would still be there—invisible and ever present, essential to life in Grandmother's house, like oxygen in the air.

And such tantrums did nothing. Last year Eliot had wanted a radio for his birthday, just for news he'd claimed. He promised there'd be no music. He had tried pleading, logic, and finally he had told Grandmother that *he* would buy a radio, and he didn't need her permission.

Grandmother didn't say a word. Instead, she halted his tirade with a single "sharp" gaze.

It was the same look she had last night. He'd forgotten that he had been on the receiving end of that look. It had felt as if his heart had stopped . . . not literally, but he recalled that he'd forgotten to breathe he'd been so absorbed by her fathomless gray eyes.

After what had seemed like minutes, Grandmother blinked, and he inhaled.

The "discussion" about his radio was over. Forever.

Angry all over again—Eliot yanked open his bedroom door.

In the darkened hallway Fiona's door yanked open at the same time, with exactly the same force, spilling another dim parallelogram of light into the shadows.

They stared at one another, then she said, "Happy birthday."

She was doing it again: that pretend twin synchronicity thing to bug him. One day he'd figure out how she did it.

Eliot's anger dimmed a little, though, as he recalled her present last night: the chocolate. Now that he thought about it, it was twice the gift that he had realized. He liked chocolate as much as the next person, but Fiona *loved* the stuff. How could one person be so nice one moment, then a total brat the next? Guess that was the short definition of a sister.

At least she hadn't escaped fashion disaster, either. Fiona also wore her Cecilia-made birthday outfit: a pink dress, misaligned at the seams, tight across the chest, and loose at the waist. A pink bow and sash about her middle cinched it awkwardly together. And a pair of white sneakers from the secondhand store had been colored with lavender marker in an attempt to make them match. She looked like a crumpled bubble-gum wrapper.

Fiona tried to smooth out the wrinkles and bunches in the fabric to no effect. She shot him a glare and said, "What are you staring at? Are you feeling okay? Hypoxia? Or anoxia?"

"I'm getting plenty of oxygen to my brain."

Fiona had been favoring medical terms in her openers for vocabulary insult. Good thing he had reviewed the premed texts on the bathroom shelves recently.

"You should switch from angiology to a field of study closer to your mental consistency," Eliot retorted. "Limacology."

Fiona's dark brows scrunched together.

He had her with this one. The *ology* part—"study of"—was a give-me. The *lima* though . . . that would get her. Even by *their* standards it was obscure. This would be one of the shortest games of vocabulary insult on record.

Eliot left her there to ponder his riddle and strolled down the hall, practically walking on air.

Behind him, Fiona whispered, "A lubricious puzzle from your equally slippery gray matter."

Eliot stopped. The grin on his face faded. She got it? So quick?

He turned. "How?"

Eliot closed his mouth, but it was too late. The damage had been done. He'd committed the one foul in vocabulary insult: asking for an explanation.

It was Fiona's turn to smile. She tilted her head and explained, "You had me for a second. I thought it was *lemma* as in the Greek for 'proposition,' as in *dilemma,* the decision between two propositions."

She was lecturing him. He loathed this but it was her right to claim— the only real prize in their game.

"But it was your clue about 'mental consistency' that really helped. I figured it had to be something slimy or sticky . . . which made me remember that *Limax maximus* is the leopard or common garden slug. After that it was easy." She snapped her fingers. "Limacology, the study of slugs. Good one. I hope you weren't saving it for a special occasion."

"Whatever," Eliot mumbled. "Score's still nothing to nothing."

She caught up to him, and together they walked into the dining room. They stopped on the threshold, however, stunned by what they saw.

The table, normally obscured with a layer of papers and books, had been cleared. The wood surface was polished to a dark mirror finish and draped with a lace tablecloth (that didn't fit). Four china plates were set out with linen place mats, napkins, and silver forks.

Across the picture window, a banner hung between the bookcases. It had been taped together from newspaper strips. On it, a laundry marker had been used to print HAPPY BIRTHDAY. The last few letters, though, shrank at the end as the calligrapher had run out of room.

Only there weren't supposed to be decorations in Grandmother's apartment.

Cecilia had made them cards last year. Each had tiny silhouettes of their faces on the outside, cut with exacting precision from black cardboard. Eliot couldn't imagine how Cee had done it with her trembling hands. It must have taken her forever.

Grandmother, however, had taken the cards and they'd never seen them again. She had said it violated RULE 11.

> **RULE 11:** No painting, sketching, drawing, doodling, sculpting, papier-mâché, or anything in any way attempting to re-create nature or abstract themes with artistic methods (traditional, modern, electronic, or postmodern "interpretive").

That was the "no arts and crafts" rule.

Didn't this banner count?

Beyond the swinging door to the kitchen, Eliot heard humming and detected the odors of baking bread, caramelized sugar, and citrus wafting into the room. Cee was cooking.

He glanced down the hallway. No one had yet seen him. He could dart back to his room, pretend he'd overslept, then run off to work—before he had to eat whatever "special treat" Cee had whipped up for them.

Fiona set her hand on his arm and whispered, "Don't. She tries so hard."

He exhaled. Cee did try . . . and he loved her for it. He wouldn't disappoint her.

The kitchen door swung inward and diminutive Cecilia backed into the room. Today she wore her good white dress with lace cuffs and petticoats that rustled under the wide skirt. She turned and they saw the triple-layer strawberry shortcake in her withered hands. She beamed at them and set it unsteadily on the table.

Cee was a sweet old lady, but her sense of smell and taste had dried up sometime around the Second World War, and as a result the things she cooked could taste like anything: limes, sea salt, or with equal probability Worcestershire sauce.

"Happy birthday, my darlings." She presented her culinary creation with a flourish. "I found this recipe in the *Ladies' Journal* and made it especially for you." Cecilia shuffled closer and hugged Fiona and Eliot together.

"Thanks, Cee," they said.

She released them. "Oh, dear," she whispered. "I forgot the pineapple and walnuts. And the candles! Stay right there." She trundled back into the kitchen.

Eliot and Fiona stared at the cake. It was lopsided.

"You try it," he whispered.

"No way. It's your turn."

Eliot sighed and took a tiny step closer. Pink and purple icing oozed from the cake's layers. From the lower edge he scooped a fingerful.

The icing was gritty. Strawberry seeds? The cake part had the spongy consistency of cake . . . but you could never be too careful with Cecilia's cooking. He smelled it: citrus and something else his nose couldn't identify.

He braced himself and popped the bite into his mouth—quickly before he chickened out.

Thankfully the grittiness in the icing *was* strawberry seeds. It tasted good, tangy and sugary the way it ought to be . . . but then the icing melted, and his face involuntarily puckered. The cake was salty and sour: unmixed baking soda and a chunk of orange peel.

Cecilia pushed through the kitchen door with two bowls balanced on one arm, and a fistful of birthday candles and a box of matches in the other.

Eliot had no choice. He swallowed and smiled.

"Can I give you a hand?" Fiona offered.

"No, no, no." Cecilia shook the box of matches at her. "Just stay there while I finish. No cheating and eating." She dealt slices of pineapple onto the cake and sprinkled crushed walnuts over that. She then punctured the frosting skin with candles, carefully counting out thirty. Fifteen for Eliot. Fifteen for Fiona.

Cecilia could have skimped and just put one set of candles on the cake, but she was always trying to make them feel that they both got what they deserved.

"Thank you," Fiona said.

"Yeah," Eliot added, clearing his esophagus as best he could. "Thanks, Cee."

"Now fire." She slid open the box of matches, fumbled one out, and struck it with a shaking hand. The flame reflected in her dark eyes.

Eliot said, "Maybe you better—"

"Let me do it," a voice behind them commanded.

Eliot and Fiona turned together as Grandmother entered the room.

"Good morning, Grandmother," they said in unison.

Grandmother looked different today. Her short silver hair had been brushed to a silk sheen. She wore a red linen shirt with a button-down collar, khaki explorer pants, and midcalf black boots that were a shade less severe than the combat boots she usually favored.

She smiled at Eliot and Fiona, then glanced at the banner over the window. She said nothing and strode toward Cecilia, who shrank back, still holding her burning match.

Grandmother snatched it from her hand and quickly touched it to all thirty candles, lighting them. The match burned perilously close to her fingers, until she rolled it, squeezing the fire to a hissing ember.

"There," Grandmother said. "Now both of you wish for happy tidings."

Eliot mentally chalked off another year when there would be no singing "Happy Birthday" thanks to RULE 34.

Eliot and Fiona stepped up to the cake and leaned closer, inhaling at the same time.

They shot a quick look at each other. He knew Fiona was wishing for more chocolate.

Eliot wished for a stereo, guitar lessons, and rock-concert tickets. This was more like "praying for a miracle" than a "birthday wish," but what the heck; it was worth a shot.

They both closed their eyes, blew for all they were worth, and extinguished every flame.

"Very good," Grandmother said.

They turned just in time to get a flash in their faces from Grandmother's antique windup film camera.

"One next to the cake, please," she told them. "Together."

Eliot and Fiona scooted closer—even though this violated their mutually agreed-on one-foot minimum distance from each other.

Cecilia sidled next to Eliot and put her arm around him.

Grandmother frowned. "Not you, Cecilia. I only have two shots left on this roll of film. We can't waste any."

"I'm sorry." Cecilia backed into the corner.

Eliot forced a smile as Grandmother snapped the shot.

As if she could manufacture the perfect family if she got enough photos and stuck them in an album. Funny, now that Eliot thought about it: Grandmother's assertion that all the pictures of their parents had sunk on that ocean liner didn't ring true. She was always taking pictures of them. Why didn't she have any pictures of her own daughter?

Cecilia reached for the cake platter.

"Presents first," Grandmother said. She went to the china cabinet, whose shelves were filled with volumes of St. Hawthorn's Collected Reference of Horticulture, and pulled out four paper bags.[5]

This was different. Usually Fiona and Eliot got a single present each.

Grandmother set the bags on the table. They had been stapled shut. Her wrapping wasn't much in the way of festive, but it was effective.

If Eliot didn't already know they contained clothes (what they got every year), he'd never have been able to guess.

She handed one bag to Eliot and one to Fiona.

---

5. St. Hawthorn's Collected Reference of Horticulture (complete title on the inside page reads St. Hawthorn's Collected Reference of Horticulture in the New World and Beyond). This nineteenth-century manuscript catalogs many plant species not found in the modern world. Many scholars claim such entries as the "Venom Creepvine of Louisiana" are pure invention. Others speculate these might now be extinct species. The last of these volumes were seen at auction in 1939, where they sold for £40,000. Victor Golden, Golden's Guide to Extraordinary Books (Oxford: 1958).

He hefted his: heavier than he expected, too dense to be a new shirt or slacks. Fiona held hers up, and one brow rose in puzzlement.

"Go ahead," Grandmother said, the slightest enthusiasm creeping into her voice. "Open them."

Eliot tore into the bag.

Inside, wrapped in a plastic sleeve, was an old book.

He hid his disappointment as best he could. When you lived in an apartment filled with thousands of books, the only thing less wanted than hand-me-down clothes was another book.

This one had a scuffed green leather cover and three ridges across the spine. As Eliot turned it over, he saw in faded gilt letters *The Time Machine* by H. G. Wells.

He glanced at Fiona, and she stared with mouth agape at the book in her hands: *From the Earth to the Moon* by Jules Verne.

Eliot was speechless.

While the apartment *was* full of books, they were moldy century-old plays, desiccated histories, thick science textbooks, and biographies of people no one had ever cared about.

The book in his hand was . . . forbidden.

There was RULE 55, the no-made-up rule.

"These are classics," Grandmother explained. She set one slender hand on each of their shoulders to reassure them. "Not first editions, but still printed in the nineteenth century, so take good care of them."

Eliot marveled at his book. He'd seen this novel referenced in commentaries on great literature. He knew the basic premise. It was something he'd never had before: a science-fiction story he could escape into.

And if H. G. Wells was considered a "classic," did that mean Mary Shelley and Edgar Allan Poe were up for grabs, too?

Eliot looked into Grandmother's eyes to see if she was serious, that this was for real. There was no heart-stopping, fathomless gaze there. She looked pleased that he liked her gift . . . and oddly a little worried, too.

"This is great," he said. "Super. Thanks a lot."

"Thank you, Grandmother," Fiona said. She held her Jules Verne to her chest.

Grandmother's thin lips parted in a restrained smile. "You're quite welcome. This is a special year for you two. You're growing up faster than I ever imagined."

"Cake anyone?" Cecilia said.

Grandmother turned to her and narrowed her eyes.

"I . . . I just thought," Cecilia whispered, "it might be a good time to eat?"

Grandmother considered, then said, "Yes, go get a knife, please."

Cecilia nodded and ambled into the kitchen.

"Now," Grandmother said, "you should open your other present before you go to work."

Eliot exchanged a glance with his sister. This was weird. Grandmother giving them a gift they'd actually enjoy, and now two gifts?

He wasn't going to ask questions. Too many questions irritated Grandmother, and her good moods were as fleeting as a rainbow in a hurricane.

Eliot grabbed the second paper bag. It was light and soft. It had to be clothes.

Cecilia returned carrying a stack of extra napkins, and a long chef's knife from the butcher's block. She set everything neatly on the table. She gazed lovingly at Eliot and Fiona.

"Well, go ahead," Grandmother said to her, irritated at this delay, then raised her camera to take another snapshot. "Cut the cake while the children—"

There was a knock at the front door. Three strong raps.

Grandmother frowned and the temperature in the apartment seemed to plummet ten degrees.

Cecilia paused, knife held over the cake. "Should I get that?"

"No." Grandmother lowered the camera and slowly turned. "Whoever this is better have an excellent reason for interrupting."

Eliot looked at Fiona, and she looked at him, shaking her head. Only one thing was worse than provoking Grandmother's anger, and that was finding her in a good mood and *then* provoking her. Whoever was at the door . . . Eliot pitied the poor guy.

6

TRAIL OF BREAD CRUMBS

Marcus Welmann thought the cinder-block apartment building was odd. Its second floor was shorter than the first floor by two feet. He paused to catch his breath on the stairwell landing and noticed the third story was shorter still, as if the place were shrinking.

He rubbed his face. He had to figure out why this Uri Crumble was so interested in the Post kids . . . and what the connection was to the lady he was looking for: Audrey Post.

The building that matched the address in the lawyer's file had been painted brown to look like wood (it didn't) and had a quaint Bavarian façade out front. Just the kind of tacky you'd expect in a Californian wine-country tourist trap.

There had been no *Post* on the mailboxes in the lobby, however, so he decided to try the building manager to see if he could get a forwarding address.

Welmann went up the steps and marched down the hallway to the manager's apartment, 3A.

Digging into his pocket, he grabbed his fake police shield. He then checked his Colt Python in its holster. He paused to make himself presentable—as much as anyone could in camo sweatpants and a black T-shirt. He zipped up his light polyester jacket.

He knocked, three times, hard, like a cop in a hurry.

Welmann waited and shifted his weight.

He hoped Robert made it back to the boss, and that the Mercedes was in one unscratched piece.

The kid had a good head, but there was too much "rebel" in Robert. He'd wash out of Driver's training, which might be a good thing. Sixteen-year-old boys ought to worry about "kid" stuff: sex, drugs, and rock and roll . . . not becoming some hero.

Welmann heard footsteps and saw the peephole go dark. The door opened without the usual unlocking of dead bolts and unlatching of security chains.

He puffed up his chest and furrowed his brow. He'd need a good head of steam to blow at this manager—impress upon him that withholding a forwarding address would be obstructing justice. He looked up, fake shield in hand . . . but the bluster stalled in his throat.

The woman who answered was tall. How old? Fifty? Sixty? Hard to say. A mature woman, but with looks like hers, she could have been on magazine covers. Her cropped silver hair was elegant, and Welmann easily imagined her as the femme fatale in his favorite noir flicks.

"Can I help you?" she asked, studying him like a smear of dog poop on her boot.

Welmann had that elevator-going-down feeling—just enough to throw off his equilibrium.

He glanced into the apartment. There were a billion books: shelves on every vertical surface and stacks that overflowed into neat piles. They were real books, too, with leather and gilt letters; not a *TV Guide* in sight.

Whatever was bugging him, he didn't see it . . . but he felt it: his skin itched and he fidgeted. There was *something* dangerous here.

"I'm looking for—"

Then he spotted them: at the end of the hall, sitting at a table, were Eliot and Fiona Post. They blinked at him with the same deer-in-the-headlights look as in their photographs.

The uneasy elevator feeling in Welmann halted—as the elevator snapped, and his stomach leapt into his throat.

He connected the dots. The manager in 3A. Post kids in 3A. No *Post* on the mailboxes because they were being hidden by the woman who stood in front of him. The woman he'd been trying to track down: Audrey Post.

Welmann looked into her gray eyes and only then *really* saw her.

He couldn't pull his gaze away. There was power there—not like the shadowy illusion printed on Crumble's business card, either. This was the roar of the ocean surf, an inexorable tide that sucked him deeper.

He was drowning. Couldn't breathe.

"Looking for what?" she asked. "Mister . . . ?"

His trance broke and he found his voice. "Welmann," he whispered, and cleared his throat. "Marcus Welmann." He gave her a slight bow, which was the jerkiest thing he'd done in a long time. Somehow, though, it felt like the only thing to do.

Her gaze hardened and she opened the door wider. "Come in, Mr. Welmann."

When his boss had given Welmann this mission, he had been crystal clear: find Audrey Post, report back, and do not under *any* circumstances engage.

Here he was engaging.

Welmann could sort this out—but he'd have to talk his way out of it . . . and that wasn't his best thing.

Audrey Post led him inside.

He smelled something baking and the overpowering scent from the molding pages of all those books.

He saw a very old woman in the dining room, hovering over the children. She wore what might have been a costume from *Gone with the Wind* and looked ancient enough to have worn it during a real Civil War cotillion. She glared at him.

The boy and girl clutched books in their laps, and they stared at Welmann with that mix of annoyance and curiosity that was pure teenager.

Behind them, draped over the window, was a banner with HAPPY BIRTH-DAY on it. Marcus was interrupting in a big, awkward way.

Good investigative technique—barging into the middle of these kids' party. Nice and inconspicuous, he thought. Still, better him than Crumble.

"Children," Audrey Post said, "this is Mr. Welmann, an old friend of the family."

Welmann slipped the fake police shield back into his pocket. So much for that dodge. Audrey Post was playing another game, one where he didn't understand the rules. Best go along for now.

The boy and girl exchanged looks and then stared at him. They were a year or two younger than Robert.

"Friend of the family?" Fiona leaned forward. "Did you know our parents, sir?"

"Shush," Audrey Post told her. "Go—you're late for work, both of you." Her voice softened a bit and she added, "We'll finish this later. I have business with this gentleman."

Both kids glanced at some paper bags on the table, then said together, "Yes, Grandmother." They rose, nodded at Welmann, and retreated into the shadows of the apartment.

. So Ms. Audrey Post was their grandmother. That made sense. Welmann listened, but detected no one else in the apartment. Where were the kids' mom and dad? Parents normally didn't miss birthdays. The girl, however, had asked him if he had *known* her parents. As in past tense. As in dead now.

Audrey Post turned to the old woman and said, "Cecilia, bring tea, please."

The older woman hesitated, opened her mouth as if to tell her something, but then backed into the kitchen, all the time watching Welmann.

The children reappeared and headed for the front door with lunch sacks. They each gave their grandmother a polite kiss on the cheek.

"It was nice to meet you, Mr. Welmann," Fiona said.

"Nice to meet you, too," he said.

Sweet kid. Polite. You didn't see that much anymore today. All the more reason to figure this out and move them somewhere safe from Crumble.

The kids left and closed the apartment door behind them. .

"Now," Audrey Post said, "we will talk."

Welmann felt his equilibrium shift a few degrees more . . . as if the entire room had just tilted. He would have preferred a mano a mano with Mr. Uri Crumble. That would have been a lot safer. Audrey Post had power; any person with a blink of the sight could see that.

"You were sent to find me?"

Welmann wasn't stupid enough to lie. "Yes, ma'am."

"You are a Driver, correct?"

She could have picked up that cake, candles and all, and smashed it into his face, and that would have been less of a surprise.

Welmann felt an instinctual urge to take a few steps backward, but he held his ground, steeled himself, and nodded.

If she knew he was a Driver, and more important *what* a Driver was, then it followed that she knew his boss and probably why he was interested in her . . . which was more than *he'd* been told.

She didn't look the least bit worried about any of this, either. "What did they tell you about me?" Her gray eyes narrowed a bit.

Welmann swallowed, his throat bone-dry. So she didn't know everything. Good. The clairvoyant ones were always a pain in the ass.

"They said not to talk to you."

Audrey Post cocked her head as if listening for something, then glanced out the window to the street below. Marcus looked, too.

The kids appeared on the sidewalk. She turned back to him. "Do you know who I am?"

Was that a trick question? "Audrey Post," he offered.

This seemed to be the right thing because she smiled. It was a nice smile, and Welmann found himself relaxing a notch. He shook off that creeping complacency. He had to keep his guard up. This wasn't a game.

She eased into one of the seats at the dining table as gracefully as a lotus blossom settling onto a reflecting pool.

"Please"—she gestured to the opposite chair—"sit."

Welmann, far from being a gentleman, was no idiot. You didn't stand when a lady of power offered you a place at her table. He sat and the chair creaked from his generous frame.

The kitchen door swung inward, and the old woman backed into the dining room holding a tray with tea service.

She set it on the table and whispered, "Why are you talking to him?" She scowled at Welmann, then made a throat-slitting motion.

Welmann liked this full-of-venom little old lady. He quashed his chuckles, though; she wasn't kidding. Sweat trickled down his sides.

"The tea will be all, Cecilia."

Cecilia's gaze dropped to the floor. "Yes, yes, of course." She stepped back into the kitchen.

"How did you find me, Mr. Welmann?" Audrey Post asked.

"Your grandchildren."

Her eyes became slits and her lips compressed to a single line.

That struck a nerve. So no one was supposed to know about the kids? Maybe that was the card to play. "Eliot and Fiona," he said, "ages fifteen, twins."

Her delicate jaw clenched. He was definitely on the right track.

"My employer respects you. You two should talk." Welmann reached into his jacket for his cell phone.

"Put that down."

Welmann's hand immediately obeyed and dropped the phone. That was a nice trick. Audrey Post had the juice all right.

"Look." He leaned forward. "I'm just a Driver, but if you're in trouble, I can talk to them for you."

She closed her eyes. "So sincere," she whispered. "That is sweet. But your employer and the rest of his family—I need not their favor, tolerance, or permission to do anything."

Welmann didn't get that. People didn't come to his boss's interest unless they merited favor or punishment. Both of which he knew how to do very well.

"How, precisely," she said, "did you discover the children?"

Welmann was no genius, but the lightbulb finally flicked on in his head. Were the kids what this game of cat and mouse between all the players was about? Sure, he'd been sent after the grandmother, but maybe—as impossible as this sounded—his boss hadn't known about the two kids.

He knew the smell of pay dirt, though, and those kids were *it*.

Welmann sipped his tea, chamomile in bone china. He was a black-coffee guy, but this was nice, too. It served as a much needed pause while he studied her and figured this all out.

Audrey Post shifted in her seat, her feathers ruffled.

"I didn't find out nothing. A guy named Uri Crumble did the legwork."

One of her eyebrows arched. "Crumble? Another Driver?"

"I don't think so. At least not one who works for *my* people."

Her smooth olive complexion paled and her lips parted in astonishment.

Apparently Audrey Post had a clue whom Crumble worked for, too. And if they were half as nasty as he heard they were, he could use that to flip her to his side.

"These are not guys you want to mess around with. They don't exactly play by rules."

She drew her hands together in a steeple. "Of course . . ." Her gaze drifted far away, deep in thought.

If Welmann had any advantage, he had to press it now. Make a connection with her and get her to trust him—for her own good. Sure, she had power; anyone could sense that. But no one had enough power to tangle with Crumble's pals . . . or for that matter his boss.

"You and your grandkids are in danger," he said with genuine concern. "I can help. The people I work for can help."

"I know they can," she whispered. She blinked rapidly, reached for her teacup, and sipped. She then stared into the bottom as if she could read the dregs.

The moment stretched into a vacuum of uncomfortable silence.

"Not to be rude or anything," Welmann said, "but time is running out. With Crumble involved, the sooner we move the better."

Audrey Post snapped out of her fugue and looked up.

She reached for a plate, picked up the eight-inch knife, and sliced the cake. "Would you like a piece, Mr. Welmann? Cecilia's cooking usually leaves something to be desired, but today she's made an effort."

Whatever connection Welmann thought he had made a second ago was gone. "I don't—"

"Understand?" A wry smile crept across her features. "This is, undoubtedly, for the best."

The danger he had felt before came rushing back. He flexed his ankle and felt the reassuring weight of his PT-145; he shifted forward, opening a gap between the chair and his spine so he could quickly draw his Colt Python if necessary.

Audrey Post inhaled deeply. "As you said, time is a consideration." She wiped the frosting off the kitchen knife with a napkin. "Now, you need to go, Mr. Welmann."

"If you don't let me help you, they'll find you."

"'They'? Which 'they,' Driver?" She pointed the knife's tip at his heart. "I think 'they' have already found me. You would have never come here without reporting in, would you?"

He stood, held up his hands in a universal nonthreatening gesture, and took a step toward the door. "Okay, lady. Take it easy."

Welmann saw his reflection in her knife. That was bad luck. He was sweating so much now his shirt clung to his chest. But what was the worry? There was no way she could reach across the table. And he had two guns. He had to get a grip and make as graceful an exit as possible.

"Maybe like you said," he whispered. "I should go."

"You must do as your nature dictates and serve your master." She rose from her chair, still holding the knife. "As I must do as it is in my nature to do: protect my children."

He suddenly smelled death in the room: the corpse-dry paper from all those books, a formaldehyde scent, and somewhere . . . blood.

Welmann drew his Colt Python and aimed at her center of mass.

Audrey Post didn't blink; she didn't even look at the gun. She dimpled the cake with the tip of her blade. "You never said if you wanted cake."

"What?" Confused, he lowered his aim a notch. "I thought you wanted me to leave."

"No. I said you needed to go." She looked up, locking stares with him. "As in 'be removed.'"

Instinct took over. It had saved his skin a dozen times before.

No thinking. The meat part of him knew to move before she spoke again, and the nerves in his arm and hand squeezed.

Welmann fired three times.

He blinked at the muzzle flash.

It took a split second for his vision to clear, and when it did, he saw a blur of steel arc at his throat.

No one could move that fast, not unless—

Audrey Post's knife slashed through his carotid artery and severed his spine.

7

MORE BIRTHDAY SURPRISES

Fiona pushed through the side door of Oakwood Apartments. She paused on the sidewalk and tugged at her dress—pulling it down and across her torso—trying to straighten out the pink fabric. It had all bunched tighter during her sprint down the stairs.

It was warm already. The late-summer sun blazed low in the sky. Fiona squinted at it and wished she could have worn shorts and a T-shirt today.

Eliot banged through the door behind her.

"No fair," he panted. "You . . . took off before . . . done tying my shoes."

"I won. Get over it." She frowned. "Who do you think that Mr. Welmann was?"

Eliot shook his head. "Grandmother said a 'friend of the family.' But she's never had any friends just drop by like that."

Grandmother, in fact, had no friends that either of them knew of.

Fiona walked up Midway Avenue and Eliot fell in at her side. "You think he knew Mom or Dad?"

"Why else would we be hustled out so fast?" she said.

Opening old wounds, Fiona thought. That's what Cecilia always told them when they brought up their parents. Thinking about the past when there was nothing to learn, she said, you might as well be picking at a scab.

But Fiona wanted to know something—anything—*everything* about her parents. They were this gigantic jigsaw puzzle, just waiting to be put together . . . only the entire box of pieces had been set on a shelf by Grandmother just out of her reach.

"Does it matter?" she said. "What would it change if we heard a lousy story from that Welmann person?"

"Nothing," Eliot replied in a faraway voice.

She touched the slick, too shiny fabric of her birthday dress. It was poofy around her hips, corset-tight across her chest. She looked ridiculous. She glanced at Eliot: a collection of seething stripes. At least he'd be in the kitchen where no one could see him.

Clouds crossed over the sun and a breeze stirred the leaves in the gutter. Fiona welcomed the shade. She flipped her hair off her neck, her skin already tacky with sweat.

Fiona concentrated, bringing into focus all the things that hadn't fit in her metronome-regular life: no homework last night; the Jules Verne book Grandmother had given violating her own rule; the broken teacup last night . . .

Cecilia's hands always shook but she never dropped anything. At 104 years old, that blanking out could have been a stroke. Fiona couldn't imagine life without her great-grandmother. More accurately, she couldn't imagine life *alone* with Grandmother.

"You think she's okay?" Eliot asked.

"Cee? Yeah. She's a rock."

"How'd you know I meant her?" Eliot asked irritated.

Fiona shrugged. "Just wondering about that busted teacup."

"You saw how Grandmother looked at it?"

How could you miss it? Grandmother had stared at that cup with an intense laserlike focus . . . as if she were counting out the individual molecules in the ceramic shards.

Chill bumps rose on Fiona's forearms, and the world seemed to tilt; the clouds overhead darkened.

"Listen . . . ," Eliot whispered.

Fiona didn't hear anything, though. It was as if someone had flipped a switch. No cars, no birds; even the hum of the power lines overhead had ceased.

There was a thumping, however; Fiona felt this rather than heard it, pulsing in the pit of her stomach.

Then tiny tinkling notes plunked over this, a jaunty rhythm just ahead: it echoed from the alleyway.

Eliot moved toward it, quickening his pace.

Fiona hurried to catch up—her disorientation increasing with every step.

She had the strangest urge to start skipping. As if she were a little girl and this was some extended game of hopscotch.

Eliot skidded to a halt at the alley's entrance.

The old bum sat there, cross-legged, smiling, playing his violin. About him lay tiny envelopes with violin strings uncoiling from a few. He had no bow, so he had the instrument in his lap and one hand slid over the neck; the other plucked the violin's new strings with great flourish as if his fingers were tiny Cossack dancers.

Eliot stepped closer to get a better look—near enough so the old man could have reached out and grabbed him.

Fiona touched Eliot's shoulder and gently tugged him back. She had wanted to yank him far from this bum, but she, too, felt like moving nearer, as if the sidewalk sloped precipitously toward the music, making it easy to move closer, harder to move away. Only her sisterly instinct to protect her brother held her back at all.

The old man looked up at them. His smile grew. The tempo of his tune increased.

The notes danced on the edges of her memory: a nursery rhyme. That was impossible because there were no nursery rhymes in Grandmother's house. This was older, though, *before* Grandmother. A tune someone had murmured to her when she was a baby.

Sleep, little baby, dance in your dreams, flowers and sunshine float down a stream.

The chill bumps on her arm were pebble hard. The music was the beat of her heart, the pulse of her blood; it made her sway; she tapped one foot.

Fiona smelled roses and freshly turned earth. She saw herself dancing around a whitewashed pole, colored ribbons about her, other children all laughing, singing, prancing round and round a maypole in an endless spiral.[6,7]

---

6. One legend regarding the Children's Crusade of 1212 is of a German shepherd boy having a vision of Jesus dancing around a maypole. This led the boy to inspire thousands of other children to march to the Mediterranean, where they believed the sea would part and they would journey to the Holy Land. When the sea failed to part, many children, without guidance or provisions, were subsequently sold into slavery by Roman traders. *Gods of the First and Twenty-first Century, Volume 2: Divine Inspirations,* 8th ed. (Zypheron Press Ltd.).

7. "Round and round the pole we go / dancing to a seraphim's song / with angled harp and bended bow / a merry tune and we skip and sow." Nursery rhyme from Father Sildas Pious, *Mythica Improbiba* (translated version), c. thirteenth century.

The air was a blur around her and the alley melted away as watercolors in a rainstorm.

She distantly felt her hand slip off Eliot's shoulder.

The only things that remained in focus were the violin strings, but even those were a smear—plucked so fast they were a haze of vibrations.

She took a deep breath, half inhalation, half sigh . . . and caught the scent of sardines, perspiration, and sulfurous burnt matches. *Unclean* was the word that rose to the forefront of her fading conscious mind.

And as she watched the vibrations fill her vision, another word came to her: *chaos*.

Even more than the thought of the unwashed old man, the thought of chaos, never-ending turmoil, strife, out of control and wild, washing her away . . . for a reason she couldn't articulate, it made her mad.

She glared at the strings, focused on just one, as if she stared hard enough—like Grandmother—she could stop this out-of-control feeling.

With a twang, the string snapped.

The old man's hand flew from his violin, and he sucked the index finger. After a second, he withdrew the finger and she saw blood welling where the string had cut.

The old man looked at Eliot, then Fiona, still smiling, and said, "Well, I'll be damned."

His voice was a rich and resonant alto. It wasn't what Fiona expected from someone who looked so shabby.

"That was great," Eliot breathed.

The man nodded at Eliot and took a little bow. He reached into the folds of his ragged coat and withdrew a wax-paper envelope. Inside were coiled strings. He gestured to the package like a stage magician, then smoothed one hand over the wood of his battered violin.

Fiona tapped her brother's shoulder and gently pulled him back. To the old man she said, "We have to get work . . . thanks." Her icy tone, however, effectively communicated that "thanks" was the last thing she meant.

The bum's smile faded a bit. He bowed again to them and started unwinding the broken string from the pegbox.

"Come on." Fiona pulled on Eliot.

Her brother whirled around and his eyes narrowed.

"If we're late two days in a row," she said, "Mike's really going to lose it."

Eliot's expression of annoyance melted into one of concern. "Yeah." He glanced back at the old man and waved. The man's full smile returned.

"Wasn't that the coolest thing?" Eliot whispered to her.

"No," she flatly replied. "It was kind of creepy."

Fiona did, however, begin to understand Eliot's fascination with music. It had taken her someplace else. Would it have been so bad if Grandmother let Eliot have a stupid radio? Or was she right? Would it have been too much of a distraction?

They hurried around the corner and found every parking spot near the intersection of Midway and Vine occupied with gleaming SUVs and Mercedes convertibles.

Tourists. Ringo's was going to be packed.

They crossed the street and ran up the stairs to the Pizza Palace.

Eliot held the door open and a blast of air-conditioning hit her. She shivered.

Mike was at the cashier's counter. He had just handed off a party of four to Linda to seat. He took one look at Eliot and Fiona and the color drained from his face.

"You've got to be kidding," he said. "Today's the start of the pinot noir festival in Napa—the place is jam-packed, and you two decide it's time to raid the Goodwill Dumpster for their costume rejects?"

Fiona flushed so hard that even in the air-conditioning she started to sweat again.

Eliot stepped forward to defend them. "Hey, don't—"

"The squirt," Mike said, cutting Eliot off, "can dress like whatever freak he wants to. But you." He looked Fiona over, disbelieving. "Wear that and everyone's going to lose their appetite."

This confirmed everything she had feared: her birthday dress really did look like a bad Halloween costume, all wrapped in a bow to put the finishing touch on her gift of humiliation.

She hated being in this family—with their rules, handmade clothes, never going anywhere. Tears blurred Fiona's vision and made the pink satin of her dress look like cotton candy.

"Wear this." Mike reached under the counter, grabbed a Ringo's T-shirt, and threw it to her. It hit her chest and fell to the floor.

She knelt, blinking as fast as she could to get rid of her tears, and picked up the shirt. An iron-on Uncle Sam smiled at her.

"I'll take it out of your paycheck," Mike told her.

Eliot's hands clenched.

"Okay," Fiona whispered. "No problem."

"And get one of the big heavy aprons from Johnny," Mike said, "to cover up the rest."

She nodded and her gaze dropped to the slate floor, no longer able to look Mike in the face. Her eyes and cheeks burned.

But she couldn't move. She didn't want the dress to rustle satin over satin and draw even more attention to it. And even if she could muffle the fabric, how was she going to cross the dining room to the kitchen with all those people watching her?

She froze there. Mortified.

Mike moved around the counter and grabbed her by the arm—his thumb digging into the crook of her elbow. Electric pain lanced down her forearm.

"Come on," he growled. "Get—"

She wrenched free of his grasp. That hurt even more, but she ignored the pain, her head snapped up, and she stared him directly in the face.

"Don't!" she hissed through gritted teeth.

Her humiliation had been a wounded animal, curled into a fetal ball . . . but it had been provoked one too many times—and it uncoiled, rose up, and bared its fangs.

She sensed Eliot close at her side . . . ready to try to punch Mike in the nose. It was good to know he was there for her when it counted.

Fiona let her tears fall without blinking and continued to stare Mike down.

"Don't," she whispered. It wasn't a whisper of shame, but one of barely contained rage. "Don't ever touch me again."

Mike's mouth opened, as if he were going to say something, but no words came out. He slowly nodded, held up both hands in a "calm down" gesture, and slowly backed away.

"Whatever," he breathed. "Just get that apron and get to work."

But he didn't look away . . . somehow still caught in Fiona's glare. He twitched and his lips curled into a grimace, as if it hurt to remain there under her withering gaze.

The bell over the door jangled, and a couple entered.

She blinked. The spell broke.

Mike turned to the customers and his smile snapped into place. "Table for two?"

Fiona took a deep breath. She turned, then she and Eliot marched through the dining room to the kitchen.

If anyone stared at her dress, snickered, or pointed, she didn't see. Her eyes were firmly fixed upon the floor again.

She pushed through the swinging doors and examined her throbbing arm. Where Mike had grabbed her, fingertip bruises dotted her skin.

"You okay?" Eliot gently asked.

"Yeah. Sure." For the first time in her life she had felt like hitting someone other than her brother. No . . . not just "felt like." She would really have done it.

For a split second Fiona had focused her hate to a white-hot intensity. For a moment, she had wished that Mike Poole would never touch her, or anyone else, ever again. She had wanted him dead.

8

MIKE'S HAND

Eliot stood before the vast double-basin sink, one side drained, one side filled with murky water, suds floating on top like clouds.

This job sucked.

But Eliot was no quitter. He finished whatever he started, even if there was no way of winning.

Working at Ringo's, though, wasn't just another game—like a vocabulary insult or a race down the stairs. Nothing was worth Mike's abuse every day. He didn't mind the bullying so much; he could take it, but what Mike did to his sister . . .

Eliot imagined plunging his boss's head into the sink and giving him a good dunking . . . drowning him.

He inhaled, startled that his fantasy had turned so dark—more startled that it gave him a real sense of satisfaction.

Eliot sighed. At least the lunch shift was almost over.

He gazed at the water and his fingers unconsciously tapped the basin. That nursery-rhyme tune was still in his head. It played over and over and he imagined shapes in the suds. A violin coalesced, then a smile, a flock of white crows, and a hand. That hand reached out, and spinning slowly in the water, the fingers grasped and closed about an unseen object . . . then the fingers writhed in pain.

Johnny called from across the kitchen, "Hey, you okay, amigo?"

Eliot shook his head to clear the music. "Zoning out. Long shift."

Johnny dumped a bag of frozen wedge-cut potatoes into the deep fryer. Boiling grease hissed and popped. He stepped back and lowered the splash guard, but not before drops spattered the concrete floor. Johnny frowned at this. He kept the kitchen antiseptic. He looked for a bucket and mop to immediately clean it up.

Fiona pushed through the kitchen door. She looked on the verge of tears.

Sweat soaked through the layers of cotton T-shirt, apron, and pink dress. Marinara sauce spattered her from chin to knees.

"Double table of *Lord of the Flies* kids," she said, and took a deep breath. "I'm ready for a break."

"I was just about to step out back," Eliot told her. "Get some fresh air."

She nodded, and they moved to the back door.

He'd broach the subject of Mike outside. They'd come up with some plan to get him off their backs.

Mike slammed into the kitchen. "Fiona wait," he called after her.

She stopped and turned, her hands clasping each other so tight they were white.

Mike with his wavy, combed-back hair and his strong chin looked clean, fresh, and honest—everything he actually *wasn't*.

"I wanted to talk to you," Mike said. He glanced at Johnny and Eliot. "You guys give us a second?"

Johnny rubbed his face. Eliot could tell he didn't want to leave Fiona alone with Mike. But Mike was the boss, and Johnny had a family to support with this job. He pulled the basket out of the deep fryer so the potatoes didn't burn. A few more drops of grease spattered onto the floor. "I'll take a smoke out back."

Eliot crossed his arms over his chest. There was no way he was leaving Fiona alone.

Mike glared at Eliot for a full five seconds.

"Okay," Mike said with a sigh, "you might as well hear this, too, squirt."

Fiona stood as tall as she could and stepped closer to Eliot, but her eyes couldn't quite rise off the floor. "What do you want?" she said.

Mike held up both hands, again in his patented "calm down" gesture. "I wanted to say I'm sorry. I didn't mean to grab you like that."

But Mike's right hand involuntarily flexed, and Eliot wondered if he was remembering how he took his sister's arm. From the glint in his eyes, it looked as if he had enjoyed it.

Eliot wanted this creep gone from their lives. Forever.

The little singsong nursery rhyme pranced through his mind.

"Let me take a look at your elbow." Mike came closer. He had on his most charming smile. "Is it bruised?"

Fiona curled her arm protectively to her body. "Stay away from me."

Mike halted and the warmth dissolved from his features. "If you two are thinking about telling Ringo anything—I was going to try and talk some reason here, but I think you don't want to be reasonable." His lips pursed. "You know what? Forget it. Both of you just grab your things and go."

"You . . . you're firing us?!" Fiona gasped. "For what?"

Eliot knew for what. So they wouldn't tell Ringo that his manager had assaulted one of his employees. Mike would fire them, and if they said anything, it would seem as if they were trying to get even. At least that's what Mike could say and get away with.

People like him *always* got away with it.

Mike's lips curled into a cruel smile. He was enjoying this.

"Why?" Mike said to Fiona. "Because you're both geeks. Because no one here wants to work with you. And because I *say* you're fired."

At that moment, Eliot had never hated anyone so much in his entire life. He wished Mike were dead.

Mike moved closer, maybe to better intimidate them, and stepped into a grease spot on the concrete floor.

He slipped and pitched face-first toward the deep fryer. One arm shot out to stop his fall—

—and it plunged into the boiling oil.

Mike screamed.

He rolled away. Fuming oil coated his arm up to the elbow, and the skin cooked and blistered.

He writhed on the floor, pulled his arm to him, then flung it away as the heat burned his chest.

Eliot and Fiona watched, horrified and dumbfounded for a heartbeat, then darted to his side.

The panic that had locked Eliot's brain vanished. He knew what to do. They'd both read and reread *Marcellus Masters's Practical First Aid and Surgical Guide*.[8]

8. Commissioned by Napoléon Bonaparte for his field surgeons. Bonaparte subsequently ordered all copies burned, proclaiming if such knowledge fell into the hands of his enemies, they would "gain miraculous powers to rejuvenate their front lines." Masters was made inspector general and was allegedly responsible for saving thousands of French soldiers. Four copies of the manual are known to exist and reported to have equivalent, in some cases better, advice to that in modern first-aid guides. Victor Golden, *Golden's Guide to Extraordinary Books*. (Oxford: 1958).

"Water," Fiona said.

"The sink," Eliot replied. "Careful. Don't touch his arm."

They lifted Mike by the armpits. He moaned and shivered. They dragged him to the sink and leaned him over the edge, his burned arm dangling into the basin.

Johnny ducked inside from the alley, cigarette dangling from his open mouth. When he saw Mike, he crossed himself.

"Call 911," Eliot shouted at him. "Now!"

Johnny sprinted to the phone on the wall.

Eliot swiveled the faucet over Mike's shoulder and turned on the cold water.

Mike screamed anew as water flowed down and over his burns. He tried to pull it out of the stream.

"No," Fiona whispered. "Keep it there or you could lose the arm."

"It's still burning," Eliot told him. "The grease is in your sleeve. We've got to cool it down."

Mike kept crying, whimpering, but he ceased trying to yank his arm away. He hung limp, sobbing, between them.

Eliot looked at his sister, and she looked at him. He knew that Fiona was thinking the same thing he was: that Mike had burned his *right* hand—the one that had grabbed her.

9

VACATION INTERRUPTED

$\int$ealiah lounged under a palm canopy on her private beach on the island of Bora-Bora, her home away from home.[9] The locals feared this place, claiming it was full of "bad magic," for when maritime disasters struck, the currents inevitably washed the bloated bodies onto this shore. Of course, she did nothing to dissuade these rumors; privacy was a thing to be treasured and, when lost, mourned.

The gold sun reflected off talc-white sand. Even filtered by the canopy and mosquito netting, it toasted her body. Her skin was the color of molten bronze, and a rope of wet coppery hair twined around her neck and throat in a serpentine embrace. She was full of form but slender enough to have been a model, which she might have considered as it would have served her unquenchable vanity . . . but men and women already fell at her feet.

She sponged off her brow, which was still wet from this afternoon's skinny-dip. She had played with the docile gray reef sharks and whipped them into a feeding frenzy until the waters were red and clouded with bits of the once-living. She licked her lips, tasted blood, and this blossomed into a rare smile.

It had been a delightful afternoon . . .

. . . about to be interrupted.

9. Although the proper pronunciation of this entity's name (title?) has mutated through all of history, most scholars cite the common ancient use of "say-lay" as the most accurate. *Gods of the First and Twenty-first Century, Volume 13: Infernal Forces,* 8th ed. (Zypheron Press Ltd.).

An intruder was on her beach.

Her eyes opened to slits, and in her peripheral vision she saw a shadow on the path where sand met jungle. Whoever cast this shadow obviously wanted her to see it as it swayed back and forth.

Sealiah toyed with the emerald that nestled in her navel and pretended to ignore the dark visitor. Perhaps it was a curious tourist who would grow bored and leave.

But it stayed there, wavering . . . waiting.

"Come," she said with an expelled sigh.

Why were these moments—just as she was about to fully and completely relax—always, without fail, with set-your-atomic-clock-by-it precision, interrupted?

She sat up and was, save for the emerald in her navel and the knife strapped to her calf, still nude from her earlier swim.

Her last lover had bragged to his friends, describing her as "raw with feral beauty." She had appreciated his compliment, but not so much appreciated his lack of discretion, and soon thereafter said lover learned exactly how feral she could be.

The shadow skulked from the jungle, resolving into a Samoan man in a black silk windbreaker, shorts, and baseball cap. He fell at her feet, worshipful, his face nestled an inch from her toes, which, had she allowed, he would have kissed.

"Enough." She waved her hand. "Up, up. Say what you came to tell me and then depart."

The man stood, towering two heads over her. He was Urakabarameel, sometimes Mr. Uri Crumble, or just Uri when she was in a familial mood, her second-in-command of special operations.

He backed away a respectful two paces, and with eyes cast to the ground he reached into his jacket and withdrew a tiny black book that bulged to the bursting point with extra pages and a rainbow assortment of sticky notes. He opened it, seemingly at random, and read.

"M'lady Sealiah," he said in a rumbling baritone voice, "the London Exchange dropped eight percent on opening. Our associates in Oxford are nervous. They demand you shore up the investment."

"Really? Well, 'demands' in the middle of my vacation are not granted." She crinkled her nose. "Sell my shares. I'll take profit today."

"That will cause a run on the three banks in—"

"I said *sell.*"

Uri bowed. "As you command."

"Let Britannia burn and sink into the sea for all I care. Next?"

"A minor thing: the ambassador from Manila has sent you a gift of three Andalusian mares. I did not know what you wanted done with the animals. He also wishes to schedule lunch at your earliest convenience."

"Oh, how wonderful," she cried with joy. "Andalusians are not animals, Uri. They are treasures to be loved." She tapped her lip with a curved, red fingernail and thoughtfully hummed. "Have stables constructed at the Subic Bay villa, and I will teach these magnificent ladies to gallop in the surf of the South China Sea. Tell the ambassador, Saturday, New York. At Mit-sukoshi's."

"Very good." Uri bowed again and started to back away.

"Was there anything else?"

"Nothing. Only a trivial matter that her ladyship need not bother with." He closed his book and tucked it into his jacket.

She grabbed his wrist, digging in her nails. He flinched.

"Show me."

Uri handed her his black book, and she flipped it open with her left hand. She continued to hold him with her right.

"It says, 'Post children.' Do we know them?"

"A low-level surveillance operation. A dead end. Two little nobodies."

"Oh?" She released her grasp and ran her index fingernail up his arm, tracing a bulging vein—then dug it into the crook of his elbow joint, breaking the skin, but not the blood vessel.

"Then why," she purred, "is it in your oh-so-important black-operations book?"

He fell to one knee and the impact sent a tremor through the sand. To his credit, however, he did not cry out in pain.

So Sealiah twisted her grasp—squishing vein and nerve bundle.

"A far-fetched clue," he grunted. "We thought it might lead to our long-missing cousin."

She released Uri. "Ah, yes, I recall. Something about a trust fund?"

"Yes, m'lady." Uri held the inside of his arm; a trickle of blood oozed and dripped upon the sand.

He stared at her navel and the emerald there; the glint of it reflected in his eyes. He coveted her power, of course; it was the way of her kind to take whatever they had the strength to hold. But couple such a gaze with the obfuscation of these Post children . . . and she smelled treachery. It made her pulse pound with anticipation.

Uri looked away, his face burning.

Or perhaps, to her great disappointment, there was no conspiracy. Nothing on Uri's part but a moment of wishful thinking. What a pity that he would ever only be her faithful lapdog.

"What about them?" she asked.

"We intercepted a money transfer from what we thought an old double-blind account of Louis's. We were able to trace the originator of the transfer: a lawyer's office in central California. I retrieved the pertinent files personally. Trust fund for two children. It is unrelated to our case."

Uri reached deep into his windbreaker and drew out a slim laptop computer. He opened it, turned it on, and presented it to Sealiah.

She sat, waiting for the file to open.

Uri rifled again through his jacket, deeper, losing his entire right arm into its folds, and removed a card table, which he set up and placed before her.

She set the computer on the table. On-screen, two high-resolution scans appeared. A boy. A girl.

They had smiles as if someone had a knife at their backs and had forced them to grin. Siblings obviously. Possibly twins.

Uri fumbled about within his windbreaker, and there was the clink of ice in crystal and the slosh of liquor. He set a Bloody Mary on the table.

Sealiah took it and sucked the salt off the rim.

"There was only one minor complication," Uri admitted. "A Driver appeared at the same office. I made sure these files were destroyed before he got there . . . but still, the coincidence is interesting."

"Driver," Sealiah whispered. "What would a Driver be doing fumbling about on this matter?"

"He could not. If I understand the pact correctly, they are not allowed to interfere with our affairs. As we cannot theirs. As I said, a mere coincidence."

"Indeed . . ."

She looked again at the children. There was something familiar.

Sealiah increased magnification on the boy's eyes. Mixed in with the swirls of gray, blue, and green, a hint of nobility was reflected in the windows of his soul.

She returned to normal magnification and squinted so her acute vision blurred.

Yes, the boy's eyes, the slender but strong bridge of the girl's nose, the high cheekbones and arching brows on both. How could she have missed it? Whoever had camouflaged them had done a masterful job: they had transformed divine into dull.

She looked up and pinned Uri with a hard stare. "And is there any update on the whereabouts of Louis Piper?"

"Nothing after the last sighting in Albuquerque. He was living in a cardboard box."

"Yes . . ." She traced her fingernail over the girl's strong chin. There was something else about these children. Something *not* connected to Louis, but an influence just as powerful.

They were *not* two little nobodies. These two were definitely involved, and possibly of great value.

"Is he connected to this?" Uri moved to get a better look at the computer screen.

It was an outside, remote, astronomically distant possibility. But when any such possibility was the only one that accounted for the known circumstances—a boy and a girl that bore no small resemblance to the man who had been her most powerful adversary, and a Driver who worked for those wielding power equal to her own—such things could simply not be ignored.

Nor could such a possibility be confronted alone.

"Summon the Board of Directors."

"I'm sorry, m'lady," Uri said, coughing a slight chuckle. "For a moment I thought you said 'summon the Board.'"

She narrowed her green eyes to slits and looked deep into his so there could be no miscommunication. "That is precisely what I ordered."

Uri backed away three paces. "I shall do as you command, as ever, but I remind you that the Board will demand tribute if so summoned by a non-Director."

"Yes, and you will see to that personally."

Uri bowed so she could not see his face, but Sealiah nonetheless sensed his apprehension.

"It shall be as you say. And the children?"

"Find them," she said. "Shadow them. Report to me the moment you see or hear anything."

Uri was as loyal as any of their kind could ever be. As tribute to the Board, he would be her eyes and ears to its inner workings . . . losing him, however, would be like cutting off a limb.

She had to send him, though. Whom else could she count on to double-deal and backstab on her behalf?

Meanwhile she had to prepare for the gathering of the Board. There were weapons to sharpen and armor to mend.

She looked back at the smiling children on the computer screen.

Indeed, one did not face one's brothers and sisters without taking careful precautions against carnage and bloodshed.

SECTION

II

FAMILY

10

A DOG IN THE ALLEY

The paramedics closed the back of the ambulance and pulled out of the alley behind Ringo's. Eliot and Fiona stood to one side, staying out of the way. They watched it roll around the corner and then were alone.

Eliot felt sick. He swallowed, but it did little to help.

There'd been a crowd of customers at first, but they'd left after they had seen Mike writhing on the gurney, saw his gauze-swathed arm . . . and got a good whiff of deep-fried flesh.

That smell was stuck on Eliot, too. That's what was making him sick. Oil permeated his shirt and pants—all of it laden with the burned-skin and french-fry scent.

Johnny pushed through the back door, balancing a load of abandoned pepperoni pizzas and fettuccini Alfredos. He tossed them into the Dumpster and slammed shut the lid with a bang.

He turned to Eliot and Fiona and said, "I called the owner. He's going to the hospital and then coming here to check the kitchen . . . see exactly how this happened." Johnny took off his gloves. Emotions quavered over the large man's face and he looked exhausted. "You didn't see what Mike slipped on, did you?"

Did Johnny think they had anything to do with the accident? Eliot had wanted something bad to happen to Mike. But *wanting* something to come true was a lot different from *making* it happen.

Besides, Mike had gotten exactly what he had coming to him. Eliot's mouth went dry and he felt ashamed, but that didn't change that he also considered this poetic justice.

Fiona moved to Johnny and set a hand on his shoulder. "What happened wasn't your fault."

Eliot then understood Johnny's question. Johnny thought *he* was to blame, that Mike had slipped on a grease spot on the floor because he hadn't mopped it up.

"There's no way anyone can blame you," Eliot chimed in. "You keep everything in the kitchen, well, clean enough to eat off of."

Johnny nodded, but the large man looked on the verge of crying.

If this was anyone's fault, it was Mike's, hustling Johnny out of the kitchen before he could clean up the very grease Mike had slipped on.

Johnny shuddered out a huge sigh. He focused on Fiona and then Eliot. "You two go home. I've closed the place for today." He wandered back to the kitchen door, paused as if he wanted to say more, but instead just slammed the door shut behind him.

"Poor Johnny," Fiona said.

"You don't think anyone's going to get into trouble?"

Fiona turned to Eliot and slowly shook her head. Was she thinking it, too? That they *were* to blame? Eliot couldn't stop remembering the pictures he'd seen in the soap suds before this all happened—a smile, a flock of crows, a hand that writhed in pain and then melted.

"We better get home," Fiona said. "Grandmother's going to wonder why we're late."

Something behind the Dumpster moved: with a rustling of clothes, a man stepped from the shadows. It was the bum with the violin; although to Eliot's disappointment, he didn't have his instrument. The old man opened the Dumpster, rummaged around, and retrieved a slice of pizza.

Eliot had never seen him standing before. He was taller than he thought he'd be. Despite the rag of a trench coat he wore, he stood straight, even looked regal somehow as he brushed aside the tangles of yellowed-white hair that fell upon an acne-scarred face and the cold pizza he munched.

Fiona snorted with disgust and started back to Ringo's, but Eliot stayed. He wanted to talk about music. Maybe even hear more.

"You know," the old man said, and paused to swallow, "you two were very brave."

Fiona halted, turned, and crossed her arms over her chest. "That pizza you're eating—that's stealing."

"I'm sure the landfill will miss it." The man ripped off a hunk and ad-

mired the sardines and crust. "Ah, bread and fishes; there is no finer meal."
He chewed and mumbled around the food, "Did you know pizza comes
from Naples? Originated in the 1800s?"

"That's not right," Fiona said, slipping smoothly into her lecture voice.
"Cato the Elder in his *Histories of Rome* wrote about flat bread baked with
olive oil, herbs, and honey." One of her brows arched. "That was the third
century BC."

"Or seventy-nine AD," Eliot added, not wanting his sister to show off without him. "There were shops in Pompeii that were supposed to be pizzerias."

A flicker of annoyance crossed the old man's face, then his blue eyes
sparkled with amusement. "Marvelous. You are both so smart."

He took another bite. "Do you suppose while Pompeii was being covered with scalding ash"—he threw one arm over his head—"her citizens
engaged in one last orgy of pizza consumption?" He dramatically flared
his fingers upward. "Before—poof! I have seen the body casts. No one was
eating."

Eliot looked at his sister, who stared back at him, her mouth open.

The old man licked the grease off his fingertips. "Which brings us back
to the events of today: you two should be proud of yourselves, rescuing
your friend from the fire."

"It wasn't a fire," Fiona muttered, and her gaze dropped to the street.

"He wasn't exactly our friend, either," Eliot said.

"All the more reason for congratulations." The old man wiped his nose.
"Even seasoned doctors sometimes cannot stand the smell and the sight of
skin sloughing off like a rotten sweater sleeve." He smiled, showing yellow
teeth and goocy dough.

Fiona made a tiny strangled noise. She moved to Eliot and said, "Let's
go. This guy is weird."

He *was* weird. And he scared Eliot, too. But the old man fascinated him
as well. He didn't seem like the same broken man they'd seen every day on
their way to work. Something had brought him back to life.

"Your music," he said to the man. "The tune you played this morning."
Eliot crept closer to him.

Fiona hissed a sigh of exasperation.

The man focused on Eliot and his grotesque smile faded. "You remember that?"

"Remember? Yeah!" To actually have someone play music. *For* him.
That was the best birthday present anyone had ever given him.

Eliot hummed the tune. His hand tapped the rhythm on his pant leg, mimicking the finger action along a pretend violin, even with little vibrato motions as if he were actually playing. It was silly. He wasn't really playing. He'd never played a musical instrument in his entire life.

Eliot expected the old man to laugh, but he didn't.

The old man's eyes widened as he scrutinized Eliot's playing motions. "Most cannot remember. I mean, it's such a trivial tune—in and out of one's head like a noble sentiment." The man snapped his fingers and narrowed his gaze at Eliot. "But, indeed, you do remember . . . and more."

The man considered Eliot a long moment, seeming to decide something, then said, "The song was a child's song. It is called 'Mortal's Coil.'" He glanced at Fiona. "Did you enjoy the song as well?"

She shrugged. "It was okay." Fiona looked past them to the entrance of the alley.

Eliot looked, too.

A dog stood there sniffing the air. It was tall like a Great Dane but as hefty as a rottweiler. Its brown fur bristled, and its giant head cast back and forth along the asphalt, snorting and sniffing. It wore a collar studded with green rhinestones.[10,11]

Eliot imagined that dog grabbing him and shaking him like a squeaky toy until the stuffing fell out. Something instinctive told him to run. Now.

That was stupid. The dog was after the leftovers in the trash. That's all.

The old man took two steps forward, placing himself between Eliot and the dog. He held one hand back to warn Eliot to stay behind. With his other hand he reached into his coat and pulled out a scrap of newsprint, holding it toward the animal.

Eliot craned his head to see.

Printed on the paper was a design that looked like a dozen geometric

10. "Benedictine monk Kay Allenso dug at the Oracle of the Dead's shrine at Cumae looking for an entrance to the underworld and the riches of the dead. Find it he did, but barring the way were three hounds. One black as pitch; one golden as flax and snorting fire; and the largest bristled chestnut fur and wore a collar of green stones. This beast beheld him with eyes dull that drowned his soul. Allenso escaped, but he was a man be-damned." Father Sildas Pious, "The Damned Monk's Tale," *Mythica Improbiba* (translated version), c. thirteenth century.

11. "Dogs of sins chase man of cloth / bite and shake for what he 'roth / Beg for mercy, none do hear / dragged and torn to bits, my dear." Translated (Greek) handwritten annotation in the Beezle edition of *Mythica Improbiba* (Taylor Institution Library Rare Book Collection, Oxford University), Victor Golden, *Golden's Guide to Extraordinary Books* (Oxford: 1958).

proofs—all overlaid upon one another. The harder he stared, the more lay-ers appeared. There were tiny symbols as well; Eliot recognized Greek let-ters, cuneiform, and others unknown to him that floated in a swarm of elusive meaning.

Maybe it was a hologram, having the illusion of depth when you held it just right, but really only two-dimensional.

Eliot blinked and pulsing afterimages swam across his vision.

The dog's head snapped up and it glared at the paper. It sniffed more vigorously than ever; a trickle of snot ran from one nostril. Then it shook its head and wandered away.

"Dogs," the old man muttered. "One can never be too careful with them. Personally, I'm more of a cat person."

He wadded the scrap of paper and tossed it away, but not before Eliot saw that the design he thought he had seen was gone.

The old man turned his attention back to them. "Now, what were we talking about? Pizza? Or music?"

Fiona sidled closer to Eliot, nudging him with her sharp elbow, and jerking her head back toward Ringo's.

Eliot saw the shadows in the alley were long. The sky overhead was al-ready the lead gray of afternoon as the coastal clouds covered Del Sombra like a blanket.

He shook his head, clearing the cobwebs; he felt disoriented. It must be the shock of everything that had happened today. He felt dirty, too; his clothes were still soaked with sweat and grease and a burnt scent that he never wanted to smell again.

"We better go," he told the old man. "Sorry, our grandmother will—"

Fiona tugged him along as she headed for the door.

Eliot saw curiosity and shock register upon the old man's face.

"Pass along my regards," he said, giving them a short bow, then returned to the Dumpster. "We will meet again, no doubt."

Eliot hoped so. And he hoped next time the man had his violin.

Fiona and Eliot moved quickly through the kitchen. Puddles and smears of congealed grease covered the floor. Eliot noted palm prints frozen in the stuff where Mike had thrashed about . . . and he felt a sharp pang of guilt.

Fiona continued without pause and he followed.

The dining room was deserted, which never happened this late in the afternoon. With the tables half-cleared, it felt haunted.

Johnny was at the front, locking the door.

"See you tomorrow," Fiona said.

"Sure," Johnny said, and shook his head.

Eliot wanted to tell him again that it wasn't his fault, that Mike had slipped; it was a simple, stupid accident.

Johnny seemed to sense this and tousled Eliot's hair. "Go home, amigo. No worries, huh? Everything will be okay. You'll see."

Eliot nodded and gave him a little wave as he and Fiona walked away. He didn't believe everything was going to be okay. Sure, what happened was really an accident. But people got blamed all the time for things that weren't their fault. Eliot was intimately aware of how that worked.

They turned onto Midway Avenue. The oil in Eliot's sneakers made a squishing noise as he hurried to keep up with his sister.

He only now noticed that she still wore the heavy apron and T-shirt over her pink birthday dress. Probably because everything she had on was saturated with grease, too. It would be a race for the shower when they got home.

The sun broke through the clouds and lemon-gold shafts played a game of tag up and down the street.

"You think . . . ," Eliot started.

"Yeah," Fiona said, "we got the arm cooled down before the burn went too deep." She slowed almost to a stop. "There'll be scars, though. Up to the elbow." She had a faraway look in her eyes, probably seeing Mike struggle and writhe, holding his tortured arm out in agony.

"Kind of weird," Eliot whispered.

"What's weird?" Her voice had a defensive edge. She turned to face him, concern wrinkling her forehead.

"Just everything today. Those books from Grandmother. The music that guy played. What happened at Ringo's."

Fiona chewed on her thumbnail. "Did you . . . I mean, I wanted something bad to happen to Mike, you know?"

Eliot nodded. "Same here. But we didn't do anything wrong. He slipped. That's all."

"But it was his *right* hand." She took her finger from her mouth and fidgeted her hands.

Eliot saw Mike's arm in his mind; it had been burned up to the exact spot where he had grabbed Fiona. Chill bumps popped over his skin.

"So what?" Eliot told her. "He's right-handed. Makes sense he would hold out that hand to brace a fall."

The faraway look in Fiona's eyes remained. "This is the worst birthday ever." Her gaze dropped to the sidewalk. "Grandmother's going to do something when we get home, I bet. Extra homework for being late. Some new rule for ruining our clothes. It's so unfair."

Eliot felt it, too: a sense of their impending doom. He could imagine a double load of geometry and essays tonight. And the worse thing was they'd have to go back to work tomorrow. He'd have to spend the day in the kitchen, smelling the same scorched scents.

If this was how fifteen was going to start, he wished his birthday had never arrived.

Not knowing how to lighten their mood, Eliot decided to try to annoy his sister. It might distract them both at least. He opened his mouth to call Fiona an *Orycteropus afer*—because of her long face. She'd know it, of course; *Orycteropus afer*, or the common aardvark, started almost every dictionary they'd ever read. But before he could speak, he sensed the light change behind him; he turned and halted midsyllable.

A shadow slinked around the corner of Midway and Vine, half a block back. It was that dog, the same monstrous canine that had been in the alley.

Fiona looked and saw it, too.

The dog's nose huffed over the concrete, leaving smears of drool as it advanced.

"Come on," Fiona said, and walked briskly away from the animal. "Don't run. That'll just make it chase."

Eliot fell in next to her.

A beam of sunlight appeared and disappeared through the clouds; the dog cast multiple shadows, angled this way and that, seeming to have a dozen shadow heads.[12]

Whomever that dog belonged to should have kept it tied up. An animal that big could hurt someone. Eliot again had that vision of the thing grabbing him in its jaws and shaking.

The dog looked up and saw them, started trotting, still sniffing, but now with its head up, catching the scents on the air.

12. Cerberus, or "demon of the pit" in the original Greek, is the iconic three-headed canine reputed to guard the entrance to hell. Of note are variations on this beast having fifty, or as many as one hundred, heads. The myth lives on in modern times, transmuted into a similar dull brown or black dog, albeit with a single head, who appears as a harbinger of death and misfortune to all who see him. *Gods of the First and Twenty-first Century, Volume 6: Modern Myths,* 8th ed. (Zypheron Press Ltd.).

"Run," Eliot whispered. "We can make it. We're almost home."

They had less than half a block to get to the apartment building. They could slam the steel security door in that thing's face.

Fiona nodded and they broke into a sprint.

The dog scrambled to find purchase on the concrete and ran after them.

It was faster than Eliot thought it would be, closing the distance like a greyhound. As it crossed from light to shadow, it seemed to flicker, brown fur blending in perfectly with the dark as if it vanished and then reappeared.

Eliot stumbled and landed on one knee, scraping his skin. The knee exploded with pain. The rest of his leg went numb.

Fiona grabbed him and, without pausing, pulled him to his feet.

The dog was forty feet behind them. It would be impossible to outrun it now.

"Go," he told Fiona. "I'll be right behind you."

"No way."

The dog accelerated, growling as it sensed the end of its chase—and its prize.

But then it skidded on the concrete, claws screeching and scrabbling for purchase, and came to a halt.

The dog sniffed the air, bobbing its massive head about.

"Shoo!" Fiona shouted.

It glared at her, eyes flashing red as they caught and reflected the light.

Eliot couldn't believe his sister had the nerve to do that. But if she could, then so could he.

"Go home!" Eliot yelled.

The dog stared at him, too—seeming to stare *through* Eliot—but then it blinked, woofed once, and quickly turned and trotted away.

Eliot watched it go and exhaled, not believing it had given up so easily. Relief flooded through his limbs. He and Fiona turned and he half walked, half limped toward their building.

A dozen steps and he could stand on his own. His knee hurt with each step, but it was getting better.

Then Eliot noticed an odd car parked in the shadow of the building. He hadn't seen it at first because it was midnight black. It was as big as a limousine—not that Eliot had ever seen one for real—but it also had the low-slung, stylized curves of a racing car. His eyes slid off its mirror finish. The motor purred, idling.

The tinted back window hummed and thunked closed.

Had someone been watching them?

"Come on," Fiona told him, "let's get inside."

Eliot realized that maybe he and Fiona hadn't been the ones to halt the charging dog, after all. Maybe the person inside that car had somehow stopped it.

And for some reason, that worried him.

11

THE SILVER UNCLE

The instant Fiona opened the door to the apartment, she forgot about Mike, the dog, and the old man in the alley. Something was different in here.

When Fiona was three years old, Cecilia had brought home a stack of magazines filled with nearly identical side-by-side pictures and captions that read, *Spot the difference*.

Eliot could always find the missing elements, but Fiona had a talent for spotting objects that had been altered—the stripes on a curtain that had changed to spots, for example.

She stood, staring, sensing something similarly "off" in the apartment.

Fiona called out, "Cee?"

There was no answer.

The dining table had been cleared. The cake, tablecloth, banner, and books that had been there this morning were gone. The surface, even the hardwood floors around it, had recently been polished.

High on the bookcase by the window, however, was a glob of birthday-cake icing. It had dried there, no longer looking strawberry pink, instead now ruby red.

Odd that Cee would miss something like that.

Fiona carefully approached the offending particle and reached out to touch it.

Cee entered from the kitchen, huffing with exertion as she carried a large cardboard box.

"Oh," Cee said, blinking at them. "You're home."

"Let me help you." Eliot took the box from her and buckled, barely able to turn and set it with a thud on the table. Inside were books.

"We're late," Fiona admitted. "Sorry."

They were supposed to have been home at four thirty. It was five now. But Cee was so distracted that she hadn't even noticed their oil-soaked clothes.

Cecilia glanced at the grandfather clock in the hallway, then at the still open door. "Oh, yes, of course, you're late." She moved to the door, closed and locked it, then turned to them and clapped her hands together. "Your grandmother and I have another surprise for you." A smile fluttered to life on her thin lips.

"What's that?" Fiona asked.

"A trip. We're going away for a tiny bit."

"Where?" Eliot asked. "What about work?"

Cee's smile faltered. "Ah . . . *where* is a birthday surprise. You'll enjoy this. And we won't be gone too long." She left his question about work unanswered.

Fiona's feeling of something "changed" here sharpened. She concentrated as if this were one of the old spot-the-difference pictures, and she realized it felt as if something had been *cut* from the picture with surgical precision.

She blinked and the feeling vanished . . . but she did see one thing that didn't fit: a cake crumb on the floor.

Cee followed her gaze. "Oh, clumsy me." She bent down and plucked it up. "Now, you two go pack. You'll need clothes for three days. And don't forget your toothbrushes." She handed a paper grocery bag to each of them.

Fiona unfolded hers. The bag would be her luggage.

"When are we leaving?" Eliot asked.

"And where's Grandmother?" Fiona said.

"Soon," Cee told Eliot. "And your grandmother is just making a few final arrangements."

"I've got to take a shower," Eliot muttered, and started toward the bathroom.

Fiona gave her great-grandmother a glance, searching for answers, but Cee's smile brightened and deflected the stare. Fiona turned and caught up to her brother.

"Subtraction," Fiona told him.

Eliot halted. "Even," he said with a sigh.

"Okay, one, two, three—"

"Seven," he said.

At the same time Fiona blurted out, "Three."

Eliot smirked. The difference was four, an even number. He'd won. Humming, he entered the bathroom. "I'll make it quick," he called back.

She wondered if any hot water would be left.

From the closet she grabbed their worst towel, so worn you could see through it, and ran it through her oil-smeared hair, sponging out the worst of it.

Inside her bedroom, Fiona closed the door and flipped on the single shaded lamp in the corner. The one window in her room had been built over with bookcases. Usually her books gave her a measure of comfort, but tonight they felt smothering. She passed by her globe and gave it a spin.

Fiona stripped off the apron and T-shirt, then removed her birthday dress. The pink fabric peeled off her skin, clinging with a layer of semi-congealed grease. She wiped it off with the towel.

A mirror sat on her dresser and she caught a glimpse of herself. Her skin glowed. Her hair, normally a mass of frizz, curled into ringlets around her face.

For an instant, at this particular angle, she thought she looked normal— not a geek supreme at all.

She turned this way and that, fascinated at the way her hair looked. It was dark and glossy like black ribbons, and set against her pale olive skin, her face didn't seem too long, either.

She almost looked beautiful. Even for an instant in just the right light, was that possible?

Before she could decide, her hair fell into her face, ruining the look.

Fiona changed into clean underwear and a new bra and slipped on gray sweatpants and shirt.

She carefully avoided looking into the mirror again. She wanted to remember the moment when she had fooled herself into thinking she looked normal.

With a deep sigh she gathered clothes and set them into her paper bag.

She also grabbed the rubber band stretched over the dresser handle. She had liberated this from a bundle of asparagus. The purple band looked good against her skin. She had to be careful though; there was RULE 49 to remember.

RULE 49: No rings, earrings, chains, medallions, amulets, or any ornamentation of metal, wood, bone, or likewise contemporary polymers classified as "jewelry" (piercings are also similarly forbidden unless proscribed by a licensed acupuncturist).

Sometimes she took the rubber band to work and wore it like a bracelet, fully aware that she was breaking a rule. It made her feel like a rebel, flaunting one of Grandmother's rules for the entire world to see.

Fiona wrapped the band around a bundle of socks to secure them—just in case Grandmother asked, she wouldn't have to lie what it was for . . . just not tell her the entire truth.

But where were they going? Would she even have a chance to wear the rubber band?

Fiona drifted to her antique globe. It was old with yellowed oceans and faded polar ice caps. Alaska was called "Russian America," Hawaii the "Sandwich Islands," and Texas was half-filled with stripes showing it as "disputed territory" before it had officially joined the States in 1845.

She loved her globe. Her fingers smoothed over its curve, hoping this surprise birthday trip would take her far away. She brushed over Africa and landed in southern Europe. So unlikely.

Cecilia and Grandmother probably had a weekend trip to San Francisco in mind. Still, it would be different from stale old Del Sombra.

She needed her toothbrush, so she marched into the hall and saw that Eliot had uncharacteristically vacated the bathroom in a timely fashion. A cloud of steam roiled along the ceiling, leaving little hope there was hot water left. She grabbed her toothbrush and tossed it into her bag.

From the front door came a knock: four polite taps.

Fiona stopped and waited for Cecilia to come out and answer it as she usually did.

"Cee?" she called.

Four knocks again.

Fiona went to the door, threw the dead bolt, and opened it.

A man stood before her. He was tall and lean and wore a gray sports jacket and black turtleneck. He was as old as Grandmother with silver hair shorn along the sides and a thick wave across his brow.

He smiled at Fiona as if he knew her.

Fiona looked away. "My grandmother isn't home, sir. She should be back in a few minutes."

"Of course." His voice was liquid velvet. "But I didn't come just to see her, Fiona. I came to visit you and your brother as well."

Fiona looked up.

Three things struck her simultaneously.

First, the intensity of the man's light gray eyes reminded her of Grandmother's. But where Grandmother's stares could be razor-edged, this man's eyes were just as intense while somehow inviting.

Fiona realized that she had stared far longer than was polite, but she couldn't help herself.

Second, the way he stood in the doorway reminded her of Mr. Welmann, the man who had come earlier today. Fiona had completely forgotten about him. What *had* he and Grandmother talked about?

And last, he made her think of the old man who had played his violin for them this morning—in that they were exact opposites. The man before her was refined and scented with spicy cologne. While Eliot's friend was rough, ill-mannered, and reeked of sardines and sulfur.

Fiona rarely met anyone new, yet today she had bumped into three strange men.

"Third time is the charm," the man told her.

She blinked, startled. "I beg your pardon, sir?"

"Yours was the third apartment I tried. I suspected Audrey would have roosted in one of the top corners of this fine establishment. I was not wrong."

Fiona found herself smiling at the man, blushing at the same time, but not looking away as she might normally do. It was as if he were an old friend, although she wasn't quite sure how that felt since she had no "old friends."

"May I come in? I am your uncle Henry. Henry Mimes."[13]

Grandmother had never mentioned any uncles, aunts, or cousins. Fiona

---

13. Henry Mimes (aka Horatio Mimes, H. M. Seers, and Hernandez del Moro), the alleged uncle to the Post twins, appears in hundreds of paparazzi photos starlet-draped and flesh pressed with technology moguls and the dictators of budding tropical "republics." Brought in for questioning by Interpol and the FBI a dozen times, he has never officially been charged with any crime. IRS probes found him the CEO, CFO, and president of hundreds of dummy corporations shielding no apparent assets. His age and nationality remain undetermined. The only thing that can be determined about Henry Mimes is that he is elusive, mercurial, and nothing is certain about him. *Gods of the First and Twenty-first Century, Volume 11: The Post Family Mythology,* 8th ed. (Zypheron Press Ltd.).

knew this man spoke the truth, though. How else could she explain the resemblance and the feeling that she had known him for a long time?

She stepped back. "Of course, please come in."

Normally strangers were not allowed inside, but Fiona didn't give it a second thought. The man who claimed to be her uncle—whom she *knew* was her uncle—radiated authority and warmth. She couldn't let him linger in the hallway.

As he crossed the threshold, the clouds outside parted and silver light streamed through the window.

He gazed at her. "You look so like your mother when she was your age. Her hair curled just as yours does, and it drove all the young men wild. Although, I have to admit you are a tad lovelier than she ever was."

Fiona's face heated to fever intensity. She wanted to drop her gaze, but Uncle Henry smiled and made her feel so at ease, her embarrassment was instantly quenched.

"You knew my mother?" This was the stupidest thing she had said all day. He had to know her. He would have been their mother's brother.

Uncle Henry's smile never faltered, but Fiona thought she saw a slight mental pause, then he said, "Oh, yes, we were very close." He looked about their apartment. A crinkle of puzzlement crossed his otherwise smooth features. "You said you lived here with your grandmother? Audrey?"

This question confused Fiona. If he was their uncle, that made Grandmother *his* mother. And for some reason that sent a chill down her spine. How could someone not know where his own mother lived?

With a casual wave he forestalled her unease. "I see you don't understand. Your grandmother and I go way back, but not as you are thinking. Your mother and I were *half* brother and sister. Same father. Different mothers."

Fiona's lips formed a perfect O, but made no sound as a thousand new questions flooded her mind.

She saw he was waiting for her to say something. "Would you like to sit?" she offered. "Are you thirsty? We have milk or juice."

"I am fine, thank you. I drank, quite a bit actually, on the journey here." He turned to the kitchen door as it swung inward. He spotted Cee and cried, "Cecilia!"

He moved to her and embraced the old woman.

Cee stiffened in his arms, her mouth open and her eyes wide. She disentangled herself. "You . . . !"

He held up a finger. "Say not another word, sweet lady of the Isle of Eea. Let us savor this moment of reunion."

Cee shut her mouth and her eyes narrowed.

Uncle Henry cooed, "Yes, you are just as I remembered. Not aged a day in . . . what has it been? Ten years?"

"Sixteen," Cecilia whispered. "Audrey will be here soon, fool. I suggest you depart."

Uncle Henry's jovial features flattened and the room seemed to chill. He tilted his head and looked past Cecilia to the bookcase and the smudge of congealed strawberry frosting. He touched it, then lifted the finger to his nose.

"Really?!" He laughed, wiped his finger on a handkerchief, then set one hand upon her shoulder. "Such the joker. I love you for it, too."

But Cee wasn't joking. Something was obviously wrong.

Fiona edged toward the front door, as Eliot emerged from his bedroom. He paused at her side. "I heard voices . . ." He stared at Henry.

"Our *uncle*," Fiona explained.

Eliot searched her eyes, seeing uncertainty there.

Uncle Henry turned and his face brightened again. "Eliot!" He took Eliot's hand into both of his and shook it as if they were the best of friends.

"Uh . . . hello, sir," Eliot managed.

"Please, if you must be so formal, call me Mr. Mimes. Although I prefer 'Uncle Henry' or just 'Henry.' I have so few living relations who can call me that. You would do me a great honor."

His smile was infectious and Eliot was charmed by it, smiling in return.

Cecilia snorted. "You have so few relations for good reason."

Fiona wanted to trust Uncle Henry, but she, of course, trusted Cee more. Great-Grandmother's hand drifted protectively to her throat—a gesture she only made when Grandmother was displeased with her.

Something was *very* wrong.

"*Mimes*," Fiona repeated. "Is that French?"

"Our family is from France," Uncle Henry told her, "and many other places. We have cousins, aunts, and uncles in all parts of the world."

Fiona blinked. "We have *more* family?"

"You know them?" Eliot asked. "Did you know our mother, our father?"

Henry tilted his head, thinking, then said, "Oh, yes. Although your father"—he shrugged—"not so well as your mother. There was quite a scandal when they fell in love." He shot a playful glance at Cecilia. "Shall I tell you how they met?" He pulled out a chair and sat.

"No," Cee said. "Tell them nothing."

"Why not?" Fiona asked.

Maybe the thing she sensed that was wrong was that no one had ever told them anything about their family. Fiona wanted to know, even if it meant defying Cecilia . . . even Grandmother.

Uncle Henry craned back to Cecilia. "Yes, why not tell them?"

"I . . ." Cee stepped back.

"Ahhh," Uncle Henry said in a soothing tone. "See? There is no reason."

Cecilia crossed her arms over her chest, but added no further protest.

"Go on," Fiona said. "Tell us."

Uncle Henry rubbed his hands. "It was in Venice many years ago during the city's carnival. This was a grand celebration, dancing and festivals in the street, parties all day and night, and everyone wears a mask. Some masks are plain leather, others encrusted with gold leaf and silver dust, jewels, and feathers from exotic birds. This is where your mother and father met—both in disguise." He held out his hand with fingers splayed over his face for dramatic effect.

Fiona was captivated. She could almost hear the crowds in the street and the slosh of boats on the canals.

"As I said," Uncle Henry continued, "I did not know your father as intimately as your mother, but I do know he cut a dashing figure, he was a polo player, and always immaculately tailored. They said his smile was irresistibly sly. And although I have this secondhand, they said no woman could resist him once he settled his gaze upon her." Uncle Henry seemed to be looking at some faraway place, then he came back. "Quite the ladies' man . . . which was sometimes the problem, I would imagine."

"How is *that* a problem?" Eliot asked.

"Imagine everyone always liking you the instant they met you. Imagine them falling in love with you because of the shape of your nose, or the style of your hair. No, he was a lonely man, for no woman actually *knew* his heart, his desires, or his dreams." Henry patted his chest. "So your father came masked. Hiding his face and covering his smile to avoid the attention, and yet drawn to the crowds all the same, seeking companionship. That is where he found your mother."

"Was she beautiful, too?" Fiona asked.

Henry sighed. "More lovely than I can say with mere words, child. Men fought duels over who would have the honor to ask for her hand. All of whom she turned down, of course. Secret admirers showered her with anonymous gifts, but they meant nothing to her. She thought romance a trivial thing for trivial people, and those in love nothing more than fools."

Fiona would have given anything to get a gift from a secret admirer . . . just once. What would it feel like to be the center of someone's world?

"But if she wasn't interested," Fiona said, "why did she go to the festival?"

"She didn't believe in love, but she *wanted* to," Henry explained. "She was a woman of intellect and purpose, but also very lonely. She once told me she went to parties to watch people fall in love, wonder at their imprudence, but also envied them their happiness . . . no matter how temporary." A flicker of sadness passed over his face and he leaned closer. "It was something she never thought she would understand, let alone experience— but she was wrong."

Fiona and Eliot sat on the floor, huddling closer to Uncle Henry.

"She saw your father at a ballroom dance. He sat as she did watching the others. They were the only two there not enjoying themselves . . . which is when he noticed her and approached.

"He had seen this masked woman reject every request to dance, so he told her he only desired her conversation and perhaps learn why so many people behaved like idiots.

"She acquiesced, and they discovered they had much in common: their philosophies; both had traveled the world and spoke many languages; and both, while being loved by many, had never themselves been in love. They strolled cobblestone streets, rode gondolas, and observed lovers, no longer ridiculing them as they had earlier, but studying them and questioning why the human heart was so easily captured . . . and then inevitably broken.

"They rested at a little café overlooking the Canale Grande and sipped minted coffee as the moon set and the stars wheeled overhead. There were lemon trees in planters nearby scenting the air with their perfume. As the sun rose over the water, your father gently removed her mask and she undid his.

"They stared into one another's eyes. All talk of the affairs of the heart, sharing their loneliness, finding a like intellect, stopped in that moment. What would have been impossible had they knowingly set out to do it had occurred by accident: they had fallen in love."

Fiona rocked onto her heels, entranced by the tale. "What happened next? Where were they married?"

"I believe so, in Paris," Henry said, looking past her, remembering. "I know not the entire story."

Fiona looked to Eliot puzzled, then Eliot asked the question on both their minds: "How could you *not* know?"

Uncle Henry let out a long exhale. "That is where their story becomes complicated. Your father's family and our family were not on speaking terms then; in fact, they made the Montagues and Capulets in *Romeo and Juliet* look like they were throwing a friendly bar mitzvah. There was an agreement that one family would never meddle in the affairs of the other, and this certainly qualified as—"

His words died as if the air had been sucked from his chest.

A shadow fell upon Uncle Henry's face.

Fiona and Eliot turned.

Standing in the doorway, holding the knife that had cut their birthday cake . . . was Grandmother.

12

FISH IN THE SKY

Eliot looked back and forth between Uncle Henry and Grandmother.

Eliot had to have gotten up too quickly. With the blood draining from his head, it seemed that Uncle Henry and Grandmother cast shadows *at* each other. But the only light was from the dining room window—to Uncle Henry's right . . . so neither shadow was cast at the correct angle.

Eliot blinked, but the darkness remained. He stepped closer to Fiona until they bumped elbows.

There was something else between Grandmother and Henry—like clear glass, straining under pressure. He felt it pinging and crackling in the air, about to snap.

He had to do something.

"It's—" His voice broke, so he cleared his throat and tried again. "It's Uncle Henry," he told Grandmother.

Light and shadow returned to their proper angles.

Grandmother sighed. "So I see." She half closed her eyes as if staring into a bright light. "And, as usual, telling tall tales."

"Simple embellishments," Henry replied.

"There are no lemon trees along the Canale Grande," Grandmother told him. "And their father was no polo player."

Henry shrugged and looked like a boy caught with stolen cookies, but he quickly sobered. He stood and his hands spread apart in conciliation. He tried a smile, but decided against this, and it faded. "I've come to talk."

"Something you are exceedingly good at." Grandmother's words were dead, cold things that made Eliot shiver. She held the knife, point down, gripped firmly.

"Just talk," Uncle Henry said.

"I should have known you would show up," she said. "Drivers never work alone. While Mr. Welmann 'talked' to me, he sent his partner to you." Grandmother arched one eyebrow. "And no one is quicker than you, are they?"

Uncle Henry's gaze drifted to her knife. "Very few."

The hair on the back of Eliot's neck stirred. The way Grandmother held that knife, her arm tense, it looked dangerous even tip down. As building manager she carried around hammers, pry bars, even knives to cut away old, moldering wallpaper. This knife, however, was the one Cecilia had out to cut their birthday cake. It looked different from this morning. Darker. Wrong.

Fiona must have sensed something amiss as well because she moved away from Uncle Henry to Cecilia.

Cee encircled her protectively with one arm and beckoned to Eliot.

Eliot moved to her side. He was apprehensive, but he stood just far enough away to avoid her embrace. He didn't want to look like a baby.

Uncle Henry glanced at them, then said, "They are wonderful, Audrey. Smart. Polite. Pristine. Everything I expected."

Eliot stood taller, taking great pride at this summation of his character; although he was unsure what to make of *pristine*.

How exactly did Uncle Henry fit into the family? Eliot had overheard him say that he was half brother to their mother. So he wasn't related to Grandmother?

That didn't *look* right, though. As they faced one another, it was easy to see Uncle Henry and Grandmother had the same silky silver hair, smooth olive skin, slender noses, wide eyes, and commanding presence.

"Are you going to stab me?" Uncle Henry said. "Or shall we talk?"

Grandmother said nothing.

Eliot heard his own heartbeat. Surely Uncle Henry was kidding.

Yet Grandmother didn't move; her face was a stone mask; her eyes were two shards of broken razor-edged mirror.

Eliot kept his mouth shut, listened, and watched.

Next to him, Fiona trembled but kept silent as well.

"Will you do to me what you did to Welmann?" Uncle Henry made a throat-slitting motion.

Mr. Welmann was dead? Killed by Grandmother? The thought horrified Eliot.

"I am no easily replaced Driver, though," Henry continued. "In fact . . ." His face split into a devilish grin. "I am utterly irreplaceable, loved by the entire family."

Grandmother snorted. "As a *jester.*"

"Perhaps." Henry made a flourish with one hand. "But should anything happen to my handsome fool head, the League would act. They would find you and the children." His smooth voice cooled to ice. "Then, there would be *no* talking."

Eliot felt sensation draining from his arms and legs. He took a numb step back, closer to Fiona and Cee.

"Well played," Grandmother said deadpan to Henry. "Of course you would not appear without other pieces on the board to protect you."

He tilted his head, acknowledging the compliment. "You must come with me. Tonight. They want to see you . . . and them. That's what I came to say." Uncle Henry held up both hands. "Kill not the messenger, my dear."

The knife in Grandmother's hand shuddered as her grip tightened.

Eliot no longer heard the clock in the hallway ticking. There was only silence and the palpable tension of Grandmother and Uncle Henry staring at each other.

Then Grandmother exhaled and nodded.

"Good," Uncle Henry said.

Grandmother dropped the knife and it clattered onto the floor. She moved to Fiona and Eliot.

Uncle Henry plucked up the knife and set it high atop a bookshelf. "My car is waiting."

Grandmother knelt before them and took their hands. Her fingers were ice-cold. "We are going on a trip. Right now."

Eliot had never before seen Grandmother give in to anyone. She looked older than she had a moment ago. It felt as if she held his and Fiona's hands to draw strength from them, as if she might never get up.

He wanted to comfort her, hold her, but was afraid she would pull away. It was the only time that she had touched them this way or seemed the slightest bit vulnerable.

"Where are we going?" he asked.

Grandmother ignored him and asked Cecilia, "They are packed?"

"For a weekend trip," Cecilia replied. "I thought we . . . but what does it matter what I thought? I will get a few of my things." She gathered herself as tall as her frail frame permitted.

Grandmother stood as well. Her strength returned; Eliot felt it flow back into her limbs as she dropped his hand.

She glanced down at Eliot and Fiona. "Say good-bye to your great-grandmother, children." Then to Cecilia she said, "You will not be coming. There is no room in Henry's car."

Cecilia's face fell.

Eliot and Fiona went to their great-grandmother and hugged her.

She hugged them back so tightly that Eliot thought she might break bones. She gently pushed them away. Tears were in her old eyes. "Be brave," she whispered. "Do no let them separate you. You are stronger together."

Eliot saw an intensity he had never before seen in Cee's gaze—as if she had so much to tell him . . . but no time left to do so.

Grandmother ushered them to the front door, which Uncle Henry held open.

"This is the right thing to do," Henry said to Grandmother as they passed into the outer hallway.

"Do not patronize me," she replied. "It is the *only* thing to do without spilling a river of blood. And that has yet to be seen."

Eliot looked back once at Cee. She waved at him with shaking hands.

Uncle Henry closed the door and asked them, "Bathroom? This might take an hour or so."

They both shook their heads.

Eliot was quiet as they marched downstairs. Fiona wasn't even trying to get ahead of him as she usually did. He was dying to talk to her and find out everything Uncle Henry had said before he started to listen, but he dared not say anything in front of Grandmother while she was in this mood.

Once on the sidewalk, Uncle Henry motioned for the sleek black limousine-racing-car amalgam parked in front of the building. It rolled silently toward them.

He opened the back door for Fiona and waved for Eliot to follow her inside.

Grandmother nodded, confirming this was okay.

Still, Eliot had the feeling once he got inside he might not ever come back here. He glanced up at the sky; clouds obscured the setting sun and it looked like a bank of smoldering coals.

Eliot reluctantly ducked into the car.

Inside it was larger than he thought possible. Two sets of seats faced each other. He slid in next to Fiona so they both looked forward.

Grandmother and Henry eased in, opposite them.

Henry closed the door.

A partition between the back and front section slid down. The driver craned around. "Where to Mr. Mimes?"

This driver was only a year or two older than Eliot. He wore a black leather jacket, gloves, and cap. His hair fell into his face as he gave Fiona a quick once-over, glanced at Eliot, then warily focused on Grandmother.

"The island, Robert," Uncle Henry told him. "Take the northern route. No one is in the mood for sightseeing."

"Yes, sir." The boy driver turned around. The partition slid up.

The car smoothly accelerated away from the curb, and Eliot sank into the padded seat. Del Sombra became a blur of storefronts as they sped over rolling hills. Black oaks and fields of sunflowers flashed by. They had to be going ninety miles an hour.

Grandmother sat unimpressed with this reckless velocity. "What are they going to do with us?" she asked Uncle Henry.

Henry flipped open a compartment. Within were crystal decanters and glasses. He sloshed amber liquid into a glass, dropped in ice cubes, swirled, and offered it to Grandmother.

Eliot smelled the odor of alcohol and smoke.

Grandmother didn't even look at the proffered drink.

Uncle Henry shrugged. "I have no idea what they're going to do. They've never known how to deal with you." He toasted her and took a sip. "It's really the children that intrigue them—which, of course, you already knew, or why go to all this trouble?"

Eliot couldn't stand it anymore. He'd been taught never to interrupt when adults were talking; but they were talking about his sister and *him*.

"Who's 'they'?" he demanded, surprised how forceful he sounded. "You're talking like we're not even here."

Grandmother quirked one eyebrow at this outburst, but otherwise appeared deep in thought, digesting Henry's words.

Uncle Henry smiled at Eliot and Fiona and made a little "calm down" gesture with his hands. He turned to Grandmother and spoke a language Eliot had never heard before.

Fiona cocked her head, listening with intense concentration. She was good with foreign languages; maybe she'd decipher it.

Yellow streaks outside caught Eliot's attention. Beyond the tinted windows he saw the orange-vermilion steel cables of the Golden Gate Bridge. The nighttime lights of the bridge flickered on. The car sped through the automated FasTrak toll lane without slowing.

More time had to have passed than he realized. Had he nodded off? It had only been a minute.

He nudged Fiona and nodded outside.

She stared, astonished at faraway Alcatraz island. She shook her head and whispered, "Did we even slow down in San Francisco? For traffic?"

"I . . . don't remember," he said. "I don't think so."

Eliot watched the Pacific coast race alongside his right, a steep drop into churning, dark waters. It was impossible to tell how fast they were going. This car took curves labeled with twenty-mile-an-hour warnings without a bump or slide and passed other cars as if they were frozen.

Grandmother interrupted Uncle Henry's rapid-fire talk with her own alien-sounding words.

Henry nodded and held up seven fingers. He ticked off one finger and spoke one word for each as he did so.

Grandmother grimly nodded.

At the last finger he pointed at himself.

Grandmother patted his hand and squeezed it.

This surprised Eliot. Her gestures of affection were as rare as passenger pigeons—at least toward him and Fiona.

Fiona nudged him and nodded out the window.

Eliot turned and almost jumped, because now they plowed through a snow-covered road; granite cliffs stretched upward on one side, endless pine forests on the other. The thing that made his heart pound in his throat, however, was the sun . . . still ablaze on the horizon.

But he'd seen the sun set in Del Sombra a few minutes ago; it had been night. There it was, though, hovering along the edge of the earth.

"North," Fiona whispered. "That's where they said we were going."

He understood what she meant, but it wasn't possible.

During the summer, the farther one traveled north, the later the sun set, sometimes remaining aloft all "day." For that to make sense, however, they'd have to be where? Alaska? Past the arctic circle?

The car slowed and turned right onto a dirt track.

He strained to see more, but the sky darkened and fingers of frost spread over the glass. Warm air blew from a vent onto Eliot's feet and he wriggled his toes.

"With that look on your face, I'd say you've become ranivorous," Fiona said.

Eliot tore his gaze from the window and looked at his sister. She tried to smirk, but it trembled uncertainly on her lips.

He appreciated the attempt to start a round of vocabulary insult, trying to spin a protective cocoon of normalcy between them . . . on what was turning into the weirdest birthday they'd ever had.

He didn't feel like playing, but he couldn't help it, either. He wasn't going to let her just win.

"Maybe I turned into an eater of frogs," he replied, "because of Cecilia's cooking. Better ranivorous than larvivorous."

Fiona wrinkled her nose, so Eliot knew she got it. *Larvivorous* meant feeding on larvae.

She opened her mouth to reply, but said nothing. She instead stared past Eliot.

The frost had melted off the car's windows, and beyond was a luminescent curtain of candy-apple red wavering against the night. Fringes of ghostly green flared, and the entire display shook like a sheet of sparkling stars.

"Aurora borealis." Eliot spoke as if he were reading it from an encyclopedia. It was easier to fall back on book knowledge because it always made sense . . . even if the context was insane.

To see the aurora, they had to be *very* north.

It had only felt like fifteen minutes, but Eliot worked through the math. California to the north pole? To travel that far they'd have to be going faster than the speed of sound. He would have noticed a sonic boom.

They watched the lights shimmer like a moonlit tide overhead.

Uncle Henry switched to English and spoke to them. "Did you know there is an old Scandinavian translation of *aurora* that means 'herring flash'? The old Vikings believed that schools of the tiny silver fish reflected moonlight into the sky to create this spectacle. Even today some think they can see fish in the sky."

Eliot looked again to see if that was indeed what this aurora looked like, but the silhouettes of mountains now blocked the view.

The car wound along a serpentine road, made a right, and slowed, entering a town lit with neon and pools of amber from shaded lampposts. The houses here were old stone and plaster, jammed wall to wall, four stories tall, and on each floor were picture windows reflecting a harbor and boats with jewel-like lights.

Eliot fixed upon a white sign with red letters: HOVERCRAFT FÄRJA I KM.

The partition lowered and the driver asked, "The long way around, sir?"

"A boat ride, I think," Uncle Henry said.

The car maneuvered onto a ramp and rolled past other cars waiting in line to board a ferry. Uncle Henry's car was waved ahead and parked on the prow.

The boat cast off and powerful fans roared to life. From their forward vantage, it seemed as if the car flew over the moonlit waves, only a slight pitch and roll to their motion.

"That sign was in *Swedish*," Fiona told Eliot. "It said 'hovercraft ferry.'"

"I can see," he replied, slightly annoyed.

Then he understood what she was trying to tell him: they were *in* Sweden.

He traced the only route that made sense. Up the coast of California to Alaska—that accounted for the later sunset, then crossing the arctic circle and down through Scandinavia—which explained the auroras.

That trajectory fit the known facts . . . but it didn't fit the laws of physics. He touched the butter-soft leather seats of Uncle Henry's car. This was a car, a fancy, powerful car to be sure—but still powered by gasoline and limited by ordinary thermodynamics.

Eliot desperately wanted to talk this over with Fiona and see if she had come to the same impossible conclusion.

One glance at Grandmother and Uncle Henry, however, stifled any comment from him. They placidly watched the water roll by, unperturbed by having just crossed the world in an hour.

They docked and Uncle Henry's car rolled off first and sped onto a six-lane highway. The limousine blasted past Porsches and Ferraris—flashing headlights so they moved aside.

"We're almost there," Uncle Henry assured them.

Eliot glanced at Fiona and they shared the same unspoken question: where exactly was "there"? He wasn't sure he was ready for an answer.

The highway turned into a two-lane road, then a single cobblestone lane winding alongside white stone cliffs. More water appeared on his right, gray under a colorless sky.

The car stopped at a set of steel gates. Beyond was a park and a building that looked like a museum. The gates parted and they eased onto the property.

As Uncle Henry's car moved closer, Eliot studied the architecture of the main building: it had two wings and a dome of gold in the center. Scrollwork and carvings of gods and spirits embellished its columns. It reminded him of the Capitol in Washington, D.C., a little smaller, but somehow grander.

The car halted. The driver hopped out and opened the back door on Grandmother and Fiona's side, offering his hand. Grandmother moved past him as if he weren't there. Fiona clasped his hand, smiled, and looked down.

Eliot clambered out after Uncle Henry. "Where are we?"

"My humble home," Uncle Henry replied, inhaling deeply and spreading his arms wide in a theatrical gesture. "Isola del Bianco Drago."[14]

The sea sparkled in the distance as the sun climbed over the horizon and left a red-gold smear upon the waters.

It was sun*rise*.

The only way that was possible was if they were half a world away from Del Sombra.

The bright light cleared the fog from Eliot's mind. The dreamlike car ride and everything that had happened since he got up this morning— those things no longer mattered. He sensed something else was about to happen to him and his sister . . . something bad. Like when Mike burned his arm.

"What now?" he whispered to Grandmother.

"Now," she said, shielding her eyes as she gazed at the sun, "I suspect you will meet your relatives. Prepare yourselves for the worst."

14. Isola del Bianco Drago (Island of the White Dragon), aka Bianco Drago (White Dragon), does not appear on any map or satellite photograph (although it is referenced in several Post Family memorabilia). Though it is often suggested as lying near Crete or Sicily, the Greek and Italian governments deny the existence of this semilegendary island. *Gods of the First and Twenty-first Century, Volume 11: The Post Family Mythology,* 8th ed. (Zypheron Press Ltd.).

13

BLOOD AND LAW

Audrey and Henry marched through a covered walkway outside his mansion. Seamless white marble mirrored their steps so it looked as if they walked upon clouds.

On one side there were alcoves with works of art: a Greek vase; a bronze Babylonian winged bull; and a life-size Chinese clay Han warrior.

These relics sat protected from the salt air behind glass, which is where the past belonged: contained and protected, but with an understanding that it was dead and too fragile to be touched.

Audrey knew that too many of her kind dwelled on ritual, superstition, and the old ways—when all their concerns ought to be firmly fixed upon the future.

The other side of the walkway was open to the sea. Water churned upon the rocks below in sympathy to her agitation.

"They will be safe where they are?" she asked Henry.

"Of course," he said, feigning offense. "You have my most solemn word. They will be treated as if they were my own children."

Audrey halted and frowned.

"I mean," he said, "better than my own."

Henry had had two sons. Neither had lived long . . . or well.

She continued walking, quickening her pace. "Remind me why I didn't kill you?"

He ignored this and said with sobriety, "They are safe for now, but I cannot guarantee this after the Council's interview."

"Interrogation," she corrected.

"As you say."

A balcony jutted over the cliff, and Audrey paused there and let the sea spray her face and the winds ruffle her short hair. She inhaled. The Aegean was swirls of turquoise and foam.

"So unlike the Pacific," she said. "I have missed these waters."

Henry joined her, perching precariously on the railing. "I'm sorry that you left us. I know you had to . . . try I mean." He looked at the water a hundred meters below. "I'm sorry that you return to us under a cloud. I will stand with you through this trial."

Audrey took a careful look at the Fool. He was as handsome and as polished as sterling. He was the closest thing she ever had to a brother, yet that meant so many different things to their people . . . none of which translated into trust. She loved him, but Henry had to be handled as one would a rabid wolf.

It was ironic that he of all people offered to stand by her. Henry continued his adventures and sexual exploits without consideration of their ramifications. His greatest gift seemed to be escaping the responsibility of his actions. Whereas Eliot and Fiona were the result of a single mistake: long ago a man and woman thought they loved each other.

It was a mistake Audrey had devoted the last sixteen years of her life trying to resolve.

She turned away from the comfort of the sea and continued along the walkway.

They turned a corner and faced the arching bridge that connected Henry's estate to a finger of stone rising from the water. Unlike the surrounding white cliffs, this stone was black.

On top were low hills and an orchard of wind-bent olive trees. Nestled in the center were a series of descending concentric rings, an amphitheater. Audrey had seen Sophocles and Shakespeare here and listened to the poetry of Jim Morrison under the stars.

There would be no poetry today.

Instead there would only be the Council, judgment, and a good chance that blood would be spilled upon the ancient stones.

Audrey hesitated before stepping onto the bridge.

Was she ready? After sixteen years of hiding and restraint? It was such a short time . . . but so much had changed. Could she face them? If this didn't go her way, was she ready to kill Henry and the others? *All* the others?

She decided in an instant: if Eliot's and Fiona's lives were at stake, yes, she could. She would.

Henry spoke and the winds seemed to tear the words from his lips. "I urge caution, at least until you see who is here."

That sounded very much like a threat from nonthreatening Henry. She didn't like that.

She stepped onto the bridge. There was no going back now. The winds ripped at her clothes and made the stones in the span resonate as she walked over them.

As she set foot on the sliver of land, the winds died.

It was like a sealed chamber, silent; the air was not only still, it felt dead upon her skin.

Audrey held her head high and descended the steps of the amphitheater wearing her usual mask of ironic composure.

Waiting for her, sitting on the inner ring, were four people.

Her eyes fell upon a man with broad shoulders, wearing a leisure suit and white shirt unbuttoned to the middle of his massive chest. His face was chiseled and tanned. Long, dark hair curled about his shoulders, and a Genghis Khan mustache draped over his square chin. He was ferociously attractive . . . not that he understood relationships of that nature. He was Aaron.

Audrey instantly understood Henry's warning.

Aaron could stop her if she moved against the Council. Few could match her skills. He was one of them. If they clashed, they would both likely die. And with her dead, the children would be unprotected.

They had checked her power.

Aaron's black eyes met her steel gaze with a mixture of appreciation and determination. He understood that she understood that he was willing to die if required.

She exhaled, controlling her fear and rage, trying to keep her head figuratively and literally.

How had they made Aaron part of this? Bribes, blackmail, or bullying? He hated the Council's politics almost as much as she did.

On Aaron's right was an old man, his head ringed with a circle of snow-white hair. He wore flip-flops, shorts, and a Grateful Dead T-shirt. He sat cross-legged, and about him were scattered notebooks and astrological charts. He smiled and nodded with a practiced naïveté that Audrey knew he had never possessed.

This was Cornelius, a perennial member of the League Council, one of the wisest among their numbers. He kept that wisdom to himself, however, for his own inscrutable purposes.

Audrey considered him neither ally nor enemy.

The man on Aaron's left was Gilbert, an athletic man with golden hair and beard. He stood to greet her, his thick arms thrown wide for an embrace.

Audrey held up one hand and stopped him.

It was genuine affection, she had no doubt, but she could not tolerate another's touch now. Gilbert had once loved her, and it would be all too easy to let herself fall into his strength . . . and let go of hers.

He nodded and bowed, seeming to understand.

Gilbert occasionally dabbled in politics, but never seriously. He rarely took anything seriously. He would only be here to debate such a serious matter if he had been pressed into service.

He looked uneasily over his shoulder at the fourth member of the Council: a woman.

She sat apart from the men. Her age could have been twenty or forty; she had a timeless beauty that seemed to defy age—as long as she hid it with makeup. She wore a black dress with embroidered red roses. A small black hat sat upon her dyed red hair. Her face was pale, lips the same rose red as in her dress, and light brown eyes set into an appraising gaze that gave away nothing.

She was Audrey's younger sister, Lucia—lovely, hateful, and scheming.

Audrey already knew what she was thinking. The black dress and hat gave it away. Lucia wore her emotions upon her sleeve: the black dress was for a funeral.

"I am so glad you could join us this morning, Sister." Lucia's voice was smooth and musical. Men adored it, but it grated upon Audrey's ears. "And the children?" Lucia asked Henry.

"Being fed and safely sequestered on the estate," he said.

"Good," she purred. "I cannot wait to meet them."

The enmity between Audrey and her sister was timeless. And unlike Eliot and Fiona, they would not be settling their differences with a game of vocabulary insult.

Lucia had to be after the children. Audrey took two steps toward her. She vowed if any were to die today, Lucia would be the first.

She then noticed something. "There are only five of you. Where are the other two Council members?"

"En route," Lucia assured her. "We decided to start as this matter is most pressing."

Henry left Audrey's side and sat between Lucia and the others. "We do have a quorum," he said.

Technically this was true. Five Council members could pass binding resolutions. This was rarely done, however, as it was perceived as subverting the normal process, one that had been designed to be thoughtful and slow.

Lucia would never attempt such a thing unless she knew the outcome. She had to have leverage on Aaron and Gilbert. Henry's allegiance, however, was like the winds, ever changing and unpredictable. And old Cornelius would be impervious to her charms or blackmail.

That gave Lucia three out of five votes. So was this already decided, and debate merely a formality, an opportunity for her to watch Audrey squirm?

Not if she could outmaneuver her little sister.

"Let us begin." Lucia rang a tiny silver bell. "I call this session of the League Council of Elders to order. All come to heed, petition, and be judged. *Narro, audio, perceptum.*"[15]

"I move we skip the reading of last session's minutes," Henry said with hopeful raised eyebrows.

"Seconded," Aaron immediately added.

"So moved," Lucia noted, and set her hands upon her lap. She looked meaningfully at the Council members and then at Audrey. "Today we seek guidance on how to deal with a delicate matter. My oldest sister has in her care two children of questionable origins."

Audrey didn't like this dancing about, nor did she appreciate the not-so-subtle insults. She kicked sand at her sister, showering her dress.

Audrey caught Aaron covering his lips to hide his pleasure at this act of rebellion.

"Too many words fill your mouth," Audrey said. "Simply make your proposition: you want them killed."

Lucia smiled—all fake sweetness. "Still the knife, Sister? Cutting to the heart of the matter and ignoring all the nuance of a situation."

Audrey had a smile of her own for her sister. This smile, however, was

---

15. Latin for "Speak, listen, learn."—Editor.

one born from imagining cutting out Lucia's heart and dropping it onto the lap of her funeral dress—an artistic still life of rose red and fresh blood.

Lucia's smile withered.

Gilbert asked, "Are they of age? Before I judge them, I would know if they are mere children."

"We decide this *before* they reach adulthood," Lucia said. "That is when the trouble begins."

Henry chimed in, "Their ages are irrelevant. Others will take action before such considerations as puberty."

Aaron crossed his arms over his chest at the mention of these "others," and old Cornelius looked up from his notebooks, worry creasing his already wrinkled brow.

In comparison to the "other" family, the troubles of *this* family were mere squabbles.

Audrey replied, "Fiona is barely a woman. Eliot is on the cusp of manhood."

"When were they born?" Cornelius held a pencil over a notepad. "The precise time if you would, please."

He was going to chart their stars. Audrey welcomed this delay. It would give her time to think.

"Fiona was firstborn," she said. "Fifteen years to the day at eight thirty-four in the evening, Paris time. Eliot entered this world ten minutes later."

Cornelius scratched his ear as he jotted a few figures. "Leos," he murmured. "Many planetary bodies in conjunction. The girl is the dominant of the pair. Very strong. Both of them. The boy will be an artist." He flipped through several books and charts, pages fluttering under his touch.

"These children are no threat," Audrey said. "They have been isolated from the families and from their potential. They are perfectly normal." When she thought about everything Eliot and Fiona had already given up, and now to have all their sacrifices end here—it seemed terribly wrong.

"How could they be 'normal,'" Gilbert asked, "with such an extraordinary mother, and such a fiend of a father?"

Henry gave an indifferent wave of his hand. "To be fair, they are intelligent, polite—but true, otherwise rather dull."

"It is not their age or their power that is the problem," Aaron said. "It is their lineage." He pinned Audrey with his dark stare. "The fact that they are from *both* families—that is the only issue here."

"You make a good point," Lucia said. "What does it matter how they were raised? I am sure you did a superlative job, Sister. But this comes down to *our* contractual obligations and *their* blood."

Cornelius set his calculations down. "Their stars are aligned in a most confusing pattern." He nodded at Henry. "Even more so than yours, I'm afraid."

"Stars," Gilbert muttered, "have never led me to truth. What does it mean, old man?"

"It means they are in balance," Cornelius told them, "scientifically equivalent, poised to tip one way or the other." He fumbled in his pocket for a box of matches. He struck one and set fire to his calculations. "They will·be a great boon for *one* family."

Gilbert asked, "Then should we not exploit them?"

"If a weapon can be so easily turned against you," Aaron replied, "best to destroy that weapon."

"Should we not first consider the treaty?" Henry asked. "If the children favor the mother genetically, then they are ours to judge. The Council must enforce the law. . . ." He let these last words trail off and glanced at Lucia.

This was theater. Audrey sensed the veils of deception, layers piling one over the other to smother the truth. What Aaron had said about their lineage and Cornelius about their being in balance, however, stuck in her head.

Lucia said, "What if they favor neither mother nor father? Some hybrid as Cornelius suggests? What if they are balanced between the two families? What are our legal options then? One family may not meddle in the affairs of the other. That is the law."

"Half of one family, half of the other," Cornelius mused. "A loophole?"

"Those two could open a door for the other family," Gilbert said. "They could use them to *legally* meddle in our affairs. There would be new alliances, power shifts, and possibly war."

"All they have ever wanted is the tiniest opportunity to wreak havoc upon us," Aaron added, and turned to Audrey. "Much more is at stake than two children."

Lucia stood and brushed the sand from her dress. "I am sorry, Sister, but the Council must act for the good of the family, for everyone. The children must be removed." She hesitated, licked her lips, then asked, "Shall we put it to a vote?"

They were silent, waiting for Audrey to act . . . or not.

Audrey knew this conclusion was already foregone, for her benefit so she would perceive this as rule of law and not seek a vendetta.

Two words turned over in her mind: *blood* and *law*. Concepts strong enough to kill Eliot and Fiona . . . or perhaps strong enough to save them?

"So then," Lucia said with a dramatic sigh, "all in favor of removing Eliot and Fiona Post—"

"Wait," Audrey said. "You cannot."

Aaron shifted, and his powerful legs tensed. He was ready to move, to fight if need be.

"You must allow the Council to vote," Lucia purred. "No one, not even you, is above the law."

"I agree," Audrey said. "Even you, Sister, are not above it. You may not take action against the children *because* of the law."

Lucia narrowed her eyes. "What trick is this?"

Cornelius murmured, "Oh, interesting. I see your point, yes. Our treaty with the others."

Henry leaned back, crossed his legs, and smiled.

"You wish to protect this family and preserve our neutrality with the others," Audrey said. "In fact the Council is legally bound to uphold our neutrality treaty with them." She took a step closer to Lucia—who backed away. "You, in fact, are not allowed to interfere with the others because of that treaty."

Aaron's face brightened. "There is a third possibility to their heritage."

"Yes," Audrey continued, "if they favor their mother, then they belong to our family and may not be influenced by the others. If they are part of each family . . . then that raises many unpleasant possibilities such as a treaty loophole. But if their genetics favor the others, then you may not touch them. They are shielded by the same treaty you seek to preserve, Sister. You must first determine what they are: ours, theirs, or something of both."

Lucia's pale skin flushed and she glared at Audrey. "Very well then. Bring them. Let us see Eliot and Fiona Post. Let them be judged."

14

THREE HEROIC TRIALS

The room in Uncle Henry's mansion where Fiona and Eliot had been left was bigger than an entire floor of their apartment building. Fiona looked up at the ceiling: twenty feet high and covered with a mural of clouds and cherubs that either played a game of hide-and-seek or lay in ambush for one another.[16,17]

Sunlight streamed through floor-to-ceiling windows on the southern wall. Beyond, the sea churned and layers of stratocumulus streamed across the horizon. Eliot stood there next to a table covered with food and a tea service. He picked at the morsels and stared outside.

Fiona studied the portraits on the walls: lords and ladies with frilled collars and velvet cloaks that belonged to another age. Yet they belonged in this place, too. They had strong jaws and smooth skin; about their eyes were laugh lines; some had ears that stuck out like Eliot's. They were relatives.

Their painted stares, however, were too fixed upon her, so Fiona looked away and crossed the room to Eliot.

16. Cherubs were not originally thought of as an angelic order. In ancient Assyrian-Babylonian works they are depicted as large birds, bulls, or sphinxes with human faces. They are first mentioned as angels in the Old Testament, guarding the Tree of Life with flaming swords. Only in recent history have they been depicted as harmless and childlike. *Gods of the First and Twenty-first Century, Volume 2: Divine Inspirations*, 8th ed. (Zypheron Press Ltd.).

17. Once glorious with four eagle wings, sword of living flame, Beelzebub of the Cherubic Order rebelled against the Light and fell with his brothers into damnation. Father Sildas Pious, *Mythica Improbiba* (translated version), c. thirteenth century.

"How can you eat?" she asked.

He washed down a mouthful of sugar-dusted orange with a cup of tea. "We missed dinner. It was a long trip."

Fiona conjured the details of that trip from memory, but it was a blur . . . everything except the driver who had opened her door. No one had ever opened a door for her before or offered a hand to help her out. He had smelled of leather and cloves, and she remembered his smile. It was a nice, uncomplicated smile. She had felt a magnetic pull from her center to his. "Robert," Uncle Henry had called him.

Eliot set his tea down. "Are you okay?"

"Yes. But it doesn't make any sense how we got here."

"It makes perfect sense, if you break Newton's First Law." Eliot picked up a finger sandwich, inspecting its contents: salami and provolone.

"And you're okay with that?"

He shook his head. "No way. But when I think about it, the only logical answer is that something is wrong with me, like I'm dreaming . . . or crazy."

Fiona grew cold despite standing in the warm sunlight. "I'm scared," she whispered.

"So am I."

Fiona was scared not because of the strange journey, but rather the *reason* for it. Why were they here?

"It's like we were kidnapped or something," Eliot said.

"Grandmother and Uncle Henry in that standoff. I thought she was going to—"

"Use that knife?"

"Yeah."

"Do you think," Eliot asked, "like Uncle Henry said, she killed Mr. Welmann?"

For Fiona's whole life she had felt threatened by Grandmother, although she had never so much as raised a hand against her or Eliot. But seeing her holding that knife, Fiona knew Grandmother knew how to use it (for more than slicing birthday cake). She knew she *had* used it, too.

Footsteps echoed along the adjoining hallway and Uncle Henry appeared in an archway. "I hope you've had a chance to eat," he said, crossing the room. His walk was smooth and liquid as if he had somehow absorbed part of the room's polished marble and burnished gold.

"Where's Grandmother?" Eliot asked.

"Waiting. Shall we join her? Do you need to use the bathroom?"

He had asked them when they had left Del Sombra. Did he think they were little kids whose bladders exploded when they got excited?

She glanced at Eliot; he shook his head. "We're fine," she said, managing to sound polite.

"Good," Uncle Henry said. "Are you frightened?" It was a simple question, one with no judgment.

"It's a little strange," Eliot offered.

Fiona held her head high and looked Uncle Henry straight in the eyes just as she had Mike earlier today. "I am."

"I am glad you can admit it," Uncle Henry replied. "You are strong and honest like your mother. That's good because you are about to meet more of the family."

Fiona felt her confidence drain. "More?" she whispered.

Uncle Henry looked at her and Eliot, seeming to decide something, then said, "They're going to test to see if you belong with us."

"And if we fail this test," Eliot asked, "we go home?"

"No," Henry said flatly.

The chill spreading through Fiona crystallized into a lump of ice in her stomach.

Without further explanation Uncle Henry strode toward the hallway. "Come, there is no turning back now."

Fiona looked at Eliot. "I think we have to," she said.

He nodded.

Together they followed Uncle Henry.

He led them through a study filled with stuffed trophy animals: Kodiak bear, a lion, a dodo, and mammoth tusks—into a glass-walled atrium where they crunched over a Zen gravel stream—then they passed into Uncle Henry's library.

It was three stories tall with wrought-iron balconies, wall after wall of books, rolling ladders of brass, and covered catwalks. It stretched into the distance; it must have had *millions* of volumes. Fiona smelled the paper, and the leather, and the scent of age. Like home. She could have spent a decade exploring the place.

Uncle Henry didn't let them dawdle, though; he ushered them through a short hallway that hissed with a pressure change, then outside to a walkway—where they halted before a cliff.

Wind whipped through Fiona's hair, blinding her. She tied it up in a knot and saw what Uncle Henry steered them toward: a slender stone bridge that arched over churning waters to an island.

As they got closer, she saw a railing on this bridge, broken in places, and far too short to stop one who stumbled.

"Is that what you meant?" she said, struggling to project her voice over the wind. "That bridge . . . is that the test?"

"Oh, no, child," Uncle Henry told her. "If you do not have the pertinacity to cross *that*, then you do not possess a tenth the backbone required to face the family."

He waved his hand, indicating that they cross . . . or not. He was giving them the choice.

Fiona looked to Eliot and he took her hand, knowing four feet on the bridge would be more stable than two. They implicitly understood that while this violated their brother-sister agreement never to touch, neither would ever speak of it.

Together, she and Eliot stepped onto cracked, unmortared stones. Wind gusted about her, so she bent her knees and took tiny shuffling steps. The span hummed under her feet, resonating in the unstable currents of air.

Fiona tried to look at her feet—which should have been easy; that's what she looked at all day at Ringo's—but she couldn't help looking at the jagged rocks and roiling waters below. Salt spray stung her eyes. She blinked away tears and kept going. She had to. If she stopped, Eliot would know she was chicken. *That* had to be avoided at all costs.

Eyes on feet, she kept moving.

Without warning the ancient stones of the bridge vanished, and she stepped onto dark sand.

She and Eliot simultaneously dropped each other's hand.

"See?" Uncle Henry skipped off the bridge behind them. "Nothing to it."

"Yeah," Eliot whispered. "It was easy."

Fiona shot him a glare for that lie.

"This way." Uncle Henry led them into an amphitheater.

The wind ceased inside, and Fiona felt as if she were inside a fishbowl. Grandmother sat on the innermost step opposite four others: three men and another woman. Grandmother blinked at Fiona and Eliot, inscrutable and rigid.

"Allow me to introduce Miss Fiona Post and Mr. Eliot Post," Uncle Henry said to the strangers. "Eliot, Fiona, these are"—he sighed—"I will drop all the confusing 'great this' and 'twice removed thats' if you don't mind."

He stepped before the woman. She was beautiful, like a model or an actress, and her smile made Fiona feel completely at ease . . . and at the same time wary.

"This is your aunt Lucia."

Aunt meant that she was her mother's sister? Had her mother been this lovely? Was it even remotely possible that Fiona could look so pretty when she grew up?

Uncle Henry next indicated the man with gold beard and wavy hair. He wore jeans, sneakers, and a short-sleeved, white shirt. He smiled at them.

"Your cousin Gilbert."

"Charmed," Gilbert said.

"Next . . ." Uncle Henry turned to a dour man who sat with his elbows on his knees. He stared at both Fiona and Eliot as if they were bacteriological specimens under a microscope. His drooping mustache reminded Fiona of pictures she had seen of Mongol warriors sweeping over Asia killing everything that resisted them.

"Your uncle Aaron," Henry said.

Henry then turned to an old man, sitting cross-legged behind this Uncle Aaron. He had notes and charts scattered about him. His eyes sparkled.

"Uncle Cornelius," Henry said.

"We're very pleased to meet you all," Fiona said.

That had to be the most brainless thing she had ever said. She wasn't pleased to be here, or to meet any of them. She should have demanded to know what they wanted. She glanced at Grandmother, who nodded. At least Fiona had managed to say *something*.

Aunt Lucia stood and her black dress flowed about her. The fabric's red-rose pattern was the same color as her lips and hair. Fiona in her gray sweats and oily, knotted hair felt awkward standing before such a sophisticated woman. How wretched must she look to all these people?

"You have had a long trip," Lucia said. "You must be tired, but please indulge us by answering a few questions."

Fiona straightened. She and Eliot were good at answering questions. If this was what Uncle Henry meant by a "test," then she knew everything would be all right. They'd been answering Grandmother's questions as long as she could remember.

Fiona glanced at Eliot and he nodded.

"We're ready," she told Lucia. "Go ahead and ask."

"I will go first," Uncle Cornelius said. He held a notebook and readied his pencil to write. "Favorite colors?"

Fiona wasn't ready for *that* question. She'd been expecting something like "What is the capital of Madagascar?" No one had ever asked what colors she liked.

"Purple," she blurted.

That was the first thing that popped into her head. Not lavender, but the black purple that was the color of the dusk or the earliest dawn. It was dark and deep and somehow sad.

Eliot's brow wrinkled with concentration. "Gray."

Cornelius scribbled this down and then consulted his charts.

Uncle Henry sat forward and asked, "When I am closed, I am a triangle. Open, a circle. What am I?"

Fiona loved riddles. Eliot and she had done them *all* when they were kids. They'd exhausted every riddle in their library and solved the ones Grandmother and Cecilia knew, too. That's why they had eventually moved on to vocabulary insult for a challenge.

"An umbrella," she and Eliot said together.

"But technically," Eliot added, "closed, you're a cone."

"And a hemisphere when opened," Fiona said.

Uncle Henry beamed and turned to Cornelius. "Note the multidimensional abstraction."

"Yes," Uncle Cornelius muttered, and scratched out several mathematical equations.

Aaron snorted and asked, "How many squares on a chessboard?"

Fiona knew a chessboard had sixty-four squares: eight by eight alternating black and white spaces. But it also had squares made up of combinations such as two-by-two or three-by-three blocks.

"Start with the bigger blocks," Eliot whispered to her.

Fiona bristled—not because it was a bad suggestion, but because he was right: it was easier that way.

"There's a pattern," she told Eliot.

"Just saw it." Now it was Eliot's turn to look annoyed because she'd figured it out first. "One, four, nine . . ."

"The square of the numbers," she told him, "ending with eight squared, or sixty-four singles. Adding it all up you get—"

"Two hundred four," they told Uncle Aaron together.

He nodded and no longer glared at them like bacteriological specimens.

Cornelius glanced up from his notes. "My calculations continue to balance. An equivalent probability of genetic options."

Aunt Lucia hissed a long sigh. "Oedipus answered the Sphinx's riddles, but that never proved a thing about his lineage, either. The children are intelligent, I grant you that . . . but *anyone* can be merely smart."

Fiona became annoyed, wondering how anyone could be "merely" smart.

Lucia continued, "Are we not looking for a spark of the transcendent?" Her jaw set. "We can take no chances with what might determine the fate of our entire family."

The others were silent, and Fiona heard her own heartbeat. Something important was about to be decided against them . . . even though she and Eliot hadn't failed any of their tests.

"There is an obvious alternative to words." Henry reached into his pocket and pulled out a pair of dice. They were red with white spots and gleamed like rubies.

The sight of them gave the adults a start.

"Where did you get those?" Lucia said, and distaste rippled across her face.

"Lake Tahoe." Henry held them out for all to get a better look. "Are there any objections?"

No one said a thing.

"Grand." He offered them to Fiona.

Fiona looked to Grandmother. She frowned, but nonetheless nodded.

A special rule covered dice in their household.

RULE 3: No dice.

It was the most curious of all the 106 of Grandmother's rules. Unlike her other prohibitions, this one forbade a *single* specific thing. There were none of the usual elaborations to avoid loopholes . . . just "no dice."

Fiona took the cubes. They were warm, but she felt nothing out of the ordinary.

"Give them a toss," Henry reassured her. "Over there on the steps."

Fiona threw them.

The dice clattered and came to rest. One showed a single pip, the other three.

Henry retrieved them and handed them back. "Toss again, please, mademoiselle."

Fiona didn't know if a three and a one was good or bad, or what she had to do now to win. She did, however, note the adults tense. Fiona squeezed the cubes; they were hot now.

She threw them. A three and four. Seven altogether.

"Crapped out!" Henry announced with a magnanimous grin.

Everyone relaxed.

Fiona couldn't believe it; it happened so quickly. No strategy was involved, either, just a randomly generated number. "I lost?" she asked, swallowing the lump in her throat.

"Oh, no," Uncle Henry reassured her. "You passed with flying colors." He turned and handed the dice to Eliot.

Eliot's hand shook as he accepted them. He was sweating. He closed his fist, swallowed hard, and tossed them.

They bounced and ricocheted. One landed cockeyed in a pit in the limestone. The other rolled against the next step, not quite flat.

Henry looked uncertainly at the dice and gave them back to Eliot. "Reroll."

Eliot grew pale. He looked as he had after he had eaten month-old pepperoncini at Ringo's and spent the night vomiting. Fiona wanted to ask what was wrong, but he was so focused on those dice, she wasn't sure he would notice her.

He threw them again.

They spun through the air flashing, landed—scattered like popcorn exploding. They spun off the stone, orbited one another, and slowly came to a halt . . . resting crookedly against each other's side.

"Fascinating," Henry breathed.

No one spoke. Even Uncle Cornelius had stopped his scribbling.

Grandmother stood. "This is a weak test," she declared, looking down at them all. "Test them. *Really* test them with deeds worthy of one of our family."

Uncle Aaron pounded the step. The impact raised dust and Fiona felt it through her feet. "Yes! Like the old days. *Heroic* trials. How long has it been since we have seen sport like that?"

Uncle Henry cocked his head, thinking. "Two millennia . . . give or take."

Fiona thought this a joke, but no one, not even Uncle Henry, smiled at it.

"Three such trials would be sufficient," Cornelius said. "All would be determined with ninety-nine percent accuracy."

The rosy tint drained from Aunt Lucia's lips, and she opened her mouth to speak.

Cousin Gilbert, however, spoke first. "A fine idea. Real tests for real potentials. I put it forth as a motion."

"Second the motion," Aaron said immediately.

"This is turning into one of our best Council meetings," Henry said. "A vote, then? All in favor?"

"Aye!" the four men said.

Lucia remained silent, but her eyes locked with Grandmother's.

After a moment Grandmother said, "Of course, we should wait for the full Council to determine the exact nature of these trials."

Aunt Lucia compressed her lips into a white line and gave her a slight bow. "Of course."

More was being communicated between them than Fiona understood, but she guessed Grandmother had just won some battle on their behalf. And Aunt Lucia had lost.

"Then we accept the Council's wisdom," Grandmother said.

"Let the record show," Aunt Lucia declared, "that we shall test the children's potentials with three heroic trials. This will illuminate their characters and determine their lineage. It will prove their possible worth to remain alive." She stared directly at Fiona, who felt the last of her strength slip away. "Perhaps even their right to be part of this family."

15

THE NAGAS OF DHARMA

Sealiah ran a crimson nail over the mirror, tracing the art deco geometry etched along its edge. The buttons of this elevator were cabochon rubies, synthetic of course, and smeared with greasy fingerprints.

The elevator was emblematic of the entire Babylon Gardens Hotel and Casino. It was a papier-mâché mask of glitz and chintz. It was the beating, bleeding heart of Las Vegas.

She hated the place. The quarter slots cheated. The shrimp cocktails were off. The drinks all watered down.

Sealiah adjusted the strap of her gown. It was gossamer scales and silver sea foam, impervious to blade and bullet. She might have gone strapless—she had no pretense of modesty save for seduction—but often these affairs turned brutal, and one could not do battle with a tangled dress about one's knees.

She leaned back, resting against the bulk of her most faithful servant, Urakabarameel. He wore his Corneliani tuxedo, looking like a mountain of charcoal gray wool, and the only color upon him was the emerald skull tie tack that marked him as hers.

"We are being watched." His voice was a subsonic rumble that she felt in her bones.

"I expected no less," she replied.

She turned into him, unbuttoned his jacket, and slipped its voluminous folds around her. In the mirrored walls she watched backward elevator numbers zigzag right to left. Nestling against his chest, she whispered, "We can speak like this."

"Will it work?" His eyes were downcast, respectfully, but to maintain secrecy, to keep his jacket shielding them, he had to encircle his arms about her. He did so and drew Sealiah a tad closer than she thought necessary.

"There is little chance of anything working as planned where *our* family is concerned."

His face darkened.

She ran a hand down her leg to the hem of her dress, then up to her inner thigh . . . stopped as she touched the cold metal sheath.

"There is no choice," she said. "Those two children may be the greatest threat, or the greatest opportunity, for us."

Uri smiled. He had never before dared smile in her presence . . . so he probably understood: this might be their last time together.

He had been with her from the start. Now to lose him because another *demanded* tribute. It seemed wrong even for their kind to do this. Yet, this was their way. If she wanted to play the game, she had to pay the ante. This didn't mean, however, she couldn't play both sides—with a pawn of *both* colors upon the board.

She unbuckled the sheath along her thigh and pressed it against Uri's chest.

His eyes widened.

This was Saliceran. Its eight-inch blade had a sinuous edge that followed the contours of the Damascus patterned metal. Between the blackened and silver layers it wept oily venom. Many claimed it was a living thing with a taste for flesh equal to its owner's.

"Take it," she said. "Quickly."

Uri gingerly grasped it with two fingers. He tucked it safely into one of his jacket's many pockets.

Sealiah glanced at the lighted numbers. Only seconds left for them. Her vision blurred with tears. How silly.

"M'lady," Uri whispered. He started to sink to his knees, but then remembered he had to remain upright to shield their conversation. He fumbled out a handkerchief with the utmost care and dabbed her cheek. "You honor me."

She sniffled, blinked, and cleared her mind. She could not afford such luxuries as feeling, now of all times.

Uri carefully tucked the handkerchief into the pocket over his heart. "Is there no other way?"

She accepted this question of her plan—not as insolence, but rather as wanting to remain and serve—so she let it pass.

Sealiah smoothed her dress and turned.

The final number lit and the elevator pinged.

"I shall miss you, Uri."

The mirrored doors pulled apart. Uri stepped off first to make certain the room was secure—an impossibility, given the circumstances, but she appreciated his futile sentiment.

Sealiah, Queen of the Poppies, then made her entrance into the Penthouse Suite of the Babylon Gardens Hotel and Casino. The walls were glass with a panoramic view: on one side the sparkling Las Vegas Strip lay before them like a buffet of jewels; on the other side, the moon cast a fragile illumination over the silvered desert.

A conference table of black basalt dominated the suite; all other furniture had been removed. There were chairs but they had been pushed aside as the gathered Directors preferred to stand.

On their feet: the better to defend themselves.

The Board members somehow seemed to absorb the qualities of darkness and light surrounding them—chameleons all—transmuting the glamour of Vegas into a living embodiment of moonglow, flash, and secrets.

Five of them had gathered.

First on her right stood Lev, Master of the Endless Abyssal Seas, older than salt, taller than her Uri, and strong enough to crush her escort with one age-hardened fist. He wore white polyester sweats that glistened from the strain of containing his corpulence. About his neck he wore a hundred gold chains encrusted with lucky charms, amulets, and medals. He looked like a thick-throated sea lion . . . which was not too far from the truth.

"Fashionably late," he said to her, and graced her with a nod that made the forty pounds of metal jingle.

"Salutations to the Beast," she replied.

To Lev's right was Abby, the Destroyer, Handmaiden of Armageddon, and Mistress of the Palace of Abomination. She wore a translucent black veil that concealed just enough of her slight albino form to entice the imagination. Smoky quartz had been woven into the gauze, artfully placed over nipple, throat, and cheek. She allowed her pet, a grasshopper, to crawl up her arm; the insect was restless and never settled.

She barely glanced at Sealiah—which for her might be considered a most generous greeting.

Sealiah let the insult go. One did not antagonize a Destroyer without good reason.

On Sealiah's immediate left at the table was a friendlier face, Oz, who ruled the Doldrums of Glamour and the Circus Damnation Extravigiganticus. Oz had long, curled hair and a meticulously groomed mustache and goatee. He wore a violet velvet jumpsuit and ruffled shirt. Too much makeup covered lovely androgynous features that needed none. This was all part of the "rock star" persona that he fancied from time to time. His smile sparkled and he held out his hand to take hers.

Sealiah knew better and curled her hand inward, feigning coquettishness. That was for the best: there would be no perceived insult . . . and she would retain her arm.

Next to Oz sat Ashmed, Master Architect of Evil. For a moment, Sealiah was actually surprised, although she expertly hid any such expression. They all respected Ashmed as he was the only one to keep his machinations entirely to himself. For him, there were no false alliances, backstabbings, or double-dealings—just an endless well of secrets.

Ashmed rarely appeared at the Directors' meetings, although he was a founding member. He was clad in a simple blue business suit, with his black silk hair crew-cut. His only extravagances were a gold ring and a smoldering Sancho Panza Belicoso cigar.

"You honor us with your presence," he said, and gave her a little bow.

"As do you, Master Architect."

And at last her gaze fell on Beal, the chairman of the Board.

She knew he would be at the head of the table, but had refrained from looking directly at him until now. He was vainglorious, and this breach of decorum was calculated to annoy him as much as he annoyed her.

Beal had cloaked himself in a mantle of feathers—fluffy ostrich, regal peacock, wild pheasant, and speckles of iridescent hummingbird.

He was bare-chested this evening. Sealiah admired his sculpted musculature and idly wondered how easily one might rip out his heart. One day it would happen; she would not be there to see it, but she would know and celebrate.

She bowed low, keeping her eyes upon all of them. "Most humble greeting to the King of the Blasted Lands, Prince of False Gods, and the Lord of All That Flies."

Beal barked a laugh. "Humble? Come Sealiah. Stand and be counted among your fellows. Genuflection does not become you."

She smiled insincerely and took her place at the foot of the table.

"You have brought tribute for this summoning of the Board?" Beal asked.

It took considerable effort on her part not to glance behind her. "Allow me to present my cousin Urakabarameel."

Uri crossed on her left, taking care so his shadow did not fall upon her, still showing her the proper respect. He set her laptop computer on the table, his last act as her servant, and marched to Beal, who made a show of examining him.

"Very well," Beal said. "I accept him."

Uri lowered his head and moved behind Beal, standing on *his* left now.

Sealiah had not imagined it would hurt so much seeing Uri next to her most hated enemy. But it had to be done.

"I hereby call this meeting of the Board of Directors to order," Beal declared.

The others laughed at his last words.

Beal smirked and withdrew a solid, sensible German Korth .357 Magnum revolver and fired three rounds through the ceiling.

This amused them all even more.

Using the pistol, he gestured at Sealiah. "You have summoned the Board. Tell us why."

"I shall show you." She opened her laptop, linked to the conference room's server, and turned on the overhead projector. "This concerns two children."

The Board's collective attention shifted to her computer files as she opened them. She led them along the trail of bread crumbs Uri had uncovered looking for Louis—the bad credit cards, the bankruptcy court transcripts, the lawyers, and the trust fund. And then she opened the file containing the photographs of Eliot and Fiona Post.

The Board members immediately recognized the resemblance, having had the clues hand-fed by Sealiah.

"Louis's progeny?!" Oz cried. "How is that possible?"

"We all heard the rumors," Sealiah said. "Him and one of the other family and their Parisian tryst."

This was an old rumor, unsubstantiated as Louis had vanished almost sixteen years ago . . . but to see proof staring them quite literally in the face was still unnerving.

"The questionable biological issues aside," Ashmed said, "is it even *legally* possible? We cannot touch them."

"Unless it was mutual," Beal offered. "Has that ever happened before?"

The Board was silent.

Sealiah decided then to share all her information with the Board. Beal would have extracted it from Uri anyway. She would save her cousin the trouble and neutralize any advantage Beal would have gleaned over the others.

She turned back to her laptop and tapped a command. Connecting lines and numeric codes flashed over the children's faces. "Interpol facial-recognition software projects a seventy-three percent probability that these *are* his children, although the issue of their mother remains open."

"Then they are ours," Abby said, "to do with as we see fit."

"Not necessarily," Ashmed countered. "If they are part Louis's and part of the others, then—"

"It's an easy call," Lev interrupted. "We hunt down these half things and kill them. If anything will bring Louis out of hiding, that will. We can have some sport. Blood will spill." He pounded a meaty fist on the table as he spoke. "I can rip them into little—"

Abby grabbed Beal's .357 Magnum before he could stop her and shot Lev three times.

Lev recoiled, gold links and medals exploding off his chest, and flopped onto the table.

Abby dropped the smoldering weapon. "Excessive violence is not always the answer, old fool."

Lev struggled and rose, blood seeping through his white polyester jacket. He brushed off the broken tangles of jewelry from his chest. "Then what," he snarled, "is the point of this gathering?"

"The point is they could be part of our family *and* part of theirs," Sealiah said. She glanced at the images of Eliot and Fiona, thrilled how they looked so much like Louis . . . and someone else.

"That is a two-way street," Abby said. "One with considerable risk for us."

Oz murmured, "But even if they are only part ours, shouldn't they be brought in? Who would stop us?"

"The others may already be involved," Scaliah said.

Uri had followed the children home, only to spot the Messenger of the other family waiting for them. So the others knew or at least suspected what the children might be.

"It is too rich an opportunity to ignore," Beal said. "How long have we watched the others prosper? Their League controls considerable assets that could be ours. This may be our chance."

Sealiah knew when he said "ours" he meant "his."

He nonetheless made a valid point. The League controlled multinational conglomerates, employed millions, subtly directed the politics of the United Nations, and influenced—with bribes to policy makers and advertising to the masses—the morals of billions. Assets most tempting. And something their unorganized organization had never managed on such a scale.

"Ours for the taking," she said, "save an unbreakable neutrality treaty."

"I still say excision is our cleanest option," Abby insisted. Her grasshopper chittered in agreement.

"Well, I say we test these two," Oz replied, "and determine where they belong—with us or the others."

The Board members tensed. This was as much discussion as they could tolerate. A decision had to be made within the next breath, or violence would certainly follow.

Ashmed held up his hands. "There is only one civil way to decide our course." He then spread both hands over the stone table and two white cubes appeared. His stage magic was as impressive as ever.

These dice were two of a matched set of five called the Nagas of Dharma. They had been carved in ancient times from the bones of a monstrous water serpent. Etched onto the faces of each was a scrimshaw head-eating-tail snake, two prancing dogs, three crossed scimitars, four stars, five hands (each making a different rude gesture), and six ravens on the wing.

The dice were legendary. They were tamperproof and renowned for being harbingers of destiny, both good and ill, within the family.

"Unless anyone has objections?" Ashmed asked.

No one would object. None could. This was their way to avoid arguments, which nearly always occurred, and to avoid the inevitable bloodshed after those arguments.

This family resolved their disputes in the time-honored fashion: by chance. God did not play dice with the universe, but they did.[18]

---

18. This common misquote originates in a letter from Albert Einstein to Max Born wherein he writes, about quantum mechanics. *"He (God) does not throw dice."* This family, who have allegedly broken all ties with God, loathe Einstein's deterministic view of reality and instead embrace quantum mechanics and its reliance upon randomness to predict the universe and their destiny. *Gods of the First and Twenty-first Century, Volume 13: Infernal Forces*, 8th ed. (Zypheron Press Ltd.).

Beal opened his mouth as if to say something, but it was too late. There could be no more debate once the dice were on the table. One either shut up and rolled or drew blood.

Beal gave a slight nod to Ashmed and said, "We will give equivalent weight to our two possible actions."

"Death," Abby said.

"Yes," Ashmed said, "death will be the odd result. But if they come up even, then we shall test the two children. Should they survive, we will decide what to do based on the results."

"Test them how?" Lev asked.

"The usual way," Beal replied. "We will tempt them. Three times. And they must survive all three."

"Oh, yes," Oz said, and clasped his hands together. "First, a girl for the boy. Sealiah can provide one, I'm sure."

Sealiah bowed. "And for the girl's temptation . . ." She looked at Beal. "Sweets?"

Beal nodded in agreement. "Of course. Traditional ways are the best."

The manner in which the children embraced or resisted these temptations would reveal their heritage. If they belonged to the other family, they would be immune as the neutrality treaty would shield them. If they were part of this family, however, they would turn temptation to their advantage. And if they belong to neither, if they were ordinary . . . they would be destroyed.

"Then all is agreed?" Ashmed scooped up the Nagas and moved to Sealiah. He stood over her shoulder, so close she could smell him: cinnamon and desert sands, cigar smoke and musk.

"As you summoned us," he told her, "the honor is yours." He set the dice before her.

Beal frowned and his cloak of feathers ruffled but he was quiet.

Sealiah picked up the dice and closed her fist about them. They were hard and radiated a cold so intense they made her bones ache. She rattled them, more to hide her shaking hand than anything else.

This is what she had wanted, wasn't it? It was the most strategically advantageous. She had to bring in the entire family. Not only did it involve all of them, but Sealiah required their help to face the might of the others. No one went to war alone. She needed an entire row of pawns to shield her and, if necessary, be sacrificed in her stead.

So much was at stake. The two families had been balanced in neutrality for so long . . . would either side even remember how to fight such a battle?

Sealiah would.

She threw the dice. They arced through the air, tumbled, symbols a blur—hit the black table, bounced, rolled end over end, a jumble of snakes and fists, swords and ravens.

Sealiah held her breath and wished upon the stars twinkling on the Las Vegas Strip at her feet.

The Nagas of Dharma came to rest. Destiny was writ.

16

TRUST NO ONE

Eliot followed Uncle Henry through his cavernous garage. It could have been an exotic-car dealership. Among the rows of gleaming fenders and headlamps was a green 1917 Buick Tourer, a Porsche 550 Spyder, and one very noncivilian version Humvee.

Fiona and Grandmother walked behind him. No one spoke.

The parabolic-shaped limousine that had whisked them from Del Sombra sat in the driveway, gleaming in the sun and purring exhaust. The sterling silver emblems on the body read v-12 and EXELERO-4X.

The driver, Robert, jumped out, snugged on his leather cap, and moved to the back door.

Uncle Henry waved him off and opened it himself. "Ladies first," he said, and motioned for Fiona to get in.

Eliot noted that Fiona looked everywhere *but* at the driver; the driver looked everywhere *but* at her.

The rest of them got in and Henry slammed the door. He rapped on the partition and the car accelerated onto the road.

Whitecapped water blurred past on the right-hand side.

No one looked at one another. Eliot could feel the tension in the air. He had a thousand questions, but hadn't been able to ask anything in the amphitheater, especially when he had held those dice. They felt charged with electricity. Something had flowed from him into the dice; something had flowed from them into him. But not a good something. More like poison.

He felt normal now, though. Almost.

Eliot turned to Fiona. She stared at fields of wheat outside. She was the one who usually started asking questions. Eliot waited and the sun dimmed, eclipsed by clouds. Fiona continued to stare, unnaturally quiet.

He took a deep breath and shifted toward Henry. "I have a few—"

"Questions?" Henry finished for him. "Life is full of them and there are so few answers." He sighed and hung his head. "I'm sorry, not everything should be a joke. I can only imagine your confusion, young man."

"Those tests. Those people. Are they really my family? They're so . . ."

"Odd? Dilettante?" Henry glanced at Grandmother. "Violent?"

"So *not* like me."

"Oh, but they are. You don't see it yet, but I do. We all do." Henry lowered his voice and leaned forward. "It might help to think of this as a custody battle, but with some very strange rules. We need to find out if you belong with us or with your father's family."

Father. The word exploded like a firecracker in Eliot's mind. He was long dead, but there was this other branch of his family that he had never met. Were they as strange as his mother's side of the family? Did they want him and Fiona, too?

He recalled what Uncle Henry had said: the two families were like the Capulets and the Montagues from *Romeo and Juliet*—two noble families at war for generations.

Had his parents really died in a boat accident? Or like Romeo and Juliet had they poisoned themselves and died in each other's arms? Or maybe they had *been* poisoned by these two families?

"No one said anything about our father at that meeting," Eliot said. "Is his family that bad?"

He wanted to ask "Was it as bad as *this* family?" but thought better of it.

Henry eased back into his seat, and he and Grandmother shared a look that appeared much like what Eliot and Fiona might exchange—a stream of unspoken information that flashed between them with a raised eyebrow and shake of the head.

"It would be best," Henry explained, "if your Grandmother answered your questions."

Eliot turned to her, hoping she might melt a tiny bit and tell him something.

Grandmother was stone. "Not here in front of this gossiping creature."

Uncle Henry set his hand over his heart, feigning hurt.

"You're not going to tell us anything?" Eliot said. "I can't believe it."

Grandmother looked away.

Fiona crossed her arms. "Stop the car."

Uncle Henry glanced outside: moonlight made the surrounding icescape sparkle. "My dear, we are in the middle of nowhere and the temperature is far below freezing."

"Stop this thing now." Fiona glared at him.

At that moment, Eliot thought she looked like Grandmother.

Grandmother examined Fiona, then murmured, "Do it, Henry. Let's see where she will take this."

Uncle Henry rapped on the partition, and it slid down. "Stop the car, Robert."

The limousine fishtailed to a halt.

Fiona opened the door. The inrushing air felt like a blast of ice water. Eliot considered going with her; he wasn't sure what she had in mind, but they should stick together. Before he could undo his seat belt, though, the door slammed shut and Fiona marched to the front of the car. She opened the front passenger's door and climbed back inside.

Shivering so hard she could barely get her seat belt on, she said, "T-t-t-too st-st-uuffy back th-th-there."

The driver looked wide-eyed at her, then to Uncle Henry.

"It's fine," Henry said. "Just continue and spare not the horses."

"Keep this partition down, young man," Grandmother ordered, "and your eyes on the road."

The driver paled, nodded, and the car jumped forward.

Eliot wanted to ask more questions, but with Grandmother's refusal, and Fiona up front, he didn't feel like trying again.

Outside there were stars in the sky but no auroras. Fields of ice turned into darkened forests; snow turned into a track, a dirt road, pavement, and then a four-lane freeway. Eliot saw the lit storefronts of Del Sombra, and the Bavarian façade of Oakwood Apartments. The car stopped.

"Shall I come up?" Uncle Henry offered. "We can share a cup of coffee. Talk about old times?"

"No." Grandmother opened the door and motioned for Eliot and Fiona to follow.

"It was nice meeting you," he told Uncle Henry.

"The pleasure was mine, young Eliot. We will see you soon."

That seemed half promise and somehow half a threat as well to Eliot.

Fiona joined them, looking one last time at the driver, and saying, "Thank you," for the ride. The driver tipped his cap at her.

Grandmother led them up the three flights of stairs. She halted at their door, examining the light filtering underneath. "Cecilia has waited up for us."

The door opened before Grandmother touched it, and Cecilia stood trembling in her long nightgown. "I'm so glad you're back. I have tea ready." On the dining table were two steaming pots, her spiderweb kettle and a chipped, blue coffeepot, as well as a dozen cups and saucers.

Cee reached out for Eliot and Fiona and welcomed them with an embrace. It felt good to be held by someone who Eliot knew loved him.

The clock in the hallway chimed midnight and Cee released them.

Eliot and Fiona's birthday was over. Maybe nothing more strange would happen. For the only time in his life, Eliot just wanted to go back to his normal, boring routine.

"I hadn't realized it was so late," Cee said. "Are you hungry? Should I—"

Grandmother closed the door and threw the dead bolt. She went to the window and looked down at the street. "Stop hovering over the children, Cecilia. It is late. They are tired."

"Wait," Eliot said. "You were going to tell us things. About the family."

Grandmother considered a moment. She then moved to the sliding double doors on the far side of the dining room and parted them. "Come."

Grandmother's office was sacrosanct. Eliot and Fiona had been in there before, but just to announce that dinner was ready or a tenant was at the door. They'd never actually been invited inside.

Her office had a single window overlooking Del Sombra's downtown— dark now save for a row of orange streetlamps. A Victorian, high-back love seat sat facing the window. On a side table was a legal pad, ballpoint pen, and yesterday's *San Francisco Chronicle*. It was the only room in the apartment with a decided lack of books.

"Sit," Grandmother said.

Eliot and Fiona sat on the love seat as far apart as they could.

Cecilia hesitated in the doorway, looking unsure if she had been invited in as well.

Grandmother inhaled and said, "We will start with the family."

Eliot knew she meant their mother's family, not his father's. He was dying to know more about his dad, but he had a feeling he'd never learn anything about them from Grandmother. But both families were connected somehow. He felt it.

"Children are rare for us," Grandmother continued. "For reasons of convenience and biology. We are not"—she paused, searching for the correct words—"there are *medical* issues."

Eliot looked at Fiona. She nodded and said, "Like the congenital defects of the seventeenth-century European dynasties?"

"Alexei Romanov," Eliot added. "He was a hemophiliac, right?"

He wished he hadn't remembered the heir to the last Russian empire. Alexei Romanov had been assassinated by the Bolshevik secret police in 1918—two weeks before his fourteenth birthday . . . almost Eliot's age.[19]

"*Not* like the Romanov's," Grandmother said quickly. "Our children have always been healthy."

"Tell them why there are so few," Cecilia said behind her, wringing her hands.

Grandmother narrowed her eyes to slits and turned. Eliot didn't see the look she gave Cee, but he saw the result: his great-grandmother withered and shrank back into the shadows.

Fiona shifted on the love seat. "So why?"

Grandmother faced them. "The reason there are so few children in this family is *because* of this family."

Cecilia slinked back to the doorway.

"The politics of our family are complicated," Grandmother said, "treacherous, and often deleterious to its younger, most vulnerable members."

"The people at Uncle Henry's," Eliot said, "they told us we had to 'survive' their trials." He shuddered, thinking of murdered Alexei Romanov. "They meant we have to live through them, didn't they?"

Grandmother pursed her lips as she was trying to hold back her words, but finally said, "Yes. And we are lucky to have the chance. Many have been crushed without so much as that."

"They are strong enough to know what they face," Cecilia whispered. "Tell them about the kidnappings, the burnings . . . the seductions." She

19. One of the legends surrounding Anastasia and Alexei Romanov (would-be heirs to the former Russian empire) is that they escaped death at the hands of the Bolsheviks and were spirited away in a forest-green 1917 Buick Tourer. The children and the car were seen in Paris, and then as the rumors spread, in New York, Chicago, and even Seattle—impossibly a day later. Recently recovered remains of the royal Russian family, however, yielded a positive identification via DNA analysis with a 98.5 percent certainty, so this legend must be dismissed as wishful romanticism. *Gods of the First and Twenty-first Century,* Volume 6: *Modern Myths.* 8th ed. (Zypheron Press Ltd.).

tried to say more but her eyes glistened with tears and her hand clutched at her throat.

Grandmother closed her eyes. "Very well. You cannot, you must not, trust your relations." She opened her eyes and her pupils were dilated as if she had been looking into the darkness. "Your dapper uncle Henry has dueled many of your cousins just come upon manhood. He employs young ladies and then 'steals' them away. This provokes a predictable confrontation—and then a snapped neck, bullet to the brain, or blade to the heart. He is a most kind assassin, as his methods are at least quick.

"Gilbert . . ." Grandmother's jaw clenched. "He has always had a predilection for the younger women in our family, sometimes seductions, and other times less than gentlemanly methods."

Fiona shifted uncomfortably on the love seat at this.

"And sweet Aunt Lucia prefers poisons. Once a young boy, your second cousin, was hidden away in an orphanage near Cork, Ireland. Lucia did not know which orphanage, so she planted swine belladonna near the local dairy farms to taint the milk. The following spring hundreds of children died the 'sleeping death.' "[20]

It seemed too weird to be true, but Eliot had never known Grandmother to lie.

The air in Grandmother's office pressed in on Eliot, smothering him, hot in his lungs. "You're saying they're going to murder us? Is that what their trials are about?"

"Yes . . . and no," Grandmother replied. "Their heroic trials will determine your lineage. If you succeed and are judged part of the family, then you have a chance. I can protect you while you learn to protect yourselves from the others."

"What if we don't pass?" Fiona whispered.

Grandmother said nothing and her gaze turned steely.

Fiona looked at Eliot. Tension creased her forehead; she was probably feeling the same thing he was: trapped.

"I don't understand why we're going through this," Eliot protested. "There are birth certificates and DNA tests that can prove whom we're related to."

20. "Leaf of blue-veined and white pucker bells be portents of eternal sleep. Taken seed from devil's spore, swollen fruit of Swine Bells brings the terror of night and Angel of Death. Fields of vile bell be purged by flame and salt." Father Sildas Pious, *Mythica Improbiba* (translated version), c. thirteenth century.

"Of course there are," Grandmother said. "The family already knows where you come from. They are not concerned with that. They want to know what you will be when you grow up, part of this family, or . . ." She shook her head, unable to finish.

"Or part of our father's family," Eliot said. "The one you've been feuding with?"

A mix of annoyance and pride rippled across Grandmother's features, and that was enough for him to know he'd hit on something important.

Fiona pressed for more as she scooted to the edge of the love seat. "Why are they like this? I thought families were supposed to take care of each other."

"Normal families do," Grandmother replied, "or they *can*. That has never been our way. In this family the weak are leveraged by the strong. Vendetta and murder are more a part of your heritage than any DNA. Only the strong survived, and only then with skill and some luck."

"Couldn't we hide?" Fiona asked, an edge of desperation creeping into her voice. "Like before Uncle Henry found us?"

Grandmother's face smoothed into its normal stony inscrutability. "It has been a very long night. You must be rested for whatever tomorrow brings. Cecilia, bring tea."

Cee, still in the doorway, vanished and returned with a serving tray and two steaming cups.

"Drink," Grandmother ordered. "And then to bed."

Eliot wanted more answers. He was familiar, though, with this routine: Grandmother shutting down, making them do homework or chores or go to bed.

Fiona took her cup first and obediently sipped.

"It's the perfect temperature," Cee told Eliot.

He sighed, took the cup, and sipped the blend of chamomile, spearmint, and honey. It was good, and before he realized it, he'd drunk it all.

Grandmother said, "We can discuss this more when the sun rises." She beckoned to them for a good-night hug. Eliot and Fiona received a token embrace, then were ushered out of Grandmother's office.

She slid the doors shut behind them.

Cecilia walked them down the hall. "Sleep is best. Rest for the body and soul. And no eavesdropping," she warned them. "Your Grandmother is in no mood for your usual tricks."

They halted at their bedroom doors. Fiona shot Eliot a look, then nodded toward the floor.

"Good night," Eliot said to Cee, and gave her a kiss on the cheek.

"G'night," Fiona echoed.

Cee shooed them into their rooms.

Only after Eliot had closed his door did he hear Cee's steps retreating down the hallway.

He waited a moment until he couldn't hear her anymore, then moved to his bed. He pulled a wool blanket off and, draping it over his head, lay flat on the floor, his face over the vent.

"You there?" he whispered.

Fiona's tinny voice drifted from the grate: "Yeah."

Eliot had a million things to talk about, but he'd start with the obvious: "You okay?"

"I don't know. I feel like I'm going to throw up—no, like I'm going to wake up from a dream and *then* throw up. You?"

"I feel like that time I hit my head on the sink at Ringo's. You think it's true? Everything Henry and Grandmother said?"

"It's so weird, it has to be true. And when has Grandmother not told us the absolute truth?"

"Well, she sure has kept secrets," Eliot shot back. "Homicidal cousins? One side of the family at war with the other? Us in danger our entire lives?" This isn't what he wanted to talk about, so he tried to change the subject. "I still don't understand the ride to Uncle Henry's island."

"Wait . . . so you don't think we can trust Grandmother?" An edge crept into Fiona's voice.

"Of course we can trust her . . . Maybe. I don't know. She said not to trust anyone in the family. I mean, she could have really killed that Mr. Welmann guy."

A wave of heaviness passed through Eliot's body: Cee's chamomile tea working on him.

"Whatever she's done," Fiona said, "she's done it to protect us. Can't you see that?"

"I just wish she'd told us earlier so we could have figured this out for ourselves."

"Figure out what?" Fiona asked angrily. "If we'd been kids when we met Uncle Henry and the others, what then? Kidnapped? Killed? Worse?"

Just as Eliot had known Uncle Henry was part of the family when they'd first met, he now felt an instinctual mistrust of him and the others. Just as when he saw a brightly colored spider; it was pretty, but he knew it had a venomous bite.

"I guess so," Eliot replied. "I just want to think for ourselves—not take everything Grandmother says as the absolute truth."

"Think whatever you want, but Grandmother has always taken care of us. She always will." A long sigh echoed through the heater vent. "I'm tired. I'm going to sleep. We can figure out what we're doing in the morning."

It was after midnight and technically it *was* morning. Fiona should have known that. Eliot felt a spike of irrational irritation that his sister was being so stupid.

He wanted to talk more, but Fiona's presence on the other side vanished, and a hollowness filled the vent.

"Fiona?"

Neither of them just left a conversation like that—not without a quip, some obscure reference. But she hadn't called him so much as a *Stapelia gigantea*.[21]

Eliot wanted to shout through the vent for her to come back, but that would only attract Grandmother's attention and might get them a new rule prohibiting "clandestine intraventilation communications."

He got up and rolled onto his bed, not bothering to take off his clothes.

Eliot stared into the darkness and wondered about his father's side of the family. Why was no one talking about them? Uncle Henry, Aunt Lucia, and possibly Grandmother had murdered. Could the other family be somehow . . . worse?

---

21. *Stapelia gigantea*, the zombie or starfish flower, is a succulent plant native to South Africa. The large starfish-shaped flowers exude a "rotting flesh" odor that attracts flies to transfer its pollen. *St. Hawthorn's Collected Reference of Horticulture in the New World and Beyond*, 1897 (Taylor Institution Library Rare Book Collection, Oxford University).

17

THE MANUFACTURE OF TEMPTATION

Beal Buan, Lord of All That Flies, piloted his Sikorsky S-92 helicopter into an updraft and soared over the icy Swiss Alps. The sun warmed his face, and he floated beyond all cares.

In that instant he was free from his responsibilities as chairman of the Board. Of course, without his iron rule they would have fallen upon one another in open civil war. He was, as they say, a necessary evil.

He drew strength from the air, drew it deep into his center, and cherished the moment of peace. Beal then spotted his destination and the moment passed.

He tapped Uri, who sat in the copilot's seat, and pointed.

Nestled upon a rocky ledge a thousand meters below was a fortress with high spires and stained-glass windows that would have looked more at home in a snow globe.

"Le Château de Douleur Délicieux," he said into his throat microphone.

Uri furrowed his brow, his French apparently rusty, then said, "The Castle of Delicious Pain?"

"It was an abbey in the Middle Ages. We converted the facilities and monks to bolster our Foods Division."

Uri grunted and looked uneasy in the turbulence.

Beal had gladly accepted Uri's service; he was an unparalleled intelligence operative. But Beal also knew Uri was part of some trap Sealiah had set. He welcomed the opportunity to expose her treachery. For too long she had hidden in the shadows of the family, gathering power.

Golden eagles flanked the Sikorsky, gliding at a discreet distance from its whirling rotors.

Beal smiled at the raptors who had come to be his escort. The creatures of the air were the only things that had never betrayed him.

The birds scattered, signaling a change in the winds.

Beal braced.

The helicopter plunged and spun in a chilled downdraft.

Uri clutched at his harness.

Beal released the controls and let the craft pitch toward a rock wall. Granite and ice and sky flashed by in a dizzying blur.

He laughed and rammed the power to full. The helicopter's nose snapped up; the craft rotated once and featherlike touched upon the landing pad outside the castle's walls.

"You will come to trust my maneuvering skills," he assured Uri, hoping his double meaning was clear.

"Yes, sir," Uri said, and smoothed out the wrinkles in his black windbreaker.

Beal looked into the cargo bay. Pallets of plastic-wrapped burlap sacks sat waiting. "See to the beans. Make sure they are untouched by human hands."

Uri gave him a slight bow, and Beal noticed that his ever-present emerald skull pin was now a blue star sapphire. He let the minuscule size of his emblem pass. In time Uri would learn to love him as much as his former mistress.

Beal removed his sunglasses and checked his leather jacket, sky-blue silk shirt, and polished boots. Appearance was important to one's underlings. Image *was* substance.

He jumped onto the landing pad.

The master confectioner was there to greet him. The man's head and eyebrows had been shaved so no stray hairs could accidentally fall into his creations. His skin was so taut it gave him a near skeletal appearance. He wore the black robe of a Roman Catholic monk, but carried neither rosary nor crucifix; instead a silver chain and water-blue stone encircled his neck.

"My lord, Mr. Baun." The master confectioner knelt and kissed Beal's ring.

Beal accepted the gesture of supplication and then, annoyed at the delay, withdrew his hand. "All is ready?"

The master confectioner flinched as if he'd been struck. "Yes, my lord. Save the beans. The quantity of silver palm required is beyond our means."

"I have brought them."

The master confectioner stood and murmured an inaudible prayer of thanks. His eyes widened as he watched Uri wrestle pallets off the Sikorsky, each containing one hundred twenty-gallon sacks filled with silver palm cacao beans.[22]

"They have been prepared?"

Beal nodded. "The fermented pods have been dried in the equatorial sun."

The master confectioner gestured for him to follow, and they passed through the raised portcullis and into the reception hall. Beal halted, inhaling rich butter, cream vanilla, a hint of ginger, almonds, and peppermint. His skin pebbled with gooseflesh at this olfactory seduction. He grinned knowing Le Château de Douleur Délicieux was prepared for full production.

They entered the grinding room, where stainless steel hoppers fed a succession of rotating spiked gears. Acolytes in pink jumpsuits unloaded the first pallet and with care poured glistening white husks into the contraption.

Husks were shredded and separated and the dark beans within whisked into finer grinding chambers. From the other end poured a brown sludge that smelled of smoke and citrus: the cocoa liquor. This collected into a silver urn that the master confectioner took into the next chamber.

This room was a converted chapel. It was sweltering and Beal removed his jacket. Red-tinged sunlight streamed through stained glass. From the rafters hung dozens of silk tubes, each tied at the bottom.

Two assistants filled one of these socks with cocoa liquor, then hoisted it aloft. From a side passage a choir of boys entered and began singing to these elongated chocolate sausages. Their soprano voices intoned the

22. The silver palm cacao is a near extinct subsubspecies of the more common cacao (*Theobroma cacao*). Found only high in the Andes, it is notoriously difficult to cultivate and used exclusively for worship ceremonies of the Mesoamerican gods. The conquistador Hernán Cortés once stole a sip of silver palm cocoa. Accounts from his officers relate that he said all other cocoa in comparison tasted as dirt. *St. Hawthorn's Collected Reference of Horticulture in the New World and Beyond*, 1897 (Taylor Institution Library Rare Book Collection, Oxford University).

"Hymn of Dark Sweetness," then "The Chant of the Rum-Sugar Plum Fairy."

Beads of oil appeared, dribbled along the length of the tube, and dripped into crystal dishes. This was the cocoa butter.

Beal withdrew a cigar case and opened it. Within were dried blood-red blossoms. "From the Lady Sealiah's fields," he said, and offered the case. "Crush them and sprinkle the powder into the butter."

The master confectioner bowed so his forehead scraped the cobblestones. "A tremendous honor," he whispered.

Beal watched as gallons of the cocoa butter collected, and the crushed poppy dust was sprinkled over the precious substance.

The family had pooled resources to expedite the testing of the Post twins. Cooperation? Hardly. It was the calm before the storm, the maneuvering of one another into the proper backstabbing position.

But, of course, the ends justified any means. In this case the twins might give the family an excuse to unite . . . something that had only happened once before.

Beal felt a tug at his heart, a feeling he had not experienced since he was a child: hope.

When enough cocoa butter had collected, it was combined with cane sugar and fresh vanilla from the castle's hothouse orchids.

Milk was added to a portion of this mixture to make a snow-white chocolate. A portion of the original liquor was added to produce a milk chocolate. And a last portion was created with the cocoa butter, sugar, vanilla, and the original liquor to create Beal's personal favorite: dark chocolate the color of night.

These varieties, while smelling divine, congealed into unappetizing clumps. They were scooped into ceramic drums the size of cement mixers and hundreds of gold beads poured over them.

The electric mixers rotated, starting the "conching" that would grind the larger particles of chocolate so small they would elude detection by the human tongue and thus be silky smooth to the palate.

After this, the chocolate was tempered in copper kettles to make it resistant to crumbling.

The moon was high in the stained-glass windows when the first batch was ready to sample. The master confectioner scraped a block of chocolate with a tiny knife. He dropped the resulting curl into his mouth. He trembled and his eyes turned into his head from sheer delight.

He spat into a handkerchief and regained his composure. "Perfection," he announced with a sigh.

Beal longed to taste it—just one tiny bite; what could it hurt? He had breathed roasting cocoa all day and it had filled him with desire. He caught himself and laughed at his near disastrous error.

The master confectioner snapped his fingers. "Gather the chocolatier chefs," he shouted. "Assemble the prepared ingredients."

He gestured that Beal join him on the observation catwalk. Beal climbed up the stairs that led to the open walkway with an aerial view of the final assembly line.

The smell was overpowering: orange zest and espresso bean and lavender, champagne bubbles, strawberry and cinnamon and vanilla, and, of course, coating it all was a smothering vapor of chocolate.

Below them dozens of chefs stood ready at tables with mixers, double boilers, and bowls. A conveyor trundled down the center of the hangarlike room.

The master confectioner handed Beal a breathing mask and a pair of Zeiss binoculars. Beal strapped on the mask and peered through the binoculars to watch each tiny confection handcrafted.

There were delicate shells filled with Dom Pérignon truffles, sprinkled with sugar crystals; dark eggs overflowing with Sicilian lemon crème; milk chocolate diamonds with frosty peppermint centers; cups of ebony black with frozen cappuccino froth; spheres of white and brown swirls containing cherry cordial; walnut clusters, squares with caramel curlicues on top; honey-filled confections plastered with pansies; one chili shaped, its tip fluorescent red; and on and on they paraded past along the conveyor . . . hundreds of them . . . thousands.

Would it be sufficient? "Enough" was never enough when it came to temptation. After all, it was possible he targeted one of his own with this ruse—and *their* appetites were insatiable.

The master confectioner handed Beal a clipboard with inventory and bill attached.

Beal raised his eyebrows at the exorbitant cost, but then again, how could one put a price on reuniting a family and leading them victorious to war?

"Delivery form underneath," the master confectioner said.

Beal filled in the address Uri had provided, double-checking numbers and the Del Sombra, California, zip code, and making sure all names were correctly spelled. After all this effort to have it delivered to the wrong person . . . well, as they said, the devil was in the details.

"And the card?"

The master confectioner handed him a blank note of creamy hand-pressed paper.

Beal wrote: *To my dearest Fiona . . .*

18

SELECTING A TEMPTRESS

Sealiah was home—the rocky hills and fetid valleys that bore such names as the Shadow of Death, the Dusk End of Rainbow, Venom-Tangle Thicket—the Poppy Lands of Hell.

She rode one of the white Andalusians that had been a gift from the Philippine ambassador. The animal was spirited and sensitive to her every command. She wished she had a hundred like her.

Ahead on the bluff was her villa, Doze Torres.[23] The pink stucco walls and sunset-hued spires beckoned to her, its color contrasting with the perpetual iron-gray sky.

She could have flown to the summit but she had wanted to ride, think, and decide how to choose among the thousands of applicants for the new position in her organization.

Already the line of interviewees snaked from Doze Torres to the base of its hill. More were streaming from the jungle-filled vales and fungus-lined caverns—like insects swarming toward a single crumb of cake.

Most wore traditional slave robes, but some had their period costumes: lace and parasols, slinky cocktail dresses, latex bodysuits. Perhaps they thought this would improve their chances . . . as if Sealiah didn't already know their reputations and abilities.

Sparkling like stars among the common seductresses were Cleo, who managed to look radiant in rags, and Margaretha Zelle (not so pretty but nonetheless exuding a confident sensuality), demure Norma Jeane, Janis, and Eva.

23. Portuguese translation: Twelve Towers.—Editor.

They were all so desperate; it filled her with disgust.

And really, how qualified did one have to be to seduce a single boy on the cusp of his manhood? Any girl could do that. Yet Sealiah needed something more: she needed a woman capable of seducing a boy in *this* family. That would take a different breed entirely.

She wished Uri were here. With his little black book, he would have found some determining factor to separate the chaff.

One of the girls in line spotted her and abandoned her place, walking quickly away.

Sealiah didn't give the waif another thought and encouraged her mare into a trot. She rounded the walls of Doze Torres to where her garden grew wild and the cliff's edge overlooked the Valley of the Shadow of Death.

Below were colors that van Gogh could have painted: poppies covered the lowlands and the silver sinew of the Laudanum River wound through them. There were countless red and white and pink dots, the traditional opium poppies, and the yellows and black-and-white stripes and indigo-blue varieties that she had bred. The winds smelled of honey and freshly turned earth . . . and mixed in with this, the delicious echoes of the screams of millions who lived and died, and died again.

She loved every blossom in each of her valleys. They were tiny budding vessels of decadence and dream.

Sealiah indulged in the view a moment—then recalled the girl who had left the applicant line. It had not been the fear Sealiah usually inspired. This girl had a glare of hatred . . . intriguingly directed at *her.*

She wheeled her mare about and broke into a gallop down the hill. Before thundering Andalusian hooves, slaves scattered, and Sealiah applied her riding crop to their backsides.

That made her feel a tad better.

The waif she wanted was almost down the hill, sprinting before her. It would have been easy to run her down. Sealiah, however, had business with this one . . . so such pleasures would have to wait.

The girl was slender and strands of hair whipped about her head.

Sealiah galloped ahead and reared back before the girl.

She fell to her knees.

Smart girl. Had she continued to run, Sealiah would have lost her composure, pursued, and trampled her. There were limits to her patience, after all.

She dismounted and rubbed the flank of her mare, calming the creature.

"Stand," Sealiah commanded the girl.

The girl did so, keeping her gaze respectfully in the dirt where it belonged.

"Look at me."

The girl obeyed. There was no fear in her eyes; instead, they smoldered with anger.

It was delightfully refreshing.

This one deserved a second looking over. She wore a tight spandex top with a radiation warning symbol silk-screened on it. Stenciled under this were the words ATOMIC PUNK. Tattered black-and-white-striped stockings clung to her legs. Combat boots armored tiny feet, and a dog collar encircled her throat. Razor-wire-motif tattoos were inked on skinny biceps. Her hair had once been blond, but was now streaked with pink and black and greens. Beneath far too much makeup was a heart-shaped face, full cheeks, and perfect lips. Pretty enough.

"Why did you leave the line?"

"I don't like to play unless I know I'm going to win . . . ma'am." The girl's voice was honey-thick with an American Georgian accent.

She had spunk—but was a poor liar. A potentially fatal flaw.

Sealiah subdued her irritation. "I will tell you this just once, girl: never lie to me. I can tell you are a gambler . . . for money . . . and other pleasures. Not a very good one, either, or you would not be here."

The girl narrowed her eyes and spat out, "I left because the job you're offering is a trick, isn't it? That's what you people do. Get our hopes up and crush them."

The girl's voice trailed off, and her anger vanished as she realized that she had perhaps gone too far—that many things were worse than death—and that she stood in front of one of them.

"We do not get anyone's 'hopes' up," Sealiah cooed. "You do that all by yourself."

She took the girl's hand, pulled, and twisted. A procession of needle tracks punctuated the girl's inner forearm. "As I said," Sealiah murmured, "you gambled for just a little more pleasure . . . and lost." She released the limb. "Tell me your name."

The girl curled her arm close to her chest, and a bit of the smoldering hate rekindled in her eyes. "I'm Julie Marks, ma'am."

"Julie Marks, formerly what? A sixteen-year-old prostitute? Late of some back alley in Atlanta?"

Julie's face reddened.

"Well, I may have a job for you, Miss Marks, one with rich rewards, and no tricks—but first a question to gauge your sensibilities. What is a woman's most valuable bodily asset in seduction?"

Julie looked surprised, but recovered quickly and examined her figure, thinking. Her body was full in all the right places, lean in the others.

Sealiah could work with such material. Remove the makeup, pale her up a bit, and lose the tattoos . . . she could be just what was needed. Possibly even irresistible.

But she was taking so long to answer. Sealiah feared the girl might say her most valuable asset was "her brain," in which case it was best to put the foolish thing out of her misery.

Julie's eyes widened and her black fingernails touched her throat. "The neck?"

Could the child actually know something? "Why?"

"The other parts," Julie replied, "they're what get looked at first. Too obvious. But there's kind of a language to seduction. You get a man close, expose the neck, and that's like an invitation, isn't it? And they're such wolves . . . especially the 'gentlemen.' It's in their blood to go for the throat."

So she did understand a bit. Apparent supplication. The instinct to bite and conquer. It made for a potent trap.

And Julie Marks did have a lovely neck. Sealiah ran one finger across it. The girl stiffened, but dared not move. She had the kind of translucent flesh and delicate bones that Michelangelo would have burned his soul to capture. "You may do."

"Yes, ma'am," Julie whispered with restrained rage. Her mouth worked without words, then she found the ability to speak: "My auntie was a witch. Creole. And as old as the swamp. She said you could sometimes make a deal with the devil . . . by winning against him at dice."

Sealiah's annoyance flared. Swamp witch! This sounded like one of Louis's mythical encounters. If she knew him, there was likely some seduction involved, as well.

It was outrageous that this common Julie Marks asked for dice and terms. The girl had no affiliation to any Infernal clan; she had no right to roll. Sealiah's hands clenched into fists so tight, the nails cut her palms.

Her emotions subsided like the ocean calming after a hurricane. But then again, there was no reason *not* to let her roll, either. Julie Marks was providing an entire afternoon of entertainment—that alone was reason to see where this led.

"By requesting dice, and me accepting, you have locked us into a time-honored ritual," Sealiah said. "I have asked you to do a job for me; you asked to roll for terms. I will set the terms of the deal if you lose; you set the terms if you win."

Julie swallowed. "I can ask for anything?"

Sealiah nodded.

"Then I want out of hell. I mean . . . I want to live again. Can you do that?"

This girl had iron in her. She would indeed do nicely. "You may ask for that," Sealiah replied. "But in turn, if I win, I may ask for any terms I so desire."

Julie Marks trembled, but nodded.

Sealiah pulled out a Naga of Dharma from her pocket. Ashmed had given her one of the legendary dice after the Board meeting. *It is an extraordinary gift,* he had said, *for an extraordinary woman.* She held the die out to Julie.

She took it. "I just throw it?"

"Not quite. This is my domain, so the odds are mine to set. I give you one chance in six. The other five chances are mine. Pick your number."

Julie paled. "Okay. . . . It's more of a chance than I had a second ago." She turned the die over and looked at the scrimshaw pips. "This one." She held out the face with six ravens for Sealiah to see. "I like the birds."

"Birds of black. Carrion eaters, razor-eyed, bringers of wisdom. A good choice. Go ahead, child."

Julie swayed as if she might faint. She opened her hand . . . and let the Naga of Dharma fall.

The cube hit the dirt, bounced with a puff of dust, and rolled to a stop.

Six ravens landed faceup.

Sealiah felt a flutter of wingbeats thrum through the air; a black feather drifted and settled next to the die.

"I won," Julie said, and her eyes turned up to the overcast sky. "Screw this place—I am *so* out of here."

Sealiah picked up the Naga. "Not yet." She set a hand on Julie's shoulder and the girl flinched. "There is the small matter of the task you must first perform: a young man to seduce."

Julie was suddenly all business. "Right. I'm ready. What's his name?"

"Eliot. Eliot Post."

THE FIRST HEROIC TRIAL

19

BROKEN

Fiona moved before she woke up, making her bed and laying out her clothes. A lifetime of schedules had been ingrained in her: she knew how to work even semiconscious.

She must have slept wrong, however; her arm throbbed. Rubbing her elbow, she went to review her homework. Her essay on Isaac Newton sat on her desk—only half-done.

Panic fluttered through her heart. Grandmother did not tolerate unfinished work. There'd be penalty assignments and extra chores.

No . . . there wouldn't be. Fiona was suddenly ice-water-splashed-into-her-face awake. There were reasons her homework hadn't been done last night.

She examined her arm: bruises dotted the elbow where Mike had grabbed her.

Fiona moved to her globe and traced their limousine ride—up the California coast to the north pole and then down to the Mediterranean.

She picked up the sweatshirt she'd worn yesterday and held it to her nose. It smelled of deep-fryer oil, car leather, and sea salt—evidence these events hadn't been a dream.

An entirely new family was in her life now, people who wanted her and her brother dead unless they passed their "trials." She had a feeling no one would be asking them mathematical puzzles or Zen koans, either. What had Uncle Aaron called them? "Heroic trials"?

How did you prepare for something like that?

She scratched her head and recoiled, disgusted with the greasy texture.

Whatever these family trials were, she wanted to be clean when she faced them.

She marched into the bathroom before Eliot got there.

Fiona halted in front of the mirror. Her hair curled into helices. She twined a finger through it and sighed. It had to go. It looked amazing, but she couldn't stand the unclean feel.

She twisted on the shower faucet and stepped in. The cold water shocked her, but she relaxed as it heated. It wouldn't last long. You'd think as building manager Grandmother could have arranged for them to get all the hot water they needed. No such luck.

Fiona opened a bottle of Cee's homemade shampoo. Sharp antiseptic vapors filled the air. Cee made the stuff by rendering animal fat on the kitchen stove, adding raw industrial-strength lye, then lacing it with toxic herbs and alcohol. Nauseating. It did, however, clean to the pores, stripping away dirt, oil, and a few layers of scalp. She scoured off the stink of Ringo's until her skin reddened.

One good thing had come out of this new family and their trials: Fiona wouldn't have to go to work today.

Uncle Henry had said that this was like a custody battle. But a battle occurred between two or more sides, so where were her father's family in all this? Why hadn't they sent a letter or called?

The water cooled. Fiona stepped out and rubbed herself dry.

She wiped the mirror and saw that her hair had curled into black ribbons even more luxuriant than before. It would frizz into a mess as it dried, she was certain, so she vowed not to look into another mirror today.

She pulled on corduroy pants, a white shirt, and boots. These were her most "adventuresome" clothes. They made her look like Grandmother and made her feel as if she could take on the world.

She *could* take on the world.

Fiona opened the door, stepped into the hallway, and almost ran into Eliot. "Hey," Eliot said, yawning. "Any hot water left?"

She opened her mouth to call him an *Eudyptula albosignata*.[24] She stopped, though, remembering how angry she was with him. He didn't deserve a clever insult like that.

They'd fought last night because Eliot didn't trust anyone—as if this

24. Commonly known as the white-flippered penguin. It is the smallest member of the penguin family, only thirty centimeters tall (twelve inches) at maturity.—Editor.

were some sort of Machiavellian plot. He didn't even trust Grandmother of all the stupid things.

Fiona moved past him, bumping him rudely in the shoulder.

She looked back and he just stared at her, eyes narrowing . . . and more important, not so much as one syllable of insult for her in return.

He was still mad at her, too. Good.

This was precisely what Fiona wanted, although she was unsure why. Maybe it was because he had doubted Grandmother, the *only* constant thing in their lives. Hadn't she tried to protect them from Uncle Henry and the others for the last fifteen years? Hadn't she raised them after their mother and father died? Not trusting Grandmother was like not believing the sun was going to rise.

Fiona sat at the dining table and the angry thoughts in her head vanished.

She smelled bacon.

Cee entered with a tray of toast, juice glasses brimming, a coffeepot, sliced fruit, and what must have been two pounds of crisp bacon. Beaming, she set it on the table.

"Heroes must start with a good breakfast," she said.

The toast was buttered and golden. There were grapefruit halves and tangerine wedges, bunches of wine-red grapes and slivers of apple. Fiona picked up a slice of bacon and greedily stuffed it into her mouth. It was smoky and crunchy and decadently rich. She grabbed more with one hand, a stack of toast with the other.

Miraculously, nothing was burned. But the only thing she had ever seen her great-grandmother make before without burning was tea. And bacon? When had they ever had that?

Cee poured her a mug of coffee.

"Wow, this is great, Cee," she said, mouth half-full.

. Cee smiled and patted her hand. "Save some for Eliot. Both of you will need your strengths today."

Fiona stopped chewing, recalling what Cee had said before they'd left for Uncle Henry's. *Do no let them separate you. You are stronger together.*

They *had* been better together yesterday. When they had crossed that bridge holding hands, and when they had answered the family's questions. She couldn't have done those things without Eliot by her side.

Fiona was mad at him for not trusting Grandmother, but wasn't she doing the same thing by not forgiving and trusting him? She wasn't sure.

They'd fought before, but this felt different, as if something between them had broken.

How was she going to cope with an entirely new family when she couldn't even get a handle on just her, Eliot, and Grandmother?

Eliot appeared, hair still wet, and sat at the opposite side of the table, pretending not to see her.

"This is amazing, Cee," he said, and started to eat.

Halfway through his third piece of toast he looked up at Fiona, and she shrugged at the bounty of food. He nodded, acknowledging the strangeness of the breakfast.

They still had nonverbal communication at least.

The door to Grandmother's office slid open and she entered, holding a sheaf of papers in one hand. She wore black combat boots, jeans, and a flannel shirt buttoned all the way up. Her silver hair radiated from her head in tiny spikes.

"Good morning, Grandmother," Fiona and Eliot said.

"I hope you slept well." She set the papers on the table. "Bacon, Cecilia?" She took a piece and experimentally nibbled. "It *is* bacon, isn't it?"

"Of course," Cee replied. "What else would it be?"

Grandmother reexamined the bacon and set it back down. She then tapped the papers on the table. "There will be a grace period for yesterday's assignments due to extreme circumstances. But I expect you to complete today's assignment as well."

"But the trials," Fiona said. "We're supposed to be tested today."

"Or the Council may take weeks to decide what form the trials may take," Grandmother replied.

Eliot dropped his toast onto his plate.

The iron determination Fiona had earlier felt liquefied and drained from her body. They might have to wait *weeks*? That was like they'd been told a tidal wave was coming . . . but then asking them to build sand castles as if nothing were going to happen.

"Life will go on," Grandmother explained. "I will not let the family interfere with your previous responsibilities."

Certainly Grandmother couldn't mean what Fiona thought she meant. She glanced at the front door and saw two paper bags. Cee had made them lunches. Fiona's heart sank and settled into her lower intestine.

They were going to Ringo's today. As if they didn't have enough to worry about with three trials that would determine if they lived or died—she'd have to bus tables and deal with greasy disasters in the kitchen, too.

Eliot saw the paper bags as well. "It's not fair," he whispered.

Grandmother raised an eyebrow. "Nothing is fair where this family is concerned. These trials will test who you already are; there is nothing you can do to prepare. You must simply be yourselves and live your lives." She glanced at her watch, and a second later the hallway clock chimed the quarter hour. "This includes work."

Fiona sat and stewed, working up her courage to demand that Grandmother tell them more about the family. Why did working at a pizzeria matter anymore?

Eliot stood. "See you later," he muttered. "Thanks for breakfast, Cee." He marched to the door.

Fiona was dumbfounded for a moment—then raced after him, but not before he'd grabbed the larger bag.

She shouldered past him and tore down the stairs. It felt good to run (and to beat her brother), but as she pushed through the steel security door and out into the open, she saw that he wasn't running behind her.

He ambled outside and shuffled down the street without a word to her. She marched alongside him.

The arguing she could take. Their insults were as much a part of their morning as breathing, but this silence was something new for him. Fiona didn't like it.

Of course, if push came to shove, she could be quiet, too—and for much longer than Eliot. She could be silent the rest of her life if she had to.

"You're just so stubborn," she muttered.

He shrugged and kept walking.

"But maybe you're right," she said. "This new family does feel a little Machiavellian. Hey, there's that folio in my room, *Discorsi su villainy*. We should read that tonight and see if there's any advice that applies to us."[25]

---

25. Among the more curious surviving artifacts from the Post apartment are three unburned pages of *Discorsi su villainy* (Discourses on Villainy). This is a collection of notes predating the writing of Niccolò Machiavelli's *Il principe* (The Prince). Contained therein are unflattering references to the Medici and other rulers of the age. Handwriting experts agree that most of the notes are not Machiavelli's—indicating either the folio is a fraud, or, more intriguingly, someone gave these notes to Machiavelli and inspired his later, famous work. *Gods of the First and Twenty-first Century, Volume 11: The Post Family Mythology,* 8th ed. (Zypheron Press Ltd.).

"Sure," Eliot said noncommittally. He finally looked at her. "You think the other side of the family, our father's side, will show up? Like Uncle Henry did?"

Fiona glanced down Midway Avenue, half expecting to see another limousine, half hoping it would be Uncle Henry to come get them. Maybe this time she'd have the nerve to say more than "Thank you" to his driver, Robert. She bet he could tell her a few things about Henry and the others.

"I don't think so," she said. "I think Grandmother's stopped them." Fiona halted and looked around, imagining that some magnetic field emanated from their apartment building, repelling all danger. "Maybe it's not such a bad thing to get out of the apartment. It'll give us a chance to think a little."

"So you're not completely trusting Grandmother anymore?"

Fiona glared at him. "I still believe she has our best interests in mind, but it might be smart to do a little digging on our own, I guess, on both families."

She wasn't prepared to entirely concede the point from last night. Eliot would be impossible to live with if she did.

"While we're at it," she told him, "we better have you checked for rhinotillexomania." She'd found that one in the *Journal of Clinical Psychiatry*. Habitual nose-picking.

"No thanks. I use a handkerchief." He reached for his back pocket. "Want to see?"

She crinkled her face in disgust. So he figured out the root *rhin* for "nose"—that was too easy.

"I think you better stop indulging in omphaloskepsis," he said.

Fiona didn't know the word, but she could work it out. The *skepsis* part meant an inquiry or the act of looking. The *omphalos* was Greek for "boss" or "center"—no, it also meant "navel." So *omphaloskepsis* meant "contemplating one's navel." Clever.

This was good. Good insults. Good stretching of their vocabularies. Things were falling back into their normal routine.

But Fiona found her thoughts sluggish now and failed to form an appropriately nasty reply.

Instead her feet stepped forward . . . on their own, little skipping steps. Vibrations ran through her body, rhythmic, as if her pulse pounded through her blood—only this was different, melodic, happy and sad at the same time.

Her ears finally heard what her body felt. Half a block ahead in an alley stood the old man who had stolen pizza out of the Dumpster yesterday . . . playing his violin.

20

YOUNG MAESTRO

Eliot wanted to run to the music.

The old man now had a bow for his violin, and he drew it back and forth over the strings, weaving the sweetest tones, which could have been the centerpiece of a classical symphony.

It thrummed along every nerve of Eliot's body. But he couldn't run; his feet insisted on keeping measure with the beat.

The old man stood tall, his head not crooked over his instrument, but rather, the violin lay loosely on his shoulder as his fingers ran over frets like river water over stones. His tangles of ivory hair had been combed back, revealing a widow's peak and streaks of black. His eyes smoldered like two blue coals. He smiled as he played.

Eliot smiled, too, and practically skipped toward him.

Midway Avenue, the buildings, Ringo's, even Fiona by his side, tunneled to a distant point, and there was only the man and the violin, and the strings . . . and then just the music.

Eliot wanted to dance and sing, which would have been the most mortifying thing he had ever done, so he checked his mounting excitement, but kept moving nonetheless forward.

He recognized his music. He had almost missed it because it had so many layers. It was the same song the old man had plunked out yesterday. What had he called it? "Mortal's Coil"?

Eliot thought it a nursery rhyme, so infectious was the melody, like "Twinkle, Twinkle, Little Star" or "Old MacDonald Had a Farm." Only this felt older. Eliot thought that he'd heard it before; that someone might have sung it to him when he was a baby.

His hand moved, trying to plunk out the notes for themselves—as if he held his own violin. But that was stupid. He couldn't play. He'd never even touched a real instrument, thanks to Grandmother's RULE 34.

Eliot imagined he could play, however. He would have composed it differently, a little slower, a different variation here and there. He dreamed he saw a crowd of children prancing about him, a maypole woven with a rainbow of ribbons, heard laughter, and a choir singing along:

> *Young girls and boys run far too fast, wheel o' life turns but never lasts, too soon grown and knowing sin, that's when the fun really begins!*

Fiona touched Eliot's shoulder and he snapped out of his daydream. They stood at the mouth of an alley off Midway Avenue.

Eliot would have shrugged his sister's hand away, but for the fragile truce in effect from last night's fight. If they were going to pass the upcoming trials, figure out anything about their family, they'd have to stick together. Besides, his mind didn't wander when she was this close.

The old man finished the music with a wild flourish and bowed.

Eliot clapped. Fiona let go of him.

"That was the nursery rhyme you played yesterday," Eliot said, "but all twisted and layered, right?"

The old man tapped his lip contemplatively and his smile faded. "Yes, yes. You have excellent ears to decipher the tune."

Eliot wondered if that comment was directed at the dorky angle his ears stuck out from his head, but decided that it was a simple compliment.

He reached forward. He didn't know what he was doing. It was instinct, the way a plant turns to the sunlight, as unconscious an action as drawing a breath—he reached for the violin and bow.

"May I try, sir?"

Eliot flushed. What was he thinking? Didn't you need years of practice with a violin to make it even sound like cat claws torturing a blackboard?

"What are you doing?" Fiona hissed behind him. "You've never even touched one of those things before."

The man looked disappointed. "You don't know how . . . ?"

Sure, Eliot had never touched a violin before, but he desperately wanted to. Why was Fiona always ruining everything for him?

"I've never tried," Eliot admitted.

The old man pulled the violin away.

Eliot quickly added, "So I don't know if I can or not."

The old man snorted, and a smile quirked at the corners of his mouth, which for some reason made Eliot uncomfortable. The old man then sobered and stared at Eliot the way Grandmother could, looking right into his center.

"Then perhaps you should." He handed Eliot the violin and bow.

"The rules," Fiona whispered. "Grandmother is going to—"

"—never find out," Eliot muttered. "*If* we don't tell her."

He took the instrument.

It felt light and heavy in his hands, too big and too small for his grasp, both awkward and a natural extension of his body.

"Be careful with that," the old man told him. "It is one of a kind."

Eliot examined the violin.

It was battered, chipped, and as dull as ordinary wood could possibly be, and yet there was something about it, something deeper than he could see.

He propped the violin on his shoulder as he had seen the old man do and cautiously drew the bow over the strings. A sound like grinding glass on crackling high-tension wires shrieked from the instrument.

The old man flinched.

Overhead, crows cawed in protest.

Undaunted, Eliot relaxed his grip and let the bow's weight do most of the work. The sound calmed to a swarm of angry bees, then settled into smooth tones.

"Ah," the old man sighed, looking impressed.

Eliot repositioned the bow and plunked the strings. To his delight simple but steady notes resounded. After a dozen of these notes, he reassembled their order in his mind and plucked out the nursery rhyme.

The old man applauded. "Bravo, young maestro!" He leaned closer. "So much talent in such delicate hands."

Under normal circumstances that comment would have made Eliot blush, but his hands *were* delicate, too small and too slender—but maybe for an instrument this size just right.

Eliot held the violin and tried the song again, this time bowing. A shaky noise—all scratches and warbles—came at first, but he kept going and it relaxed.

He played.

He no longer saw the alley or the old man or Fiona. Eliot was some-where else with another audience around him: a thousand silent held breaths in a packed concert hall, the shrieking laughs and padding feet of children dancing about him. The air itself circled, driven to frenzy by his song, and Eliot smelled fresh flowers with every note.

He finished with a little uncertain vibrato flourish and withdrew bow from the quavering strings.

Eliot panted. Not a car drove on Midway Avenue, not an insect buzzed over the nearby trash cans; Eliot couldn't even hear his heartbeat. There were only the faintest, dying notes still vibrating deep within the violin.

"*Magnifique!*" The old man clapped Eliot on the shoulder.

Fiona stood staring, her mouth open. Eliot had never seen this expres-sion on his sister before: something between astonishment and anger.

Or was it jealousy? She'd never been jealous of him before. She was always better—at everything.

Fiona composed herself. "We better go. We're already late."

If they were late, maybe Ringo's would call Grandmother. And if she found out about this music . . . Eliot wasn't sure what she would do.

Eliot grudgingly handed the violin and bow back to the old man. "Thank you, sir. Very much."

"Thank *you*. It was an honor to witness your first performance. I hope one of many more to come." He gave Eliot's shoulder a squeeze and took the violin—although the instrument stuck to Eliot's fingers as if it didn't want to leave.

He wanted to play more. This wasn't like work or writing an essay. Eliot had created something all his own.

"I really better go," Eliot said, his eyes still on the violin. "There's work . . . and Grandmother's rules. I'm not supposed to play."

"A rule against playing music?" the old man said. "Really? Even in the Dark Ages they had music—not very good music, but music nonetheless. Even the Nazis liked music. What a ridiculous rule."

"Yeah," Eliot whispered. "Maybe it is."

Fiona led the way back onto the sidewalk.

On the street six crows clustered about some roadkill; they looked up and stared at them.

Back in the alley, Eliot heard the old man whisper after him, "Promises, hearts—*everything* was made to be broken, young man . . . *especially* rules."

21

UNDER THE INFLUENCE

Eliot tried to outwalk his sister—an impossibility given that her legs were three inches longer than his. Instead all he managed was to march in lockstep with her down the street.

"We need to talk," she said.

"About how I *can't* play the violin?"

Fiona frowned and sighed. "You shouldn't have done that."

"Because Grandmother has some rule so I don't miss my homework?"

"There's probably a *better* reason than that—like all the things she did to keep us hidden and safe from the family."

"I think," Eliot said, "she's making us work and has all these rules just to keep us from asking more questions about the family."

"Of course she is. She's kept them a secret to protect us."

Eliot slowed. "But wouldn't it have made more sense to *tell* us about them? Like teaching us how to cross a busy street? Or to stay away from drugs?"

"Maybe," Fiona murmured, slowing as well.

"Now we're not protected *and* we don't know anything. Like how these people—our so-called relatives—might kill us if we fail their trials? How can they get away with that? Are they like the Cosa Nostra?"

"We should definitely check those Machiavelli papers tonight. There might be something we can use in there." Fiona halted. "But in the meantime I want you to stay away from the old guy with the violin. We don't know him. He creeps me out."

"He's a great musician," Eliot muttered.

"He's an old homeless guy."

Eliot was done talking. He'd wanted to figure out what they were going to do about their family and the trials, but Fiona was apparently jealous that he could play the violin, and that's all she was thinking about. She had a talent with foreign languages, and no one had a rule forbidding that. What harm could there be in playing a violin? Millions of people played musical instruments—famous, respectable people. They didn't turn into ax murderers.

He turned toward Ringo's. Cars were double-parked on the street. Over the entrance was a banner that proclaimed UNDER NEW MANAGEMENT. NEW AND IMPROVED MENU!

"That was fast," Fiona said.

"Does that mean Mike isn't coming back?" Eliot asked.

Six people sidled past them into the restaurant.

"We better get inside," Fiona said. "Yesterday was busy. Today looks insane."

Together they pushed through the doors.

Eliot blinked, seeing double. Two Lindas stood by the cash register, helping the people that had come in ahead of him.

He quickly realized as one spoke that they were two different girls. This other girl was blond and the same height as Linda. Eliot hadn't met many girls, but Linda had always been his top pick for beauty—not that he had ever dared look at her too long. But now, Linda's good looks only served to highlight what *real* beauty was.

The new girl glowed, her skin pale and lustrous like marble. Her hair was tousled and curled. Her cheeks and lips and eyes were so fascinatingly animated that Eliot couldn't pull his gaze away. His heart hammered in his chest.

The girl looked up and smiled. It hit Eliot like a punch in the stomach.

"That's them," Linda said, then helped seat the party of six.

"Oh, wonderful," said the other girl. She moved from behind the cash register. "I'm Julie Marks, the new manager. It's nice of you all to show up early. We could sure use the extra help."

She spoke with a honey-sweet Southern accent. She wore a dress with lacy ruffles at the hemline and neck. It was old-fashioned and not the least bit revealing, but the way it moved over her was so hypnotic that Eliot felt dizzy.

"No problem," Fiona replied.

Eliot nodded. It was all he could do because his mouth was too dry to form words.

"Dishes already piled up in back."

Eliot smiled as if Julie had just asked him out.

She said to Fiona, "Help Linda today. Take a few orders, all right?"

Fiona tried to say something, but more people came in and Julie greeted them.

Fiona pulled Eliot into the dining room and whispered, "She seems a little young to be a manager."

Eliot cleared his throat. "Seems fine to me. Anyone's better than Mike."

Fiona stiffened. "I guess so." A crash of dishes came from the party room. "I better go. Try not to drown yourself, okay?"

"Yeah." Eliot failed to think of a quip back. He was too busy counting people in the dining room. Every table was full. Extra chairs had been brought out from storage—all of which meant more dirty dishes.

He pushed through the doors into the kitchen.

Johnny stood before the stove—all burners lit—explaining to a new assistant how to fry up the chicken parmigianas. Johnny wore a white chef's uniform and looked like a pro.

"Hey, amigo." Johnny gave Eliot a little wave. "Business is good today, huh?"

The kitchen had been changed. The deep fryer was gone. A rack of copper pans, steamers, and kettles hung over the stoves. Everything was sparkling clean . . . except the washing sink in the back.

Eliot's gaze drifted over the unassailable peaks of filthy dishes and scorched pots.

"Anyone say how Mike is doing?" Eliot asked.

Johnny's face contorted as if he had never heard of Mike before, then recognition dawned. "Oh, he's fine, but out for the summer. But, hey, we got a new boss lady and owner. They're going to remodel the entire kitchen."

"That's wonderful." Eliot worked up a smile, but he felt ill as he approached the same chipped porcelain sink he'd washed dishes at for the last year.

He sighed, donned his apron and rubber gloves, and plunged in. *Hard work is the cornerstone of character,* Grandmother had always told them.

Hot water and soap sloshed together into a lake of suds. All Eliot could see, though, was Julie Marks's snow-white face and the lacy cuffs of her dress.

He wanted to dream up adventures of them sailing a clipper on the blood-warm Java Sea. Sometimes his daydreams were the only thing that kept him sane—but there were too many other things he *had to* think about.

Like a family that might kill him and Fiona if they failed to pass some heroic tests.

And more immediate: there were a half ton of dishes to clean.

He was worried, scared, and more than a little annoyed that he was literally up to his elbows in filth. Eliot's hands angrily tapped on the side of the basin. That nursery rhyme tune was right at his fingertips.

There was only one thing to do: he grabbed a dish. Scrubbing and tapping and humming away, he got the plate clean in no time.

One down and a few hundred to go. He'd have to pick up the pace.

He thrummed a staccato beat and imagined the music in his head jump in tempo. The water splashed in response.

As Eliot worked, he watched the patterns in the soapsuds. Bubbles coalesced into dozens of tiny hands, some waved hello or good-bye, but most postured rude gestures. He kept washing, rinsing, and then grabbing the next dish. He made the music go faster and saw in the suds flocks of white crows, disembodied smiles, and tiny, swirling galaxies of bubbles.

He sensed someone behind him.

"I know you're busy . . . it's Eliot, right?" Julie Marks's voice was at his shoulder. Her breath tickled the back of his neck.

"Ah-huh," Eliot murmured. He wanted to turn and talk, but the music kept him going; he couldn't drop the beat.

"There are going to be a few changes around here. All for the better, and I wanted to talk to you about them. Later maybe?"

"Sure. Maybe."

"How about now?" Her voice was no longer honey-sweet.

Eliot kept washing. "Later . . ."

He was just echoing her words. He hadn't meant that as an insult, but it *did* sound that way.

The presence at his shoulder left; only her perfume lingered.

He felt bad, but he couldn't stop. He focused, and the music settled to a standstill in his mind.

But it was there still . . . waiting. It was as if he weren't standing in front of a sink, but a conductor's stand, and a hundred musicians were poised in anticipation of his commands. Eliot didn't dare keep them all idle.

He moved his hands, splashed into the water, and waved dish and sponge as if they were batons. French horns blared and rows of cello swelled to life. Harps and kettledrums then joined.

Eliot whipped the nursery rhyme into a full symphony, twisting and turning the melody and making it his. It wasn't as good as the old man's solo performance. He was a master of his craft and Eliot was just beginning, but this was a start.

Fiona came and spoke to him, wanting to talk about Grandmother and the others.

He said something in response—he wasn't even sure what—and after a while, she went away.

She was in another world for all he cared.

His eyes locked upon the water and the vibrations that bounced and rebounded off the walls of the basin. They made crisscrossing patterns, lines of force, threads of destiny that overlapped to make a tapestry. This was the big picture. His life set before him with all its possibilities: triumphs, dead ends, his birth, and his death. It was all there.

The music was there with him, blasting chords and harmonies, choirs of voices and clashing percussion, up and down the scales, a thundering mix of divine and diabolical.

It was out of control . . . but that was part of the wonder of the piece. It was like weather—sometimes a breeze, sometimes a hurricane.

The tempo slowed and the last note wavered and died.

Dripping with sweat, Eliot lifted his pruney hands from the water and looked up.

Every dish and pot was cleaned and dried and stacked.

But more than that: the plates at Ringo's were glazed stoneware that had been scratched dull over the years. These plates, though, were as reflective as if they'd just been removed from a kiln. And the pots—dull and battered before—now shone like the chrome grille of Uncle Henry's limousine.

His fingers started tapping again.

Eliot willed them to stop.

Julie, the most gorgeous girl he had ever seen, had come and talked to him—and he had ignored her. He added this to the list of stupid things he'd done in the last few days.

Fiona had wanted to talk, too. He couldn't even remember what she had said. But they had to talk about things that were life-and-death important.

Eliot looked at the water: it was gray and still. There were no longer stars and lines of force. Had it all been a daydream?

He looked at his "conductor" hands and then balled them into fists.

He believed he had been in control of the music . . . but maybe it had been the other way around. Maybe the music had been controlling *him*.

Eliot wondered about Grandmother's RULE 34. He'd thought her forbidding music was arbitrary or meant to keep him focused on homework. Was there more to it? Was it possible music, for him, might somehow be dangerous?

22

SECRET ADMIRER

L et's talk," Fiona whispered.

Eliot washed dishes and said nothing. He'd plowed through half of the piles in front of him. Fiona had never realized that Ringo's had that many plates. But they had much more important things to talk about than clean dishes.

"Shift is almost over," she said. "I never got my break, thanks to our new manager. Take yours now and we can get a plan together for tonight."

"Uh-huh." Eliot's hands flashed underwater, suds danced on the surface, and he remained at the sink.

Fiona waited and glanced over at Johnny and his new assistant. They were busy, too, but a weird kind of busy. They artistically arranged food on dishes, tossed pizzas, shook copper pots over the flames, moving together as if they were dancing to music. She couldn't hear anything, though.

She nudged Eliot. "Come on."

"Later," he murmured, and kept washing.

Okay, so she deserved a little cold shoulder for giving him a hard time about that stupid violin, but this was silly. They had real issues to sort out: namely, these family tests. What was he thinking? Was he that much a baby that he was going to hold a grudge and get them killed?

Julie Marks sashayed into the kitchen. Under one arm she had a square box the size of a medium pizza.

Fiona disliked this new boss. The girl looked as fresh as she had this morning after hosting all afternoon as well as helping her and Linda wait and bus the tables.

Johnny and the new guy looked up, smiled, and waved at Julie. Why were all the guys treating her like some queen bee? She wasn't *that* pretty. Was it the Southern accent?

Julie moved to the sink. "I know you're busy . . . it's Eliot, right?"

"Ah-huh," he murmured, and continued working, not even turning around.

Why was he acting like such a jerk? Eliot was shy—but this was way beyond simple bashfulness.

Julie tried again to engage Eliot, but he just mumbled a halfhearted reply, totally absorbed in washing the dishes.

A shadow crossed Julie's porcelain features, and a flicker of anger smoldered in her eyes . . . but this vanished as quickly as it had come. She turned to Fiona. "You did great today, honey. A few broken dishes and misorders—but that's to be expected first time out. You really came through for me. Thanks."

She handed Fiona an envelope.

Fiona looked inside: there were five-dollar bills, a ten, and a twenty.

"Your share of the tips," Julie explained. "Easy money from happy tourists."

Their paychecks had always been sent by mail and deposited by Grandmother into a college fund. Fiona never had cash of her own. She ran a finger over the bills, wondering what to do with them.

"Oh, almost forgot." Julie handed the box under her arm to Fiona. "Delivery truck dropped this off for you."

Fiona took it. International customs stamps plastered the box.

"See you tomorrow," Julie said. "Eliot, honey?"

He washed, oblivious to the world.

Julie glared at the back of his head, then tromped out of the kitchen.

Well, Eliot could be rude to everyone and keep scrubbing dishes until tomorrow if that's what he wanted.

Fiona took her package into the women's changing room. She had the place to herself; Linda had already left.

She set her box down. A card was in the plastic wrapping. She hesitated, her fingers on the plastic, feeling static electricity crawl across her skin, then she cautiously slid out the card.

It read:

To my dearest Fiona,
My heart is full for the loveliest creature that walks the earth.
                                                    Worshipfully,
                                              A Secret Admirer

Lovely? Her? She felt dizzy. Was this right? She read it again.

She then checked the name on the delivery label: *Miss Fiona Post c/o Ringo's All American Pizza Palace.*

Was it from Uncle Henry? That would account for the international stamps. Or maybe it was from his driver, Robert?

She smelled the card. There was a faint scent of men's cologne. Her heart skipped a beat.

Robert had barely looked at her the entire drive. Then again, she hadn't dared look at him, either, and here she was thinking about him.

Still, a real secret admirer, any admirer—Fiona took a moment to catch her breath—just as her mother had.

She opened the package. Inside was molded Styrofoam, with a red satin heart-shaped box nestled in its center. She pulled it out. It was much heavier than she thought it would be. She rapped the side: solid wood, not cardboard, under the fabric.

She ran her finger over the luxuriant pleats on the lid, then curled over the lid's edge to pull it off . . . and froze.

What if *this* was the first heroic trial?

She imagined the box full of venomous centipedes. The way Fiona's life worked, that would be more likely than getting a gift box from a secret admirer.

She lifted the box and sniffed. The scents of peppermint, almond, ginger, and chocolate curled through her nostrils.

Fiona's hands seemed to move on their own, opening the lid and tearing off a layer of tissue paper. Her breath caught in her throat.

A dozen chocolates sat in frilled silk cups: fat truffles, solid medallions, foiled balls, creamy white stars, and puckered heart shapes. Not one was the same. Her fingertips hovered over them.

She again considered the possibility of these being poisoned, some sort of test, but that was silly. She wasn't going to ruin her first secret-admirer gift with paranoia.

Her mouth watered. It was no longer a question of *if* she should eat one—but *which one* to eat first.

She closed her eyes and pointed to the exact center: a milky oval with dark tracery that looked like a piece of abstract art. She plucked it up and the smell of rich chocolate tickled her nose. She salivated so suddenly that she had to wipe her mouth.

Fiona then lifted the confection to her lips: a tiny bite. It felt like a kiss. And *not* like a good-night kiss on Grandmother's cheek, either. This was long and deep and touched her center, the way she imagined kissing Robert would be.

Butter-smooth citrus and smoke-tinged cocoa spread over her tongue and down her throat. She took another bite, and honeyed apricots coursed over her palate . . . along with a surprising sharpness of brandy.

Fiona's heart squeezed blood into every capillary, flushing her skin to crimson.

She'd never felt so warm, inside and out—never felt so alive.

She devoured the rest of it. There was no need to nibble when she had so many.

The intensity of the chocolate overwhelmed her; she sat, and every square inch of her flesh pebbled with chills and fire.

Fiona swallowed the last of it. She rested, caught her breath.

Her mind flew over clouds, racing ahead of her thrumming body at the speed of sound. Sparks and aurora flashes filled her thoughts.

She figured it out then—understood what she had to do to get everything done tonight.

Fiona set the lid back and stuffed the box of chocolates into a plastic take-out bag. This she slid down her shirt. She inhaled and crossed her arms over her chest. If she kept moving, there was a good chance no one would see it.

She marched out of the changing room—

—and straight into Eliot.

"I'm finished." He seemed exhausted as he peeled off his soggy apron and unplastered his hair from his face. "So . . . I thought we'd talk on the way home."

"Then let's go home. Stop dawdling." Fiona sidled past him and without looking back went out the back door.

She power-walked out of the alley to the sidewalk. Eliot jogged behind her to keep up.

"So where do we start?" he asked. "Hey—can you slow down already?"

"No. We've gotten a slow enough start today. We start by looking at the

Machiavelli's *Discourses on Villainy*. I have a hunch that those medieval Italian princes were a lot like our mother's and father's families." The plastic under her crossed arms made a slight rustling sound as she increased her stride.

"What do I do? I can't read Italian or whatever that thing is written in."

"You have your talents," Fiona whispered. "I have mine."

"What's that mean?"

They arrived at Oakwood Apartments and Fiona entered the stairwell and sprinted ahead of her brother, easily leaving him and his silly questions behind.

Inside Cee waited with tea and mangled homemade cookies. Fiona blew past her, saying, "Homework—no time to chat." She breezed into her room.

She closed her bedroom door and twisted the tiny lock under the knob. She had made it.

Her finger lingered on the lock, though. She'd never really shut her brother out like this before. But Eliot's head after that music wasn't in the right place to help. He meant well, but she'd work faster, and probably better, alone. It was for the best.

She withdrew her box of chocolates from under her shirt and set it on her bed.

She'd eat a few of these, recapture that feeling of being able to see the horizons, and dive into her homework and that folio—figure out their plan of action.

She opened the box and plucked out another chocolate: an explosion of mint, ginger, and dark chocolate boosted her senses and made her tongue curl with ecstasy.

Everything was so clear.

She reached up and got a collection of rubber-band-bound parchments from the bookcase. She blew off the dust and saw script lettering: DISCORSI SU VILLAINY, *Niccolò Machiavelli*.

There was a knock on the door.

"Let me in," Eliot said, muffled, on the other side. "I can help."

"Go away!" she shouted through the door. "I need to concentrate."

"We should talk."

"Later."

She felt a little satisfaction at throwing the same careless refusal at Eliot that he had used on her earlier today.

Eliot said more, but she tuned him out, focusing instead on which chocolate to eat next. She picked a triangle of red-and-black chocolate. Inside was a cinnamon ganache that smothered her with spice, velvet warmth, and amber shadows.

Then to the folio.

She transcribed Machiavelli's handwritten notes onto three-by-five cards—taking care not to smudge the original document.

Italian was easy for Fiona; it had so many Latin roots. Medieval Italian, however, should have been entirely another story. The meaning of the cramped handwriting, though, was as illuminated to her as stained glass lit by a noontime sun. It had never been like this before.

She read what Machiavelli really thought of the princes of old Italy. Foremost he was terrified that he wouldn't be flattering and he'd be tortured (again) or killed.

There were anecdotal notes that the princes' parlor-room wars often turned inward. The children of these royal families fared the worst in politics. Many failed to live long enough to compete with their elders for power. He called them an "army of pawns" that were used and sacrificed . . . but never, ever allowed to completely cross the board.

Fiona didn't even know which side of the board she and Eliot were supposed to be on: their mother's or their father's side. But that wasn't what their trials were about. Or was it? She wondered if there was more to Uncle Aaron's chess-permutation riddle than she'd first imagined.

She rubbed her eyes and saw her alarm clock blink: 8:30 p.m. Time flew when you were reading about medieval mayhem and murder.

She reached for another chocolate. Her hand cast among discarded silk cups, feeling nothing but paper.

Her stomach sank.

She grabbed the box and brushed out the wrappers.

Gone—all the chocolates. She'd eaten them all and not even realized it.

A cold, drowning sensation filled her.

Besides Grandmother's and Cee's weird gifts, this had been the one thing someone had given her because he or she liked her. She should have savored them. Saved at least one for tomorrow.

She squeezed her eyes. She would have given anything to have more. She'd been so stupid—eating while she worked.

She picked up the box to throw it across her room. Something inside shifted.

Fiona halted and returned the heart shape safely to her lap. She held her breath. Her body trembled.

Inside there was a layer of waxy rice paper . . . which she gingerly lifted.

It was as if the sun had risen again in her world. Relief flooded back into her and she smiled.

Within the box was a *second* layer of chocolates.

23

KILL NOT THE MESSENGER

After Eliot had woken up, he waited fifteen minutes in the hallway for Fiona. He'd even tried knocking once, but she hadn't answered.

She'd never been so late.

From the dining room there were hushed voices. Grandmother and Cee were probably waiting, too. Eliot made sure they couldn't see him. He didn't want to face them alone. He'd done a horrible job on last night's homework: an essay on Napoléon at Waterloo.

Why had Fiona shut him out? Sure he'd been a jerk at Ringo's—totally distracted in his music—but that was no reason to lock her door. Last night he'd called to her as loud as he dared through the heater vent, but she either hadn't heard him or had ignored him.

Maybe she'd gotten caught up in the translation of the Machiavelli folio.

But it didn't change that Eliot was angry at her, too—for being angry at him.

They were supposed to stick together when things got tough, and for the first time the opposite seemed to be happening.

He rolled his essay into a tube and nervously tapped his thigh. Tinkling music pranced at the edge of his mind: that stupid nursery rhyme again.

He stopped his hand and forced his thoughts to be still.

Where the morning light cut the shadows in the hall, dust swirled. These motes looked like tiny birds on thermals and then notes of printed music . . . that he could *almost* understand.

Eliot looked away.

He would stay in control of the song today—not the other way around. He'd had his doubts after yesterday: almost blacking out while washing dishes. But he'd practiced last night, stopping the music every time it crept into his head.

It hadn't been easy. He had *wanted* to listen, but he was afraid he'd lose himself . . . and something a lot weirder than a few dirty plates getting antiseptically cleaned would occur.

He added that to the growing list of hard-to-explain things that had happened recently: the hand he'd seen in the suds before Mike got burned, the gigantic dog that had chased them, and Uncle Henry's limousine ride across the world.

"Come on, Fiona," he whispered at her door. "Get up."

If he waited much longer, Cee or Grandmother would come looking for them.

They'd be late for Ringo's, too. Eliot assumed they were working today. Why not? Grandmother would expect them to work during a ten-point-oh earthquake while California sank into the Pacific Ocean.

He cocked his head and listened, now detecting a third voice in the dining room.

Another relative? He wasn't about to miss another conversation as he had when Uncle Henry had arrived.

Eliot took a deep breath. He wouldn't need his sister to face them this time. He marched down the hall.

Grandmother and Cee sat at opposite ends of the table, and between them was Uncle Henry's driver. Only a year or two older than Eliot, he was a head taller and was twenty pounds heavier. He wore a black leather biker jacket, faded jeans, and white T-shirt. His hair fell into his eyes as if it had never been brushed.

This was how Eliot sometime imagined he looked in his daydreams: part pirate, part secret agent, and all rebel.

"Hi," Eliot said. "It's Robert, right?"

No one spoke. Robert sat bolt upright, his hands on the table and feet poised on boot tips. Cee twisted her hands together. Grandmother's glare was locked onto the driver—pinning him like a beetle to an insect collection board.

"This is Mr. Farmington," Grandmother said.

" 'Robert' will be just fine, ma'am."

Eliot was impressed that he could correct Grandmother. He had a slight accent. Midwestern? A little German thrown in? Fiona would have been able to figure it out.

Eliot held out his hand for Robert to shake.

Robert looked surprised, but he rose, never taking his eyes off Grandmother, then grasped Eliot's hand.

Eliot briefly wondered what it would have been like to have a twin brother instead of a sister. Someone not so emotionally volatile. Robert's grip was politely firm, but the muscle behind it was iron. If he'd been his brother, there'd likely have been more physical instead of mental sparring . . . so maybe things were better the way they were.

"Pleased to meet you," Eliot said.

"Likewise." Robert examined him and the wariness on Robert's features softened.

"This is about the tests, right?" Eliot asked. "Are we beginning?"

Robert gave a shrug that seemed to say that the situation was far more complicated than a cool guy such as himself could ever explain—too many words. "I'm here to meet everyone. Mr. Mimes thought you'd feel more comfortable with me as your Council messenger."

When he said *Council,* much of his coolness evaporated.

Eliot remembered something Uncle Henry had said to Grandmother: *Kill not the messenger.* Was that what had happen to Mr. Welmann? Had he delivered some unpleasant news?

"None of them has courage to face you," Cee whispered to Grandmother. "So they send a boy."

Robert flushed and worked hard to look neither at Cee or Grandmother as he said, "I wouldn't know, ma'am. I just go where I'm told."

Grandmother steepled her hands. "Then go. You've introduced yourself. You are dismissed. We have nothing to communicate to the Council at this time."

He bowed, acknowledging Grandmother's order, but remained where he was.

"There is more?".

"Yes, ma'am. Mr. Mimes wanted me to explain the general nature of the trials. He said that would be only fair."

"Fair indeed," Cee muttered. "Send my lambs to the Wolf for advice."

Robert's jaw clenched as if he were about to say something, but instead he exhaled and kept his mouth shut.

"I'd like to hear it," Eliot said.

Robert nodded, relieved that at least one person wasn't giving him a hard time. "The Council wants the trials to have meaning for you," he said to Eliot. "I mean killing Hydras and dragging Cerberus back from hell . . . who cares about those things these days?"

Robert halted, looking as if he'd just said something wrong. He dared glance at Grandmother.

She nodded and leaned forward. "Continue . . ."

Robert licked his lips. "So the trials are going to be based on *their* myths. Urban legends. Like Bloody Mary in the mirror."[26]

"Bloody who in the what?" Eliot asked.

RULE 55 forbid any reference material on myths and legends like that, urban or classical. Eliot had a sinking feeling that the Council had picked one of the few subjects that he and his sister knew nothing about.

"Oh, dear," Cee whispered, echoing Eliot's thoughts.

Grandmother shot a look that silenced her.

Robert continued. "They thought it was the only fair thing to do. Mr. Mimes said, 'The children's own mythology will bridge their mundane world to the fantastic where they belong.' Or something like that."

Behind Eliot, Fiona said, "I don't think I like Uncle Henry calling me a 'child.'"

Eliot whirled about.

His sister looked as if she had just stepped from the shower. Her hair curled around her face in dark ribbons, not frizzed as usual. She wore her corduroy pants, work boots, and a green shirt and had a frayed canvas book bag slung over her shoulder. These were her least geeky clothes.

She held herself straight and head high and looked confident. She could almost have been a younger version of Grandmother.

"You look nice, sweetie," Cee cooed. The quaver in her voice, however, indicated otherwise.

---

26. A ghost summoned by chanting her name before a mirror often by candlelight and/or being spun about thirteen times. This spirit has many alleged origins: a child murderer (or a wrongfully accused child murderer), a witch, even Queen Mary I. She maims or kills the summoner—although some claim she gives a glimpse of one's future husband (or a skull if one is to die before marrying), making this game popular among adolescent girls. The hallucinations are explained by suggestion; poor lighting, and the dizzying antics that "prepare" the summoner. *Gods of the First and Twenty-first Century, Volume 6: Modern Myths*, 8th ed. (Zypheron Press Ltd.).

"Indeed," Grandmother remarked without emotion.

Robert stared, looking Fiona over, then regained his train of thought. "I'm just telling you what he said, miss."

"I'm Fiona."

She'd seen him before on the ride to Uncle Henry's, but Fiona nonetheless offered her hand as if they'd just met—a gesture halfway between a handshake and a daintily held out wrist that someone was supposed to kiss.

Why was she acting so weird all of a sudden? Eliot's sister didn't speak to strangers, especially boys. And never in front of Grandmother.

Robert took her hand and held it a moment.

Fiona's eyebrow quirked up just as Grandmother's did when she was irritated or interested.

After an uncomfortable few seconds of silence, Grandmother said, "Well, Mr. Farmington, you have come, introduced yourself, and delivered your message. I think it is time you left."

He released Fiona's hand. "Yes, ma'am. You have my number and e-mail if you need me."

Grandmother narrowed her eyes, which Eliot knew meant that she would not need Robert Farmington's services now or anytime in the future.

"I'll see you out," Fiona offered.

"He doesn't need help out," Cee said, covering up her discomfort with a dry laugh.

"It's the least we can do," Fiona said. "Mr. Farmington has come so far to talk to us."

Grandmother gave her a tiny nod.

Fiona led Robert to the door.

"It was nice to meet you," Eliot said.

Robert gave him a casual salute, then bowed to Cee, then bowed lower to Grandmother.

Fiona walked him down the hallway and closed the door behind them.

"I don't like her alone with that boy," Cee whispered.

"She is growing up," Grandmother replied, and took a sip of tea. "Perhaps she will be able to find out more. What is sweet tempts the lips, no?"

Growing up? Is that what Grandmother thought was going on with Fiona? Eliot felt a dozen different things pulling and pushing on them both, forces he didn't understand . . . or like.

24

ONE SMALL, IMPORTANT TRUTH

Fiona walked Robert to the stairs.

Her blood was hot and pounded a drumroll on her chest. She had never been so nervous.

She was getting used to it, though. All she had to do was hold on . . . and not slip back into the ground-staring dork she usually was.

She had stayed awake most of last night, eating the second and third layers from her heart-shaped box (how many chocolates could they cram into the tiny container?), reading Machiavelli, and learning what he thought of the medieval Italian princes—and more important, how to survive them.

Robert paused at the door to the stairwell, pretending to read the USE IN CASE OF FIRE sign there.

He was taller than her and she was unaccustomed to looking up when she spoke to boys. It was a nice change. The smell of his leather jacket was intoxicating.

"Thanks," he said. "For being nice. They told me what to expect from your Grandmother, but"—he glanced back at the apartment door—"she's beyond scary."

"I know."

Grandmother was a terrifying force of nature like a hurricane or earthquake when she wanted to be. You couldn't fight her; you could only survive her. But, oddly, Fiona wanted to tell Robert that she could be kind in her own way, too. She'd protected her and Eliot and had always looked out for their best interests.

Robert brushed the dark hair from his face, and for some reason the gesture made Fiona's heart pound even harder.

"Well, thanks again." He opened the door to the stairwell and started to leave. "See you around."

"I'll walk you all the way. It's no problem."

Robert smiled that simple smile she'd seen before. It was nothing like Uncle Henry's or the other family members' smiles, laced with hidden meaning. It was honest.

Robert held open the door for her. "Cool."

They spiraled down the stairs, and despite being alone with a boy for the first time, Fiona could think only about Grandmother. Was there more than authority and attitude to her being scary? She'd never lifted a finger against her or Eliot. But Uncle Henry had said she *killed* that Mr. Welmann. Did Robert know that, too?

And if Welmann had been killed, why wasn't Grandmother worried about the police? For that matter, why hadn't anyone suggested going to the police to protect them from the rest of the family? They were acting as if the law didn't apply to Grandmother or the family. And this from the woman who demanded they wait for green lights and use crosswalks when going to work.

Fiona decided to test this curiosity on Robert. "Do you think the police will get involved?"

"The cops?" He stopped on the second-floor landing, looking at her as if she had just told a joke. "No way. What could *they* do?"

Fiona didn't want to seem completely ignorant, so she just nodded, and they continued their descent. She trusted Robert's answer. Uncle Henry was rich and likely influential, but how could anyone be entirely above the law? And how could Grandmother, who was just an apartment manager?

"What's it like working for Uncle Henry?"

Robert's features clouded. "It's hard sometimes. Dangerous." He smirked. "And it's a nonstop roller coaster that I wouldn't give up for anything in the world."

That sounded like the complete opposite of her existence . . . well, until recently. Fiona wasn't sure she could handle a "nonstop roller coaster" for the rest of her life. Her knees trembled as she took another step, and she felt drained.

The sugar from her chocolates had worn off. She'd eaten so many this morning as she'd distilled the last of Machiavelli's private thoughts onto index cards. Each time she ate another truffle or caramel, the flush and rush from it was smaller.

But she couldn't falter now. Not when she was alone with Robert. Not when she had some control of her life and for once felt confident.

It wasn't just the chocolate, was it? Part of this *had* to be her.

"So you're Uncle Henry's driver?"

Robert glanced up the stairwell and all traces of his smile evaporated. "I guess I am now."

Fiona walked closer to him, brushing against his leather sleeve so lightly that he didn't notice. She ran her fingertips over the grain, thrilled at the rough texture.

"Maybe you could teach me? How to drive?"

She couldn't believe she had dared say such a thing. No—she could have kicked herself for being such a coward. She *had* meant to say exactly that.

Fiona flushed but didn't look down the way she had been doing all her life. She wasn't embarrassed. She was *emboldened*.

This felt exactly like when she had eaten that first chocolate yesterday.

Was Robert the "secret admirer" who had sent the box of chocolates in the first place? She didn't want to ask . . . not yet. She wanted to keep the secret a mystery a bit longer.

Robert looked at her appraisingly and his simple smile returned. "I could teach you, but I don't think you'll ever have to drive for yourself when you grow up."

She returned his smile, but inside, she turned cold.

When she grew up? She was almost as old as he was.

He pushed open the outer steel security door for her. "Ladies first."

Outside, sunlight washed over concrete and asphalt and made the California air waver with heat.

She and Eliot were going to be late for Ringo's, but for the first time in her life she didn't truly care.

Fiona glanced up and down Midway Avenue. Uncle Henry's limousine was nowhere in sight.

Robert nodded to a motorcycle angled against the sidewalk. "That's my ride."

The bike's frame was a sinuous curve of matte black that ended with dual chrome pipes. Cradled in the center were twin-V pistons that radiated power even still. Stenciled on the gas tank were silver wings.

Of course Robert rode a motorcycle. She imagined herself on the back of that bike, her arms encircled around his leather-clad waist, the wind rushing through her hair.

"Thanks," she whispered, then blinked the fantasy away. "For coming. It couldn't have been much fun to sit with Grandmother."

She wanted to say so much more. And she wanted to ask a million questions, starting with his phone number—but her energy waned . . . and she felt like the old Fiona.

It took all her willpower to keep from looking down at the sidewalk, to keep her gaze locked onto Robert's eyes.

"We'll study those urban legends like you said. It's kind of hard, though, not knowing what the family expects. Kind of hard not to be scared."

Robert studied her face and took a step closer.

Fiona's heart fluttered.

Robert looked up at her third-story apartment, then turned back to her and whispered, "Be ready for water—get waders, wool clothing, that kind of stuff. It'll be dark, too. You'll need flashlights. Get a gun if you can." He glanced up at the sky. "I could get in a lot of trouble if anyone found out what I just told you."

She took his hand and squeezed it. "No one will know. I promise."

He gave her a tiny squeeze back, held her hand a second, then let go. He held up both hands in a "surrender" gesture. "I've got to go. Me alone with you: not such a great idea."

Robert mounted his bike. He pressed the ignition and thunder rumbled along the streets of Del Sombra.

"What do you mean?" Fiona said, raising her voice over the noise.

"There are rules about a guy like me with a girl like you." Robert opened the throttle and revved the engine. "I'm just a Driver. But your mother was a *goddess*. That's what this is all about. They think you might be one, too."

Robert rocketed away, leaving a cloud of dust and exhaust . . . and a bewildered Fiona.

25

MOSTLY LIES

Fiona stepped over moldering cardboard and tiptoed around a tangle of rusted rattraps. She waved her flashlight, illuminating stacks of turn-of-the-century magazines, jars of tomatoes, and porcelain doll heads that stared back.

An overabundance of treasure, junk, and "treasured junk" was in the basement of Oakwood Apartments. The room stretched the length of the building.

They'd found flashlights and rubber boots by the door on the workbenches, but the more interesting stuff was deeper inside.

Fiona glanced back and saw Eliot as he high-stepped over marble slabs encrusted with fossilized fish.

"Did you believe him?" he asked her.

"No way. How could our mother be a *goddess*?" Fiona covered her mouth, gagging on the dust she'd kicked up. "I'd be more likely to believe it if Robert said she was a pink elephant."

Besides, if their mother was a goddess, that meant Fiona's brother could be a young god. Eliot tripped on a mound of Navajo blankets, and a cloud of moths took wing. There was no way— Eliot was barely human.

And Fiona felt even less than that. The sugar rush from this morning's chocolates was gone. Everything itched, and she wanted to punch someone.

Waving away fluttering insects, Eliot said, "What about RULE fifty-five? All references to the fantastic, to gods and goddesses, erased from our books."

"That's so we're not distracted with that kid stuff. That makes a whole lot more sense than our mother having been divine."

Of course they knew what a god was, RULE 55 or not. Grandmother couldn't remove every reference. There were passages in *Hamlet* such as:

> What a piece of work is a man! How noble in reason! How infinite in faculty! In form, in moving, how express and admirable! In action how like an angel! In apprehension how like a god!

There was no escaping the capital-G God, either. Every day they passed Disciples of Light, a Christian-studies store on Midway Avenue, and a Unitarian church was on Vintner Street. Eliot and Fiona had long ago filled in the blanks of what a god was: a divine superbeing, part legend and the foundation of human-controlled religious power bases throughout history.

"Let's just get the stuff Robert told us to and get out of here," Fiona said. "I can barely breathe."

"That's one thing we agree on," Eliot muttered. "We're going to be late."

Fiona had stopped caring about Ringo's. Why Grandmother insisted they still go to work while trying to pass the family's potentially fatal tests was beyond understanding.

Eliot still cared about work, though. And Fiona felt bad about shutting him out of her room last night, so she was going to make it up to him.

She pushed farther into the basement and spotted a dog sled and rotten silk parasols. She pulled out a cracked whaling harpoon.

"I can see us dragging this into Ringo's," she said, experimentally hefting it.

"We'll stash the boots and flashlights in this." Eliot held up a canvas backpack covered with faded Boy Scout patches. He frowned. "What Robert said does make *some* sense, though. A family that ignores the police? Uncle Henry's car violating the laws of physics? That all seems beyond normal, doesn't it?"

"Uh-huh," Fiona said, ignoring him now. Her brother was entering his own personal daydream world.

"You think this is part of the trial? Robert dropping hints? Us finding what we need?"

"Or a trick."

Fiona wanted to believe Robert's comment about goddesses wasn't a joke. He had seemed so serious, but it couldn't possibly be true. Or could *goddess* be slang for something else?

A glint of metal flashed in her light.

She pulled out a steel tube wrapped in oilcloth. It was a sawed-off shotgun and a bandolier of shells. The gun was a break-action model, barrels side by side, with tarnished silver plates riveted between the triggers and strike box. Engraved was a faded name: WESTLEY.

Holding the gun sent an electric thrill up Fiona's hands. She checked and then doubled-checked that it wasn't loaded.

Eliot and Fiona had written a report on the history of firearms last year. They knew how to load, clean, aim, and fire a wide variety of pistols and long arms . . . at least in theory.

"Put it in that sack of yours," she told Eliot.

He stared at the shotgun as if it were a writhing viper. "What's the matter with *your* book bag?"

"Fine." She swung her bag around and slid the shotgun snugly next to the box of chocolates. She smoothed her thumb over the red satin. All she had to do was make it to Ringo's, then she could eat a few more. Fiona picked her way over wagon wheels and broken garden statuary toward the light of the open door.

Eliot, however, remained where he was. His flashlight pointed into the corner illuminating a shrouded shelf.

"This is something," he whispered so softly that Fiona barely heard him.

She moved to her brother's side. She felt something, too; her skin prickled as she neared the covered shape.

Eliot reached for the tarp. A geological layer of dust shuddered free. Whatever was under there had been undisturbed for ages.

Fiona felt an odd urge to take out the shotgun, but resisted. It wasn't loaded, and if it were, she wasn't sure she wouldn't blow off her own foot.

Eliot rolled up the tarp, revealing rows of books. Some were paperbacks, some hardcover, and as Eliot unveiled the last, there were older editions bound in increasingly darker leather. The last was the size of an encyclopedia with a hand-tooled spine that looked disturbingly like its human namesake.

Most were in shockingly bad condition.

Books were sacrosanct in the Post family. Cee took meticulous care of each volume in their apartment, repairing torn pages and rebinding when necessary. Even Grandmother treated them like priceless Ming vases. To leave these down here at the mercy of mold and insects was a crime.

With the greatest respect, Fiona lifted a paperback: *Childhood's End* by Arthur C. Clarke. The old acidic paper crumbled. It was a tragedy.

Eliot, his head turned, read the titles out loud, *"The Modern Prometheus* . . . twelve volumes of something called *The Golden Bough* . . . *Bulfinch's Mythology* . . . *Traditional Knitting of the Westerfield Witch Clan* . . . *Lost Celtic Weavings."*

Fiona's insides crawled. RULE 55 forbade science fiction, fantasy, and mythologies. RULE 11 prohibited arts and crafts. If Grandmother ever caught them with these . . . They'd never broken *two* rules at once before.

Eliot reached for the oldest volume on the end.

"Don't," Fiona said.

"It's just a book."

Fiona bit her lip. Of course it was just a book, but if they were harmless, why were they down here?

Still, she was curious, too.

"Okay," she whispered. She glanced back at the open door—half expecting to see Grandmother's silhouette.

Eliot pulled out the book. He opened it and creamy vellum pages turned under his fingers. The letters were the pristine work of a monk, and every other page had illuminations, woodcuts, or hair-fine diagrams.

"Text is . . . what?" His brow crinkled. "Medieval German?"

Fiona leaned closer. "Old or Middle English maybe."

"There are notes scrawled all over the margins," Eliot said, pointing out the obvious. "This one is in Latin. Another's in Greek."

"Different handwriting. Not Grandmother's or Cee's."

"Different inks, too. Some have faded . . . some written over."

Eliot flipped through more pages, past a gold-and-red mosaic of Arabic script, a diagram of a dissected human hand, then he paused at a woodcut of a medieval piper as he danced and led a procession of children and rats.

"This one has a note in modern English," he said.

Fiona peered closer. In neat cursive it read, *Pied Piper of Hamelin.* Under this were five parallel lines and a bunch of meandering dots. It meant nothing to her.

Eliot ran his finger over them. "Musical notes," he murmured. "So cool."

Fiona inwardly groaned: make that breaking *three* rules at once. "What's this thing called?"

Eliot flipped to the front. There was no title page, and the first page had large letters so thick with embellishments that it was impossible to read. Alongside this, however, penciled in neat block letters was "*Mythica Improbiba*. Mostly lies."[27]

Fiona had been fascinated by, in love with, bored from, but never physically nauseated by ordinary paper and ink—even the autopsy instruction manuals—until now. Something about this thing made her want to throw up.

"Put it back," she said. "I've got a bad feeling."

Eliot closed the volume and smoothed his hand over its cover. "Is this rhinoceros hide?"

Fiona started rerolling the tarp onto the shelf. If anyone gave it more than a cursory look, they'd see that it had been disturbed. There was no way to replace the dust. She hesitated, waiting for Eliot to put the book back.

"No." He slipped it into his pack. "I want to take a closer look at it later."

Fiona sighed. She didn't want to get in an argument here. Grandmother or Cee could come through the door at any moment. She covered the last of the shelf and moved out of the basement.

"Whatever," she said.

Eliot followed her and they paused in the stairwell. She handed him her flashlight and he stuffed it in his pack along with the rubber boots they commandeered . . . next to that stupid book.

They then ran up the stairs and pushed through the steel security door. No racing today; they just both wanted outside.

The air was deliciously fresh and dust-free, and they took a moment to clear their lungs.

They then fell into their usual we're-late-for-work stride—although today that seemed to be the *only* thing so far that was normal.

Fiona snuck a glance at her brother. Dirt smeared his pants and shirt and his face; his eyes were focused on his feet.

---

27. Written by a thirteenth-century monk of questionable sanity, Sildas Pious, this collection of late-classical and early-medieval legends provides as many insights as it does lies and illogical conclusions. It is, however, the only source for many tales of deities and demons. Only eight (each slightly different) volumes are known to exist. They rarely remain in private collections. Owners claim poor luck, nightmares, and other undocumented paranormal phenomenon . . . which ironically only increases *Mythica*'s value at subsequent auctions. The one publicly available edition resides in the Beezle Collection (viewable by special appointment), Taylor Institution Library Rare Book Collection, Oxford University. Victor Golden, *Golden's Guide to Extraordinary Books* (Oxford: 1958).

"I'm sorry," she said, "about last night."

She wanted to be decent to her brother. She knew she'd hurt him.

Her stomach rumbled, and she found it hard to concentrate. She should have eaten something solid; she'd skipped dinner and breakfast . . . and eaten how many chocolates? Three layers from the box?

At least one layer was left—a treasure trove of sweets in her book bag, inches away. Her mouth watered thinking of the caramels and truffles.

She wouldn't delve into them now, though. Eliot would see. He'd want one, or a few, or half—which was fair. She *should* share them. On the other hand, they were from Fiona's "secret admirer." Sharing them would be like sharing a kiss. Yuck.

Fiona cleared her throat. "So I shouldn't have locked my door. We're supposed to stick together. Like Cee said."

Eliot nodded, graciously not saying anything, although there was an obvious opportunity for an easy insult such as calling her a *Tenodera aridifolia sinensis,* the Chinese praying mantis, whose first meal was often its own just-out-of-the-egg siblings.

He didn't take the gibe and Fiona appreciated it.

"I just needed to think alone," she said. "The medieval Italian, it's not that easy to translate."

It *had* been easy for her, but one tiny lie wouldn't hurt.

"I get it." The hurt in Eliot's voice was worse than any insult he could have hurled at her.

They walked for a while and then he asked, "Did you find out anything useful?"

"There was plenty about family clans fighting. A lot of people in sixteenth-century Italy got tortured and murdered."

"And that helps us how?"

"The kids in those noble families . . . they were like chess pawns, meant to be pushed ahead into danger. Tactically placed to protect the bigger pieces."

Eliot licked his lips. "Did Machiavelli have any advice for a 'pawn'?"

"Yeah. Get to the other side of the board."

"Live long enough to be an 'important' piece, right?"

When pawns made it all the way to the opposite side of the chessboard, they got promoted to a queen, rook, bishop, or knight.

Fiona nodded. "I wonder if that's what Aunt Lucia meant when she said that the trials might prove our 'worth to remain alive,' and *then* she said they might even prove our 'right to be part of this family.'"

"I'd wondered about the order she said that, too. Like being part of the family was more important than living."

"Machiavelli wrote, though, that the promoted pawns were damaged. He didn't say how, just that they lost something."

"Given the option I'll cross the board . . ." Eliot's voice trailed off and he stared ahead.

Fiona followed his gaze.

Someone stood in the alley a quarter block up the street.

It took three full seconds to register that this someone was the bum that had lived in this alley for the last few months. He wore a new gray trench coat. His hair was cleaned and pulled into a ponytail of silver and jet-black. Even his ratty sneakers had metamorphosed to polished loafers. He waved and beckoned them closer.

Eliot veered toward him.

"Oh, no." Fiona grabbed Eliot's arm. "I've already had my recommended daily allowance of strange today."

Eliot yanked his arm free. "I want to talk to him."

Fiona let go and looked at her hand. Mike had grabbed her exactly as she had just grabbed her brother.

"I'll wait for you." She moved on and didn't make eye contact with the old guy. There was no way she was going to listen to them talk about music and Pompeii and whatever demented things filtered through that bum's alcohol-sponge of a brain.

As soon as she passed the alley, Fiona shifted her book bag and undid the snaps. She glanced back: Eliot and the old weirdo were talking. He wasn't grabbing her brother and dragging him into the alley. So far, so good.

Fiona slipped her hand into the heart-shaped box. She plucked out a chocolate. It was textured like a tiny tangerine and sprinkled with orange zest.

She bit it in half. It was laced with particles of orange and grapefruit swimming in a bouquet of smoky cocoa.

Her blood warmed and raced and she felt alive again.

Through half-lidded eyes she watched Eliot. Still talking. Still safe.

Her thoughts drifted to Robert, and she remembered his last words about her mother being a goddess. That couldn't be true because there was only *one* divine thing in the world . . . and she held it between her fingers.

26

MORE THAN ONE KIND OF "PLAYED"

liot couldn't believe the man in front of him was the same person who had lived in this alley for the last six months. He looked a half foot taller and part of his hair had ungrayed and was now as black as midnight. He wore a new trench coat, pleated slacks, linen shirt, and shiny leather shoes.

Cee told Eliot people never changed, that they were what they always were (and that, much to his annoyance, he would always be her "sweet" Eliot).

The man's sparkling blue eyes were identical, though, and when he smiled at Eliot, he knew it was the same person. Maybe *this* cleaner person was the man he had always been, and the homelessness was just a phase.

The man nodded over Eliot's shoulder. "I see your sister still thinks me an escaped mental patient."

Eliot didn't remember telling the man that Fiona was his sister. He looked back and saw Fiona watching him . . . as she chewed something.

"She's just shy."

The man raised an eyebrow. "Aren't we all?"

"You look so . . . better."

Eliot couldn't believe his lapse of grammar and talent for stating the obvious. He knew so many words. Why did he have such a hard time speaking them sometimes?

"Better, yes. Thanks to the miracle of a YMCA shower, soap, and a stiff brush." The man paused. "No, actually I only have you to thank, my young prodigy."

"Me?"

"*You* woke me. I am Lazarus." He curled his hands into fists and raised them over his head. "Christ arisen from the grave! Donald Trump refinanced!"

Maybe Fiona had been right about the man's mental state. Eliot took a step back, glanced over his shoulder, and spotted his sister . . . which reassured him. "Do you mean the music?"

"I do." The man turned to a shopping cart by the alley wall. "And such a miraculous restoration deserves a reward."

Eliot took two steps closer and asked, "Another lesson?" He could feel the violin under his fingertips: vibration and pressure, rhythm and crescendo.

The man scoffed. "I would sooner whitewash the *Mona Lisa*." He rummaged through the cart, retrieved a battered and lidless red Macy's box, and thrust it into Eliot's face.

Eliot took the proffered box. The instant he felt the weight, he knew what it was . . . but dared not believe it. The box was stuffed with plastic grocery bags. He dug deeper, touched wood, and pulled out the man's violin.

"The only thing you now require," he told Eliot, "is practice."

Eliot turned the instrument over and over, amazed. No one had ever given him anything like this.

The man handed him the violin's bow. "Let us not forget this."

Eliot's fingers rested on the strings. They seemed to resonate with a slight vibration all their own.

He wanted more than anything else to play, but he held back. Yesterday he'd almost lost himself in song. Today he couldn't. He had to focus on too many other things: work, life-and-death trials, and a new family.

"I don't know what to say."

"Say nothing." The man touched his index finger to his lips, making a *shh* gesture. "The look on your face is enough. Besides, words are the tools of fops and fools."

"But I can't."

That was the last thing that Eliot wanted to say, but he had to. One of Grandmother's life philosophies was to never accept extravagant gifts. *Too generous presents come with strings,* she had told him. *They'll spoil you.* And the never-repeated-often-enough *Hard work is the cornerstone of character.*

So what if he got spoiled just this once? The violin felt like his already. And just imagining breaking a rule . . . it made his blood race.

But Grandmother's ideals—like them or not—had been fused to Eliot's character.

"I can't," he whispered. And then, although it was the hardest thing he had ever done, he handed the violin back to the man. "You'll need it a lot more than I will."

All animation drained from the man's face, and even though neither of them had moved, he now seemed to be looking down at Eliot.

"Will I?" The man snatched the instrument and set it into the shopping cart. "On the contrary, I am leaving these luxury accommodations and abandoning my misery." He stroked the violin. "Alas this has too many sad memories now to keep."

"You're just going to leave it there?"

The man's eyes narrowed and glimmered with mischievousness. "Perhaps it will be found by some homeless match girl and she will burn it to keep warm. Or an insane street lady will use it like a ukulele. Or perhaps . . ." He set it in the gutter in the center of the alley. "A delivery truck will crush it." He raised his foot.

Eliot had never moved so fast—he grabbed the violin and cradled it to his chest.

"So . . . you've changed your mind then?"

"Yes." Eliot felt his heartbeat reverberating through the wood and the strings. He wasn't sure how he was going to hide this from Grandmother, but he couldn't let it be smashed into splinters.

"I will sleep better knowing she is in a master's hands." The man knelt and touched the violin. "Look, I will show you à secret." He scratched at the wood, and tape peeled away. "I had to disguise her. Had any of my neighbors seen her true nature . . . well, possession as they say, is all."

Scabs of Scotch tape dotted the body of the instrument. Each had been blacked with marker, scratched, and dulled with grime. They camouflaged pristine lacquered wood underneath that had the look of liquid gold and sparkling topaz.

Eliot could see his face reflected in the grain. He felt as if he were melting into the mirrored, smooth surface.

"It's beautiful."

"She. *It* is a *she*. And *her* name is Lady Dawn." The man spread his hand over the violin theatrically. "Crafted by Antonelli Moroni in the sixteenth century; all others compared to her are mewling harpies. Treat her with the respect that she demands."[28]

Treat her with respect? Eliot started to protest that the man had almost crushed the violin under his heel.

But the man held up a finger. "You will learn that musical instruments are not the only things that can be played."

He'd *meant* for Eliot to take the violin the entire time. His face flushed.

The man stood and brushed off his coat. "Now I must leave this golden palace of open-air urinals and rodents and never return."

He held out his hand for Eliot.

Eliot looked back out the alley. Fiona waited for him on the street and made a "hurry up" gesture. Her warning that the man was crazy echoed in his thoughts, but Eliot turned and reached out to shake his hand anyway. It seemed to be the only polite thing to do.

It was like when he shook Uncle Henry's hand: the man's skin was warm and firm. But when Eliot squeezed, he found it unyielding like stone. The man could have grabbed and crushed him like a soda can.

The light faded . . . and although Eliot could not tear his gaze away from the man, he saw in the periphery shadows on the walls: people crowding to get a better look, and the silhouette of a large, sniffing dog.

The man let go.

The shadows vanished.

"A fine grip. You will be stronger than I am when you grow up."

"Thanks," Eliot said, looking at his small hands and doubting that very much.

"I'm Eliot."

"Louis. Louis Piper. Nice to make your acquaintance. I hope we meet again under different circumstances."

"Yeah." Eliot glanced at Fiona waiting. Her arms had crossed her chest and she glared at him. "I better go."

But the man had already turned and strolled halfway down the alley, whistling to himself.

Eliot went to his sister.

Fiona's eyes locked onto the violin. "What are you going to do with *that*?"

---

28. Antonelli Moroni may be related to Anna Moroni, who married Alessandro Stradivari. In 1644 they had a son, Antonio Stradivari, who became the world's most renowned violin maker.—Editor.

Eliot unhitched his backpack, shuffled the contents, and slid Lady Dawn carefully into a rubber wader. "There."

"And what about Grandmother?"

"I'll figure that out later. I *had* to take it."

Fiona sighed and shook her head. She looked flushed with exasperation as she turned and walked away.

He slung the pack and caught up to her. "You're not going to tell, are you?"

She halted. Her mouth dropped and she rested a hand on her heart—as if he'd stabbed her.

Fiona might have tried to drive him crazy, dreamed up the worst insults in the world to throw at him, but she'd never in a million years have snitched on him. Not that she *had to* snitch. Grandmother usually figured out everything they did anyway.

"Sorry," he whispered.

Fiona chewed on her lower lip. "Don't worry. I'd never tell."

They stood a moment, both looking at the sidewalk, neither saying a thing.

Fiona then started walking, slowly crossed Vine Street, and waited for him on the steps to Ringo's.

Eliot followed. Only half as many cars were parked outside as yesterday.

Together, he and his sister entered.

The clock on the wall informed him that they were twenty-five minutes late. A new record.

Mike would have docked them a half day's pay—threatened to fire them, too. Eliot wondered how he was doing. When or if Mike was coming back. If he'd lost his hand.

Julie leaned on the cash register. She said nothing about their being late and just gave them a little bored wave. She wore a fuzzy sky-blue sweater with a plunging neckline and a lacy white skirt that fell to her knees.

"Party room got used last night," she informed Fiona.

Fiona hung her head.

"But I came in early and got it for you," Julie said. "Would you wait tables later today, honey? Linda has a dentist thing."

"Thanks." Fiona blinked unbelievingly. "Uh, sure."

Julie moved from the counter and flashed a hundred-watt smile at Eliot. "I've got something to show you in back."

Eliot followed her through the dining room and into the kitchen, unable to tear his gaze away from her liquid motions . . . and feeling embarrassed by this new boldness.

Julie waved hello at Johnny. Johnny waved back in between a pizza toss.

Eliot spotted a new stainless steel cabinet next to his washing sink.

Julie opened the thing. Inside were jet nozzles and metal racks half-filled with dirty plates. It was a dishwasher.

"Your new best friend," Julie said. "It does sixty racks an hour—faster than you can load it."

"Does this mean"—Eliot swallowed—"that I'm out of a job?"

Julie giggled. It sounded like sleigh bells. "You dreamer. Every plate and pot still needs to be scraped, loaded, unloaded, and racked, but it will make your job a thousand times easier."

"Wow—thanks."

"You'll have some extra time, so I want you to help Johnny. He needs a new assistant."

"Assistant chef? Me?"

Eliot had always wanted to cook. Cee had, however, shooed him out of the kitchen whenever he tried to do more than gather ingredients for her to burn.

"The new guy didn't work out." Julie looked around as if someone else might hear. "I fired the cad."

He wondered what the new guy had done to warrant that. Eliot had shown up nearly a half hour late . . . and got a promotion.

"In fact, you'll have so much free time, you might want to ask me out for coffee on our break." Julie grinned and her cheeks dimpled in an enchanting way.

She flounced off and Eliot watched, fascinated.

Johnny whistled low. "Listen, amigo." He crept closer and wiped flour-dusted hands on his apron. "You better listen to that new boss lady. Stuff like that doesn't cruise into your life every day."

"I know."

In point of fact, Eliot did *not* know. Stuff like this never happened to him, the prince of all nerds. Only in his daydreams were there music and girls who asked him out. His entire life had been turned upside down, and not necessarily in a bad way. He could get used to it.

But he was breaking Grandmother's rules 34 and 106 (music and dating, respectively) . . . and she always found out.

"What happened to your assistant?" he asked Johnny.

Johnny shrugged his hulking shoulders and stirred a pot of meatballs in marinara. "Just didn't show up today."

Funny, Julie said she fired him. That meant she talked to him, right? Something seemed wrong with that, but Eliot was sure she had a good reason.

Johnny checked on his pizzas in the oven and the flames lit his face. "So what are you waiting for? Lady gave you an engraved invitation."

Eliot went to the new dishwasher and pressed the START button. It whirled to life.

It was too easy. Grandmother's voice echoed in his thoughts: *Hard work is the cornerstone of character.* What would she say about this?

The dishes done, he left the kitchen to take his break.

In the dining room he spotted Fiona taking orders from a tourist couple. She smiled and almost looked happy talking to total strangers.

This day just got more and more weird.

Julie waited for him by the cash register, bouncing on one foot. "You asking me out to coffee?"

"Who's going to run Ringo's?"

"Fiona's taking orders, and Linda's covering for me." Julie twined a finger around a wisp of honey-blond hair. "It's not like we're running off to Hollywood."

Eliot's head felt like a helium balloon. He couldn't believe this: a girl was interested in him.

"There's the Pink Rabbit across the street," he said, trying to sound as if he did this all the time. "They have juice and coffee."

"Sounds dreamy. Let me grab my purse."

The phone buzzed. Julie snapped up the headpiece and held up one finger, indicating this would only take a moment.

Eliot saw that she'd chewed her nails to the quick.

"Ringo's All American Pizza Palace. How can I help you?" Julie's face went slack and she stared at a distant point, concentrating. "Yes, they're both here. May I ask who is calling please?" Her eyebrows shot up and she pulled the earpiece from her head. "Same to you!" She handed it to Eliot.

No one had ever called for him at Ringo's.

"Hello?"

"It's Robert Farmington, Eliot. They've decided. Your first trial has started."

27

TEATIME OMENS

Audrey listened intently to the phone.

She then hung up, left her study, and sat at the dining table.

Cecilia had outdone herself today for teatime. Coffee crumble cakes had been set out along with tiny plates of Waldorf salad (both ordered from the Pink Rabbit's Organic Delicatessen and Bakery), and there were three teapots: one filled with her chamomile blend, one Darjeeling, and her spiderweb pot with plain boiling water nestled in its crocheted cozy. Cecilia had prepared for any eventuality.

"It has begun," Audrey told her. "Their first trial."

Cecilia rose from her seat. "That was the boy on the phone?"

"Our Mr. Farmington, yes."

Cecilia gathered her shawl about her shoulders and twisted its ends nervously. "Did he say what? Or where?"

"I did not ask." Audrey settled into her seat. She poured a cup of the Darjeeling.

Cecilia blinked at her. "We *are* going to do something, aren't we?"

"Of course we are. We are going to have tea."

"Yes, yes." Cecilia's eyes clouded milky white. "I shall start the ritual. There is much we can divine and then influence from here."

Audrey made a cutting motion with her hand. "I meant we will have tea, and that is all. We have done too much already. It is up to the children now."

"There must be more. We can—"

"Do no more. Otherwise we risk the Council detecting our help. They would summarily judge against the children."

"You talk as if this is a game," Cecilia said. "As if two points would be deducted instead of Eliot and Fiona ending up . . . end up . . . I cannot even speak the words."

Audrey narrowed her eyes. "I know what is at stake."

Cecilia sat hard in her chair, appearing, if possible, even more frail than normal. For someone masquerading as a centenarian, this was considerable.

Audrey added creamer to her tea, spooned in heaps of sugar, and stirred. Cecilia's theatrics were working, however; doubt and guilt yipped at the edges of Audrey's thoughts. She hated her for that.

"Everything has been done to tip the scales in their favor," Audrey said. "Did I not intimidate Henry into sending Mr. Farmington? And then maneuver the boy into revealing as much as he dared?"

"You mean Fiona maneuvered him."

"Yes . . . that was unexpected." Audrey realized that she still stirred her tea and stopped.

"She grows up faster than you think. Like her mother after she learned of love."

Audrey dropped her spoon with a clatter and Cecilia recoiled.

Why did she keep this old crone? One day she would push too far and Audrey would impale her bloodless heart—put Cecilia out of the world's misery.

Audrey sipped her tea. "Did we not leave them all the tools they'd need in the basement?"

"The product of a quick and shoddy divination that left them *half* what they need," Cecilia murmured. "Supplemented with a collection of *lies* disguised as a book."

Audrey shrugged. "They would never have accepted the truth if it were told to them. The book, though; they love their books, do they not? They believe anything that is written."

Cecilia's thin lips twisted into a cruel smile. "Henry would die if he knew anyone read his old writings."

"I do not think we are that lucky."

Cecilia considered this and her smile faded. "Eliot and Fiona are not ready: fifteen years and so innocent. You have suppressed all they could have been."

"They are smarter than any children in or out of this family. That shall have to be enough."

Audrey wished Cecilia would be silent. More doubts surfaced in Audrey's mind. Had it been the right thing to hide them? What choice had there been? Eliot and Fiona were powerless, true, but had they been trained, the families would have found . . . and consumed them.

The families. Plural.

That her side had discovered the children was bad enough. If their father's family found them, it could be the end of the long truce between the clans.

Cecilia dragged the spiderweb teapot close and poured steaming water into a china cup. Her face puckered into a defiant expression.

Audrey sighed and nodded. She would allow her a simple divination, but no more.

Cecilia mixed snow-white petals and a pinch of belladonna to the water and stirred with her finger. Vapors rose from the cup. Her dim eyes kindled as the mists thickened and braided into strands.

Cecilia's problem was that her sight was shortened by her strong emotions—emotions that ironically also made her Audrey's greatest asset.

One of them had to feel.

Audrey longed to love—unconditionally, unyieldingly, and irrationally—but she had long ago chosen to sever herself from those possibilities. She had decided to keep her head, calculate and recalculate, and survive. Regardless of the cost. That is what their kind did.

The tendrils of fog that spilled from Cecilia's cup slithered over the tablecloth. Poised upon this smoke sat a vaporous spider that tested each thread with tremulous legs.

"What do you see?" Audrey asked.

Cecilia and her spider spoke together, one croaking, the other squeaking. "Danger. There is hunger in the water, and I hear . . ." She inhaled, surprised. "Music!"

Music was a black omen. It likely indicated the other family.

Audrey wanted to touch the web, but stilled her hand. With one finger she could bring the entire probability grid into focus. She could pull strings and destroy forces aligned against the children . . . but with a single touch, the Council would be alerted to her influence.

"Try to sense more," she urged.

Cecilia reached for the spider and stroked its thorax. It elongated and sprouted cellophane dragonfly wings and flitted among the foggy threads.

Audrey squinted at the leaves floating in Cecilia's teacup: they looked like a hundred tiny eyes, then coalesced into teeth that opened and snapped shut.

"Another danger awaits them," Cecilia whispered. "A trap. More than one, and then *only* one. Smaller . . . and then much larger." Her eyes widened and the milky film covering them cleared. She snatched her dragonfly and held it to her chest. "Reptile," she murmured trancelike, then started breathing heavily. "A river of teeth. Eater of the innocent."

Audrey waved her hand.

The web of fog condensed into fine strands of ice—hung in the air for a heartbeat—then fell and shattered upon the table.

"Enough. They must finish this alone."

The danger was too great. While Audrey could not feel love, per se, she could feel her protective instincts roused. If Cecilia told her more, she would act and destroy any chance, however slender, Eliot and Fiona now had.

Cecilia glared at her. "How can you be so cold?"

"What would you have me do?"

"You could kill the Council. All of them. Quickly."

Audrey quirked one eyebrow at Cecilia's bold suggestion. "I am not so certain I could best Aaron."

"You would have *tried* in the old days," Cecilia hissed.

Audrey took a deep breath, stilled herself, then said, "There were no children in the old days. Begin a blood vendetta and they will make sure Eliot and Fiona would be the first casualties."

Cecilia worried her hands. Her spider—now dragonfly—was once again ceramic and perched atop the teapot.

"Better to have kept running," Cecilia whispered.

"Cease your prattling lectures on how you think I should run my family."

Cecilia's lips trembled. She said nothing, but hatred smoldered in her eyes.

Audrey felt like kicking something helpless, so she added, "You had three sons once. Did not one of them kill their father?"

Cecilia looked as if she'd been struck. "May all our children be so cursed."

This touched one of Audrey's last exposed nerves. It was a sensation so sudden that Audrey, even with faster-than-lightning reflexes and a clockwork intellect, was blindsided. She had protected herself from any attachment surrounding the children, but their father . . . he was entirely another matter.

Audrey stood and her chair fell over.

Her shadows multiplied, crossed, and crisscrossed. Darkness spread across the hardwood floors, up the plaster walls, and enveloped the midday light in the window.

Power collected about her, a hurricane of spinning razor shards that cut the air.

"You wish me to act?" Audrey said in a whisper that resonated through every atom in the room and shook the windows.

Cecilia backed into a corner and huddled, arms over her head, whimpering in the storm.

"You wish death?" Audrey said. "If Eliot and Fiona fail, if the Council or their father's family take them, then I will destroy everyone. Everything."

If Audrey unleashed her vengeance, no creature or Council law would stop her. To do so, however, she would have to utterly give herself over to it; she would have to sever all ties to pity, remorse, and friendship. All human ties.

And Cecilia was her last link to that humanity.

"If the time to kill comes," Audrey said, "you, old woman, will be the first to go."

28

A HUNDRED HATE-FILLED EYES

Fiona and Eliot made it to the Del Sombra city limits where Robert had asked to meet. Despite the chocolates she had eaten at Ringo's, Fiona was dead tired after the fifteen-minute speed walk.

This far off the main tourist avenue there wasn't much: an abandoned housing development; the Oro Recycling Plant, with its mountains of cardboard and plastic bottles; and little Franklin Park.

They waited on a park bench in the shade of a eucalyptus tree. Cicadas buzzed. Next to the bench was a terra-cotta fountain that hadn't run in years because of water conservation efforts. The wind shifted and brought with it the scents of melted plastics and wet pulp.

It would have been peaceful here if it weren't for the trembling tension running through Fiona's core.

She wanted to get away—as far and as fast as she could. But even Grandmother had given in to the Council's demands that they complete these tests . . . tests where their lives might be at stake.

"You're sure he said here?"

"Yeah," Eliot replied, wiping sweat from his forehead. He fished out a bottle of water he had filled at Ringo's and offered it to Fiona.

She accepted it and drank deeply. All that chocolate had gone down butter-smooth, but the sugar had made her throat raw.

"Any idea what kind of heroic trial could be here?" he asked.

"Urban myths, Robert said." Fiona glanced at the recycling center. Maybe move one of those cardboard piles? Turn it all into what? She searched for some trace of a childhood fairy tale—something every kid picked up just by breathing. Had there been a story about turning straw into silver? Or was it paper into gold? There was nothing. Grandmother had done a superlative job of keeping that stuff out of their lives.

She shook her head and sighed. Everything that had happened since their birthday two days ago had taken on a skewed reality. Or maybe their lives *up to* that point had been the unreal part. With Grandmother keeping them in the dark, how. could they be sure what was going on, or who they really were?

Eliot got a take-out bag from his pack and dug out a hunk of garlic bread. Julie had wrapped it up for him before they left. "You want some?"

"Not hungry."

Eliot munched on the butter-slathered bread.

Fiona's stomach twisted. What she needed was a few more chocolates.

She wished she had more time at Ringo's. She'd only had three: an almond cluster with tiny marshmallow bits; and two truffles, a lime ice that actually chilled her tongue, and the other a rich crème de cacao. She remembered each delectable bite.

But then Eliot and Julie had found her and said there was a "family emergency." Eliot said they had to leave. Julie had ordered Linda to reschedule her dentist appointment and Johnny to load the dishwasher after lunch. Mike would never have done that for them. Was Julie being so nice because she actually liked Eliot?

Something was so wrong with that picture.

In the distance a deep-throated motorcycle rumbled, and all thoughts of her brother and Julie and chocolates vanished.

Fiona and Eliot stood, shielding their eyes from the sunlight.

Robert raced toward them. At the edge of the park he skidded to a halt and dismounted his motorcycle. He didn't bother to take off his leather jacket or skullcap helmet.

"This way." He started walking. "There's not a lot of time."

His features were set in cast-iron determination. The way he just turned his back to Fiona made her wonder if she had done something to make him angry.

They followed him out of the park and into the deserted housing development—through tumbled-down cinder-block walls, bare concrete foundations, and cracked asphalt.

Robert halted in a patch of sand. The only thing nearby was a tumble-weed. He flipped open a phone and said, "We're there. . . . Yes, sir, right away."

He pocketed his phone and then kicked at the sand. Buried underneath was a manhole cover.

"This was going to be a huge housing tract," Robert told them. "Some con artist made off with the money, though, but not before roads were built, a few foundations poured, and they put in sewage lines."

"Our 'heroic' trial is in a septic tank?" Eliot asked unbelievingly.

"Sewer," Robert said. "Big difference."

"So, besides the obvious, what's *in* the sewer?" Fiona asked.

"An alligator."

Fiona and Eliot exchanged a blank look.

"Don't you guys know this urban legend?" Robert asked. "Kid bought a lizard in a pet store, but it never stops growing. His dad flushes the thing down the toilet, and a few years later, bang—alligator in the sewers of Del Sombra."[29]

"You're kidding," Eliot said.

Robert shook his head.

"Our trial is an alligator?" Fiona said. "What do we have to do? Take a picture of it and prove it exists?"

"The Council already knows it's down there. They want you to . . ." Robert looked at the sand, unable to meet her gaze. "Their exact wording was 'vanquish the beast.' And you've got to get back to the surface with proof in two hours."

Fiona couldn't believe this. *Vanquish* was just a fancy word for kill. How were she and Eliot going to kill a real alligator? Shotgun or not, they weren't hunters—she'd never killed anything on purpose before. Even the spiders she found trapped in the bathtub she gently removed and set on the windowsill before turning on the water.

---

29. The first record of large reptiles in sewers comes from the Byzantine Empire. Guards routinely scoured the sewers of Constantinople hunting crocodiles (although this legend may have been started to dissuade would-be invaders from attempting to gain access in this fashion). The first modern reckoning is from 1935 in New York City, when an alligator escaped from a ship hailing from the Florida Everglades. The unfortunate reptile was discovered by two boys disposing of snow down a storm drain and beaten to death with their snow shovels. In reality alligators are prone to disease and therefore it is highly unlikely that any would survive long in such conditions. *Gods of the First and Twenty-first Century, Volume 6: Modern Myths*, 8th ed. (Zypheron Press Ltd.).

Robert unstrapped his watch and handed it to her.

She took it and slipped it on next to the rubber band on her wrist. The watch was a stainless steel Rolex with three chronometers. It was heavy and too big, but she wouldn't have taken it off for the world.

Eliot whispered, "What if we can't do this?"

"Man, I don't know," Robert said, but his conciliatory tone made it clear that he knew exactly what would happen.

Prove their possible worth to remain alive, Aunt Lucia had said. And after everything Grandmother had told them about the family—how they killed off all those other children—Fiona knew they had to succeed or meet a similar fate.

Eliot swallowed and said nothing.

Fiona wondered why anyone thought they could kill an alligator in water, an animal bred for millions of years to prey on clumsy land dwellers like themselves. Unless they thought there was something special about her and Eliot.

"When you told me that our mother was a 'goddess,'" she said to Robert, "that wasn't slang for something else. You meant she was really a . . ." She couldn't say it; it was so impossible.

Robert took off his helmet and scratched his head, looking confused. "Didn't anyone tell you about her?"

"No one tells us anything," Eliot said.

"Well, maybe that was the right thing," Robert replied. "Your family has money, political connections, and is smarter than anyone I've ever run across. They're like that because they're all old—hundreds of years, maybe older. But they're not like the gods in the movies or comics with lightning bolts or stuff like that. More like . . ." His lips moved but he failed to find the right words.

"Italian princes?" Eliot suggested. "The Cosa Nostra?"

Robert nodded. "Yeah. Part mobsters, part worldwide conglomerate, but one hundred percent dangerous."

Fiona didn't want to accept any of this . . . but there was Mike and his hand getting burned after he'd touched her, and Eliot's talent with that violin. Were those parts of them inherited from some preternatural family?

"They wouldn't have set this up," Robert said, brightening, "unless they thought you had *some* chance."

Fiona wasn't sure if that meant fifty-fifty or snowball-in-a-furnace odds.

Robert glanced at the sun. "I've said everything I can . . . and a little more than I should have." He then whispered, "Did you get everything I told you to?"

Fiona pulled the sawed-off shotgun from her book bag.

Robert whistled, impressed. "Westley-Richards. That'll do. Aim for the gator's head. Even better, wait until it opens its mouth and then shoot." He didn't look very confident as he said this, though.

He knelt and inserted a hook into the manhole cover. With a wrench, he yanked the lid free and rolled it aside. Odors of wetness and mold wafted from the hole.

Fiona and Eliot leaned closer. A ladder disappeared into the shadows.

"So we're really doing this?" Eliot asked her.

Fiona set one hand on his shoulder and squeezed. "Piece of cake," she lied. She let go and moved closer to Robert. "Thanks for everything."

She wondered what Robert had risked by telling them how to prepare. Fiona couldn't imagine what Aunt Lucia would be like angry . . . or dangerous-looking Uncle Aaron. She wouldn't have been brave enough to do what Robert had for them.

She moved closer to him.

She could be dead soon, and she wasn't about to go without ever having kissed someone other than Grandmother or Cecilia.

Fiona touched her lips to Robert's cheek, light as a butterfly landing; his skin was hot, and her lips warmed. A thrill pulsed from the touched flesh down her neck, made her flush and her heart pound.

She withdrew. The heat between them lingered.

That was better than any chocolate. *Much* better.

Robert took a small step back and stroked where her lips had been. He looked away to Eliot, and his expression sobered. "You better get going."

Eliot looked incredibly uncomfortable. Fiona wasn't sure if this was due to her kiss or because they were both about to enter a dark sewer with a man-eating reptile.

Eliot pulled on his rubber boots, got his flashlight, and peered down the hole. He licked his lips, craning his head to get a better view.

"Oh, for crying out loud," Fiona said, pulling on her boots. She grabbed her flashlight. "I'll go first."

She glanced one last time at Robert, then descended the ladder. The air grew cold, damp, and dark.

"Watch the time," Robert called down.

She climbed down fifteen feet, then splashed into calf-high water.

Fiona was in a four-way intersection and the passages stretched as far as her flashlight shone.

The tunnels were eight-foot-diameter concrete with a canal along the bottom. Suds, chucks of algae, and disintegrating labels floated past . . . refuse from the recycling center. On either side the curved walls squared to make ledges.

Eliot clambered down and stepped onto one ledge, avoiding the sludge. He held out his hand.

Fiona frowned, irritated that she needed help, but nonetheless took it and stepped up.

She shook her foot. Some of this gunk had gotten down her rubber boot. She hated wet socks.

"Alligator," Eliot said. "There are two species, *Alligator mississippiensis* and *Alligator sinensis*. We're probably looking at the American, not the Chinese variety."

"*Alligator* comes from the Spanish *el lagarto*," she added, "which means 'the lizard.'"

It was always easiest to start with encyclopedic knowledge. The real world tended to be a great deal more—she shook her boot again—messy.

"Average weight and length is six hundred pounds and thirteen feet," Eliot said, not to be outdone. "Largest ever recorded, though, was over nineteen feet."

"They're capable of sprints up to thirty miles an hour."

"More of a lunge, really," Eliot replied.

"We just have to keep out of that lunge range, then. It's not armor-plated or anything. Shotgun should do the trick."

She sounded so cool and confident. Inside, however, she shook with terror.

"Yeah, sure." Eliot's brows cinched together.

She glanced at Robert's watch. The numbers glowed.

Two hours. Would that be enough time? Fiona didn't have a clue. Any of the four passages could lead to the alligator . . . or they could lead through miles of nothing.

She and Eliot combined the light of their flashlights and scrutinized each way.

Down the north tunnel their light blinded a rat. It squeaked and scrabbled off over the concrete.

Fiona repressed a shudder. There were rats in their basement. Even with her traps and poisons Grandmother couldn't get rid of them all. This rat, though, was the size of a dachshund.

"Genus *Rattus*," Eliot offered. "Not sure of the species."

This time Fiona's encyclopedic knowledge didn't help. She could only think of how rats carried the black plague and hantavirus. They were unclean, rabid animals that swarmed over one another—all teeth and claws and gleaming red eyes.

She exhaled. She had to keep her cool. It was only one rat.

"You know," Eliot said, "a rat wouldn't be down here unless there was something to eat."

"Like alligator leftovers?"

"Have a better idea?"

She shook her head and they started after the rodent.

"Shouldn't we get out the gun—just in case?" he asked.

Fiona opened her book bag. The half-wrapped shotgun was there. Of course, she'd be doing the shooting. Eliot hadn't even wanted to touch it before. Sometimes he was a child.

She reached for it . . . paused. In reality, she was scared of the thing, too.

How hard could this be? A shotgun versus one lizard with a brain the size of a plum? With double barrels she wasn't likely to miss.

Fiona grabbed the gun, set down her flashlight, loaded the shells, and snapped it shut. It felt natural, as if she'd done this before.

She then stuffed the oilcloth back into her bag and her fingertips brushed the red satin of her chocolate box. Fiona reached inside and grabbed one—popped it into her mouth without even seeing what it was.

She crunched milk chocolate, chopped hazelnuts, and granules of butter toffee. It warmed in her and liquid energy spread to her fingertips and toes.

Now she was ready.

"What was that?" Eliot asked.

"Chocolate." She chewed the last of it. Toffee stuck to her molars. "Robert gave it to me."

At least, this was the most likely explanation. She didn't have the time to explain the entire "secret admirer" story to Eliot, who would have asked endless questions. Nor did she particularly want to think too hard about how the slender box could have had three . . . or was it four layers inside?

"Oh," Eliot said, sounding a little disappointed.

She hefted the shotgun and awkwardly balanced her flashlight on top.

Before Eliot could ask for a chocolate, she took the lead. "This way. Keep your light ahead of me. I might have to drop mine in a hurry."

They moved to where the rat had been. Tiny tracks headed back, criss-crossing over the original trail.

Fiona followed the rat prints along the concrete shelf, down one block, then right at the next intersection.

She double-checked that they could follow their own tracks back. The concrete was mold- and algae-spotted, and their rubber boots left an easy trail. The last thing she wanted was to get lost down here. Part of the test, after all, was *getting back*.

Another rat flickered into view, caught by the beam of Eliot's flashlight. No, three of them scampered ahead.

Fiona's first instinct was to blast them. She raised the shotgun, but held off.

They were just rats. Even a dozen couldn't hurt her.

The rodents peeped and their fur ruffled as they stared down the barrel of her gun. They ran off.

Fiona pressed on, but Eliot hesitated.

"What?" she asked.

"Did those rats seem, I don't know, like they knew what we were doing?"

"They're *rats*. You're imagining things."

Fiona reached into her bag, grabbed another chocolate, and stuffed it in her mouth: a caramel and marshmallow amalgam, sticky and wonderful.

"How many of those things are you going to eat?" Eliot hissed over her shoulder.

"What do you care?" she said, chewing. Fiona marched ahead.

Another rat crossed just five feet ahead of her, then two more flitted past. These seemed even larger than the first ones . . . but Fiona couldn't be sure; they moved so quickly—a dart of gray fur and whip of a tail.

Eliot said, "I can hear them behind us."

Fiona listened, strained to detect anything over the gurgling water, and the pounding of her own sugar-charged heartbeat.

There was faint scratching. Then a peep that ranged into the ultrasonic range . . . not only behind them, but to either side, and now ahead as well.

"We've got to be getting close," she whispered.

She took three careful steps into an intersection. Old brickwork started here. There were different smells, too: earth, rotting meat, urine.

"I don't like this," Eliot said.

Neither did Fiona. The hair on the back of her neck prickled. But what choice did they have?

Eliot suddenly removed his light from the path ahead and swiveled right.

Fiona stopped short, fumbled to grasp her flashlight, then turned to see what he was doing.

There were more rats.

Not three or four—but forty or fifty, all piled on top of one another in the adjacent passage. Their whiskers twitched, and a hundred hate-filled eyes stared at her and Eliot.

These were intelligent eyes. Hungry eyes.

Eliot turned his light down the left passage.

With great effort Fiona pulled her gaze away and followed where her brother now looked.

More rats were there: dozens of them, each three times the size of any rat she'd ever seen.

Fiona slowly backed up until she bumped into Eliot.

"Go back," she whispered. "Carefully. Very slowly."

All they had to do was keep their heads. There was nothing to worry about. Just go back the way they'd come.

Chittering squeaks came from ahead—so loud Fiona almost dropped the shotgun to cover her ears. Then she heard a thousand whisperlike scratches of claws on concrete.

She shone her flashlight farther down the old brick part of the passage. There was a seething carpet of moving fur, black glares, and whipping tails.

Fiona turned to run; so did Eliot.

But hundreds more rats were blocking their escape.

Fiona turned to face the onrushing rodents and cocked both barrels of the shotgun.

29

THE PIPER'S SONG

One especially bold black rat darted forward. Eliot kicked it into the water.

Fiona cocked the hammers of the shotgun.

That gun could kill lots of rats, but no where near enough. They were surrounded by *hundreds* of them.

The rats slowed, confused by the light, pressing closer, climbing over one another, squealing louder.

Fiona raised the shotgun—fired one of the double barrels.

A flash and thunder filled the tunnel. It left Eliot blind and his ears ringing.

Rats cried in pain, surprise, and outrage. It sounded like a million tiny nails on a blackboard.

Eliot blinked and saw the rats running in every direction.

It worked.

Eliot stepped over one creature chasing its own tail. They could get out of here while the rats were stunned. He took two more tentative strides back the way they'd come. Fiona followed.

The rodents slowed, however; they sniffed the air and peeped to one another.

Then every one of them turned toward Eliot and Fiona.

Eliot froze. It wasn't going to work, after all. Shooting wouldn't have worked if they had a hundred shotgun shells; there were too many of them.

He played his flashlight down the tunnels—looking for a way to escape. As far as his light penetrated: all rats, a tide of them rushing in.

"They smell that bread you have," Fiona hissed at him.

Of course. A rat's nose, its stomach, the instinct to eat—that's what was driving them.

"They can have it." Eliot reached into his pack and grabbed the foil parcel. He pulled it apart and flung the bread into the channel. The pungent smell of roasted garlic permeated the air.

Rats surged toward the free meal.

A narrow opening on the ledge cleared.

"Hurry." Eliot pulled his sister along. "This way."

Fiona cocked and fired the other shotgun barrel.

The percussion in the enclosed space made Eliot dizzy. He nearly fell into the water.

Why was she doing that? It just made them angrier.

Six steps and rats again blocked his way. One dashed forward and bit into his rubber boot. Chisel rodent teeth sliced the material; Eliot's toes instinctively curled away as he tried to kick it free. The rat held on—teeth clamped.

In the darkness the hiss of claw on concrete and chittering was deafening.

There had to be something else they'd want to eat more than him and Fiona.

"Your chocolates," he screamed back at her.

"What? No!" Fiona yelled.

Despite her protests, though, Eliot felt her dig into her book bag and hurl handful after handful at the water. The scent of milk chocolate and caramel filled the tunnel.

The rat on his boot released and scampered into the water . . . as did others. Driven insane by this new odor, the rats pushed and ran over one another to get to the candy.

The way was clear.

Eliot ran. Fiona was right behind him.

Their flashlight beams bobbled ahead . . . until he saw an intersection.

A rat clung to the corner—head height—glaring at him.

Eliot slowed and played the beam back and forth over the ledges and walls. His heart skipped a beat. Rats were everywhere—clinging, crowding, some climbing so high they lost purchase and splashed into the water.

It'd take too long to reload the shotgun, and they'd run out of food to throw. There was only one thing left for the rodents to eat.

Fiona bumped into him. She trembled. Or was that *his* body shaking?

She fumbled and found his hand . . . gave it a squeeze.

Eliot squeezed back.

Of all the ways to die: killed by a hundred not-so-tiny bites. He wished Fiona weren't here with him. He'd rather die than see his sister devoured before his eyes.

Was that an option? He could throw himself at the rats and give Fiona a chance to get away.

The rats inched forward, sensing lunch close and helpless.

Any theoretical heroics evaporated in a flash of white-hot panic. Eliot tried to scream but his lungs were vapor-locked.

The rats pushed and climbed over one another to get closer.

Eliot had, however, seen this exact thing before.

He'd seen it recently, too . . . in a book.

Rats ran over his boots, scampered up his pant legs.

Fiona screamed.

But the rational, encyclopedia-loving part of Eliot's mind spoke to him again: rapidly sifting rodent facts and statistics—which halted on a wood-cut picture of a man surrounded by rats.

He had that picture with him.

Eliot pulled a rat off his backpack. He plunged his hand inside and withdrew the heavy leather book they'd found in the basement. He cracked it to the last page that had been opened.

A rat tore at Eliot's shirt; its claws raked his back.

Eliot resisted the impulse to whirl about and get the creature off. He couldn't. He had to focus on the handwriting he'd seen in the margin.

Balancing his flashlight, he saw the woodcut of a handsome rake playing a recorder—surrounded by a thousand rodents, sitting up on their hind legs obedient.

And penciled in alongside this: musical notes.

Eliot had never read music before, but the dots on the higher lines and spaces had to correspond to higher-pitched notes. It seemed so easy . . . as if the ability had been written into his genetic code.

He dropped the book—grabbed his violin.

A dozen rats ripped at the hem of his pants.

He experientially plunked out the music.

The air stilled.

Every rat simultaneously stopped squealing. Claws on concrete quieted. Tiny furry ears ticked forward.

Eliot didn't dare move . . . as if it would break the spell.

Behind him Fiona leaned closer and over ragged breathing whispered, "Keep doing that."

He nodded and plucked out the tune once more.

The rats on his body clambered off and sat on their hind legs.

He slowly knelt and retrieved the violin's bow from his pack. He drew it over the strings. It skittered and scratched, making the wrong notes squeal.

The rats hissed and nipped at one another, shuffling anxiously.

Eliot closed his eyes and forced himself to relax his hold on the instrument, let the bow flow over the strings.

He played.

The song from the book was a simple tune like Louis's nursery rhyme, but whereas that music made Eliot think of children dancing in a circle, this song was for marching—forward it moved, ever on.

He opened his eyes and saw that every rat watched him, enraptured.

Fiona tapped him on the shoulder. "Let's get out of here while we can. Can you walk and play at the same time?"

He wasn't sure. Until yesterday, Eliot hadn't even known that he could play at all. He nonetheless nodded and took a few steps along the ledge, careful not to squash the becalmed rodents.

They let them pass but turned in unison and followed.

It was just like in the picture. He could lead the rats anywhere and momentarily distract them from eating them . . . but that wasn't good enough.

Eliot halted. "This isn't getting us any closer to finding that alligator. We need to stay."

"Are you crazy?" Fiona said. "We stay and we're rat kibble."

"And if we don't find the alligator? Finish the test?"

He paused in the song. The rats instantly grew restless . . . so he started once more.

"I'll take my chances with Aunt Lucia and the Council," Fiona said, and looked at the rats as they again settled. She shuddered.

Eliot struggled to keep his arm and fingers moving. His body shook with spent adrenaline, and he wanted to sit down—to laugh or cry—he wasn't sure which.

But he was sure what would happen if they failed the test. He felt it in his bones. He knew his newly discovered family were more dangerous than a million bubonic-plague-ridden rats.

"Uncle Henry, Aunt Lucia, they're not going to let us off the hook. Run if you have to. I'll stay." The resolve in his voice surprised him, but he meant it. He was going to finish this, one way or another.

"You can't do this alone, moron." Fiona exhaled her patented why-do-I-always-have-to-put-up-with-my-brother sigh. "So other than serenading rats all day, do you have an actual plan?"

"Start with the book. What else does it say about the Pied Piper?"

Fiona set down the shotgun and picked up the *Mythica Improbiba* volume. "I cannot believe I'm reading this stupid book surrounded by a thousand rats about to eat us," she muttered. She scanned the page. "It's in Middle English—bad Middle English. Just about every other word is misspelled."

Eliot kept playing. His arm wasn't used to the bowing motion. It burned with fatigue.

The rats' eyes were fixed upon him, a sea of glassy stares in the shadows as far as he could see.

"According to this, the piper charmed the rats away from a village, but he didn't get paid as promised. So he charmed the village children away to extort a payment . . . no, wait." Fiona squinted at the page. "There's another part that says there were never any children taken. That the piper sent the rats back to the village to steal their silver."[30,31]

"How'd he do that?"

She adjusted the flashlight. "It says he played the rats 'notes of silver' to give them the idea."

"Is there anything in the margin? More music?"

She flipped the pages back and forth. "Nothing."

Eliot thought he understood what the piper had done. Not understood as if he'd read about it, but understood as if it were hardwired into flesh and bones, knowledge that was literally at his fingertips.

"I'm going to try something," he said. "Get ready."

Fiona reloaded the shotgun. She picked up their packs and flashlights. "Okay."

---

30. "Silver notes played by full moon / swarm a thousand crooked tails / Piper paid none too soon / strings broke and maidens wailed." Father Sildas Pious, *Mythica Improbiba* (translated version), c. thirteenth century.

31. Variations on the Pied (or Paid?) Piper tale include cleansing the village of rats, wolves, or bats. Alternative versions have the piper lynched; made mayor; or absconding with the village's silver, children, and/or virginal maidens as his payment. *Gods of the First and Twenty-first century, Volume 4: Core Myths* (Part 1), 8th ed. (Zypheron Press Ltd.).

Eliot slowed the song as he considered what an "alligator" would sound like. He made the notes darker, minor, flowing together snakelike through the uncharted waters of his imagination, then added a light pizzicato phrase like jagged, zigzagging teeth.

Fiona's mouth opened. She slowly closed it and said, "That does sound alligatorish. How'd you—"

The rats peeped excitedly. They jumped on top of and over one another. Some scattered. Some darted into cracks in the walls. But hundreds turned and ran deeper into the sewer.

"Forgot how. Look! They're going to find it. Like the silver in the story."

Fiona watched them for a moment. "Keep playing. I'll go first. She propped a flashlight atop her shotgun and moved cautiously after the stream of rodents.

Eliot followed, alternating between the beguiling song in the book and his improvised alligator tune. He increased the tempo. The rats ran faster, growing wild. His feet skipped in time to the beat.

Smooth concrete walls became older cinder block, then age-crumbled brick.

"The music is creepy," Fiona whispered. "I've heard of it soothing the savage beast, but making them fetch?"

Eliot agreed it was weird. Like Uncle Henry's wild limousine ride or Robert's claim that their family were a bunch of immortals . . . these things danced on the edge of his reality. Not quite impossible—not quite possible, either.

The rats led them left and right and left again, spiraling down, and the water flowed faster in the channel, rippling and churning. The old brick walls became reinforced with beams of solid rust.

A new scent was in the air, an animal smell, part blood and part dung.

The rats halted before a large arch. They squealed in protest and turned rather than continue, but there was nowhere else to go and more rodents crowded the ones that had halted—as if they had all hit a glass wall. They splashed into the water and swam upstream.

Eliot stopped playing.

The rats were no longer interested in his music, no longer interested in lunch, either. They just wanted to go.

"I . . . guess that's a good sign," Fiona whispered.

Eliot nodded.

She focused her flashlight on the arch's keystone. It read DSSS 1899.

"Del Sombra Sewer System?" he said.

She angled the beam lower.

Past the arch was a lake with no discernible shore. Sunlight filtered in from a hole above, and water dripped in continuous streams. Trash floated by: pulpy paper, plastic bags, and a squad of drowned green plastic army men.

Eliot picked up the other flashlight and added its light to the search.

He spied an island in the shadowy center of the lake. This patch of land was made from a few telephone poles, tires . . . but mostly bones— slime-covered, broken to suck the marrow—cow and rabbit and human.

Curled upon the center of this grisly mass, watching them, was the alligator.

30

VANQUISHED

Fiona added her light to Eliot's beam—but almost pulled away when she saw what the extra illumination revealed.

The reptile was covered with black scales that could have been fittings of cast iron. It blinked; nictitating membranes slid over golden pupils and retracted. The creature looked directly at them.

"The narrow snout," she whispered to Eliot. "And see both exposed upper and lower teeth?"

"It's not an alligator," Eliot replied.

"Crocodile," they said together.

This was bad. Crocodiles were far more dangerous than their alligator cousins. They were bigger, faster, and meaner. They had been reported attacking lions, tigers, and even sharks. Every year they killed—and presumably ate—dozens of people in Africa and Southeast Asia.

A chill spread through Fiona's arms, and the shotgun felt as if it weighed a hundred pounds.

"How did a crocodile get to America?" Eliot asked.

"Like Robert said, it was a pet and got flushed down the toilet."

This specimen didn't look like any picture of crocodiles she'd seen. Its neck seemed longer. The eyes were bigger, too. Or maybe that was because it still had them locked in its glare.

"Part plesiosaur?" Eliot said, unsure.

Plesiosaurs were a family of aquatic Jurassic- and Cretaceous-era dinosaurs. Impossible that one could still be alive, but he had a point about this thing looking more primitive than any other creature she had ever seen.

"Don't be stupid," she whispered. "Focus. We have to come up with a plan to get close enough to shoot it."

She couldn't believe she'd said those words—especially since she was the one most likely to be using the shotgun.

What had Robert said? Wait for it to open its mouth? The chill in her arms spread to the rest of her body, and she found it hard to breathe. She would have to be almost on top of it to aim down its open maw.

The crocodile's jaw worked side to side. It hissed a bassy rumble that rippled the water. It sounded like . . . words.

Eliot looked at her. "Do you hear—"

"Shhh."

She strained and listened. There were variations and intonations, but they couldn't be words. It was just her mind playing tricks. Animal sounds like a birdcall.

Eliot tugged at her sleeve. "In the limousine, when Grandmother and Henry spoke."

Fiona connected the two events, then and now, in a flash. When Grandmother and Henry hadn't wanted them eavesdropping, they switched to a language Fiona hadn't recognized.

This reptile spoke the same language. She couldn't decipher it then, nor could she now, but she sensed it was old, and something full of secrets.

"There's no way that's real," she whispered.

The crocodile's eyes widened a fraction and then it said, "English. How distressing. You wish to discard tradition, very well."

Fiona stared at the animal. Her mind refused to accept what she had heard. Its mouth *had* opened, though. The sound *had* come from it. Still, such things didn't happen in this world.

She turned to Eliot. He trembled and stared at the animal.

Fiona felt—of all the ridiculous things—as if she were going to faint.

"So death finally comes to the eater of death," it said.

In the years to come, this would be the moment that Fiona would look back on and acknowledge as the turning point. Her reality changed in that instant. Staring into the eyes of a talking crocodile—nothing could be the same afterward.

She struggled, however, to hang on to her old, nonfantastical world and cast about for an explanation. There must be gas in this sewer causing hallucinations such as rats that obeyed violin music and speaking reptiles. That was the only reasonable thing, wasn't it?

But the deep voice of this crocodile was no illusion. It spoke with the weight of the ages, like Grandmother. As if it had spoken to hundreds of girls before her . . . telling them to be calm and walk into its gaping jaws.

She shook her head to clear those thoughts.

She had to face this. She had to face everything. Maybe her extended family would really kill her. Maybe her mother had been a real goddess. And maybe a crocodile really was talking to her.

"It just sits there," Eliot said. "Why isn't it swimming toward us?"

The crocodile lay its head upon the bones. They crunched from the weight.

"If I had wanted you dead," it replied, "you would be. Come closer. Let us end this."

"It's a trick," Eliot whispered. "Remember it's fastest at short range. It lunges at prey."

"I don't think it's a trick," Fiona whispered back. She cleared her throat, then addressed the beast: "We don't *want* to kill you, and we won't . . . unless we have to defend ourselves."

The beast snorted. "I have read the signs. I know you come to vanquish."

Fiona squinted. Were those tears in its eyes?

The crocodile shifted upon the island, revealing its shoulder. A shaft of metal pierced its stubby arm and left the limb swollen, gray, and limp. Fiona could see teeth marks dotting the metal—above and below—where it must have tried to chew it off. Black blood welled and dripped from the wound onto the bones.

She could only imagine the pain it was in.

"It would be one thing if it were attacking," she whispered to Eliot, "but to just blow its head off, that would be . . ."

"Murder?" Eliot said. "Isn't that what we came here to do? The only way to pass the test?"

They were quiet a moment.

"You know what Machiavelli said about pawns?" she asked him. "How they had to change to survive?"

Eliot nodded.

"I don't think I can become someone who kills just because they're told to."

"Me neither." Eliot glanced at the shotgun and then at her. "So what do you want to do?"

"I'm not sure, but there has to be another way. I mean, this *is* an intelligent, talking creature."

Eliot fidgeted, looking uncertain and uncomfortable.

"We can try to help it," she said. "Remove that thing from its arm. It might know our family. It might help us figure out how to survive."

Eliot took in and exhaled a slow breath to steady himself. "Maybe I can make it docile with music. You could get closer—either to help it or . . . whatever."

Fiona pressed her lips together, trying to imagine herself voluntarily moving toward the animal. She couldn't.

She nodded, stood straighter, and again addressed the beast. "We'll help you. Get that thing out of your shoulder. Then maybe we can talk."

The crocodile considered her a moment with its gold-and-black, unblinking eyes. "Very well. Come end this."

"That sounds like an invitation," Fiona said to her brother.

"Or a trap," he replied.

If that was the case, then Fiona still had the shotgun . . . but even with it she wasn't sure she could kill the thing. Anything but a head shot would just wound an armored animal that size.

But Fiona had to do *something* before she lost her nerve. She was still a little dizzy . . . disoriented enough so the fear had yet to rush in and fill her. But she knew it would come soon enough.

She reached into the book bag, into her heart-shaped box, fumbled, and found a chocolate. She'd thrown handfuls of them at the rats, but thankfully the box seemed as full as ever. She popped it into her mouth.

Bittersweet chocolate and raspberry cordial melted over her tongue. Warmth spread throughout her body and steadied her shaking hands.

Fiona shone her flashlight into the water.

It was three feet deep. The current was strong, but it eased off once it flowed into the larger "lake" room.

She stepped off the ledge. Her boots filled with water. It was cold, but the effect of the chocolate she had eaten repelled this chill. She hated wet socks. The discomfort, though, would keep her mind off the insane thing she was about to do.

Wading forward, she made sure the shotgun was held high—well away from her splashing strides.

Eliot stepped in after her, but veered toward the curved wall. He started

playing his violin, a slow song that was half the reptile tune he had in-
vented . . . and half dreamlike meander.

Fiona blinked, surprised to find herself yawning. It was working. What
else could her brother do with his music?

The crocodile yawned as well.

This instantly sobered Fiona. The beast's mouth had more spike teeth
than she had ever seen on any animal—hundreds of interlocking ivory dag-
gers.

Fiona then grasped the proper proportion of things. It had been hard to
make out the dimensions of this chamber outside, but inside she saw the
room was fifty feet across with a central shaft filled with misty light.

The island in the center was larger than she had realized. It stretched
twenty feet across. How many things had died and been eaten to make
that pile of bones?

No—best not to think about that. Better to focus on moving ahead.
Keep the shotgun ready, finger on the triggers.

Then the last dimension of the scene clicked into place: the crocodile.
It wasn't just large. It barely fit half-curled upon the island, and its tail
trailed into the water.

Fiona had read that some record crocodile specimens had been twenty
feet long. This animal was *twice* that size.

She halted, suddenly feeling the fear she had managed to keep at bay so
long. The joints in her arms and legs locked.

Did it really matter how big it was? A twenty- or forty-foot reptilian eating machine—it would kill and eat her just the same, right?

She took a deep breath and reached for another chocolate. Fiona forced
herself to stop.

The last thing she needed was to have that thing charge when her hand
was stuck in her bag. She had to have both hands free for the flashlight and
shotgun. She'd have to do this without eating another chocolate.

Fiona licked her lips, marched to the edge of the island, and crunched
onto the bones.

The crocodile didn't stir, appearing half-asleep, eyes just slits.

Her heart raced. She was certainly inside its "lunge" range.

She kept the gun pointed at its head, waiting for it to strike.

She glanced at Eliot playing. If this didn't work, if the crocodile turned
on her and she failed to stop it . . . her unarmed brother wouldn't stand a
chance.

She gingerly stepped over rib and skull and hip bones around to the far side to the protruding sliver of metal. Both ends had indeed been chewed away. Fiona could only imagine the jaw pressure needed to do that.

She inched closer.

One crocodile eye rotated, tracking her.

To pull the metal free she'd need both hands; she'd have to set her shotgun down. This close, however, she might never get a better shot at the creature. She could aim for the eye. Point-blank, surely that would penetrate the skull through the occipital orb, pulp the brain—kill it.

That's what they were supposed to do, wasn't it?

But why? This thing was alive and intelligent. Yes, it killed, but to eat, not because someone had told it that's what it had to do to pass some stupid, arbitrary test.

Shooting it in self-defense would have been a different story. She almost *wanted* it to turn and lunge.

Grandmother would have shot it. She would already have done it. She wouldn't be wasting any time thinking about it.

So Fiona decided. She decided that she would not take a life without a better reason.

She set down the shotgun.

Her pulse pounded so hard she no longer heard Eliot's music. Her vision narrowed on the metal shard, the animal's shoulder, the black blood oozing.

The only way to get the metal shard out would be to pull or push straight through.

She reached for it, but paused when she saw its jagged edges. She had to be smart about this or she'd cut herself to ribbons.

And how docile would the crocodile remain if it smelled her blood?

She picked up two femurs and set them into teeth-made indents in the metal. The fit was good.

The crocodile shifted as she did so.

Fiona froze. It was too late to reach for the gun. If it wanted to, it could turn and snap her in half before she'd react.

The crocodile settled.

Fiona took a deep breath. She counted: one, two, three! She pulled up with all her strength.

The metal spike resisted—then wrenched free, metal grating over the tendon and bone. It tore out of the flesh with a sucking sound and a splash of blood.

The crocodile roared and spun.

Its tail swept out her legs and it pinned her with one clawed foot.

Directly over her was death: an open maw filled with a hundred teeth . . . and beyond a blackness so profound she knew it stretched forever.

She couldn't do anything but stare into that emptiness. Every thought froze in her brain. Petrified.

Darkness swelled around her. A chill penetrated her soul. She felt as if she were falling.

"Fiona!" Eliot yelled. There was a distant splash in the water.

She hoped he wasn't idiot enough to try to do something. He had no gun. And she very much doubted a lullaby was going to calm a now enraged two-ton reptile. What was he thinking?

At least contemplating how stupid her brother was got *her* brain working again.

She could barely breathe with the weight on her chest, but she did see the shotgun on the ground next to her. It was just out of reach.

If she could stretch, just a little, she might be able to grab it—shoot straight up into the crocodile's open mouth as Robert had told her.

But this was wrong.

Why wasn't it eating her? Crocodiles weren't known for taking a few moments to savor the quality of their dinners before devouring them.

Was it testing her? Waiting to see if she would go for the gun? Give *it* a reason to kill *her*? Not that it needed one. But still, it hadn't moved a muscle after knocking her down.

She waited, too.

The only detectable motion was Fiona's heart: a rapid-fire, machine-gun drumroll beat in her chest.

The pressure eased and the crocodile stepped off her. It closed its titanic black hole of a mouth.

Fiona blinked. Light and warmth seemed to flood back into the world. She slowly sat up.

The crocodile regarded her with hypnotic golden eyes and said, "Thank you."

Eliot sloshed onto the island, his violin and bow held high. He was so foolish sometimes, or was he just foolishly brave? She was glad he was here.

He knelt next to her. "You okay?"

She probed her ribs—tender, bruised—but not broken. "I'll be fine."

He helped her stand and they faced the crocodile.

"You're welcome," she said to the beast.

It gave a little shake of its head. "Most odd," it murmured. "My readings are never wrong. I scry the trash that floats by as a Gypsy might read tea leaves."

The crocodile opened and closed its mouth—a quick smacking snap that sent a chill down Fiona's spine. "The signs said that two heroes would come to end my misery."

"Yeah," Fiona replied, "that's what we just did."

The calm in her voice surprised her . . . but then speaking to a giant, intelligent reptilian oracle didn't feel much different from speaking to Grandmother.

The crocodile breathed out a long, contemplative hiss. "A literal reading is rare in my line of work. You must be strong to so influence omens." It bobbed its head, the equivalent of a bow, Fiona guessed. "Souhk, I am called. I am in your debt."

That sounded promising, as if maybe it wasn't going to eat them.

She did her best to approximate a curtsy (not an easy thing to do in rubber boots and with bruised ribs).

"This is my brother, Eliot. And I'm Fiona. Fiona Post."

"I foresaw the coming of children from two great families. Momentous things are writ in your destiny. Terrible things. Or perhaps nothing if you fail tests and temptations."

Why was everyone always referring to her and Eliot as "children"? Fifteen years old—you'd think someone might call them teenagers.

"You're talking about the Council's heroic trials, right?" Eliot asked.

Souhk nodded. "I worked for them long ago. There is nothing more loathed than a middleman, no?"

Fiona took a tiny step back. "This is very awkward, sir, but we were sent to . . ." How to politely explain that for them to live, they had to kill their new acquaintance?

"'Vanquish' me," Souhk finished for her. "An unlikely outcome for two children." He snorted a great blast from his nostrils at the shotgun on the ground. "Even with such an instrument."

"Then we lose," Eliot whispered.

Souhk's mouth cracked open into a terrifying crocodile smile. "Oh, no, child. You have won."

Fiona and Eliot looked at each other, puzzled.

"One definition for *vanquish*," Souhk said, "is to defeat in war. Another, however, is to demonstrate superiority in contest or argument . . . or in your case, with kindness."

"I don't get it," Eliot said.

"No, I do, listen," Fiona said. "Robert said we had to 'vanquish the beast.' And we did. We made him our friend."

Souhk's smile widened. "Temporary allies is closer to the truth. 'Friends,' however, will carry a certain sentimental shock value when this is told to the Council." It chuckled.

Relief washed through Fiona. They had found a way to pass the trial without killing, or getting killed.

But a new doubt tugged at her. "Will the Council accept this? I mean, I'm pretty sure they meant for us to kill you."

"So they did. They will most certainly look up the definition of *vanquish* in many dictionaries before they allow it. Allow it they will, though. The Council adheres to their laws . . . to the very letter."

The crocodile shifted and pointed toward one of the passages that led into the Del Sombra sewers. "I am filled with hunger," Souhk said in a deeper, more primal voice. "I must feed."

The wound in its shoulder healed before Fiona's eyes. The puncture closed. Clear scales grew and darkened to match the cast-iron black of the rest of its body.

Fiona took another step back and pulled Eliot along with her. "Maybe we should be going."

Eliot yanked free of her hand. "But I have a million questions. Who *is* our family? Where do they come from? What about our father?"

Souhk turned and stared at them, so long that she wondered if the intelligent part of its mind had submerged, and they now faced a hungry reptile—not their new friend. Maybe Souhk was both.

"*I* must eat first," it growled. "*You* must survive the other trials . . . and your families. Ask me questions after that." It lumbered toward the water, each weighty step shifting the bones of the island. "Return in a year. I will have finished then."

A year? How much food did Souhk need? And *what* was he going to eat? She glanced at the hill of bones at her feet; a human skull stared back. Fiona didn't want to know.

"Just one question," Eliot called after it. "Please."

It paused and turned.

"Please," he repeated in a tiny voice.

"Very well, ask one question then, maker of music."

Eliot puffed out his chest.

That's all her brother needed, someone calling him a musician. If Grandmother ever found out he had that violin . . . she'd what? What could she do to them now that they'd faced a giant crocodile?

"Ask him about the next trial," Fiona whispered.

Eliot shook his head. "We know about our mother's side of the family. That we have to somehow grow and become like them to survive . . . but what about our father's family? Will they get involved? How do we contact them?"

Souhk rushed toward Eliot and Fiona—a sprint much faster than either could believe—it skidded, sent bones flying, and halted only an inch away.

Eliot and Fiona instinctively drew closer together . . . as if this could possibly protect them.

"That is *more* than one question," it hissed.

Souhk cocked its huge head, angling its stare at them both. "I see them in you. There is more danger in dealing with your father's family than your mother's. Few survive their interests. Avoid them at all cost."

Souhk glanced about the room. Fiona thought this gesture unmistakably one of fear. It then turned and slid into the water without a sound. With one great swish of its tail it propelled itself out of the room.

"They are the Infernals," Souhk said. "Mortals call them something else, though . . . the fallen angels."

PAWNS IN PLAY

31

FAMILY GATHERING

Riding in a tanklike ice crawler, wrapped in a down-filled cocoon, Sealiah considered her journey—a private jet from Los Angeles to Reykjavík, helicopter to the interior of Iceland, followed by crawler ride when the winds proved too fierce . . . all to get to one of the last untainted Old Places.

Iceland . . . had there been anything wrong with warmer Las Vegas (apart from the antiseptic absence of good taste)? Or had Beal's overdeveloped sense of drama gotten the better of him? Surely there was no practical reason to drag them here, other than to prove that he *could* drag them all here.

Still, it had been ages since she had seen the place.

Her skin prickled. They were close.

Beyond the crawler's windows, halogen headlights punctured the blackness and illuminated swirls of snow.

The global-positioning display on the dash beeped. They were near sixty-four degrees north, seventeen degrees west: dead center in the middle of nowhere.

The driver said, "I'll get the cold-weather suits, my lady."

Sealiah cast off her blanket, opened the door, and jumped three meters to the ground.

Her boots shattered the ice on impact and sent the scale armor covering her thighs shivering. The howling winds flash-chilled the mail on her chest and shoulders and whipped the arctic-fox-fur cape behind her.

She took a deep breath and let the cold freeze her blood. Thinking of her cousins made her boil, and she could not afford the pleasure of a blind rage tonight.

Sealiah marched to an outcropping of rock. A dim red glow emanated from the far side, and she saw men.

She checked her blades, Exarp and Omebb, to make certain they were not frosted in their scabbards.

The guards held Kalashnikov machine guns. They raised their aim at her approach, but lowered them when they saw that she wore only bits of choice metal in the subfreezing weather.

They bowed deeply before her.

Splashed upon the ice was blood. Apparently one of them had not bowed low enough for her cousins.

A dozen ice crawlers sat close, their engines idling. News of the Post children must have spread to have attracted so many to this remote location.

Perhaps Beal was not the fool she had thought. Convening the Board here limited the number of family members attending and gave him a chance to retain control. Or was "control" the last thing he had in mind?

She approached the statues that flanked the subterranean entrance. They were vague shapes of black stone. One could still make out the chiseled square-tip swords in their hands, however.

Sealiah bit her thumb and smeared blood upon each sword. Not even she dared enter this place without the proper respect.

She descended the spiral of stairs.

Warm air rushed past and melted the ice that clung to her. She smelled hot iron and sulfur.

She emerged in a large cavern. To her right a frozen wall glistened amber. Ice stalactites dangled a hundred feet above her head. Paving the floor were hexagonal basalt tiles. A dozen paces in, this floor tilted and submerged into a lake of molten stone. Pillars rose from the boiling lake. Once there had been faces of heroic proportions carved upon them. Gods before there ever was a word for "god" or a humanity to worship them.[32]

What would Sealiah have given to coax these Ancients to whisper their secrets? But, alas, time had caught up and overtaken even them.

32. "In the cave were gods before God, locked twixt stone ice and flame / Blind and deaf until the end of days / Tread with care traveler / Let titans sleep until the stars fall." From the "Saga of Yorik Bloodied Beard" in Father Sildas Pious, *Mythica Improbiba* (translated version, Beezle edition), c. thirteenth century.

A narrow wedge of stone thrust out precariously over the molten lake. Upon it a slab of basalt served as a table.

Most of the Board had already arrived and stood at their places.

Abby wore pink for the occasion, a thin ribbon of silk wound about her slender form. She stood at the far right of the table, one step from the edge—as if daring anyone to push her in. A red-and-black centipede curled up her pale arm, eating something bloody from her hand.

Lev stood opposite her in the same polyester sweat suit he had worn last time, the outfit living up to its name: soaked with his perspiration. His corpulent chest heaved, panting in the heat. He fanned himself with a hubcap-sized medallion strung about his neck.

Ashmed stood next to Abby, close to the foot of the table. He wore an immaculately tailored gray suit and silver tie that glowed in the molten illumination. He nodded at Sealiah, a small sign of respect, or interest, which sent an unexpected thrill through her.

How she wished there were no layers of politics between her and her cousin. She would like to know him without the constant undercurrent of suspicion, intrigue, and danger that was more intimately bound to their character than the DNA in their cells. Even such thoughts were dangerous, as they could be detected and exploited . . . which made this fantasy all the more stimulating.

Oz turned and beckoned her to stand near him. He wore the leather fetish gear of a Hells Angel and had his hair curled like an eighteenth-century Parisian whore's. A beauty mark was on his powdered cheek.

"Greeting to Queen of the Poppies," he purred, and gestured to the foot of the table.

Sealiah moved to join them . . . but slowly. She took her time and carefully glanced about the cavern. It was always wise to examine treacherous terrain.

Many of the Board members had brought their entourages. Gathered on the far side of the cavern where the air was cooler and breathable, men in tuxedos and women in cocktail dresses sipped champagne in carved-ice flutes. Shadow bodyguards slithered upon the walls, gathering whispers and spying on spies.

Almost unnoticed, disguised as the catering staff, or standing with a nonchalance that dared any to see them, were other family members. Samsawell, the Ever Hungry (who she heard now called himself Sam); vulnerable-looking, old Mulciber of the Infernal Eternal Bureaucracy; and even reclusive Uziel, the Golden Child, Prince of the Killing Fields—all represented powerful non-Board clans.

Predators and scavengers alike were gathering. Each pretended not to notice her noticing them.

Beal made his entrance, contriving to time his appearance with a pair of exploding jets that geysered from the magma. Molten droplets and sparks filled the superheated air—reflected and magnified on the distant walls of ice.

Beal took his place at the head of the table outlined by fountains of fire. Sealiah had to grudgingly admit it was a fine effect.

He wore a tuxedo with black shirt and a cape of ostrich feathers. The only color was his blue eyes and the fist-size sapphire that dangled on a leather thong about his throat. In his hand he cradled a black rat.

"Let us begin," Beal said. "I will only lie to you with the truth."[33]

He pretended to just now notice Sealiah. "Very good, the Poppy Queen has joined us. Although not part of the Board, I thought it apropos to have you here to report on the progress of your temptress."

She tilted her head in faux appreciation and checked her rage at his mocking. She had already made her report to him. Julie Marks was ready to make her move: a lion pouncing upon a kitten. Sealiah understood why she was really here. To be watched.

"The honor is mine," she replied. Her smile wiped the joy from Beal's features.

Beal set the rat on the table and gestured. Porters in silver heat suits carried a laptop and wide-screen plasma viewer to the table. "I have called us here to discuss developments in the Post case," he said.

The Board exchanged glances, save Ashmed, who sat still.

The rat leaped to the floor, and mighty Uri stood in its place, smoothing his tuxedo. He did not look at Sealiah.

Her heart ached to have him so near again. He was her knight disguised as a pawn upon the board. But he was in play; she could not pull him back now . . . so she made her heart ice once more.

---

33. Traditional Infernal greeting. Infernals lie to suit their own end, but according to myth they can unfailingly detect any falsehood. Therefore, it is considered the gravest of insults for one Infernal to *simply* lie to another. This greeting assures Infernal kin of their respectful intentions, i.e., only lying by omission or twisted fact. Experts consider it emblematic of their warped values. *Gods of the First and Twenty-first Century, Volume 13: Infernal Forces,* 8th ed. (Zypheron Press Ltd.).

Uri tapped on the computer keyboard and the display flickered to life. "The League has decided to test the subjects as well," Uri explained.

The Board members shifted. Any mention of the others made them uncomfortable. Even little Abby's albino body rocked back and forth. Sealiah, too, wished she could act against their old enemy, but they were all bound by an unbreakable neutrality pact.

"It was a simple matter for me to follow the children and observe," Uri continued.

Video appeared on-screen: a black-and-white blur that focused into a ground-level view of a sewer tunnel and a hundred rats that jostled the lens. Squealing and scratching noises blared from the speakers.

"The video quality of this bit is poor, but the interesting part is the audio." Uri adjusted audio sliders at the bottom of the screen.

The rat noises faded and the sound of a violin playing resolved.

The Board members stilled.

The music was faint, but each note was crystal clear in Sealiah's mind. It was an old song. A nursery rhyme. One of *their* songs.

"That is 'The Piper's Song,'" Ashmed said, and stroked his fine beard. "Have you found our long-lost Louis?"

Uri shook his head. "It is Eliot Post that plays."

A fifteen-year-old boy who played like a master? Sealiah closed her eyes and indulged a moment; she had not heard this song since she was young and foolish and in love.

On-screen the rats quieted and sat on their hind legs. Some pawed at the air trying to catch the music.

The melody slowed and changed so a new tune interwove through the first—darker notes that slithered and coiled.

"Reptile," Lev murmured, and leaned closer, pressing his head to the speaker. "That's a summoning!"

"A human child could not know such things," Oz said. "Louis must have taught him."

Ashmed shook his head. "We do not know if Louis is alive. We have discussed this many times: if he lives, why can we not detect him?"

Abby nervously twisted her centipede in her hands. The insect hissed.

"Listen to the music," Lev growled. "Only the Deceiver plays like that. Louis lives, I tell you."

The rats scampered down the tunnel. The picture then froze and a mass of rodent blur filled the screen.

Beal nodded to Uri. "Fast-forward. There are more interesting bits ahead."

Uri tapped controls and the screen refocused to a wide-angle view of a flooded room, an island of bones, and a crocodile.

"This is the League's test," Uri explained.

He flexed one massive hand, a gesture Sealiah recognized as nervous concern. Had direct exposure to the music affected him? Could he actually care what happened to the Post children?

"So typical of the other family," Oz remarked. "A classic beast-vanquishing. I'm astonished they did not give them a white horse to charge in on."

Lev leaned back. "At least we'll see a little blood spilled here." He snapped his teeth at Abby.

Beal stood impassively, observing the Board's reactions. Sealiah wondered what game he played.

She noted Ashmed, as well, watched Beal instead of the video. Ashmed then glanced at her and gave her the slightest of approving nods.

Abby stepped closer to the screen and touched the image of the crocodile. Her nails left tiny indentations on the glass.

The animal spoke to the Post children: "So death finally comes to the eater of death."

Oz perked up and leaned forward. "Is that actually . . . Sobek?"

"You will find this interesting," Uri said, and zoomed in on the girl, Fiona. With a hand trembling she delved into her book bag, retrieved, and then devoured a chocolate.

"Note the stilling of her body after she eats it," Beal said. "The flush reaction. She is obviously addicted."

"A mortal if I ever saw one," Lev growled.

They watched Fiona warily approach Sobek.

"Brave though," Ashmed noted. "There may be yet something to her."

Lev snorted. "I'd be brave, too, high on those things."

Uri adjusted the audio so that Eliot's lullaby flooded the chamber and they listened with rapt attention.

Sealiah inhaled and held her breath. She blinked rapidly to clear her head and noted that even the bubbling lava had stilled.

Oz trilled, "Oooo, I have goose bumps. He must be one of us. Let's grab him now."

Abby set her centipede down and shooed it away. Her pink eyes reddened with blood. "These were *not* the terms we rolled on. We let the three temptations run their course."

"I agree with Abigail," Ashmed said. "If the boy is Louis's and the other family is involved, we must proceed with care. One misstep and we may lose him to them . . . as well as any chance to break the treaty."

"No—this smells of Louis," Lev told them, raising his voice. "He's out there. Pulling strings and laughing at us."

Sealiah watched the screen as Fiona pulled the iron spike from Sobek. It turned and crushed her under one claw, but then it hesitated . . . poised to consume her soul.

Miraculously it allowed her to live. It let her up, then spoke to the children.

They had charmed the monster. Impressive.

The Board, however, failed to notice this as they continued to argue.

"Louis alive is an impossibility," Abby stated. "He would have been found."

"So how did he die?" Lev retorted. "No one here claimed the kill. That leaves the League . . . which means they got around our 'unbreakable' treaty first to slit Slyboot's throat? I don't believe it."

Beal nodded to Uri.

Uri bowed to the Board (they ignored him) and departed.

Beal followed, smiling.

"Bring the boy in," Oz said. "Let me question him. I'll get to the bottom of it."

"Enough talk!" Lev gripped the table and braced; his sweat suit ripped. The massive stone cracked. "I've got a better way to settle this." He grunted, picking up the three-ton hunk of basalt.

The debate was over. It appeared that the Board would skip rolling dice and go directly to the violence portion of the agenda.

Sealiah surmised that Beal had engineered this squabble to distract the Board . . . long enough to let him do whatever he wanted to the Post children. Had he summoned her hoping to involve her in the conflict, as well?

How dare he think her easily led. Oddly, however, their goals of chaos were in alignment. Sealiah could live with that irony, as long as in the end she won.

Abby jumped on top of the table—now held precariously by Lev—and leapt at him.

Lev flipped the stone, slapped her out of the air, hurling her into the lava.

He waddled to the precipice and dropped the massive stone, yelling, "*That's* what I think of your ideas!"

Far below Abby screamed, her anger now loosened. Gouts of flame leapt upward and licked the ceiling.

Oz meanwhile, crept closer and pushed Lev over the edge. He hurled smaller rocks down at his cousins . . . as well as some amazingly archaic insults regarding their romantic preferences.

A wave of magma splashed up and covered Oz. He shrieked as his leather accoutrements sizzled off.

Gunfire, shattering glass, and screams erupted across the cavern. The Board members' entourages were not going to stand idly and watch. Following their masters, they were going to try to kill one another.

Sealiah loosened her blades and backed away.

Ashmed brushed soot from his suit and came to her. "Brilliant, no? Beal seems to win again."

"Does he?"

Ashmed smiled. "Shall we discuss it all over a glass of champagne? I saw a case of Bollinger Vieille Vignes Françaises as I came in." He cast his gaze through the murderous crowds. "Ah, yes, there. Unbroken for the moment. Shall I fetch us a bottle?"

She tilted her head. "How could any refuse you?"

"They cannot." He smiled and left her side.

Abby crawled up over stone ledge. Her pale body glowed with orange heat and her eyes blazed. Poison dripped from her taloned hands and sizzled where it touched the stone. She roared liquid fire—no longer Abigail the diminutive, but gigantic Abaddon the Destroyer, frightening to all.

Beneath her in the molten lake raged the Beast . . . not Lev, but rather the serpent called Leviathan.

The earth shuddered as Leviathan struck the edge of the stone. It crumbled under Abaddon and she plunged back into the molten pool.

The lava boiled and erupted as they fought.

Sealiah backed to the far wall. She had no desire to get between two of her most physically intimidating, if somewhat mentally diminutive, cousins.

A shadow stood near her. As she had hoped, Uri had momentarily slipped away from his new master.

"M'lady," he whispered.

She heard it all in his tremulous voice: how her mighty Uri missed her. Her heart of ice stirred, but not enough to thaw.

"There is little time," she said. "What game does the Lord of All That Flies play?"

"It is Louis. He has sniffed a trace of his power in the city where the children live."

Could Louis truly be alive? This complicated her plans . . . or did it present a new facet for her to exploit?

"If Beal attempts to contact him," she told Uri, "offer to speak in his place. Say the Deceiver is too dangerous. Louis may yet be the key for *us*."

Uri nodded and faded. "He calls me. I must . . ."

How she wished he could have lingered, but even the few seconds they had had together was fraught with danger. It had been worth it, however. Louis was back in play? It made the game all the more dangerous and exciting.

Ashmed returned with a bottle. "It sadly is warm. Shall we open it outside?"

He offered her his arm and she took it. Together they strolled to the stairs, stepping over the bleeding and broken bodies of very foolish mortals.

32

A KING ONCE MORE

enry watched his cousin lean against the railing. Aaron looked so somber that he seemed to drag the black clouds looming on the horizon ever closer.

They rode upon Cousin Gilbert's zeppelin, *The Akkadian,* sailing high over the North African coast: whitecaps and lapis waters on one side, golden gleaming desert on the other, and in the sky cumulus humilis clouds like so many puffs of cotton.

Aaron wore worn jeans and boots and, of all the ridiculous things, a rattlesnake-banded cowboy hat. Next to him, propped against the railing, was a metal bar with either end chewed.

Henry joined him and leaned recklessly over the edge. "You look like you have swallowed a skunk."

"The Council speaks," Aaron replied, "but through layers of meaning meant to hide their hearts."

"That is the short definition of politics."

"I thought you said politics was 'the art of getting everything from everyone using the illusion of compromise.'"

"That is *also* its definition," Henry said. "There are thirteen if you'd care to hear them all."

"I grow tired of the games." Aaron spat over the edge and watched it fall. "Where do we belong? In the clouds? Down there? Or perhaps we have no place at all to call our own."

"Do not be so morbid." Henry handed him a handkerchief to wipe the spittle that clung to his long mustache.

How many of their kind had simply wandered off when taken with these moods? Direct men like Aaron were the most susceptible. Like Poseidon, perhaps the strongest of them all, who ended his days snorkeling too close to the Bikini atoll in the spring of 1954.[34] It was odd how the simple ones always sought such dramatic ends.

This is why Henry considered it his duty to stir the pot. His role in the family was that of a hurricane, disrupting the normal course of things (with him, of course, in the calm center). How else would any of them survive the boredom?

He felt a twinge of jealousy, however, that the Post children were the most exciting thing to happen in decades—and none his doing. Audrey of all people had managed it, the last he ever expected to be so rebellious.

Still, he adored Eliot and Fiona; they reminded him that their kind could be innocent . . . at least for a time.

From the apex of the zeppelin a silver bell chimed.

"Let us get the talking over with," Henry said, and set his hand on Aaron's shoulder. "And then we can get drunk in Morocco."

Aaron laughed. "Another adventure, old Wolf? Very well." He plucked up the iron spike.

They strode up the curve of the airship to the observation platform perched on the very top.

Gilbert had insisted they meet here, "a proper venue" he claimed. He had gathered leather couches and tables of food and drink so they would have every comfort as they soared through the clouds.

Gilbert greeted Aaron and Henry with hardy claps on their backs. His golden hair and beard had been immaculately braided. He wore linen and a coat of gold as he used to in the old days.

Something had changed in Cousin Gilbert. He seemed more alive than Henry had seen him since he lost the woman he loved and his best friend so long ago. Had recent events rekindled the sparks of his once kingly greatness? Was Cousin Gilbert again Gilgamesh?

"There's Ström vodka and beluga caviar," Gilbert said.

"Little eggs are hardly a meal for men," Aaron muttered.

"We go to Morocco after this," Henry said. "Join us?"

Gilbert tilted his head. "Yes. Today, I feel ready for anything."

---

34. On March 1, 1954, a hydrogen bomb, code-named Bravo, was detonated on the surface of the reef in the northwestern corner of Bikini atoll.—Editor.

Aaron exchanged a look with Henry, as surprised as he was by Gilbert's willingness to have a little fun. It had been a long time.

Aaron took Gilbert by the arm and they moved to the tables. "Then let's start. Vodka's better than nothing."

Henry stayed behind. There were regrettably still serious matters that he could not face with a head full of liquor.

He surveyed the platform. They had a proper quorum: seven Council members.

Lucia wore a white silk dress that flowed about in the breeze like the petals of an intricate orchid. She sat apart from the others, a large book open in her lap, its pages fluttering.

Cornelius sat cross-legged on the platform's edge. The old man had no papers—they would all have blown away. Instead he favored a half dozen tablet computers, which surrounded him in an arc, aglow with simulations and spreadsheets and NASA star charts.

And the two Council members who had missed their first meeting on the Post children were here, sitting side by side upon one couch.

Dallas had come from St. Petersburg, where she spearheaded its burgeoning avant-garde film industry. She wore a tiny fur hat and a matching mink miniskirt. Adorable. She was dangerous as well, and she reminded Henry of this by smiling at him, flashing her dimples, making his pulse quicken . . . and making him forget all for a moment.

He held up his hands. "Please, madam, your charms can wound the unprepared."

She giggled, and the sound was like crystal ringing.

Next to her was Kino, skin the color of ebony slate—and so tall that even sitting he was the same height as Henry. He had left his island paradise to be here. He looked none too happy about it.

Kino tipped his top hat at Henry and rapped his cane twice on the platform. "Are we to start?" he demanded. "I am eager to hear more—especially since I have missed so much of this theater with Audrey and her children."

"By all means," Dallas said, crossing her long legs. "What have you found, Lucia? Do you need help with the big words?"

Lucia removed her reading glasses and looked up from her book. "I am just on the last entry. *Vanquish* apparently has a half dozen meanings."

Henry spared a glance at poor Robert.

His new Driver sat on the opposite side of the platform, alone on a love seat, looking as uncomfortable as any boy could after he had made his report. Well, it was his job to report these things to the Council. Robert would survive the process . . . or not.

Of course matters were a tad more complicated: Robert was in play now. Audrey had a knack for drawing Henry's minions into her games. She had killed Welmann and, with the help of Fiona's unwitting and naïve charms, had made a pawn of Robert. How many more would Henry have to sacrifice to the Cutter of All Things?

He felt for the boy. A hero's job was difficult. He'd have to give Robert a long vacation after this.

Lucia slammed shut volume forty-eight of *Sanswret's Unabridged Dictionary* and tossed it onto the platform.[35]

"It is as they say." Lucia shot a glare at Robert, and he squirmed in his seat. "The second entry for *vanquish* is to overcome an opponent by means 'other than physical.'"

"Then it's settled," Henry said, clapping his hands together. "They 'vanquished' the beast with an act of heroic kindness and a song. They passed."

"Not so fast." Lucia narrowed her eyes, "Our intent was that they slay the old wyrm—not loosen him again upon the world. Do you know the trouble he has caused us?"

Henry shrugged. As far as he was concerned, a little trouble was a good thing, but he knew better than to say this when Lucia was in a volatile mood.

Cornelius cleared his throat. "It is a technical win by the most microscopic of margins." He consulted his spreadsheets. "As with previous calculations regarding these two—they balance on a razor's edge. And I agree with Lucia, they perverted the *intended* objective of the test."

Aaron tossed back a shot glass of vodka. With face flushed and still holding the iron spike, he stepped forward. "A warrior's greatest achieve-

---

35. This unusual set of dictionaries contains a lexicon of modern English, but in addition also a heroic effort to list all words lost from usage as well, including but not limited to names banned by the early Egyptian dynasties for offense to the gods; magical phrases reputed to set the speaker aflame; and an entire volume dedicated to the words of the barbarian shamanistic tribe of the Utites destroyed by the Romans in 120 C.E. The collection was commissioned by the Carolingian dynasty in the eighth century, but oddly then ordered burned by Charlemagne after he was crowned Emperor. One incomplete set survived and was reprinted in 1922 by Hafterberry Brothers of London. No more than a dozen of the seventy-two-volume sets were ever produced. Victor Golden, *Golden's Guide to Extraordinary Books* (Oxford: 1958).

ment is to make an ally of an enemy. The children clearly won. Or do we only follow our laws when it suits us?"

"We follow them," Lucia said in a calming voice as if she spoke to a contrite child. "But Fiona and Eliot are not yet part of this family. They are not subject to the same exactness of our rules."

Dallas stood and smoothed her miniskirt. "I think *you're* the one playing with words now. The kids won. You're just sore because you didn't want them to."

Did Henry's ear deceive him? Or did he detect a hint of auntly protection for Eliot and Fiona? Or was it just Dallas's instinctive reaction to oppose whatever her sister favored?

Kino stood and drew himself up to his full height. "No. It is as Lucia states. This is ambiguous. Our rules do not yet apply to these two. That is what the three trials will settle." Kino turned to Aaron. "You jump ahead of things."

Aaron locked eyes with him and flipped the iron spike end over end as if it were a toy baton.

"I agree," Cornelius chimed in. "As far as I am concerned, we judge them as if they are outsiders until *proven* otherwise."

Gilbert laughed, attempting to diffuse the building tension. "I think we're missing the point here. They *are* part of the family. Audrey is our kin and has—"

"No," Lucia said. "This is the heart of the matter. The trials will prove them part of this family, as ordinarily mortals, or belonging to that other, lower family. Only then can they be judged by our laws."

"Yes," Kino said, crossing his arms.

Aaron gripped the iron spike so tightly that the metal popped. The wind stilled, seeming to hold its breath. "Fine," Aaron said. "Then let us determine what their next trial shall be."

"I do not believe," Lucia said, "that we have come to a consensus *if* they passed this first one."

Henry saw Robert working himself up to stand and say something on the twins' behalf. He caught the boy's eye and gave him a subtle shake of his head.

Robert obediently sank back into his couch.

Brave boy. But foolish to open his mouth. Henry had no desire to find yet another new Driver.

Besides, more talking would only polarize them now. Henry would have to work hard to blur the political lines being drawn here today.

"I move we vote on this matter," Henry said. "Can I have a second?"

"You've got it Silvertongue," Dallas said before Lucia objected.

Lucia tilted her head at Henry. "Excellent timing," she whispered. "Very well. I vote no. The twins failed to perform as we wished."

Aaron snorted. "They passed. That is my vote."

"I disagree. They did not pass the trial as specified," Kino said with a conciliatory note. He removed his top hat, smoothed his bald head, and gave a short, apologetic bow in Aaron's direction.

They all turned to Cornelius. He waved his hand over his computers and they shut down. "I must abstain. All is in balance within a slight margin of error. The truth cannot be determined."

Dallas swayed a bit as she danced to music only she heard. "Yes," she said, "of course they passed."

Two against and two for the children. So far a tie.

Lucia sighed and looked at Henry. "I suppose I know your vote."

Henry's mind churned—so many delightful variables to this. His aim was neither to win nor lose, but merely to prolong the game and enjoy himself as long as possible: chaos with a purpose.

"The day you are able to predict my actions, my dear Lucia, will be the end of days." He smiled. "The childrens' fate is not to be determined by me: I also abstain."

Lucia registered shock for only a split second, then delight rippled over her features.

Aaron's mouth dropped. He looked as if Henry had stabbed him in the heart.

At least no one was bored.

"Well then . . ." Lucia turned to Gilbert. She practically glowed in anticipation of victory.

Gilbert the Once King had only been elected to the Council because Lucia had engineered it. He was a blatantly unpolitical creature. When he bothered to vote at all, he always sided with her.

But Lucia had not seen what Henry had seen in Gilbert . . . something of his old self.

Gilbert cleared his throat and emotions played over his face: worry, frustration—and then the resolve that he had possessed millennia ago as

Gilgamesh, First King. He stepped to the center of the platform. A change welled up from within him. He stood taller. The wind blew about him. His deep laugh lines vanished and his face took on a serious cast.

"I will not do it." He turned and faced Lucia. "I will not side with you on this. I must vote with my heart. And it says the children passed."

They were silent a long moment and only the winds spoke.

Lucia stood impassively, her gaze turning upon Henry . . . knowing he had won a much greater victory today than this one vote.

Then she said with a great inhalation of breath, "So be it. We next take up the matter of the twins' second trial. We must be specific with our language and make it something of a challenge this time."

Aaron slammed his spike into the deck, embedding it a foot through the teak planks. "I will have no part of this. You sent two children to clean up a mess we left long ago—and they only failed you because they did not die."

"Hardly," Lucia murmured.

Aaron held up one finger, warning her into silence. In his eyes was the glint of violence. "I will have no part in this debate of lies."

He turned and stalked off.

"Where are you going?" Lucia called after him. "The Council has not dismissed you."

"To help my kin," Aaron told her.

Lucia pursed her lips, irritated, and nodded to Cornelius. "Let the record show that Council member Aaron left these proceedings—"

"Left them under protest," Dallas corrected, shooting her sister a puckish look.

"Yes, left under protest," Lucia added, "but that the Council maintains a quorum. We shall continue with the task at hand: the twins' second heroic trial."

Gilbert moved close to Henry and whispered, "There goes Morocco."

"Much more than that goes," Henry whispered back as he watched Aaron descend belowdecks.

What would Lucia make of this? Aaron now strongly aligned against her will? Audrey poised to destroy the Council. And what of the real issue? The children? Were they something delightful and new? Or the means to unravel the treaty that had protected them all from the Infernal clans? Indeed, so many variables to keep spinning the air. . . .

33

A TINY REBELLION

nd then I pulled the spike out," Fiona explained, pantomiming the motion to Cee, who sat wide-eyed at the dining table. Fiona felt the thrill again as she relived what had to have been the most dangerous thing she'd ever done.

"It was this big." Eliot spread his arms as wide as he could. "I can't imagine how that spike got stuck there in the first place."

Grandmother sipped her tea, listening without comment.

Fiona had purposely omitted the part about the rats. That would have required that she tell how they survived those rats . . . which would entail explaining the book from the basement, the violin, and Eliot's miraculous talent.

All these were violations of rules on the List. Successful trial or not, it would have landed them in hot water.

"You were *so* brave." Cee patted Fiona's hand. "My little darlings, I cannot believe they sent you down there." Cee looked at Grandmother for confirmation of this sentiment, but Grandmother sat just as impassive as if Cee had just commented on the weather.

"It's okay," Fiona reassured Cee. "We made it."

"And then?" Grandmother asked. "Did this talking reptile, Souhk, just *let you* pull the spike out?"

Fiona steeled herself. "It did. I think it wanted the thing out."

This, technically, was not a lie. It did, however, leave out the vital detail that Eliot had been playing to first lull the creature into complacency.

The lie of omission was to protect her brother. He really loved that stupid violin. And Fiona had to admit he had a talent she didn't understand. It had certainly come in handy, and she was sure it would come in handy on the last two trials. If Grandmother found out, however, she would have confiscated the instrument.

But why even bother to try to hide the truth? Grandmother *always* knew when she wasn't getting the entire story.

Fiona held her breath . . . waiting for Grandmother to demand the rest of the tale.

She said nothing.

"Then it spoke to us," Eliot said. "It told us that we were heroes. That it could read the trash floating by like a Gypsy fortune-teller reads tea leaves."

Cee shifted in her chair. "How silly," she murmured.

It stuck Fiona as odd that Cee didn't believe *that,* but *could* believe in a two-ton, talking crocodile.

"Did it foretell anything?" Grandmother asked.

"It said great things would happen to us."

"And terrible things," Eliot added.

"I don't think it was sure," Fiona said, "that we'd survive the next two trials."

"I see." Grandmother looked distracted. "As Cornelius indicated, much still hangs in the balance." She turned her attention back to Fiona. "Did it say anything else?"

Fiona shot a quick glance at her brother.

He gave a shake of his head—so slight that she almost missed the subtle motion.

"He said stuff that didn't make any sense," she told Grandmother. "It was that language you and Uncle Henry spoke in the limousine."

Again, this was not a lie—not exactly, anyway; it was just part of the truth, and out of chronological order.

She and Eliot had agreed not to reveal what they had learned about their father's family. Grandmother had gone to such great lengths protecting them from *her* side of the family . . . if she knew what Souhk had told them, there would be at least one full page of new rules added to the List.

Infernals.

She and Eliot had barely understood the reference, shielded by RULE 55, but as with the meaning of gods and God, they had absorbed enough from everyday sources to understand that fallen angels were part of the societywide mythology of evil: demons and devils.

Did she believe it?

Talking crocodiles? A family of immortals? It wasn't a big leap from these to accepting fallen angles as aunts and uncles.

And this new fact fit what little she knew about her mother and father. There was Uncle Henry's account of them meeting in Venice and falling in love, then fleeing because of their warring families. And then what? An accident at sea? Both drowned?

Or murdered by families who wouldn't let them be together?

Just as the Council was figuring out if they would live or die because of their mixed blood.

She suppressed a shudder.

Fiona looked to Grandmother, waiting for her to ask for the whole story . . . free of omissions and twisted facts.

"Very well," Grandmother said, "and then what?"

Fiona was too stunned to reply. She had actually gotten away with a lie to Grandmother. How was that possible?

"We dragged the spike up to the surface," Eliot said. "It was heavy and we almost got lost on the way back—but we made it just before the time ran out."

"Mr. Farmington took the spike with him?" Cee asked, sounding disappointed.

"Proof for the Council," Eliot said. "It had a lot of blood on it."

Fiona remembered the smell of Souhk's blood, like hot metal. There was strength in that blood. Had she fooled Grandmother because she was growing strong, too? A pawn turning into something else?

"We passed the Council's trial and we didn't have to kill anything," Fiona said. "Do you think that's enough for them? Will we have to go through with the other two?"

Grandmother considered this, and her head tilted. "The Council will rule and let us know."

"But you could ask," Fiona said. "Maybe even convince them?"

"Oh—a marvelous idea," Cee said.

Grandmother closed her eyes, deep in thought for a moment, then she opened them, her face that curious combination of inscrutability and irony. "You must complete all three trials. They reveal much of your characters"—one of her eyebrows arched—"apparently things that even I had not been aware of."

She looked at Fiona.

Fiona was suddenly sure Grandmother knew about her lie of omission . . . sure she knew everything.

Grandmother looked at Eliot, and he also withered under her gaze.

But Fiona's willpower rekindled. The next two trials might *kill* them—didn't Grandmother understand that? Fiona stepped closer to her brother, feeling stronger even than when she had faced Souhk.

"The household rules," she started, and her voice quavered. She cleared her throat, wishing she had eaten a few chocolates before this. "I want to talk about them."

"Oh?" The slightest ripple of interest appeared on Grandmother's face.

Cee clasped her hands and inhaled.

"Yeah," Eliot whispered. Then he, too, found his voice and said, "They were meant to keep us safe from the family, right? Make us seem . . . normal? But they know about us now, and we know about them, so what's the point?"

".We were thinking," Fiona said, "that maybe it's time to relax a few of the rules."

"You think that's all the rules are for?" Grandmother said. "*Your* protection?"

For the first time in her life Fiona dared to ignore a direct question from Grandmother and forged on. "We think it's time for a change."

"We've done everything you've asked," Eliot said, his tone now growing irritated as well. "And we've passed the family's first test, too. Doesn't that mean we're responsible enough to make some of our own decisions?"

Fiona wasn't sure what the intense expression on Grandmother's face meant. Could she actually be uncertain?

Outside, clouds covered the setting sun. The room got cold.

Grandmother half closed her eyes and her face hardened into a mask. "It is true you are on the cusp of adulthood, but now more than ever you must have no distractions. The rules shall remain." She made a cutting gesture to emphasize that the discussion was over. Her decision final.

Fiona trembled. She couldn't believe that just this morning she had actually defended Grandmother and her rules to Eliot. She wanted to shout that this wasn't fair.

But she already knew what Grandmother's reply to that would be: *Many things in life are not fair.*

She stared into Grandmother's eyes, wanting some small victory . . . even if it was making her blink first in a duel of glares.

It was like staring into steel-gray clouds, thunderheads upon the horizons, and Fiona had about as much chance as influencing Grandmother as she had reaching up with her hand and affecting the weather.

The phone rang, breaking the one-sided contest of wills, and Fiona looked away.

Cee picked up the receiver. "Hello? . . . Yes? . . . Oh, yes—one moment please."

She offered the phone to Fiona, and then Eliot, looking unsure whom it was for. "It's work."

Grandmother nodded to Fiona. "Get them off the line. We are expecting a call from the Council."

Fiona hissed a great sigh. She was tired of people telling her what to do every moment of her life. She disobeyed Grandmother and stalked to her bedroom—brushing past the stack of homework papers on the table and scattering them onto the floor.

She needed her chocolates to help her deal with this family.

Fiona didn't care anymore about homework or Ringo's or even Grandmother. What did it matter if they passed the Council's trials if they were only going to remain prisoners in their own family?

34

GOOD LITTLE BOY NO MORE

liot took the phone. Grandmother looked after Fiona as she stormed off. He thought Grandmother was going to order her to come back and pick up the papers.

She said nothing, though. Her eyes followed Fiona, seeming to bore through the walls after she slammed her door.

Without turning to look at him, said she, "Well, Eliot? Answer the call."

"Hello?" Eliot said into the phone.

Julie's sweet voice filtered through the receiver. "Are you okay? Your family emergency . . . ?"

"It all worked out." Eliot pressed the phone into his ear, hoping Grandmother couldn't hear.

"Thank goodness," Julie said. "You looked so freaked-out when you left. I was worried about you. And Fiona, too, of course."

Her words moved Eliot. Cee had made much over him and Fiona when they had returned from the sewer . . . but it felt rehearsed, as if Cee had already known they'd succeeded.

Julie's concern was somehow more real.

She sighed through the phone and Eliot imagined her breath on his neck. Gooseflesh coursed over his skin.

He had to be careful and not let Grandmother know this was a personal call . . . from a girl no less.

There was a rule.

RULE 99: No use of electronic communication devices, specifically, but not limited to, telephones or telex apparatus. Exceptions include use directed by an adult or for emergency medical, police, or fire assistance. Incoming calls of a personal nature must politely, but immediately, be terminated.

He hated these restrictions, but he wouldn't let his temper get the better of him as it had Fiona. He had to be smarter.

He had more to lose.

"If everything's okay," Julie said, "then you're coming in tomorrow? We're still on for coffee?"

Eliot's heartbeat quickened. "You bet."

"I've been thinking about it all day."

Grandmother finally turned and glanced at the phone. No more warning was required.

"You probably can't talk," Julie said, a slyness creeping into her voice. "I understand. I'll let you go . . . for now."

"Thanks," Eliot whispered. "We'll be in tomorrow. No problem."

"See you then, honey." She hung up.

Eliot replaced the phone in its cradle. "That was work. We left in the middle of our shift. They wanted to know if we were okay."

"That's nice," Cee said.

Grandmother said nothing and stared at the phone as if she could peer down the line and see Julie at the other end.

"Dinner is in an hour," Grandmother said. "Tell your sister, if she is interested in joining us, that is."

Grandmother retired to her office and slid the doors shut behind her.

Eliot breathed a sigh of relief.

Cee set a trembling hand on his. "Do you need to tell me anything?" she whispered. "It can be a secret."

Eliot knew he could trust Cee, but he shook his head. The last thing he wanted was to burden her with his secrets. All that would do was land her in hot water when Grandmother found them out.

And Grandmother always found out.

Cee stepped back and sighed. "We can have a little party to toast your success. We have cake from the Pink Rabbit."

Eliot glanced down the hallway at Fiona's closed bedroom door, knowing there would be no celebration tonight. "That sounds good. I better get cleaned up."

He knelt and straightened the papers Fiona had scattered. There was a page of logarithm exercises and a writing assignment on Cape Town, South Africa. Half their normal homework. Grandmother was being generous.

Cee's hands curled inward and she reached for him. She looked as if she wanted to tell him something. Instead, though, she smiled her tremulous smile and said, "You go then, darling. Get clean. I'll have the food ready soon."

Everything in Eliot's world had turned upside down, but Cee was the same: always there for him. A little senile, maybe, but loving.

She ambled into the kitchen.

And yet Eliot had the feeling that she wasn't exactly part of the family—not like Uncle Henry, Grandmother, or Aunt Lucia. She didn't act like the rest of them.

But that was stupid. She *was* his great-grandmother, as much a part of his family as Fiona. Wasn't she?

Eliot picked up his canvas pack and marched to Fiona's door.

He gently knocked. "Fiona?" he whispered.

There was no answer.

He slid her homework under the door and retreated into his room.

Eliot closed his door and locked it. The tiny lever made a grinding sound as it engaged. He'd never used the lock before—but then again, he'd never had secrets like *this* to hide.

He tossed his homework on his desk. He was so obedient. Cecilia's "good little boy." He hated that.

Eliot got as mad as Fiona—maybe even more—he just didn't show it. What was the point? Fiona had had to run off to her room because no one could stand up to Grandmother.

Still, it had been something: the world's tiniest rebellion. There were other ways to rebel, though. Quieter and more effective ways.

Their studies of history showed that underground insurgencies could lead to big revolts . . . the toppling of empires. That's what Eliot was doing starting tonight—organizing his own personal revolt against the family.

The alternative was to continue being a "good little boy" . . . a possibility perhaps *before* his fifteenth birthday—but not anymore.

He set his pack on the bed, pulled off both pillows, and sat on the floor by the heater vent.

"Fiona?" he whispered into the grill.

Silence.

He'd sit here all night if he had to.

They'd been so happy only an hour ago. When they got out of the sewer, gave Robert the proof of having "vanquished" Souhk, and told him how they'd done it. They thought they'd won.

But all it meant was the chance to do it all over again for the second and third trials.

And when and if they passed all the tests? Would they be accepted into the family? Would there be even more rules and restrictions?

He was tired of being shoved around.

Eliot rummaged into his pack and touched the violin nestled in the rubber boot. Its strings vibrated to the beat of his fingertip pulse—something that could only be felt. Still, with Grandmother's sharp ears he wasn't sure, so he withdrew.

He pulled out the *Mythica Improbiba* book next and ran a hand over its rough leather cover.

Fiona had insisted that he hide it in the basement, but he'd only pretended to do it to shut her up. Something attracted him to this forbidden book.

He opened to a random page and gazed at an ancient diagram of a clockwork sphere with orbiting planets and moons, stars, and comets. In the center of the mechanism sat a man cross-legged, observing. Crammed alongside the diagram on the page were notes in Greek.[36]

It was amazing, but the Greek was meaningless to Eliot.

He suddenly had the feeling he was being watched. He looked up, listened intently, and scrutinized the gap at the bottom of his door.

No shadows moved. No one was there.

Well, if someone came in, he was reading a book—that's all. He could close it and it would look like any other of the thousands of volumes in his room.

He flipped through the pages. They weren't paper, but vellum, calfskin of remarkable thinness.

---

36. The Sphere of the Celestials is described as the Wonder of the Ancient World *that never was*, said to have been almost completed by Archimedes and an unknown assistant, during the last thirty years of his life. According to legend, even partially constructed the Sphere had the power to predict eclipses, comets, and even foretell earthquakes, volcanic eruptions, and the fall of empires. *Gods of the First and Twenty-first Century, Volume 5: Core Myths* (Part 2), 8th ed. (Zypheron Press Ltd.).

Eliot stopped on one page with Middle English scrolled upon it: a tale of the God of the Seas, Poseidon, and a group of Vikings. Poseidon led the Vikings over the Atlantic Ocean to the New World. The story read like one of his daydreams. There were adventures with mermaids and sea serpents, wild storms, and Indian princesses.[37]

Most intriguing, there was a tiny line drawing of Poseidon on his water-borne chariot leading the Viking longboat over a stormy sea. There wasn't much detail, but the chiseled features and the intense eyes were cast from the same mold as Uncle Henry's or Grandmother's.

Or Eliot's.

He felt a connection to this person . . . to something long ago and far away. For a heartbeat, Eliot believed there really had been gods and goddesses and that their blood, no matter how diluted, ran through him now.

He delved deeper through the book, searching for more.

What would it mean to be a part of this family? He was no longer sure. But he was sure he could be a lot more than a pawn.

And what about his father's side of the family?

As if summoned, he turned the page to a woodcut of the devil, tormenting medieval peasants with fire and pitchfork.

The image repulsed Eliot. He couldn't be related to anything like this. And yet he found his fingertip tracing the bat wings, horns, and barbed tail . . . fascinated by this being's obvious power.

He bet no one had ever called the devil a "good little boy."

37. Poseidon and Odin both appear after a Viking band made an appropriate sacrifice. The gods were drunk and Odin appears to pass out, inebriated, but Poseidon continues with the group. This is the first tale from the late classical period in which *two* gods from different pantheons appear together. From handwritten notes in the Beezle edition of *Mythica Improbiba* known as "The War Song of Poseidon and Yorik the Bloodied Beard." Father Sildas Pious, *Mythica Improbiba* (translated version), c. thirteenth century.

35

JULIE'S SONG

Eliot inhaled deeply, savoring the smell of freshly pulped carrots, oranges, and clove cigarettes in the Pink Rabbit coffee and juice café.

He tried to read the menu, but couldn't see the fine print. He'd strained his eyes last night scanning the nearly microscopic writing of "The Lost Maiden's Tale" in Mythica Improbiba.[38]

His blurry vision hadn't got any better that morning—nor at breakfast, nor on the walk to Ringo's, nor during the five minutes at work before Julie dragged him across the street for their coffee break.

He blinked and looked up at Julie, sitting across from him.

Sunlight streamed into the Pink Rabbit from skylights overhead and made her blond hair a halo of gold. The light also made her blue cotton summer dress enticingly translucent.

"What are you looking at?" Julie asked.

Eliot glanced away. "Just the stage," he lied, and nodded to the center of the room. "Must have been a big party last night."

The Rabbit hosted musicians every Friday night—strictly a local affair

---

38. The tiny print of this passage in the Beezle edition of *Mythica Improbiba* is obscured by a stain of ancient origins. A few words are revealed with ultraviolet light—enough to piece together "The Lost Maiden's Tale," in which the trickster god Loki Laufeyjarson and Saint Vladimir Sviatoslavovich the Great both try to win the love of the young girl. The amalgam of pagan and Christian mythologies was dubbed (ironically) the "Chimera Heresy" by the Papal Inquisition of 1230. It was punishable, if the author recanted his sin, by wearing a yellow cross for life. If the author failed to recant his sin, he was burned at the stake with all copies of his works. *Gods of the First and Twenty-first Century, Volume 5: Core Myths* (Part 2), 8th ed. (Zypheron Press Ltd.).

for the resident artists and hippies and connoisseurs of homebrewed ales. Onstage were tribal drums and a pair of guitars. The bartender sat there tuning one. He strummed a chord and Eliot noted the way he held it, how it was similar and different to how he held his violin. The man then set the guitar down and went back to work.

Julie turned to look at the stage, and as she did, Eliot admired the lines of her neck and slender shoulders. She was like a Michelangelo statue: perfect proportions and flawlessly smooth. He imagined running a hand over her skin, and his pulse quickened.

Their waitress came, blocking the sunlight and startling Eliot.

"Sunrise Butter, please," Eliot said.

This was a mix of honey, ginger, carrot and orange juices, and it tasted great . . . but it was a kid's drink. Nowhere near sophisticated enough for someone on a coffee break with the most beautiful girl in Del Sombra. Why was he *always* doing the most uncool thing?

Julie didn't seem to notice. She glanced at the back of her menu at the selection of wines and beers. "Got any of the White Rabbit Ale left?"

Their waitress pursed her lips and crossed her arms, not even bothering to ask for ID.

"Just kidding." Julie flashed her hundred-watt smile and the waitress relaxed a notch. "Coffee, please. The Sumatra, if you don't mind, miss."

Eliot should have thought of that: coffee on a coffee break.

"So tell me about yourself, Mr. Post." Julie leaned invitingly forward.

What could he say? Everything about his life sounded crazy.

Well, Julie, I've spent my entire life sequestered with my grandmother and great-grandmother, and, oh, by the way, part of my family thinks they are— and might actually be—gods and goddesses. My father's side of the family, however, could be fallen angels. The really odd thing is that my sister and I are in the middle of heroic trials trying to figure out which side of the family we belong with, or if we belong with anyone at all . . . alive.

"My life is just full of the normal dull things," he said. "You know: homework, more household rules than air molecules, and any free time I might have had—until recently—was spent washing dishes."

She snorted. "Sounds like my life. Only throw in a few dysfunctional brothers and a stepmother from hell."

All traces of her smile faded and she rubbed one arm.

Even Eliot, who wasn't good with people, could tell that she had exposed something real, and very wrong, in her life. He wanted to ask about her family and if there was anything he could do to help. That seemed stupid, though. Why should she trust him? She hardly knew him.

But maybe she *needed* his help, so badly that she was willing to reach out to a stranger.

If only he could talk to her like a real person, instead of wondering what was the right thing to say, or how to say it, or worrying so much about sounding like a dork.

"You can tell me," he whispered. "Anything. Really. I'm a good listener."

Her smile returned, this time used as a shield to ward off any awkward questions. Her lips trembled. "I just wish . . ." Her hand moved forward a little as if she were going to reach across the table, but she hesitated, then withdrew the unsure gesture.

Eliot didn't know what to say to get her to trust him. What could he do? Quote some fact from an encyclopedia? Or dazzle her with his obscure medical vocabulary?

But there was another way to communicate. It was right in front of him: the just-tuned guitar on the stage.

"I want to do something for you. Give me a second?"

Julie looked around, following his gaze, confused as if she were missing a joke. "Sure, what?"

"Just wait."

Eliot got up and marched onto the stage before he lost his nerve. This was like "The Lost Maiden's Tale"—or something he might do in one of his daydreams: win the heart of a lovely girl with a serenade.

Only this was real.

He was suddenly so nervous that he'd look like an idiot, he felt like throwing up. But he wasn't about to back down now; that's not how you won the hand and heart of a young lady . . . at least, in all the books he'd ever read.

He sat on the stool and picked up the guitar. He wanted to lay it flat like his violin, but resisted that instinct and instead rested it upright in his lap, holding the neck as he'd seen the bartender do.

He strummed the steel strings, slow and evenly.

The notes, however, warbled and slipped out of his control as if they were squirming things.

The Rabbit's patrons glanced up. The bartender and waitress scowled at him. Julie's face crinkled and she looked like someone watching a car crash in slow motion.

Eliot flushed. Perspiration beaded on his neck and hands. Great. Sweaty palms. That'd just make the strings harder to control. He looked at his fingers, and suddenly his blurry vision snapped into focus.

He could do this . . . as he had with the violin.

But he had seen Louis play entire songs on Lady Dawn before he tried to copy him; he'd only seen the bartender strum a few chords with *this* instrument.

Eliot molded his fingers around the fret and thumbed once more over the strings. The sound was no better—exactly like someone playing a guitar for the first time.

He felt the customers' annoyance heat about him; it made his skin prickle. In his peripheral vision he saw the bartender wad his dish towel and stride toward him. Eliot didn't look up, but he knew Julie was wondering why she'd bothered with such a weird little kid in the first place . . . probably sneaking out of the place right now.

His fingers were wooden, his muscles jelly, his mind blank. How had he ever played music? *Had* he ever really played . . . or was it some sort of daydream?

No. He had. He could. He would.

Eliot was alone. No stage, no Pink Rabbit café, just him and the guitar, and somewhere in the dark a different audience waited and listened and trembled with anticipation. The stars and shadows watched him.

The universe held its breath.

One good note. Just one. A start. That's all he needed.

His index finger pinned a string and his thumb flicked.

The sound was pure and perfect and all his. It rolled through the dark, bounded and rebounded, echoing back to him. Eliot sensed space and time and the vast empty corridors of fate that stretched in all directions from where he sat in the center.

He strung more notes together, flowing smooth and effortless. It was the first song he had learned, the nursery rhyme, "Mortal's Coil."

In his imagination a choir of children sang along:

> *Spinning faster round the pole. Soon too old from chasing gold.*
> *Young hands wrinkle, hearts to stone. Dust to dust and ashes*
> *cold.*

Eliot's hands moved faster, formed chords, improvised, and layered in textures. The music vibrated through him and the wooden stage and out to the audience.

He opened his eyes and looked up.

The bartender stood at the edge of the stage, frozen, mouth agape. Every customer faced him, rapt.

Julie stared wide-eyed.

He added a phrase as he thought of her. The notes turned lighter and sounded like her lilting Southern accent. The sunlight streaming through the skylights tinged pink and warmed.

Eliot eyes locked with Julie's.

Her entire being opened to him, and he read her as easily as he had the musical notes in *Mythica Improbiba*. She was honey-sweet and perfect . . . but that was just the surface layer; deeper, there was more: darkness and sadness and pain.

He shifted to a minor key and found new phases within Julie, pouring from her heart, an inversion of the nursery rhyme, and anguished chords so low in the guitar's register they were felt more than heard.

Julie's song yearned for release from pain and the notes wavered and ran together. Eliot felt pinpricks on his arm, but resisted the urge to itch. He forged ahead, following the spiral of tragedy and regret into the shadows, until the music ended in a pulsing heartbeat . . . notes that faded to nothing: the sound of a young, strong heart broken.

Shadows flitted over the skylights, and there were thumps upon the roof.

No one took notice of the noise overhead. Every eye in the audience glistened. Tears streamed down Julie's cheeks. No one moved.

But her song *couldn't* end this way. It was almost as if she had died.

Eliot wouldn't let that happen.

The music was his to make and control—not the other way around.

His fingers reversed and made the heartbeat come back, faint at first, then stronger, and bridged back through minor keys with a complex set of harmonies that nearly made his hand cramp—ended back at the sweetness and light and innocent happiness where she had started.

Julie blinked and wiped away her tears. She smiled. It wasn't the hundred-watt grin she seemed able to summon upon command. This was real. No glamour, but simple joy. And it was just for Eliot.

He ended with a flourish that echoed the nursery rhyme; it sounded like . . . hope.

The sunlight pouring through the skylights brightened.

Eliot set his hand on the steel strings to still their insistent vibrations.

The world seemed normal again.

The customers clapped, stomped their feet, then got up and gave an ovation.[39]

Eliot had never had anyone applaud anything he'd done. It was almost better than making the music. Almost.

He could have stayed up there all day, entertaining them, just so they would fill him with their praises.

Julie, however, was not one of the people clapping. She stood and stared at him intently, looked fascinated and somehow horrified, too.

She beckoned to him.

Eliot then understood that there were more important things than the adulation of strangers.

He set the guitar on its stand.

The bartender clapped him on the back and said he could come back and play anytime.

Eliot muttered his thanks and moved to Julie.

She embraced him, gripping him hard, her tears wetting his shoulder. She sniffled and wiped her face on his shirt, then pulled back so she could look at him.

For a moment, she seemed like a little girl. She looked so desperately grateful, as if no one had ever given her anything in her life.

"That was for me?"

"It's your song," Eliot whispered.

She trembled. "It's not supposed to go like this." Her voice was different. The Southern accent was still there, yet without the honeyed smoothness. She looked away. "You weren't supposed to make *me* . . . I can't do this."

Julie pulled away and turned to the waitress. "Make those orders to go, miss."

"I thought we were going to talk," Eliot said.

39. When the survivors of the Del Sombra conflagration were later interviewed, many cited the public demonstration of Eliot Post days before as a transformative experience. It was not the most technically proficient performance, but all the interviewees agreed that it was the most heartfelt music they had ever heard. More than one person said, "It sounded like angels sang with him." *Gods of the First and Twenty-first Century, Volume 11: The Post Family Mythology*, 8th ed. (Zypheron Press Ltd.).

Julie straightened and blinked and smoothed her dress. Confusion rippled over her face, but quickly set into a mask of determination.

"Coffee break is over, Post. We're going back to work." She strode to the exit.

Eliot wasn't sure what had just happened. Had he offended her? How could he mess up everything—even the things he was good at like music?

He fumbled out the money Fiona had lent him, leaving enough for their drinks and the tip, then ran after Julie.

He caught her in the doorway.

Julie whirled on him. "Don't." The iron in her features melted a little and she tried, but failed, to smile. "I like you, but I can't do this to you . . . not today."

She pushed through the door.

Do *what* to him? She was making less sense than Fiona.

He followed her outside. Julie had frozen stock-still on the sidewalk. In fact, several cars on Vine Street had halted in their tracks.

Crows roosted on the telephone and power lines overhead, crowding them so they bowed from their collective weight. Some of the birds, however, were on the sidewalk and in the street, flapping confusedly, recovering from flying into the Pink Rabbit.

There were *hundreds* of them.

Eliot grabbed Julie's hand and took a step backward, pulling her along, remembering how the rats in the sewer had tried to eat him and Fiona.

Every crow turned and pointed its beak at him, cawed, beat its wings, and yet remained in place.

Eliot didn't move, terrified that they might take wing and swoop down upon them. But none of them moved. It was almost as if they were applauding.

36

Fiona forced herself to smile as she sat the couple at the best table in Ringo's. They asked about today's lunch special. She recommended the meatballs.

As she did this, she felt as if someone pulled strings that controlled her. And why not? She had been Grandmother's puppet for fifteen years, doing everything she wanted, thinking it was all for the best. And now she was the Council's puppet—jumping when they yanked her cords.

Fiona the Marionette, that's what she should call herself.

She still couldn't believe that Grandmother had refused to step in and at least *ask* the Council to stop. She realized that she was the only one she could count on now . . . well, and Eliot; he'd always be there for her.

But her brother had two new distractions in his life: that stupid violin, and their boss, Julie Marks.

Julie had snatched Eliot the instant they'd got to work. A "coffee break" before he'd rinsed a single dish. In her sweetest voice Julie had ordered Johnny to cover the dishes (admittedly a lot easier with that new behemoth of an automatic dishwasher, but still, it was Eliot's job). Then she had Fiona cover *her* hostess duties.

She should have picked Linda. Fiona hated talking to people. It wasn't natural for her.

Linda hadn't said a word, but from her nonstop glares, Fiona knew what she thought of her being replacement hostess.

How could Julie be so bossy *and* so nice at the same time? That irritated

Fiona more than anything else. With her Southern accent, her quick smile—she must get her way all the time.

Fiona settled behind the cash register, waiting for more customers, bracing herself to be pleasant.

What was Eliot thinking, running off? The next trial could come at any time.

She reached into her book bag for her chocolates. She pulled out a truffle and admired the crushed hazelnuts covering it. She bit into it and tasted creamy coffee and nibs of lavender. The texture was a wondrous juxtaposition of silk smooth and granularity. She shuddered with a chill of delight.

Then she devoured it.

Linda looked in . . . probably to give Fiona another drop-dead glare.

Fiona was sick of being blamed for Julie's decision, so she blasted Linda with a hate-filled glance of her own.

Linda went white and her gaze dropped.

"Johnny's slowing down on the orders," Linda said. "Customers are complaining . . . a little." She hurried back into the dining room.

Fiona felt ashamed. Linda had only come to tell her about Johnny.

Why was she mad at everyone? Fiona peered into her book bag and the half-opened chocolate box. Could it be all the sugar?

It then registered what Linda had told her. Johnny was never slow with orders. Maybe the new automated dishwasher had blown up. Fiona marched back into the dining room and told Linda to cover the front.

Linda brightened and unstrung her apron.

Fiona passed into the kitchen.

There were pots with boiling marinara sauce, pasta draining, dishwasher churning . . . but no Johnny. Fiona went to the men's changing room and knocked. No answer.

Johnny wouldn't leave stuff unattended on the stove unless there had been a good reason.

She turned off the burners.

The back door opened. Johnny stood in the doorway. He looked like someone who had narrowly missed getting hit by a truck.

"*Madre de Dios*," he whispered, then saw Fiona. "I was just coming for you, *señorita*. There's a man in the alley. He said"—Johnny's face crinkled with worry—"he knows you."

"Oh." Fiona's anger rekindled. "Him."

It was the old, creepy guy back for more free pizza. Or maybe he wanted to hassle Eliot again. She'd give that bum a piece of her mind, maybe call the cops.

To tell the truth, Fiona *wanted* to be mad at someone. Linda, Johnny, even Julie, it wasn't fair to be mad at them. Even Eliot, although he was a pain sometimes, didn't deserve her unjustified wrath. But the old bum— she could be mad at *him* and no one would care.

She pushed through the back door, her irritation feeling like a million army ants crawling under her skin.

The old man stood with his back to her.

The door banged shut and he turned.

He wore a long black leather coat, tight jeans, a T-shirt with the words DONE TAKING NAMES. I'M HERE TO KICK ASS, and a cowboy hat with snake-skin band and rattlesnake tail tassel.

This was *not* the old bum. Every flicker of fire inside her cooled to ashes.

"Uncle Aaron," she whispered.

Was he here to announce their second trial? Wasn't that Robert's job? Or had the Council some other, more unpleasant announcement? Like they hadn't really passed the first test and had sent Uncle Aaron to . . . what? Kill her and Eliot?

Her fight-or-flight adrenaline reaction flooded her body. She licked her lips and tasted chocolate.

She'd fight.

She was tired of being pushed around. Even if Aaron *was* here to do something horrible—she'd make sure she stood tall when it happened.

She stared into his bottomless brown eyes.

Aaron likewise regarded her.

His face was rugged and chiseled. His mustache drooped over either cheek. Despite his country-western attire, Fiona still thought he looked as if he should be leading a Mongol-horde charge on horseback.

He'd never blink.

Well, neither would she. She had looked into the infinite eyes of a crocodile who had called itself justifiably "the eater of death." After that, Aaron couldn't scare her.

"I have come to *help* you, child," he growled. "Check your adolescent attitude."

"Help?" she said, unsure.

"Had I known you had a shotgun on the first trial, I would have made sure you knew how to use it."

Fiona stiffened. "I could have used it *if* I had needed to. And how do you know that I don't know how to shoot a gun?"

"The way you stand," he said, narrowing his eyes. "It is obvious that you have spirit. Equally obvious that you have never spilled blood."

She set her hands on her hips.

It was true. She'd never fought, not even wrestled with Eliot, whom she could have trounced. The only thing that had come close was Mike's recent escalation of his standard sexual harassment . . . a problem that had taken care of itself.

Fiona dropped her arms. "So you're going to show me how to fight?"

The corners of Uncle Aaron's eyes crinkled. Fiona guessed this was the closest thing that passed for a laugh with him.

"I have come to see if your abilities match that attitude. If they do, I may be able to show you something."

"Eliot's across the street. I'll get him."

Aaron held up a huge hand. "No."

"What do you mean no? You just said you came to help."

"*You* are the warrior." Aaron glanced down the alley to the Pink Rabbit. "Your brother is a poet."

"That's unfair. Sure, he's a little short for fifteen, but he deserves a chance to learn how to defend himself, too."

"So loyal. I see now why some on the Council fear you two together." Aaron held his hands out in a "peace" gesture. "But you misunderstand me. With his music, Eliot is already armed. I only wish to make you his equal."

Eliot *had* done some amazing things with that violin—even his knowing how to play the thing defied logic. Still, Fiona didn't like Uncle Aaron's offer. She and Eliot were stronger together, just as Cee had told them. This felt like a trick to split them apart.

"Forget it. If Eliot's not part of—"

Aaron knelt and unrolled a bundle that had been in the shadows. Metal glinted.

Fiona stepped closer and knelt. "What's this?"

"*Our* instruments."

In orderly rows on a black cloth were knives and swords, spears and clubs, pistols and shotguns and rifles, *shuriken* and darts, even a set of brass knuckles—every handheld weapon ever devised to slice, chop, crush, or otherwise hurt another living creature.

The array of razor edges and spikes and polished wooden handles fascinated Fiona. She saw her face reflected in a hundred surfaces.

"Do you feel it?" Aaron whispered. "The gravity they possess?"

Fiona moved her hand closer, not touching any of the weapon because she was a little scared, but drawn to them nonetheless. Is this what Eliot had felt the first time he'd seen his violin?

One weapon looked out of place: a wooden yo-yo. It was a little larger than a normal one—but still a toy. She remembered reading something about Polynesian tribes using them to crush heads with deadly accuracy.[40]

At the end of the cloth Fiona spotted the spike she had pulled out of Souhk. "That was yours?"

"It moves very fast for a lizard. I missed its thick skull, impaled the shoulder." Aaron pushed back his sleeve, revealing a saw-toothed scar on his arm. "In return, it gave me this."

Fiona marveled that Souhk hadn't completely severed his arm.

"You got away?"

Aaron's eyebrows rippled with amusement. "Not exactly. The lizard was the one to first show its tail."

Fiona plucked nervously at the rubber band she wore today on her wrist. How could one man, even one such as Uncle Aaron, beat a two-ton crocodile? And yet, he had nearly killed Souhk with that spike. Whoever could do something like that had to be more than a man.

Aaron asked, "Why didn't *you* kill the beast? You had a chance. And your life and your brother's hung in the balance."

She shrugged. "I couldn't."

It wasn't right that they'd tried to make her and Eliot kill. Her anger rekindled, but not as hot as it had been earlier. This anger was ice-cold.

"Making it an ally took a hundred times more courage than using a shotgun," Aaron said.

40. While true that Filipino tribesmen were seen using yo-yo-like devices as weapons in the sixteenth century, the documentation of this coincided with the development of the modern yo-yo in Europe and is therefore suspect. Modern records have been discovered of one Hernandez del Moro, a toy manufacturer, traveling to the Philippines in the 1930s and subsequently credited with all photographic anthropological "evidence," which happened to be used in an advertising campaign for his company's ZIPP-brand yo-yo. *Gods of the First and Twenty-first Century, Volume 6: Modern Myths*, 8th ed. (Zypheron Press Ltd.).

"I'm not a butcher," she whispered. "Isn't that *your* job? I mean, if we fail the Council's trials?"

Aaron was silent a moment, then finally said, "Should you fail, the Council will certainly destroy you."

The Council? Not him? Was it possible that Uncle Aaron, like Souhk, might be turned from an enemy to . . . what had Souhk called it: *temporary allies*?

Aaron got up and waved a hand over his arsenal. "Pick one that calls to you, child. We will see what you know."

Fiona gazed over the weapons and felt a curious thrill . . . almost as if she were looking into her box of chocolates, trying to decide which would taste best.

Something nagged her about that: how many layers of chocolates *had* she eaten? Eight? A dozen? Certainly more than had a right to be packed inside one box. She shouldn't question such a great gift. Still, Grandmother's voice echoed in her mind: *Overly generous presents come with strings*.

She'd think about the chocolates later. She had to focus on other things.

Fiona smoothed her hands over the weapons, and they came to rest on the handle of a silver rapier. Its gold filigreed hilt was scratched and the jewels on the pommel were chipped. It was nonetheless beautiful.

She picked it up. It was light and responsive and, she believed, deadly. She liked it.

Fiona turned and raised the tip at Uncle Aaron's eyes.

Aaron shook his head slightly. "Not for you."

"I've studied everything there is to know about swords. Prehistory flint knives—the first bronze castings—modern Damascus steels—all of it."

"You talk too much. Choose another."

What Fiona hadn't told him was that she'd written papers on Olympic fencing, Kendo, and Miyamoto Musashi. All encyclopedic knowledge, true; but how different could the theory of sword fighting be from its practical application?

She'd give him a nick—just a touch—something to make him appreciate that she wasn't helpless.

She lunged at Aaron.

His movement was slight, but enough of a side step to let the rapier slide past his elbow.

His jacket billowed and Fiona got a glimpse of the man inside: solid slabs of muscle that flexed and bulged.

Aaron stepped in close—clamped her hand on the weapon's ivory grip. With his other hand he pulled the blade up and around, levering her arm over her head.

Her shoulder joint strained . . . almost popping from the socket. Fiona grunted in pain. Her face heated, embarrassed at how easily he had deflected her attack and immobilized her. As if she were a child with a toy.

He gave her arm a shove. Pain screamed down her stretched tendons, but she didn't cry out.

"Good," he whispered. "So you don't do everything you're told . . . like your mother. But, I wonder, you do have her patience, too?"

He released her, pulling free the rapier and setting it back in his collection. Fiona glared at him and rubbed her arm.

"Pick another," he said. "See if you can do better."

Fiona marched back to the weapons and reached for a snub-nosed pistol.

"No guns," he told her with an icy finality. "You will only hurt yourself."

Fiona hesitated. She wanted to grab it—just to worry Uncle Aaron. She'd never really shoot him in a million years. She knew, though, that if she moved a hairbreadth closer to the pistol's grip, something bad would happen to her.

She instead picked a pair of nunchaku: two black plastic bars joined by a length of chain. Fiona had never studied the weapon, but its flexibility intrigued her. Mainly, she didn't want Aaron grabbing her hand again and completely nullifying her attack.

She picked it up and experimentally spun one of the handles, increasing its momentum until it was a blur.

"Better," Aaron remarked, "but still not for you."

She considered attacking him anyway—a quick burst of speed and a flick of the wrist would send the handle at his head. But the pain in her shoulder reminded her how fast Aaron was.

She sighed and set the nunchaku back.

Maybe there wasn't a weapon for her. Maybe she wasn't really a warrior as Aaron thought, but just fighting because she had been thrust into an impossible, dangerous situation.

Didn't warriors *want* to fight? All Fiona wanted to do was stay alive.

Overhead she heard wings flapping. A flock of crows, actually called a "murder" of crows, flew past and landed on the power lines on Vine Street.

She returned her gaze to the weapons, and her eye lit upon the wooden yo-yo. Something about it fascinated her, even more than the nunchaku. There was certainly nothing more flexible in Aaron's arsenal.

She didn't make a move for it, though. She wouldn't give Aaron a chance to tell her no. She'd plan what to do first, then just do it. Maybe this time surprise him.

Fiona took a deep breath—grasped the string and flung the heavy wooden part at Aaron's head.

He ducked.

She registered a flicker of astonishment in his eyes as she whipped the yo-yo around and back in a fast-spinning arc, building momentum.

Aaron backed off two steps, crashing into the Dumpster, denting it.

Fiona followed him, changed the angle of the whirling weapon, and sent it whipping at his head.

Aaron rolled to one side—drew a short sword from his jacket. He lashed out.

The tension in the yo-yo's string vanished, and it fell limp.

The now freed wooden disk careened through the air, bounced off the brick wall, and rolled down the alley.

Fiona let out a heavy sigh. "Guess that one wasn't 'for me' either."

Aaron, however, was no longer concerned with her. He craned his head around either side of the Dumpster.

"Guess again," he murmured. "You have inherited your mother's talent."

He touched the corner of the Dumpster.

A section of the corrugated steel an arm's span across slid free and crashed to the alley. The edges of the cut metal were mirror smooth as if they'd been severed with a laser.

Fiona approached and stared at this curiosity, trying to understand what Aaron meant . . . and how this had happened.

She traced the angle of the cut metal: it matched the angle of her yo-yo's trajectory.

Aaron faced her, smiling broadly. "Try again, child. It is important you understand when you can and cannot do this. What frame of mind you must be in to cut."

Was he suggesting that she had *cut through* metal with a string? Was that any stranger than a talking crocodile?

Yes, very much stranger, in fact. A talking reptile might be explained by mutation or some never discovered line of reptilian evolution. But a cotton string cutting steel? That violated the laws of physics.

She looked at the string in her hands, then to Aaron. He wasn't kidding.

So, although it felt silly, she held out the length of string and approached the iron drainpipe running down the wall.

She hesitated. "If this works, wouldn't it cut me, too?"

"Only if you let such a thing happen," he said.

Fiona tensed and pressed the string to the pipe, lightly at first, then harder.

Just as she thought—nothing happened. The length of cotton fiber was no more likely to pass through solid iron than a pat of butter could pass through a brick wall.

"Remember what you felt as we fought," Aaron said.

Felt? Fiona hadn't felt anything . . . other than being sick of being pushed around. By Grandmother. By the Council. And hadn't she wanted to hurt dear old Uncle Aaron? Just for a fraction of an instant? Hadn't she wanted to bash his brains in with that yo-yo?

The string glistened.

It snapped taut on the far side of the pipe.

The motion was sudden and as impossible as a stage magician's sleight of hand.

Aaron gently pulled her aside.

The pipe groaned; the top section slid free and clattered onto the asphalt.

Fiona stared dumbfounded at the cut. She reached to feel the edge, but stopped, knowing it was sharper than any razor.

"You said my mother could do this, too? With just string?"

"Cut through anything when she put her mind to it," he told her. "So you *are* her daughter, after all. And my niece."

She looked at him. He was the same mountain of a man, still tougher and scarier than anyone she had ever before seen, but his gaze had softened as if something about her now didn't completely repulse him.

Shadows flickered through the alley and Fiona glanced up. A hundred crows were airborne, circling. Some dived at the Pink Rabbit, bouncing off its skylights and walls.

"Listen," Aaron whispered. "Your brother tests his arsenal as well."

Fiona was about to ask him what he meant, but Johnny banged open the back door.

"Fiona," Johnny shouted. "Phone—some boy."

She turned and shouted, "Okay, hang on."

She turned back to her uncle. She had more questions for him.

But the bundle of weapons and Uncle Aaron were gone.

37

LANCELOT COMPLEX

Robert Farmington rolled his Harley to a halt next to three dusty Cadillacs with Baja license plates. He stripped off his leather jacket to his sweaty T-shirt underneath.

It was funny that so many locals were at the cantina. It was a sweltering afternoon—prime time for a siesta on this sleepy Mexican coastline.

He glanced over the cliff at the village of Puedevas, nestled by the ocean. A few savvy fishermen knew about this place . . . and too many smugglers.

Robert cruised down to Puedevas whenever he could. The señoritas always smiled at him, the lobster enchiladas were heaven, and most important, the cantina served him cervezas.

He strolled toward the entrance, but halted. The CERRADO sign sat in the window . . . but the door was ajar. It had to be a mistake. The cantina made a point of staying open in the afternoons for the rich American fishermen looking to quench their thirsts.

Robert pushed through. Inside, the adobe walls were covered with turquoise paint and ceiling fans pushed the hot air to little effect.

Eight local men sat at the bar, reeking of three-day-old perspiration and a hint of cordite from recent gunplay. They wore cheap leather jackets, even in this heat, and Robert noted the bulges of obvious handguns.

These were middle-management thugs between drug kingpins and their distributors on the U.S.-Mexican border. Robert classified these types as "banditos."

They were easy to deal with one at a time, but not like this. They were like a pack of hyenas . . . and even lions backed down from too many hyenas.

He was about to back out, but he spotted Theresa, the cantina owner's daughter. She was a sweet girl, maybe eleven years old, and she stood in the corner like a trapped animal.

She gave him a shake of her head.

The message was unmistakable: *Get out while you can.*

Her dark eyes, though, were wide with panic and they had an equally clear message: *Save me.*

Robert smiled. Marcus Welmann had always told him that he had a thing for "damsels in distress." He also told Robert it would get him killed one day.

Marcus had never understood, though, why Robert had taken this job in the first place. Damsels in distress, danger, adventure, never having to grow up—who cared about your life span when you had all that?

Besides . . . who was still alive, and who was now dead?

He nodded to Theresa and then sauntered to his favorite booth in the back. He'd be able to watch the banditos from there.

They could see him, too. This would make them feel at ease, like they had him right where they wanted.

And so what? Maybe they did.

The banditos looked him over, murmured something, and laughed. A few of them helped themselves to more beers from behind the counter. No bartender in sight. That was not a good sign.

One of them went to the front door and slid the dead bolt. He grinned at Robert and stumbled back to his barstool.

Yeah, they were going to get good and drunk, then the fun would begin. They'd take care of him first . . . then, he guessed, Theresa.

Robert held up a greasy menu with one hand while his other hand slid to the holster in the small of his back. He pulled out his Glock 29 and set the tiny gun on the bench next to him.

Theresa came to the table. "Order, señor?" she said, loud enough so the banditos could hear.

"Lobster enchiladas and black beans."

"Go," she whispered. "Quickly—if you can."

Robert smiled even wider. "And *dos Coronas, por favor.*"

She sighed and moved to the kitchen.

Eight against one. Robert would soon be dead unless he found some angle. For now, though, he was happy to let them drink and let their reactions degrade. From the way those guys were tossing back the tequila and beer, he figured he had about ten minutes before they were liquored up enough to do whatever they were working up to.

He had, as they say, "time to kill."

Robert grabbed a salt shaker and sprinkled the table. He traced a map of the world. He smudged the approximate center of North America.

He had lived most of his life in Arkansas off Country Road 32. He'd worked the fields with his family and caught a little school in the afternoons. One day after stepfather number three had taught him a lesson for "back-talkin'" that gave him a split lip, Robert decided he'd had enough.

He kissed his mother good-bye as she slept and headed to the crossroads where Highway 20 turned into 43. Robert had heard that if you waited at such a place, at midnight the devil would come and you could sell your soul.

Midnight came. The devil never showed, but the Greyhound bus had, and that was good enough.

He traced an arc in his salt map to the Atlantic.

Robert was big for his age and a fair liar. Still, the Virginian shipmaster had to know he was only fourteen. He let him work, though, for his passage. Robert picked up some Spanish on the voyage, then jumped ship in Barcelona.

He drew a big line across the ocean and a bunch of zigs and zags over Europe.

That year had been crazy. Robert had almost died while he learned his new trade: thief of fine art.

That stopped in Turkey, though, when he crossed paths with Marcus Welmann.

Robert sighed and blew away most of the salt.

What good was all this remembering? Marcus was dead. Sure, he had hassled Robert, but he'd also taken care of him, shown him how to ride, fight, and think . . . which was more than any of his mom's boyfriends had ever done.

"It's not the punks that'll get you in this business," Marcus had once told Robert. "It's our bosses. You start thinking of them as people—that's dangerous. They're more a force of nature than flesh and blood. Lose sight of that, cross them once . . . and you might as well try talking your way out of a tidal wave for all the good it'll do you."

Which is what had happened.

Marcus had crossed Ms. Audrey Post. No one had told Robert that, but it's the only way his mentor's disappearance and Robert's replacing him made any sense.

Robért had tried to hide his feelings when he'd delivered the Council's message to the Posts. Ms. Post, however, had looked straight into his soul and seen it all. Any plans for revenge he had, had been snuffed out in that instant.

But those were problems in the past. His troubles in the here and now had reared their collective ugly heads: the eight banditos turned on their barstools.

"Hey, *chico*," one of them said. "Come over here. We talk with you."

If Robert made his move now, they'd all start shooting. But if he played along, all sorts of unpleasant things were likely to happen.

Not much of a trade-off.

He reached for his gun.

The front door slowly swung open. The sunlight made them all blink, Robert included.

The banditos turned—even drunk they realized something was wrong. That door had been bolted. It shouldn't have just opened like that . . . at least, not without getting kicked off its hinges.

Standing in the doorway was an American tourist in a Hawaiian shirt, khaki shorts, flip-flops, and a ridiculous straw hat.

"*Buenos tardes,*" the man slurred. He stumbled in and let the door slam behind him.

He flopped onto the bar and pounded his fist. "Bartender, *cervezas y tequila!*" He reached into his pockets and pulled out fistfuls of twenty-dollar bills.

When no bartender showed, the man shrugged, reached behind the bar, and grabbed a bottle of Cuervo and a shot glass.

He turned to the banditos, staggered, and fell into their group.

They shoved him—he struggled between them, accidentally bumping his elbows into their ribs.

"A *thousand* pardons. Have a drink on me, amigos." He dropped a few more crumpled bills on the counter.

The stranger then staggered to Robert's table.

The banditos laughed, scooped the money off the counter, and decided to watch what this rich American fool would do next before they pulled his arms out of their sockets.

"Good afternoon, Robert," the man said, perfectly sober, as he settled in opposite Robert. "How are you?"

The man before Robert changed his name as often as other men changed their clothes. He had been called at various times the Big Bad Wolf, Loki Sly Boots, Hernandez del Moro, or just plain Hermes—but they were all his boss, Mr. Henry Mimes.

Robert wasn't exactly sure how he did stuff like this—finding him during his off hours and opening bolted doors from the other side. And why in the world if he'd wanted to talk to him hadn't he just used his cell phone?

All he knew for sure was that Mr. Mimes was good at finding things . . . especially trouble.

"Do you need to be driven anywhere this afternoon, sir?" Robert asked.

Robert kept one eye on the banditos, who whispered among themselves. Although he seemed to amuse them, this American tourist complicated their plans. Rich Americans tended to, also like hyenas, travel in packs.

Mr. Mimes glanced at the salt scattered on the table. "Reminiscing? A habit I try not to indulge. It leads to moroseness, which is on my list of distasteful behaviors next to nose-picking and crying at weddings." He flashed Robert a smile and tapped the dot that represented Istanbul. "Do you know what I liked about you most when we first met?"

"No, sir."

"Unlike most art thieves, you didn't melt your treasures for the gold. You always took the risk to sell them intact."

Robert shrugged. "They were too pretty to break."

Mr. Mimes's gaze wandered to Theresa, who stood in the corner. She clutched a stack of menus to her chest, watching the banditos watching them.

"There are too few lovely objects in this world," Mr. Mimes said. "I agree, they should be protected."

One of the banditos moved to the cantina door, inspecting the dead bolt and confirming it was *still* thrown. He looked extremely confused. He turned to his pack and they discussed this. One of them made the sign of the cross. The oldest, largest bandito, however, slapped him in the face for such superstitious nonsense.

"I hate to interrupt whatever you are up to," Mr. Mimes said with a careless wave of his hand, "but I thought it time we had a chat about your future."

Future wasn't a word that Marcus had ever used when talking about this job. Something more than a driving assignment was on Mr. Mimes's mind today. Robert had a nasty feeling it might be something worse than his about to be getting shot by drunken drug dealers, too.

"I don't understand, sir."

"Do you like working for me?" Mr. Mimes's smile was still there, but his eyes had hardened.

Robert was about to reflexively answer yes, but hesitated. Mr. Mimes had asked a serious question, so Robert would carefully consider how he really felt.

There were downsides to being a Driver for Henry Mimes. Missions were often high risk. You had to operate without the assistance of, and sometimes on the wrong side of, the law. And as Marcus had pointed out, their boss was part of a League of Immortals, who were unstable and always lethal, sometimes even to the hired help.

But this job had plenty of upsides, too. Robert could ride anywhere he wanted on his time off. He'd been taught a dozen languages. He had an expense account most Fortune 500 CEOs couldn't even dream of.

Pretty good for a sixteen-year-old high-school dropout.

Most important, though, there was the adventure. He was never bored.

"Working for you might shorten my life span," Robert finally said, "but at least I have a life worth living."

Mr. Mimes brightened and squeezed Robert's shoulder. "My dear boy, I couldn't have said it better. Well then, I have a new mission for you—a secret one involving a pretty girl. I want you to get to know her and help her if you can."

"A spy deal?" Robert asked, intrigued. He felt something hard and cold solidify in his gut as he understood what Mr. Mimes was asking. "You mean Fiona Post."

Mr. Mimes raised an eyebrow. "Did our dear departed Mr. Welmann teach you to read minds?"

"No, sir. But with everything that's happened the last few days . . . who else?"

"Marcus said you could sometimes see to the heart of the matter. She *is* something special, is she not?"

A girl that could quick-talk a monster alligator into being her friend? And barely batting an eye as she and her brother related the tale, handing him the thirty-pound iron spike she'd pulled from the creature?

"Yeah, she's something," Robert said. "But I'm not allowed to 'get to know' anyone even potentially in the League."

"I would never ask you to break the rules," Mr. Mimes said, feigning offense. "That would be wrong. But if you were to break the rules on your own, well, that would be something I could have not foreseen . . . nor be blamed for."

Robert swallowed. He got the gist of this. If it went bad, Mr. Mimes was throwing him to the Council as a sacrificial lamb.

He'd read how the Council punished rule breakers. One guy got his liver (and a bunch of other stuff) torn out every day for a thousand years by some bird—then the organs would grow back . . . just in time to get ripped out the next day.

And the Council had liked that guy.

"Yes," Mr. Mimes said as if reading Robert's thoughts. "The Council does love their rules."

"But—" Robert started.

Mr. Mimes held up a finger, indicating silence. "One moment. There is a bit of unpleasantness to deal with."

Robert had, if only for a few seconds, forgotten the banditos, but he saw them now as they stood and faced him.

Robert tried to stay cool. He couldn't afford a shaking hand now. He'd only get a shot or two off before they returned fire.

The banditos grinned as they reached for their pistols.

Mr. Mimes set a hand on Robert's hand and shook his head. "Let them try," he whispered.

Robert reluctantly overcame his instinct for self-preservation; Mr. Mimes had given him a direct order. And weighing the two parties— understated Mr. Mimes or eight armed killers—Robert knew who was more dangerous.

The banditos' fumbled as they grabbed at empty holsters.

With a clatter Mr. Mimes dropped a double armful of pistols onto the table.

Their drunken smiles evaporated.

Robert remembered how Mr. Mimes had bumped into each of them. He must've lifted their weapons.

But eight guns? And not one of them had felt a thing? That was a world-class bit of pickpocketry.

"Marcus was always saying that you had a Lancelot complex," Mr. Mimes whispered to Robert. "Charging to the defense of damsels in distress. I definitely approve."

Mr. Mimes plucked up a snub-nosed .38 and shot the largest bandito in the stomach.

The man crashed into the barstools, clutching his midsection.

Mr. Mimes waived the gun at the others. *"Vamos, perros."*

The banditos, now utterly sober, went slack-jawed and wide-eyed at this American who had shot their boss. Four of them knelt as if to carry him off.

Mr. Mimes shot two more rounds through the roof of the cantina. "Leave him . . . or join him."

The banditos moved, almost breaking down the door as they fumbled with the bolt.

As Cadillacs screeched out of the driveway, Mr. Mimes turned to Theresa. "Call the *policía*, señorita. There is a reward for the one I shot—more alive than dead—so hurry."

"Sí, señor." Theresa disappeared into the kitchen.

"Now, where were we?" Mr. Mimes set the pistol down. "Ah, yes, the lovely Miss Fiona Post, our damsel in the greatest distress of all. I am merely suggesting that you do what you would do anyway: get close to her and help her survive the last two trials. But also listen and learn what happens within her immediate family."

He was right. Robert did want to help Fiona, but there were rules . . . and more than that, punishment for breaking the rules. It was too much to risk.

"I sense equivocation," Mr. Mimes said. "So let me put your mind at ease. I know you have already broken the rules: letting her and her brother know what to take into the sewers."

"How did you—" Robert shut his mouth.

How did he know? Well, for one thing Robert's reaction had just told him he was right. Second, Mr. Mimes just knew things—the same way he walked through bolted doors, sped across the world in a few hours, or stole the guns from eight banditos right under their noses.

Marcus's voice echoed in Robert's mind: *You start thinking of them as people—that's dangerous.*

Theresa and three men came from the kitchen to examine the bleeding bandito leader. The men with her had been beaten and tied up. They wanted some revenge, but Theresa restrained them and explained about the reward.

She then brought Robert and Mr. Mimes their beers and thanked them again and again.

"Con mucho gusto," Mr. Mimes told her. "When you see your mother, tell her the Old Coyote sends his affections."[41]

She gave Mr. Mimes a curious look, nodded, and left them.

"Well, Robert? What shall it be? Danger, intrigue, and romance? Or ordinary driving jobs for the rest of your simple, dull life?"

Robert grabbed his beer and took a long pull. "I need a raise."

"And you shall have it when this is over. A promotion and a long vacation as well, I promise."

"How do I start?"

"Do what all boys your age do. Call her and ask her out on a date."

41. While the Coyote of Native American myths is known for his cleverness and trickery, he was also known for his sexuality (and sexual exploits). These stories, however, were sanitized by conservative European settlers, who may also have discouraged the indigenous populations from retelling them. *Gods of the First and Twenty-first Century, Volume 4: Core Myths* (Part 1), 8th ed. (Zypheron Press Ltd.).

38

THE SHADOW CABAL

eal Z. Buan, Lord of All That Flies, was far from the open skies he so loved. He was in the living room of a vacated house, the so-called Devil House, which stood among the many flattened buildings of the abandoned suburb of Love Canal in Niagara Falls, New York.[42]

A sharp metallic odor and the sweet smell of benzene seeped from the basement, and Beal inhaled deeply, almost seeing the concentrated vapors curl about him.

The furniture had been cleared and the carpet torn off the plywood floor by Uri. Beal had had him sweep away the multitudes of dead cockroaches. Beal required a pristine surface.

He knelt and retrieved a razor blade from its cardboard sleeve. He then used the blade to etch a large circle in the plywood. As he completed the figure, he slit his wrist and let his blood dribble out.

It seeped along the razor's track . . . diffused into the filaments of the plywood, tattooing tiny dots, squares, triangles, and cuneiform letters. The pattern radiated out from the circle and traveled up the Sheetrock walls and overhead until it met in the center of the ceiling.

---

42. Love Canal is infamous for the toxic contamination that prompted the evacuation of hundreds in 1980. Local legends relate that the Devil House is haunted by those fatally poisoned. Adolescents often challenge one another to spend the night in the building, although none have ever lasted the entire evening, and many have been hospitalized for pulmonary edema (chemically induced pneumonia) from the noxious vapors present on-site. Hallucinations from these influences may account for the numerous spirit sightings. *Gods of the First and Twenty-first Century, Volume 6: Modern Myths*, 8th ed. (Zypheron Press Ltd.).

Beal then held his wrist and stanched the wound. He scrutinized the surrounding network of ancient symbols and was satisfied.

"All eyes and ears are blocked," he announced. "We may speak."

Uri resolved from the shadows, stepping into the circle of silence to attend his master.

Beal did not trust his lesser distant cousin, but it gave him great pleasure to have him near, knowing that he had taken the oath of binding and could not betray him—not even for the sake of his former mistress, the Queen of Poppies.

"Let me stress," Beal said to the darkness, "that the nature of our treachery this evening is extreme. We subvert the terms determined by the roll of dice most sacred. The Board would be well within their rights to declare a vendetta and destroy us." Beal smiled and spread his hands in an expansive gesture. "But the rewards if we succeed are equal to this risk."

One of the shadows stepped into the circle, clarifying into a gaunt man in a gray suit. "Ain't that always the way with anything worth doing?" he said, chewing a peanut-butter-and-jelly sandwich. He was Samsawell, the Ever Hungry.

Mulciber crossed over next. He was a small, old man with gnarled hands perpetually curled into fists. "To clarify," he whispered, "we all get *equal* shares of this reward?"

Beal must take care to offer this old one every courtesy. Mulciber's temper was as great as his wisdom. Once roused, he never forgave.

"Of course," Beal said, and bowed.

The last of their cabal entered, and the shadows seemed to cling to this one, refusing to relinquish their embrace. He was a boy of fifteen in cutoff shorts and a tank top. Only his pale eyes betrayed the cunning contained behind the innocent façade. "You have engineered a most ineffective Board of Directors," Uziel said, and tilted his head. "I marvel at your machinations."

They stood at equidistant positions about the circle, the five prescribed points to strengthen the silence. Beal felt the air coalesce, and crackling, it solidified about them.

Beal nodded to Uri, who withdrew a card table from his coat and set it up. Upon this he unrolled a large aerial photograph.

"A satellite map of Del Sombra," Beal explained. "There is a single arterial road that runs through its thirty-odd businesses, mostly restaurants and tour shops, catering to wine enthusiasts."

Uziel peered down. "I had a look at this place once. A Gold Rush boom-town that survived by making wine and beer for travelers."

"You didn't notice the place for the local charm," Samsawell muttered around his sandwich. "What really gives?"

Uziel leaned forward and gold hair fell into his face. "It is between places of power, elemental, good, evil, astral, disjunctive. And like equal but opposite water waves meeting, they cancel."

"Del Sombra," Mulciber said, and came closer to examine the map. "It means 'of the shadows' in Spanish."

"A perfect place to hide," Beal said.

He nodded to Uri, who overlaid a plastic sheet upon the map. Translu-cent red and green colors shaded the streets and buildings.

"The green regions," Beal said, "are controlled or patrolled by League forces." He tapped one building. "This Oakwood Apartments complex ap-pears to be a concentration of power."

Mulciber smoothed his gnarled hands over the plastic. "The red areas . . . ours?"

"We have agents there. Watching. Taking no direct action."

"What are these?" Samsawell touched several small uncolored regions, leaving a sprinkle of crumbs.

"Those are the interesting bits," Beal said, pausing for dramatic effect. "I believed they are caused by Louis."

Uziel flipped the hair from his face. "Louis is dead."

"Is he?" Beal said. "No one has ever confirmed that. He simply vanished sixteen years ago in that business with the woman from the other family."

"I always thought it curious," Mulciber remarked. "A power like his cannot just vanish. It would be as if a star went missing from the sky."

Beal motioned to Uri, who removed another tube from his jacket, un-rolled it, and overlaid one more plastic sheet upon the map. Tiny lines and cuneiform covered it.

"These are the power sources we have detected," Beal told them. "All the usual probes and countermeasures . . . save this." With his pinkie, he tapped the center of a dark patch—a dancing collection of stick figures and spirals.

"That's the Ritual of Theophilus," Uziel said.[43]

43. Theophilus of Adana (died c. 538 CE), later known as Saint Theophilus the Penitent, was an Orthodox cleric who made a deal with Satan to become a bishop. He later confessed his sins, recanted his association with the devil, and had a legitimate bishop burn his Infernal

"That's one of ours, then?" Samsawell asked.

"It's our engineering, no doubt," Mulciber replied. "But it's a mortal channel. Someone begs for power."

"I believe it is Louis," Beal said. "Who else would know the ritual? Who else would be there . . . near his children?"

"Why use such a low-order ceremony?" Samsawell asked.

"Trying to *quietly* leverage his children?" Mulciber said, and rubbed his chin with one curled hand.

Uziel stood taller. "We came here to discuss the boy child. What is your interest in Louis?"

Beal smiled. "Louis, if he is indeed alive and needing power, is the key to our plan."

"I see what you're thinking." Uziel's eyes brightened and cast a pale blue illumination over the map. "You believe that something tragic happened to the great Louis Piper sixteen years ago—that he was not destroyed, but somehow . . . what? Stripped of his power?"

"So what?" Samsawell wiped his mouth with a napkin, now so engrossed that he had actually stopped eating. "He comes back to watch his kids grow up? Make sure they are safe? I don't think so."

"What would be more likely," Mulciber said, "is that Louis circles like a shark, waiting for an opportunity, some way to use them to regain what he lost."

Beal nodded. "I propose this is how we outmaneuver both the Board of Directors *and* the League Council. We use the greatest user of us all: Louis."

"If he's really powerless," Samsawell said, "the League and the Board might never notice such a small fry."

"And if he is the boy's father," Uziel whispered, and touched the dark region of the map, "I would bet he has already made contact . . . preparing the boy for some bit of his own treachery."

"Louis wants power," Beal said, "so we will give him that. We can offer him amnesty for his past transgressions as well. In exchange, he will lure Eliot away from the protection of the League and deliver him to us."

"It's too easy," Samsawell said, licking his lips. "Louis makes plans inside

---

contract, whereupon Theophilus expired from the joy of being released from his burden (or as others theorize, his soul was then actually forfeited to the Dark). Considered to be the first documented account of a pact with Infernal forces. *Gods of the First and Twenty-first Century, Volume 13: Infernal Forces,* 8th ed. (Zypheron Press Ltd.).

plans like those little Russian dolls—one inside the others. What makes you think this isn't all a setup?"

"And his involvement with the other family," Mulciber murmured, "with that woman. Could he be working with her?"

Beal shook his head. "Whatever the details, we are protected. Louis is outcast among us due to his very involvement with this woman. If his attempts to get the boy for us are discovered by the League or the Board, they will destroy him. As he will be working alone, with no immortal attachments, there can be no repercussions to us."

"Like a damned circuit breaker," Samsawell said, and stuffed the last of his sandwich into his mouth.

"We are in agreement then?" Uziel looked to his fellow conspirators. "We answer Louis's summons and make him an offer he can't refuse?"

Beal bristled. He did not like that Uziel now directed his meeting. It was undoubtedly a portent of treachery. He knew it had been a mistake to invite one so clever and ambitious into his cabal. Some unfortunate accident must be arranged for Uziel, but later—after he had Eliot for himself.

"A fine plan," Beal declared. "It has all the hallmarks of excellence: extortion, kidnapping, and duplicity."

Mulciber huddled over the map and a scowl creased his weathered face. "Could this be a trap *for us*? Louis is clever . . . too clever to be so easily cornered."

"Unless he has lost everything," Samsawell replied. "Wouldn't you risk everything only if you had *nothing* to lose?"

They all paused and considered.

Beal sensed their reluctance . . . and he felt it now as well. The problem was Louis. Even without power, he was sure to retain his razor-edged cleverness. He had made fools of them all many times before. To think the Master Deceiver now helpless, well, it was unthinkable. He would always be dangerous.

Uri cleared his throat and whispered, "He does have something to lose, my lord."

Beal turned to his servant, so quiet, he had nearly forgotten him. As he looked over the mountain of a man, he realized that he indeed had a solution to the immediate problem of Louis.

"Go on," Beal said.

"He has his son and daughter to lose," Uri explained. "If he has long been powerless as you believe, then his emotions might have weakened him. He may actually care for them."

Mulciber scoffed.

Beal moved closer to Uri. "All the better. We can threaten one or the other to obtain leverage on Louis." Beal placed a hand on Uri's huge shoulder. "And as you seem to have insights into this emotional weakness . . ."

Beal reached into his pocket and withdrew the Infernal Board Seal of Power. It was a sphere the size of a baseball. One hemisphere was inscribed with ancient iconography and encrusted with the gemstones of their various clans. The design moved as political powers waxed and waned. Presently Beal's teardrop sapphire sat in the center of this glittering constellation. All others orbited it. And nowhere to be seen was Louis's diamond—as it should be.

"You shall go as our representative," Beal told Uri. "Make a deal with Louis—or whatever is left of Louis."

Uri flinched. "It would be an honor, my lord." A tiny bit of fear was in the man's massive rumble of a voice, and this pleased Beal.

He handed the seal to Uri, and he took it reverently with both hands.

If Uri was caught in some web of deception or discovered by the other clans or the other family . . . well, then Beal would claim Uri was acting on his own, or better yet, on Sealiah's behest; after all, who could resist her charms?

Samsawell waved at Uri with a ham-and-Swiss sandwich. "Good luck, buddy!"

Beal leaned closer to Uri. "Listen to his lies," he whispered. "They will point the way to the truth."

"Yes, my lord." Uri backed to the edge of the circle, and with a mighty sigh he stepped into the shadows and vanished.

39

FOOL'S BARGAIN

ouis touched the glass. He had painted every window in this basement apartment black so there was nothing to see, but he could nonetheless feel the notes resonating through the pane. He understood what they meant: a song for a girl named Julie.

It was a deliciously sad piece, and then, in the last notes, an unexpected twist of hope . . . something he would never even have attempted.

Eliot had the potential to one day be *better* than he was.

His son.

Louis's heart would have burst with pride if that particular organ had actually been intact. But even if he had a heart, what use would it have been? Louis Piper, the once great, was now lower than dirt.

And yet, could not even dirt change? With heat and pressure it could metamorphose into marble and be chiseled into the pillars of society. Empires were built from such stuff! Was he not still the penultimate bluffer? The Master Deceiver? Crafter of lies most exquisite?

Perhaps . . .

He turned from the window and surveyed his work. Yesterday this low-rent basement apartment under the Christian-studies store, Disciples of Light, had been furnished with 1970s avocado-colored furniture and an orange shag rug.

Last night he painted the windows. The decor had all been tossed into the kitchen. Butcher paper had been taped to the floor and covered with symbols and the tiny angles of cuneiform—not quite the scrawlings of a madman . . . and yet a truly sane person who stared too long at them would see the lines twist *into* the air and *deeper* into the concrete.

He flexed his cramping hand. He should've used blood instead of a Sharpie permanent marker. He had learned in the last fifteen years, however, that he had limitations. Losing more than a pint of blood was one of them.

Besides, if anyone bothered to show up and complain about it, he'd consider it a victory.

The Ritual of Theophilus was the lowest order of summoning, a whisper into the aether. He dared no more. True, he'd need help to survive the imminent clash between the two families—but help always had a price . . . and he had so little to pay with.

All that he really wanted was an insignificant shadow to answer his call, a fool that he could fool.

It had been six hours since he'd finished. What was taking so long? Or had he not even the power to cry for help like some fatted and hobbled lamb?

He looked at his hands—all flesh and blood—so weak. How had he survived this long after trying so hard to kill himself with booze and misery?

How did any human survive?

Well, of course, ultimately *none* of them did.

Louis laughed and poised his arms dramatically for his nonexistent audience. "'What a piece of work is a man!'" he said, overacting. "'How noble in reason! . . . How infinite in faculty! In form, in moving, how express and admirable!'"

"'In action how like an angel!'" the shadows said, finishing the *Hamlet* for him.

"Ah," he said, turning to the darkness. "I knew the irony would be irresistible."

But the smile forming on Louis's face froze.

This instinct had served him well in the past. He could conceal his emotions as he worked out some complication.

Only this was no mere complication. It was, perhaps, the end of his life.

Part of the shadows detached and stepped over the lines and symbols, which should have prevented just such a thing from occurring. The blackness resolved into a man twice the width of a professional wrestler, with more beef filling out his black windbreaker and polyester dress slacks than an entire herd of longhorn cattle. His broad Samoan features were unmistakable.

He was Urakabarameel, Master of Shadows and Whispers, the Hound of Hades, chief intelligence officer for the Queen of Poppies . . . and Louis's third cousin.

Uri had the power to crush him with one flexed bicep. And for what other purpose could he possibly have been sent? His mistress was among Louis's most bitter enemies.

He was glad she had not come herself. How embarrassing would it have been in this slovenly mortal shell to have thrown himself prostrate before her irresistible beauty?

But Uri . . . he had fooled him many times in the past. He needed no special powers for that.

"Greetings, Cousin," Louis said, managing to sound normal, as if this were some chance meeting in the park. "Destroy everything you touch."[44]

Surprise registered on Uri's face. "Lies and salutations to you as well, Cousin." His lips curled slightly with revulsion. "So it is true. You live." He sniffed. "But as a mortal?"

"Just when all thought I could fall no farther . . ." Louis gave Uri a slight bow. "I do so enjoy disappointing the family."

Louis sniffed the air as well, although not as conspicuously. He detected fried chicken, burning metal, and the faint gangrenous scent of Sealiah's poisoned blade, Saliceran. Odd that she would allow Uri to carry one of her most prized possessions.

"I surmise the situation at home has become *interesting* in my absence? Or are you here for some trivial personal vendetta?"

"Interesting, yes," Uri rumbled. "Vendetta, unfortunately no. We have business."

"Oh? What business could the Queen of Poppies desire with me, the lowly dirt?"

Uri flinched as if mentioning her were a physical blow. He then clum-

---

44. Traditional Infernal greeting/departure. This phrase has become an often heard parental colloquialism to naughty children: "Must you destroy everything you touch?" Many experts associate this with the now less popular counterresponse: "The devil made me do it." *Gods of the First and Twenty-first Century, Volume 13: Infernal Forces*, 8th ed. (Zypheron Press Ltd.).

sily attempted to change the subject. "How did you . . . ?" He waved one of his massive hands about. "Become this?"

Louis paused, wondering if he could possibly craft a sufficient lie, but decided against it. The truth would serve better to confuse. "Quite simple: I fell in love with a woman. I'm sure you've heard all the rumors. She, metaphysically and metaphorically, ripped out my heart. I was as surprised as anyone to find out that I actually needed it."

"I see," Uri said, clearly not understanding.

"I know you can relate to the trials of love gone sour."

Uri's brows bunched.

That smell of poultry intensified, and Louis remembered where he had last detected that particular acrid avian scent.

"Beal," Louis muttered. "So you come on *his* behest? What has befallen your precious queen?"

Uri's eyes widened, his hands curled into fists, and he stepped closer, crinkling the butcher paper underfoot. Louis could feel the vibrations of power and rage radiate from him.

"You always talked too much, Louis."

He grabbed Louis's arms and squeezed, picking him up off the floor. The bones strained and popped—not quite breaking, but not quite intact anymore either.

The intense pressure forced the smile back to Louis's lips. "My apologies, Cousin," he grunted. As his last breath was forced from him, he squeaked, "You mentioned business?"

Uri hissed, gave him one last flex—which cracked a few ribs—then released him.

Louis dropped to his knees.

He admired his cousin, truly, but Uri was a blunt instrument, never the scalpel. This confirmed Beal's involvement. Who else would have been foolish enough to send him to deal with Louis?

And yet Beal possessed the beloved servant of Sealiah, which indicated a significant shift in the architecture of power back home.

"So your new master has gotten himself invited onto the Board of Directors?" Louis whispered, and carefully got to his feet.

Uri crossed his arms and the plastic of his windbreaker rustled. "Always too clever, Cousin," he growled. "Only this time, cleverness will be of no use."

"The *chairman* of the Board?"

Uri's face froze in disgust.

The multitude of his other relatives Louis could handle; he even grudgingly respected their treacheries . . . but Beal? This would be a problem.
That particular tyrant had not a shred of style.

Uri unzippered his windbreaker and his entire arm vanished within its
infinite folds. Louis spied Saliceran, sheathed over his heart. A weapon
that had brought down popes and kings, so deadly it had destroyed Titans
and monsters alike . . . reduced to a mere love token?

Louis noted the Queen of Poppies also still appreciated irony.

Uri removed a folding chair for Louis and battered card table and set
them up. "Business," he said, and threw down a file folder.

"What is it the Board wishes?" Louis asked, sitting. "My soul? My undy-
ing, unwavering loyalty? Shall I be their puppet, too?"

Poor Uri. This was like teasing a pit bull on the other side of the fence.
Dangerous . . . but fun.

Uri glowered as he sat on the floor. His head was now level with Louis's.
He flipped open the folder and removed two photographs: Eliot and Fiona
Post.

"The primary interest is the boy."

The family knew of his children?

The picture of the situation shifted in Louis's mind. He saw himself as
a small wheel between two much larger gears—his family and the League.
He had to leverage himself a better position or be crushed.

"What precisely is being offered here?" Louis asked.

Uri chuckled, and the deep rumble roiled through Louis's stomach like
nausea. "You make this so easy. You are but a man. And what does any man
desire? Power? Fame? Wealth?"

"Yes . . . ," Louis murmured, hoping to get a few more seconds to think.

No matter how desperate his situation, Louis had always managed to
wiggle free, always emerged from dung heaps smelling of roses. Save for
once, of course; but that involved a love most treacherous—so it didn't really count.

Louis also had his reputation to consider here. He couldn't allow his
cousin to best him in a simple brokerage for power. He would never be
able to live with himself.

He blinked and considered the photograph of Eliot. It had been taken
perhaps a year earlier. He was so young and so talented. Louis caught himself reaching out to touch the picture.

What was this? Was he feeling pity for the boy? How odd. How distressing. And yet, something else churned inside him, a new emotion—soft and unpalatable—some vague desire to protect the child.

"Power," Louis whispered without taking his eyes off the photos. "Make me the world's most powerful practitioner of the dark arts."

Uri sighed, sounding disappointed. "I expected so much more from the Master Deceiver." He dug through his jacket and retrieved a tablet computer. "It shall be so: you will be made the world's most powerful mortal."

Of course that was the catch: mortal.

Louis would never regain his former glory, unless he could rob one of his cousins of his or her power . . . but that would be like a gnat bringing down a bull elephant.

"And what does the Board want in return? Specifically?"

Uri checked a few boxes on his tablet computer, filling out the form contract. "They specifically want you to deliver the boy, intact body and soul, for the usual rituals."

The "usual rituals" would remove Eliot from Del Sombra. If he was human, body and soul would be torn asunder. If he was part of the family, the rituals would cement his fate and translocate him to another realm where Beal no doubt had plans for Louis's son.

For a split second Louis wanted to kick over the table, grab Uri by the throat, and demand that he leave his children be.

How foolish.

He'd known his mind had gone soft—it was, after all, only flesh and blood now, and addled from years of drinking. Still, something about these new emotions Louis could not ignore.

"You find something disagreeable?" A faint smile played upon Uri's lips.

If Louis refused to negotiate a deal, then the fence separating him from his pit bull of a cousin would be removed. Uri would take his time tearing him into tiny pieces.

"Just considering the options. What is your timetable?"

"No longer than three days hence at sunset will we require the boy. Else you default on the contract—with the usual consequences."

Louis gave a careless toss of his hand. "Yes, of course. Soul dragged to hell. Eternal damnation. Blah blah blah." He leaned closer, reading the upside-down contract. "I was more interested in my payout schedule."

"What payout schedule?" Uri looked up, now confused.

"You don't expect me to pluck the boy from the army of League agents with my bare hands? I was thinking half down now, and half upon delivery."

Uri snorted. "You have your wits, Deceiver; that is all you ever needed. Giving you half the power now makes you all the more slippery and untrustworthy."

Louis spread his arms in a deprecating gesture. "You honor me with your implications, Cousin. But half it must be. If this task were easy, then why are you so desperately employing me in the first place?"

Uri tapped a photo of Eliot. "Because you know him. He trusts you."

"Yes, of course . . . you need a betrayal." For some strange reason, it hurt Louis to say these words.

Uri stopped fussing with the form contract, sensing something wrong, too. "Is there a problem with that? You have betrayed us all a dozen times before."

"No. No problem at all." Louis flashed his armored smile. "What problem could there possibly be? Other than our terms . . . which apparently are at an—"

"Impasse." Uri set the tablet down.

They stared at one another. The air grew still and heavy.

"You leave me little choice, Cousin." Uri started to shrug off his jacket—so no blood would spatter it. Dry-cleaning the nearly infinite inner surface would be dreadfully expensive.

"Always the brute." Louis waggled a finger at Uri and set a pair of dice on the table.

Uri halted.

"We cannot come to an agreement," Louis said. "So shall we roll?"

Uri snatched the dice. From his jacket he removed calipers and a scale that measured their dimensions and weight. "Very well. If I lose on my first toss, standard craps rules—you shall have half your power."

Louis opened his mouth to argue. One could only lose at craps on the first roll if the dice came up double ones or double sixes. Lousy odds.

But then he realized Uri didn't technically have to roll for anything. He was, in fact, being generous. The tradition of dice in deal making only applied to *family members* . . . of which Louis had departed when he unwillingly joined the human race.

So why offer him *any* chance?

Unless he actually wanted to give him some edge against Beal? Was Uri still loyal to his beloved Queen of Poppies?

This would make Louis, by proxy, Sealiah's pawn . . . but he could live with that. A pawn was *in* the game, after all—which was a huge leap forward from where he'd sat only a few days ago pissing himself in some alley.

"I accept," Louis said. "Let us see if chance favors fools."

Uri shot him a grin. He shook the dice and the motions of his massive arm moved the air. He tossed them against the far wall, where they impacted with a crack and bounced to a halt.

Snake eyes.

"I lose," Uri said unperturbed. "You win."

Louis smiled like an idiot. He would have half his power now. He could actually do something other than skulk in alleyways.

But his smile faded as his gaze fell upon the photos of Eliot and Fiona, and something stabbed the spot where his heart had once been.

What had he done?

40

SMALL AMONG GIANTS

Fiona dismounted and pulled off her borrowed motorcycle helmet. She shook out her hair.

Her body thrummed from the ride up the coast. Robert's Harley had the speed and power of a rocket. She had clung to him—totally scared out of her mind, thrilled, too.

He'd picked her up from Ringo's only fifteen minutes ago, and there was no way they could have made it so far up the coast. Yet, as with Uncle Henry's limousine ride, they hadn't seemed to go that fast, just that everyone else on the Coast Highway had seemed slow in comparison.

What bothered Fiona more, though, was when Julie and Eliot had returned from their break. Julie looked as if she'd been crying. Eliot looked bewildered (as usual). She'd wanted to ask him what had happened, but then Robert showed up . . . and she'd left.

Robert got off his bike and stretched his leather-clad body. All other thoughts faded from Fiona's mind.

After holding on to him for so long, smelling leather, she wanted to go back and cling to him some more.

Was this really a date? So many things had happened so quickly, and little of it made any sense. But did it have to make sense for Fiona to enjoy herself?

And if this was her first date, she didn't want to blow it. She unthinkingly brushed her fingers through her hair, worrying the ends. She forced herself to stop. She didn't want to look like a nervous little girl.

"This way." Robert strode toward the trailhead.

Surrounding the tiny gravel lot where they had parked was a forest of shadows, ferns, and wildflowers. The sign by the trail read REDWOOD NA-TIONAL FOREST INTERPRETIVE TRAIL 0.6 MILES (LOOP).

"Just a sec," she said.

Fiona set her book bag on the bike and reached inside for her chocolates—just two or three to perk her up. Her hand wavered, however, over the heart-shaped box. She'd never felt more confident. Did she *really* need them? She'd never before been able to talk to anyone other than Grandmother, Cee, or her brother. Had she changed? Or was it just the sugar?

What if this wasn't really her? What happened when the never-ending box of chocolates . . . ended?

Maybe it was time to find out.

Fiona zipped up the bag and trotted after Robert.

The instant they stepped onto the path, the sounds from the road vanished. Insect buzz, birdcall, and the nearly imperceptible sound of the air moving filled her ears.

She'd seen the huge trees before in books, but now just a few steps from them, it felt different. These redwoods were giants—all silently looking down and watching her.

"There are sequoias in the mountains that are more massive," Robert explained in a reverent whisper, "but these redwoods are the tallest trees in the world. Some grow over three hundred feet."

They walked solemnly along the trail, and Fiona craned her head upward, trying to find the treetops. The redwoods filled the sky. Layers of fog drifted in and out and added to the illusion that she was in a private world, alone with Robert.

"I must sound like a dork, quoting facts like some encyclopedia."

"No," Fiona said, her head still angled up. "I like it." Uncharacteristically not looking where her feet were, she stumbled.

Robert caught her, and suddenly his face was close to hers. The earth seemed to spin and her heart pounded.

Robert inhaled sharply, hesitated, then helped her stand.

"I come here whenever I can," he said. "Makes me feel calm, you know?"

Calm was the last thing Fiona had felt in his arms.

But he was now acting withdrawn from her as he had before . . . outside the apartment building. What had he said? That he was a driver and there were rules about "a guy like him being with a girl like her"?

The last thing Fiona wanted to do was ruin the mood and jinx her first date, but Robert knew things *and* was willing to tell her. She had him alone now, far away from Uncle Henry and Grandmother. What was more important? Ruining the mood and getting real information about her family? Or trying to nurture her nonexistent love life?

She licked her lips, desperate for a bite of cinnamon truffle.

Fiona glanced again at the towering trees. Giants. Like Uncle Aaron, Grandmother, the rest of the Council, watching over her and Eliot.

"Are Eliot and I the only ones? Kids, I mean. In our family."

Robert blinked and thought about this a moment. "I'm not sure. There are about a hundred members total in the League."

"The League? That's our family?"

"The League of Immortals."

"But they don't really live forever . . ."

"I know it sounds crazy, but they might. They know things and they can do things." Robert looked away, unable to hold her penetrating gaze. "But no kids . . . at least none I've ever personally met."

"Then there have been others before? Henry and Grandmother said there were, but said that things happened to them, too."

Robert looked back. "You should know the truth. Know that the Council's tests are life-and-death serious."

Fiona wondered what kind of trouble Robert could get in by telling her these things. What would Grandmother do to him if she found them in this forest together, alone, revealing family secrets?

The air stilled and fog settled about them.

"There were others like you and Eliot," Robert whispered.

"Are they close? Do you think we could talk to them?"

"I said there *were* others. They're all dead. Or grown-up and in the League for longer than I've been alive."

She moved closer to him. The fog chilled her. She felt the heat from his body. "So some of them *did* survive?"

Robert reached out to her, but stopped himself. "I'm not going to candy-coat this for you. For every one of their kids that lived long enough for history to notice—Hercules, Horus, Tantalus—there were supposedly hundreds, maybe thousands, that didn't make it."

"Grandmother told me," Fiona whispered. "The kidnappings . . . and the poisonings." She felt weak in the knees. She needed her chocolates.

"Maybe I've said too much," Robert whispered.

"No." Fiona took his hand and squeezed. "I understand. Thanks for telling me the truth."

She appreciated the warning about her family—she just couldn't stand to hear any more. It was all too much.

They walked quietly along the path through the fog.

So she and Eliot were sacrificial pawns in a game. The stakes were clearer than ever. Before Robert had spelled it out for her, she had hoped that the Council was bluffing with their "life or death" threats—just trying to scare them.

But they weren't.

Robert stepped closer to her and gently tilted her face toward his. "Don't worry. You have a real chance. What you did to that alligator . . ." He whistled low. "I couldn't have done that. Most professional hunters wouldn't have even found it."

Fiona remembered the raw power of the oracle crocodile. How he had knocked her over and almost devoured her with his black hole of a maw.

And she remembered what it had said: that her father's family was even worse than the League. Fallen angels . . . they seemed more improbable even than gods or goddesses.

"There are other families?" she asked. "Like the League?"

Robert cocked his head, thinking. "Yeah. There are others—some hippie writers in Seco County, New Mexico; the Scalagaris of Sicily; and the Dreaming Families . . . but none of them has half the power of the League."

"What about the Infernals?"

The blood drained from Robert's face. "Those are very scary individuals. Where did you hear about them?"

"They're in competition with the League, aren't they? At least that's the way Uncle Henry talks about them."

"They don't exactly compete." Robert looked around nervously. "If they did, it'd be all-out war. There's some treaty. From what I understand, they can't even touch each other."

"Do *they* have kids?"

Robert shrugged.

A breeze cleared the fog. The trail widened and a tall log-cabin structure stood to one side. It bore the dual pictogram for male/female.

Robert nodded at it. "Do you mind? I'll just be a second."

"Oh, sure."

She watched him enter the outhouse, almost happy that he was gone. She needed a break from all this truth.

Fiona suddenly didn't like these trees. They were majestic, awe-inspiring, but alone with them now, she felt as if they had all taken a giant step closer to her.

She felt so small among them.

She backed to the opposite side of the trail. There, lying on its side, was a fallen log approximately the size of a truck. A sign explained how fallen trees like this were called nursery logs and provided nourishment for younger trees in the forest as they decomposed.

Draped completely around the circumference of the downed tree was a hemp rope. It had a mark each foot along its length and a placard at eye level that read:

California (or Coast) Redwood (*Sequoia sempervirens*). 20-foot circumference.

Fiona reached out and took the rope in her fingers.

So she had to become like the rest of the family? Kill or be killed? She had found a way not to kill on the first trial, though. Could she do the same for the last two?

Her hand wound the rope, tightening it in her grip.

But was it worth taking the risk? Or was it better for both of them to change and live? Not be pawns anymore?

And become what?

She wanted to go back to the way it was: homework, a normal job, reading—no trials or murder, no gods or devils.

An image of Eliot, beaten and bloodied, flashed through her imagination—and her only thought was to protect him.

She yanked the rope.

It ripped free without resistance—cutting effortlessly through the tree's width.

A sixty-foot-long section of the downed log cracked and rolled onto the trail, tons of wood easing to a stop, crushing the gravel underneath.

Robert tore out of the bathroom, cell phone in one hand, gun in the other.

"What . . . ?" He looked confused at the displaced log, then back to her.

"That was me." Fiona sighed and looked at her feet, feeling once again like some dorky little kid. She then looked up at the sky. The edges were tinged yellow and orange.

"You better take me back," she said bitterly. "Grandmother will be expecting me home soon."

An extremely confused-looking Robert holstered his gun. "Grandmother . . . right."

"I'll explain about the tree on the way home." Fiona went to him, leaned against him, and they walked back down the trail.

41

DALLAS

liot would never understand girls.

As he walked home from Ringo's, Julie had started walking with him up Midway Avenue.

"I'm in Hillcrest Apartments," she explained without breaking her stride. "A few blocks past Oakwood."

Earlier, Julie had wanted to have coffee with him. He'd serenaded her and made a connection.

Why she had pulled away and said that she "couldn't do this"? What did that mean?

Eliot had been raised by women . . . you'd think he'd have some clue.

He watched her walk. Julie had her own music, one that didn't require an instrument. The curves of her pale skin, the flex of taut muscles, every liquid motion, even the downy blond hairs on her arm, seemed to sing to him.

"How'd you know I live at Oakwood?" he asked.

"Your employment application."

Great. If she had read that, then she knew that he and Fiona were weird, homeschooled shut-ins.

A hot breeze swirled about them and made Julie's dress flutter. It was the most entrancing thing he'd ever seen.

He should just ask her why she ran away at the Pink Rabbit. Was there something terrible about her family that she couldn't share? Eliot bet he could match her family—terrible secret for terrible secret, and then some.

What would be the point? She wouldn't believe him. *He* hardly believed it.

Maybe some people were just destined to be alone because of the truths they thought no one else would believe . . . when, in fact, they all had similar things to hide.

Or maybe she was still freaked out by the hundreds of crows that had been outside the Pink Rabbit, watching them, cawing at Eliot, what he thought was a cry for more music.

He wasn't sure where those birds had come from. He hadn't exactly been scared of them, but hadn't felt entirely comfortable with two hundred solid black eyes staring at him, either. When Eliot had shooed them away, however, they had taken to the air—a tornado of feathers and caws.

Eliot stopped on the sidewalk. Julie kept walking for a few paces, halted, and looked back at him.

"What?" she asked.

"Whatever I did at the café . . . I just wanted to apologize."

Julie opened her mouth—closed it. She looked as if she might cry again, but then her brow crinkled. "Forget it." She started walking.

She stopped, whirled about, and came back to him. "The problem is you're too nice," she said, sticking her face into his. Her eyes were narrow slits of pure hatred. "Has anyone ever told you that?"

"I was just trying to help," he whispered. "If it bothered you, I'm sorry. I'll just—"

The expression in Julie's blue eyes changed, and something entirely different smoldered within. Something primal.

She touched her lips to his. Her flesh was hot.

His arms found her waist and drew her close. This seemed as instinctive as his heart beating or inhaling his next breath.

His bewilderment dissolved. Everything was liquid and flowed between them. This moment was all there was—him and her—nothing else in the entire universe.

And while he wasn't sure exactly *why* this was happening or if he would *ever* understand girls in a million years—he knew it was best not to ask any stupid questions.

Julie pulled away. She smiled and bit her lower lip.

He would've done anything to continue that kiss, but he relaxed, worried that if he pushed too hard, he might scare her off.

"Like I said," Julie purred. "You're too nice."

She started to move closer—but hesitated and quickly turned her head, listening.

Eliot heard something as well: a rumble that echoed down Midway Avenue.

Julie disentangled herself from him.

A motorcycle flashed around the corner. It was a blur of black metal and curling exhaust that skidded to a halt next to them.

There were two riders. The one on back dismounted and removed her helmet. Fiona shook out her hair, looking like a wild creature. Dark circles were under her eyes. But it *was* Fiona. She had her book bag bulging with the box of chocolates she thought was so hidden, and she still wore her silly rubber-band bracelet.

Fiona shot Julie an annoyed glance, then softened. "Sorry. I didn't know how late it was getting."

"It's cool, honey." Julie blushed but did not look away. "There were only a few customers. Nothing Linda and I couldn't handle."

Fiona looked at Eliot. She was curious, but didn't ask what Julie was doing walking him home . . . or why they both looked so obviously guilty.

"I'm Robert," Robert said to Julie. He tipped his skullcap helmet.

"Julie Marks." She gave him a charming half curtsy.

Something weird passed between Robert and Julie—a tension that made the air itchy with static. Or maybe Eliot just imagined that.

Still, the way they held each other's gaze a bit longer than normal seemed odd to him. As if they knew one another, or more accurately, they *thought* they should know each other.

"We have to get home," Eliot said, "but maybe you both want to come up with us?"

Robert straightened. "No," he said quickly. "I mean thanks, but Mr. Mimes probably needs me."

Of course. Eliot had (as impossible as it seemed) actually forgotten about Grandmother and her effect on their "houseguests."

Julie shook her head so vigorously that a mass of her half-tangled curls fell into her face. She blew them off her forehead. "I have to get home. I've got family stuff, too. Maybe next time?"

She smiled, and it seemed to hold more light and promise than sunshine. She nodded at Eliot, Fiona, then her smile faded as she nodded to Robert. "You'll all excuse me?" She trod past them down Midway Avenue.

"I'll be in touch." Robert moved toward Fiona, but then saw Eliot . . . and just smiled at her. Fiona smiled, too, and gave him a little wave. He revved his bike and peeled out the opposite way down Midway.

In a moment both Robert and Julie were gone. Eliot and Fiona stood alone on the sidewalk—walking home as usual from Ringo's as if this had been another boring day.

"So," Eliot asked, "good ride?"

Fiona shrugged. "Sure, I guess. Hard day at work?" It was a fair question, but the way she asked it was laced with venom.

"What do you have against Julie?" Eliot asked. "She's nice to you."

Fiona started walking. "Nice to you, too. Don't you think it's odd her showing up just like Uncle Henry and the others have?"

"So you think she's—what? Like a cousin?"

Fiona shook her head. "No, just something. I get a funny feeling when I look at her."

The real problem was that Fiona was jealous. Like when Louis had given him the violin. She hadn't liked that, either.

And he hadn't said *one* word about her stupid chocolates. Even now, she dipped into her pack and grabbed another one of the things—popped it into her mouth while trying to keep it hidden.

"Shouldn't you be rolling those on the ground, *Scarabaeus sacer*?"

Scarabaeus was the scientific name for the scarab, or the dung beetle, which rolled its excremental prizes along the ground to their nests.

Fiona reddened, but couldn't immediately reply as she had to chew the gooey confection.

Eliot knew she knew that word. No points in vocabulary insult for that one. But seeing her struggle and not get any enjoyment from the chocolate was almost as good as winning.

On Midway Avenue the peach trees in their planters shuddered in the warm breeze. Blossoms fell, took to the air, and it looked as if it were snowing in the hot California afternoon.

That shouldn't be, though.

Those peach trees had already flowered months ago, and their tiny, rotten fruit had been spattered on the street like abstract art.

Fiona finally managed to swallow. "I see you're intimately familiar with the food source of *Scarabaeus,* being an ampulla varices.[45]

Eliot knew what she meant, but his mind was no longer in the game. Something weird was happening on Midway Avenue.

---

45. *Ampulla* refers to a dilated tubular (anatomical) structure, and *varice* refers to a distended submucosal vein. In this context, a hemorrhoid.—Editor.

"Did they replace these trees?" he asked.

Fiona stared ahead, but not at the trees. Her attention riveted on the old Volkswagen Beetle parked in front of their apartment.

It didn't belong there. Eliot knew every battered car that parked on Midway. It really stuck out because of the rainbow tie-dye paint that swirled into a peace sign on the hood. A bumper sticker proclaimed LOVE YOUR MOTHER and had a picture of the planet Earth.

"Uncle Henry's?" Fiona whispered.

They looked at each other—then raced for the side door of the apartment building. Maybe the second trial had started. Or maybe Grandmother had spoken to the Council and got them to bend on the next two tests.

Either way, Eliot would be the first one upstairs.

He pushed past Fiona. He wasn't faster, but her book bag got hung up on the railing. Once ahead, he didn't let her pass—blocking her way with his elbows.

He shouldn't have done it. It was a dirty trick. But as he tore down the hallway and for once got to their door first, he felt good.

Fiona caught up an instant later.

They took a moment to straighten their clothing, and Fiona slipped her rubber-band bracelet into her pocket.

Eliot reached for the doorknob, but halted. Someone was laughing inside.

Laughter wasn't something they heard in their home. This was a woman's laugh, but not from Grandmother or Cee (not that Eliot had ever actually heard Grandmother even chuckle). This laugh was full of life.

"That's not Uncle Henry." Fiona nodded at the door. "Go already."

He pursed his lips and opened the door.

Eliot blinked at the sunlight streaming through the dining room window. Three figures sat at the table. It was just like yesterday when Robert had been there, Grandmother on one end, Cee sitting on the other . . . but this time, sitting in between them was a girl.

She looked perfectly at ease. In fact, she sat close to Grandmother, her hand resting next to hers. If anything, Grandmother was the one who looked uncomfortable.

The girl was older than Julie, but not by much. She was maybe eighteen. Her hair was honey blond and the same color as the intense sunlight.

Grandmother wore her customary mask of stone and regarded them in the doorway.

"Children, come in," Grandmother said. "I would like to introduce your aunt Claudia."

The girl perked up and smiled at them. Her features were like Aunt Lucia's or Grandmother's: smooth skin, wide eyes, and the high, expressive forehead. Only on this girl they were full of animation, whereas on Grandmother they had solidified.

She crossed the room. She wore a tight tie-dyed blouse, a miniskirt, and slender sandals.

"Call me Dallas." Her voice was musical and she had an accent: Italian or Russian, something exotic. "'Aunt Claudia' is so"—she rolled her eyes— "ancient, you know?"

Dallas took their hands and drew them into an awkward embrace. She smelled of peach blossoms.

She stepped back and looked them over. She ran a hand through Fiona's hair. "Lovely. You and I have to talk later. Girl stuff, okay?"

Fiona, usually adverse to anyone touching her, grinned. "That would be great."

"And dashing Eliot!" Dallas placed one hand over her chest. "I'm sure all the ladies chase you. So many hearts you're going to break."

Eliot found himself smiling, too.

As when he'd first met Uncle Henry, something instinctively told Eliot that he could trust her with his innermost secrets, but also that given a good reason, she could be a formidable enemy.

"Come." Dallas dragged them toward the table. "So many things to show you." She looked about the apartment. "Don't you have a couch, Audrey? Something comfortable?"

Grandmother's frown deepened. "We have what we have. If you do not like the accommodations, you are free to leave."

"Are you really our aunt?" Fiona asked. "It's hard to get a straight answer from anyone in this family. You were actually our mother's sister?"

Dallas laughed again, and it sent goose bumps down Eliot's arms.

"Perfectly put. The family is not known for answers, only questions. But, yes, I am your mother's youngest sister. Shall I tell you about her?"

How old was she? She looked young, but if Robert had told them the truth, then these people didn't age normally. Dallas could be eighteen or one hundred and eighteen.

"The children have no time for such fairy tales," Grandmother said.

The perpetual smirk on Dallas's face faded. "As you wish, 'Grandma.' Business first, it shall be."

She took Eliot and Fiona by the hand and beckoned them to sit on the floor in the square of sunlight. "I'm going to teach you something," she whispered conspiratorially. "It might help you pass your trials."

"Direct help is forbidden," Grandmother said, half rising from her chair.

"I think it's up to the Council to decide that," Dallas told her. "And since I'm a member of the Council and you're not—*shush*."

Grandmother sat, but looked extremely irritated.

"Besides," Dallas said, "I'm just showing them what they should already know. If they *are* my sister's children, this is as much a part of them as their bones or blood."

"Semantics," Grandmother grumbled.

Dallas ignored her and turned back to Fiona and Eliot. "This is just a simple, silly trick, but comes in handy more times than you'd think."

She pulled the thread from the frayed hem of her miniskirt.

"What are you going to do with that?" Fiona asked, looking a little scared.

Dallas twined the thread about her pinkies. "Oh, it's nothing. Just the future."

Eliot felt movement in his stomach as he gazed at the string—a vibration that set his teeth on edge.

Dallas patted his hand. "Relax," she cooed. "This is like sleight of hand. Stage magic. Like any fortune-telling it's just a way to talk with a primitive part of your brain that never learned how to speak."

Eliot tried to relax, but so many strange things had happened, he wasn't sure if this string would turn into a snake, a balloon animal, or become a lit stick of dynamite.

"Look closely," Dallas urged. "Sink into the groove. . . ."

Eliot and Fiona leaned in closer. The string was white cotton, tiny threads curled about one another . . . and it caught and held the sunlight, looking like gold and rippling water.

Eliot focused on this thread—only this thread—and the rest of the apartment fell in the shadows.

From someplace distant he heard Dallas whisper, "Look along its length now. From here to there. Now to later."

Eliot's gaze moved down the string. The single thread became part of a weave, a web that glistened with silver and rusty iron the color of blood.

He imagined that he ran a finger over these and felt ice and sandpaper, tasted sea salt and kiwifruit, and the smoky sharpness of whiskey.

He tried to see where this string ultimately led. It was far longer now than the arm's length Dallas had pulled from her skirt. In fact, it stretched as far as he could see—past the walls of their apartment, past the horizon, past the sun . . . to the stars.

Eliot blinked and found himself sitting back on the apartment floor, slightly dizzy.

Fiona blinked as well, looking intrigued.

"Sometimes you see things," Dallas explained. "Other times, you might sense things: a noise, a glimpse, a taste." She shrugged. "Some in the family have a talent for it. Others, like me, just muddle along."

"It's cool," Eliot breathed.

"I'm glad you think so." Dallas's catlike eyes widened. "Because now it's your turn."

"You go too far," Grandmother said.

Cee worried her hands over one another. "Oh," she whispered. "I'll have to fix their clothes."

Dallas made a disgusted sound deep in her throat. "These clothes need to be *burned* . . . but we'll get to that soon enough. Maybe a shopping trip in Paris?" She patted Fiona on her knee.

"If you're going to do it," Grandmother said, "then best get it done quickly before the sun sets."

"So right." Dallas sobered. She pulled Eliot's arm straight and found a loose thread in the cuff of his shirt. She ripped out a long string, which she handed to him.

Dallas found a similar loose thread from Fiona's khaki pants.

"Hold them taut," Dallas instructed. "And like you did before, sink into the groove. Wait for the sensations to come to you."

Eliot held his string and let his eyes wander its length.

As the sun set, his thread shimmered silver and twisted with deepening shadows. Other colors appeared: bronze and cast-iron black that braided and frayed and branched.

He felt them vibrating and wanted to touch them, play them like his violin . . . but he followed Dallas's instructions and just watched.

He heard a song from the strings. Not like his violin. It was a funeral dirge of church bells.

And even though he wasn't touching them, he felt glass shattering and fire.

He tasted blood and smelled brimstone.

Something terrible was going to happen . . . soon.

He dared look as far as he could. The threads wove back and forth into a confusing tangle that grew more confused the farther he focused.

Eliot wasn't sure what any of it meant, but he did know it scared him.

He blinked and was back again in the apartment. The string he held between his fingers was just string again.

He wanted to explain what he saw, tell Dallas and Fiona how weird it was, but the words died in his throat.

Fiona sat next to him. Her thread wasn't the arm's length that Dallas had originally handed to her. It was a nub that extended just past her fingertips.

"It's so cold," Fiona whispered.

Dallas scrutinized the string. All joy on her face vanished and she said, "That's because you're going to die."

42

ONE DAY TO LIVE

Fiona knew something was wrong the instant she touched the thread.

At first she had been worried that she'd focus on it the way Uncle Aaron had showed her—accidentally cut with it. But it hadn't been like that. The way Dallas had her focus wasn't really focusing at all; it was more like pressing your face to a blurry window trying to get a better look outside.

Her string went slack. It shrank as she watched.

Fiona imagined warm liquid pulsing between her fingers . . . then it congealed and cooled.

It was blood. Her blood.

Blood that was going to be shed soon.

"I'm sorry," Dallas whispered so softly that only Fiona could hear. "A day. Maybe a little longer. That's what it says you have left."

Fiona glanced up. Everyone was giving her a weird look.

"I don't get it. A day until what?"

But she knew. The ticks and tocks left in her life were crystal clear along the string, measured out . . . and then they stopped.

"The strings have been wrong before," Dallas said, and looked back to Grandmother, "at least once or twice."

Fiona examined the thread. It was again just a piece of string. No blood. No impending portents of doom. And yet, she had the taste of ashes in her mouth. She dropped it and watched it spiral to the floor.

One day? Maybe a little longer? That was nothing. And now when everything was supposed to change—a new family, Robert—things Fiona had only dreamed about her entire life.

How could they let this happen? Grandmother and Cee stared back at her helpless. They didn't care. They could've done something to stop this . . . at least try.

And Dallas? Fiona wished she had never met her.

Only one thing could make any of this better.

Fiona ran to her room. She slammed the door and locked it.

She threw down her book bag, reached inside, and dug out a fistful of truffles. She jammed them all into her mouth. Seven or eight: dark and white and milk chocolate, toffee, lemon, and vanilla, hazelnut and caramel.

She chewed and chewed and half choked swallowing it.

Her pulse pounded and her blood roared like a tide—but the panic and anger churning inside didn't dull.

She hammered her fists on her desk in one last futile gesture, then fell still.

Was this how she wanted to spend her last day? Throwing temper tantrums and pigging out on chocolates?

She heard a knock—not on her door, but on the apartment's front door. There were footsteps and new voices in the dining room.

After a moment, there was a gentle knock at her door.

"Fiona," Eliot whispered. "It's me. Are you okay?"

That was a titanically stupid question, but Eliot's heart was in the right place.

She tried to answer, but her throat was too parched from the chocolates.

"Robert is here," Eliot said. "The Council has started our next trial."

If the thread was right, if she only had a day or two left, then she'd use them. Maybe she'd live, maybe not, but she had to help her brother make it through this.

Fiona marched to her door—halted, then went back and grabbed her book bag.

There was one thing she had to do first, though.

She opened her bedroom door, walked down the hall and through the dining room—ignoring everyone there, even Robert—and marched straight into the kitchen.

She got out the heart-shaped box . . . the still *full* heart-shaped box. It was the best gift she had ever received.

Fiona opened the trash chute, but froze, unable to move the box any closer.

How could she throw them away? They made her feel *so* good.

Those feelings weren't real, though. If she only had a day left, she wanted to live it as herself, not hopped up on sugar and chocolate-triggered endorphins. She wanted to be Fiona Post . . . whatever that was . . . shy and awkward . . . scared . . . but herself.

She forced her hand to move the box past the lip of the trash chute.

Fiona then let go.

She watched her red satin heart fall . . . and vanish into the dark.

THE SECOND HEROIC TRIAL

43

TEST OF DEATH

Eliot had never seen so many people in their dining room—not even when the pipes had busted, flooding the second floor.

Robert stood at the table flanked by Grandmother and Aunt Dallas. He looked scared but resolute—as if telling them about a test that could kill them were all in a day's work.

Fiona emerged from the kitchen, looking pale, tears staining her cheeks.

Eliot wanted to tell her it was all going to be okay. That he didn't believe in Aunt Dallas's predictions, and neither should she. That they would deal with this test, just as they had with Souhk.

Before he could speak, though, Robert cleared his throat. "Sorry about the short notice. The Council wanted it that way."

"I should not be here for this." Dallas went to Fiona, took her hands, and kissed them. "My blessing upon you, child."

Dallas turned to Eliot and drew him aside. "My blessing upon you as well, noble born."

She kissed his forehead.

It felt like a brand and made his brain flash with kaleidoscopic colors. Eliot wanted to scream, but all he managed was a startled gasp.

Aunt Dallas withdrew and the sensations vanished. She went to Grandmother and they embraced. Grandmother squeezed her with genuine affection, which surprised Eliot almost as much as the kiss.

Dallas then moved to the door, but lingered near Robert. "I was not here," she whispered to him. "Tell not even the moon if it asks." Her tone was light and lyrical, but also managed to convey a threat.

Robert swallowed. "Yes, ma'am."

Fiona stiffened and her eyes narrowed at this exchange, and she watched with an intensity Eliot had never before seen in his sister.

Dallas left and closed the door; the light from the sunset seemed to depart with her.

Cee turned on the dull, yellowed overhead lamp.

Robert looked to Grandmother, who gave him a nod to proceed. "The Council wants someone's blood spilled this time. Mr. Mimes calls it *l'essai de la mort*."

"That means 'the test of death,'" Fiona whispered to Eliot.

Eliot shifted from foot to foot. "We'll just outsmart them like last time."

"It may not be that easy," Robert said. "There's an abandoned carnival near Mount Diablo State Park. A crazy guy has kidnapped a little girl, and he's going to kill her at midnight if you don't rescue her."

Eliot gripped the edge of the table. "What are you talking about? What does some girl have to do with us? Why involve her?"

Fiona moved to Eliot's side, leveling her intensity at Robert as well. "Is this for real?"

Robert stepped back from them and held up his hands. "It's real—very real for that kid. And for you."

Grandmother nodded. "It would not be the first time the Council has involved innocents."

Eliot knew that he and Fiona were being treated as disposable pieces on the Council's chessboard, but how would they treat people not even related? A shudder crawled down his spine.

The clock in the hallway chimed.

"Midnight in six hours," Eliot noted.

"Shouldn't we call the police?" Fiona protested. "No test is worth someone getting killed over. Maybe *that's* the test: to see if we do the right thing."

Cee patted her arm. "The morals of the family, my dove, are entirely different than what you and I think of as 'right and wrong.'"

How could that be? All their lives Grandmother and Cee had taught Eliot and Fiona right from wrong. Did those lessons mean nothing now?

"Calling the police won't help," Robert said. "Even if they found him before midnight, the crazy guy has radio scanners. He'd know they were coming. He'd finish and be gone before they could stop him."

This was horrible. The stakes of the first test had been dire: Eliot's and Fiona's lives. But this . . . the Council involving a little girl. It wasn't fair.

"I hate them," Fiona whispered.

Eliot wondered if Aunt Dallas knew about this. Was that why she'd left so fast?

"Let's just try and figure out this trial," he told Fiona. "We'll worry about the Council later."

Fiona nodded. "So who is this 'crazy guy'?"

"It's the classic urban legend." Robert pantomimed a downward slashing motion. "Insane guy with a big knife. Or in this case, I think he burns things."

Eliot and Fiona both shook their heads, not getting Robert's "classic" reference.

"It's in every slasher-summer-movie, group-of-teenagers-gets-killed-off-one-by-one film that's ever been," Robert said. "There's a guy who's unkillable? Goes on a rampage?"[46]

Eliot looked for a pad and pen to take notes. "What else?"

"How do the teenagers in these movies win?" Fiona asked.

Robert shrugged apologetically. "I've told you everything the Council gave me orders to."

"We understand," Grandmother said in a chilly tone.

Robert rummaged through his motorcycle saddlebag and pulled out a tiny laptop computer. He set it on the table. "I did some digging around, just for my own curiosity. Guess if I *accidentally* left this here, no one would notice. There's probably nothing that would help you anyway."

Robert held Eliot's gaze a moment, then looked meaningfully at Fiona. He nodded to Cee and then Grandmother. "Ma'am, I can wait if you need a ride."

Grandmother tapped the laptop with one finger, thinking. "Thank you, Mr. Farmington." Her tone had slightly defrosted. "I think you've done enough for us this evening. You may go."

Robert glanced one last time at Fiona and left.

"A computer?" Cee crept closer, reaching out but not touching it. "It violates the household rules . . . thirty-four, fifty-five, and ninety-nine."

---

46. A subgenre of horror cinema where an insane killer relentlessly pursues a series of young adults. The killer can withstand being shot, stabbed, etc., and continues to stalk his would-be victims. Decried by film critics, these films, others note, are a metaphor for uncontrollable evil rather than a commentary on human morals and are comparable to (the equally graphic) late medieval fairy tales. The origin of the genre is generally recognized as Alfred Hitchcock's 1960 film, *Psycho*. *Gods of the First and Twenty-first Century, Volume 6: Modern Myths*, 8th ed. (Zypheron Press Ltd.).

Grandmother stared at the carbon-fiber case. "Indeed it does, but perhaps this once." She lifted the lid, turned it on, but halted at the start-up screen.

Eliot and Fiona moved closer.

The screen glowed with a redwood forest scene of such depth and color it looked real. A tiny box with PASSWORD blinked in the center.

Fiona stared at the familiar trees and then elbowed Eliot aside. "I think I know the password."

She typed in *Sequoia*.

The computer beeped. Colorful icons appeared. Each had labels: DIABLO STATE PARK TOPOLOGICAL MAP, PATIENT RECORD 0478, and CALIFORNIA HIGHWAY PATROL INCIDENT REPORT DF-4829.

Eliot noted a cluster of musical notes in the corner, and an antenna symbol broadcasting waves.

Robert's computer connected to the outside world. It had to have music, movies, people to chat with—everything. Eliot would give anything for five minutes alone with the thing.

He shook his head and remembered what was happening. "Try the police report first," he told Fiona.

Fiona's hands froze over the keyboard. "How do you work it?"

Grandmother looked to Cee, and she shook her head.

How stupid could they all be? Robert had literally handed them everything they'd need to know about the upcoming trial—had probably risked his life doing so—but none of them knew how to work a computer?

"Let me try," Eliot said.

Fiona's jaw clenched in annoyance. She nonetheless turned the computer toward him.

Eliot smoothed his fingers over the keys, getting the feel of the thing, but not pressing any of them. Below the keys was a smooth rectangle. He brushed his thumb over it and an arrow appeared on-screen that mirrored his motion. He swished it in a wide arc, delighted.

As with the violin and the guitar, Eliot got a sense of this instrument just by touching it . . . not mastery by any stretch of the imagination, just a tickle in the back of his head.

He zipped the cursor to the police file and double-tapped it as he would have fingered two notes on his violin.

A report opened. There was a mug shot of a man. He was five foot six, had brown hair, brown eyes—nothing out of the ordinary—until Eliot saw the scars on one side of his face and the burns that had liquefied his left ear.

"Perry Millhouse," Fiona read over his shoulder. "Multiple arsons, felony endangerment, first-degree murder . . . sixteen counts."

Millhouse had locked the doors to a school, then set it on fire. Eliot felt sick as he read this. Millhouse had been caught, tried, and sentenced to death. On appeal he was found mentally unfit and the ruling was overturned. He was remanded to a state facility for the criminally insane.

Eliot tabbed ahead to another police report. This one detailed how Millhouse and two inmates torched the hospital, killed two guards, and escaped. They were tracked to the foothills near Diablo State Park. Two of the escaped inmates were shot—but Millhouse eluded capture and took refuge in a cabin.

Before the police could get him, he set fire to it . . . while he was inside.

The police watched him burn.

"If he's dead already," Fiona asked, "then who has the little girl?"

Grandmother scanned the report over their shoulders. Her expression was inscrutable as usual, but Eliot thought he detected a shadow of what? Recognition?

"There is one more police file," she told him.

He opened it.

This report was of an ongoing investigation. Last year three kids had disappeared near Diablo State Park. The last, Amanda Lane, had gone missing yesterday.

There was a picture of her. She had just lost her baby front teeth, and she grinned proudly in the photograph.

Fiona whispered, "It's like the pictures we had taken. That police program at the supermarket, remember?"

Eliot touched Amanda's picture with his fingertip. "Yeah."

He glanced back at the clock. "We need to get going. We should have taken Robert's offer for a ride."

"I have a car," Grandmother said. "I will get you there just as fast."

Eliot looked at Fiona, puzzled. Grandmother had a car? She could drive? She always walked or, in extreme cases, took the bus.

"Okay, great." Eliot gathered up his courage and told her, "We'll need to get some stuff, though. Gear we used in the sewer. It'll just take a minute."

Grandmother stared at him a moment, then said, "Hurry. I will meet you out front."

"Should I pack some food?" Cee asked. "I can be ready to go in moments."

Grandmother regarded her with narrowed eyes. "You know there will barely be room for the three of us in my car, Cecilia."

Cee dropped her head, disappointed.

Eliot turned to Fiona. "Basement?" he asked her, and grabbed his backpack.

They raced downstairs—not competing to see who would be first—all that childish stuff was gone, replaced by a wrenching anticipation of what might happen tonight.

L'essai de la mort. The test of death.

Eliot hoped Uncle Henry was wrong about that.

44

THE ONE THING THAT MADE HER STRONG

Fiona wrapped her handkerchief over her face. The dust in the basement made her gag. She retrieved her Westley-Richards shotgun and a box of shells from a pile of yellowing newspapers.

The weight of the weapon reassured her. She ought to permanently keep it in her book bag with all the weird things happening.

Did she look like a criminal? Shotgun in hand and mask on her face. Or did she look a little like Robert? A rebel.

In the far corner of the basement, Eliot plunked his violin, tuning it. She waved her flashlight at him. He was so deep in concentration he didn't notice.

Motes of dust jumped into mosaic patterns with his every note.

She marveled at this display . . . and felt a twang of what? Jealousy? Maybe.

He'd taken to the violin as if he'd been born with the thing in his hands. He had tamed rats, quelled Souhk, and now apparently made even the air dance. What else could he do?

And what could she do? Regurgitate facts and figures like some living encyclopedia? Bus tables? What good was that when they had to face an insane arsonist tonight?

She could cut.

Fiona pulled on and snapped her rubber-band bracelet. It stung her wrist. She halted, horrified, and examined her hand.

She had to be careful. If she had been in the wrong frame of mind when she did that, she might have severed her hand . . . and bled to death.

So that was her talent? Destroyer of things? Cutter? Was that a gift or a curse?

She stretched the rubber band to a taut line and shoved it at a nearby garden statue. It sliced through the concrete cupid as if it weren't there.

The cherub's head thudded to the floor, its childlike face staring back at her.

That felt good.

If she put her mind to it, she'd be able to cut through anything. No one would be able to stop her. Not even imposing Uncle Aaron. Not even Grandmother.

That thought stopped her cold.

No, she'd never be able to cut anything *alive*.

She knelt and touched the cherub's face. "Sorry," she whispered to it.

Her stomach rumbled and her blood ran cold. She needed to eat.

She tasted chocolate on her lips, but her truffles were long gone. Hadn't she decided she wouldn't rely on them? She'd just need more and more to get the same sugar rush.

Eliot stopped tuning his violin and turned to her. "I'm ready."

"Go ahead. I'll be right up."

"You okay?"

"Sure." Fiona stood slowly. "No problems. I just need a second."

Eliot nodded. "I'll tell Grandmother you're coming." He hesitated as if he wanted to say more, as if he could sense that she was in trouble. But then he turned and ran up the stairs, his flashlight waving crazily through the dark.

One day left to live—how could that possibly be right? Aunt Dallas thought it was true, though. And when Fiona concentrated on what she had seen and felt prophesied from the thread . . . she knew it was true, too.

She really needed a truffle: one taste of chocolate cream, butter toffee, cherry cordial . . . just one.

And why not? Why be just plain old Fiona Post? Look-at-the-ground, never-speak-up-for-herself Fiona Post. Wasn't a little girl's life at stake tonight? Not to mention hers and Eliot's.

Shouldn't she be doing *everything* in her power to be the best she could?

When it came right down to it, wasn't she being selfish to throw away the *one* thing that made her strong?

And if she only had a day left . . . why deny herself any of life's pleasures?

She took a deep breath. She knew what she had to do.

Fiona plodded upstairs and outside into the alley—running to the Dumpster where the building's trash chute ended.

She lifted the lid and clambered into the container.

She gagged from the smell: diapers and barbecue, seaweed and a hint of gasoline. She reeled back from the odors and almost fell out.

She pressed her handkerchief over her nose and panned her flashlight back and forth.

A rat blinked back at her, unafraid, then went back to devouring a moldy jelly doughnut.

What was she doing? Rummaging through a Dumpster at night? Looking for something she wasn't entirely sure was good for her? Holding up the second trial . . .

But she couldn't stop, either.

Her beam landed on a blood-red heart. It was covered with fast-food wrappers. She grabbed the box, brushed off grease and mayonnaise, and cradled it to her chest. She firmly secured the lid and tucked it into her book bag.

Perfect.

She climbed down and brushed herself off.

A shadow glided to the mouth of the alley and honked twice.

She sprinted to Grandmother's car—ready now to face death.

45

MADHOUSE

Eliot sat jammed in next to Fiona as Grandmother raced down the street. Her car (which neither he nor Fiona had *ever* seen) was a Jaguar XKSS. The midnight blue marvel was mostly a curve of aerodynamic hood that stretched out in front of the cockpit. Eliot wondered how Grandmother saw the road at all. There were only two leather seats, and no backseat.

Where were they going to put the little girl when they rescued her? Of course, he wasn't certain they'd even get that far tonight.

As they rounded a curve, Eliot slid into his sister. Fiona elbowed him back.

She smelled of eggs and grease. What had Fiona done in the few minutes he had left her alone?

"Do you know Perry Millhouse?" he asked Grandmother.

Grandmother drove in silence. They bounced and slung up and around the rolling foothills. The twilight made eerie silhouettes of the black oaks dotting the landscape. Shadows stretched and thinned and crowded out the light.

"I knew the man before he lost his mind," Grandmother finally replied. "Now he is an animal. No more."

"But why would he do such terrible things?" Fiona asked. "Kill people? Burn buildings? Kidnap a little girl?"

"Do not think of that." Grandmother flicked off the headlights. The outline of the road faded to a barely visible edge. "Think only of your task: find the girl and get out. Do not cross his path if you can help it."

"Yeah, no problem," Eliot whispered.

"If you do," Grandmother said, "do not hesitate to act. He will destroy you if you let him."

Eliot glanced at Fiona. She looked as if she might throw up. He swallowed, suddenly unsettled, too.

Grandmother turned onto a dirt road. A sign lit with a dim forty-watt bulb read:

HALEY'S TREASURES
Carnival, Fun House, and Entertainment Resale Antiques!
(inquire at office)
(OPEN 9AM to DUSK)

"If Millhouse operates anywhere near Diablo State Park," Grandmother whispered, "it is here. He enjoys such places."

In the distance loomed the shapes of cargo trailers and carnival rides that in the gloom looked like metal dinosaurs.

Grandmother cut the Jaguar's engine, shifted into neutral, and rolled toward the chain-link fence.

"But what *is* Millhouse?" Eliot whispered. "Part of the family? Something like Souhk? Just a crazy guy?"

"None of those," Grandmother said. "He took something, and it changed him."

"What?" Fiona asked. "And what did it change him into?"

Grandmother frowned, thinking, then told her, "He took some fire. That is all you need to know right now."

Eliot didn't understand. Fire? Why did someone need to *steal* fire? You just struck a match or turned on the stove and you had fire.

The car stopped.

Eliot knew he had to get out and save that little girl's life, but he felt stuck to the leather. He was scared.

Grandmother turned to him. Her hand lifted off the wheel as if to reach out to comfort him, but then it dropped back.

"I have raised you both to be polite, gentle, and thoughtful," Grandmother whispered. "But you cannot be those things. Tonight you may have to kill."

Eliot's skin crept with gooseflesh.

Fiona shook her head.

"The Council has declared this a test of blood," Grandmother said, trying to sound conciliatory. "They will have engineered it so there will be no choice: someone's life will be taken. So grasp the initiative, and if it comes to it, make sure the life taken is *not* yours."

"There has to be another way than killing," Fiona whispered.

Eliot knew they would find a way. They did it with Souhk. They could do it here, tonight . . . somehow.

Grandmother considered them in the dark. "Stay to the shadows."

Fiona opened the door. "Come on." She grabbed Eliot's hand.

Normally this would have violated their brother-sister-never-touch-me agreement, which had been in place since they had been toilet trained. But tonight, Eliot let her.

"I shall be here," Grandmother said from the dark. "Waiting."

Eliot waved to Grandmother, unsure if she saw.

Fiona marched ahead, leading him to the fence. There was a rustle, then she pulled apart a portion that had apparently already been cut.

Four lamps atop telephone poles flickered to life. A sickly glow washed over the lot.

The scrapyard was set up like a real carnival, albeit a rotten, never-used-in-the-last-thirty-years carnival. Beyond this were cargo trailers stacked precariously, and along the far fence stood behemoth thrill rides—the Zipper, the Whiplash, Avalanche, Spinout—all rusting and long dead.

The lights overhead seemed bright, but by the time the illumination filtered to the ground, shadows pooled everywhere.

Eliot and Fiona wandered inside and kept to the darkness.

They paused by a merry-go-round with brass calliope tubes sprouting from its center. Snarling horses with chipped and fading paint chased one another. They gave Eliot the creeps.

"What do you think Robert meant by 'slasher' movies?" Eliot whispered. "You think Millhouse has fire *and* knives?"

Fiona shrugged.

Had the Council known they'd never seen a movie before? That to understand urban myths, you probably had to have contact with the world? By keeping them "safe" and isolated, Grandmother might have cut them off from the very information they needed to survive.

"He said something about kids dying at summer camp," Fiona said. "I didn't get that reference. Maybe it's some sort of fairy tale meant to scare people."

Eliot nodded and wondered how the people in those "slasher" movies survived.

They came to a lane of gaming booths. There were shooting galleries, baseball pitches, plastic clowns with open mouths and squirt guns, rope ladders, and beer-bottle ring tosses.

"So what's the plan?"

"I don't know." Fiona shot Eliot an irritated glance. "Just keep your eyes open and stop talking so much."

"Those trailers in the back," Eliot whispered. "I bet that's where Amanda is. You could lock someone up in there."

"Or the sales office." Fiona looked around, uncertain where exactly that might be. She reached into her book bag and popped a chocolate into her mouth.

"You're eating those things now? Are you crazy?"

Fiona's face bunched and she looked unsure. "Yeah," she muttered around a mouthful. "It helps me." She threw up her hands, exasperated. "Okay . . . let's check the trailers."

They turned to backtrack through the gaming lanes—but halted. A glow flickered to life thirty paces away, blocking their path.

It was a tiny flame, but so intense that Eliot had to blink as his eyes struggled with the illumination.

The fire came from a silver lighter, polished so that it reflected the light.

Holding it was a dirty hand with torn nails.

And attached to the hand was a man in a blue-gray jumpsuit.

Fiona stepped closer to Eliot so they were elbow to elbow, hidden in the shadows.

The man brought the flame to his face and puffed a cigarette to life. He looked normal . . . at least on the right side, but he turned and Eliot got a better look.

Eliot's breath caught in his throat.

On the left side all the man's hair was gone. His face was melted. His left ear was missing, and one eye was white and blind.

It was Perry Millhouse.

"I heard you," he rasped. "I've been expecting you both. I know you're there somewhere."

Eliot saw now that in his other hand Millhouse carried a gallon milk jug. Eliot could smell the stench of gasoline.

"We have to run," Eliot whispered.

"You think after what they did to me that *you* can kill me?" Millhouse turned to his left. "You think *I* haven't tried?" He turned around and shouted, "Come out! Come out! Wherever you are!"

"If he's out here," Fiona murmured, "then the little girl . . ."

"Has to be alone," Eliot said. "Let's go."

"Wait." Fiona pulled out her shotgun.

Millhouse released a great sigh. "Okay . . . so we do this the easy way. That can be fun, too."

He pocketed his lighter, reached up, and wrenched an old-fashioned two-pronged electrical switch. Sparks crackled as it made the connection.

The shadows vanished. The carnival lit with a thousand blazing globes that strobed and raced one another and made the faded colors pop with intensity.

Millhouse turned and spotted them. "I have fire. That means heat, children . . . and light."

In the light Eliot could see that Millhouse's coverall was unzipped. His chest and stomach were a mass of scars—not burns, but as if he had had a hundred operations, and no one had bothered to properly sew it all up.

Eliot's heart hammered, but he finally found his breath. He turned to Fiona. She was too terrified to move.

He grabbed her hand and ran, pulling her along. This broke her trance.

Hand in hand, they sprinted down the lane of carnival games.

The flashing lights made Eliot dizzy. The colors blurred together. He dropped his gaze to the straw-covered ground and kept moving.

Behind them, he heard the sloshing jug and the man wheezing—getting louder.

"Shotgun . . ."

"I can't just shoot someone," she said, half-pleading and half-panting.

Eliot risked his balance and looked over his shoulder.

Millhouse was only ten steps behind them.

"He's going to catch us! You have to."

They kept running, sprinting as fast as their legs would pump.

Millhouse sounded close enough to reach out and grab them.

Fiona suddenly stopped—whirled about, raising her shotgun.

She screamed and fired.

Twin flashes belched from the double barrels and the recoil knocked her over.

Millhouse fell backward, rolled, and skidded to a stop.

The milk jug bounced in front of Eliot—and he kicked it away, not wanting that gasoline anywhere near him.

The jug spun across the lane; its cap popped off and gasoline glugged out.

Fiona's face was frozen, horrified as she looked at the crumpled man. She dropped the smoking shotgun and got to her feet.

"I killed him," she whispered. "I didn't mean to."

"We'll call 911," Eliot said. "The police can help us find the girl." He took a step closer to Millhouse's prone form, wanting to somehow help—but afraid to touch him. "Maybe it's not too late for him, either."

Millhouse coughed and, laughing, rolled over. "It's far too late for me, junior."

A shotgun-blast pattern peppered the front his coverall, but there was no blood. Instead the tiny chest wounds erupted with jets of flame that sputtered a thick napalm fluid onto the ground . . . igniting the straw . . . then the puddle of gasoline.

Millhouse stood and then reached out to the fire. It crept toward him, licking up his left side, melting the polyester fabric of his coverall.

Flames collected in his hand, and he held it out, the fire curling and blazing and popping hypnotically.

Eliot couldn't move, too fascinated by the dancing flames to think.

Millhouse took two steps closer.

There was a whoosh and a sudden wave of heat.

The jug of gasoline had melted and released its contents; flaming liquid flowed to the baseball-toss booth and set the plywood ablaze.

The sudden noise and heat broke the trance Eliot and Fiona were in.

They ran.

Behind them, Millhouse laughed.

The lane of carnival games twisted right—and dead-ended.

Blocking their way were trailers that had been cobbled together into a single sprawling mass of glittering glass and polished steel. Over this, blazing in neon was:

MADHOUSE!!!!

It was a maze of mirrors. There was no way to get around it. No way to climb over it.

They were trapped.

Eliot turned, his heart hammering in his throat, but his hands balled into fists. He didn't stand a chance; nonetheless, he was ready to fight.

Millhouse strolled toward them, trailing fire, and grinning. He knew he had them.

Eliot spotted the shotgun—far away where Fiona had dropped it. Not that it had done much good . . . but it had slowed Millhouse down a bit.

Fiona whipped her head around. "Come on." She pointed. "Look. There!"

Out the other side of the mirror maze were stairs. A way out.

Eliot had done a thousand maze puzzles when he was a little kid. He was good at them, even the three-dimensional ones where the paths crossed over and under one another. Maybe they could lose Millhouse in the maze.

Fiona led the way, running up the stairs to the madhouse entrance.

Eliot was right behind her.

Inside, however, the walls were clear glass and perfectly reflective mirrors—as Eliot found out as he ran straight into one.

That dazed him for a second.

"Move!" Fiona shouted at him. "This way. To the left."

Eliot shook his head, clearing the minor concussion. "No, go right!"

Most mazes had a right-hand path solution. It was always best to try the obvious one first. He felt in front of him, making sure there were no more invisible barriers.

He turned.

Fiona *hadn't* followed him. Stubborn as usual. She had taken the adjacent passage.

"Turn around!" he shouted through the glass.

Millhouse thumped up the steps and stood at the maze entrance. In his hand he still clutched fire.

Eliot smelled burning hair and charring skin.

Fiona instinctively tried to move toward Eliot. She put both hands on the glass between them helplessly. "Go!" she shouted.

There was no way Eliot was leaving her.

Millhouse entered in the maze, turning down the path Eliot had taken—coming for him.

But there was no way Eliot could stay, either.

He ran.

46

TIES OF ADDICTION

Fiona watched Millhouse pause at the maze entrance. He looked at her . . . looked at Eliot, then plodded down the passage after her brother.

Eliot ran away—jackrabbit quick.

Millhouse passed Fiona in the adjacent passageway a hand span from her on the other side of the glass. His flesh burned, fell away, regrew, and reignited.

She felt the heat from his fire. She wanted to scream but found herself too frightened to even breathe.

Millhouse held up one flaming finger, grinned, and mouthed, *You're next*.

He turned and continued after Eliot.

Fiona helplessly watched. Her brother moved effortlessly through the invisible twists and turns, avoiding the dead ends in the maze.

Millhouse moved just as fast, though, as if he had the maze's solution memorized.

Fiona had to help. She reached for her shotgun, but it wasn't there. She had dropped it when she thought she had killed Millhouse. She wished she had. Wasn't killing for self-defense okay?

If only she had the shotgun now. A point-blank shot to the head would stop him . . . at least long enough for them to get out of here.

Her hand brushed against the box of chocolates. She should eat one so she'd be stronger, think clearer.

No way. She was going to waste time eating truffles? She had to get to Eliot first. They were stronger together; he'd need her to face Millhouse.

Fiona sprinted back toward the entrance. She'd get the gun and—

She ran headfirst into an invisible glass corner.

She bounced off and fell. The edges of her vision dimmed and blurred, and her body went numb. A high-pitched ringing echoed in her head . . . that faded to a dull whine.

Her vision cleared a bit and she rubbed her head. It was wet. Must be sweat . . . or had it been raining outside?

She looked at her hand. It was covered in blood.

"Oh," she said, realizing in a calm, abstract sense what she had just done. At the very least she had a concussion. Maybe a genuine skull fracture.

She pressed her palm to her hairline and felt blood ooze.

Smoke curled along the wooden floor. She saw the path Millhouse had taken over the plywood was on fire.

Her head cleared a bit.

She remembered: Perry Millhouse, the little girl they had to save by midnight, her brother in mortal danger.

Fiona stood, got dizzy, and sat back down—hard.

Her head throbbed so badly she thought it would split. Blood trickled down her forehead and into her face.

She spotted her book bag, its contents spilled. Her box of chocolates was missing its lid and the glazed contents glistened in the firelight.

Yes, that's exactly what she needed to snap out of this: a sugar boost, some courage, the willpower to get up and get that shotgun.

She crawled toward the heart-shaped box, stretching her hand for one of the milk chocolate diamonds . . . or the toffees with the candied roses on top . . . or an almond cluster.

Her mouth watered.

Some of the nuts, however, moved.

She froze, her hand almost touching.

Bugs.

Bugs were on her chocolates: crawling flies and wriggling grubs. They had to have gotten in when she tossed the box into the Dumpster. How stupid could she have been?

She *needed* them.

Fiona pulled out a red chocolate strawberry. Tiny cocoa nibs had been arranged to look like seeds . . . but it was also covered with squirming maggots.

Her tongue curled to suppress her gag reflex as she brushed them off.

Minuscule holes were burrowed into the candy. There had to be more inside. It was so gross.

But she had to eat it. For Eliot's sake. How else was she going to get back on her feet?

The flames made a nearby glass pane fracture with a loud crack.

Time was running out. She forced herself to bring the chocolate to her mouth. Something moved under her fingertips.

She pulled away. She couldn't do this.

Why didn't she have the willpower to get up on her own? Wasn't she strong enough?

She licked her lips, imagining the richness of the chocolate. She wanted it . . . even covered with maggots.

She stared at the truffle. Yes, she wanted it. She hated herself for it, too.

She was weak. The chocolates had so much power over her. It was as if she weren't eating them. It was as if they were somehow *eating her*.

She focused intently on the chocolate and saw a thread dangling from it, spider-silk fine; it undulated in unseen air currents. She tilted her head and saw that it arced to her wrist.

Was it from one of the bugs?

Upon closer inspection, she saw a microscopic dimple on her skin. It looked as if the line of silk actually penetrated her flesh there.

She tugged at the thread and felt it pull *inside* her arm.

Was this a concussion-induced hallucination? Or was it maybe one of the threads that Aunt Dallas had shown her?

Did that mean her destiny was tied to these chocolates? That she wanted them so badly they had become a part of her life?

Or did it mean that *they* had attached themselves to *her*? . . . Like a parasite.

She tugged harder on the thread. It pulled deeper and painfully inside her.

Smoke swirled about Fiona's ankles. She coughed.

She had to figure this out quick or she'd sit here going back and forth trying to decide to eat the chocolates or not . . . while her brother died, and this place burned around her.

She could do this. All she had to do was stay calm.

Fiona stared at the thread until it became the only thing she saw.

She pulled on it gently . . . drawing out the entire tangle of threads that represented her life: it was a snarl of lines and knots and snags that extended an arm's length.

Fiona traced the line from the chocolates as it entered the weave. It corkscrewed through fibers that looked like spun glass, human hair, hemp twine, and helixed about others that gleamed gold.

The fiber ultimately attached to a single fat tube—a vessel that throbbed like an artery, but instead of blood it pumped dark sludge.

What aspect of her life was this supposed to represent?

It didn't matter. She'd just cut the line from the chocolate and be rid of them once and for all.

She pulled the rubber band encircling her wrist so it was taut. She pushed this toward the tiny spider-silk fiber. It would be easy to cut.

She pressed hard.

The nearly invisible line shimmered . . . but the rubber band refused to go through.

Fiona tried again, frustrated. Nothing.

She had cut iron and steel. This was one silly thread. It should work.

Uncle Aaron had told her she'd be able to cut through anything . . . but he also said that she had to *want to* cut. That was the reason her fingers didn't amputate when she held the cutting edge.

That had to mean on some level she didn't want to cut herself free from the chocolates.

She still wanted them, even covered with maggots, and even though she could die here in the fire. She wanted more, right now. Not just one chocolate, or three, or seven—she wanted every last one of them.

Tears blurred her vision. Fiona had never before given up, but now she felt that she had to. She was strong, but her desire was stronger.

She hung her head and her gaze dropped to the tangle of threads heaped in her lap . . . the thick pulsing artery the chocolates had latched onto sat coiled on top.

She had no idea what that was, but maybe not knowing would work in her favor. Her subconscious mind wouldn't allow her to sever the line from the chocolate, but what if she severed what they had bonded to?

She pulled out a loop of the unknown tube. Inside, more gelatinous sludge pushed through. It was disgusting. Certainly she could do without *this* in her life.

But still, she'd be cutting part of herself.

What choice did she have?

She steeled herself and stretched her band—snapped it across the thing. The rubbery vessel cut through with only a buttery resistance.

Sludge poured out in pulses. It smelled of bile and blood and chocolate.

Fiona instinctively held her arm far away. A river of the stuff sloughed out from her, covering the floor, her book bag, and the heart-shaped box with thick, steaming goo.

At first she thought it was blood.

But she wasn't getting weaker—in fact, the more of the stuff that pumped out of her, the *stronger* she felt.

The flow lessened to a trickle and she stood.

She stared at the half-congealed mess at her feet. She never wanted to eat another chocolate again. In fact, if she never ate anything again, that would be fine with her, too.

She no longer felt weak and helpless—she was mad.

Whoever had given her the heart-shaped box had known what it would do to her. She promised she'd find out who had done this and get even.

But first, there were more important things to do.

Fiona turned toward the maze exit. That's where Eliot had gone. That's where Millhouse had followed as well, his path clearly marked by the trail of fire blazing over the floor.

There was no time left to make her way carefully through the maze, so she stretched out her rubber band and took three steps forward.

At the first glass barrier she snapped the rubber band.

The pane shattered into a thousand pebbles that bounced about her feet. The plastic-coated safety glass didn't cut her, but the bits that she had sliced through were razor sharp.

Slivers embedded in her arm. Droplets of blood welled. It felt like a dozen stinging wasps.

She ignored the pain; that didn't matter now. Nothing did except getting out.

Cutting as she walked, Fiona left a trail of shattered glass and severed steel frames.

She didn't look back at the chocolates, not even once, and vowed never to let anything control her like that again.

Fiona moved forward, unafraid, avoiding the spreading fire until she emerged on the far side of the maze. She hopped to the ground.

The trailers behind her were completely engulfed in flames.

Now she had to find that little girl and Eliot.

And if she had to, she'd deal with Millhouse, too.

47

FIRE SERENADE

Eliot jumped off the top of the stairs and tumbled onto straw-covered ground.

Millhouse emerged from the maze a moment later and limped down the stairs after him.

"Stay," Millhouse hissed. "I have things to tell you, kid. Things you'll *need* to know."

Eliot sprinted for the shadows, toward the cargo containers along the back fence. He wouldn't be caught by such a simple trick.

After a minute of running, Eliot stopped, caught his breath, and looked back.

Millhouse was a smoldering dot, still coming for him, but far behind— far enough so Eliot could stop and think again.

From the mirror maze flames spread to the concession stands. Would Fiona be okay? She could get out easily; she was right by the entrance . . . but then what? Would she circle around to meet him?

He wished he had a cell phone like everyone else in the world.

He couldn't wait for her. He moved at a brisk pace to the cargo contain-ers. There were at least a hundred of the trailers, stacked three high in places like building blocks. The little girl could be in any one of them or, as Fiona believed, none of them.

"Amanda?" he whispered. "Amanda Lane?"

He didn't dare yell loudly enough for her to actually hear him—that might give away his position to Millhouse. But if he didn't shout, he'd have to search each container, and that could take hours.

There had to be a quicker way.

Eliot spied a ladder and clambered on top of some containers. From this vantage, he saw several small fires flare across the lot.

Would anyone see these blazes from the road and call for help? He doubted it. On the drive up here there hadn't been any other cars.

The fear he had managed to outrun caught up with him. He had almost been trapped inside the maze, until he figured out to look at the floor, spot the glass and mirror frames that had blocked his way, and avoid them.

Millhouse had still gotten close enough to grab at him—singeing his shirt. His body shook. He stopped it, but then it started again.

He had to get a grip on himself. If Millhouse didn't find him, he'd probably go back for the little girl. Time was running out for them all.

It was unfair to put Fiona and him in mortal danger for some test, and doubly unfair to involve someone *outside* the family.

How was he going to find Amanda Lane?

Before, when he had to find Souhk in the sewers, he'd used his music. Could he use a similar trick now? There were no rats to lead him, but maybe the music could find another way.

He knelt and retrieved the violin from his pack. Resting Lady Dawn on his shoulder, he strummed her strings.

Eliot played. He started where he always did, with the simple nursery rhyme that Louis had taught him. His fingers leapt over the strings; his bowing was a natural part of him, like his heartbeat, smooth and regular.

The world faded and far away he heard the now familiar choir of children singing along:

> *Babies born in blood and pain; loved or hated, rich or lame; coos*
> *and cries and hungry smiles; not prepared for life's cruel trials.*

He closed his eyes and thought of the photo of Amanda Lane he had seen on Robert's computer. Just a kid. Missing her two front teeth—and looking darn proud about that.

More thoughts came unbidden to him: *daddy's little girl . . . growing up strong and tall . . . a silk ribbon in her dark hair*.

His music became a simpler melody, trickling along as if skipping, happy—and then Eliot felt something else.

Rough hands had grabbed her, tape wound about her wrists and ankles, and there were hot tears.

His fingers plucked pizzicato notes, dissonant, and leapt upward like sparks of fire.

He played louder and cast his song out into the yard.

He opened his eyes.

The scattered fires danced to the rhythm of his song. Electric lights pulsed; every booth and stand and ride flickered to life. A Ferris wheel lit with spokes of neon and began to turn. A roller coaster grumbled as a car clacked to the top of its rails, then plummeted to the ground with a tremendous crash. The Zipper, the Avalanche, the Gold Rusher—all moved now with creaking and screeching metal, sparks and wild gyrations. The arm of a giant octopus whirled about, detached, and smashed through the flaming mirror maze.

A spike of panic pierced Eliot. Fiona *had to* be out of that place. There was no way she would've stayed inside.

Apart from bringing the entire place to life, though, had his music worked? He rested his hand on the quivering strings of his violin.

He didn't sense anything as he had with Souhk. He hadn't expected rats to appear and show him the way to the girl . . . but something . . . anything.

Eliot then heard an echo of his song, higher in tone, and far away.

It was by the entrance: the carousel they had passed on the way in. The ride was lit and turning. From the center, its calliope piped out his song. It changed the melody, improvised, and seemed to be singing, *Here! Here I am! Come play with me.*

It was Amanda's song. He was certain. She had to be there.

Eliot packed up Lady Dawn and clambered down the container.

He ran back through the rows of blazing carnival games. He instinctively raised his hand over his face to shield him from the heat.

Beyond the crackling and popping of the fire he heard metal grinding and breaking apart. The crashing and sparking sounded like music. His music.

Eliot had done this. He hadn't actually started the fire—that was Millhouse's fault—but his music *had* somehow encouraged it to become a raging inferno.

And it seemed angry.

Where was Fiona? He wanted to call out, but he wasn't sure anymore where Millhouse was, so he kept his mouth shut and kept running.

Eliot skidded to a halt before the carousel.

It spun faster than any merry-go-round he'd ever seen; only it wasn't exactly spinning. The base was indeed turning, but that didn't account for the rapid pace of the horses.

The carousel horses ran.

He saw their legs tramp and gallop . . . just couldn't quite believe it. In a slow-motion gait, they raced one another—pink and purple and cream-colored ponies with eyes that gleamed black and mouths that foamed. As they ran and dodged the brass poles in their path, they nipped at one another, snarled, and whinnied.

Eliot blinked.

Mesmerized rats, talking crocodiles, a drive halfway across the world—those were all weird, inexplicable things.

This was a step beyond.

But he accepted it. He had to, at least for now.

The calliope continued to echo his song and the little girl's desperate call for help.

His eyes focused past the moving wall of color at the carousel's center section. That part didn't turn. There was a door there. Inside had to be the motor and the steam-powered organ . . . and he'd bet anything that's where Amanda was, too.

Eliot took three deep breaths and slowly approached the carousel. If he timed it just right, he could jump onto the spinning platform.

Horses snapped at him, then wheeled around out of sight.

Eliot stepped back.

Those animals would be another matter, however. He'd have to jump onto the carousel and dodge them as they ran past.

Fiona was better at this kind of stuff. He glanced about once more, but there was no sign of her or Millhouse.

He had to do this. But how? The instant he was up there, he'd be trampled . . . and that wouldn't help anyone.

Eliot imagined himself as the swashbuckling hero of his daydreams. He would've jumped up there, dodged and weaved—heck, he might even have jumped *onto* one of the animated horses and ridden it. He would've saved the girl, saved the day.

He swallowed, then he did what he thought was the bravest, and the most stupid, thing he'd ever done in his fifteen years.

He jumped for the carousel.

Eliot soared through the air . . . and only then realized his mistake: the carousel turned far too fast to just jump straight onto it. He should have jumped at an angle.

The instant his feet touched the wooden planks the carousel's centrifugal force wrenched his legs and flung him off.

With both hands he made a grab for a brass pole; one hand slipped; the other held—and he swung around, nearly pulling the arm from the socket, and landed.

Eliot heard thunder. He turned in time to see a silver stallion galloping straight for him.

He pulled himself close to the pole.

The beast sprayed him with spittle and froth and clipped him with a hoof, slicing open his thigh.

The pain was electric. There was blood.

Eliot heard more horses—didn't bother looking—and flattened himself to the pole and grit his teeth as three more stallions raced by on either side in a cloud of angry snorts and blurred gold paint.

Eliot saw a break in the herd and leapt to the next pole, caught it, spun around on his uncertain leg—into the path of a black charger he hadn't seen coming.

It caught him square in the chest and knocked him to the floor.

A tangle of legs and flashing hooves passed over his head, then it was gone.

Eliot rolled onto the center of the platform—where he skidded to a halt on the ledge.

He lay there a moment, panting. He smelled blood. He was pretty sure he'd just got a million splinters in his backside . . . but he'd made it.

Eliot patted his body. His backpack was gone.

He looked on the ledge nearby. Nothing.

Then he saw it pass just out of the reach on the moving part of the carousel.

The black charger ran over the pack, making it spin in place.

Lady Dawn was in there, and the mythology book, too. One hoof making contact and the violin would be crushed.

Eliot reached out—pulled back when the black horse returned—then he darted out and grabbed his pack.

He cradled it to his chest. With the greatest care, he checked inside. Inside its protective rubber boot, his violin was miraculously intact. He exhaled.

Eliot got to his knees and turned to face the door of the carousel's enclosed center section. It had a dead-bolt lock but it wasn't engaged and it
yielded to his touch.

Inside it was dark, save for a few sparks. His eyes adjusted and he saw a
generator, a diesel engine, and a large steam vessel that pumped a sputter-
ing atmosphere through a network of pipes.

The sound from the calliope outside was loud—inside the center section it was deafening.

He fumbled out his flashlight and snapped it on. Against the far wall sat
Amanda Lane, bound and gagged with duct tape. Her eyes were wild and
defiant. She wasn't a little girl, however. That photo on Robert's computer
had to have been taken a long time ago. She was maybe thirteen or fourteen, and almost as tall as Eliot.

Eliot held up a finger, indicating that she wait. He went to the machinery. He couldn't think with that song repeating over and over and the
carousel rumbling around him.

A yellowed page of instructions had been taped to the machinery, but it
was blurry. He squinted and worked out where to find the kill switch. He
flicked it.

The steam vessel gave a great hiss and died; the notes faded; outside
Eliot heard the protesting neighs and hoofbeats of the horses stop.

He knelt by Amanda and ripped the tape off her arms. She hugged him.

"It's okay," Eliot said, gently pulling her arms away.

He then reached for the tape on her mouth—tore it off in one quick
pull. It had to hurt, but she didn't cry out.

"You're Eliot, right?" she asked. "He said you'd come. He said he was
counting on it."

"'He'? You mean Millhouse?"

A line of light appeared on the wall, an arc that ran through wooden
panels and steel struts. This section of wall fell in with a crash.

Fiona stood silhouetted by firelight.

Eliot didn't know how she had done that, but it didn't matter. He'd
never been happier to see his sister.

Blood was trickling from her head, though, and she looked angry. Her
gaze softened a bit as she saw him and then Amanda.

"We have to move fast," she said.

48

FIRST BLOOD

Fiona had been ready for anything when she cut through the carousel's wall, but she exhaled a huge sigh when she saw Eliot inside—not Millhouse as she'd expected.

The girl was there, too. Fiona hadn't let herself hope that they would find her. She had just wanted to find Eliot . . . alive.

This didn't feel right. Millhouse had said he was expecting them. Why hadn't he caught Eliot? Why leave Amanda Lane where even her brother could discover her?

"Nice work," Fiona said to Eliot.

She offered her hand to the girl. Amanda took it and didn't let go.

Fiona wondered for a split second what it would have been like to have a twin sister, instead of a brother. She would probably have stolen all her clothes.

"Come on," Fiona said. "I saw Millhouse a minute ago. Lost him. Then I saw you running this way."

Eliot looked at a section of the wall. "How'd you—"

"Later. Let's get out first, then I'll tell you about it."

Fiona ran, dragging the girl behind her. Eliot caught up, grabbed Amanda's other hand, and together they half pulled, half lifted her along.

On either side mechanical rides on fire clattered along, and the concession stands crackled and collapsed into smoldering heaps.

They sprinted to the nearest exit: the front gate of Haley's scrapyard. The gate was a mock-up of a carnival entrance with turnstiles and two large plywood clowns that flanked the ticket booth. Outlining the clowns were a hundred brilliant bulbs—half of which were dead.

The clowns stared at them with mocking smiles that gave Fiona the creeps. If she had had the extra time, she would have cut their eyes out.

Where had *that* thought come from? She hated fighting . . . now she was thinking about cutting people's eyes out?

She had to stay focused. Get out of here. Save all their lives. Win.

Behind them was a thunderous crack.

Fiona turned.

The flaming Ferris wheel tore loose from its support frame. Four stories of circular steel teetered and tottered and then rolled—smashing game booths and ticket stands, leaving a wake of fiery destruction.

She stopped. So did Eliot. They stared, helpless before the wobbling mass. It came straight for them.

Amanda screamed. Eliot dragged her along. Fiona was right behind them.

Closer to the front gate, she saw it was chained and padlocked. She could cut through, but that would take time. Just a few seconds—that's all it would take for the Ferris wheel, though, to catch up and crush them.

She glanced back: the wheel bashed into one side of the lane, destroying a lemonade stand, teetered to the opposite side, flattening the ring toss—back and forth, blocking any escape.

She grabbed Eliot's shoulder and jerked him to a stop.

"Can't outrun it," she panted. "We have to dodge it."

He turned and watched the flaming wheel bear down on them, transfixed, then he snapped out of it and nodded, understanding.

Fiona tried to judge the wheel's momentum, but it wobbled crazily right and left, then right over an ice cream truck, ricocheting back to the left.

"Go!" she yelled. "Now—to the other side."

They ran across the lane.

Tons of flaming metal screeched and sparked past them.

Fiona smelled burning hair—hers. Eliot turned and shielded Amanda.

Then the heat was gone. It had passed them . . . and while the flames had singed a little, it had thankfully not burned any of them.

The wheel hit the front gate, crashed through the turnstiles, barreled into the barbed-wire-and-chain-link fence, slowed, stopped . . . stood there for a heartbeat, then teetered and fell with an agonizing crash.

Flames and sparks leapt into the sky. The grinning plywood clowns caught on fire.

And Millhouse's hissing laughter filled the air.

Fiona spun around.

Millhouse stood a dozen paces from them, blocking the way back. Half his body was somehow still burning. It should have been reduced to ash long ago.

Fiona wanted to move, but there was nowhere to run. Everything was on fire.

Millhouse took a step closer. "Right where I wanted you," he whispered. "In the middle of my ring of fire."

"You planned this?" Fiona yelled.

She should've been terrified. Why wasn't she? Something felt wrong inside her . . . broken or missing.

"They said you would come. So I got it all ready." As Millhouse spoke, he exhaled wisps of smoke. "It's going to be okay. I'm going to set you free. Something I wish they'd done to me a long time ago."

"Shotgun," Eliot whispered to Fiona. "Tell me you've got it."

She shook her head.

Fiona, Eliot, and Amanda took three steps back, but the heat from the fallen Ferris wheel was too great. Any farther and they'd be roasted alive.

Millhouse advanced on them. He brought his right hand to his left, and it ignited. He screamed and laughed.

"Your violin," Fiona said to Eliot.

"Yes!" Millhouse shook one leg in a parody of a dance. "Play me a jig, devil boy. I like your music. So does the fire."

Amanda buried her face in Eliot's shoulder and whimpered.

There was no time for music. By the time Eliot got his violin out and started playing, Millhouse would be on them.

Fiona took a step in front of her brother, placing herself between him and the burning monstrosity of a man.

"The brave one," Millhouse sputtered, now completely engulfed in flames. "They said you might try to fight."

"I'm not going to *try* anything."

"Are you crazy?" Eliot whispered. "What you doing?"

Fiona's pounding heart slowed and the heat inside her cooled. No creep was going to hurt her or her brother. A chill spread through her body, the same sensation she'd felt when she had tried to brain Uncle Aaron with that yo-yo.

But she wanted to do a lot more than that to Millhouse: she wanted to stop him. Permanently.

She pulled the rubber band on her wrist, stretching it the length of her arm.

"It's going to take more than that to slow me down, girl." Millhouse shambled toward her, fire dripping from his reaching arms.

"No!" Amanda cried.

Fiona darted forward. She ducked inside his reach.

All Millhouse had to do was close his arms around her. She'd be cooked.

A split second before that, however, the leading edge of her rubber band caught him. It made a line from his left shoulder, across his body, to his right hip.

Fiona pushed through—*all the way*.

Millhouse's skin, muscle, and bone offered no more resistance than a whisper of spider silk.

49

SOMETHING VERY WRONG

Fiona slammed the door to her bedroom shut and caught her breath.

They had dutifully reported the rescue of Amanda Lane from the scrapyard as Grandmother drove them back home. Fiona and Eliot had unceremoniously been dumped at the Oakwood Apartments, while Grandmother and Cee had taken Amanda Lane to the hospital.

Grandmother ordered the two to rest. She would take the news of their success directly to the Council.

Fiona ran all the way up the stairs to get away from them and be alone. Neither Grandmother nor Cee had even asked how she had stopped Millhouse. Did they already know? Or did they just not care?

She surveyed her room: a globe, three thousand books lining her walls, and her desk with neat rows of sharpened pencils and a blue Corona manual typewriter.

She hated it all. Fiona had spent her entire life in here, reading and learning . . . and what did any of it mean? What did passing the Council's test mean? According to Aunt Dallas's threads she was supposed to die in less than a day.

Maybe it was all meaningless. Everyone died in the end, right? Even the unstoppable Mr. Perry Millhouse.

Especially Millhouse.

She couldn't stand to think of him or what she'd done.

Fiona knocked over her globe and it rolled to the far corner—Antarctica faceup. She went to her desk and swept off the papers, reference books, and pencils with a grand gesture. The typewriter tipped over, hit the floor, and pinged.

That felt good. She didn't have to think. Papers and pencils didn't fight back . . . or bleed.

She moved to her bookshelves and pulled out armfuls of histories and biographies and ancient never-before-published manuscripts—tossed them all into the center of her room.

There was a scratching at her door. Eliot, puppylike, was waiting for her out there.

She opened her mouth to tell him to go away, but as she did this, she tasted chocolate—and felt bile rise in her throat.

She jumped across her room, fumbled with the lock, brushed past Eliot, and threw herself into the bathroom.

She got the door locked behind her and the toilet seat up just in time.

Her stomach heaved, and a river of black fluid spilled from her open mouth and spattered the porcelain.

She shuddered and curled into a ball and the stuff poured from her— gallons and gallons of it.

She reached up and barely had the strength to flush.

"Fiona?" Eliot asked from the other side of the door.

"Go a—"

She threw up again. There couldn't possibly be room inside her for all this.

The smell of it was unmistakable: vanilla cream, cherry cordial, peppermint glaze, hazelnuts . . . but more than anything else, milky curds of chocolate.

It was as if every truffle, toffee, and butter cream she'd eaten since she had first opened the heart-shaped box had stayed inside her—and was now vacating the premises.

Well, good. She didn't want that stuff inside her. The way they had made her feel had been great for a few moments, but it was unnatural, unhealthy, and something else was very wrong about them.

She heaved again.

This was the same fluid that had oozed out when she cut that arterylike fiber. Had she damaged something inside herself? How could that be? The threads were just in her imagination, weren't they?

The chocolates, though, had attached themselves to those imaginary threads . . . linked themselves to her destiny. What choice had there been other than to cut them away at the point of attachment?

Just as there hadn't been any choice when she turned and faced Millhouse.

Dizziness washed over her. She didn't want to remember this. She wished the memory of the fire and the blood would just go away.

Fiona had had to do it to protect Amanda and Eliot.

She had stretched the rubber band out before her in a taut line—so taut that it had become a nearly invisible edge as she focused on it.

There had been one thought in her mind: cut.

Millhouse moved toward her, his arms outstretched. He wanted to pull her close and let his fire catch.

But Fiona had been faster.

She darted inside his reach, pressed her rubber band to his chest, her arms wide enough so the line made an angle from his shoulder across his torso to his hip.

Cross my heart and hope to die if I should ever tell a lie.

She cut him.

The rubber band penetrated the melted layers of his coverall, the outer charred skin, muscle, popping organs, bones—all soft and without resistance—then passed through his spine and out the other side.

The only evidence of cutting through his body had been a faint thrumming in the rubber band.

He grabbed her arm and brushed her hair, singeing it. His other arm grabbed her shoulder, burning through her shirt and leaving blisters . . . before his arms had fallen away—his top half cleanly severed from his bottom.

Blood gushed from his body and extinguished his flames, but Fiona only vaguely remembered that part.

What had been burned into her mind more than anything else was his smile. As if he were one of those stupid clowns at the entrance. As if he'd been *happy* to die.

Fiona tore off her rubber band and flushed it. She never wanted to see it again. It had killed someone.

No . . . *she* had killed someone.

The Council had been trying to get her to do that all this time. They'd changed her from a pawn into a killer. But the final decision had been hers, hadn't it? It had been a simple choice: become a murderer or be killed.

Her hands trembled. All the color had drained from them. She'd never seen her skin so pale before.

She wanted to pass out and forget everything, but her body wouldn't let her. She turned back to the toilet and more chocolate came from somewhere deep inside her.

Eliot knocked again gently on the door

Fiona gasped for air. "Go away!" she screamed. "I never want to see you again."

50

BEING THERE

liot's hand hovered over the bathroom doorknob. His sister needed him. She was sick and crying. But he'd never heard her so angry before.

Who could blame her for being angry? Grandmother had barely batted an eye when they had returned with Amanda . . . with the entire carnival burning to the ground behind them. She hadn't asked how they got away. She hadn't asked about Mr. Millhouse, either. She probably already knew everything.

Grandmother and Cee had left them at the apartment. Amanda had to be taken to the hospital, then probably reunited with her parents. He wondered if he'd ever see her again. She had clung to him and Fiona all the way on the ride back—and had to be torn away by Cee.

And while Cee took care of Amanda, Grandmother was probably halfway to the Council by now to report that they had passed their bloody second trial.

A leaden feeling settled in Eliot's stomach as he realized that meant there'd be a *third* trial. He didn't know how they'd make it through another one.

He remembered how Fiona had stood up to Millhouse at the last moment. He should have faced him with her. He was ashamed that he'd just stood there, frozen, terrified, like a complete dork.

While Fiona had cut Millhouse in half.

He was sure that's what he had seen; that wasn't an optical illusion. He hadn't lingered afterward because the place was burning, but it was obvious that the top half of the guy had fallen one way and his lower half had fallen the other way.

And the blood . . . there was so much. Enough to finally extinguish his fire.

Fiona had cut through the carousel, too. He hadn't seen any knife. Although now that he thought about it, it would've taken a blowtorch or buzz saw to slice through as fast as she had.

He had a million questions for her. Again his hand rose to the bathroom door, but inside he heard her crying.

Not yet. She needed time.

He turned to leave and give her some privacy, but halted. It felt wrong to leave her alone, too.

Eliot sighed and sat quietly on the floor

"I'll be right here if you need me," he whispered. There was no way she could have heard him, but just saying this made him feel a little better.

He couldn't leave his sister when she needed him so much. As Cee had said, they were stronger together. Maybe it counted even if Fiona didn't know he was here.

He crossed his legs and inspected his backpack. There were scuffs on the canvas where the black horse had almost trampled it. He checked the violin again. Yes, she was reassuringly intact.

He then pulled out the heavy *Mythica Improbiba*.

Eliot glanced over his shoulder. The apartment was empty, but he checked anyway. If Grandmother came in and found him with this particular book—successful trial or not, it would have been confiscated. And he *needed* it. It had answers about the family.

He flipped it open and reexamined the medieval woodcut of the devil. It seemed to be grinning at Eliot as it poked peasants with its pitchfork. Creepy stuff.

He turned the page and found the next entirely covered with strange lettering. Each character was composed of fine lines and tiny open circles and squares and little curlicues. It wasn't like anything he had ever seen before.[47]

---

47. This passage in the Beezle edition of *Mythica Improbiba* is a variant of the sixteenth-century artificial language developed (discovered?) by magicians of the era, often called the Alphabet of the Angels. The lettering in *Mythica,* however, does not match any previous version of this code and remains to this day undeciphered. Victor Golden, *Golden's Guide to Extraordinary Books* (Oxford: 1958).

There were more pages of this weird lettering so Eliot quickly flipped ahead. As he turned the vellum, he smelled the dust of a thousand miles and the sweat of all the hands that had turned these leaves before him.

His thumb brushed the edge of one page that was warm to the touch.

He backtracked and found the page. The body contained Latin that ran together in one long stream of letters, no spaces or punctuation. It had been illuminated with crying saints, their halos tilted.

On the edge of this passage, however, was something entirely different: a line of seven tiny, stamped images. These weren't like the fine woodcut he'd seen before; these were rougher, like ancient pictograms one might find on a Neanderthal's cave wall.

In the first one, stick figures huddled together, obviously cold. In the others, a man left the group and headed up a mountain . . . up to the sun . . . he reached out and touched it . . . his left hand ignited . . . he ran back to the group. In the last pictogram all the figures sat around a campfire.

As Eliot ran his finger over these pictures, the ink warmed. Or had they been warmer than the surrounding pages to begin with? The one where the man reached out and touched the sun was particularly hot.

It had to be his head playing tricks with him.

He turned the page and the pictograms continued.

Unhappy faces appeared in the sky over the group . . . the one man with the burning hand stood alone before them.

Eliot knew how the man felt, because this reminded him of how he and Fiona had stood before the Council.

The next block showed the man tied to a rock . . . a large blackbird landed upon him . . . and fed. Strangely his hand *still* burned.

Just like Mr. Millhouse.[48]

Eliot closed the book.

It was just a fairy tale, but part of it felt real: the part where the gods were cruel.

48. The fire-bringer legend is ubiquitous in many cultures, in which heroes/gods endure trials or engineer trickery to bring the gift of fire to humanity. Many of these heroes are revered, but many others are punished. In Greek mythology, Prometheus for his crime was chained to a rock and every day an eagle would rip out his liver, which regrew overnight, which was to repeat throughout eternity. It is considered an apocryphal lesson to teach primitive man not to meddle with the gods. Yet without the gift of fire, where would mankind be? Many anthropologists wonder if this tale is not actually a propaganda piece, martyring those who have defied the gods. *Gods of the First and Twenty-first Century, Volume 4: Core Myths* (Part 1), 8th ed. (Zypheron Press Ltd.).

Would something similar happen to him and Fiona if they failed the Council's last test?

Just a few days ago he was daydreaming of adventures and heroics. He ran his hand over the rough rhinoceros-hide cover of the book. There was a lot more to being a hero than he had ever realized. Right now, he would have given anything to go back to his old life.

Eliot hadn't heard any noise from inside the bathroom for a while. He reached for the door to knock, but he didn't have to.

From under the door, fingertips reached out to him.

Somehow Fiona had known he was there.

He touched her fingers. They were ice-cold. He squeezed them and their warmth returned.

"I'm here," he whispered. "I'll always be here for you."

Behind the door, Fiona quietly started to sob again.

Eliot didn't let go.

51

EVOLUTION

Henry was worried. The world was changing. And while he enjoyed change (in fact, he lived for it), this was the kind of change where people died. He could feel it coming in his bones. Heightened security, no one smiling, and worst of all—no one was drinking.

Well, one person was drinking: Aaron. The one among them who *shouldn't* be.

They had decided to meet this time on Henry's ship, *Wayward Lost*. She was a sixty-foot yacht of teak and polished brass, powered by sail, and crafted with love.

He settled next to Aaron on the stern and asked, "Do you have a glass for an old friend?"

Aaron glowered and thrust a bottle at him. "No glasses."

Aaron had not changed clothes, or his sour mood, since the last meeting—quite the binge he had embarked upon.

Harry sighed and took a delicate swig of the 1890 Napoleonic brandy. It was a crime to not let it breathe properly, but also a crime to let Aaron drink alone on such an occasion. After all, if the end of the world was nigh, one should not face it sober.

The *Wayward Lost* rolled gently up and down on the waves *inside* an iceberg. This particular ice hollow bobbed in the waters near the Diomede Islands between Russia and Alaska. It had been carved by wind and water into delicate scallops that towered over them more glorious than any manmade cathedral. Intense arctic summer light filtered through—golden and blue and wavering with reflected water lines.

They were completely hidden here from spy satellites and prying eyes.

The waters nearby bubbled, and Gilbert's finned submarine, *The Coela-canth*, surfaced. The craft could have sailed directly out of the pages of a Jules Verne tale. This submarine, however, was powered with a *real* nuclear core.

Hatches opened, gangplanks extended, and the Council came aboard.

Dallas wore a dainty sailor's uniform. Kino had donned a black suit, overdressed as usual. Cornelius looked as if he had not slept in days, eyes ringed with shadows and his MIT T-shirt rumpled. Lucia wore red capris and a white halter that accentuated her graceful motions. Gilbert wore jeans, a sports jacket, and thick chains of gold about his wrists and throat, just as he had in the old days.

They took their places next to Henry and Aaron on teak benches.

Lucia settled on the center seat and rang her tiny silver bell.

"I call this session of the League Council to order," she said. "All come to heed, petition, and be judged. *Narro, audio, perceptum.* Let us dispense with the formalities and proceed directly to Henry's report."

There were too many of them, too close. Henry knew what happened when one tried to contain so much power and politics in a compressed space.

He noted that Gilbert sat far away from Lucia, next to Dallas. This was likely a result of the last Council meeting, when he had voted against Lucia. Had politics seeped into their bedroom as well? Or had Dallas managed to worm her way between them?

Henry stood and bowed. "There are three items of interest with regards to the twins' second heroic trial."

He clicked a remote control and a hidden projector flashed light onto the mainsail. A photograph of a blackened human skeleton on an autopsy tray appeared.

"First," he said, "we have this gentleman. DNA analysis confirms it is our Mr. Perry Millhouse. Note the clean, laserlike separation across ribs and spine."

"So he is finally dead," breathed Cornelius. His frail hand covered his mouth in horror.

Aaron muttered, "More of our mistakes cleaned up by children."

Lucia perked up. "I think we can all agree on the cause of death."

"Wait a second," Dallas said. "If he's dead, what happened to the little girl?"

"A happy ending." Henry flashed a smile. "Reunited with her parents. Traumatized, but nothing hypnotic suggestion couldn't set right."

"Let us not lose focus." Kino stood and smoothed a hand over his bald head. He moved to the picture, drawing a line from shoulder to hip bone. "A single cut. Absolutely straight. One of the children did this with no training?"

"That remains an open question." Lucia looked pointedly at Aaron. "At least the training."

Aaron took another swig of brandy. "The girl was born a warrior. Any *fool* could see that."

Lucia raised one eyebrow. "So it would seem." She turned to Henry. "Did Audrey mention this in her report?"

"She only gave me barest facts. Laconic, I'm afraid, as usual."

"Audrey should be here." Gilbert tugged at his beard contemplatively. "After all, we're talking about her charges."

"No, Audrey complicates this entire affair," Lucia said. "The less she is involved, the better. Now, about Fiona's ability to cut—"

"Oh, who cares *where* she learned it?" Dallas said. "The point is she can, and that proves Fiona is one of us."

Cornelius poked his tablet computer. "I find myself in agreement. Molecular disjunction is a genetic trait only found within your family tree."

Lucia inhaled and then expelled a sigh. "Very well, we shall concede the point. But genetics are only a small part of this, and it hardly proves she belongs in the League."

All nodded, except Aaron, who simply drained his bottle and tossed it overboard.

Kino pursed his lips until they whitened. He had much more to say, Henry could see, but he held it back, waiting for the right moment.

"The next item of interest," Henry said, and advanced the projector.

A shard of mirror appeared on the sail. The surface was visibly warped, its edges distorted by heat.

"My team found this in the remains of a mirror maze," Henry explained. "It is remarkable because it fluoresces in the presence of aetheric radiation, indicating it has been exposed to great power."[49]

That shut them up.

Power this great was the upper limit of what mortals could manipulate.

---

49. Aetheric (also *etheric*) refers to an elemental life-force. Plato first proposed such a material, which he called *quinta essentia* (the fifth element). Aristotle later introduced aether in his classical system of elements as a substance that had no material qualities and was incapable of change. Medieval philosophers believed aether filled the universe above the terrestrial sphere and, as such, was beyond the reach of mere mortals. *Gods of the First and Twenty-first Century, Volume 3: The Pseudosciences,* 8th ed. (Zypheron Press Ltd.).

It indicated either an extremely skilled practitioner of the arts . . . or an immortal testing a newfound ability.

"Exposed to extreme heat," Henry continued, "this piece was imprinted, much like a piece of steel in the presence of a strong magnetic field. Scanning with lasers we translated the following."

Henry punched a button on his control and sound came from the cabin speakers.

A single violin played.

"That's not a human song," Lucia said, sitting upright.

"Oh, parts of it are," Henry said. "Parts are something older and foul. Parts are something entirely new."

"Played by whom?" Gilbert asked.

"I suspect Eliot Post, based on the fragmentary report Audrey gave. Although, obviously, we will need to follow up on this."

Cornelius wordlessly made notes on his computer.

"The girl has power," Aaron said. "So does the boy. Let us move on—you said you had *three* items to show us."

Henry hesitated. He had hoped there would be some way to delay this. He sighed and flicked the control and a new image appeared: a charred wooden box in the shape of a heart, and about it what appeared to be congealed tar.

"This was also found in the mirror maze," Henry explained. "Fiona's fingerprints are all over it."

"What we looking at?" Dallas wrinkled her nose. "It's gross."

"Chemical analysis reveals this is mostly high-grade chocolate. However, we have extracted two interesting trace elements: spirituous alkaloids, and alkahest."[50,51]

---

50. Spirituous alkaloids where isolated in 1855 by the renowned alchemist and medium May Mortimer from a specimen he named the Tortuous Lilly Poppy. On a visit to the Louisiana bayou, Mortimer met a witch who claimed to have found the river Lethe. Upon a sandbar on this cursed waterway, the witch maintained a garden of rare herbs and flowers of "horrific beauty." Mortimer took several specimens to London, but set aside his alchemical pursuits when his fame as a spiritualist climbed to stratospheric heights. He died of opium addictions in 1857. His notes and an illustration of a poppy with extraordinarily convoluted petals were discovered, but none of the original specimens remained. *St. Hawthorn's Collected Reference of Horticulture in the New World and Beyond,* 1897 (Taylor Institution Library Rare Book Collection, Oxford University).

51. Alkahest is the mythic universal solvent. Medieval alchemists claimed it would dissolve any substance on contact. If such a material did exist, paradoxically no container would be able to hold it. *Gods of the First and Twenty-first Century, Volume 3: The Pseudosciences,* 8th ed. (Zypheron Press Ltd.).

Cornelius's eyes widened. "Spirituous alkaloids are only used by one entity, the Queen of Poppies."

"So these are an Infernal concoction," Aaron growled.

"Then they know of the children." Lucia stared at some distant point, thinking. "They are testing them as well."

Gilbert got to his feet. "Honestly, Henry, why didn't you show this to begin with! It changes everything."

Henry shrugged, feigning innocence.

"They must be protected," Aaron said. "The other family must not be allowed to get their hands on them."

Kino stood as well, towering over them. His expression was more funereally somber than usual. "On this I agree with you. The children must not be allowed to be used by our ancient adversaries. They are precisely the tool they need to break the neutrality treaty that has protected us for centuries."

"Then there is no time to waste." Aaron fumbled at his cell phone. "We will move them to a safe—"

"No," Kino said. "They will *never* be safe. Don't you see? There is but one way to protect us all."

The two men stared at each other. Kino was absolutely still. Aaron remained seated; his hands flexed.

Cornelius cleared his throat. "We've all known that if, hypothetically speaking, one of the children has mixed lineage, this would produce a loophole in the treaty. Conceivably, one of the children backed by the might of the other family could remove us one at a time."

"Then there is no choice," Kino said. "For the entire League's safety, they must be killed."

"No," Dallas whispered.

Gilbert said nothing but took her hand.

Lucia sat impassively, waiting.

"The League's safety?" Aaron muttered. "Why should I be concerned with protecting a league of *cowards*?" He stood and stared up at Kino. Aaron's bloodshot eyes narrowed to slits. "If it is killing you want, then this is a good place to start."

Although many would disagree with Henry, he was not entirely a fool: he knew this had to be stopped.

Aaron and Kino would kill one another, or worse, they would wound one another and this would spiral out of control as they gathered supporters and waged a full vendetta within the League.

And yet, if Henry stepped between these two predators in an attempt to quell the violence, he would be cut down.

So he did not attempt such a heroic maneuver . . . hence the not-being-an-*entire*-fool part of his self-assessment. No, there was another, better-qualified person to handle this situation.

Henry turned to the lovely Dallas. She sat watching the two warriors, her hands worrying into knots.

She noticed Henry.

He tilted his head at her and his darling cousin understood him completely.

She stood and interposed her slight figure between the two giants. Dallas smiled at Kino—dimples and all—and his pantherlike stance eased.

She then turned to Aaron and held out her hands in a little pleading gesture. Aaron took a step back and unclenched his fists.

"I'm starved," she announced, and looked back at Lucia. "How about a break for lunch, Sis?"

The tension in the air abated a notch.

Kino exhaled. "Yes . . . a break. Perhaps that would be wise."

Aaron grumbled something unintelligible, but he let Dallas wind her arm through his.

"Where can a gal get something to eat on this tub?" she asked.

"I have a little sideboard set up in my cabin," Henry replied. "There's a bottle of Lemon Hart rum there as well."

Aaron paused as Dallas led him past Lucia. "This is not over," he told her.

"Of course not," Lucia replied, unfazed. "We shall pick up the debate in half an hour, as I said."

Dallas then pulled Aaron belowdecks.

Gilbert pretended to stretch nonchalantly. He was no actor, though, and Henry could see that the Once King Gilgamesh shook slightly. Had he been prepared to do battle as well?

"I'll have my chef on *The Coelacanth* whip up something," Gilbert said. "Please, everyone is invited aboard for lunch."

Kino bowed to Lucia and took his leave.

Cornelius whispered to Henry, "I would like to see your molecular analysis of the chocolates and the mirror."

"I have placed the relevant files on the League's computer."

Cornelius accessed the files on his tablet as he followed Kino and Gilbert aboard *The Coelacanth*.

Lucia waited until the deck was clear before she said, "I know you enjoy dancing on the edge of ruin, Henry, but was it absolutely necessary to offer Aaron *more* liquor at a time like this?"

"It was my duty as a host. Besides, that particular bottle of rum is laced with enough haloperidol to sedate a bull elephant. Our pugnacious cousin should sleep the rest of the afternoon."

"Ah . . ." She removed the band that held up her silky red hair and shook it out. She then held out her hand to Henry. "May I?"

"Of course." He gave her the remote.

Lucia flipped through successive photos of the destroyed carnival until she came to mug shots they had seen before of Eliot and Fiona. "What do you think of them?"

"I like them."

"You like everyone. I mean . . ." She struggled to find the right words. "Beyond all the politics and the games you play with the Council. What do you think they are? Off the record. Our family? Or the others?"

Henry sat next to her. "I think they are the coming storm."

"So you believe Kino is correct? Remove them—to be safe."

"I might have thought that a week ago when this started. It's too late for that now."

"Surely they cannot be so powerful. Even with Audrey hovering over them as protector."

"Audrey is the least of our worries. The children are still weak, I agree . . . but that is their greatest strength."

Lucia turned to him, her eyebrows angled together. "Must everything be subterfuge and Zen riddles with you?"

Henry shrugged. "Very well, I shall speak plainly, for once. Aaron has bent our rules to unlock Fiona's abilities. Someone in the other family has done the same for Eliot and his music. I even have intelligence that dear little Dallas paid the children a visit. One can only imagine the mischief she has tangled into the weave of fate."

Lucia considered this. "They seem to be having an influence on some of us. All the more reason to act quickly."

Henry set his hand upon hers—a gesture part consolation and part, he hoped, seduction. "There was a time," he whispered, "when we found ourselves in the same situation. When powerful forces polarized around us—some wanting us dead . . . some willing to be similarly influenced by our better natures, and they raised us among the stars."

Her mouth opened, forming a little *o* as she remembered.

"When we were young," Henry continued, "*we* were the mixed breeds, the innocent, and newfound in our powers."

"But we grew, learned everything so fast, and . . ."

"Killed the Titans," Henry said, "and then we took their place."

Lucia sat pondering this for a moment as the waves lapped at the hull of the *Wayward Lost*.

"Evolution may have finally caught up with us," Henry said.

At this Lucia stood and pulled Henry up with her. "We must go. Now. You and I to see them."

"And the Council?"

"I think we are past the Council," she said. "It is time I took matters into my own hands. We must not let the other family have such power over the future. We must make those children *ours*."

"And failing that?"

"And failing that . . ." Lucia suddenly looked sad and tired. "Failing that, I will kill them myself. Audrey and Aaron can have their vendetta upon me, but the family will survive."

Henry exhaled. Sometimes he wished he were half the romantic fool he dreamed he was, because right now, to his utter disappointment, he found himself in complete agreement.

52

A BANNER OF WAR

Beal Z. Buan, the Lord of All That Flies, was rarely surprised. The last time it had happened he had arranged for a double to replace Archduke Franz Ferdinand, only to have the man assassinated in front of him by a Bosnian Serb student.[52]

Of course, the family had rallied to turn those regrettable events to their advantage. That had been Louis's plan, but Beal always thought his original strategy would have turned out better.

This morning he had received a message that the Board was convening for brunch, a meeting called by its members—not him. It was technically allowed, but had never before been done. It was the chairman's function to call the meetings. The Board's general function was to argue and eventually fight over the scraps of power *he* left behind.

"Drive faster," he told Uri.

Uri floored the accelerator and the Cadillac limousine raced over the dry lake bed and dunes of the Mojave Desert.

Las Vegas wavered in the distance behind them in the morning light. Upon the opposite horizon a tiny square of color fluttered: a circus tent. Uri angled toward it, slowed, and parked next to the Humvees arranged in a haphazard line.

Beal was fashionably late. Usually, that would've been fine. Not today. Someone on the Board was trying to outmaneuver him, a someone whom he would make pay.

52. The event often cited as sparking the start of World War I.—Editor.

He jumped out of limousine before Uri could open the door and strode to the tent. Desert winds blasted him with sand.

With a flourish, he parted the tent flaps and entered—ready to tear into the ones who had arrived before him.

The interior was carpeted with ancient Persian rugs, and the air was thick with incense. A side table offered poached ostrich eggs, bison bacon, kiwi flown in from New Zealand, and a selection of pastries from Poujaran in Paris. Along the opposite wall were video displays showing images of a circus. Fires raged on several of the screens.

Beal stopped . . . surprised for the second time today.

The *entire* Board sat about the conference table. They had been talking as he entered and, remarkably, even laughing.

All conversation stopped and they turned to face him.

No . . . the entire Board was not here. Oz was missing. And Sealiah sat in his spot.

Lev rose and gestured magnanimously at the head of the table for Beal to join them. Lev wore a patch over one eye and was missing one of his front teeth. He smiled anyway.

"Hope you don't mind," he told Beal. "We started without you."

Beal smiled back as he palmed a transmitter from a hidden pocket. He flicked off the remote detonator's safety. He had come prepared (as unlikely as it had seemed this morning) for a coup attempt.

Within his limousine's trunk were enough high explosives to level a city block . . . which he would happily detonate if they moved against him. Or he would at least threaten to do so, which usually did the trick.

None other than Lev rose, however. There was no overt threat yet.

Beal moved with deliberate grace and settled at the head of the table as if none of this bothered him.

He opened his mouth to protest calling a meeting without the chairman's authority, but he checked that impulse. To do so would come perilously close to claiming there were rules, or more ridiculously some point of order, to the Infernal Board. When in reality there had only ever been a fine tradition of *dis*union and *dis*order.

"What is this all about?" Beal asked with deliberate calm. "Who called this meeting?"

Abby set her pet scorpion on the table. It waved its stinger dangerously about. "*What* is a review of the latest League trial of the Post twins." She nodded at the displays.

"An impressive performance," Ashmed added as he brushed sand from his jet-black suit. "And as for *who* called the meeting . . . well, I suppose we all did."

Beal looked at each of them, his gaze lingering upon Sealiah. She sat opposite him at the foot of the table, a desert blossom in a gossamer wisp of a silk dress.

"Where is Oz?" Beal demanded.

"He's a little under the weather today," Lev explained.

Did that mean he was dead? No, Beal would've heard if that were the case. There would have been Oz's domains and power to fight over. More likely Oz had been grievously wounded at the last meeting and hid, licking his wounds.

"You have seen this video?" Abby asked.

Beal looked at the displays: extreme-long-range shots of Eliot and Fiona Post running through a carnival, dodging flames and whirling animated rides, and some League fire assassin chasing after them.

It looked like the material Uri had obtained in California last night. How the Board had managed to get these shots was something he would like answered. He would review the security of his computer networks after this.

"Of course I've seen them," Beal replied.

The "wrongness" of the situation crystallized in his thoughts: no one was fighting.

There was not a single word of dissent over the twins. Beal would have expected blood to have already been spilled—especially after he had engineered such brilliant animosity among them all at the last meeting.

Beal smiled and looked from Abby to Lev. "Well then, I think we can all agree that their performance against the League champion was nothing less than spectacular. And I'm sure we can all agree on our next course of action."

He hoped these comments would spark the usual dissent between these two. They never "agreed" on anything.

Instead, they said nothing.

"Quite," Ashmed said. He turned and reflected Beal's smile to Sealiah. She sat and continued to coolly stare at Beal.

"Oh," Ashmed said, "I hope you don't mind. We all decided that since Oz was indisposed, dear cousin Sealiah would sit in on his behalf."

Beal nodded, kept smiling, but his mouth became as dry as the desert about him.

Was this disastrous calm her doing? Certainly it was her style . . . move in silently and slit her opponent's throat before he knew what had happened.

"I would like to hear the audio file again, if you don't mind," Sealiah said.

Abby tapped the remote control.

A sweet violin solo rolled through the tent: Eliot Post's music.

It was appreciably better than the last time Beal had heard it. The ancient notes stirred long-forgotten emotions. His breath caught in his throat, and he remembered older, better times . . . when he had been young . . . before life had become so complicated.

A new phrase in the music reminded him of little girls, and then a distant calliope answered in its own singsong voice.

"Wonderful," he murmured.

"Yeah," Lev said. "I could listen to it all day."

Ashmed cleared his throat. "I propose that this song and the subsequent life-force infusion of the carnival rides constitutes proof that young Eliot belongs to us."

Abby interrupted. "A powerful mortal with the proper training could also do this. Which leaves—"

"Eliot's temptation to prove it one way or the other," Lev said. "We oughta move up the timetable on that."

Sealiah nodded. "My agent is in position. She is ready to make her move."

"Then move," Beal said more forcefully than he intended.

Sealiah narrowed her eyes and replied, "It shall be done tonight. If successful, Eliot will be tempted, pulled from the protective arms of the League, and delivered to us—either as a dead mortal, or a very much alive Infernal."

Beal's hand curled tighter about the detonator. It would be so much simpler to trigger the delay mechanism, excuse himself from their presence, and take his chances. Violence was always easier than subterfuge.

But he had his own plans in motion for collecting Eliot Post, a plan involving his now mortal father, Louis. Perhaps Beal could accelerate his timetable as well . . . or better yet, delay theirs.

"One fifteen-year-old boy," Abby said, and twined her scorpion's tail playfully about her pinkie, "hormonally poisoned by near puberty and enticed by Sealiah's handpicked seductress . . ."

"Yeah," Lev muttered, "it'll be a kick in the pants to see how he turns her around."

"What do you mean?" Beal's hand loosened about the detonator. They knew something he did not. "What chance can Eliot possibly have?"

"About the same chance that Fiona Post had of surviving *your* tempta-tion." Sealiah nodded at one of the displays.

Abby clicked a button, and one video appeared on every screen.

Fiona sat in a mirror maze. The place was on fire. She was on the floor near the open heart-shaped box.

Abby zoomed in and pressed another button. "Looking now with aetheric-spectral filtering."

Invisible lines of force resolved on-screen, shimmering rainbows and shadows. Fiona's hands ran over them, then she teased a thread out from within herself.

"Gives me the chills every time I see it," Lev whispered. "Kid's already almost a pro."

Fiona attempted to cut the line of power from the chocolates . . . but she failed. Naturally. Once attached, lines of addiction never loosened their hold.

But Fiona didn't give up.

She pulled out a part of herself—the part where the chocolates had attached—and cut that.

"Her appetite," Abby explained. "She could not overcome *your* power, so she cut away *her* vulnerability."

"That took a lot of moxie," Lev added.

Beal watched the video replay, hardly believing what he was seeing. No one had ever broken free of one of his temptations, especially *after* be-coming addicted to them.

"The point is," Sealiah continued, "that the weaker of the two children managed to overcome your best effort."

Beal bristled at this. He wanted to cross the room and wrap his hands about her lovely throat.

"Of course," he said. "And this is most welcome news, is it not? More proof of their power?"

Ashmed held up a finger. "Hold that thought. More on that in a mo-ment. Fiona's disjunction of the chocolates and her resistance to tempta-tion is actually evidence that her genetic makeup favors the League . . .

and yet, if she has but a drop of Louis's blood in her veins, it will ultimately corrupt her—"

"And she will be ours," Abby said as her eyes reddened with bloodlust.

"Let's be clear what we are talking about," Sealiah said, setting her hands on the table. She appeared so perfectly at ease that Beal felt, if only for a moment, that he sat at the foot of the table and she sat at the head. That she ran this meeting.

Sealiah continued. "Our neutrality treaty, the Pactum Pax Immortalis, states that neither family may harm each other bodily—even touch one another—or harm the interests of one another. The legal language is airtight."

"Unless," Lev interrupted, "there's mutual consent."

"That was the only loophole in the document," Sealiah said, ". . . until now. If one or both children have dual lineages, they can inflict harm on anyone they please . . . and we can use them to attack the League."

Ashmed reached for the remote and tapped another button. The displays played video of Fiona and Eliot cornered by burning wreckage. "Here, the League's flame eater closes on them."

Fiona stepped forward. The audio was lost among the crackling flames, but it was clear from her tone and stance that this young girl was actually issuing a challenge.

She took a step forward. The flame eater charged her.

Her hands were a blur of motion as she and the flame eater fell upon one another.

Fiona remained standing.

The man fell away—cut in half.

"I love that part," Lev whispered. "Play it again."

"Impressive," Abby whispered.

"This is the kind of power we can amplify to our advantage," Ashmed said. "Imagine Fiona and Eliot, backed by our family, finding Henry Mimes in some dark alleyway. What chance would even the Fool have to escape? What chance would any of them have?"

They all nodded, except Beal.

They were moving too fast and would get to Eliot first. He had to stop them.

"There is but one problem," Beal said.

The Board turned to him.

"We rolled for terms. All here agreed to *three* temptations to thoroughly test the twins. While I would love to advance things"—he shrugged—"the dice have decided."

It was the one thing the family never argued over. Once you rolled, the terms of the deal were set. No one welshed after rolling.

True, that was what *he* was trying to do via Louis, but his scheme skirted the razor edge of a technicality. Louis was mortal. Their rules no longer applied to him.

Lev sighed. "That was what we were discussing when you came in: what to do for their third temptation?"

Beal flicked the safety back on the detonator and slipped it into its hidden pocket. A new plan had taken root in his mind.

"As I watch these videos, I recall their first trial. It appears the twins are more powerful together. Providing Sealiah's attempt fails"—he nodded appreciatively in her direction—"I propose that we use the third trial to both test *and* separate them so they are easier to bring in."

Ashmed tapped his lower lip contemplatively. "How precisely do you propose that we do these things simultaneously?"

"The Valley of the New Year."

"Ah, yes." Ashmed stared at some faraway space.

"That will take time to set up," Abby stated. "All the doors to that place were closed when the Satan departed."[53]

"Is there a better way to lose oneself?" Beal asked. "Has the Valley ever failed to separate loved ones, family, or friends? And even if the twins manage to stay together . . . they will at least be out of the League's reach."

"I agree," Ashmed said. "The Valley has the added bonus of making them forget. They will be all the more ready for us to mold."

"I know where to start." Lev stood and shrugged so the many pounds of chains about his throat shifted. "I know a guy who paints doors. I'll get the ball rolling."

Beal observed his cousins. This had been the strangest Board meeting

---

53. Lucifer, Beelzebub, Mephistopheles, and others are often mistaken as synonymous with Satan. Satan, or more precisely "The Satan," was originally a rank of significance in the celestial order of angels before the Infernals' fall from grace. The Satan led the fallen angels for millennia until he became irritated with their civil wars and left to explore realms unknown. The title, since retired, remains unclaimed. *Gods of the First and Twenty-first Century, Volume 13: Infernal Forces,* 8th ed. (Zypheron Press Ltd.).

he had ever attended. There was neither fighting nor political maneuvering (save his own).

Something had changed. The Post twins represented a new family dynamic. They had always schemed and fought among themselves for power . . . but for the first time they were planning *together*.

Could these children unite them?

Beal considered, and his blood warmed to the possibility of the twins leading them (secretly controlled by him, of course) against the Immortals . . . under a banner of war.

53

A DAYDREAM IN THE LIFE OF ELIOT POST

Eliot chewed a slice of four-cheese pizza.

He and Julie sat under a eucalyptus tree in Franklin Park having a picnic lunch. It was overcast today in Del Sombra so the heat wasn't too bad, and the wind blew *away* from the Oro Recycling Plant so there wasn't any stink.

It was just him and the prettiest girl in town with leftovers from Ringo's. Life was good.

She poured grape juice into a plastic cup and offered it to him.

Eliot took a sip—almost coughed the stuff out his nose.

Julie giggled. "I'm sorry. That's some of Ringo's house pinot noir. I should have warned you."

The warmth of the red wine spread through Eliot's chest. "No problem. It's cool."

There was of course a rule for alcohol.

> **RULE 62:** No distilled spirits, beer, wine, or other ethyl-alcohol-based intoxicants. Most notably restricted are the use of fermented materials in combination with singing or dancing (see RULES 34 & 36, respectively). Exceptions limited to medical uses as prescribed by a qualified physician.

Eliot took another sip and managed not to choke this time. The stuff tasted horrible. It didn't matter, though; he had to look cool in front of Julie no matter what.

Julie poured herself a cup and sipped along with him, draining hers. The wine stained her lips blood-red.

She looked great today, but not dressed the way she normally did for work. She wore tight, faded jeans, flip-flops, and a T-shirt with a flying scarab and the word JOURNEY printed on it.

Eliot thought it a funny coincidence; he had just called Fiona a scarab the other day. He would never have guessed that Julie was into entomology, too.

Her hair wasn't so neatly curled this morning. It just kind of hung loose and framed her face. She brushed it back behind one ear. The simple gesture made his heart race . . . or maybe it was the wine.

They could relax because there was no work today. When Eliot had shown up at Ringo's, Julie had been outside waiting for him. Ringo's was closed. A sign on the door explained the place was being renovated.

It was odd that no one had told them about it earlier, but he wasn't about to question a day off alone with Julie—and most important, with no Fiona, Grandmother, or Cee looking over his shoulder.

He felt as if he was getting away with something—a different, but not entirely unwanted, sensation.

Julie had such a sly grin on her face, he almost wondered if she had engineered Ringo's closing. That was nuts, though. The owners made those kinds of decisions. If Julie's family owned Ringo's, she wouldn't be living at the Hillcrest Apartments complex. That place was a dump.

What was it like at her home? She had tried to tell him the other day in the Pink Rabbit, but couldn't. It was selfish of Eliot to think he was the only one with family problems.

"You look so serious, honey." She punched him in the shoulder. "Lighten up. It's a play day."

"Just a little worried, I guess."

"About Fiona? I couldn't help notice you came alone to work. Is she all right?"

He shrugged. In fact, Eliot hadn't been worried about her, and that made him feel guilty. He'd said he would stay with Fiona as long she needed him . . . and then he'd left her this morning.

She'd been asleep after a long night of sitting by the toilet puking. What was she going to think when she woke up and he wasn't there?

She'd be okay. Probably.

"Fiona has the stomach flu."

Julie crinkled her nose. "I should've told her yesterday to wash her hands. When you hostess, you touch all those grimy menus that everyone else has touched. You pick up some of the nastiest germs."

Eliot nodded. Great. Now he was thinking about Fiona and the next heroic trial that would probably kill them both because she was sick.

"I know what we need," Julie said. "Play something." She reached into his pack and pulled out the rubber boot where he kept Lady Dawn.

Eliot took the boot, a little annoyed that Julie had touched his violin.

Had he told her about it? He didn't remember. He took another sip of wine, grimacing the stuff down. He must've told her.

He stroked the grain of the wood. It looked like fire, and he remembered last night and how the carnival had come to life. Was that because Mr. Millhouse had thrown some master electrical switch? Or had it been his song? It was a crazy thought, but that's what it had felt like. And the way the calliope had answered his music . . .

"I better not."

Julie's smile faded. "Oh, okay."

They both sat a moment, the only sound the hot breeze rustling eucalyptus leaves on the ground.

Fiona told him last night how Uncle Aaron had showed her how to cut. It must be scary to know that you can cut through anything. Fiona had then started crying again, thinking how creepy Mr. Millhouse had died— how she had cleaved him into two pieces.

That had been the grossest thing Eliot had ever seen.

He couldn't begin to imagine what his sister felt like.

He set his wine down, suddenly not thirsty at all . . . and certainly not for blood-red wine.

"Still thinking about Fiona?"

"Kind of. Weird family stuff."

Julie sighed. "I know how you feel. Sometimes even a perfect day, a bottle of wine, and a cute guy can't make me stop thinking about them."

Had she called him "cute"?

But it was too late. He'd done it: ruined the picnic with his melancholy mood.

Maybe that was okay, though. Maybe Eliot could turn this into a real chance to talk with her. Help her.

"So what's it like for you? I mean, your family?"

Julie stared at the leaves and bit her lower lip. She then opened her mouth . . . but closed it and slowly shook her head.

He should go first and share something about his family. "I know how you feel. Sometimes I think there's no one who'd believe half the stuff that goes on at our place. Like my grandmother has this list of rules that are eight pages long—typed! One hundred and six regulations."

Julie looked up, astonished. "Sounds like a prison. How can you even remember half of them?"

Eliot shrugged. Of course he remembered them. He'd lived with most of the rules since he'd been able to read. It was as if he and Fiona had come with an instruction manual.

"And then there are my aunts and uncles." What could he tell her about them? Even he wasn't exactly sure *what* they were. "They're larger-than-life, but not in a good way. It feels like Fiona and I are always getting shoved around by *someone* in the family."

Julie looked away and blinked quickly. Without meeting his gaze she pulled her T-shirt over her shoulder. Three finger bruises marked her pale skin.

"That's from my stepmom," she told him so softly that he barely heard her. "I'm not the only one that gets it. I had three brothers . . . one of them got pushed down the stairs."

She didn't speak for a moment and her face quivered. She was valiantly trying to hold back tears, but they nonetheless tumbled down her cheeks. "The police believed her when she told them that he fell."

Eliot gently set his hand on her back. You didn't have to be involved with gods and devils to have your life entirely messed up. All it took was one bad person.

She turned to him and his arms folded around her. Julie cried against his chest.

He wished he knew what to say to make her feel better. Or was this something even the right words couldn't fix?

"Hey, I know, how about I play some music for you?"

She sat up and nodded, wiping her face with the heel of her hand. "That would be wonderful."

Eliot pulled out Lady Dawn and the bow and experimentally strummed his thumb over her strings. Microscopic vibrations ran along her length.

A corner of his mind whispered that this was precisely what Julie had wanted in the first place—that all this was a trick to get him to play.

How could he even think that? Julie had real problems. A nice girl like her would never manipulate him to get something so trivial. Eliot flushed, ashamed at his suspicions. Dealing with the Council was making him paranoid.

He set the violin under his chin and brought up the bow. He started with the familiar "Mortal's Coil" singsong nursery rhyme.

The key, however, shifted under his fingers to something dark. The shadows cast by the eucalyptus tree deepened, and Eliot found himself in a tiny circle of dim light.

Only Julie remained, kneeling next to him.

This isn't what he wanted. He was trying for something light and fun to cheer her up.

He gazed at her tearstained face. That's where this darkness was coming from. It was as if when he was around her, his music became a magnifying glass on her soul.

The words Eliot always imagined he heard along with the nursery rhyme came:

Now you're dead and buried long. Is there light or is it gone?
Flames and pain for all your wrongs. Spirits lost and all alone.

He pressed hard with his fingers and forced Lady Dawn to play what he wanted—bridging her back to a major key. He forced the song to become a light jig. He tapped his foot and felt alive again.

The sun emerged from behind clouds. Wind stirred and a thousand slender eucalyptus leaves took to the air and danced about them in time to the song.

Julie laughed with delight.

Children get their just rewards. Welcome light or point of sword.
Kind or cruel life's too brief. Dead or not there's no relief.

Eliot's stomach turned. Something wasn't working with the song; light and dark notes mixed in a way he didn't want. Even though the sun had come out, he could have sworn he saw stars as well now in the sky.

The ground thundered. A deeper power stirred and tried to accompany him, a rumble too deep to be felt . . . but nonetheless triggering an instinctive reaction to run away and hide.[54]

Eliot finished the jig with a quick flourish.

Julie clapped and cried, "Wonderful!"

The stars in the sky faded. The earth fell quiet. The leaves and wind settled. Eliot exhaled. It was almost as if the music had fought him, running away from him again, alive, with a mind of its own.

Julie sat closer and stared into his eyes. "You're the most amazing boy I've ever met," she whispered.

Eliot didn't have a clue what to say. Things like "I like you, too" came to mind, but how dorky did that sound? Instead he just smiled. Maybe being stoically silent would work for him.

"Listen . . ." She scooted closer. "I've been planning something for a long time. I wasn't going to tell anyone, but, well, then I met you." Julie sat up straighter and her face scrunched in concentration.

"You can tell me." He set aside Lady Dawn and took Julie's hand.

"I'm leaving," she sighed. "Ringo's. Del Sombra. My stupid stepmother. Everything."

Eliot didn't understand how a person could just leave. "When?"

"I know some people in Los Angeles. I'm going tonight before my stepmother gets drunk and pushes *me* down some stairs, too."

Julie closed her eyes. Tears squeezed out from under her eyelids. She withdrew her hand from his and quickly wiped them away.

"I understand," he whispered.

"You do?" She looked genuinely surprised. "I thought you would try and talk me out of it."

"The last thing I want is to see you leave, but if you think it's the right thing to do, then it probably is. I'd do the same thing if I could get away with it."

54. The Oro Recycling Plant was spared the fire that razed Del Sombra, however, it closed soon thereafter when the Environmental Protection Agency cited it for numerous pollution violations. Interviewed workers claimed the plant was clean—that nearby Franklin Park was the source of increasingly strange phenomena: mutated lizards, cracks in the earth, and expelled sewage. Many claimed that ghosts dance every night in the park to some unheard song, but this has never been confirmed as the EPA quarantined the region and declared it a Superfund cleanup site. *Gods of the First and Twenty-first Century, Volume 11: The Post Family Mythology*, 8th ed. (Zypheron Press Ltd.).

She grabbed his hand. "You can come with me. I've got a job lined up. A place to stay. We can do it together."

Only in Eliot's daydreams did things like this happen. He didn't know how to answer. Naturally he wanted to run off with Julie, the prettiest and nicest girl he'd ever met. And, sure, there was nothing more he wanted than to get out of Del Sombra—away from the rules and restrictions and Grandmother.

But some microscopic portion of him would actually miss Grandmother, and Cee, and of course Fiona.

Who would help his sister? How was she going to get through the last heroic trial without him?

Did Fiona really need him, though? If she could cut through anything, what was going to stop her?

Eliot remembered her on the floor of the bathroom, crying, so weak she could barely lift her head to the toilet.

She needed him.

But didn't Julie need him just as much?

He was forgetting one thing, though. Running away wouldn't get *him* off the hook for the last trial. Uncle Henry and the others had found him once. How hard would it be for someone with all that money and power to track him down again?

He did, however, have a few tricks of his own. He touched the smooth body of Lady Dawn, then carefully slid her back into the boot.

"If only you were leaving a few days later," he said. "So many complicated things at home would get settled."

"I can't wait a few days. I'm scared." She squeezed his hand harder.

Eliot wanted to go with her more than anything else in the world—and not just to run away from his problems. He would be running *to* something as well: a new life.

But there's no way it would work. He had too many responsibilities.

And how fair would it be to drag Julie into *his* family's problems? If Uncle Aaron and Aunt Lucia were prepared to kill him and Fiona . . . would they even blink before hurting Julie if she got in their way?

Julie reached up and stroked his cheek. "It's okay. Don't burn out all those brain cells thinking about it." She released his hand and poured more wine. "Just spend the afternoon with me."

She offered him a full cup.

He took it and sipped. The wine tasted better this time.

"Just . . ." She hesitated.

"What?"

"Come say good-bye to me. Tonight at the bus station. Five thirty."

Eliot mentally rearranged his chiseled-in-stone schedule. He'd call from Ringo's around four thirty and tell Cee he had to clean up the back room—that would let him do whatever he wanted until at least six.

"No problem. I can do that."

He slipped into daydream mode and imagined that he'd grab his extra set of clothes from his locker at Ringo's, meet Julie at the bus station, and leave everything behind. In a few hours they'd be in Los Angeles, two people among millions. Uncle Henry would never find them.

Julie finished her wine and drew close. "Shhh. I told you," she whispered. "Stop thinking so much."

She brought her face close to his.

The line separating reality and daydreams blurred, and Eliot found himself living in his fantasy.

He wasn't sure what would happen tonight when he met Julie at the bus station . . . but he was 100 percent sure what he was going to do right now.

He kissed her.

54

WHAT WAS CUT AWAY

Fiona lay on the bathroom floor. Her stomach was hard and concave, as if her insides had been scooped out. Maybe they had.

She rolled over and opened her eyes. Blankets had been thrown over her and a pillow had been pushed under her head.

Now she remembered . . . Eliot had brought her these last night when she had refused to move. She'd been too weak to get up and walk the six steps to her bedroom.

Cee had come by, too, and tried to get her to swallow some of her homemade remedies—but all that had done was made her throw up more.

Grandmother had not checked on her once.

For the first time in her life Fiona wondered if Grandmother was really their grandmother and not some caretaker appointed by her real mother before she died. Sure, Grandmother looked like Fiona and the others in the family, but even Uncle Henry had showed them more feeling—and he might end up *killing* them.

She wanted someone to hold and comfort her. She wanted her real mother.

But that wish was a distant candle flame in her mind, winking out, and buffeted by the hurricane of recent events. No one was here to take care of her, and that wasn't going to change.

She slowly got to her feet. Her body felt as if it weighed half as much as it did yesterday.

Dreading what she would see, she turned to the mirror.

A gaunt slip of a girl stared back, eyes wild and bloodshot, hair a rat's nest, skin the color of chalk. What did she expect from someone who was supposed to be dead soon?

She ran the faucet and scooped a handful of water to her mouth. She managed to swallow a tiny sip. The act was mechanical and didn't quench her thirst. She splashed her face, pulled her hair back and tied it in a knot—hideous, but it kept it out of her face.

With her hand flat on her stomach, she closed her eyes and tried to sense what was going on inside her. It was still and quiet. The bout of gastric distress she'd had last night was over. She wasn't hungry, even though she hadn't eaten any real food for days. Breakfast was as abstract a concept as logarithms to her.

Last night every chocolate she'd eaten from the heart-shaped box had been purged. It seemed impossible now, but she had to have devoured ten or twelve layers of truffles from the box. And yet remembering the sheer volume of the gunk she'd upchucked—the rancid curdled-chocolate and syrupy taste—that was the only thing that made sense.

She licked her lips, tasted cocoa, and her gag reflex clenched.

No. She'd be okay now. She was never going to eat another chocolate. Ever.

Fiona knelt, picked up the blankets, and folded them. She'd had these wool blankets for ten years, and they had been softened by a hundred hand washings. She didn't want to lose them, which is what would happen if she left them on the floor. There was a rule.

RULE 16: No disorderly accumulation of personal property. Any pile or mishmash of said property will, after twenty-four hours, and without prior notification, be permanently removed from the premises.

Grandmother had clarified that one when it had been added to the list. Fiona and Eliot were only four years old. She called it the "clean up your mess or I will throw it away" rule.

That scared them, and they tried, but they were only four years old . . . so things got messy again. That's when Eliot's collection of bottle caps and the clothespins Fiona had been using to build castles had been scooped up by Grandmother. She tossed them down the trash chute while they were forced to watch.

They had cried and pleaded and promised never to do it again, but they might as well have tried to ask the sun not to set for all the good it did.

The only indication that they had gotten through to Grandmother was her telling them to "do better next time."

The only exception to RULE 16 was for books. Books were *never* thrown away, but if found scattered or in disorderly piles, Grandmother would sequester them indefinitely in her office. Somewhere in there were copies of Louisa May Alcott's *Little Women* and James Herriot's *All Creatures Great and Small,* taken from Fiona and Eliot when they were seven.

Speaking of missing things . . . where was Eliot? He had promised to stick around in case she needed him.

And right now Fiona could've used someone, even her brother, to talk to.

She glanced down the hallway. The apartment looked empty. Burning odors wafted from the kitchen, however. Fiona guessed that Cee was cooking up a batch of her infamous chicken soup—charred poultry skin and all—just for her.

Eliot probably got distracted with his violin or that book. So typical.

Her annoyance evaporated, though, and she wondered if something else had happened. Maybe the Council's third trial had come and Eliot had foolishly tackled it alone.

No, even he wasn't that stupid.

But what if the Council hadn't liked the job they had done on the second trial? What if they wanted to question him and had taken him away?

Fiona remembered with crystal clarity what they had done to pass the Council's last test. She relived the moment—pressing her stretched rubber band into Millhouse's coveralls . . . how the shimmering line cut through dirty blue fabric and skin and meat and bone and snapped out the other side.

Fiona felt nothing. She remembered crying last night over him, and over what the Council had made her do, but this morning she felt no remorse.

She inhaled and forced herself to focus on the here and now.

Eliot was probably at work. She couldn't imagine Grandmother would let him stay home today. Her precious work ethic demanded that they go to Ringo's with anything less than a 102-degree fever (not that either she or Eliot had ever had such a fever).

Fiona paused, realizing something was indeed wrong.

Grandmother hadn't made *her* go to work. Did that mean she was really sick? Apart from the hollow feeling inside her, though, she didn't feel any different.

Fiona went to Eliot's bedroom door and knocked. There was no answer, so she entered.

Eliot wasn't here and his canvas pack was gone.

Fiona immediately sensed something off with the place . . . like one of those spot-the-difference pictures.

She spotted it: a new book had been added to the shelves, a fat volume of gray leather that couldn't look more out of place than if it had flashing red warning lights. It was that *Mythica Improbiba* thing he'd found in the basement.

She told him to keep it downstairs. If Grandmother found it here . . . she'd what? Take it away? Punish them? So what?

Maybe Eliot was right to rebel and keep it near him, even right to keep it a secret from her. Her little brother was sneakier than she had realized, and she kind of admired that.

She moved to the volume. It still gave her the creeps. She felt its pull, felt, too, the waves of revulsion from it as if it were a magnet that couldn't decide what polarity it wanted to be.

She closed his bedroom door and came back. She ran one finger down the book's spine and felt a tingle. It reminded her of the first time she'd touched her heart-shaped box of chocolates.

What if this book was a similar trap?

If it was, she knew how to deal with it. A few cuts and it could be a pile of confetti.

She removed the book from the shelf and sat cross-legged with it on Eliot's bed. She opened it and flipped through perfectly preserved vellum sheets. It had to be fifteenth century or earlier. Maybe much earlier. Books this old were extremely rare, and despite her apprehension she handled it with reverence.

There were pages with Greek writing, Latin, Arabic, and several with primitive pictographs that she didn't recognize. It was weird. More like a collection or a journal than a single cohesive narrative.

Fiona noticed a tiny slip of paper marking one page. She turned to it. There was a woodcut of a monster poking terrified medieval peasants with a pitchfork. The caption identified this creature as the devil.

Eliot must've been doing a little research on their father's side of the family. It scared her, but she was glad he was learning about those relations in case they showed up, too.

She wrinkled her nose at the picture.

That couldn't be real. More likely a distortion of whatever they really looked like . . . if they were real at all.

There was another slip of paper. She turned to the spot.

This was a story about Vikings in the New World. Line drawings showed heroic battles and Indians and mermaids—just like her brother to find some daydream fantasy to escape into.

She flipped ahead, past star charts and long passages in cuneiform, then paused when she found an illuminated section. Framed in red-and-gilt filigree a nude woman stood surrounded by creatures of the forest: bears and wolves, foxes and squirrels and rabbits, finches and hawks. The woman held out her hands to the animals, letting them smell her—or it almost looked as if she was blessing them.

Fiona had seen this gesture recently, and she struggled to remember where, but no insights came.

She translated the Latin text on the reverse page:

> Lady Nature anoints the animals of the woods, gifts them with claws sharpened, noses and ears and eyes keen, and the kiss of Winter Sleep.

Fiona snapped on Eliot's bedside lamp, and the illuminated manuscript glimmered with gold and rich colors. Lady Nature's face was lifelike. It was Aunt Dallas.

Fiona quickly closed the book. It was one thing to look at a tasteful nude picture. It was quite another to see your own aunt naked . . . and with perfect features that made yours seem like, well, what they were: the inadequate features of a just recently postpubescent fifteen-year-old girl.

Fiona crossed her arms over her chest, holding the book there, and feeling her cheeks burn.

It was just a picture. The artist could have drawn it—embellished it—any way he had wanted.

She opened the book again, focusing this time on the words.

There was a story about Lady Nature and her adventures in the Forest of Shadows. She helped the animals trick the hunters. She also had several encounters with a woodsman, fisherman, blacksmith . . . all of whom seemed to fall in love with her. They also seemed to . . . Fiona reread these passages with great care, not quite sure she'd ever run across these particular Latin words before.

The context, however, was clear. Aunt Dallas, at least in the story, was having sex. Lots of it.

Fiona flipped to the next page to see where this was going. Another illuminated picture was here: Dallas and Aunt Lucia danced about a maypole.

In the margin of the page was a handwritten note in Greek:

> *Seasons cycle, come and go. Clotho, Lachesis, Atropos.*
> *Two sisters welcome, one is not. Sister Death is best forgot.*[55]

At the mention of Sister Death, chill bumps pebbled Fiona's arms.

Lachesis. That was close to *Lucia.*

Clotho? That wasn't even close to *Dallas,* but hadn't Grandmother introduced her as "Aunt Claudia" before Dallas had amended that?

What kind of name was *Dallas* anyway?

It struck Fiona how curious this was: here was a picture of two women—her aunts, so they claimed—put on this page five hundred years ago. Could it be a fake? This felt like a real medieval book. Smelled like one, too, with that distinct centuries-of-mold-and-dust odor about it.

But what if they weren't her aunts? What if . . .

Fiona marked her spot in the book with her hand and went to the bathroom, closing and locking the door behind her.

She reopened the book to the first illumination of Lady Nature. She propped it up as best she could and leaned closer to the mirror, placing her face next to it.

It *did* look like Aunt Dallas. Exactly like her.

It also looked like Fiona.

They both had the same high forehead, the same eyes (although Dallas's were a little greener). Her hair had the same waves as Fiona's had, too; although in the picture hers looked a million times better and was blond.

Fiona flipped ahead and compared her own face to Aunt Lucia's.

They looked alike as well: the same lips, the same chin, but . . .

She turned back.

She looked more like Aunt Dallas . . . Claudia . . . Clotho . . . whatever her real name was.

The people in this family seemed to lie about so many things. Was it

---

55. The three mythical Fates, youngest to eldest: Clotho, Lachesis, and Atropos.—Editor

possible they could've lied about being her aunts, too? Not that Fiona had any doubt they were related, but what if instead of being her aunt, Dallas was something else?

Fiona touched the image of Dallas reflected in the mirror.

Her mother?

Dallas had certainly had the opportunity to have children if she behaved as she did in the story. But why tell her and Eliot that their mother was dead if she really wasn't? Didn't she want them? Or was it to keep their identities a secret? Hand them off to "Grandmother" to raise them away from the family for their own protection?

And hadn't Dallas come back when they had needed her the most? To teach them how to use the threads to read the future. Wasn't that the act of a protective mother?

Fiona had been so stupid to run out when she'd discovered how little time she had left. She should've talked to Dallas. She could have found out so much.

Or was this all wishful thinking?

Maybe Dallas was just their aunt, and their mother was really dead.

She set the book in her lap and touched the illuminated illustration. Longing stabbed her heart.

Fiona gently closed the book. It hurt too much to think about this. She supposedly had less than a day left—according to her threads—and she had one more heroic trial to get through. She had to think about that first and foremost.

She took the book to Eliot's room and slipped it back on the shelf.

She went out into the hallway and heard pots clattering in the kitchen. Maybe she should talk to Cee. She always listened to her . . . but how could she understand what she was going through? She wished Eliot were home.

She sighed and went back into her room and locked the door.

All her problems centered on threads: the thread from the chocolates that had parasitically attached to her; the fact that her thread ended, indicating she had only a little time left to live; and whatever had she done the other night in the mirror maze—cutting away a part of herself. That had been another thread.

Or had that been a trick of her mind? She had, after all, just taken a nasty blow to the head.

She touched her scalp and winced. There was a bump and a scab.

What if she had only seen these mythical threads *because* of Dallas's hypnotic suggestions or under the influence of a concussion?

There was one way to find out.

She wriggled out of her singed and dirty clothes and got into more comfortable sweatpants and a T-shirt. From her elastic waistband she pulled a thread, snapped it off, and held it before her.

Fiona could cut with this thread, but that's not the frame of mind she needed. She was supposed to be focused . . . but not completely, like when you stared cross-eyed at something and it suddenly doubled.

There: the thread appeared to coil back inside her . . . and end a tiny bit from where she held it.

It wasn't elastic anymore. It was red and pulsed. A drop of blood beaded at the end. Her life's blood.

So—unless she was in a constant state of hallucination or waking dream—this trick with the threads did actually work.

A little scared, but excited, too, she ran her forefinger and thumb backward along the fiber until it crossed tangles and knots that became a weave. As she touched this, sensations flitted up her arm: the taste of Ringo's salty pepperoni, the dust of old books that made her cough, the sharp pine odor of Cee's homemade cleaner, and the softness of her washed-a-hundred-times wool blankets.

This was the pattern of her for the last fifteen years—sleep, clean, work, and study—repeated over and over.

She moved back up to the tangles.

Dark fibers were woven into her life here: cold and slick, sticky in patches. *Evil* was the word that came to mind. There were also threads of pure gold. One was leather and smelled faintly of motorcycle exhaust. That was Robert.

This was her life.

But as she continued forward, to what she assumed was the present, her fingertips ran over a bump.

She focused and found the blood-vessel-like tube spiral from that point in her life—one end going into her body, the other end cleanly cut and hanging limply.

This was the line she had severed last night.

What exactly had she done to herself to break free from the chocolate's influence?

Dizziness washed over her and she felt as if she were going to be sick again.

She let go of that severed part.

Maybe she could find the other end and glue them together.

She moved back, searching for a loose thread. This took more energy than she thought it would, as she separated fibers. The farther back she moved, the more the threads stiffened, as if they had been set in concrete.

She spotted one silver thread that ran through every part of the weave. She hadn't noticed it before because it was so intricately bound . . . so much a part of her that it blended completely.

But at the very beginning of her pattern this silver thread became a separate thing: frayed, tattered, almost broken.

She gently touched it and found it as resilient as steel wire. It was cold and clear and pure. This had to be Grandmother's thread.

Her focus wavered and she let go.

There was too much here to sort through.

Whatever she had cut out of herself last night would have to stay cut for now.

And what would she do if she even found the other severed end? She didn't know how to sew things together—she only knew how to cut.

There was a knock at her door. Cee's quivering voice filtered through. "My darling dove? I have soup for you."

"That would be great," Fiona said, and started to get up.

But those words never came; they floundered on her lips. Her entire face went numb . . . and as she got up, the world spun, and her legs turned watery.

The floor rushed up to meet her.

Her head hit and bounced and everything settled into a black so deep Fiona was quite sure she would never again awaken.

THE THIRD HEROIC TRIAL

(and Transformation of Eliot Post)

55

SYMPHONY OF EXISTENCE

Eliot stood in front of his open locker at Ringo's.

He was at a crossroads. Go one way—run off with Julie to a new life—or stay at home, face his troubles, and probably get himself killed for being so responsible.

Eliot had left Julie in the park an hour ago. She had to get a few things from home while her parents were out, but he had a terrible feeling something was wrong.

He could call the police. They might not be able to solve *his* family problems, but they'd be able to help Julie.

Or maybe it wasn't Julie's problems that filled him with unease. Eliot had plenty of his own to think about: the next heroic trial and his sick sister.

That was the real issue. He couldn't decide whom to worry about more, Julie or Fiona.

He'd come to Ringo's in case he was really leaving. He wanted the extra set of clothes stashed here. Neatly folded at the bottom of his locker was a pair of Cee's home-sewn pants. If checkered corduroy ever came back into style, he'd be ready.

He wished the *Mythica Improbiba* volume were here, too, but he'd left it in his room. Reading about both families had intrigued him—especially his father's side.

According to *Mythica*, the fallen angels were divided into thirteen clans with leaders such as Satan, Lucifer, Beelzebub, Leviathan, and Azmodeus. Those names tolled like funeral bells in his mind, familiar, and shaking him to the core.

Eliot laughed.

Who was he kidding? Really? Running off with Julie was just another of his wild daydreams.

Fiona needed him. She couldn't face the third trial alone. No matter how much Eliot wanted, he wouldn't turn his back on his sister or his responsibilities.

He slammed his locker shut—angry at having to do the right thing—and wandered back into Ringo's dining room.

The tables and chairs had been removed. Sheets of plastic draped over the salad bar and the soda fountain. The plastic rustled as the kitchen door swished closed behind him.

Eliot thought he saw the shadows move.

"Hello?" he whispered.

No one replied.

Eliot hurried to the lobby. He didn't like being alone in here.

He picked up the phone and dialed home. He should've called earlier to check on Fiona. She probably had the stomach flu or just eaten something bad—and with Cee's cooking this was highly likely.

Now that he thought of it, though, Eliot didn't remember Fiona eating or drinking *anything* for the last two days except those stupid chocolates. No wonder she had thrown up.

The phone connected and rang.

In the dining room the plastic sheets continued to rustle . . . although no door was open to make them do so.

No one answered the phone.

Eliot hung up, marched to the front door, squeezed through, and let it lock behind him.

He didn't look back and quickly marched up Midway Avenue. The walk home felt dangerous without his sister's company. As he passed the alley where Louis lived, however, Eliot stopped.

He called into the shadows, "Hey . . . Louis?"

Eliot wanted to talk to him. He had questions about the music. The last time he'd played Lady Dawn, the earth had moved as his song ran away from him. And in the carnival—he was certain he hadn't imagined it—he had brought the place to life. Those horses on the carousel had chased him, almost trampled him to death. All because of his music?

That was crazy.

Even eccentric Louis would think he'd lost his mind.

It was getting dark, unnaturally so for a summer evening. Midway Avenue was deserted. Eliot imagined every demon in the *Mythica* book lurked in the shadows.

He nonetheless took a step into the alley.

There were piles of pizza boxes, discarded crusts, mounds of fast-food wrappers, and everywhere lay empty screw-top bottles. No Louis, though.

As his eyes adjusted to the weak light, Eliot saw graffiti on the cinder-block walls. It wasn't ordinary, normal spray-painted letters, either. In crayon and felt-tip pen and drippy paint were straight lines, tiny circles, arcs, and triangles.

It looked part geometric proof, part puzzle, and part poetry. Those pages in *Mythica Improbiba* that Eliot hadn't been able to read, they had looked like this.

Eliot felt static electricity—lightning about to strike—the sensation strongest in the soles of his feet.

He glanced down. Weird writing covered the asphalt, too.

Had Louis drawn this all? In places it looked as if he had written over it many times, making the already jumbled symbols a riot of abstract patterns.

One section, though, near the cardboard boxes, was different. There were parallel chalk lines, then dots and arcs scribbled over them. It was musical notation.

Eliot reached out to touch it, but stopped, realizing he'd only smudge the notes.

As he stared, however, some notes seemed to penetrate deeper into the street while others rose over the asphalt.

He blinked. It must be a trick of the fading light.

A lightning flash reflected off the walls and thunder crackled.

Eliot didn't flinch. His entire focus was on the music.

The notes started simple, then increased in complexity until they became a tangle at the end.

The last bit was only a blur of pink chalk. It looked as if new notes had been written over that part many times, smeared again, and then there was one last frustrated indecipherable scribble.

Eliot went back to the beginning and read the first bit. It was "Mortal's Coil," the very first thing Louis had taught him.

Eliot hummed it and traced the notes with his finger.

New phrases and inventions were quickly introduced, music that he had used in his own compositions.

As he neared the end, the music became wild. The last part didn't fit the style of the earlier sections. It sounded . . . wrong.

Eliot stared at this part: dots and arcs represented highly contorted finger motions. Some of these seemed to need six or eight fingers to attempt to perform.

But then at the end—as the piece built to a climax—it fell apart. The last phrases blurred into a chaos of Louis's half-erased scribbles.

Eliot desperately wanted to hear the whole thing.

Maybe he was trying too hard. Maybe he had to relax the way Aunt Dallas had shown him, let his mind wander *with* the music as a willing partner.

As he tried this, however, raindrops fell, dotting the asphalt.

Eliot panicked and huddled over the chalked lines to protect the music from being washed away.

He couldn't cover it all, though. He grabbed a cardboard box and used it as an umbrella, but before he could, a few drops spattered onto the piece.

Eliot froze.

While the raindrops obliterated parts of Louis's frustrated smears . . . in doing so they ended up looking like notes themselves.

The *right* notes.

Fascinated, he watched as more raindrops appeared.

Yes. He heard the music in his head . . . that last bit, and it felt correct.

As before, he imagined a choir of voices singing along. Gone were the childlike voices, though; these were panicked and mingled with shrieks.

> *Nothing left and lights all gone, Music lingers echo song, God*
> *lies down and fades to dust, Darkness and Death's end a must.*

It was dangerous music; Eliot felt this deep in his bones. It was a symphony of sorts, and Eliot knew what it was about: everything.

"Mortal's Coil" had a simple beginning. That was about creation and youth and innocence.

The middle part was about life and love and growing old.

The last bit was about the end. The end of one's life. The heat death of the universe. The end of days.

Raindrops pelted the music and washed it away.

It didn't matter. The symphony burned in Eliot's mind. He could never imagine having the courage to play the entire thing . . . but he would never forget it, either.

Rain soaked his shirt. Shadows enveloped the alley, and he felt watched again.

He left the masterpiece to melt and wandered to the sidewalk. Shafts of sunlight struggled to break through the thickening clouds. Lightning flashed on the horizon. Three crows sat on the telephone lines, cawed, and took to the air.

"Mortal's Coil" echoed through his mind.

What if it was all true? That you only got one life to live, and there was nothing after? Forever?

Why *shouldn't* he make the most of the one life he got? Find love and adventure while he could. Tomorrow he might be dead.

Actually, in all likelihood, tomorrow he would be dead.

He wasn't sure what to do anymore. He was sure, though, that he was going to the bus station to see Julie one more time . . . even if it was only to kiss her good-bye.

56

LEFT BEHIND

Eliot entered the lobby of the Del Sombra Greyhound bus station—ready and willing to start a new life. Two hippies with long beards stood by a vending machine. One other man was sitting near the restroom, a newspaper covering his face. He wore a black suit.

Julie wasn't here, though.

Eliot sat on one of the wooden benches. He noted the time on the clock over the ticket counter. Ten minutes until their bus left.

He imagined himself on a Hollywood street corner, playing his violin or maybe even a guitar. Could you make a living doing that? The people in Los Angeles must be nicer than in Del Sombra. They'd have to be; so many people living so close together. Otherwise, everyone would get on each other's nerves.

They'd pay him to play in a club. Everyone would applaud.

He made himself stop.

This was just another fantasy. Becoming a star wouldn't be easy. It'd take a lot of work, but he thought there was a chance . . . especially with Julie at his side.

It was unusually dark outside now. Streetlights flickered on and made orange cones of illumination.

Eliot pulled out his violin and stroked the strings. The hippies looked at him. The guy with the newspaper set it down. Eliot plunked out a few notes from the middle section of the symphony.

Young girls and boys run far too fast, wheel o' life turns and never lasts, too soon grown and knowing sin, that's when real fun begins!

That was the good part. Life was worth living. You had to take a chance . . . or have no chance at happiness at all.

For the first time in his life he was taking control. No more rules. No Grandmother. No one telling him what to do.

He felt a stab of guilt about Fiona and a third heroic trial. She'd do okay without him, but still, the weight of this all-important decision seemed to crush something inside him.

But this was about *him*. *His* life.

And Julie's.

Five minutes to go. Where was she?

Eliot touched the strings of his violin again: just a few notes from "Julie's Song." He played the phrase about how there was still hope in her life.

Sunlight broke through the clouds for a moment.

Eliot stopped and slipped Lady Dawn back into the rubber boot, then into his pack.

The hippies and the guy in the suit got onto the bus.

The bus driver came out of the bathroom and paused by Eliot. "Getting on board, young man? Or waiting for someone?"

"Both I guess."

The driver tugged on his cap. "We're leaving at five thirty, sharp."

"Yes, sir." The clock on the wall read 5:28.

Julie had to be close. He could almost feel her.

He got up and poked his head outside the bus station. The sidewalks were empty.

He darted back in, ran to the women's restroom, and whispered, "Julie—you there?"

There was no answer.

Behind him he heard the doors to the lobby swing open. He turned around, hope rising in his chest like a bubble. . . .

But it was only the driver leaving and getting onto his bus. He looked at Eliot expectantly.

Eliot shrugged.

The driver nodded, closed the bus's door, and started the engine. With a squeak of released air brakes, the bus rolled onto Vine Street and was gone.

She hadn't come.

Eliot imagined the worst: something had happened to her at home. But, of course, there was a more likely explanation: Julie had already left.

The crushed feeling he felt a moment ago intensified, squeezing his lungs and heart so it was hard to breathe.

Maybe she hadn't gone home after the park—just come straight here and left on the four o'clock to Oakland. Maybe she finally realized what a total nerd Eliot was. . . .

Why would a girl like Julie Marks hang out with him in the first place? None of it made sense.

The only thing that Eliot really understood was that he had turned his back on his family, that given half a chance he would have left Fiona neck deep in hot water.

Dejected . . . lonely . . . overwhelmed with guilt, he hung his head and left the bus station, going to the only place that would have him. Home.

57

THE SECOND DEATH OF JULIE MARKS

Julie Marks strolled toward the Greyhound bus station. She had taken care to pick the right outfit for the occasion: a black T-shirt with a few rhinestone sparkles (low neckline, of course), skintight jeans, and black boots. Nothing flashy, but nothing too timid, either.

Certainly nothing a fifteen-year-old boy could resist.

This was the moment she had been working toward for the last three days—three glorious days alive and in the light. She wanted an entire lifetime of days like these.

She had been clever to earn Eliot's trust, play the friend, the tease, and finally the wounded bird. He was hers to do with whatever she pleased.

Julie thought they'd have given her something hard to do in exchange for her freedom, but this was like shooting catfish on the sidewalk.

She slowed.

Eliot was nice, though; not like every other man who had been in her life . . . when she had been alive, that is.

But wasn't that the point of all this? A gamble to escape hell and earn her life? There was no way she was going back.

Julie approached the glass door of the bus station and reached for the handle.

Three men were inside.

The one reading the newspaper was an Infernal agent. Best not to make eye contact. They all looked the same to her. If she crossed paths with the wrong clan, they'd as soon eat her as say hello.

The two hippies, she got no vibe from. They were likely what they appeared to be; although, in this town, it paid to be cautious.

On the bench in the middle of the station, so small and unassuming that she had missed him at first glance, sat Eliot.

He hadn't seen her: Bambi in the headlights of an onrushing eighteen-wheel truck.

God, could she really do this to him? Hadn't she messed up enough lives? Hers first and foremost?

She rubbed her arms. The needle tracks were no longer visible, but they still ached.

Mama's voice whispered in her head: *You had your life, child—tossed it away, overdosed in some Dumpster in Atlanta. White trash in every sense.*

Yes, she was doing this. She got herself dead—out of the frying pan and into the fire literally. This was her one chance to crawl out.

She checked her curls in the reflection of the glass. She was the perfect candy-coated bait.

Inside the station, Eliot had his violin out. He plucked a few notes.

The glass rattled in the doorframe.

Julie withdrew her hand.

Her boots tapped as if they wanted to dance. The hairs on the back of her neck stood . . . as if she were his instrument. As if *he* were playing *her*.

Well, there was no way in hell that was happening tonight. Death sucked. For now she was alive, and she planned on staying that way.

Julie shook her head to clear it and pushed on the door.

But Eliot played again.

The sound turned her arms to Jell-O. She stood helpless and listened. He played *her* song.

With a few notes he conjured her past: parents that weren't so bad . . . just never really understood; friends promising a new life . . . then stealing everything; on the streets having to do terrible things . . . and the end.

White trash in every sense.

Eliot managed a new end, though. He turned it all inside out and made her feel something that she hadn't felt since she was a little kid.

Hope.

Was there hope? Really?

She believed once, but there had been so much pain. She had learned there were things that could make the pain go away: wine, cocaine, and then heroin.

They had worked, too. They'd been great. No pain. Job accomplished.

But after the pain had been blotted out, she always found herself in the same spot . . . only with less hope.

Until it had all gone.

Was that what she felt beating in her chest now? That no matter how badly she had messed things up, there was still a chance to do the right thing?

How dare he throw it back in her face like this. Hope wasn't something you got from a song. People like her didn't have hope. They took what they could, and . . .

And what? Overdosed and died? Went straight to hell?

Eliot finished with a pizzicato flourish and tucked his violin away.

No matter what she was thinking, though, hope was inside her once more, warm and strong and comforting. The feeling that had long been buried and presumed dead, Eliot had resurrected.

"No, no, no," she whispered to her reflection in the door. "Don't do this to yourself, Miss Julie Katherine Marks. You all are smarter than that."

She put one hand over her chest. Unfortunately smarts didn't have anything to do with how she felt.

She dreamed that there could be another way. Another life. Another way to love. It was like a sunrise during an endless night. If she had to . . . she could make that transcendent moment of hope last forever.

It was nothing short of pure magic.

In one glorious instant Eliot had given her more than all the lies the Queen of Poppies could promise her in an eternity.

Sealiah had brought back her flesh, but Eliot Post had made her *feel* alive. If she betrayed him now, she knew the feeling would fade forever.

And that might be worse than death.

Julie pressed her palm to the glass, and despite the hope her heart ached. She couldn't tell him good-bye. What could she say? How could she avoid being seen by that man in black?

Julie turned and quickly walked away—before she changed her mind.

She glanced down the street and spotted a 1974 Plymouth Duster. That would work. It was more rust than steel, but it had V 8, and no fancy alarm system.

Ten seconds and one smashed window later, she was in the car, crossed the ignition wires, and coaxed the engine to life.

She floored the accelerator. The more distance she put between her and in-the-middle-of-nowhere Del Sombra, California, the better it would be for her.

Could she really do this?

Maybe. Sealiah wasn't all-powerful . . . not here. In the world of light their kind had money and influence, but they needed people like her to do their dirty work. If Julie ran far enough fast enough, it was possible she could escape. She hoped.

She snapped on the radio. Elvis warbled through the speakers, crooning about true hearts and how his life sucked. Join the club, King.

Twelve miles and she got onto the Coast Highway. She'd have to ditch the Duster and find another ride.

There—she spotted a flickering neon sunset and two dozen Harleys parked underneath. The tavern's sign read LAST SUNSET TAVERN.

She'd been to places like this before. The pool tables, jukeboxes, sawdust and peanuts on concrete floors, had been a second home.

Julie found a parking spot in the shadows and killed the engine.

She got out and marched to the women's restroom. She'd worn a little makeup for Eliot tonight, but to get inside the bar and find a protector and new transportation, she needed war paint.

Julie fluffed her hair. She slathered on lipstick, a color that would've made her mama blush.

She sighed and fogged up the mirror. She wished she were with Eliot. What would it have been like to hear him play every day?

What if she had just told him the truth?

Could Eliot forgive her? More important, would he believe her and be able to *protect* her?

Sealiah had spoken of his family—how they were so powerful that the Infernals had to dance around to get a chance to grab Eliot.

Of all the places in the world she could go, Eliot's dingy, little run-down apartment, smack in the middle of boredom on earth, might just be the safest place, after all.

Would his family even listen to her, though, a spy for the enemy? And if Sealiah was so scared of them . . . shouldn't she be, too?

She wished she had had time to think this all through. Eliot would be back home by now. If she was going to try this crazy plan of telling the truth, she'd have to do it quickly.

Julie wiped off her lipstick. She decided: back to Del Sombra it was.

Maybe it was Eliot's song making her think crazy, but she'd give the truth a chance . . . even if it killed her.

Julie trotted back into the parking lot. A group of guys by the bar spotted her and called out, but she ignored them. She was getting out of here just in the nick of time. It would've been all too easy to slip back into old ways. And look where that had landed her.

She hurried to the Duster, not making eye contact with the bar creeps. She heard them walking after her.

She opened the driver's-side door, got in, and slammed it shut. In the rearview mirror, she saw the three of them stop . . . whisper to each other, then back away, almost running to the bar.

Julie exhaled. Too close.

Funny, she thought she'd smelled the leather of their jackets. But they hadn't got that close, had they?

She held up her hand. It shook. She tried to make it stop. That's all she needed now was to get pulled over by a cop for driving like a drunk.

A slender hand clamped onto her arm.

"No need to tremble, my pet," cooed a velvet voice.

Julie jumped.

Sitting next to her, perfectly still and silent, was Sealiah, Queen of Poppies, Mistress of the Many-Colored Jungles, the Lady of Pain. She wore snakeskin pants and an oversize black biker jacket. The smell of reptile leather and perfume was overwhelming.

Julie turned and pulled on the door handle.

Sealiah yanked her back—nearly pulling her arm out of its socket. With a blur of motion, the door's lock smashed down into a blob of metal.

"There has been quite enough running for one evening, I think." Sealiah released Julie's arm.

Julie's parents had made her watch nature documentaries when she was a kid (partially to compensate for all the school she skipped). She remembered what happened when a lion or pack of hyenas caught up to a gazelle. The animal would scream and kick, but then it gave up, eyes glazed over . . . and it would let them eat it *still alive*. As if some part in its brain started turning off the lights before it fully checked out.

That's where Julie was at this exact moment.

Trapped. About to die. Strangely calm.

Or was that Eliot's hope still inside her? She snorted a laugh. As if one silly emotion could help her out of this mess. She had been such a fool to believe.

"Much better," Sealiah said. "I'm glad you've decided to be reasonable. I have just a few questions."

"Yes, ma'am." Be polite. Mama always told her politeness would take her further than her looks.

"I'm not angry. I admire your spirit." Sealiah stared at Julie a moment, examining her, then asked, "I want to know why you left. By all reports, you already had our young Eliot Post for the taking."

Julie dared not lie. "Yes, ma'am, I did."

"A girl like you wouldn't have been scared. There were no League agents present. Why depart at the moment of your victory?"

Sealiah lifted Julie's chin with one pointed fingernail.

Julie had no choice but to look into her emerald eyes. Sealiah was beautiful. Her features reminded her of a predator cat, sleek and dangerous.

"I . . . I couldn't do it to him."

"Surely you did not fall in love. I *know* you are smarter than that."

Julie struggled to keep her feelings to herself. She didn't want to share them with this monster. The words came nonetheless, pulled from her unwillingly.

"He gave me something," she whispered.

Sealiah's hand drifted between Julie's breasts.

Julie's heart beat fast and erratic as if it were being torn from her chest. She gulped in air, but it didn't help.

"I can hear it," Sealiah whispered. "A song just for you. Powerful magic. Oh, yes, an extraordinary gift." She withdrew her hand and wiped it on her pants. "Did you know that people can go their entire lives, and most actually do, without ever feeling that? I am almost jealous, child."

Julie folded her arms protectively over her chest.

Sealiah set her hand on Julie's arm again, holding it lightly, but her pointed nails dimpled the flesh. "So I don't blame you. If I were you, I might've tried the same thing."

"Really?"

"I can see that you did your very best with Eliot. Who could have ever imagined he would be so clever."

Julie felt hope again. She heard Eliot's music inside her. "So I can—"

"Go?" Sealiah's hand tightened on Julie's arm. "Of course not. I said I *understood*. I did not say that I was an utter fool."

Julie's hope dimmed to a faint ember, not completely extinguished, but it would never blaze again as it had when Eliot had first played her song.

"No need to take such a somber attitude. I like you. I've come to give you the easy way out." Sealiah opened the glove box, removed a leather wallet, and unfolded the flap. Inside was a length of rubber tubing and a syringe.

Julie stared at it, horrified. "No . . . ," she whispered.

"It is the best. I saw to its procurement myself."

"I . . . I can't." Julie tried to pull away, but Sealiah's hand was immovable and her nails drew blood.

"There are harder ways, my dear. Much harder. I shall not be so generous again."

Julie stopped her struggles and touched the syringe. It was ice-cold.

No. Never.

But she couldn't take her hand off the thing, either. It would feel so good. It would take away the pain, make her forget . . . just for a while.

"This is something you must do for yourself," Sealiah said. "I cannot help. There are rules about these things."[56]

Just as before . . . Julie would kill herself. *Cross my heart and hope to die.*

She let the truth of the situation settle about her like concrete. She had set the terms of their agreement—binding no matter what the outcome. She had gambled for her life and soul . . . and lost both.

She picked up the tubing. Like the half-eaten gazelle, she would have to check out. The easy way or the hard way, but she *was* going.

Mechanically, she tied off her arm. The veins bulged.

She hated herself for being weak, for not even trying to be strong in the last moment of her life.

There was still some hope . . . wasn't there?

She should fight . . . She should . . .

One pinprick.

"There," Sealiah whispered. "That's a good girl."

Eliot's song faded. Numbness washed over Julie, and Sealiah drew her closer.

Drowning in euphoria, Julie squeezed the last tears from her living eyes. Her heart slowed. As blackness took her, she felt the Queen of Poppies take her and rock her to sleep.

---

56. The angel Sealiah was responsible for teaching agriculture to humanity. When she fell from grace, she made a gift of poppies to mortals and taught all their nefarious uses. She has dominion over all who sin with and die from such opiates. *Gods of the First and Twenty-first Century, Volume 13: Infernal Forces,* 8th ed. (Zypheron Press Ltd.).

58

A CURE FOR THE BLUES

liot could see the Bavarian façade of the Oakwood Apartments ahead, but he dawdled. He didn't want to stay outside, but he didn't want to go home, either.

It felt as if someone had taken a spoon and scooped out his insides. Julie was gone.

Clouds rumbled overhead, rain fell in patches, and light broke through here and there.

Why had she asked him to go with her if she hadn't meant it? Was it possible she was just playing with him the entire time?

He shuffled through a pile of shattered safety glass on the sidewalk. It looked as if a car window had got busted out.

On the other hand, maybe it was best not to know why Julie had left without him. Instead, Eliot wondered if something might have forced her to leave early. She could be just as broken up about it as he was. It was as if fate had kept them apart.

He slipped into a daydream, one where he found clues to where she had gone, puzzled out the mystery, and fought the bad guys—

Eliot stumbled into a man on the sidewalk.

"Oh, sorry, sir."

"They are called the blues, young man."

Eliot looked up, surprised. He recognized the voice . . . although not the man who had spoken.

This person was as tall as Grandmother, slim, but somehow managing to block the entire sidewalk. He was an older gentleman. His black hair was streaked with silver at his temples, combed back, and flowed over his shoulders. He wore black slacks and a cornflower blue shirt that matched the twinkle in his eyes. He had expensive alligator-leather shoes and a camel-hair overcoat.

"You might as well be playing a funeral dirge upon Lady Dawn. Your face is so long it practically drags on the sidewalk." The man drew his hand over his chin, pretending it was ridiculously elongated.

Eliot recognized him. It was homeless Louis, now transformed. "You look . . ."

Louis smiled at Eliot with brilliant white teeth. "No longer like an alcoholic bum urinating on himself in the corner of an alley? Selling his blood by the pint to pay for fortified spirits to blot out the indomitable pain of life?"

"I was going to say, you look good, sir," Eliot said.

"Well, thank you." Louis's smile faded a bit. "You should watch where you're going. You could have wandered into the street and been flattened by some careless driver."

Funny . . . but now that Eliot thought about it, he hadn't seen a single car or person since he had left the bus station. It was as if everyone in Del Sombra were on vacation.

"I'm sorry for running into you. I was thinking about someone else."

"Never apologize twice for the same thing. It transforms politeness into weakness. There is nothing to apologize for. You are a young man with deep thoughts, an admirable trait."

"I guess so."

"So tell me about this girl."

"How did you know . . . ?"

Louis placed his hand over his chest. "I have worn the look on your face many times." He gestured back up the street. "I was walking this way. Would you care to accompany me? We can talk for a bit."

Eliot glanced toward home. Grandmother and Cee were probably wondering where he was. And Fiona surely needed him.

But Eliot had needs, too. And right now, he needed another guy to talk to about Julie.

"Okay," Eliot said. "I can only stay a few minutes, though."

"That will do."

Louis turned and Eliot followed. Louis walked at a brisk pace and Eliot trotted to keep up.

"So there was this girl. I thought she and I . . ." The words stuck in Eliot's throat. "But she never showed up."

Louis's smile vanished and his lips pursed. "Hold a moment." He stopped. He placed his long hand upon Eliot's chest like a doctor performing a checkup. "Your heart yet beats," Louis whispered. "It is wounded, but strong. You'll live."

He turned and they continued to walk, but slower.

"You may not believe it now," Louis said, "but in a week the pain will lessen. In a month, it will still hurt like hell, but it will be more memory than real."

Eliot could *almost* believe that. Louis seemed to know what he was talking about. Certainly he had dealt with women before, too.

"She was special . . . different. A girl like that has never even given me a second look before."

"She was beautiful?"

"The prettiest girl who's ever come to Del Sombra."

"Really?" Louis stroked his chin. "Pretty *and* new in town?" His eyes narrowed and his face darkened. "Of course they would tempt you."

Eliot didn't like this look on Louis. He'd seen him crazy and confused. He'd seen him in loving concentration when he had played Lady Dawn. But never before had Eliot considered Louis dangerous, until now . . . his eyes smoldering.

Eliot changed the subject. "I found the music you left for me."

This snapped Louis out of whatever thoughts clouded his mood.

"In the alley. Chalked on the sidewalk," Eliot explained. "I found it just before the rain washed it away."

Louis smiled, but it was as if the grin had frozen on his face, and behind it something else was going on.

"How fascinating," Louis said. "How lucky for you."

Twilight shadows flooded the street, and the concrete sidewalk ahead became squares of solid gloom.

Louis set his hand on Eliot's shoulder. "Let's discuss this music before we go farther."

Louis knelt next to him. He drew a set of lines and dotted notes on the sidewalk. It was the nursery rhyme he had taught him.

"'Mortal's Coil,'" Eliot said.

"Indeed. It is the first part of the *Sinfonia di esistenza;* that's Italian for *The Symphony of Existence.*"

, "I saw the rest, the middle, and even the end. Although that last part was a bit smeared. I figured it out, though."

Louis's smile completely faded. "Did you?"

"Sure."

The raindrop-painted notes blazed in Eliot's memory. It was tremendously complicated, but he nonetheless tried to reduce it so he could hum it for Louis—prove that he knew it.

Louis held up one finger. "There is no need for that. I can see it like a bonfire burning in your thoughts."

He stared deep into Eliot's eyes. It was like one of those soul-penetrating gazes Grandmother gave him when she was displeased . . . only this was something Eliot had never before seen. Louis actually looked proud.

"You have done something even I could not have." Louis squeezed Eliot's shoulder. "You are already better than I."

"There's no way." Eliot felt himself blushing—and embarrassed by this, he blushed even harder.

"Do not be modest. Ever. People will always try to make you less than you are. Do not assist them." Louis got a faraway look. "Yes, a violin. Naturally, strings. I should have foreseen that you would inherit great gifts."

"I don't understand, sir. I'm sor—"

Eliot was about to say again he was sorry, but then remembered Louis's admonishment to stop apologizing for everything. That was Grandmother's and Cecilia's influence on him: always their "good little boy." Maybe Louis was right; he had to stop feeling so worthless.

"When I play, it's like . . ."

"Like the world listens? The sky and the earth accompany you? That the entire universe is your audience?"

Eliot nodded. "There were these rats in the sewer, and a calliope in a carnival . . ."

"I know. I have heard every note, carried to me by the winds."

That wasn't possible. Louis was talking crazy now.

And yet he was the one who had showed Eliot how to play Lady Dawn in the first place, the one who had brought his talent to the surface.

Louis wasn't normal. That was for sure. But just how *un*normal was he?

He wasn't like Uncle Henry or Grandmother or anyone else in the family. He wasn't like any person he'd ever met, sane or otherwise.

"Who are you?" Eliot's question came out as a squeaky whisper, as if asking it broke some unspoken cosmic rule.

Louis's mouth worked but no words came. He finally managed, "I am someone who cares very much about you." He sighed. "Apparently even more than *I* realized."

Louis looked up and Eliot followed his gaze.

The shadows that seem to be absorbing the sidewalk crept closer.

"We don't have much time. There are plans to consider." Louis looked again at Eliot, emotions fighting for control of his features. "And plans to *reconsider* as well." Louis stood and turned his back to the darkness. "I must get you home. It is late to be in this part of town."

Eliot didn't want to go home. Louis knew things about music. Did he know about the family, too? The Council? How could someone who lived in an alley know anything?

"You know what's happening, don't you? My family . . . the trials . . ."

"I will never lie to you, Eliot. Yes, I know, part at least."

"Who are you? Really?"

Louis hurried Eliot along. He was stronger than Eliot imagined, forcing him to walk back the way they had come at a brisk pace.

"I have had so many names." Louis glanced over his shoulder. "All you need to know is that I'm your friend, maybe the only one who places your well-being before their own."

"Please tell me. I'm a great listener."

"I'm sure you possess that rare talent as well." Louis stopped. "But, alas, here we are . . . as far as I'm permitted to go."

They stood at the exact spot where Eliot had bumped into him.

Behind them, the darkness was somehow . . . darker. As if part of Del Sombra had been swallowed by a void.

But that was silly.

Streetlights flickered on overhead, casting pools of illumination along Midway Avenue up to Oakwood Apartments. The other way, however, back toward Ringo's, the streetlights were broken. All of them.

"There is so much I want to tell you." Louis cocked his head as if he heard something far away. "But there is no time. They are already coming for you."

Finally, someone who actually wanted to tell Eliot something. "So tell me," he pleaded. "Quick."

Louis's lips fused into a single white pressure line. "Do you trust me?"

Of course Eliot did, and he started to tell Louis so . . . but something inside him hesitated.

He looked carefully at Louis—really for the first time. Before, his features had been obscured by tangles of hair and half-shaven stubble, but now he saw Louis had a sharp, pointy nose and his ears stuck out . . . a bit like Eliot's.

Could he be related? Like Uncle Henry, but not from *that* side of the family, rather from his father's people?

"Do you trust me?" Louis repeated.

Eliot took a tiny step backward. "No . . . yes. I'm sorry, sir, I don't know."

Louis nodded. "Honesty between us will be best. Always. Go with your first impulse."

"I want to."

"Tut-tut . . ." Louis's face brightened. "There is one thing I can tell you." He gently tapped Eliot in the center of his chest. "In here you are strong—despite the vagaries of women who will doubtless plague your life. Your sister is strong, too, but in another way. Together you are more than the sum of these strengths. Stay with her, for now."

"Fiona? What does she have to do with you?"

"Oh, regrettably, everything." Louis looked down the street.

Along Midway Avenue a black shape rocketed from the shadows. A gleaming silver grill and mirrored chrome rims reflected the orange streetlight.

The car headed straight for Eliot.

Louis wrapped his arm about Eliot's shoulder, draping his camel-hair coat over him.

Closer now, Eliot glimpsed a silver v-12 emblem on the car's hood. He froze in its high-powered halogen headlights.

The tires of the limousine smoked, skidded to a halt, and parked perfectly at the curbside.

The driver's door popped open. Robert leapt out.

Robert stayed where he was, though, keeping the bulk of the car between them.

"Get away from that creep," Robert ordered Eliot.

Eliot blinked, recovering from the shock of almost getting run over. "What are you doing? You could've killed us!"

Robert shook his head, but otherwise didn't acknowledge Eliot. His eyes were locked on Louis.

Louis stared back. He held up one hand. His other arm and camel-hair coat, however, still wrapped protectively around Eliot.

"Get away from that guy," Robert repeated. "He is a black hat."

Eliot didn't understand. Louis wasn't wearing a hat. Or was that another popular-culture reference that any ordinary person would have understood?

"In this particular drama," Louis said, "I wear neither white nor black hats." He withdrew his arm from around Eliot and stepped away. "But I do have better things to do, so I will have to say good-bye for now."

"Wait," Eliot said. "We were going to talk."

"And we will. Soon. I promise."

"Don't listen to him," Robert said. "All his kind can do is lie. Just get into the car."

"No." Eliot wheeled on Robert, the anger in his voice surprising them both. After surviving two heroic life-or-death trials, Eliot found that he had more than enough willpower to stand up to cooler-than-humanly-possible Robert.

"Go on," Louis whispered. "Remember what we talked about."

"I think I'm old enough to decide what to do on my own," Eliot said.

Louis nodded at him. "So you are. But I believe your young Driver friend has yet to tell you something."

Robert licked his lips. "You *have* to come with me, Eliot," he whispered. "It's Fiona. She's in the hospital . . . dying."

59

FATAL DIAGNOSIS

Eliot stood at Fiona's bedside and held her right hand. Cee was on the other side of the bed, clutching Fiona's left hand, careful not to tangle her IV lines.

His sister looked as if she had been bled dry. Her arm was limp and ice-cold and felt a good deal lighter than normal. Eliot had never in his worst nightmares imagined that Fiona, so strong and active, could look so frail.

He glanced about, hoping someone could tell him what had happened to her.

Robert stood in the corner of the private hospital room, arms crossed and eyes riveted on Eliot's sister . . . all his bravado and coolness useless now.

Grandmother stood at the foot of the bed, poring over the doctor's notes.

If Eliot hadn't left Fiona this morning, maybe he would have been there when she needed him—prevented this.

Grandmother looked up. "This is not your fault," she said drily to him, then her eyes flicked back to the pages. "Your sister's clinical diagnosis is severe malnutrition and dehydration."

"How is that possible?" Eliot asked. "She's been eating . . ."

Eating those chocolates. Tons of them.

Had they been poisoned? Eliot had always known there was something weird about them.

Grandmother ignored his question and continued to read the doctor's notes. "Intravenous rehydration and feeding tubes have been used, but to no effect. Her body rejects food and water."

That couldn't happen. Eliot knew that was cellular-level chemistry, not a conscious decision.

"There's more to this than medical science," Eliot whispered, "isn't there?"

Cee leaned over and touched his arm consolingly. "It's best to focus happy thoughts towards your sister, dear."

Grandmother turned to the hallway door. She dropped the notes on the bed—and a scalpel appeared in her hand.

The door opened and Aunt Lucia and Uncle Henry entered, both halting and staring at Grandmother's hand and the knife.

Eliot was just as startled. Grandmother looked (if this were possible) even more threatening than he thought she could.

No one moved or spoke for a moment, then Uncle Henry whispered, "Please, Audrey. We're here to help this time."

"How typical," Lucia said, narrowing her eyes. "Make sure you kill *all* who love you."

Grandmother sighed. The scalpel disappeared.

Eliot didn't see where it had vanished to.

Lucia moved to Audrey and hugged her. Grandmother halfheartedly returned the gesture.

Uncle Henry nodded at Robert, then stood behind Eliot, setting his hands on his shoulders. "We pieced together what has happened," Uncle Henry told them, "and came as soon as we could."

"I could strangle Dallas," Lucia muttered, "for showing them the threads so early."

"Fiona had no choice," Grandmother replied. "There was an external influence. If she had not made the cut, she would not have even lasted this long."

"Can someone please tell me what this all means?" Eliot demanded.

Grandmother pierced him with a stare, but Eliot mustered his resolve and didn't blink.

"It was as you saw," Grandmother said. "That afternoon when Dallas showed you the threads, we saw Fiona's end. She has only a handful of hours left to live, and there is nothing anyone can do to prevent that."

Eliot went numb. He couldn't imagine life without his sister.

"This may not be entirely true." Lucia pushed the medical charts aside and forced Grandmother to look at her. "We think we may have a way to save her."

Grandmother raised one eyebrow, for the first time showing a glimmer of interest.

"Yes," Uncle Henry said, "with the twins' third heroic trial."

60

AN APPLE A DAY

Fiona was air. She was dust and light and spread so thin her thoughts drifted.

Then her mind settled into a heaviness that crushed her and made every breath a struggle.

She opened her eyes.

She was in a strange bed. Grandmother stood to one side in the shadows. Aunt Lucia stood on the other side bathed in the moonlight that streamed through the open window.

Their hands moved over the covers. Among the rumpled bedsheets were a tangle of multicolored cotton fibers, plastic twine, leather thongs, glimmering silken strands, and lines of gold. There were stranger things as well: threads of smoke and shadow, and serrated razor wire.

Fiona struggled to sit up and realized all this material came from *inside* her.

Grandmother and Lucia had opened her up—her insides pulled out in piles. The two women tugged at sections of the weave and tied knots. Every motion pinched and hurt.

Waves of nausea washed over Fiona and she drew in a deep breath to scream.

But then there wasn't a weave anymore, only Grandmother and Lucia straightening her bedcovers, smoothing the sheets with practiced hands.

A nightmare?

She didn't think so. That was the same weave she had seen in the mirror maze. The same fabric of life she had examined before . . . she what? Blacked out?

She hadn't expected to wake up, she remembered that much.

Fiona touched her throbbing forehead.

"Did I fall?" she asked.

She looked around, her eyes finally able to focus.

An anxious-looking Eliot stood next to Grandmother and he tried to crowd closer.

It annoyed Fiona that her brother hadn't been there for her earlier. Nonetheless, she reached for him, and he took her hand.

Cee was right behind Eliot, smiling, and wringing her hands. "We thought we'd lost you, my dove."

Grandmother glared at her and Cee stepped back.

Fiona's heart skipped a beat when she spotted Robert in the corner of the room.

He looked uncomfortable, arms crossed over his chest. He gave her a little salute . . . as if everything were normal, as if she were in this hospital room because she had a hangnail. His eyes gave him away, however: bloodshot and nervously glancing toward Uncle Henry.

Uncle Henry settled on the foot of the bed and crossed one leg over the other, completely at ease in this weird situation.

That both Uncle Henry and Aunt Lucia were here chilled Fiona. Did that mean the Council was about to do something to them again?

"What's going on?" Fiona asked.

"If the child is well enough to ask," Uncle Henry said, "then I suggest we tell her."

"We have shored up your strength," Lucia explained gently.

"I . . . I think I saw that. The weave."

Lucia and Grandmother exchanged a glance, then Grandmother said, "Very good. Then you know that when you cut yourself before, you damaged the pattern."

Fiona nodded.

"You severed your appetite," Lucia continued, "when you freed yourself from . . . external influences."

The chocolates, that's what they were talking about. Fiona's hand rose to her throat.

"I had to," she whispered.

"Of course you did," Grandmother said. "No one questions that decision. But there were consequences."

"Appetite in excess is disastrous," Lucia said. "But *no* appetite is—"

"Fatal," Grandmother said without emotion. "Your body now refuses to take in food or water."

Eliot tightened his grip on her hand. Fiona could see he was scared, too. "It's going to be okay," she told him.

The situation, however, was far from "okay," but Fiona wasn't about to show the fear taking root in her. Instinctively she knew that showing weakness in front of so many family members would be a mistake.

"That's what Dallas was trying to show to me the other day," she said. "My thread—the one leading into the future was short. Less than a day left."

Fiona looked about the room for Dallas, the woman who might be her aunt or might possibly be her mother. She disappointingly wasn't here.

"No longer a day," Grandmother said. "Six hours, perhaps less."

"We have given you the strength, at least," Lucia said, "to stand on your own for the remaining time."

Cee whimpered, but thankfully didn't start crying. If someone started crying now, Fiona wasn't sure she'd be able to keep her tears in check, either.

"This sucks," Fiona said.

"An accurate summation," Uncle Henry said, and flashed a smile. "But worry not. We have a plan."

Henry pressed his palms together as if cupping some invisible sphere. He twisted his hands back and forth, feigning concentration, then astonishment. With a great flourish, he revealed a Granny Smith apple, which he presented to her.

"Thank you, Uncle Henry, but I'm not hungry."

"Really, Henry," Lucia said. "Try, for once, to have a modicum of tact." Henry shrugged and took a bite of the apple.

"The way they've come up to help us," Eliot whispered, "is our third trial."

There was an edge to Eliot's voice, warning her that whatever it was, it wasn't going to be as easy as eating some stage-magic conjured fruit.

"It is no ordinary apple that you will need," Lucia said, "but a Golden Apple."

Fiona looked to Eliot, but he just shrugged. Fiona turned back to Lucia. "Is that like a Golden Delicious?"

Lucia sighed. "You really have kept them in the dark about *everything*, haven't you, Audrey?"

Grandmother tilted her head so she seemed to look down upon her sister. "Apparently, not enough in the dark . . . or they would not be in this predicament."

"Ladies, please, bicker later." Uncle Henry tapped his wristwatch. "The sands of time slip away."

"You are correct for once, Henry." Lucia smoothed out her dress and turned back to Fiona. "The Golden Apples you seek are not to be found at your local farmer's market. These apples have great life-giving powers. So prized are they that wars have been fought over them."[57]

Fiona swallowed hard. The thought of eating anything made her want to throw up. "What's the catch?"

"Ah, good, your mind is undiminished despite the recent blows." Uncle Henry patted her knee. Grandmother glowered at this display of affection, so he immediately withdrew his hand. "Yes, there is a catch."

Across the room, Robert shifted, looking even more uncomfortable.

"Years ago," Lucia said, "pieces from a single apple fell into hands we never intended."[58]

"So we took steps to ensure they would be safe." Uncle Henry reached up toward the ceiling. "And we set them among the stars."

"A satellite receptacle," Lucia explained. "Completely undetectable."

"Alas," Henry said, "we failed to consider the vast amounts of man-made space junk. Collisions eventually nudged our satellite out of orbit and back to earth."

"So it's buried somewhere?" Eliot asked. "In some impact crater? And we have to find it?"

"It has already been found," Henry told him. "We never bothered getting it back, because they'll never open it in a thousand years . . . and

57. So-called Golden Apples appear in many mythologies. The Norse Aesir retained their immortality by eating such fruit. The goddess of discord rolled one such apple inscribed with FOR THE MOST BEAUTIFUL among Hera, Athena, and Aphrodite—which ultimately precipitated the Trojan War. The Celts tell of such an apple feeding a person for an entire year. A hypothesis among mythohistorians is that the Golden Apples of legend were actually oranges (not commonly introduced to Mediterranean regions until the eleventh century). In many languages *orange* is etymologically equivalent to *golden apple*. *Gods of the First and Twenty-first Century, Volume 4: Core Myths* (Part 1), 8th ed. (Zypheron Press Ltd.).

58. One little-known urban myth is that slivers of magical apple appeared in late 1960s and early '70s, and that certain individuals ate the fruit and went on to found record and computer corporations taking this fruit as their symbol. Many dispute this legend, but others claim the two corporations' meteoric rise, power, and wealth was nothing less than "magical." *Gods of the First and Twenty-first Century, Volume 6: Modern Myths*, 8th ed. (Zypheron Press Ltd.).

they have it in a very safe place: the Air Force Flight Test Center in Nevada.[59]

"Air force?" Fiona asked. "The *United States* air force?"

Uncle Henry nodded.

"So it's going to be guarded," Eliot said.

Henry gave a careless wave and let out a sigh. "Oh, yes . . . vaults, guards, trained dogs, perhaps even patrolling stealth helicopters."

"So this is your third heroic trial," Lucia told them. "Enter the base, steal the apple back . . . and eat part to save your life."

"Or get ourselves shot trying," Fiona muttered.

"We can do it," Eliot told her in a whisper.

She nodded to him.

She didn't believe in a million years they had a chance. This wasn't one crazy guy in a carnival . . . or even a talking crocodile. There would be hundreds of guards with guns on a military base. There'd be electronic doodads and experts trained to look for people like her and Eliot trying to sneak inside.

Or was there perhaps a *tiny* chance?

She could cut through anything: barbed-wire fences; cinder-block walls; or even, she bet, a hardened-steel vault door. And was there anything Eliot couldn't do with his music?

Still, Fiona didn't buy Uncle Henry's explanation about their leaving the apples there because they were safe. She had a feeling they left them because even the League *couldn't* get to them.

Robert stood straighter and took a step toward Fiona. "Let me—" He cleared his throat and tried again. "Let me go for her. You've let others use champions."

"No," Lucia said coldly, and glared at him.

Robert halted dead in his tracks.

"I like this one," Grandmother said to Henry. "Brave, kind, but your Drivers do seem to have a regrettable tendency for suicide by bravado."

The color drained from Robert's face.

Henry grinned at him as one might at a puppy trying to charge a fully grown bull mastiff. "Thank you, Robert, but I'm afraid not. Proxy champions are only allowed for League members, not *potential* League members."

Robert nodded and took a step back.

59. Aka. Groom Lake, Paradise Ranch, or Area 51.—Editor.

"I must go and deal with loose ends," Grandmother said. "Children, I want you ready to leave in thirty minutes."

"Yes, Grandmother," Eliot and Fiona said together.

Fiona bristled. They *still* followed her orders. She glared at Grandmother as she left the room.

"We could die and she's not going to help us, is she?" Fiona said. "None of you are."

"There are rules, my dear," Uncle Henry said, and he glanced at Lucia. "And we all follow them."

Lucia sighed. "You may give them a ride to the base's perimeter," she said without looking his way. "Ask no more."

Fiona could understand Lucia and Uncle Henry . . . a little. The Council was out to prove something about them using brutal traditions. But what was Grandmother's excuse for being so cold and callous?

"I hate her," Fiona said.

Cee sidled next to her. "My darling, you must not say that."

"It's true."

Cee's lips quivered as she whispered, "Others have make sacrifices and done dreadful things. You are not the only one who's had to cut herself." Cecilia's eyes were teary. "You may never fully understand your grandmother, but you must trust that she is doing the right thing for you. Always."

Fiona nodded. She would never trust Grandmother. She couldn't. Not after fifteen years of lies. But she wasn't about to argue with poor doddering and loving Cee.

Besides, Fiona was busy processing what Cee had just told her: Grandmother had cut herself, too.

What had she severed? Her sense of humor? Her pity?

"You should tell them about the others," Robert said to Uncle Henry. "They're close. One of them was with Eliot when I picked him up."

Lucia took a step toward Robert. "Go fetch the car, Driver, while you still can."

Robert gulped and whispered, "Yes, ma'am." He spared an anxious glance at Fiona and hurried from the room.

"What 'others'?" Fiona asked. "The other family?"

At this Aunt Lucia's eyes widened.

"Who was with you?" Fiona asked Eliot.

Eliot features bunched together. "It was Louis. Robert might be right. Louis, I think, is with the other family."

Fiona laughed, even though this hurt her stomach. "No way. Louis the bum? Dirty, psychotic, pizza-stealing Louis?"

"Hush, child," Uncle Henry said, shaking his head. "Even if that *is* true . . . you must not speak that way of your father."

SAND AND FOG

Eliot, Fiona, and Uncle Henry rode in the back of his limousine. Robert had driven them down the California coast and across the Mojave Desert.

Eliot had wanted to ask Uncle Henry about Louis back in the hospital room, but Aunt Lucia had spoken to Henry first—in rapid-fire Italian. Eliot didn't understand Italian, but he got the gist of it: there would be no more talk of *that* side of the family.

How utterly typical.

Once more they were keeping the one thing he most wanted to know from him and Fiona. As if their knowing about their father and his family might somehow hurt them . . . when they were about to face death for the *third* time this week.

He stared out the window. The lights of Las Vegas glimmered in the distance. It looked like a carnival, and that thought caused a shudder to run down his back. It had been less than a day since he and Fiona had been trapped in the flaming scrapyard, since he had rescued Amanda Lane, and Fiona had killed Mr. Millhouse.

Had that only been *last* night? He felt like a different person.

The thrumming power from the Maybach's fuel-injected cylinders relaxed to a purr. "Slowing down a bit, sir," Robert announced from the driver's compartment. "We're close to the base, and I'm not sure what their radar will pick up."

"Quite right," Uncle Henry replied. He looked distracted for a moment, then said, "Where was I?"

"You were telling us about the base's security," Fiona replied.

Eliot's sister sat unusually straight. She was pale and looked weak, but her eyes burned with determination.

"Let me start from the beginning." Uncle Henry swirled the contents of his highball glass: ice and some pungent liquor whose fumes made Eliot's nose crinkle. "First, there are patrols along the perimeter. Guards will have night-vision gear. Computer-controlled motion and thermal sensors will be the next obstacle to overcome. They are located on base and monitor via telescopic imaging—very difficult to get around."

Eliot wondered if Uncle Henry spoke from firsthand experience. He seemed to know an awful lot about this.

"If you are detected," Uncle Henry continued, "it will trigger a massive response: all-terrain vehicles, and if necessary, aerial reconnaissance."

"Can we stow away on a truck?" Eliot suggested.

Uncle Henry flashed a pitying look at him. "They check each vehicle by weight. The more secure areas, which you need to get into, use X-ray machines. There are trained dogs as well, who are harder to fool than machines."

"Assuming we somehow can get onto the base," Fiona said, "what's there?"

Uncle Henry casually waved his hand. "A few high fences. Some sections are mined. There are security cameras. And, oh, there will be an organized tactical-response team to deal with intruders . . . they will shoot to kill."

Eliot felt a momentary spike of panic, but it faded. He recognized the potential lethality of these obstacles, but oddly such things no longer paralyzed him with fear.

Recklessness and bravado stirred within his soul—feelings that would a few days ago only have existed in his fantasies. Now they seemed real.

"Where are the apples?" Eliot asked.

"How silly of me. Of course, the most important detail." Uncle Henry looked at his drink, then set it aside. "Building 211. It appears as any other office building, but is actually a camouflaged long-term-storage vault."

He reached into his pocket and unfolded a tiny blueprint. Etched upon it was a picture of what looked like a Fabergé egg with intricate jewel-like electronics and cuneiform captions.

"The satellite vessel," he explained.

Fiona pointed to the thick outer shell. "What's it made out of?"

"The outside is a ceramic alloy impervious to man-made laser, bomb, or edge."

"Can *I* cut it?" Fiona asked.

"I honestly don't know. But you'll have to try because the satellite weighs a considerable amount and will be impossible for you two to simply carry off."

"Five minutes," Robert called from the front.

The lights of Las Vegas were long gone. They were on a dirt road, and the limousine's headlights illuminated sagebrush and dust clouds.

"I guess that's enough about the base," Eliot said. "I wanted to talk more about our father, though."

Uncle Henry found a handkerchief and dabbed his lips. "Oh, that was a slip of the tongue. I shouldn't have said a thing about that. Really, it is for your grandmother to discuss."

"And where is she?" Fiona asked.

"Dealing with a few loose ends," Henry said. "Some bad people were following you, and we couldn't allow that."

"They're not 'bad people,'" Eliot said, anger creeping into his voice. "Don't treat us like kids. We know they're the other side of our family. I want you to tell me more about Louis Piper."

Uncle Henry looked out the windows. "I suppose this is no longer news," he quietly said. "Louis met your mother at the Venice carnival. I told you about the carnival? They wear these masks—"

"You told us that already," Eliot said. "Stop avoiding the issue. Everyone said our father was dead. Instead, he's some homeless person? How did that happen?"

Uncle Henry scooted backward in his seat, making the leather squeak.

"Eliot, my dear boy," he whispered. "Please, do you know what your Aunt Lucia and grandmother would do if I spoke of this?"

Eliot and his sister together glared at him.

Uncle Henry blinked, then with a great sigh said, "Oh, very well, life is too short to keep such secrets." He leaned forward. "Your mother felt that Louis was a threat to you, but she still loved him and thus could not bring herself to actually kill him. A very foolish sentiment, I might add." Uncle Henry finished his drink. "So she merely removed his power—cast him down in a lower form to the mortal world."

"Why didn't someone offer us *that* option instead of the heroic trials?" Fiona asked. "I'd rather be normal than dead."

Her suggestion made Eliot's stomach turn. He loved his music. Was it his own natural ability, though? Or something supernatural? Was it worth risking his life for?

"Alas," Uncle Henry said, his features becoming uncharacteristically stony, "this is a trick only your mother could perform. One she never shared with the League or anyone else."

"So Louis is *just* human now?" Fiona asked.

"Human, but hardly 'just.' He possesses many lifetimes of knowledge and has ties to the other family, which make him dangerous. I urge you to avoid the man. Certainly never trust him."

"Because he doesn't have our well-being in mind?" Eliot retorted. "Like he might send us on near suicidal tests to figure out which side of the family we belong to?"

Uncle Henry's gaze fell to the floor, and he looked wounded. "Have I not bent every rule I could to help you?"

Eliot felt the ire drain from him. He was about to say he was sorry for ever doubting Uncle Henry, but halted . . . remembering Louis's advice to stop apologizing so much. Did Uncle Henry really care anyway, or was he just manipulating them?

Robert killed the limousine's headlights, slowed, and pulled off the dirt road. "This is it. The shortest way to Area 51 is southwest from here— about a six-mile hike. Sorry, it's the closest I can get you." Robert got out and came around to open the door on Fiona's side.

Eliot slid out after her.

It was cold. Uncle Henry handed them both fleece-lined windbreakers.

"Thanks," Eliot said, and pulled it on.

Fiona embraced Robert. "Thank you for everything," she whispered to him. "If I don't see you again . . . I just . . . I just wanted to say . . ." She touched her forehead to his.

Robert whispered something back to her. Eliot couldn't make it out, but Fiona shook her head.

Eliot looked away, embarrassed. It made him uncomfortable to see his sister all clingy, but he understood. If Julie were here, he would have wanted the same thing.

He wondered where Julie was now. He scanned the southern horizon. He hoped she was safe in Los Angeles.

"Move quickly," Uncle Henry said. "Remember your past successes. I know you can do this."

Eliot nodded. He slipped on his backpack, making sure Lady Dawn was secure and his flashlight ready.

Fiona detached herself from Robert and marched into the desert.

Eliot hesitated, looked one last time at Uncle Henry and Robert. Robert gave him the thumbs-up sign.

Eliot turned and followed his sister into the dark. "Hey!" he hissed. "Wait up."

Fiona didn't slow down, but rather increased her gait, slogging through sand and onto a hard, dry lake bed.

"I wouldn't have to slow down," she muttered, "if you weren't such a *Partula turgida*."

Eliot remembered that one. A *Partula turgida* was a snail, a particularly slow one. Nice colors, but supposedly extinct now . . . maybe because it was too slow? Nice double meaning.

He didn't have it in him to come up with a good comeback insult, so instead he asked Fiona what was really on his mind. "How you feel?"

She walked for a few moments, then replied, "Okay, I guess. A little weird inside. It's hard to explain. I'm just angry."

"At who?"

"I don't know." She sighed. "Everyone. Grandmother for not caring, or at least never showing us she does. Henry, Lucia, and the Council for putting us through this. Louis? I don't know if I should feel sorry for him or mad that he never told us who he really was."

Something crashed through the sagebrush. Eliot fumbled out his flashlight and clicked it on.

A jackrabbit bounded over the brush and vanished.

Eliot exhaled and turned off the light, hoping no one had seen it.

"Do you think," Fiona said, "Louis was in the alley all this time just to watch us? Isn't that kind of creepy?"

"I think he cares about us. There's nothing 'creepy' about that."

He wanted to tell her how Louis had been earlier tonight—a transformed, powerful man—but he wasn't sure where to start . . . and it felt like a secret between him and his supposed father.

"If he is a fallen angel, I bet he was the one called Lucifer," Eliot told her. "That's one of the names I found in *Mythica Improbiba*."

"Louis Piper," Fiona whispered. "Lucifer—makes sense."

"One of thirteen Infernal clan names. There are others: Leviathan, Azmodeus, Beelzebub, and Mephistopheles. Those could be our cousins."

"It feels weird. Do you—" Fiona's mouth worked for a moment without words, then she said, "This sounds so stupid."

"What?"

"Do you *feel* like a god? Or an angel?"

They walked in silence and Eliot thought about it.

The moon rose and made the desert a pale silver landscape. It was peaceful. Funny that just ahead was a military base full of secrets. That's how Eliot felt about his life. It seemed so ordinary a few days ago . . . but it turned out there were fences and guards and minefields he was about to stumble across.

What if Uncle Henry had never found them? Would he and Fiona have continued living with Grandmother? Homeschooled, working part-time jobs, and then what?

"No," he finally answered. "I don't feel special."

"Just ordinary, nothing's-changed Eliot Post, then?"

"Ordinary would be a step up." He sighed. "I know all these things from books, but it's nothing practical. I don't have any friends. I'd be happy just to be able to go to school and experience what every other person gets to."

The possibility of having a normal life seemed astronomically remote tonight. Eliot imagined that he and Fiona were walking on the surface of the moon—might as well be for all the connection they had to the real world.

"How about you?" he asked.

"I don't know how to feel when everything I've been told is a lie. Is Grandmother really our grandmother? Henry our uncle? Our father turns out to be alive and evil incarnate. Is it possible that our mother is alive, too? Am *I* really who I thought I was?"

"You think we're even brother and sister?"

"I'm *sure* we are," she muttered. "I'm not that lucky." She suddenly halted. "Shhh. Listen."

Eliot strained his ears. There was a car, a big one, running over the dry lake bed. To the right.

He heard another to their left.

And two more in the distance . . . straight ahead.

"I don't think those are the routine patrols Uncle Henry mentioned," Fiona whispered. "Wouldn't be so many—coincidentally *surrounding* us."

"Should we run for it?"

"No. Play something."

Eliot stepped away from her. "What do you mean? Play what?"

"I don't know . . . you got a million rats to lead us to Souhk. Can't you make a few jeeps stall? Or hide us somehow?"

Eliot rubbed his fingers, thinking. The last two times he'd played, the music had fought him for control. There had been an earthquake in Franklin Park. The fire in the carnival had come to life and spread, almost consuming them before they got away. He loved playing his violin . . . but its music was beginning to worry him, too.

"There might be something," he whispered. "Something I just learned. But it'd be hard to do."

Fiona squeezed his shoulder roughly, then let go. "Better decide if you want to try that or try to outrun all-terrain vehicles, little *Partula turgida*."

Her sarcasm was laced with poison barbs, suggesting if they got caught, it'd be his fault for not trying.

Eliot wanted to throw that back in her face and tell her to cut those vehicles in half if they got too close.

But she was right. Once they were on the base, she would be able to get them into the vaults and the satellite casing.

Out here—it *was* up to him.

He could've kicked himself; he should've been thinking about this as they walked, not about the family.

He pulled out Lady Dawn and rested her on his shoulder. Her strings vibrated in anticipation.

"Stand behind me," he told her. "Close, but don't get in my way."

He set bow to strings and played.

He didn't bother warming up with the nursery rhyme "Mortal's Coil." There was no time. The sound of the trucks was close. He jumped right into the middle of the symphony he'd seen in Louis's alley—a part where the music twisted around in ever increasing complexity.

Eliot played faster, and his fingers moved over blurred strings until they were blurs, too.

He operated on instinct, feeling the musical notes, then seeing them in his mind as they had been on the pavement.

The song became a wild thing he barely contained.

Around him the air moved in gusts—this way and that. Sand stung his face. Clouds obscured the moonlight. He smelled the ocean and seaweed and heard cries in the dark that were not human voices.

And in the back of his mind was the singing:

Running through life chasing dreams. Nothing's ever what it seems. Meaning lost and never found. Damned souls wander round and round.

The violin's vibrations layered upon themselves and echoes hung in the thickening air. It sounded as if an entire row of violins accompanied Eliot, all playing furiously.

He saw the next section of the symphony in his thoughts. It was *more* complex. The finger positioning stretched to impossible lengths.

And the melody turned darker: a weave of shadow and pain.

He wouldn't play it; it scared him.

This would have to do.

He stopped . . . or rather he *tried* to stop. The music had a mind of its own, though, and he continued to play; minor keys and deeper notes that dragged his fingers along.

This wasn't the way it was supposed to work. He was the player. Not the instrument.

He fought, stiffening his fingers, pressing harder to make them hold fast.

Lady Dawn flexed as pressure built within her body. Eliot felt tiny cracklings within the wood.

He pressed harder, though. He *had* to be in control.

A string snapped and cut his finger.

Eliot immediately pulled the violin off his shoulder. He stuck his index finger into his mouth to suck the blood.

Fiona moved closer to him and whispered, "What have you done?"

Enveloping them was fog and swirling sand suspended in the air and shimmering with moonlight.

It wasn't a cloud. Layers were moving over layers. When Eliot tilted his head, he saw passages through the mists . . . like the mirror maze they had run through at the carnival. Only these walls undulated, pulled apart, and closed again.

"There were words that went with the symphony," he whispered back to her. "They talk about wandering forever . . . through this stuff, I think."

"Nice going," she hissed back. "I asked for a little cover to hide in. Not something that would get us stuck, too."

Lights appeared in the silent storm: indistinct blobs of color, what might have been headlights—several of which moved toward them. Men called out to one another, obviously lost in the stuff.

"They're close," Fiona whispered, "but I don't think they can see us."

Eliot squinted at the vapors. He thought he saw the outline of someone . . . but it twisted, becoming bones and a grinning skull that peered back.[60]

He blinked, but the image didn't vanish in a puff of smoke as he'd hoped it would. Instead more things appeared in the mist: claws and eyes and one large moving silhouette that might have been the shadow of some great extinct dinosaur.

Eliot was scared, terrified, actually . . . but somehow he forced himself to think.

This was only water vapor and dust. They could plow right through the stuff—Eliot was sure of that. But he was also sure that he could hear distant screams. Real screams.

Stepping into the stuff would be easy. It was getting out once inside that he wasn't certain about.

But he had made this. He should be able to unmake it, too.

He slid a fingernail along Lady Dawn's remaining strings, producing a scratchy sound. A slender passage parted before them, the mist on either side boiling.

"This way," he said, and walked ahead of Fiona.

As in the fun-house maze, Eliot kept his eyes on the ground, only looking up when absolutely necessary. Fiona stayed on his heels.

They emerged on top of a low hill. Behind them was a sea of mist, rippling under the moonlight and lapping at the hillside. In the middle of this he saw flashing lights and heard distant gunshots.

"What's happening back in there?" Fiona asked. "I thought I saw . . . things."

It had been a long time since Eliot had seen his sister scared, but she looked scared now.

"I don't know," Eliot admitted. "Something tried to take over my music. I fought it, but not before . . . I don't know . . . not before I brought it all here."

He hoped it was just a smoke-and-mirrors trick. That no one was getting hurt inside the fog he'd conjured.

---

60. "Conjure thrice-damned sea of mists. Be upon sand or fjord or pasture pristine. Evil's taint come to thee. Spirits lost only vengeance find." From "Contritions of the Rose-Mired Witch," in Father Sildas Pious, *Mythica Improbiba* (translated version), c. thirteenth century.

But he wasn't about to go back inside to find out.

Fiona chewed her lower lip. "Okay, maybe you better not do that again. How's your finger?"

It was a simple cut, deep, but not bleeding. It hurt like crazy as Eliot flexed it, though. "I'll live."

Ahead of them lay the outer boundary of the air force base. A double fence was topped with concertina wire. Guard towers stood ominously along the perimeter. Beyond were buildings and aircraft hangars. Jeeps and Humvees raced out the front gate, but none moved in their direction.

"I think I can get us in from here," Fiona said. "Cutting through the fence—that'll be easy, but it might set off alarms." She glanced back at the fog. "On the other hand, we can take advantage of the confusion while it lasts."

A small sun appeared in the sky, directly overhead.

Whirlwinds materialized around Eliot and Fiona, pelting them with sand.

Eliot looked up, shielding his eyes with both hands from an intense halogen spotlight.

In the center of the glare a dark helicopter hovered in silence. Silhouetted men dropped from it, looking like tiny spiders on silken lines.

"*Hold your position,*" boomed a voice over a loudspeaker. "*Or we will open fire! Get on your knees. Hands on your head.*"

62

THE FIRST MORAL CHOICE OF ELIOT POST

Eliot felt terrible. He and Fiona had failed the third trial. Fiona would be dead soon. Eliot, too, probably after the Council got done with him. He couldn't imagine how things could get any worse.

He sat in a small room with green walls. His right hand was handcuffed to a steel table. A large mirror faced him on the opposite wall.

Sitting next to him was an air force doctor, called Miller. He had sandy hair and laugh lines radiating from the corners of his eyes.

"Lucky I got to this," Miller told him without looking up. "See this red line spreading up from your finger? That's a heck of an infection."

It couldn't be an infection; at least no infection Eliot knew of could spread that far in a matter of minutes.

"Yeah, I'm lucky," Eliot replied, his sarcasm barely contained.

He had been grabbed by military police, zip-tied, hooded, then separated from Fiona—photographed, fingerprinted, and brought to this place.

While Eliot had waited in a jail cell for someone to come get him, his finger and hand swelled. After a minute, a red line had appeared, moving up the cephalic vein in his arm.

Lady Dawn's snapped string had cut his finger. It had only been a tiny wound. Eliot could've kicked himself for sticking his finger into his mouth; that was probably how this started.

He'd immediately been moved into this room, and Dr. Miller had come. He'd swabbed the cut, drawn blood, and injected Eliot with antibiotics and tetanus boosters.

None of it seemed to be working, though. The red line kept moving higher—almost to the elbow now.

Eliot had read *Marcellus Masters's Practical First Aid and Surgical Guide* cover to cover, so he knew infections like this could turn deadly. But severe infections usually had other symptoms.

"Do you think it's septicemia?" Eliot asked Dr. Miller.

Miller looked up and one eyebrow quirked. "No." He smiled. "You don't have any fever." He looked back at Eliot's arm and his smile vanished.

"Bacteremia then? Or cellulitis?"

Miller shook his head, then blinked and gave Eliot a funny look. It wasn't the first time an adult had been surprised by his vocabulary. "We're going to get you to the base hospital. You can ride with the young lady you came in with."

Fiona was going to the hospital, too? Was she sick again?

The door to the tiny room unlocked, opened, and another man entered. His name tag read FREEMAN.

He looked angry; his features bunched about two tiny black eyes. He could've given Grandmother a good match in a staring contest. He wore the double-bar insignia of a captain.

Freeman set a plastic bag marked EVIDENCE on the table. Inside wrapped in individual plastic bags were Eliot's pack, his flashlight, and, swaddled in bubble wrap, his violin and bow.

Eliot wanted to reach out and touch Lady Dawn, but he resisted that impulse.

"How is he?" Freeman asked Miller.

"He'll be fine. I want to get them both checked into the hospital . . . just in case." Miller gave Freeman a tiny shake of his head.

"The girl?"

"Tox screen was negative. Can't keep her blood pressure up, though. Ambulance is on its way. There have been delays. Busy night."

Freeman grunted and then finally looked at Eliot as if just seeing him for the first time. "You're staring at me, young man. Do I look funny to you?"

"No, sir."

Eliot started to look away, but he realized that's what Freeman wanted. It's what a "good little boy" would do. This was a contest of wills, and if Eliot dropped his gaze, he'd be admitting Freeman had the power here.

So Eliot kept staring and did his best imitation of Robert Farmington, easing back in his chair.

Freeman pursed his lips. "Go ahead and play the tough guy. We don't need you. The girl told us everything."

The coolness drained from Eliot and he sat up straight.

"After you're checked out at the infirmary," Freeman told him, "you'll be taking a long bus ride to Nellis Federal Prison Camp."

Eliot's composure crumpled; he opened his mouth to tell Freeman that he and Fiona hadn't meant any harm, but they just needed one thing, and that they . . .

But he stopped himself. Shut his mouth.

Freeman was just trying to get him to talk.

"My sister would never tell you anything," Eliot said. "And you can't send a fifteen-year-old to a federal prison."

Freeman wrote on a little pad, *Sister. Fifteen.*

"You may think this is some joke," Freeman growled, "but you're lucky you didn't get killed tonight. Besides almost getting shot while trespassing in a high-security region, you and your sister walked through a rocket-testing zone in the middle of a fuel dump . . . right through a cloud of toxic fumes."

That was a lie. Eliot knew—he wasn't sure how, but he knew. Not the part about almost getting shot; that was likely true. But the part about the fuel test. That wasn't right.

First, Eliot had caused that fog with his music.

Second, Freeman just *sounded* wrong when he said it.

But why bother to lie at all? Because Freeman couldn't explain the sudden appearance of a cloud in the middle of a desert on a summer night?

What was so important about the fog that it was worth lying about?[61]

Eliot remembered hearing men screaming in the mist and seeing all

61. That summer afternoon a rocket-test site on Nellis Air Force Range allegedly leaked toxic fuel fumes. It was assumed to have quickly dispersed, but a local pressure inversion forced it to remain undiluted at ground level. As military patrols unsuspectingly passed through the cloud that evening, hallucinations were reported and friendly fire taken. When the cloud crossed over the Air Force Flight Test Center, Detachment 3, dozens of military personnel had to be hospitalized and five died. Before dawn, the cloud passed over the nearby town of Rachel. Inhabitants reported the dead rising and walking among them, and that aliens had escaped from Area 51. *Gods of the First and Twenty-first Century, Volume 11: The Post Family Mythology,* 8th ed. (Zypheron Press Ltd.).

those weird things: claws and skeletal figures and giant shadows. "Was anyone hurt?"

"Yes." Freeman's glare intensified. "I have two men down. And they wouldn't have been in that area if they hadn't been chasing you."

It *was* his fault, but not the way Freeman thought. Eliot tried to swallow but found his throat too dry.

Two men down. Did *down* mean "dead"?

It had been an accident. How was he supposed to know what his music would do?

But he *had*. He knew it would be dangerous. All he'd thought about, however, had been the danger to Fiona and himself. He hadn't considered what his music might have done to the people around them.

Freeman said to the doctor, "Transport them. I want him stabilized and we'll continue this interrogation." He asked Eliot, "You want to call your parents?"

Eliot shook his head.

"I thought so," Freemen muttered. "We'll find them soon enough."

Eliot and Fiona had done those police ID kits at the supermarket two years ago—had their pictures and fingerprints taken in case they were ever kidnapped. Freeman would eventually find out who they were and contact Grandmother.

He almost laughed. What did that matter now? He was thinking like the old Eliot Post—worried about getting into trouble . . . when Fiona was dying.

There was no way they were ever getting to those Golden Apples now.

His eyes lit upon Lady Dawn.

Or was there?

He could make out, even wrapped in layers of plastic, the fine-grain pattern on his violin, flashing as if she were on fire. He saw the coiled ends of the snapped string. Could she even be played with only three strings?

He thought he could do it . . . shift things this way and that a little, changing and recomposing the *Symphony of Existence* as he went along.

Freeman and Dr. Miller started speaking about the other wounded people, but Eliot's attention remained focused on his violin.

Playing her with three strings wouldn't be *entirely* impossible.

That's not what the problem was. The problem was him.

This time if he played and summoned the fog, it would be his decision—not something thrust upon him at the last moment and done without thinking it through. He fully understood the consequences of his actions now.

He'd need a denser fog. There were more people on base to hide from; two here in this room with him.

And for that, Eliot would have to go further into the symphony to the darker places that scared him and bring to the surface . . . awful things.

People who were just doing their jobs would get caught in the mist, surrounded by those things that lived inside it . . . lost in its ever-shifting passages. Maybe people would even die.

He would be responsible.

But Fiona's life was at stake. Was it worth it to endanger so many to save one person?

That was the choice. That was *his* choice.

Eliot might as well be shooting a gun into a crowded room—not aiming, exhibiting reckless abandon for human life.

He couldn't let his sister die, though.

Maybe that's what this test was all about. Fiona had had to kill Mr. Millhouse in the second heroic trial. Maybe it was his turn now.

It was still his decision to make.

Kill or be killed. Live or die. Right or wrong.

Freeman reached over and unlocked the handcuff on Eliot's wrist. "Unless you have something else to say, young man, it's time to go."

Eliot considered—teeter-tottered over the morals of this precarious situation—and then decided.

"I know you're lying about the fog," Eliot whispered. "There was no fuel test. You don't even know what it was. But I do."

"Oh?" Freeman looked at him as if he were examining something he'd just scraped from between his teeth.

"I can show you how I did it, too."

Freeman and Dr. Miller exchanged a nervous glance.

"It would help my diagnosis," Dr. Miller whispered to Freeman, "if I knew what the heck we're dealing with here."

"Okay," Freeman said slowly. "Tell me."

"I need to show you." Eliot reached for the evidence bags on the table.

The throbbing infection in his hand subsided as he touched Lady Dawn. It was as if they were meant for each other, and this brief separation had caused the pain.

"I need to play my violin."

63

THE GOLDEN APPLE

When it started, Fiona was in the ambulance. She lay on a gurney. Both her arms were cinched tight to her sides.

Fog rushed around the vehicle like an incoming tide, and the temperature dropped to ice-water frigid.

"This is strange," the driver called back to the medical technician. The driver flicked on the lights, but this just made the pea-soup-thick mist completely opaque.

"Any word on the other kid we're waiting for?" the technician asked.

"Eliot?" Fiona asked. "He's coming with me? Is he hurt?"

The med tech ignored her.

What had they done to him? Fiona struggled against the restraints, but she couldn't get her hands free.

Something bumped the ambulance, and the pea soup outside the window swirled into shapes that looked like octopus tentacles.

Fiona had a sinking feeling that something *had* happened to Eliot . . . something a lot worse than a few air force officers pushing him around.

In the distance, men yelled. Gunshots echoed.

The medical technician grabbed a tackle box of supplies. He opened the ambulance's back doors, jumped out, and left Fiona . . . and also left the doors ajar.

The mist seemed to hesitate at the entrance, but then slowly crept inside. Long tendrils extruded and scraped, as if now solid, along the floor.

Fiona pulled at the padded cuffs around her wrists. They were tight, but she didn't care; she had to get free. She folded her thumbs against her palms, making her wrist as narrow as possible. She yanked—bracing her legs against the raised sides of the gurney.

Her skin abraded, but all she managed was to wedge her hands tighter into the cuffs.

"Hey!" the driver yelled back to her. "Stop that."

She heard his seat belt unsnap.

But before he could get out of his seat, the windshield shattered.

The ambulance rocked back and forth and the driver screamed as he was pulled from the vehicle.

There was a wet spatter, then the crunch of bone.

Fiona couldn't turn around and see what was happening.

All rational thoughts retreated from her mind. She jerked and tugged until her right hand came free.

There was blood. Hers. That didn't matter.

The mist inside the ambulance scratched and clawed alongside the gurney.

Fiona un-Velcroed the restraints on her left hand.

She managed a single coherent thought: a thread. She had to get a cutting edge.

She riffled over the blanket that had been thrown over her. It was polyester fleece. No weave to pull a thread from.

She tore at the hem of her shirt and loose threads flowered. She pulled free a length of cotton fiber—snapped it taut in her hands.

A vaporous skeletal arm reached up, curved bone spurs rasping along the gurney rail as it felt about for something to grab.

The old Fiona Post would have screamed, froze with terror, or closed her eyes and hoped the nightmare would go away.

But Fiona was long past little-kid fears like that. The sight of this monstrosity reaching for her only made her feel one thing: angry.

Fiona thrust her cutting edge—once, twice, thrice—severing the arm into chunks of bone . . . which turned into wisps of smoke and vanished.

She recovered a bit, could breathe again, and think a little.

That's when she heard the music.

It sounded like a dozen violins, echoing through the fog . . . here . . . there . . . surrounding the ambulance . . . and nowhere. It was Eliot's music, but not as she'd ever before heard it. Along with the usual sweet notes there were shrieks that sounded like a bucket of nails dumped onto a broken blackboard.

The fog moved, solidified, and parts evaporated to make a tunnel.

A shadowy figure appeared along this path, walking toward her, bowing his violin, an unwrapped bandage trailing from his hand.

Eliot looked up. He saw her and ran to her.

Fiona did something she hadn't done since she was a toddler: she embraced her brother.

He hugged her back with one arm.

She pushed away from him. Happiness that Eliot was okay was one thing; actually hugging him was kind of gross.

Plus something was wrong with him—above and beyond his usual geek factor, and that they were in some fog full of monsters. A red line of infection ran up his arm, and the skin to either side was mottled with bruises.

Rage boiled inside Fiona. "They hurt you."

Eliot curled his arm inward. "It's nothing."

Fiona was quite certain it was not "nothing," but she let it drop for now. They had more immediate problems.

"What is all this? You brought the fog again. Do you know it's killing people?"

Eliot leveled at her a glare so malevolent she thought it would make Grandmother flinch. "Yes, I know. Do you want to find the Golden Apple or not?"

Fiona had never seen Eliot like this. He was harmless, unless you backed him into a corner. And even then . . . well, it had never been possible for her to think of him as threatening.

Until now.

Something was very wrong with her brother. Or maybe the entire world was wrong, and he had just become a part of it.

"Yeah," she told him. "Let's find the stupid thing."

Eliot nodded and turned his back to her, lifting his arm to play. Fiona watched, fascinated, as the red line and bruises on his arm vanished.

He played a new song; it was soft and slow.

An image of a tiny leaf popped into Fiona's mind, struggling to reach for the sun; it had flowers and buzzing bees and swelling fruit. She smelled honey and tasted . . .

"Apples," she whispered.

The thought of food, even something as innocuous as an apple, however, made Fiona's stomach heave with revulsion. She steeled herself, swallowed, and was okay.

In response to music, the mist moved, and a new path materialized.

Eliot played and walked forward. Fiona followed.

She marveled at his growing talent. But this new appreciation vanished when she spotted a horseman galloping past in the gloom, sword raised over his headless torso. An obscured sharklike figure the size of a tugboat glided along the other side of the path.

Dull explosions thumped in the distance. There was the popcorn crackle of gunfire, too.

Fiona moved closer to Eliot and saw that as he played, tears streamed down his cheeks.

She wanted to touch his shoulder, comfort him, but she was afraid she would throw off his music. And what could she say to make him feel better? When she had killed Millhouse, she had wounded her soul as well. She knew no one could talk that hurt away.

Their path through the fog brought them to a concrete sidewalk, and they halted before a double set of steel doors.

Painted on the doors was 221.

"This is the place," Eliot told her.

Fiona stepped forward, a coiled thread clutched in her hand. The door looked thick and impenetrable with metal plates bolted over the lock. An electronic keypad and card reader glowed on the wall next to it.

How was she going to cut through a *flat* door with a line stretched between her hands?

But did she have to do it that way? With both hands? Uncle Aaron had told her she could cut anything if she just put her mind to it. He never said she had to hold the string with two hands.

She took a deep breath and pulled a span of the cotton fiber between her pinched thumb and forefinger. She concentrated upon it with such intensity that the rest of the world faded.

Fiona let go of one end.

The thread remained stiff in the air and focused into a nearly invisible line of force.

Keeping her eyes fixed firmly upon it, she moved the thread toward the steel door—and inserted it like a red-hot needle into butter. She moved it up and over and down and across, then stepped back.

The door fell inward with a tremendous crash.

Beyond stretched a fog-filled corridor.

Eliot stared at the door and at the single thread in her hand, his mouth open.

Despite everything else that was happening around them, cutting soothed Fiona. She enjoyed it and could have done that all day.

Alarms suddenly blared and red lights strobed inside Building 221.

"Which way?" she asked, shouting over the noise.

Eliot plunked a few notes of his "apple" song. The haze rippled and cleared a passage that turned left at the first intersection.

She led the way, thread held between her hands. Fiona glimpsed disembodied eyes, reflected in the flashes of red light, peering back at her from the fog.

Come and get me. I dare you.

Where was that thought coming from? The last thing she wanted was more confrontation. She just wanted to be left alone.

Or did part of her *want to* cut more? Want to fight?

They twisted through the building, then down a hallway that angled into a subterranean portion—past doors of solid steel, some with number pads, others with palm-print readers, others as thick as bank vaults.

Eliot halted before a small oval door embedded in a concrete wall. Next to this was an optical scanner and printed instructions on how to get your retina identified.

"This one," Eliot said, trying to read the instructions, squinting as he did so.

Did he need glasses?

Fiona started reading them, too, but then stopped. No lock or scanner could stop her tonight.

She stretched out an arm's length of thread, focused, and slid it through the microscopic seam of the high-security door. Steel, titanium, high-carbon alloys . . . those offered only the slightest resistance to Fiona.

She traced along the door's edge, and together she and Eliot pushed in the door.

On the other side was a room the size of Ringo's with rows of shelves that stretched to the ceiling. Upon these were crates, lockboxes, and fifty-five-gallon drums—each with a bar code and a serial number. Most bore biohazard or radiation warning stickers . . . or both.

Eliot walked directly to a drum on a lower shelf. "Here."

Fiona looked down the hallway. No creatures from the mist or military police followed them. That was good.

Or it was bad, depending on *why* no one was answering this building's alarm.

Maybe everyone was dead.

What had they done? In the first trial, she had almost died rather than hurt Souhk. And then she had murdered Perry Millhouse. Now? Eliot's conjured fog could be killing people. She just wanted it all to stop.

Fiona's strength drained from her limbs. She grasped the doorway. Her time to live was running out.

She limped to the drum and cut off the top.

Nestled within, packed with Styrofoam, was a large metallic egg. She and Eliot rolled the drum out to get a better look.

The egg was dull silver and coated with a thick lacquer. On closer inspection, she saw lines etched into the metal: veins that traced a web over the thing; in places it looked like twining vines with budding orchids; other patches appeared like a printed circuit board; some seemed like a repeating crystalline structure that then rounded into clusters of cells, frozen in middivision, chromosomes splayed out like the interlocked fingers of two hands.

The artistry of the piece took her breath away.

"What are you waiting for?" Eliot asked. "Open it."

"It seems a shame to ruin it."

Nonetheless, Fiona looped her thread around the top. Maybe she could cut off just a tiny bit. Destroy as little as possible of this miraculous egg.[62]

She tugged her string.

The thread slid partway into the metal—then caught.

She had cut through solid steel that could have shrugged off a bomb blast, but this was stronger. It was as if it were alive and fought her.

But Fiona's life was at stake, too. She had to get inside.

She tightened her grip on the thread until her knuckles whitened. She sawed back and forth, maintaining her concentration until beads of sweat dripped into her eyes.

The etched lines in the surface of the metal parted, and her loop snapped to a single line as it passed through.

---

62. Russian jeweler Peter Carl Fabergé crafted the legendary Fabergé eggs, making fifty-seven of the miniature works of art in his life. One, *Hypnogogia*, was never completed. According to his notes, Fabergé sent an expedition to the Podkamennaya Tunguska River near the site of the 1908 Tunguska impact event. From metal fragments found in river sediments he forged *Hypnogogia* and wrote, "It seems one part metal, one part living, and one part light." Fabergé left Russia during the October Revolution, and all further notes, illustrations, and the partially constructed *Hypnogogia* were lost. *Gods of the First and Twenty-first Century, Volume 6: Modern Myths,* 8th ed. (Zypheron Press Ltd.).

Air hissed into the hermetically sealed container.

The veins and flowers etched upon the egg smoldered like burning pa-per, blackened, and faded away. The metal then turned white as if rapidly oxidizing.

Eliot crowded next to her and they both looked inside.

Cradled in folds of black velvet was a single yellow apple. The size of a crab apple, it had a slender stem with a single leaf. Several tiny bites had already been taken, but its flesh was white and unblemished.

"That's all there is?" Eliot asked.

"What did you expect? They said it'd be an apple. So shockingly, it's an apple."

But as Fiona pulled it out, she saw the fruit's skin was uniformly striped with gold and silver and spotted with ruby red and jade green. It was more like a jewel crafted and faceted by a master artisan than something that had been grown. It was hard and cold. It smelled of honey and citrus.

Her mouth watered. For the first time in days she felt hungry for some-thing other than chocolate.

"What's the matter?" Eliot asked. "Eat it already."

"I want to . . . but that's the problem. I wanted those chocolates—more than anything. And look what happened. And when I cut myself, I wanted to be free from the chocolates more than anything. Everything I seem to want more than anything turns out to be bad."

Eliot gave her a puzzled look.

"It's like I'm being manipulated," she said. "Like they're making me do these things. Making me into something I don't want to be."

"Isn't that better than being dead?" Lines of anxiety creased Eliot's face. This wasn't a rhetorical question.

"I don't know," she whispered. "It's complicated. It's not just about liv-ing or dying. It's about living like *I* want to, and not becoming another Lucia . . . or Henry . . . or Aaron."

"Or Grandmother," Eliot said, nodding.

"Or Grandmother."

Eliot ran a hand over his head, tousling his hair. "I can't think anymore." He sighed and sat on the floor. He flexed his hand, set down his violin, and pushed it away. "You know, I think people died tonight—I mean, I killed them so you could get that thing." His voice had an edge now. "If you weren't going to eat it, you should have decided that before we started this."

Eliot was right; they had to get the apple. There hadn't been a choice about that. But *she* still had a choice to make. Possession of the apple completed the third trial—assuming they got off the base and back to the Council. Eliot would be safe . . . even if she died.

If she ate the apple, it would be only to save herself, and she would have to accept the consequences.

Hadn't this been predetermined? Aunt Dallas had showed her the thread of her destiny. Her life *was* supposed to end. Now.

Or could she choose another path? Choose to live instead of die? Choose not to be like the rest of the family. Be something new. Be reborn.

She took a deep breath and decided.

Fiona brought the apple to her lips and took a tiny bite.

64

MOVING VIOLATION

Robert might have gone too far this time.

He knew, though, Mr. Mimes would have his back. After all, he had ordered Robert to protect and get close to Fiona.

It was best to bend the rules when no one was looking. But at times you *had* to break the rules out in the open . . . run them over a few times for good measure . . . burn what was left, and scatter the ashes.

If he could just explain . . .

Robert's former mentor Marcus had once told him, *Start thinking of them as people—that's dangerous. Cross them once and you might as well try talking your way out of a tidal wave.*

Robert sat on a metal folding chair on the sidelines of an indoor basketball court. He'd been told to stay there by Mr. Mimes. It was uncomfortable and he had to go to the bathroom, but he knew better than to get up.

So he sat and shifted back and forth, waiting for Mr. Mimes and the one called Gilbert to finish their game of one-on-one basketball.

Mr. Mimes had stripped down to his shorts. He was whipcord lean but his body rippled with a fine musculature. His hairlessness was in contrast to Gilbert, who looked more Kodiak bear than man.

Mr. Mimes moved around Gilbert, dribbled the ball between his open legs—and bounded up the perfect shot.

When Gilbert got the ball, he played slowly and methodically, until he was five paces from the three-point line. He planted both feet and launched the ball. It arced through the air and swished through the basket.

That was the sixth shot he'd made that way, which easily won him the game.

If Robert hadn't known better, this would've looked like an ordinary game with two guys.

Start thinking of them as people—that's dangerous.

Mr. Mimes toweled off, shook Gilbert's hand, and remarked, "Hardly any fun that way."

"Hardly fun that way for *you*," Gilbert said with a smile.

Outside a torrential downpour drenched Mr. Mime's island estate. The Aegean Sea had whipped itself into a frenzy of froth and fury, and the Council amphitheater was flooded.

Which is why they were inside today.

But why Mr. Mimes had picked his indoor basketball court to meet when he had three grand ballrooms, Robert would never know. Maybe he just liked to keep people off-balance.

Maybe that's why he had Robert sitting in this stupid chair.

Most of the Council were already here on lower bleachers: Mr. Cornelius; the gorgeous Dallas, who when she glanced at Robert with her cat-like eyes made his heart beat faster; the imposing as he was tall and dark Mr. Kino; and Mr. Aaron, who sat apart from the others, dour as ever.

Something else, though, other than the weather and the location made this particular gathering of not-so-ordinary people even stranger.

Other League members were here. Robert had never seen this at a Council meeting. Men and women sat scattered across the bleachers. They appeared to be a normal businessman, a Japanese schoolgirl, a starlet in sunglasses, a surfer, one overweight, middle-aged Redskins fan, a librarian, a jogger sipping from her hydration pack, and a little girl with pigtails.

They all looked like regular people save for the one thing Robert had come to expect when dealing with the Immortals. They held themselves in a way that went beyond confidence or cool. It was as if they were always looking down at you, no matter where they were or even if they weren't looking at you at all.

This Council meeting had to be pretty important to interest the League at large. And it gave Robert a bad feeling to be singled out, sitting alone on the floor in this chair.

Mr. Mimes *did* have his back, didn't he?

Robert tried to catch his eye, look for some subtle reassuring gesture that it'd be okay. He knew Mr. Mimes liked him. Robert liked him, too, as much as he could given what he was. He'd almost begun to think of him as . . . well, not a father figure, but maybe *his* uncle Henry.

Ms. Audrey Post and Ms. Lucia Chase entered the court side by side. They sat next to Dallas. Seeing these three great ladies together gave Robert a chill. It was as if something in the universe had just clicked into place.

Mr. Mimes dropped his basketball and let it roll away. "Rematch later?"

Gilbert shook his head. "What would be the point?"

The two men took their places on the lowest bench. Neither spared a glance at Robert.

Lucia rang her tiny silver bell. "This session of the League Council of Immortals is called to order. All come to heed, petition, and be judged. *Narro, audio, perceptum.* I assume everyone has read the report?"

There were nods and murmurs of ascent.

"Unless there are any objections," she said, "we shall agree that the twins' third heroic trial was a success. Let us move on to the discussion of their lineage."

Robert didn't get it. He thought Eliot and Fiona passed the trials and were now safe. Wasn't that the deal?

Now that he thought more about it, though, it seemed weird that Eliot and Fiona had to be tested by trial to figure out which family they belonged with. Why not just do a DNA analysis? That would've resolved everything.

"I judged them to be with us," Aaron said, standing. "Fiona has the heart of a noble warrior—her mother's influence, no doubt."

Audrey Post arched one eyebrow.

"And the Golden Apple," Dallas chimed in. "Fiona took a bite. That should end any debate. I mean, her mortal life ended when she did that, and her immortal life started."

Lucia removed an apple from the folds of her green dress. Several tiny bites marked the fruit's skin. "I suppose it does."

Audrey looked at Mr. Mimes. "You expunged all evidence?"

"Of course I did. Fingerprints, photographs, statements, and recordings— all removed from Nellis Air Force Base and destroyed."

"Then the only outstanding issue," Cornelius said, "would be the boy, Eliot."

"That fog," Kino said. "None of us could have called such a thing. So full of evil."

Aaron glared at him. "The boy passed your three trials. Certainly that should count in his favor."

"I remind you that the successful passing of our tests serves only to illuminate their characters," Lucia explained. "That is the only measure by which we shall judge. An Infernal could've passed them as easily as an Immortal. It is *how* they did so that interests us."

"Another loophole in our so-called rules," Aaron growled.

Audrey Post stood and faced him. "You are wrong. I know their blood better than any here—that was never the issue. What they are will neither be determined by genetics nor their upbringing. Eliot and Fiona will ultimately *choose* what they will be."

Robert leaned forward. They got to decide which family they belonged with? Why hadn't anyone told them that in the first place?

Audrey and Aaron stared at one another.

All fell still and silent.

Looking at them, Robert felt sick. It was like standing on a bridge and watching two vast rivers crash into one another beneath him—vertigo-inducing and awe-inspiring.

He had no idea who Audrey Post was. He didn't want to speculate about it too much, either. Doing so, he knew, would only give him nightmares.

The one they called Aaron he knew a little about. At various times throughout history he had had other names: the Red Horseman of the Apocalypse, Ares Enyalius, the Charioteer, Lancelot, and the King of the Sacred Grove.

Aaron blinked and softly said, "Do you not love them, Audrey?"

"Love no longer has a place in my heart. All that remains is my duty to protect them." Audrey looked away and slowly sank back to her seat. "Even if that means sacrificing one to save the other."

Robert couldn't believe he was hearing this. Sacrifice? Did she mean kill Fiona or Eliot? That sounded medieval, but then again, some of these people *were* medieval. He'd have to warn Fiona.

Mr. Mimes cleared his throat. "With regards to the Post twins, I believe clarification is coming via the Infernal temptations. There is one left."

He gestured to the larger-than-life video monitor over center court. It flickered to life.

On that was the photograph that Robert had taken in Franklin Park the other day—Eliot and his girlfriend, Julie Marks. The telephoto lens had made it a bit grainy, but otherwise it was a nice composition. Two kids with a crush on each other having a picnic lunch. What could be more natural?

Only Robert had done a little digging around. He had lifted the girl's prints from Ringo's and found that she had a record for petty theft and drug possession—and a death certificate, dated 1981. Heroin overdose.

"The Infernal seductress," Mr. Mimes explained, "is also in my report. Eliot has thus far avoided temptation, but these things traditionally come in threes." He held up three fingers for emphasis. "I propose we wait and see how they deal with this last challenge."

"It would be valuable to collect more data," Cornelius said.

"But it would place the twins in more danger," Lucia replied.

"It would place *us* in danger," Kino said.

"There is always danger," Gilbert told them. "What difference does it make? We should decide their fate based on the existing evidence."

"I thought we were supposed to protect them from the other family?" Robert said.

He sat frozen, utterly surprised. He hadn't meant to . . . but he had whispered this *out loud*.

He'd been so engrossed in the Council's debate over Eliot and Fiona that it felt like a dream. He had forgotten the first rule of being a good Driver: keep your mouth shut.

They all turned and looked at him.

He felt his heart stop—then pound recklessly, panicked.

Robert had been told to keep quiet at the last meeting. He knew these people didn't give second warnings.

Mr. Mimes gave a great sigh. "I had almost forgotten, alas. We should deal with this matter first."

"I agree," Lucia coolly murmured. "The twins' fate shall be tabled momentarily while the Council decides the proper punishment for Henry's errant Driver."

Errant—that was another word for "rule breaker." And Robert knew what happened to rule breakers in the League. They got their livers ripped out for an eternity. Or they were turned into marble statues, then ground up to line someone's driveway.

Robert had pulled a fast one last night. Mr. Mimes had left him alone, so at sunrise he drove the car to the edge of the base to pick up Eliot and Fiona.

Fiona had been waiting for him, the base behind her, covered in mist. She looked relieved, scared . . . and she definitely looked as if she could use a ride.

Robert looked hopefully now at Mr. Mimes.

His employer clenched his jaw and gave him a slight shake of the head.

Robert felt stabbed in the chest, because he knew with that one gesture that Mr. Mimes definitely did *not* have his back.

"I don't even know where to begin." Lucia picked up the report and turned the last page. "This trial could have been ruled invalid by Mr. Farmington's actions. The twins technically had to clear the base on their own." She continued to read. "And we have rules about Drivers fraternizing with League members . . . even potential League members."

"I have heard," Mr. Mimes added, "that there may even have been a kiss."

Robert couldn't believe this. It had to be a mistake—a joke. Mr. Mimes had *told* him to do those things. Okay . . . maybe not specifically the kiss, but everything else.

He wanted to jump to his feet and say something. But Robert couldn't. He was suddenly too weak to lift his arms or even open his mouth.

Mr. Mimes walked to Robert. "I am so sorry you have to go through this," he whispered. "I must ask you to return my keys."

Robert would have felt less pain if he'd been hit with a sledgehammer. The keys were the symbol of his office. Driving was his life.

"You're . . . firing me?"

Mr. Mimes looked anguished as he took the keys from Robert's trembling hand.

"Fire," Lucia mused. "Now *that* is a fine suggestion."

"Oh, please." Mr. Mimes turned to her. "I agree the boy broke a few rules, but there was really no harm done. Let us just lock him up for a few hundred years and let him mull it over."

"Always lenient with the hired help," Lucia said. "Very well, if there are no objections . . ."

A few hundred years? Locked up? Freedom was everything to Robert. If he wasn't able to ride . . . to feel the air rushing over his face . . . to see new things . . . death was better.

"Wait," Ms. Audrey Post said. "The boy has been kind to me. I ask that we reduce his sentence."

"Audrey asking for mercy?" Mr. Mimes said, and a broad smile spread over his features. "Shall the sun turn dark as well? The moon blaze with flame?"

She glowered at him and his smile faded.

"Oh, very well, call it an even fifty years—in isolation," Mr. Mimes said. "Let's continue with more important matters."

"So be it." Lucia rang her tiny silver bell.

Robert finally found the strength to stand. He was going to say something. He had trusted Mr. Mimes. He had thought he really understood him . . . even cared for him.

But what was Robert going to tell them? Was he going to rat Mr. Mimes out?

No. Despite everything, Robert couldn't do that. He was no stool pigeon. That would be sinking to *their* level.

Instead he stood and stared at Mr. Mimes, communicating all his anguish, his disappointment, and his anger with a single glare.

Mr. Mimes stared back completely unperturbed.

As the sound of Lucia's bell faded, the world squeezed in about Robert until he could no longer see . . . or feel . . . or breathe.

65

THE NIGHT TRAIN

Sealiah crossed her legs, sank deeper into the crushed-velvet seat, and loosened her boots. She let the clicking of the train tracks soothe her nerves.

The railcar's stained-glass skylights cast weird half rainbows from the perpetually setting sun in this part of hell. Beyond the leaded windows on her left was a desert dotted with towering mesas. Clouds of carrion eaters circled overhead, waiting to swoop on those trying to escape. Occasionally the flaming fuselage of some airliner would flash past and spectacularly crash.

It was a picture-perfect postcard moment.

She had always enjoyed these little rides upon the Royal Crowned Prince. They didn't make, or break, trains like this anymore.[63]

Ruining her momentary peace, however, was Julie Marks, who sat beside her, squirming on the edge of the settee. The poor thing was unable to enjoy the luxurious surroundings because she was scared of Sealiah. Understandable.

---

63. The Austrian court commissioned the Royal Crowned Prince in memory of Archduke Rudolf, crown prince of Austria. It was an unusual act considering he was thought to have died in a double suicide with his mistress (later evidence indicated a double murder). No expense was spared upon the train, making it a hallmark of turn-of-the-century opulence. Upon its inaugural run, however, the Royal Crowned Prince tragically caught fire and ran out of control down the mountainous Arlbergline—its cars ultimately crashing. Many claim on the night of the new moon the train can be observed running wild down the mountain, on fire, its passengers screaming. It has become known as *Der Nachtzug*, the Night Train. *Gods of the First and Twenty-first Century, Volume 6: Modern Myths*, 8th ed. (Zypheron Press Ltd.).

But while she may have been scared of Sealiah, she was absolutely terrified of the others here, so much so that she refused to leave her side.

The members of the Board and some stragglers were going home. Too long had they been in the land of light. Their minds and souls were exhausted. Being among such mediocrity always did this to their kind. Having to return home was ever their curse and their blessing.

Lev lay like a beached sea creature upon two couches that he had pushed together, sipping martinis through a straw. A dozen empty glasses rolled and clinked on the floor next to him.

The wizened Mulciber sat opposite Uziel playing Rogue's Chess. As expected, the golden boy was winning, pinning Mulciber's Whore into a corner of the board with his Press Gangs.

Abby and Ashmed sat together (much to Sealiah's annoyance), engaged in an animated conversation about the scarab beetle. Sealiah only caught the occasional phrase about genetic sequences . . . longevity . . . and La Jolla biotechnology investments.

Sealiah hoped the little Destroyer was not moving too soon upon Ashmed—not that Abigail would know what to do with him if he ever paid any attention to her. Sealiah was not done with Ashmed, or his political favors, just yet.

She reached over and pulled Julie close to her. The girl resisted, but her struggling only made Sealiah enjoy this all the more.

Dark circles ringed Julie's eyes, and her skin had the pallor of the grave. Bruises mottled her arms. Beauty was a fragile thing for mortals. Age, too much sun, too much wind, not enough sleep, or death—all made their magnificence fleeting.

"Listen to me," Sealiah whispered into Julie's ear. "They may yet question you. Do not lie. They will know and not like it. But neither reveal to them everything. Do you understand?"

Sealiah released her.

Julie glared at her, nodding, rubbing her arm. A spark of defiance was still within this one.

Sealiah could feel her heart beating, feel the hope inside. Did this girl understand the magnitude of Eliot Post's gift? Even Sealiah did not fully comprehend the ramifications of infusing eternal hope within one of the eternally damned.

Julie Marks would bear watching.

The train whistle sounded—the shrieks of a hundred burning souls—and there was a noticeable deceleration. The Royal Crowned Prince pulled into a covered station. Clouds of smoke and sparks swirled about the car.

Other trains were at the station, some gilded and ornate, some levitating upon magnetic rails, and one a steaming heap of rust. From this dilapidated vehicle a dark figure emerged, and all other shadows scattered before it as it approached the Royal Crowned Prince. As this darkness stepped onto the railcar, it tilted to one side.

The rear curtains parted and Uri cautiously entered.

He bowed to all, but held Sealiah's eyes a fraction of a second longer.

She returned his ardent stare, wishing there could be more.

This matter with her former lieutenant, however, would soon be over. This was best. Uri would be hers again or forever lost—either way would release him from the torture he endured by Beal's side. How she wished there could have been some other way.

She glanced at Uziel as he took advantage of one of Mulciber's Mercantile Lords with a lowly pawn. When you played the game, pieces were inevitably lost. If one worried about loss, one should not play.

Uri reached into his midnight sports jacket and retrieved an electronic device. He swept the railcar for bugs. He then pulled out a burning incense brazier from within his voluminous folds, waved it about, sniffed, and scrutinized the patterns of drifting smoke.

Satisfied that there were no malicious devices or intentions, he stepped off the train.

Beal entered a moment later, his cloak of feathers covered with the glowing cinders that fell in this part of the desert.

Uri carefully brushed the sparks off with a brush. The feathers bristled at his touch.

Beal surveyed them. He fingered the fist-size sapphire, Charipirar, the symbol of his clan, that hung about his neck on a thong. Such an ostentatious display of power—Sealiah would dearly love to tear it from his throat and crush that jewel.

These blasted lands were part of his domain, and he was far too powerful here. Still, he had chosen not to ride until this point, which meant he only felt on equal footing with them within the confines of his realm. A definite sign he believed his power in decline.

She smiled and tilted her head at him.

He smiled at her as well, a shark's grin that faded as he spotted Julie Marks. "So your handpicked seductress was not up to the task?"

"It was all in Sealiah's report," Lev replied, and drained another martini. "Didn't you read it?"

Beal shot a quick glance at Uri, who then whispered to him. Beal nodded, frowned, then moved down the aisle, settling across from Sealiah and Julie.

"My computer network," he explained, "is having a few upgrade problems."

Abby opened her palm and released a golden scarab into the air, then she turned to speak to Beal. "The girl actually had Eliot cornered, but left at the last moment."

"It appears," remarked Ashmed, "she developed a conscience."

"Really?" Beal leaned forward. "After spending time in the Valley of the Poppies?"

Julie pressed into the back of her seat, trying to escape Beal's carrion stench. "No, sir . . . not exactly."

Mulciber and Uziel looked up from their game of Rogue's Chess, now interested as well.

"Then what exactly?" Beal set one hand on her knee and squeezed until she yelped.

"It was his music." Julie struggled to keep her tears back. The air was so hot in this realm that they dried instantly, staining her cheeks.

Sealiah felt the child's heart race within her chest . . . when it should not be beating at all.

"I could have brought Eliot to y'all," Julie said, "but not after he played for me."

"We have all heard him play," Beal said. "But if *my* soul were at stake . . ."

"It was worth it," Julie said, whimpering. "It was like there were people singing along with his music."

Sealiah froze.

This was one detail that the girl had failed to tell her of—one she wished Julie would now keep her mouth shut about.

"It was like," Julie said, struggling with her words, "it was a choir of angels."

Everyone in the railcar stopped what they were doing and looked at the girl.

Once they all could sing thusly. The memory was dear and almost forgotten, and too painful to be dredged up.

Sealiah bit her lip until she tasted blood. Here was a possibility that she had never considered: what if Eliot was indeed one of them, but free of sin? Neither mortal, nor Immortal, nor entirely Infernal because he was not damned?

Beal laughed, breaking the spell over them. "Superstitious nonsense. I had these dreams, too, when I was a boy. But that is all they were: silliness that we left behind when we grew up."

He squeezed Julie's knee. The bone broke.

Julie curled toward Sealiah. She encircled one arm about Julie, unsure whether to strangle the child to keep her quiet, or to protect her so she might be able to extract more information later.

Clouds crowded the desert horizon. The land sloped and the Royal Crowned Prince picked up speed. Twisted trees laden with creepers and moss appeared as they rushed past.

They were, at last, entering Sealiah's lands.

"I think," Beal said, glancing outside, "I would like to further examine this child. A dissection might determine what her problem is."

Sealiah lowered the window. Brimstone choked the railcar. Julie wheezed and coughed, but the stench quickly faded, and the rich scent of honeysuckle, vanilla, and vegetative rot perfumed the air.

Sealiah's land was a steam-filled jungle, full of shadows and poison-dripping thorns and blooming wildflowers.

"I think," Sealiah cooed back, "that you should have thought of that sooner, Mr. Chairman." The power of her realm boiled her blood and filled her to overflowing. "I am no longer in a sharing mood."

Beal opened his mouth to say more, glanced again outside, then nodded, conceding the point. He stood and ruffled his cloak. "I need a drink." He strode to the wet bar and poured whiskey.

Mulciber and Uziel returned to their Rogue's Chess, both of them somehow managing to keep one eye upon Sealiah.

Lev wiped the sweat as it slithered from his head and neck. "Is there air-conditioning on this thing?" He sat up and maneuvered his bulk to the wet bar. "I could use one of those," he said to Beal.

Beal grudgingly poured him a whiskey as well.

"We're ready to move on that Valley of the New Year thing," Lev said. "I found a guy who paints doors. Even dug up one of those antique brass knobs."

"Valley?" Beal asked distractedly. "What are you babbling about?"

"It was your idea," Lev muttered. "To get the twins separated, and out of the League's reach."

"Oh, yes, yes," Beal whispered. "Of course. *That* Valley."

"Is there a balance point in Del Sombra?" Ashmed asked. "That is the best place to set these things up. It extends their half-life."

"The Last Sunset Tavern," Sealiah replied. "A few miles out of town. Isolated. In between many sources of power."

"I'll send my guy there," Lev said, "unless our chairman has any objections?"

Beal waved away Lev's words.

Uri stared at Sealiah—a dangerous gesture for him in front of his ever-suspicious master. The chairman of the Board, however, was busy pouring himself another generous whiskey.

Sealiah glanced back at Uri. The thumb and forefinger on his left hand formed a right angle: sign language for the letter *L*.

What did *L* mean? And more intriguing, what would be so important that Uri risked communicating in the open?

She recalled when they had last spoken, he had told her that Beal believed their long-thought-dead cousin Louis was still alive and in Del Sombra.

Was Beal networking with Louis? That seemed unlikely, but then again, everything about the Post children seemed to invoke unlikeliness.

She had ordered Uri to contact Louis, perhaps influence him to their cause. Had that gone well? Or was Uri's signal an indication that it had *not* gone well?

Sealiah cautiously glanced about the railcar.

Abby and Ashmed had their backs to her, chatting once more. Beal and Lev likewise were too occupied drinking to observe her.

Uziel moved his Lawyer into attack position upon the chessboard, giggling with glee.

Mulciber, however, still had one of his bloodshot eyes fixed upon her. Well, even the old bat could not watch her and Uri and his game all at the same time.

She sighed and reclined and gave a minuscule shrug, making sure to make eye contact with Uri. This signaled her request for clarification.

The fingers of Uri's hand making the *L* curled inward, leaving his thumb pointing downward.

Bad news.

Sealiah waited until Mulciber had to focus on his game or lose his Whore Queen, then she curled her fingers inward—and made a quick sideways cutting gesture.

Her message: *Entice Louis to see things her way. If that failed, remove him.*

Uri nodded. He held her gaze for a moment, communicating all his longing, all his remorse, and all the anguish that this might be their last time together.

This was too much for Sealiah. She closed her eyes.

In all likelihood she'd just ordered the best lieutenant she'd ever had to his death. What choice was there? An alliance between the Great Deceiver and the Lord of All That Flies was too terrible to contemplate: brains and brawn combined. That had to be stopped, no matter what the cost.

She inhaled deeply, reveling in the rich scent of decay and growth, the complex perfumes of a thousand flowers, then she exhaled.

So be it.

Pieces were lost in the game. There was no other way to win.

The train hissed, slowed, and pulled into a station covered with creeper vines and shaded under banyan trees that stretched to the clouds.

Sealiah turned to Julie. "Our stop, my dear." She lifted Julia to her feet, and her broken bones crackled. Julie cried out in pain.

"That," Sealiah assured her, "is the very least of your troubles now."

She escorted her limping charge to the door at the rear of the car.

"Cousins," Sealiah announced to them all, "I bid you adieu and look forward to our next meeting . . . perhaps with the young Mr. Post to entertain?"

Lev raised his glass to toast that sentiment.

Ashmed stood, bowed, and told her, "I shall call you soon, m'lady."

"Of course you shall." Sealiah smiled and, still grasping Julie, stepped off the Royal Crowned Prince and into her jungle.

It felt good to be home. The air was full of steaming vapors and nectar. Tiny runners twined about her legs and curled around her wrist, blossoming with orchids and poppies—delighted that their mistress was back.

She moved to the stables alongside the station, pulling the creature that had formerly been known as Miss Julie Katherine Marks roughly behind her.

There was much to do. She would take great pleasure testing Julie's new hope—see how it fared under her delicate care. She might yet prove entertaining.

SECTION

VII

END GAME

66

EVER POISONED

Louis knew everything would change today at sunset. He either had to deliver his son to Beal or forfeit his own life and soul. Neither option especially struck his fancy.

He glanced at his new Rolex Cellinium. His fancy notwithstanding, the deal with the Infernal chairman of the Board ended in twelve short hours.

Louis stood in what had been his rented apartment under the Christian-studies store, now further remodeled to suit his needs. The carpeting, light fixtures, and wiring had been torn away. What remained were bare concrete walls and foundation. Not the ritually cleaned basalt he'd hoped for, but it would have to do.

That he stood under a store that contained a hundred crucifixes, Bibles, and beatific porcelain cherubs that stared helplessly down upon his blasphemous self filled Louis with a shudder of delightful irony . . . and he almost forgot that he could be dead in a few minutes.

He consulted his watch again and mentally strained to alter the passage of time. Alas, that power was far beyond him in this mere shell of flesh.

Ten minutes, thirty, tops—that was how long he estimated before one of his numerous cousins would try to amend his pact with Beal. Amend it, that is, by breaking his feeble body.

He was ready. Let them try.

This last bit of treachery was almost a formality before the *true* double-dealing began.

Louis knelt and checked the circle he stood in. It was immaculately clean and just large enough for his size-thirteen Italian leather loafers.

Surrounding the circle, symbols and lines flowered across the floor, walls, and ceiling—a lotus of a thousand arcs and ancient letters that twisted upon themselves. As with all his plans, this circle was not what it appeared to be.

He reexamined the edge, folding and coaxing the space with his fingertips. Even with his advanced payment of power, Louis had to take great care. It required a delicacy he barely possessed. This particular trick he had learned from the origami master Zhe the Blind.[64]

Plans inside plans. All this complication increased the odds of Louis's true schemes going awry. But what was one with so little power to do?

His hands trembled. Long scars traced along his wrist. As with all things worth doing, there had been a price to be paid for this trick. Half of the marks upon the floor had been made with pastel chalk and laundry markers . . . the rest, however, had been inked with his blood.

How he hated this feeble flesh. Yet hadn't it been that ephemeral fragility that had captured his heart so long ago? Is that what he now felt for Eliot?

Or was it some temporary weakness that would pass? Like so much gas.

No, he *was* proud of his son. The boy had stumbled across his partially reconstructed master symphony and he had finished it. Truly, what else should he expect from his progeny?

Louis curled his hand into a fist until the knuckles popped. These feelings he had for Eliot were a toxin coursing through his soul. Love?! First God, then what he had thought had been the perfect woman, and now again with his son? Hadn't he learned this lesson the hard way? Nothing good ever came from love.

Perhaps there was some antibiotic to rid himself of this diseased thinking before his limbs turned gangrenous, blackened, and fell off.

"Talking to yourself?" the shadows asked. "You sound crazy."

Louis looked up. The darkness in the corner of the basement collected into a large man. Parts of the shadow resolved into broad Samoan features

---

64. Zhe the Blind was one of the Buddhist monks known to have introduced paper to Japan in the sixth century. After folding a partially accurate (and unflattering) origami figure of a Soga clan matron, he was sentenced to death and imprisoned. When Prince Regent Shōtoku Taishi heard this, he raced to save Zhe, only to find he had disappeared from within a guarded thirty-foot-deep pit. Zhe was never seen again. In 1899, however, the *Lambent Water Scrolls*, penned by Zhe, were unearthed. A lost method of wet-paper folding was discovered, as well as diagrams that mathematicians are only now beginning to understand with modern topology and supercomputers. *Gods of the First and Twenty-first Century, Volume 8: Eastern Myths,* 8th ed. (Zypheron Press Ltd.).

and hard, glittering eyes. It took two steps toward him. The figure's black shoes sank and mingled with the symbols in the foundation as if they were mud.

Urakabarameel, Master of Shadows and Whispers—his appearance momentarily confused Louis, for he was Beal's lackey, not the third party he had anticipated come to stop their bargain.

Unless, he was *both*?

Uri's soul belonged to Beal, but his heart might still be held by the Queen of Poppies.

Louis sighed with relief. Uri was like a common chess rook. He moved with murderous efficiency, but his patterns were straight lines. So easy to predict.

Uri gestured to the mess of symbols. "Was this supposed to keep me from wringing your neck?"

Louis laughed. "Just a precaution, Cousin. You know what it's like, politics and Board members trying at the last moment to get the upper hand on one another."

Uri scowled.

"I guess you came to discuss only business?" Louis asked. "A pity. In the old days we would talk for hours."

"We never 'talked.'" Uri took a step closer, pushing against some unseen resistance in the air, dragging himself through the mire of geometry on the floor. "I only recall your endless teasing. Less talk with you is best."

Louis pretended to be hurt. Perhaps Uri, though, had learned a few things in his absence. Louis looked carefully at his cousin, trying to discern the telltale bulge of the sheathed blade near his heart.

It was there still. Saliceran, Sealiah's infamously ever-poisoned blade, a living shard of metal that delighted in murder almost as much as its mistress . . . and still over foolish Uri's most vulnerable organ.

"So," Louis said, straightening, "to business then, my laconic anthropophaginian."

Uri crinkled his forehead.

Louis must take care to use more monosyllabic words. No need to torture the poor puppy.

"Your new master has revised the deadline," Uri said. "He commands you to move immediately. Trap the girl, Fiona, in the Valley of the New Year. Then deliver Eliot to him."

"You have access to the Valley of the New Year? How interesting." Louis flashed his armored smile, behind which he hid his sudden unease. "I didn't think he was allowed to change terms. The original pact is binding. We rolled—"

"You say 'we' as if this deal is not one-sided."

Louis, of course, was expendable as far as Beal was concerned. It wouldn't violate any pact of theirs to have Louis transformed into a bloody smear.

"Yes, I understand," Louis said. "But it would help if I understood the urgency. There are so many Immortals and Infernals in Del Sombra, I can barely move without stepping on toes and talons."

"Things are complicated." Uri hesitated, considering his words carefully, then said, "What if I told you that others wished you to take your time with the young Master Eliot? And that their rewards would be just as generous as Beal's?"

This was it: Uri's counteroffer on behalf of some unnamed third party to betray Beal.

Louis continued to smile . . . and his mind raced. It would take cooperation for the Board to open a passage to the Valley of the New Year—a distressing development in and of itself. If his cousins actually worked together, there was nothing they could not accomplish.

And yet, it also appeared to be business as usual: some friendly double-dealing, a few backstabbings here and there, sharks smelling fresh blood in the waters.

Eliot and Fiona had stirred up the clans in ways he had not foreseen. They were far more dangerous than he had realized—which made his decision all the more easy. After all, if he was going to play, why not play with fire?

Uri struggled with his steps, pushing closer to Louis's circle. The symbols and lines on the concrete dragged behind him, snarled in tangles about his ankles. He grunted as the resistance increased. "Well?"

"I cannot accommodate your requests. Either of them. I will honor Beal's deal to the letter, and according to the original timetable."

Uri's muscles bulged with effort, and his massive hands clenched. The air about him rippled from the tremendous pressure he exerted.

"I gave you a chance to live, Louis. Refuse me and I will have no choice."

Louis laughed. The notion that Uri could actually *save* his life . . . how amusing. "Refuse? I shall do much more than that, Cousin."

Uri halted and his face flushed. To his credit, however, he actually attempted to puzzle it out. "Why would you tell me such a thing, unless . . ."

Louis's armored smile dissolved. "Unless I was about to do to *you* what you had to come to do to *me*?"

Uri glanced about. He stood in the center of a morass of symbols and lines that he had hauled into a hopeless knot. Then he finally understood that he had been looking at this the wrong way.

Louis allowed the layers of bent space to relax and revealed the true geometry of the room.

The normal perspective tilted . . .

. . . and the "floor" that Uri stood upon was neither flat, nor under his feet, but curved up and around him. He was inside a seamless cylinder, trapped like an insect within a web of tiny lines and symbols and letters.

Louis was above him, peering down through a tiny circle into this cocoon of his own devising. "You will find nothing to gain purchase upon."

Uri glowered up at him, his eyes blazing red, foam upon his lips. His muscles bulged and flexed to gargantuan proportions.

Louis opened his mouth to say more, but hesitated. He hated to goad Uri further. It was as foolish as standing on railroad tracks and daring the onrushing locomotive to come closer.

But he could not help himself. "Solomon used these, remember? Klein bottles with their frictionless Möbius-like surface? He trapped all those pesky jinn spirits, and they were never heard from again."

Uri roared and struggled, but all this accomplished was to further entangle himself within the snare of sticky ciphers that Louis had drawn upon the floor.

Until one taut string of symbols, drawn in lime-colored chalk (never approved for such ritualistic purposes), "pinged" from the stress.

The dots and Greek letters upon this line shuddered and fell free, vaporizing into puffs of green smoke.

All traces of victory evaporated from Louis's face.

Uri bared his teeth, half a grin, half-gritting. He grabbed the shuddering line with both hands and pulled. The construct of tangled icons twisted and resisted his efforts . . . and then the line pulled free—and the Klein-bottle construct unraveled.

Heaps of symbols and geometries inked in blood and marker and pastel chalks spilled upon the concrete floor in a tidal wave of red, black, and muted rainbows.

Louis fell, bowled over by the surge of power.

Uri remained standing, immune to the pull and the swirls of color about him as if made of immovable granite.

With three mighty strides he crossed to Louis.

Louis started to explain how this was all a mistake. Even as the words formed on his lips, however, Uri balled one of his hands into a gigantic fist and hit him.

It was everything Louis expected it would be: sledgehammer hard, an atomic-bomb explosion of pain, a semiconscious floating-away sensation— the crushing return trip to reality as he bounced onto the concrete.

Louis blinked away reddening tears. He rolled over, dazed, but not so much that he did not know what was coming next from his cousin.

Blood and mucus drooled from his nose onto his hands . . . and there germinated the seed of an idea how to squirm free. He snorted, blowing clots and snot over both arms, then rolled over just in time.

Uri loomed over him, blotting out all else.

His cousin had pulled that punch. He could have shattered every bone in Louis's body had he wanted, but his desire to play with his food was too great. Louis gave brief thanks for Uri's stupidity.

Uri grasped Louis by his shoulders and hauled him up.

Louis looked for the thing he needed to make what might be his last desperate deception work. He spotted it: the slight bulge of a knife sheath under Uri's shirt.

Louis brought up his hands, close to his own chest, so this action could not be misrepresented as anything threatening . . . only a pitiful, pleading, "have mercy" gesture. It was a ridiculous thing to do considering what he faced, but necessary to get his blood-, snot-, and sweat-soaked arms and hands into the proper position.

Louis had seen Uri kill. He liked to do it up close so he could feel his prey squirm. He enjoyed the perfume of fear.

As predictable as the tide, Uri crushed Louis in an enveloping hug.

Uri took it nice and easy—this initial embrace only made Louis's lungs collapse, and his bones pop . . . but not quite break. He could take ten seconds of this before he blacked out or his spine snapped.

Worst of all, though, Uri smelled like wet dog.

Louis kicked his feet, hoping this would appease the feral brain of his cousin . . . while his hands and arms, now made even more slippery by Uri's sweat and the increasing pressure, squirmed and wormed upward, fingertip by fingertip over Uri's chest until . . . Louis touched the hard leather knife sheath . . . then the hilt of Saliceran.

Just a bit farther.

His fingers wrapped around the knife's handle.

Uri froze and his eyes widened.

He knew he had made a mistake, but what could Uri do? If he released him, Louis could immediately draw the poisoned blade.

So Uri did the completely predictable thing: he squeezed *harder*.

Louis's spine crackled along its length. The additional force, however, propelled his lubricated hands and arms upward as if shot from a cannon.

Grasping the blade and pulling it free of the scabbard, Louis twisted it so the edge ripped through Uri's silk shirt and the jagged tip grazed his cousin's neck.

A black line appeared where the blade had cut skin—blisters blossomed along with red lines of poison that traced a web of blood vessels.

Uri screamed.

He dropped Louis in an unceremonious heap and clutched at his throat.

Saliceran's kiss was legendarily painful.

Louis still somehow held the blade. He gulped in air. The black spots at the periphery of his vision cleared.

The blade was half the length of his forearm. In the First Great War, it had been a mighty sword—broken upon the ultimate immovable object, alas. Now its pieces lay scattered among the stars. This last remaining jagged shard forever wept oily venom that smelled of honeysuckle and almonds. Runes so old even Louis could not read them were etched upon Saliceran's Damascus layers.

Uri wheezed and gasped as the poison worked deeper, ballooning the tissues of his neck.

Louis did not make the same mistake his cousin had. Without preamble, speech, quote, or hesitation he stabbed the beast in his eye.

Uri cried out. His hands slashed at the air, reaching for one last thing to grasp and crush.

Louis stepped away.

Uri blinked with his one remaining eye . . . and fell onto the concrete, shaking the foundation. He convulsed once, twice, then expelled one last great sigh and lay still.

"Sorry, Cousin," Louis whispered.

And he did actually feel sorry for Uri. He had loved Sealiah. True, in his own slavish dysfunctional way, but it was love nonetheless. And love like that deserved to survive, if for no other reason than to make both parties eternally suffer.

"You're better off this way," Louis said. "These things never work out. Trust me. I have some small expertise in such matters."

Every bone in Louis's body seemed cracked. The pain was electric along his spine.

It would pass. Physical injuries would be easy to repair once he performed the ritual to drain the last bits of power clinging to Uri's physical form.

He reached for Uri's neck to check for a pulse, but the tissues there were too swollen. So, Louis gingerly removed one of Uri's shoes and felt the artery at the ankle. There was no motion, no warmth or life.

Saliceran's poison had felled king and pope, immortal and angel—which is what it was made to do, after all.

He moved to Uri's chest, unstrapped the sheath and slid the poisonous blade back inside.

Louis turned the now covered blade over in his hands and considered. With Saliceran he had new options. To do what, though? Besting Uri was like pitting a matador against a mammoth. A highly unlikely contest . . . but one with a *slight* chance that the man would walk away.

What he was considering now would be like a mosquito jousting with a bullet train.

Unless Louis was especially, extraordinarily, and expertly deceptive.

Perhaps.

With a rag he shut Uri's one good eye, then closed what remained of the other. He patted him once on the forehead. Louis considered saying something to commemorate the passing of his cousin. What could one say? He was faithful? A good soldier to the end? A slathering puppy ever following his mistress's heel?

He decided a moment of silence would serve.

Feeling he had observed all the proper ritual and form and bestowed every drop of respect his cousin deserved, Louis unbuttoned Uri's jacket, tugging and wrestling each sleeve off his massive arms.

The jacket—like some stage magician's never-ending handkerchief—revealed itself to have enough cloth to make a circus tent. There were hundreds, if not thousands, of interior pockets. The Scalagari family tailors had outdone themselves.

He ran his hands along the silk lining. His long fingers twitched, and he delved into one pocket after another, pulling out mystical seals, a Magic 8 Ball, bells, a sextant, and a rolled-up star chart.

"No, no, no," Louis whispered.

He felt again and removed a thick manila file folder.

Opening it, he found reports on the Post twins: Eliot's newly formed musical ability, and even more intriguing, Fiona's talent for cutting.

Louis suppressed a shudder. The girl took after her mother.

There were notes on their daily activities: their work at Ringo's, their walk home, how they spent far too much time cooped up in their dreary apartment.

Until recently.

Surveillance photos showed Eliot walking and talking with a lovely blond thing. From Eliot's awkward posture and his demure eye contact, Louis surmised that she was the one who had stolen his heart.

In more photos the two of them were in the park, eating and drinking . . . embracing. The boy obviously took after his father—attracting the wrong women.

Louis expelled a heavy sigh. He must find time in the near future to school his son about the intricacies of the deadlier sex.

Next were pictures of Fiona dismounting a motorcycle, accompanied by the same young man who had fetched Eliot last night. More pictures showed these two walking in the woods, with one snapshot of them kissing on the sidewalk.

He found a separate file on this boy: Robert Farmington. There were all the relevant facts and figures. He was a Driver for the League. Interesting. Kissing Louis's daughter? He was a rebel and rule breaker. Louis approved.

He ran his fingertips over Robert's ruggedly handsome face. "You will do nicely."

Louis cleared his throat. "Robert Farmington," he whispered.

And then louder: "Robert Farmington."

He stretched his voice into something a half octave higher. "Robert Farmington." There—just as he remembered him last evening.

Down to business, then. Louis had his orders, fates to seal, and an Infernal pact to fulfill.

He would deal with his daughter first, and as requested, exile her to the Valley of the New Year.

He felt a tad guilty. Not about potentially trapping her in a shadow realm forever, but rather because he didn't feel the way for her as he did Eliot. Perhaps she reminded him of her mother too much. No matter. Once she was in the Valley of the New Year, there would be all the time in the world to catch up.

Louis found Uri's cell phone, looked up the phone number for the Posts' residence, and dialed.

After Fiona, Eliot would get his turn. No matter what Louis's personal plans entailed, he, at all costs, had to betray his son and deliver him to Beal.

The phone rang and connected.

"Hello?" Louis said. "This is Robert Farmington calling for Fiona, please."

67

TROUBLE CALLS

Fiona's room was a mess. Her possessions lay scattered everywhere, and a mountain of dirty clothes had been kicked into the corner. If anyone still enforced RULE 16, everything Fiona owned would get tossed out.

It was funny. Why was she worried about her material possessions after three life-or-death trials?

Still, it was the principle of the thing.

She picked up her collection of Roman histories and set them back on the shelf. Books deserved better treatment. Next time she felt angry, she'd take it out on something that deserved it.

But that was the odd thing this morning; she didn't *feel* anything.

Ever since she had cut herself in that fun-house maze, it had been getting harder to feel sad or scared or even happy. Anger was the only emotion that came easily. But that was no good. She couldn't run around feeling angry for the rest of her life.

If she closed her eyes and concentrated, she could feel a glimmer of happiness and hope. She and Eliot were done with the League's trials. They had to accept them as family now . . . or maybe not. She could almost hear them deliberating over them now.

At least the tests were over. No more out-of-the-blue adventures in the middle of the night.

As she thought about the League and her new extended family, she lost focus on any happy feelings.

She righted her antique globe and turned it so the Pacific Ocean and Micronesia faced her.

Was this the detachment that Grandmother always seemed to possess?
Cee had told her that Grandmother had cut herself, too. Fiona doubted
very much, though, that she had severed her appetite as well. How many
never-empty boxes of cursed chocolates could be out there?   ·

Fiona remembered what had made her feel good. She rummaged through
her dirty clothes—ripped apart her sweatpants and pulled out a single cotton
thread.

Cutting.

That would make her feel again. With increasing regularity, cutting
things gave her pleasure.

She pulled the thread taut and focused. The fiber twisted end to end,
sharpening until it seemed to vanish—a line of force that rippled through
the air.

She cast about her room, searching for something to destroy.

Books . . . typewriter . . . furniture . . . she cherished it all. She sighed.
That's all she needed was to make more of a mess.

Fiona relaxed, and the string went limp.

Maybe it was better to feel nothing than to feel joy over destroying
something precious.

She toyed with the string, draping it over both hands. It reminded her of
how Dallas had showed her the trick of looking at her life . . . and how she
had seen the end of that life.

She stared at the thread, made it go out of focus and back into view, in
that out-of-the-corner-of-your-eye way.

The thread blurred into many fibers, a pattern that stretched back into
her past—and farther ahead from where she held it—to the future. ˙

The weave in the past was the same, save for the fringe leading up to the
present. That line frayed so much that it looked as if it were about to snap.
She stared closer at this part. Microscopic tendrils wrapped about it, twined
together, and made a bridge from yesterday to today.

This was precisely when her life was supposed to end.

No . . . She squinted. It *had* ended. The original line had worn so much
that it got smaller and thinner and just disappeared. If not for this other
fiber sprouting around it, her life would've been severed.

She gingerly touched this part. It felt like wood, glimmered like soft
gold, and was warm. There was a pulse, too, strong and regular.

That had to be the doing of the Golden Apple. One life ended . . . and
now this. A new life? A second chance? Or something she didn't yet un-

derstand? Whatever it was, it moved through the present and stretched out before her. She did indeed have a future.

Both curious and cautious, Fiona cast her eyes ahead, following the twining vine. The fiber multiplied and fanned outward, cross threads interweaving; it became a fabric that branched in many directions. Here and there she could see the vine adorned with tiny leaves and apple blossoms.

What did these many paths mean? That her future wasn't set? She noted many dead ends . . . and Fiona took those at their literal meaning. Many more, however, continued on—all moving forward into the shadows.

She tentatively moved her hand up to that part of the weave, feeling wood and brick textures under her fingertips, tickled by champagne bubbles and smelling perfume and hearing laughter.

Fiona smiled. It felt like a party. She hoped so.

But farther along, these sensations turned to ice. She felt pebbled asphalt and the slick stickiness of blood . . . smelled brimstone and fire. She didn't like that part one bit.

Fiona let go of the threads.

She picked up her typewriter and papers and all of her books—just in case Grandmother came in. She scooped her clothes into the hamper, then left her room. She no longer wanted to be alone with her thoughts.

She knocked on Eliot's door, then went in—or, at least, tried to.

His door was locked.

"Just a second," Eliot said from the other side, then unlocked and opened his door. "Oh. It's you." He looked back to his bed. "Come in. Lock the door."

Since when did Eliot *lock* his door? Then again, Fiona had recently taken to locking her door, too. They all had things to hide these days . . . and she didn't think that was such a good thing.

Nonetheless, she closed and locked his door behind her.

He sat on the edge of his bed and flipped back the blanket hiding his violin. Fiona saw that the snapped string had been replaced. It looked as good as new. She wondered where Eliot had gotten an extra string.

He touched it once and then turned away, staring into space with a pained expression, his hands folded into his lap.

Fiona had a fair idea of what was going through his head: last night, the fog, all those people screaming . . . and dying.

She remembered how she had at first tried to rationalize what she had done to Perry Millhouse. Fiona had been backed into a corner, had to protect herself, Eliot, and the girl. None of those things really changed that she had killed a person.

But when it came right down to it, she had enjoyed destroying that monster.

Eliot would never feel that way, though. The people on the air force base weren't like Millhouse.

If anything, during this last heroic trial, Fiona and Eliot were the monsters.

She sat next to him on the bed and sighed.

"How do you feel?" he asked. "Can you eat?"

"I had some oatmeal this morning. It tasted like sawdust, but it went down and stayed down. Some water, too."

"What about the apple? Do you feel any different?"

"Nothing different. Just me."

Eliot nodded. "That's good, isn't it?"

He didn't sound too sure, and Fiona gave him a quizzical look.

"I mean," he said, "everything that's happened to us since our birthday turns out different than how it first looks. Presents that come with unintended consequences—a new family I thought would care about us have instead been trying to kill us—everything." He rubbed his arm.

The red line and bruises on his arm that she had seen last night were still there. An infection? Poison? He should see a doctor.

Eliot noticed her concerned look and turned away so she couldn't see. "It's nothing. Just a scratch."

"That's more than a scratch," she whispered.

Fiona stopped herself from saying more. Her brother sounded as if he was hiding something—just as she had when she had been eating all those chocolates.

She glanced at his violin. It looked normal, but something about it . . . the fiery wood grain, the way she could almost hear the strings vibrate even though nothing had touched them.

She wanted to tell Eliot that maybe he should put it a way for a while. That too much of a good thing probably wasn't.

He was so attached to the violin, though. She'd have to talk to someone else about it. Maybe Uncle Henry. In the meantime, she'd watch that arm of his.

"Is Grandmother back?" he asked.

It was an obvious change-of-subject tactic, but she let it slide. Fiona shook her head. "I guess we'll have to go in to work."

"Ringo's is closed for a week. Renovations."

That was unexpected but welcome news. She could give Robert a call. Maybe her life could actually be normal—just for a few hours.

"Are you going to hang out with Julie?"

Eliot winced and looked even more miserable. "She's gone," he whispered. "Had to leave town . . . and I don't think she's coming back."

"Oh."

Fiona wasn't sure if this was a good or bad thing. It had been obvious that Julie liked her brother. But just as there was something different about Eliot's violin, there was something strange about Julie, too. Something Fiona had never liked.

She wanted to tell her brother that it would be okay. He'd get over Julie. After all, they were tough; they'd survived everything the League had thrown at them.

Of course, there was the small matter of what surviving had cost them. Like the pawns that had crossed a chessboard, they'd changed. Or would they always be the League's pawns?

Fiona's fist clenched until the knuckles whitened, her anger easily welling to the surface of her thoughts. She deliberately exhaled and relaxed her hand.

The phone in the dining room jangled.

Fiona and Eliot jumped to their feet.

"That has to be Grandmother," Eliot said.

"I bet the Council's decided," Fiona said.

They bolted to the door. Eliot fumbled with the lock, Fiona opened the door, and they exploded into the hallway. Scrabbling for purchase on the hardwood floor, they raced for the phone.

Cee ambled steadily toward it, however, and picked up the receiver before they got there.

"Hello? . . . Good morning, Mr. Farmington. Yes, Fiona is right here. Is this a business or personal call?"

Robert was calling for her?

If it was business, that would mean something was up with the Council. Maybe they'd decided she and Eliot needed another trial. Robert always seemed to be the bearer of bad news.

If, on the other hand, he said this was a personal call, then Cee might just hang up on him. RULE 99: *No personal calls.*

Robert answered Cee. What he said exactly, Fiona couldn't tell; his voice was barely audible from where she stood.

Cee laughed, though, and blushed (Fiona hadn't even known her great-grandmother *could* still blush), then she handed the receiver to her.

Eliot hovered nearby, curious.

"Hello?" Fiona said breathlessly.

"How are you, baby?" Robert sounded cool and relaxed, as if he were basking on some beach, sipping a drink.

Fiona had the urge to check herself in a mirror. How silly. She composed herself. "I'm fine. What did the Council decide?"

He hesitated. "Nothing yet . . . but something new has popped up." He sounded a little less cool now, and a bit of urgency crept back into his tone. "Can we meet?"

The way he asked—so direct, so insistent—it caused a warmth to spread across Fiona's chest. She stepped away from Eliot and Cee, cupping the receiver closer to her mouth. "I think so. What about?"

"I can't say over the phone. It's not a secure line."

She didn't exactly know what that meant, but she trusted Robert knew what he was talking about.

"Okay. Where? When?"

"I'll cruise by the corner of Midway and Vine in ten minutes." After a pause and the hiss of dead air, he then whispered, "Come alone, Fiona. What I have is just for you."

The heated excitement she had felt a second ago chilled.

Fiona glanced at Cee and Eliot, who stared back at her expectantly. Surely Robert had meant to come alone—as in "don't bring Grandmother or Cee." He couldn't have meant not to bring her brother. It wasn't as if this were a date, was it?

She didn't dare ask. Not with Cee hanging on her every word.

Fiona wasn't sure how she felt about Robert's wanting to meet her when the Council was deliberating her and her brother's fate. As much as she wanted to be with him alone, under the circumstances it somehow seemed improper. Besides, she couldn't ditch Eliot. Not in his current depressive funk.

"Fiona? You still there?"

"Yeah, still here. I'll be there in ten minutes."

"Cool, baby. See you then." He hung up.

Fiona stared at the receiver. Since when had he started calling her "baby"? She didn't like that.

"Well?" Eliot asked.

"We're going for a walk. You better bring your pack—just in case."

The look of intense curiosity upon Eliot's face hardened. He understood: this might be dangerous . . . and he might have to play his violin again. He considered a moment, nodded, and ran back to his room.

"A walk, where?" Cee asked, wringing her hands.

Fiona didn't answer; instead, she marched into the kitchen.

Cee followed. "Do you need me to fix you a snack first, darling?"

Fiona got into the refrigerator, pulled open the vegetable crisper, and grabbed a bunch of asparagus. Looped about the stocks was a purple rubber band.

She remembered how she had used a similar band to cut through Millhouse—his limbs falling away from his torso in opposite directions.

She blinked away the unpleasant memory, grimaced, and grabbed the rubber band.

Fiona turned to face Cee, experimentally stretching the cold rubber into a taut line. "This is nothing serious, but Eliot and I need to go alone."

Fiona was sure this *was* serious. A sensation of wrongness crystallized inside her. She didn't know why . . . but she knew it was there.

"If we're not back in half an hour, call Grandmother."

Cee set a hand on her chest and started to breathe heavily. Her eyes widened and she took a step closer to Fiona. "You can't just leave."

Fiona let go of one end of the rubber band. It recoiled into her hand with a sharp snap.

Cee's hand reflexively jumped to her throat.

"Yes, we can," Fiona told her with a finality that sounded just like Grandmother.

She regretted using that tone with Cee, but nonetheless moved past her into the dining room.

Eliot was there, waiting, pack draped over his shoulder.

Without looking back, they raced down the hall, then spiraled down the stairs.

"So what did Robert say?" Eliot asked. "What's this all about?"

"If I had to guess," Fiona told him, ". . . it's trouble."

68

A DOOR TO THE NEW YEAR

liot sat in the back of Uncle Henry's Maybach Exelero and mulled the "wrongness" of this situation.

It wasn't the you're-about-to-die kind of wrong that he and Fiona had dealt with recently, but rather the kind of wrong as in those spot-the-difference pictures.

When Robert had picked him and Fiona up, the race-car/limousine hybrid looked a little off. The mirror-chrome finish was dull, and mud spattered the back panels. And most curious, a yellow smiley-face ball capped the antenna. Eliot was sure the car hadn't had this ornament before . . . or even had an external antenna.

Fiona sat up front, of course. She tried to talk to Robert, but he told her he had to focus on driving. He would explain everything when they got there.

Watching him, Eliot thought he could drive, if he had to. Not that Grandmother had ever let him try. He and Fiona had, however, studied automobiles and knew everything there was to know about motors and transmissions. He saw how Robert worked the gear selector, accelerator, and brake. It should be easy.

Eliot looked out the window. Highway 1 rolled by, and golden California sunlight sparkled on the ocean.

Why weren't they there yet? Robert had been driving for ten minutes, and he had said it was close. In Uncle Henry's car they should've been across the state by now.

The smell of the car was wrong, too. Before it had smelled of leather, whiskey, and cigar smoke. Now, only a sour scent permeated the car.

Fiona hadn't said anything, though, so maybe it was just his imagination.

The "wrongness," real or not, was a welcome thing. It kept Eliot busy trying to puzzle the mystery out, kept him from thinking about last night . . . his music and the fog . . . and all those people screaming and getting hurt inside the mist.

No, not just hurt. He was sure it had been a lot more than hurt. People had been killed.

That had been his fault. It was his choice, and ultimately his responsibility.

But if he hadn't done it, Fiona would be dead. How would he feel if he had had a way to save her and hadn't used it? Wouldn't that be killing, too?

He sighed. He'd never feel good about this—either way, he was guilty of killing *someone*. Better strangers, though, than his sister.

"Ah," Robert said. "We're here."

The car turned into a gravel driveway. A neon sign proclaimed LAST SUNSET TAVERN.

Eliot craned his head and saw a dilapidated building with a red metal roof. A few beat-up cars and a row of motorcycles were by the front door. Bottles and trash littered the parking lot.

"Looks like lots of people are here," Fiona said. "Do they serve breakfast?"

"Not really," Robert muttered. He backed into a spot far away from the other cars and bikes. "There's something inside you have to see."

"Wait." Fiona looked uncomfortable and set her hand on Robert's arm. "No one's listening over a phone line now. Tell me what this is all about. Is it dangerous?"

Robert patted her hand. He looked at it, took it in his, then kissed it. "Dangerous? Yes and no, my darling. It's about your father."

She made a face. "Oh, you should've told us that before we got here." She withdrew her hand from his.

"You wouldn't help him if he needed you?" Robert asked.

"I don't know. He's so weird." She crossed her arms over her chest. "Besides, what's he ever done for Eliot or me, besides stalking us and being a creep?"

"I'll help him," Eliot said, and opened the car door.

Eliot wanted to give Louis a chance. Bum or not, crazy or not, part of the Infernal family or not—he had shown Eliot more trust and warmth than any of his other so-called relatives.

"He's not here," Robert said to Eliot. "Not exactly, anyway. But he *is* in trouble, and you can help him . . . if you want." He glanced at Fiona and frowned. "It's going to be easier to show you, though."

"So show us," Eliot said, impatience creeping into his voice. He grabbed his pack and waited for Robert.

Robert turned to Fiona. "Well?"

She expelled a great breath. "Okay. I can't let my brother go into that place by himself." She fingered the rubber band about her wrist, then opened her door and got out.

Together, the three of them strode onto the Last Sunset Tavern's porch and through its double swinging doors.

The place was dark, punctuated by neon beer signs, a jukebox in the corner, three spotlights over pool tables, and a flickering television in the corner. The floor was covered with sawdust and peanut shells. It smelled of beer.

Unshaved men in denim and leather stopped what they were doing (mostly drinking beer) and their gazes gravitated toward Fiona.

Robert stepped in front of her and gave a nod to the bartender.

The bartender nodded back and then at the rear of the room.

The customers returned to talking and drinking and ignored them . . . mostly. A few continued to stare at Fiona.

"Don't let these jerks rile you," Robert whispered. "This way." He moved to the door in back.

Eliot and Fiona followed, trying not to make eye contact, but these people were so interesting that Eliot found it hard not to look. There were so many different tattoos. He imagined his arms covered with Celtic knots, flames, and tribal spirals . . . and liked this new tougher version of himself.

They got to the back door and Robert slid a key into its dead-bolt lock. He opened it, and they filed through. Robert found the light switch and a single fluorescent bulb strobed on overhead.

They were in a storage room with beer kegs and boxes half-filled with bottles. It was cold. A steel door to the left led to a refrigerated compartment. Another door at the back was chained and padlocked and had a darkened EXIT sign over it.

Robert locked the door to the bar behind them.

"And this is where you want to take me *alone*?" Fiona whispered to him.

"Alone?" Eliot asked.

"Never mind that. What you have to see is over here." Robert pushed aside boxes to make a path.

Old calendars littered the floor. Eliot got his flashlight, turned it on, and took a closer look. One had pictures of bass fish on it from 1979, another featured hot rods from 1963, and a third showed various covered bridges in 1932. They were all folded back to December.

Robert rolled aside one last keg. "Here it is."

A doorway stood in the brick wall.

It wasn't a real door, though. It had been painted there, and not very well painted. It had a black outline sketched with a marker. The body was red-brown—slashes and splashes that gave it the texture of roughly hewn wood.

Eliot took a step closer. It was difficult to tell, but that could be dried blood.

A brass doorknob had been stuck into the wall as well—literally just stuck there, rammed into the brick. It hung at a precarious angle, ready to fall out.

"Is this a joke?" Eliot asked.

"Not at all." Robert wiped sweat from his brow. "This leads to the Valley of the New Year. I think it's where your father has gone. It's a very dangerous place. You'll have to go in and look for him."

Fiona made a rude noise. "We've just survived three life-or-death tests. I'm not about to risk myself or Eliot for a man who couldn't bother to tell us the truth about being our father."

Robert looked astonished at her words, hurt, too.

"Wait a second," Eliot said. "Maybe there was a good reason he never told us."

"Like what?" Fiona asked.

"Well, Grandmother for starters. I bet she's been scaring him off."

Fiona pursed her lips. "So he was just clandestinely watching over us, making sure we were okay? I don't believe that. He's with the other family. I bet he wants something."

Robert leaned against the wall and glared at her, although Fiona didn't see him.

Something was "off" with Robert. Like the wrongness that permeated Uncle Henry's car, Eliot sensed Robert wasn't quite himself today.

"We should at least give Louis a chance to explain," Eliot told her.

He waited for Fiona to reply and watched as she stared at the painted door, thinking. She could be so cold, like Grandmother sometimes, then other times she surprised Eliot and was almost decent.

"Okay, you're right," she finally whispered. "Open it. Let's see this valley."

Robert brightened. "You're doing the right thing, Fiona. Family *is* the most important thing." He held up a warning hand. "Back up a bit, though. This might get tricky."

He faced the doorway and grasped the knob.

The paint crackled over the brick like water suddenly freezing. The wavering marker edges snapped straight. Bricks in the wall popped and compressed, and tiny shards of stone exploded and bit into the flesh of Eliot's exposed arms.

The fluorescent light in the room went dead, and a dim illumination appeared from the door's edges.

Robert jiggled the doorknob, straining to open it. He set one foot alongside the wall and pulled.

Eliot felt his perspective tilt as if the room slanted downward . . . toward the door . . . pitching steeper until his inner ear was sure that he stood at the mouth of a deep hole.

Fiona stepped closer to him, one hand grasping her rubber band.

Eliot felt vibrations as if a thousand microscopic strings twanged in the air about them. He could almost see space blurring.

"Threads," Fiona whispered to him. "Do you see them all?"

"No," he whispered back. "But I do *feel* them."

Robert grunted and the seams of his leather jacket ripped.

A low hiss came from the door that grew into a thunderous roar of rushing wind.

Robert wrenched the door open.

A vortex of air and fog and snow swirled about them. It settled and left the atmosphere still and crisp. Eliot could see his own breath.

He and Fiona stepped closer for a better look.

The door did not lead to the back of the Last Sunset Tavern, nor did it lead anywhere outside . . . at least not outside to sunny California.

Beyond the doorframe there were snowdrifts and a frosted forest. It was night. Aurora wavered among twinkling stars, painting the sky with violet and silver. Nestled within the forest sat a village, its church spires and rooftops decorated with Christmas lights, Japanese paper lanterns, and a thousand candles. Eliot heard people singing and laughing, horns blaring, shrieks of pleasure, rebel yells, and breaking glass. Fireworks shot into the air and exploded into blossoms of spark.

Eliot smelled spiced apple cider and fresh gingerbread, but shivered as he took the chilled air into his chest.

Fiona shivered, too.

Robert removed his leather jacket and draped it over her shoulders.

"The Valley of the New Year," Robert explained. "It's a never-ending party. They're stuck forever, just a few seconds before midnight on December thirty-first."

"Who's stuck?" Eliot whispered. He kept his voice low because he was afraid the people in the village would hear him . . . and something told him that wouldn't be such a good thing.

"They're folk who have lost their way, fallen out of time," Robert whispered back. "It's a place where the forgotten ticks and tocks collect—going back and forth, forth and back, never quite the present or the future."

"How did Louis end up there?" Fiona asked. She edged toward the door, reached out, and caught a few snowflakes.

"Louis visited a long time ago. He liked it . . . always wanted to find a way back. Everyone likes it." Robert licked his lips and glanced about the room. "Wouldn't you children like to go in and see for yourselves?"

Eliot would. He had an urge to make a snowball and plaster his sister in the back of the head. He imagined them running and sliding through the drifts. They could join the party. That cider would taste good. It would be great to just relax for a few minutes.

But how long would a few minutes be where time didn't move?

Fiona started for the door, and Eliot set one hand or her arm. "Careful," he whispered.

She shook her head, clearing her thoughts. "That was strange. I wanted to go inside . . . or outside, or wherever that is, and see it for myself."

They looked at one another, communicating their concerns with a single glance.

This was very wrong. All of it: the Valley, their father being there, this tavern, Uncle Henry's car, even Robert . . . the way he was acting and talking.

They turned to Robert. He wasn't there.

He stood behind them now. Eliot couldn't see him clearly. The fluorescent light overhead was out, but plenty of light streamed through the doorway. That should have illuminated the room, but Robert seemed covered in shadows.

Eliot got the impression that he wore an overcoat. That made sense because it was so cold in here, but he hadn't seen him bring one in, and he sure hadn't been wearing it *under* his leather jacket.

"You called us 'children,'" Fiona said, suspicion creeping into her voice.

"Well," Robert replied, clearing his throat, "you *are* a little younger than I am, my dear."

"Why do you want us to help Louis?" Eliot asked. "Last night you told me to stay away from him. That everything he said was a lie."

Behind Robert, the door to the bar rattled in its frame.

"Your father will always tell you the truth, my boy. Always." Robert quickly turned and assessed the shaking door. "I think, however, the time for talk has run out."

A fist pounded on the door. "Open up!" someone shouted on the other side. "Right now, buddy!"

Robert stepped closer to Fiona, and Eliot saw he indeed wore a trench coat of fine camel hair . . . just as Louis had the other night.

The door splintered and fell in. Three men in leather vests pushed through. One carried a baseball bat, one a jagged knife, and one a shot-gun.

The man brandishing the bat growled, "We're here to make sure nobody double-crosses Mr. Buan."

"With all the grace and impeccable timing one has come to expect from hired help," Robert said.

The three men looked puzzled.

Robert quickly whispered to Eliot and Fiona, "I will take care of this."

Robert glanced at the stacks of boxes and beer kegs and made a dra-matic motion with one arm—his camel-hair coat trailing behind in a flour-ish. He didn't touch any of it, but the entire pile tumbled: an avalanche of aluminum and crashing, smashing bottles and cardboard that buried the three men and covered the door to the bar.

Robert turned back to them. "We don't have much time. My hand is forced in this matter. Here's what I need you to do."

Fiona had her rubber band stretched between her hands. She relaxed as Robert approached, but just slightly.

"What's going on?" she demanded. "We'll need answers before we do anything."

Robert made a "calm down" gesture with his hands. "Answers you shall have, my dear." He crept closer and cautiously put one hand on her arm, smiling the entire time.

He held the smile before him like a shield . . . a smile Eliot had seen before. "Louis!?"

Robert turned to Eliot and his smile warmed. "An eye for the details, I see. It serves you well."

Robert spun Fiona around and roughly shoved her—so hard she flew into the air—through the open doorway, and she tumbled onto a snowdrift.

She sputtered and screamed, outraged, and started to get up.

Eliot took two steps toward her.

Robert grabbed him by the collar and hauled him back. He slammed the door shut on Fiona. The brass doorknob fell onto the concrete floor.

Eliot shrugged off Robert's hold, ran to the doorknob, and shoved it back into the wall, turning it back and forth.

There was no lock mechanism, though. It was just a bunch of cracked brick.

"That won't work," Robert assured him.

Eliot wheeled around. Blood pounded in his temples. "Who are you? Robert? Louis? Someone or something else?" Eliot reached into his pack for Lady Dawn.

Robert clamped a hand on his arm. He was stronger than Eliot, a great deal stronger, and he pulled Eliot's arm away from the violin.

Robert's eyes widened as he spotted the red line of infection running up Eliot's forearm. "Ah, that is an occupational hazard for true musicians, I'm afraid. Problematic . . . but fixable."

Eliot stared at his face. He looked so much like Robert . . . but he talked like Louis, and he knew about the violin's snapped string hurting him.

If it was Louis, why the pretense? Why not just come to him and explain what he needed? Eliot would've listened.

But Fiona wouldn't have.

And if Grandmother found him—Eliot could only imagine what would happen if she and Louis were in the same room.

Robert cocked his head, listening intently. "Shhh."

There were footsteps outside the storage room, lots of men, on every side, and husky whispers. The EXIT door banged as if kicked—but it held.

"I sense a thousand questions boiling your brain," Robert said, "but there is no time. We must act."

"But Fiona." Eliot turned to the painted doorway. "If you think that place will hold my sister, think again."

"Yes, she can cut, I know. But it will take a good deal of cleverness to find *what* to cut to leave the Valley."

"Why'd you push her in?" Eliot demanded.

"Because I had to." Robert roughly let go of his arm. "I made a deal." He said this as if it explained everything. Robert dug into his pocket and handed Eliot car keys and a cell phone. "Come with me."

Robert then marched to the door of the refrigerated compartment. He opened it and entered, beckoning Eliot to follow.

Eliot turned back to the painted doorway. He touched it—just brick now—but he imagined Fiona was on the other side searching for a way back.

He had to stay and figure a way to get her out . . . but how with so many people obviously intent on hurting him?

He looked at his pack and saw Lady Dawn. He could summon the nightmare fog. But even then, he might not find a way to Fiona. Robert—Louis—or whatever he really was, was the only one who knew for certain how to open that door.

Robert stood on the threshold of the freezer. "Coming?"

Would Fiona be okay in that cold? Would she survive long enough for Eliot to get back with help?

Eliot hesitated, uncertain.

"Trust me," the person who looked like Robert said. "This is the only way out for us all. I have never lied to you. Nor will I start now."

Eliot believed his words, but ironically, that didn't make him trust him any more.

A shotgun blast thundered and a dozen tiny holes appeared in the back door.

Eliot's options were shrinking by the second. He took a deep breath and followed Robert into the freezer.

Robert ran to the door in the back of the frosty compartment. It was caked with so much ice it would take a pickax to get through.

Robert kicked the door off its hinges.

Blazing sunlight streamed inside, dazzling Eliot.

"There's the car." Robert pointed.

Eliot squinted. A beat-up Lincoln Town Car with primer-painted fenders sat where Robert had parked the Maybach.

"Go!" Robert urged.

The car had the same smiley-face antenna ball Eliot had seen earlier. Apparently this car wasn't what it had appeared to be, either. He looked at the keys clutched in his hand, still unsure if it was the best thing to leave Fiona.

"We will be able to help one another," Robert whispered, "but you must go—or *I* will not live to see the end of this day." He gave Eliot a gentle, but firm, shove into the sunlight.

Eliot blinked and immediately saw a group of men rounding the corner of the building. They brandished pool cues and broken beer bottles.

Robert ran toward them.

Gunshots rang through the air. Robert convulsed, continued running toward the men, and leapt, taking down three.

Eliot's heart beat in his throat. Robert or Louis or whoever that was . . . he was going to die to give Eliot a chance to escape. He had to help, play his violin, or even use the car as a battering ram against those men.

But Robert stood up, unharmed. And the three men he had taken down remained down.

Eliot ran for the car. He'd get away—from both the bar patrons *and* the thing masquerading as Robert—then he'd call Uncle Henry or Grandmother and get back here to rescue Fiona.

He skidded to a stop at the driver's-side door. It was unlocked. Eliot slid inside, inserted the key just as he had seen Robert do, and turned it.

The Lincoln's engine coughed to life.

Eliot glanced back at Robert. He looked different now: his hair long and streaked gray, his face angled to a point. More like . . .

Louis.

The other men in the mob backed off a few paces. The half-Robert/half-Louis waggled a finger at them and smiled. His smile faded into a snarl, however, as more men ran out of the tavern's entrance. He laughed and it sounded deep and dark . . . not human at all.

Eliot felt that something very wrong was about to happen, and part of him wanted to stay and watch the carnage. His hands grasped the steering wheel until the knuckles popped.

He gritted his teeth, banished the alien bloodlust, and stomped on the accelerator.

The Lincoln Town Car jumped out of the parking lot. Eliot whipped the wheel around and fishtailed onto the road.

69

THE FATE OF THE REAL ROBERT FARMINGTON

Robert sat cross-legged in the corner, crying.

He thought he'd gotten past this. He hadn't cried since he was little kid back when his mom and dad were still together. Funny, he could hardly remember what Dad looked like. Mom always said Robert looked like him.

He laughed and wiped his tears. He couldn't even remember what had made him bawl like a baby. Then again, he had his pick of reasons.

He pounded the smooth metal walls. He had to get a grip on himself and keep sane for one more day.

Just for one more day . . . so he could go through this again.

The Council had sentenced him to this isolation cell for fifty years. At least as far as he could remember, that's what had happened. He'd blacked out during that last meeting, woken up here, and hadn't seen anyone since.

How many months had passed? Twenty? Thirty? He'd lost track.

Maybe that was the point of this place: to blur your sense of time, make you forget who you were, and slowly lose your marbles.

Robert had tried to mark the time, but the cell's walls were brushed steel, and there was nothing to scratch the surface.

His cell was ten by ten paces. The ceiling stretched up five times his height. There was a tiny window that he couldn't reach, but he heard the surf crashing beyond. Never a voice, though. Not even a gull's cry to keep him company.

The light changed; that's how he kept track of day and night. Sometimes rain fell through the window: his only taste of freedom and his only reminder that there *was* an outside world.

He'd gone through a time where he wanted to end this. No easy way to do that, though.

He wore a plasticized paper jumpsuit that was impossible to rip. The toilet and sink in the corner didn't hold enough water to drown in. No blankets for a noose, either—just a soft spot on the floor and a pillow. They had thought of everything. Couldn't let a little inconvenient suicide end his torture, right?

That bad time had only lasted a few days. Robert was ashamed to think of it now. He'd never considered himself one of those pansies that took the easy way out.

In self-defense he did the only rational thing: he checked out. He had all the freedom he wanted in his head. He was never any good at day-dreaming, so that left him with his memories.

At first, he remembered all the bad stuff: the series of Mom's boyfriends and stepdads, then the criminals he'd hung out with as he worked his way across Europe, and the long nights when he found himself alone.

But he forced himself to remember the good things, too: Marcus and the Driver training sessions they had at Thunderhills Raceway; riding his Harley down the Mexican coastline; and Fiona and how she looked and smelled and felt that last night in Nevada when he had held her.

He wondered if Fiona even remembered him.

A knock reverberated on the metal door.

Robert froze. His heart pounded in his throat.

Another hallucination? He'd heard voices before in the cell. Robert had to sing to crowd them out . . . and they had eventually left him alone.

A voice outside said, "Hello, Robert? Do you mind if I come in?"

It was a human voice, but it'd been so long that Robert hardly recognized the sound.

He struggled to stand and straightened his jumpsuit. "Y—" He cleared his throat. "Yeah, sure."

The vaultlike door cracked open, and the last person Robert expected to ever see again entered: Mr. Mimes.

Beyond being surprised, however, Robert noted with keen interest that the door had *not* been closed—freedom was just a few steps away.

Mr. Mimes wore black slacks and a tuxedo dress shirt with mother-of-pearl buttons. His silver hair was slicked back, although one curl had escaped and fell over his forehead. He smelled of cigars and a woman's citrusy perfume.

"Pardon my appearance. I've been dancing all night. Had to keep up pretenses, mind you. I hope you hadn't thought I'd forgotten you, Robert."

"Forgotten me . . . ?" Robert's hands itched to wrap around Mr. Mimes's throat, and Robert took a tiny step forward.

He hesitated. What he longed for was company, someone, *anyone* to talk to, even the person who had put him here. So he'd let him talk for a few minutes . . . *then* he'd strangle him.

"Really, Robert. No theatrics, please. I came to make peace." Mr. Mimes glanced about the cell and grimaced. "I remember these walls very keenly."

"You were locked in here?"

"Another story, for another time. I recall, though, how distressing this place can be. I hope you are well?"

"You mean, have I lost my mind?" Robert considered carefully. It was a fair question. "I don't think so. I mean, I think I'm okay . . . as long as *you're* real."

Mr. Mimes fished out a slender mahogany case and plucked out a cigarette. "Do you mind?"

"Yeah, actually I do. Besides being bad for your health, I can't stand the stink of those things."

Mr. Mimes shot Robert a quizzical look and smiled. "Quite right." He flicked the unlit cigarette away. "A disgusting habit, I often forget." He then found a hip flask, uncorked it, took a sip, and offered the silver container to Robert. "Peace offering, my boy. Go on. Take it."

Robert wanted to take it, all right—take it and throw it in his face.

He grabbed it, though, and tilted the contents down his throat.

It wasn't brandy or whiskey or bourbon. It was luxurious velvet in liquid form, and its heat exploded through Robert's chest and shot through his limbs. Smoke curled through his thoughts . . . and cleared.

Everything cleared. His mind. His eyes.

He inhaled. It felt like his first breath.

"Nothing like a little soma to get things started, yes?" Mr. Mimes retrieved his flask. "But no need to overdo things."

Robert licked his lips, tasting the last drops of the stuff. It crackled with static electricity, champagne bubbles, and the whisper brush of the last time he had kissed Fiona.

Fiona. Where was she now? And, more important, what had the Council done to her while he had been locked away?

"How long?" Robert asked. "It couldn't have already been fifty years."

Mr. Mimes nodded as if he understood the torture Robert had endured. He glanced at his watch, counted on his fingers, and said, "Eleven hours."

It took all of Robert's strength to remain standing. He struggled to fit those words with his reality. He felt as if he had been in this place for months . . . maybe years.

He touched his face. It was smooth. If he had been here that long, he would've grown a beard. There wasn't even stubble.

"Imagine what a year would've done to your mind," Mr. Mimes whispered. "Let alone fifty."

Robert wanted to scream, bolt for the open door, and get out before it shut again. Instead, he somehow found his lost cool, crossed his arms, and leaned against the wall. "What's the deal, then? Come to rub it in? Or say you're sorry for stabbing me in the back?"

Mr. Mimes snorted a laugh, took another sip from his flask, then tucked it back into his pocket. "Nothing of the sort, my boy. I came to help you escape."

Robert chewed this over. Why would Mr. Mimes get him fired and locked away in this place, *then* spring him?

A setup? Robert could only imagine what the Council would do if they caught him trying to escape. That didn't make any sense, though. If Mr. Mimes had wanted him dead, he could have arranged that—especially since the Council had wanted Robert's throat cut at that last meeting.

The Council. They were the key.

Robert remembered everything now from that last Council meeting. There was a lot of talk about that treaty between them and the Infernal clans, the Pactum Pax Immortalis. Not only *didn't* the League want to help Eliot and Fiona, but they legally *couldn't* interfere with the Infernals' plans.

And as long as Robert worked for Mr. Mimes, neither could he.

Mr. Mimes consulted his watch. "Have you got it yet? Or must I connect all the dots?"

"I got it. *I* can help them now."

A smile flashed over Mr. Mimes's lips and vanished just as quick. "I have no idea what you're talking about."

Every bit of anger Robert had for Mr. Mimes evaporated. He had to give the guy credit—he was thinking three steps ahead of everyone else.

"Where are my things?"

Mr. Mimes ducked outside and retrieved a small doctor's bag. "I took the liberty of procuring your clothes and a few other items."

Robert dug through the bag. Inside was his leather jacket, a clean T-shirt, neatly pressed jeans, and his boots. He wriggled out of the paper jumpsuit and into real clothes. He almost felt human again.

Also in the bag was his Glock 29 handgun, three clips of ammunition, a cell phone, the keys to his bike, his wallet, a stack of cash, and a set of brass knuckles that he'd never before seen. Robert slipped the knuckles on.

"Something I thought you might find a use for."

Power surged through the metal, warming Robert's hand and arm. "Might come in handy. Thanks."

Robert's phone buzzed, startling him so much he almost dropped it. "You didn't tell anyone . . ."

Mr. Mimes shook his head and arched his eyebrows. "I suggest you answer it."

Robert had a bad feeling about this, but he nonetheless did as he was told. "Hello?"

"That's weird. I didn't even dial." Eliot's voice was on the other end. "Robert? Is that you?"

"Uh, yeah." Eliot Post was the last person Robert thought would be calling him. He'd never given him his number.

There was a long pause on the other end.

"Eliot? You still there?"

"I'm here. Were you just with me a few minutes ago?"

Mr. Mimes leaned closer, listening.

"There's no way I was with *anyone* a few minutes ago. Trust me on that. Are you in trouble?"

"You could say that. First things first, though. How did you get on this line? You, or someone who looked a lot like you, gave me this phone. I just turned it on, and you were on the other end."

Mr. Mimes held up a finger.

"Hang on a sec," Robert told Eliot.

"You have been cloned," Mr. Mimes explained. "Someone has copied you to such an exacting detail that even your psychical artifacts were duplicated. This is the only way to account for this other person . . . and the phone, which apparently shares identical electronics."

"How is that possible?"

Mr. Mimes shrugged. "It should not be. The two creatures I knew with such a talent are both dead. Apparently though, one is not as dead as I believed, which gives rise to many interesting possibilities." He gestured to Robert to return to the conversation.

"What kind of trouble are you in?" Robert asked.

"It's too much to explain over the phone. I had to ditch the car. It was running funny anyway. I think they're after me."

Eliot sounded scared, but not the kind of scared where you're worried about your own skin. Something else was going on.

"Wait. Back up," Robert said. "*You* were driving?"

"You told me to—or rather some other Robert told me. I don't know. It might have been Louis."

"Louis? Louis Piper? With the other family?"

This seemed to make sense to Mr. Mimes, because he nodded.

"I think it was him," Eliot replied. "So much happened so fast, and now Fiona's stuck in this other place."

Fiona, of course. If Eliot was in trouble, she had to be, too.

"Where are you?"

"Ten minutes south of a place called Last Sunset Tavern on Highway 1."

"Okay. Sit tight. I'll be there as fast I can. Don't call anyone else."

Eliot hesitated, then said, "Yeah . . . okay. Just hurry."

Robert hung up.

"If either family is involved," Mr. Mimes said, "you must make all due haste."

"I agree." Robert held out his hand. "Give me your car keys. I'm going to have to steal the Maybach."

A Cheshire cat grin appeared on Mr. Mimes's face as he handed the keys to Robert.

There was so much more Robert wanted to say to Mr. Mimes . . . mostly that he was sorry for ever doubting him. But there was no time for that. Fiona and Eliot were in a heap of trouble.

He ran outside.

Robert had never opened up the Maybach to find out exactly how fast she could go—but he was about to find out.

70

DECIDED WITH DICE

Eliot sat on the edge of his seat. Robert decelerated the Maybach from its surreal pace.

"That driveway up there," Eliot told him. "There were at least twenty guys with knives and pistols."

Robert—the real Robert—nodded, but didn't take his eyes off the road.

At least, Eliot hoped this was the real Robert Farmington. He talked and moved like Robert. He even radiated his usual tough-guy, supercool aura. And the very first words out of his mouth when he had come for Eliot had been "Where's Fiona?"

Eliot rested Lady Dawn on his lap. Could he use his music to kill again? The notion chilled his blood.

In self-defense, yes. To save Fiona . . . well, he'd already proven he could. He'd never thought twice about playing Lady Dawn before . . . now he *always* would.

He ran a finger over her polished wood grain. When he touched her, the pain in his arm vanished. In fact, the fingers on that hand actually felt more limber.

The other Robert—Louis—had seen his arm and the poison. What did he say? *Problematic . . . but fixable.*

Robert turned off the road and the Maybach's fat tires crunched over the gravel driveway of the Last Sunset Tavern.

"Here we go," Robert whispered.

The place looked the same: a dozen Harleys and pickup trucks parked by the front porch, and neon flickered inside the darkened tavern.

Eliot, however, spotted a few critical differences. The front windows of the tavern were busted. Bullet holes riddled the side of one pickup. He smelled smoke and a curious whiff of brimstone.

Robert eased open his door. "Stay here."

Eliot gave him a look. He had to be joking. If Eliot hadn't been stopped by an ancient crocodile, a guy who burst spontaneously into flames, or an air force base full of guards . . . Robert wasn't going to pull that "it's too dangerous" stuff on him now.

"Okay, okay." Robert shook his head. "Just keep behind me." He got out, his gun in hand.

Eliot climbed out of the car and followed.

No music played from the tavern. There wasn't a single voice.

Robert halted before the porch and stared at the gravel.

A splash of semicongealed blood made a large arc across his path.

Robert swallowed, glanced around, and continued on . . . but slower.

Eliot skirted around the blood, trying not to look at it, but he failed, and his eyes riveted on the spatters of crimson brown. He tore his gaze away— creeped out by his fascination with the stuff.

Robert held up one hand and paused in the doorway of the tavern. He ducked inside, then eased back out. "It's safe. No one's home."[65]

Eliot entered. Inside was eerily silent. All the lights were broken, save a few dim lines of neon that still flashed. The tables and chairs were splinters. Oddly, the bottles behind the bar were intact. There were even filled shot glasses on the counter.

Had Louis disguised as Robert done *all* this damage?

Eliot's eyes fixed upon a pair of dice on the bar. They looked like tiny rubies . . . just like those Uncle Henry had made him toss at that first Council meeting. Eliot's fingers itched to touch them.

"Where's this room with the door?" Robert continued to look around as if someone, or *something*, might pop out of the shadows.

"By the bar."

Robert crept toward the kicked-in door. He shoved aside the mound of

65. Although the crime scene at the Last Sunset Tavern (dubbed the Sunset Tavern Massacre by the press) was destroyed by the riot that evening, the initial police investigation discovered the remains of six individuals. One severed finger matched the bouncer, a wanted felon. None of the patrons who matched the registries of the parked vehicles were, however, ever found. *Gods of the First and Twenty-first Century, Volume 11: The Post Family Mythology*, 8th ed. (Zypheron Press Ltd.).

kegs and boxes and bottles that Louis had pushed over. There was no trace underneath of the three men that had come after them.

Robert glanced over the back room, strode to the door with a shotgun blast in it, and checked that it was still bolted. He then went into the freezer compartment, came back out, and shut that door behind him, too.

"The door was over here." Eliot moved to the wall and ran his hand over the painted bricks.

He remembered how the disguised Louis had shoved Fiona through and slammed it shut behind her. That valley had been subzero cold. Fiona could have hypothermia by now.

Eliot didn't understand why Louis had done it. Was it to protect his sister from the bar thugs? If so, why hadn't he pushed Eliot through as well? But Louis had given her his jacket beforehand, as if he were really concerned for her. It didn't add up.

"It's just bricks and paint now. But it *was* here."

"I know." Robert slipped his gun into a holster. He stared at the doorknob on the ground, looking scared to touch it.

Thankfully, he didn't ask how this could have been a real doorway. He believed Eliot. Of course, working for Uncle Henry, he probably saw this stuff all the time.

And yet, while Robert was far too cool to be what Eliot considered normal, he did seem very human. It reassured Eliot to know a person could be exposed to this craziness and be, more or less, a nice guy, unlike the rest of his family. They were so cruel—and liars all.

"What's it like working for Henry?"

"What?" Robert looked perplexed. "Now isn't the time for this. We have to find a way to get your sister back."

Eliot nodded, but he nonetheless asked, "I mean, is he a good person?"

Robert sighed. "Yeah, he's the best." Emotions played over his face, then Robert finally tore his gaze away from the doorway. "Really, he is. Most of the time I can't understand half of what he does or says—but he's always been fair, even nice, to me, and I guess he's saved my skin more than once."

Eliot could tell there was a lot more that Robert wasn't telling him, but he sensed enough truth in what Robert said to be satisfied.

Eliot turned his attention back to the doorway. He picked up the knob. It was solid brass and mirror-polished. He stuck it back into the wall where it had been, but nothing happened.

"When it opened before, it looked like the door was stuck. It took a lot of strength to get it open. Maybe it'll take both of us."

"I've only heard about these things before." Robert cautiously ran one finger along the doorway's edge. "It's going to take a lot more than muscle to make it work."

"Like what?"

Robert shrugged. "Magic is more your department."

Magic? Grandmother had made sure to explain to him and Fiona that there was no such thing. It was "the primitive mind's misunderstanding of natural phenomena." That's why she crossed out all those passages in their books . . . so their reasoning wouldn't be compromised.

But what about all the things he had seen? Souhk? Mr. Millhouse? And how had he called all those rats? Made the fire sing back to him? Conjured a fog full of nightmares?

Maybe Grandmother had forbidden all the folklore and fairy tales because they *were* real. And dangerous.

It didn't matter what you called it, real or imagined, myth or science. As Aunt Dallas had told them, you just had to accept some things to communicate with a part of your mind that had no language. Learn to use and control it . . . before it controlled you.

"Okay," Eliot whispered to Robert. "Give me a second to figure this out."

Eliot propped Lady Dawn onto his shoulder and touched the bow to her strings. He tapped a rhythm to the beat of his heart. The faint vibrations cleared his thoughts.

Eliot had found the path to things before: Souhk, Amanda Lane, even the Golden Apple sealed in that container. So all he had to do was compose Fiona's song. That would lead him right to her.

But taking what he knew about his sister and turning it inside out for anyone to hear felt wrong. Music gave him power over the things he played about. No one should have that kind of control over Fiona.

He decided to work on the doorway first. Take it one baby step at a time. Find a way to bring the door back, open it, then track down his sister on the other side.

He remembered the snow-filled valley, a party in progress, people laughing and singing, and the music that accompanied them. Eliot had heard the song before (despite RULE 34), through the thin walls of the Oakwood Apartments complex every New Year.

He started humming it, but stopped, only able to remember a bit. He turned to Robert. "Do you know that song?"

"Who doesn't?" Robert looked perplexed.

"Would you sing it for me?"

"You don't want me singing *anything*."

"I need to hear it to open the door."

Robert winced, looked around, then sighed, cleared his throat, and sang.

> *Should old acquaintance be forgot, and never brought to mind.*
> *Should old acquaintance be forgot, and auld lang syne. . . ."*[66]

The tune was simple enough. Eliot reproduced the melody on Lady Dawn, then built upon it, adding a phrase for the falling snow . . . and a flourish, representing the fireworks that shot over the alpine village.

The bricks in the wall cracked. The temperature in the room dropped to icy cold.

Eliot layered in a harmony that reminded him of the laughter he had heard in the valley. He sprinkled in a few notes for the moonlight glinting on the snow and the reflection of the aurora in the night sky.

The doorway thickened: no longer mere paint on brick, but real wood and iron bindings. The brass doorknob stuck into a mortared joint rattled and straightened with a clack.

Eliot played faster and took a step toward the door.

The knob slowly turned.

But the music drifted; a single note that went down the scale when he had wanted to go up.

It was happening again: control slipping from his grasp.

Angry, he tightened his grip, wrestling with Lady Dawn, trying to master the piece.

His cut finger throbbed with pain, and he felt the hot poison push up the vein in his wrist.

What if the music knew something he didn't? Maybe it was better to let it go and ride it to wherever it wanted to take him.

---

66. *Auld lang syne* means "old long since" or "anytime but now," but earlier folk translations for this phrase suggest a meaning closer to "once upon a time," which has been a standard opening phrase (or some say evocation?) used in fairy tales since the fourteenth century. *Gods of the First and Twenty-first Century, Volume 5: Core Myths* (Part 2), 8th ed. (Zypheron Press Ltd.).

He hesitantly loosened his grip. The music transformed into a jig, and his toes started tapping. But the mood darkened. All the happiness soured to melancholy. The fun became pain. It *was* the same music, just twisted into something terrible.

The clockwork mechanism of the knob's lock clicked . . . and the door swung open.

Eliot stopped playing and set his hand on the strings.

It was probably best to only let the music take him so far.

Robert stared at the open doorway. His breath fogged as he said, "Nice work."

Beyond the doorway it looked like the inside of the snow globe. A thick layer of white covered hills and forests, and it all shimmered. The village was still there in the distance, lit with candles and blinking strings of Christmas lights. People sang that New Year's Eve song, and when it ended, fireworks rocketed into the sky.

It was all the same. Exactly the same. Like déjà vu.

The snow near the doorway, however, had scuff marks where Fiona had tumbled. Footprints circled around and around, but those impressions had nearly been filled by the falling snow.

"She must have been trying to open this door," Robert said, "or maybe she couldn't find it at all. That could be a problem."

Robert rummaged through the debris, found a crowbar, and wedged it under the door.

How long had Fiona wandered out there? Eliot stuck his hand through the doorway. Snowflakes lit on his palm and didn't melt for several seconds. It was very cold. He withdrew, curling his stiffened fingers.

"Her tracks led towards that settlement," Robert said. "I'm sure she's okay."

Eliot wasn't so sure. There was no telling how far that was. The snow muted his sense of distance, making the village seem near and far at the same time.

"We better find you a jacket," Robert said.

Eliot's pocket buzzed. He jumped.

Robert's phone jangled, too.

They both pulled out their cell phones.

"Mr. Mimes said they were the same phone," Robert explained. "It's probably for me."

"How can they be the same?"

Robert ignored Eliot and answered his phone. "Yeah?" His face immediately darkened. "No, he's not." Robert started to hang up.

"Wait. It's for me?" Eliot opened the phone Louis had given him.

Robert looked extremely unhappy about this.

"Hello?"

"My boy." Louis's voice filtered through the tiny speaker. "Would you be kind enough to tell Mr. Farmington to stop listening to our conversation? Why, I believe the League has rules about such things."

Robert steadfastly held the phone to his ear and shook his head.

Eliot shot him a glare worthy of Grandmother.

Robert frowned, but slowly folded his phone shut and crossed his arms over his chest.

"Very good," Louis said. "Gossip can be a nasty thing. Sometimes you practically have to kill people to stop it."

"It *was* you before, wasn't it?" Eliot asked, half-irritated, half-intrigued. "I mean, you were Robert . . . disguised."

"Of course."

"You said you would never lie to me."

There was a pause, then Louis said, "I did not. Did I ever *say* I was Robert? Do you think your sister would've come with us if I had appeared as myself?"

He had a point: Fiona wouldn't have.

"But why bring us to the doorway? Why am I even talking to you? Fiona could be freezing to death—and it's your fault!"

Eliot slid his thumb over the END button, but for some reason he couldn't press it.

A sigh hissed through the speaker. "Your sister is perfectly safe. Her every need will be seen to. That valley may be the *one* place where she will be safe during some very unfortunate events that must happen tonight."

Unfortunate events? That had to mean the family. Either the Council had plans for him and Fiona . . . or it was the Infernal side of the family. Eliot's anger momentarily subsided, and his curiosity took over.

"You *are* my father, aren't you?" There was a long pause this time, and Eliot thought the connection had been lost. "Sir? Are you?"

"You and I have something we must do tonight," Louis said, not answering his question. "Your sister cannot be a part of it. I will not explain any more over the phone. You must come to me. Come, and then I will answer all your questions."

"I don't think so. I'm getting my sister." Eliot hesitated, finding it hard to say the words. "I don't trust you, Louis. You've never lied to me, but somehow I don't think you've been entirely honest with me, either."

"Too much truth is unhealthy for growing boys. But I will tell you this: if you are not with me tonight, Eliot, I will certainly die."

"Die? How? Why?"

"Too many details to discuss over this contraption," Louis said casually. "Besides, it makes my ear hot. Does it have that effect on you?"

"Just tell me."

"No. Come to me, my boy. Behind Ringo's. The alley. Dusk."

"But—"

"I leave it to you to decide if my life is worth saving."

The line clicked to silence.

"Louis? Louis?!"

Eliot glared at the phone. Why was it that every adult he spoke with left him feeling utterly frustrated? Especially his relatives. He squeezed the phone until his arm shook.

"Whatever he told you," Robert whispered, "you shouldn't listen. He's dangerous."

"I know."

Eliot was so angry that for the first time in his life he couldn't think. He wanted to scream. It was as if Louis had deliberately waited until the *worst* possible moment to spring this stuff on him.

On the other hand, Louis had given him something no other adult ever had: a choice. Everyone was always telling him what to do. The Council, Grandmother—well, maybe not Cee, but she didn't count.

This was now Eliot's choice. Help his sister or help someone who might be his father.

Maybe it was like Robert said—Fiona had just walked to the village. She was probably sipping apple cider by some fire right now.

And Louis? Would he really die if Eliot didn't come to him?

"I hope you're not thinking of listening to him."

Robert had better ears than Eliot realized if he had overheard.

"There's no way I'm giving you a ride to that creep," Robert continued. "You want to help *him* instead of your sister? You can walk back to Del Sombra."

"Don't tell me what to do." Eliot's irritation flared, now directed at Robert. "I don't need you. There's a bus stop a quarter mile back. I can grab the Red Line and be in Del Sombra by dark."

Robert opened his mouth, closed it, and sighed. "You're right. It's a family thing, man. Do what you have to. But I'm going after Fiona. Come help me, and then I'll drive you wherever you want."

That sounded reasonable, only Eliot didn't know how long it would take to find Fiona. And what if they got lost on the other side of the doorway?

Robert turned and went back into the tavern.

"What are you doing now?" Eliot asked, following.

Robert paused at the bar and grabbed a handful of pretzels out of a bowl. He examined them, seeming dissatisfied.

"You're hungry at a time like this?"

"Not exactly." Robert moved behind the bar and rummaged about, pulling out a large bag of pretzels. "Hansel and Gretel."

"Huh?"

"A trail of bread crumbs. I got the feeling Fiona had a hard time finding the door—even though she was probably standing right in front of it."

Eliot knew "Hansel and Gretel" had to be some mythological or popular-culture reference that he'd never understand in a million years, but he got the "trail of bread crumbs" from context.

Robert started for the back room. "So what's it going to be? You coming with me or not?"

Eliot truly didn't know. He had to help Fiona; that was the right thing to do. But Louis said the Valley would be safe. And Eliot believed that . . . to a point. He didn't think she'd die in there, at least.

He also believed Louis when he said that he'd die if Eliot didn't come to him. It seemed outrageous, yet something about the way he said it, and the way he left it up to Eliot to decide his fate, made it seem plausible.

Eliot felt torn equally in opposite directions.

His gaze fell upon the bar . . . and the dice there. He couldn't take his eyes off their gleaming red surfaces.

He moved closer and touched them. They were plastic, nothing special. They immediately warmed, however. He scooped them up and rattled them. It felt good.

What if he let *them* decide? What harm could there be if he was truly split in his thinking?

He shook them in his closed fist, feeling the excitement build in the air around him.

It was so simple. If the dice rolled an even number, he'd go after Fiona first.

If they came up odd, then he'd help Louis.

"What are you doing?" Robert asked, the slightest edge of apprehension in his voice. "There's no time for games."

"It's not a game." Eliot's voice sounded strange to him, older and deeper and darker. "It's *never* been a game."

He tossed the dice.

They bounced and scattered along the bar, spinning to the edge, then halted . . . and forever changed Eliot's world.

A six and a one.

Seven. Odd. He'd go to his father.

71

THE LAND OF NEVER

Fiona held her hands before the bonfire, flexing her fingers. The flames gave off heat, but not with the intensity she expected from such a pile of timbers. It was as if she stood in front of a sixty-watt lightbulb.

It had taken her a while to find a fire without toga-wearing dancers whirling around it. Metal drums with burning trash were scattered here and there as well, but those had bums gathered around them, a bottle of wine in every hand.

Wasn't *anyone else* here as cold as she was?

She pulled the collar of Robert's leather jacket higher and examined the crowds.

Lots of people danced; maybe that kept them warm. A group of ice-skaters were whirling to a disco tempo. Farther from where she stood, a proper hardwood floor sat under a massive tent where men in tuxedos waltzed with women. Fiona had been tempted to go there, but she couldn't muster the courage to enter looking the way she did.

She had faced a giant crocodile, infiltrated a high-security military base, but when it came to her appearance . . . she was still such a coward.

Maybe it was all the food here that kept these people from freezing. There were tables heaped with bacon-wrapped appetizers smoldering over cans of Sterno; mountains of cheese cubes clustered about ice swans; enough shrimp cocktail to fill a small ocean; and trays with chocolate-covered strawberries. Fiona suppressed her gag reflex.

A group of boys ran past her, their faces hidden by masks. They wore doublets, fur-lined capes, sabers, and carried steins of beer. They laughed and screamed and pelted one another with snowballs.

One boy in a lion mask almost tripped as his gaze caught hers. He smiled. Fiona's face reddened.

The boy saw someone else, though. He forgot Fiona, chucked a snowball, and ran off.

Just as well. Maybe he might have helped her, but she hadn't liked the hungry glint in his eyes.

Fiona then spotted several couples walking arm in arm, some pausing in the shadows to find other ways to keep the cold at bay.

She looked away, embarrassed.

So many of them wore strange clothes. Some girls had their hair up, artfully curled, and wore dresses that looked like something Cee might've worn to an antebellum cotillion. Others had on sequined gowns and shimmered as if they'd been dipped in quicksilver. Lots of boys and girls wore sweatshirts adorned with two or three Greek letters (although they spelled nothing that made sense to Fiona).

There must be hundreds in this village . . . but she was completely alone. She crossed her arms over her chest, trying to insulate herself from the cold. Good thing she had Robert's leather jacket. It had probably saved her life.

Fiona recalled how she got here, though. Her rage rekindled.

Robert. If she ever got her hands on him again . . . well, she wasn't sure what she was going to do to him, but he wasn't going to enjoy it.

He'd shoved her through that doorway. When she'd pulled herself out of the snow and turned back to the tavern—there wasn't any tavern. Nor was there any Robert, nor Eliot . . . nor most important, any doorway back. She'd searched, but there hadn't been so much as a peanut shell in the snow.

There hadn't been a choice. It was bitterly cold, and the only place to go was this village. The tents, kegs of beer, Christmas lights draped over steep-roofed buildings—it all looked new, warm, and inviting.

Fiona stopped thinking as everyone started singing that dopey song about "old friends not forgotten" for what had to be the bazillionth time since she had gotten here.

And how long had *that* been exactly? It only felt like a few minutes, but she knew that was wrong.

Kazoos and horns sounded. Confetti, streamers, and fireworks filled the air. All the strange partygoers gave a great cheer and hugged and kissed the person next to them.

Fiona was glad she was by herself. These people were crazy.

There was a crunch in the snow. She whirled and stood face-to-face with the boy in the lion mask.

"My lady," he said, speaking with a Scottish accent. He bowed extravagantly. "Please allow me to accompany ye. No one should be alone on this night o' all nights."

The boy then did the strangest thing: he moved toward her, arms open as if to embrace.

"Hey!" Fiona raised her hand and stopped him cold.

He looked confused, but his smile never faltered. The boy brushed back his mane of blond hair. "Ah, quite right. The moment has passed, has it not? I suppose ye shall have to wait a wee bit longer."

"Who are you?" Fiona touched the rubber band on her wrist. What was she going to do if he tried to kiss her again? Cut him in half?

"I be Lord Jeremy Covington of the Galloway Covingtons." He took her hand in a silky smooth gesture and kissed it. The touch of his lips sent a shiver up her arm.

Her entire life she would have killed to get attention like this. Now that she had some, though, she had no idea what to do with it. How did normal girls manage?

She yanked her hand back.

"Nice to meet you. I'm Fiona Post. What is this place?"

"The Land of Never. The Valley of the New Year."

"Yeah, I know that. But *where* is it?"

He considered a moment, then nodded, seeming to understand. "If I not be mistaken, before we declared independence, it used to be part of purgatory."[67,68]

---

67. Sicilian navigator Ignacio Balermo (1211–58 CE), returned from an expedition to Africa claiming to have sailed past the edge of the world and explored the beginnings of heaven and hell and all the lands of purgatory between. Questioned by the Church, Ignacio revealed that purgatory was a crossroads to many lands. He was eager to return and explore. The Church refuted this account and asserted purgatory led only to heaven. Ignacio recanted his tales and yet was still subsequently burned at the stake. His maps (reported confiscated and burned as well) later appeared in the possession of the thirteenth-century Benedictine monk Sildas Pious. *Gods of the First and Twenty-first Century, Volume 2: Divine Inspirations*, 8th ed. (Zypheron Press Ltd.).

68. "Here be dragons, Minotaur and giants, saints and sinners, fear for the Lost, and revelations for the brave." Note prefacing the cartography section of Father Sildas Pious, *Mythica Improbiba* (Beezle edition), c. thirteenth century.

"Purgatory?" Fiona murmured. She'd never heard of the place—and that was saying a lot given her encyclopedic knowledge of geography, both modern and historical. "Is that in Eastern Europe?"

Lord Jeremy laughed. "No, no, purgatory—the place betwixt hell and heaven?"

Fiona had heard of *those* places, of course, even with Grandmother's rules. She doubted, however, that this place was really between the two. Then again . . . it made as much sense as any of the other strange things she had seen since her birthday.

"Ye be a newcomer then?" Jeremy's smile faded and he looked concerned.

"You can say that. How does one get out of purgatory?"

"Well, 'tis not truly purgatory as I told ye. The folk here did no like the way it was set up—all those rules and cleansing fires and ritual chanting. What bloody nonsense!"

"Someone decided to throw a party instead?" Fiona said, looking around.

"A New Year's Eve party specifically. The only wee bit o' trouble be, we never quite get to midnight. Manage to get a good running start now and then, but then we always seem to bounce off."·

Jeremy sighed. "And just like that last moment, nothing ever quite satisfies here. The drink. The food." The glint returned to his eyes. "Even the lassies. Perhaps ye'd like a taste? A glass of champagne to celebrate?"

Fiona took a step back, suddenly feeling not at all comfortable so close to young Lord Jeremy Covington. "I've had little experience with that. I'll pass. Trying to find satisfaction can be addictive."

"It can be at that." He took another step closer. "Though it do no take away the pleasure from trying."

At the edge of the village, a woman started to sing again. Bottle rockets shot into the air.

"Here we go." Jeremy dug into the folds of his doublet and pulled out a mangled twig of mistletoe. "Ye do know it be traditional to kiss on the New Year?"

"I don't think so."

Jeremy closed the distance to her faster than she thought he could move and slipped his arm around her body . . . leaning in.

Fiona didn't know what to say or do.

Her body had a pretty good idea, though: she brought up her knee as hard as she could—connecting with Lord Jeremy Covington of the Galloway Covingtons' groin.

His smile vanished, and with a great exhalation he fell to his knees.

"I like ye spirit, lass," he grunted.

Fiona's fingers twined about her rubber band. She didn't really want to do this . . . but she wasn't sure how far Jeremy intended to take that one little traditional New Year's Eve kiss. Under the circumstances, she wasn't even sure he was alive or dead, human . . . or something else entirely.

Jeremy stood. The hunger in his eyes had sharpened.

At that precise moment, however, a snowball packed to ice hardness shattered on his lion mask—with such force it snapped Jeremy's neck back and lifted him off his feet, head over heels into the snow.

Fiona turned to see who had saved her.

Robert Farmington stood ten paces away. Brass knuckles on his fingers glinted. He had another snowball ready, squeezing it tight.

"Robert! What are you doing? That's enough." Her first impulse was to check on Jeremy, at least make sure he was breathing, but then she remembered that Robert was responsible for her being here. She wheeled on him, one hand plucking the rubber band on her wrist. She wasn't sure she trusted Robert any more than Jeremy.

Robert must've seen she was in no mood for games, because he immediately dropped the snowball.

That's when Fiona noticed two things that didn't make sense. Robert wore *his* leather jacket, the same leather jacket—right down to the eagle patch and scuff marks along the right arm—that *she* had on. Robert also for some reason held a large bag of pretzels.

"I'm so glad I found you." Robert moved toward her. "I don't know how long I've been looking. This place is so—"

"Stay right there. First you better explain why you pushed me through that door."

Robert halted. "That's easy . . . it wasn't me."

He told her how Louis Piper had tricked her and Eliot, separated her from her brother, then lured Eliot back to Del Sombra.

Fiona felt dread pool in her stomach as Robert explained. It made sense. It accounted for why Robert had acted so strange in the tavern. And the two jackets . . . one was from the duplicated Robert. It also made sense because, given half a chance, her stupid brother would run off trying to rescue their supposed father and get himself into even *more* trouble.

Jeremy groaned and rolled onto his knees, shaking his head. He laughed and slowly got to his feet. "Ye have a strong arm," he told Robert. "No real harm done, though." A trickle of blood ran from the snout of his lion mask.

"Just back off, mister," Robert ordered. The hand adorned with brass knuckles curled into a fist.

Jeremy looked at Robert and then to Fiona. "Oh, I see." He bowed to Fiona. "I apologize, my lady. I had no idea ye came to the party escorted."

"We're not here to party," Robert growled at him. "Come on, Fiona, we're leaving." He shook his bag of pretzels. "I left us a trail."

"A trail o' bread crumbs?" Jeremy asked with great interest. "To the doorway?"

"You know about that?" Fiona asked.

"I know the myth," Jeremy replied. "Like the unicorn, fleeting, there one instant, gone the next. Easier to chase snowflakes." A faint trace of his smile returned. "But ye have a trail o' bread crumbs . . . that might be a different story. Fairy-tale magic be strong here."

"Fiona," Robert whispered, and held out his hand. "We should get going. I have a bad feeling about this place."

Fiona reached for him but hesitated. This was the real Robert, wasn't it? She thought so. He looked like Robert. But more than that, this felt like the real Robert: a hero.

She took his hand. It was warm and strong.

"I'm glad you came for me," she whispered.

"I would've found you no matter where you were. No matter what it took." Robert nodded at the pretzels scattered behind him. "The snow will cover them up soon. We need to hurry."

Jeremy, without saying another word, ran back to the party.

Fiona was a little disappointed, but relieved, too. Jeremy had seemed so nice, then not, then nice again. Why were boys so confusing?

She and Robert followed the trail. The pretzels were easy to spot on the sparkling snow, but after a minute, as Robert had predicted, the falling snow clung to the pretzels and made them hard to spot.

After a few minutes the trail was lost.

"Don't worry," Robert said. "We don't need the pretzels anymore. It should be just ahead."

"Wait. Did you actually *see* the doorway on this side when you stepped through?"

Robert shook his head. "I made sure to mark it, though. On the threshold, I scattered a few handfuls of pretzels."

"Which we won't be able to find because they'll be covered, too."

He frowned. "What do you want to do then? Start brushing the snow and look for every pretzel?"

Fiona heard footfalls. Jeremy ran toward them . . . along with his pack of friends. They all wore masks: rhinoceros, ostrich, hyena, and gorilla.

Robert drew his gun.

"No need for that," Jeremy said, panting. "We've come to help. The trail be lost, no? We can find it."

"Sure," Robert said without lowering his weapon.

Jeremy pointed to six of his friends, then at the snow ahead. They fanned out, searching. He pointed at the last two, then the back at the village. They ran off.

"Might as well let them help," Fiona suggested.

"I'm not so sure that's a great idea," Robert whispered.

"Here!" shouted the boy in the rhinoceros mask. "Found it."

"Good work," Jeremy said to his friend. "The rest o' ye move ahead. Maybe we get a wee bit more luck."

Fiona watched as the pack of boys spread out looking for the trail. If the seven of them turned out to be not so friendly, she wasn't sure Robert and she could defend themselves . . . at least, not without using lethal force.

She shivered. Then again, away from the fires of the village she was freezing. There wasn't much choice.

"Where'd those others go to?" Robert asked, finally lowering his gun.

"To get more help, of course," Jeremy explained. "If ye are to have a snowball's chance in . . . well, never mind. Ye know what I mean."

Fiona and Robert looked for the trail as well, and soon more people from the village joined the effort. There were more boys in masks, men in tuxedos, a group of Indians in buckskins, and a gaggle of those cotillion girls with their hoop skirts trailing behind them—dozens of them searched through the snow now for bread crumbs.

Jeremy ran ahead, seeming to intuit the path, and discovered the vast circular scattering of pretzels that marked the entrance of the doorway.

There was no doorway, though.

Jeremy, Robert, and Fiona pantomimed through the air, feeling for anything.

"Dead end, I'm afraid," Jeremy whispered disappointedly. "Rotten luck."

A crowd gathered about them, perhaps fifty people from the village. An uneasy murmur rippled through them.

So many had joined in the search . . . and it wasn't just to help Fiona and Robert. As fun as a continuous New Year's Eve party might seem, after half an eternity of dancing, drinking, and who knows what else, they all had to be bored out of their minds. They wanted out as badly as Fiona did.

"Maybe we better get back to those fires," Robert whispered to her. "While we're still unfrozen, and before the natives get ugly."

"I'm not giving up. There has to be something here." Fiona snapped her rubber band and stretched it before her, concentrating. The air crackled and popped as she moved her cutting edge.

The crowd backed off several paces. The boy in the rhinoceros mask whispered, "Witch!"

The rest of the world, however, fell away as Fiona focused on her line of force. She saw nothing, but felt textures, ripples, and bumps . . . as if the very atmosphere were permeated with threads.

Maybe it was. If her life had a weave to it, with one side that extended into the future and one to the past, why couldn't the rest of the world?

She slipped into that relaxed state of mind that Dallas had spoken of and the pattern of this place came into focus: a simple back-and-forth, over-and-under weave. It was featureless . . . save for a single seam.

Fiona moved closer, and as she did so, she saw that this seam was actually a fold in the otherwise smooth surface. A pocket of fabric had been tucked perpendicularly away from normal view.

She twisted her mind around it and saw a tapestry of an ironbound door. The door was open, and on the other side were shadows, moonlight, kegs, and cardboard boxes filled with liquor bottles.

But the edges of this tapestry were frayed and unraveling at an unnerving pace.

Whatever she was going to do, she'd have to do it quickly while there was still something here to work with.

She cut the threads tacking the doorway in place, dragged it out of its sideways orientation, and laid it flat upon the fabric of this world. This, however, only accelerated the unraveling. Maybe she'd better put it back.

A hand touched her shoulder.

She blinked and found herself back in the cold.

Robert was next to her, staring at what had once been empty space.

The doorway stood before her, open, but fast fading.

"This way!" shouted the rhinoceros boy. "It's open! Quick! Everyone through."

The crowd surged forward, pushing past Fiona and Robert, forcing them apart and knocking her to the ground.

Robert tried to help her, but the cotillion girls ran her over.

What sounded like a cannon exploded near Fiona.

All fell silent . . . until the crisp air was punctuated by the sound of steel being drawn from a scabbard.

The crowd parted and backed away.

"Enough o' that, ye rabble." In one hand Jeremy held a smoldering flint-lock pistol, and in the other his saber. "Let the lady go first."

He tucked his flintlock into his belt and offered a hand to Fiona.

She took it and stood. "Thank you."

Jeremy bowed to her. Robert glared at him.

Fiona glanced at the crowd. They looked eager and hopeful, but re-spectful now as well. Perhaps a hundred people from the village were now there, with more running across the snows to join them.

No time to ponder what they'd all do on the other side.

She turned to the fading doorway, held her breath, and stepped through.

It was dark. She knew she'd made it, though, because the cold van-ished. She inhaled the scent of old cardboard and balmy California air.

A police officer entered the storage room. Cotillion girls brushed past him. The officer looked about, utterly confused.

Robert stepped through the doorway next. He took Fiona by the elbow, sidestepping toward the refrigerated room.

"Hey!" the policeman said, spotting them. "Wait right there."

But it was too late. No one was waiting for anything anymore.

The crowds from the Valley of the New Year streamed through the painted brick wall—Lord Jeremy Covington and his boys, the Indians, men in tuxe-dos and women in sequined gowns, foxhunters on horseback, winos, and a troupe of clowns. They spilled over one another and shoved the officer out of the way, some grabbing kegs and bottles as they did so, all of them making for the open front and back doors of the tavern.

"There are more coming," Robert whispered to Fiona. "Lots more. We need to leave."

He led Fiona through the refrigerated compartment and the outer door into the parking lot.

Jeremy and his masked friends tussled with police officers on the tavern's porch. Several men in tuxedos clambered into police cars, mounted the Harleys, and drove off.

Fiona took a step toward Jeremy.

"He'll be okay," Robert assured her. "Remember, we've got our own troubles. Eliot. And Louis."

Fiona halted. Robert was correct.

They got into the Maybach, Robert fired up the engine, and they rocketed out of the parking lot, scraping past two police cruisers blocking the exit.

"Let me borrow your phone," Fiona said.

Robert dug out his cell phone and Fiona dialed home. It rang twice and was then picked up.

"Hello, Cee? . . . Is Grandmother there? . . . No? Then take a message. . . . Yes, I'll wait—just hurry."

Robert floored the gas. The acceleration squished Fiona into her seat. "We'll be in Del Sombra in no time."

Fiona glanced at the setting sun. "Good . . . because that's how long I think Eliot has."

72

A TRICK UP HIS SLEEVE

Eliot walked among the lengthening shadows. Cars drove up and down Midway Avenue in Del Sombra. Many had double-parked in front of the Pink Rabbit.

He heard folksingers playing inside, but as much as Eliot wanted, he had no time to stop and listen. It was late, and he had to find Louis before sunset.

Eliot crossed the street to Ringo's—still closed for renovations—and headed to the alley. He paused, however, to get Lady Dawn from his pack.

He flexed his hand. Would the infection take root inside him again? Louis had noted it earlier and said it was an "occupational hazard."

Eliot took a deep breath. He did not want do this alone. He believed that Louis's life *was* in real danger, but the thought of dealing with the other side of his family made him reconsider. Everyone—Souhk, the Council, *Mythica Improbiba,* even Robert—had warned him about them. Were they actually fallen angels, evil incarnate? Or was that just propaganda?

Eliot imagined he was a hero, swooping in at the last moment to save his long-lost father, who was being held in a medieval castle. There would be a duel with rapiers . . . maybe Julie would be there to save as well.

He made himself stop. Retreating into his daydreams only distracted him from what was really happening. It was little-kid stuff, anyway. Time he outgrew it.

Eliot stepped into the alley.

The shadows here were thick as black velvet. Every scrap of trash had been cleaned up. Lit candles sat alongside the walls, illuminating brick and cinder block with dancing flickers.

Louis had his back to Eliot, scrutinizing his work: a design of chalk arcs and dots and zigzags that covered the wall to the two-story roof, across the asphalt of the alley, and over the opposite wall.

It looked like a giant cocoon spun from geometry and ancient symbols. The lines pulled at the light and made everything darker about them. Looking at the design gave Eliot chill bumps—part from revulsion, part from recognition, and part from a static charge building in the air.

He turned his attention to Louis. He'd always felt a connection with Louis, even when he had thought he was only a bum.

Eliot wanted so badly to run over there and hug him, then tell him that he had hoped and had waited all his life for his father to miraculously reappear.

But he held back. He had to.

Louis was family. And all the family Eliot had met thus far hadn't exactly been nice to him or Fiona. In fact, they had almost gotten them killed three times already.

Louis cocked his head and drew in a deep breath. "So, you came." He turned to Eliot. His smile wavered with emotion.

"Something wrong?" That had to be the stupidest thing Eliot had said all week. Of course something was wrong. Louis had said his life was at stake.

"Everything is all right, now that you are here." Louis fiddled with the chalk in his hands. "As long as you trust me. Please tonight of all nights, trust me. It will be confusing. And dangerous."

Eliot's stomach fluttered. He so wanted to trust him . . . but a deep primal instinct screamed at him to turn and run. If Louis's life was truly in danger, wouldn't Eliot be in greater jeopardy?

He straightened. He'd come this far. He wasn't chickening out now. "Tell me what I have to do."

"Such bravery," Louis whispered, "clearly from your mother's side."

Eliot gestured to the tangle of lines. "You need help with this thing?"

"It's only a doodle." Louis tossed his chalk aside. "No, it is close enough for tonight's work."

"Close enough for what?"

"It is an electrical circuit." Louis pointed to symbols. "Transformer coils, capacitors, a fuse there—all of which enable a simple transfer of power."

Eliot squinted, trying to understand the pattern, but he couldn't concentrate. He hadn't come here to decipher ancient pictograms. He had come to save Louis's life . . . and to ask him one question.

"Are you my father?"

Louis looked at him a long time, almost as if he were asking a similar question: *Are you truly my son?*

"I *am* your father," Louis finally said. "Louis Piper, Lucifer, the Morning Star, and the Prince of Darkness. We share the same blood." He held out his arms, beckoning for him. "Can you not feel it?"

Eliot could indeed feel it. He knew Louis spoke the truth. A part of his life missing for the last fifteen years clicked into place, and he took a step toward his father.

This wasn't the devil portrayed in the medieval *Mythica Improbiba* wood-cut. He was Louis, clean and sober and waiting for him with open arms. He *was* his father.

But again, Eliot hesitated, because while he knew Louis told him the truth, he also sensed it wasn't *all* the truth. And that was a kind of lie, wasn't it? So many things still had to be explained.

"You left us when we were babies."

"Left? Never, my boy." Louis dropped his arms. "My leaving was entirely your mother's doing."

"Tell me. Everything. Please."

Louis checked his watch and sighed. "Is this what you want to talk about? Her? I, who know half the secrets of the universe, and you want to hear of one romance and my lapse in sanity?" He shook his head. "How disappointingly normal of you."

Eliot opened his mouth to take it back. He so wanted Louis's approval. But, no—he wouldn't be dissuaded from the truth.

"Tell me," Eliot said, his voice now full of iron. "No one ever talks about my mother. It's as if she's still alive . . . and everyone is scared of her."

"*Still* alive?" Confusion flickered over Louis's face. "I begin to see just how large this conspiracy against you and Fiona has truly been." His face brightened. "Very well, what can I say? We met, fell in love, did all the things people in love do, which precipitated you and your sister."

"Only that shouldn't have happened, right? People from the two families, the League and the Infernals, aren't supposed to like each other . . . let alone, you know."

Louis quirked his eyebrows. "So you've been told of the Pactum Pax Immortalis, have you? How open-minded of the League." He snorted. "Well, in the beginning we did not know each other's true identity. In glorious ignorance, we consensually joined . . . two months in Paris, one month in Rome, Istanbul, Cairo, Nepal, and finally San Francisco . . . the best time in my life. But inevitably the proper biology took root. That is when your mother grew suspicious I was not as I appeared."

"What were you supposed to be?" Eliot asked, confused.

"Normal. Human. And with such types, your mother's blue-blooded kind has . . . let us call them 'technical difficulties' with reproduction."

Eliot wanted to ask about all those other cousins on his mother's side of the family that Aunt Lucia had mentioned. If it was so hard to have children, where had they come from?

Louis continued, "I was similarly befuddled by passion. Had *I* known who *she* was . . ." He chuckled. "I must have truly loved her to be so blind. How else can one explain such cosmically foolish behavior? Alas, all sewage under the bridge, as they say."

Eliot didn't understand how Louis could say he had loved her one moment, then regret it so much the next. "She didn't love you back?"

"Of course, what woman could not love me?" Louis made a tiny bow to the shadows. "But upon deducing my true Infernal nature, she thought I would take you and your sister away. My people have a terrible, and highly unjustified, reputation. But whoever believes the man in such things? And whoever blames the woman for her rash, hormonally induced actions?"

"She severed you from your power."

"Such is the sharpness of a woman's anger, my boy. Be well forewarned. Better that she had killed me, so I would not have to drown in a sea of human self-pity." Louis curled his hands and folded them across his chest as if he felt this anguish anew.

Eliot wanted to put an arm on his shoulder and comfort him the same way he had when Eliot had told him about Julie.

"But I had to come back to you and Fiona," Louis said. "Where else was I to go? You two were the last bits of what I adored. If I could no longer be with the woman I was meant for . . . at least I could look upon you and remember the love we once shared."

There was more—Eliot could sense it—a mountain of larger truth submerged under an ocean of deception. Louis had told him that there would always be truth between them, but just enough truth for him to hide behind.

"And?" Eliot demanded.

"And what?"

"And what's the catch? There's usually a catch with you people, isn't there? Do you have tests and trials that Fiona and I have to pass? Or is it some different trick with this side of the family?"

A smile appeared on Louis's face. It was broad and genuine. "Of course there's a trick. There always is."

Louis looked up to the sky. There was no light. The sun had set while they had spoken and not a single star yet twinkled.

Eliot felt something near Louis—a gravitational force that tugged upon his center. He found it hard to breathe.

He squinted and saw a silhouette behind Louis in the shadows. Not his shadow. Another's. This other person must have been there the entire time, heard everything . . . that, or he had just materialized from the blackness.

The candle flames leaned toward the shadowy figure as it stepped forward.

He was a man, but much larger than anyone else Eliot had ever seen. As Louis towered over Eliot, this person towered over Louis and made him look like a child. The man held himself with a majestic ease as if he commanded everything his gaze fell upon.

He wore a cloak of feathers: ostrich and owl and eagle and peacock plumes that for an instant looked like wings on his back. He was bare-chested and muscular. About his neck was a leather thong, and dangling from it over his breastbone was a faceted sapphire the size of a grapefruit.

Eliot's vision swam in the stone's watery depths for a moment . . . lost.

Then Eliot gazed into the man's face. His features were sharp like a bird's, but handsome and perfect. Eliot sensed power about this being. It repulsed him and at the same time he wanted to step closer and bask in it as well.

Something deep within him knew what this was; it was programmed into Eliot's DNA—he knew that the creature towering before him was part of his family.

Louis prostrated himself before the cloaked figure. "All hail and tremble before Beelzebub, Lord of All That Flies, Prince of False Gods."

Beelzebub stepped past Louis without a glance.

"Our young Mr. Eliot Post." Beelzebub's voice was smooth and echoed inside Eliot's head. "You have no idea how much I've been looking forward to meeting you."

Eliot miraculously found his voice. "So you're . . . what? My uncle?"

Beelzebub laughed, a great sound that made the bones in Eliot's body tremble. "Oh, no, that would make Louis *my brother*. And if that were true, I should have to slit my throat. No, *cousin* is the closest term that applies. But you will have all the time in the world to learn about our family tree."

Eliot definitely didn't like the sound of "all the time in the world."

He remembered his manners, though, and said, "It's very nice to meet you, sir."

The faintest flicker of annoyance creased Beelzebub's thin lips. "Lie not to me, young man."

"I . . . I'm sorry, sir."

"No harm done," Beelzebub cooed. "Lessons in decorum will follow soon enough. First, however"—he drew a jagged blade from the scabbard on his belt—"one small technicality."

"Technicality?" Eliot's voice faded.

Beelzebub's blade was black-green obsidian and left a trail of shadows in the air.

Faced with this knife, Eliot's mind drained of all thoughts. Instinct took over: he backed away, toward the mouth of the alley.

Bricks and cinder block broke free of their mortar. They spun and crashed and reassembled into a wall blocking the alley's only exit.

Eliot glared at Beelzebub, adrenaline uselessly pumping through his body. There was nowhere to go now. Nothing he could do.

Beelzebub lowered an outstretched hand. "We must sever your mortal flesh from your spirit. If worthy, you shall join me in my domain. If not, well . . . this might sting a little."

He raised his obsidian blade and started toward Eliot.

Eliot's pulse thundered in his ears. He saw his reflection on the knife's chiseled surface. He saw his own death move closer.

Louis cleared his throat. "My lord, I beg your pardon."

Beelzebub halted, scowled, and tilted his head at Louis, not quite deigning to look upon him. "You dare speak, worm?"

Louis slowly got to his feet. "Regretfully."

Beelzebub wheeled on Louis, his cloak of feathers bristling. "I shall enjoy splitting you in half, my now mortal cousin."

Louis looked completely unafraid and held up one index finger. "I wouldn't do that if I were you. You have forgotten something."

Beelzebub's hand trembled, barely holding his blade back from cleaving Louis in twain.

Eliot could have cheered. Of course, Louis had some trick up his sleeve. A trap he was about to spring on this Beelzebub. His father was going to save him.

"Our deal," Louis said, "was that I separate the boy from his sister and then deliver him to you. Have I not accomplished this?"

Beelzebub lowered his knife.

"Before you take delivery of said goods," Louis continued, "you have a contractual obligation to render payment."

Beelzebub chuckled. "Of course, Louis. How foolish of me." He touched his blade to Louis's shoulder and whispered, *"Votum de Vir fio a vermis epulum."*[69]

Louis's hair glistened ebony and sterling silver. He straightened and seemed twenty years younger.

"All the power a mortal could possibly ever use. Enjoy it while you can," Beelzebub muttered, "and never cross our path again."

"It shall be as you say." Louis grinned from ear to ear. "Please, Lord, proceed."

Eliot couldn't believe it. Louis had had a trick, but it had been played upon *him*. Louis had fooled him into coming, alone . . . and then sold him off . . . for power?

Eliot was not afraid. His blood boiled and his fingers twitched with anticipation. He had never been this mad before.

Beelzebub turned to him and raised his black blade.

Eliot stood tall and set Lady Dawn upon his shoulder.

69. Translation from Latin: "Prayer of Man becomes a worm's feast."—Editor.

73

DEFIANT

ome backbone, after all?" Beelzebub whispered. The tip of his blade dipped slightly. "How delightful. And we had thought your sister was the fighter."

"She is. But so am I."

That was no lie. Eliot had been scared before. He was scared now. But he had survived three heroic trials. He'd bested one side of his family on their own terms . . . now it was time to show the other side what he was made of.

"Then let us see what you can do," Beelzebub replied, as if reading his thoughts.

Eliot quickly drew his bow over Lady Dawn's strings, playing the middle part of the *Symphony of Existence*. Mist snaked along the alley, and curtains of pea-soup fog closed between him and Beelzebub.

The giant man slashed at the vapors curling about him, but to no effect. He was quickly surrounded and obscured.

Eliot played and crept along the right side of the alley. With luck, he'd get to the back door of Ringo's, slip inside, and make a run for it. Being brave and fighting when cornered was one thing. Being stupid and fighting alone when he could run away was an entirely another matter.

Serpents slithered past Eliot in the fog, oceans of tentacles groped, disembodied eyes blinked, and ghostly hands plucked at his shirt.

Within the mist, though, Beelzebub laughed.

A wave rolled through the vapor, and the imagined creatures swirled about confused—then were blasted away as wind filled the alley.

The air pushed Eliot backward and he slammed into the dead-end wall.

Another great rush of wind, and for an instant he saw a headless horseman and air sharks and swarms of giant swimming bacteria, and then the nightmares all washed away, leaving only tiny vortices in their wake.

Beelzebub stood, his cape drawn with upraised arms. Eliot swore they were real wings . . . but he blinked. It was only a cape.

"Child's play," Beelzebub declared. "Exactly what I expected from a child." He motioned with his blade, "Come to me, Eliot. Come willingly. It will be better."

Eliot pushed himself upright, more irritated than scared now.

Louis crouched in the far corner of the alley, watching, but showing no indication of helping. In fact, he smiled as if this were some sort of game.

Eliot flexed his hand. The poison was still there, hot in his palm, pulsing with pain.

"Child's play?" he whispered. "Try this on for size, then."

He drew one slow note from Lady Dawn. The pain in his hand disappeared. This was from the last bit of the *Symphony of Existence*. The part about the death of all. The end of the universe.

Beelzebub's eyes widened.

The music was low and steady; it drew the light from the air and plunged the world into darkness. Eliot felt space pucker about him as it drew power from the very fabric of reality.

He imagined a black hole, pulling the last planets and stars and galaxies toward its ultradense core. The end of everything . . . crushed to neutron density.

Eliot tilted his violin, directing the center of the music upon Beelzebub.

Bricks in the wall shattered. The asphalt under Eliot's feet cracked. He felt the earth tilt upon its axis.

Beelzebub gritted his teeth and rushed toward Eliot.

But he was too late.

The walls of the alley collapsed—blocks and bricks and steel pipes whistled through the air, narrowly missing Eliot—all flying toward his adversary.

Stone and metal struck Beelzebub and exploded in the clouds of dust. He staggered back. He raised his arms to protect his head, but that didn't matter. Tons of material buried him, compacting under intense gravitational force.

Eliot stopped playing.

He squinted, but couldn't quite see through the dust.

Pebbles and chunks of asphalt continued to roll to the spot where Beelzebub had stood.

The air then cleared enough to see.

A ball of stone and pipes and blacktop rested in what had once been the alley behind Ringo's. The sphere was half as tall as Beelzebub. Surely he had been squashed like a bug inside. Even now the mass crackled and popped as it continued to shudder and compact upon itself.

As more dust settled, Eliot saw the walls of the alley still precariously stood. Most of the bricks and cinder blocks had torn free, but the remaining bits balanced in a skeletal lattice. It all swayed back, somehow upright.

Then Eliot saw why.

The chalk design that had been drawn upon the walls was intact. Even where bricks were missing, the lines wavered in the air like spider silk, holding it all tenuously together.

On the ground, the design remained as well, even though chunks of asphalt had been torn away.

Louis was alive, still in his corner. His hand touched the wall, seeming to give it power and stability. He still had something up his sleeve . . . something Eliot was sure he wouldn't like.

A hissing emanated from within Ringo's, and Eliot smelled the sulfurous additive in natural gas.

The ball of compressed stone continued to pop and shudder—but now as if something *inside* pushed against it . . . something inside that wanted out.

Eliot turned and scrambled through gaps in the dead-end wall. He turned back and called to Louis. "This way. Hurry!"

Louis had tried to sell him off. He didn't deserve to be saved, but he was the key to Eliot's unanswered questions. If Louis died, Eliot would never learn anything more.

Louis smiled and shook his head.

Eliot glared at him. There was nothing Eliot could do if Louis *wanted* to die.

Eliot wriggled through the break in the wall and emerged on Midway Avenue.

A crowd of people stood outside the Pink Rabbit, pointing and staring at the alley.

"Hey!" a man in the crowd called. It was the bartender who had let Eliot play his guitar the other day. "Kid, you okay?"

"The gas main!" Eliot yelled back. "It's broken. It's—"

An explosion flattened Eliot. He sprawled face-first onto the street. The wind was knocked out of him. Bits of brick whizzed over his head.

He shook off the disorientation and clutched at Lady Dawn, who had been tossed aside.

Gouts of flame spiraled skyward and lit the night, making long shadows flicker everywhere as if they danced in celebration. The alley had been blown wide-open—Ringo's had been mostly flattened, and the parts standing were engulfed in fire.

Beelzebub, Infernal Lord of All That Flies, towered among the ruins, swathed in the flame. His body was scaled, feet and hands taloned with razor claws. Wings stretched up two stories tall—a skeletal framework covered by a black membrane and a rainbow patchwork of feathers like some Jurassic-era archaeopteryx. His eyes burned with blue fire the same color as the sapphire that dangled about his throat.

The people from the Pink Rabbit screamed and scattered. Even the bartender who had been coming to help Eliot left him in the middle of the street.

A few days ago, Eliot would have run, too. But now he understood this was a family matter that only he could take care of. He stood and gently plucked up Lady Dawn.

"Enough games," thundered Beelzebub. He lifted one hand skyward. "Your flesh shall be mine, even if it be consumed by a thousand other mouths."

Eliot followed the direction of that upraised hand. All he could see, though, were the clouds as they reflected the fires below, and the first stars twinkling, which then vanished . . . blotted out.

He felt a shift in the air—not a breeze per se, but movement, nonetheless, all around him.

Eliot instinctively slapped his arm as a mosquito tried to bite.

Only there were no mosquitoes in Del Sombra so late in the summer. There was no water. Eliot suddenly had a very bad feeling about that one little mosquito.

He looked up again, squinting.

Clouds of gnats swarmed about the orange streetlamps. Wasps darted past his face, a flock of sparrows, too. A kite on fire pinwheeled by. Eliot ducked as a radio-controlled toy airplane almost took off his head.

The air changed, thick with insects, alive with the fluttering of feathered wings, floating trash, and smoldering cinders.

Eliot heard the whine of a billion hungry bloodsucking bugs . . . as they all spiraled toward him.

He knew what to do. He set his bow on Lady Dawn—quickly advancing along a scale to her highest note.

He held it and made it waver.

The high pitch made the swarm overhead buzz with agitation and lose cohesion, drifting apart as insects attacked one another.

Using what he had learned from the *Symphony of Existence,* Eliot bridged *past* the highest note possible. His fingertips touched only the blur of string, and he slipped the pitch up—a screech that pierced the night, higher still, and the sound faded into the ultrasonic and past his ability to hear—and he kept pushing higher—until he *felt* the highest impossible note shrieking through his bones.

Car windows shattered along with every storefront on Midway Avenue not already blasted out by the explosion.

Beetles and wasps and bees popped and their bits rained from the sky. Flocks of vultures and finch flew into buildings.

Eliot held the note until it felt as if his skull were cracking. The concrete sidewalk fractured. Paint peeled off walls and the nearby cars. His vision blurred.

He stopped.

Eliot's body tingled. Blood trickled from his nose and his eyes, which he wiped away.

Beelzebub held his ears and screamed. He recovered and glared at Eliot with his flame-filled eyes. "Very well, young cousin," he hissed. "You prove yourself a worthy opponent. We shall treat you as such."

He strode from the alley, swatting aside the cars in his path.

Eliot raised his bow to play once more.

Beelzebub's wings slashed forward—ripping Lady Dawn from Eliot's grasp and knocking him onto his back.

His violin bounced into the gutter. There was no way to retrieve it in time before Beelzebub could finish him.

Yet Eliot *still* refused to give up, still refused to give Beelzebub the satisfaction of seeing any fear.

Beelzebub laughed and raised his claws. "Come."

Eliot saw himself for an instant doing as Beelzebub commanded. It was a nightmare daydream of fire and Eliot leading hundreds of Infernals to war . . . and millions dying because of him.

ERIC NYLUND

He had killed before to save Fiona. But he'd never willingly help Beelzebub kill. Not in a million years.

"I don't think so."

Beelzebub glared down upon him. "So be it." He reared back one taloned
hand to strike.

Eliot looked him straight in the eye and braced . . . his final act of defiance.

He barely saw it: a shape moving out of the corner of his vision, midnight black and chrome silver gleaming, and so fast it rushed before him, a
blur—

—as Uncle Henry's Maybach Exelero-4X limousine ran over Beelzebub.

74

MAKING THE FINAL CUT

he Maybach hit something the size of a bull elephant. At the speed Robert had been driving, though, all Fiona saw was a dark shape and a pair of wings that were too big for anything that existed in this world.

The impact flung her forward, and a split second later the seat-belt harness caught.

The car tumbled end over end—airborne—there was a curious feeling of motion *and* weightlessness.

They crash-landed nose first.

Metal wrenched and squealed and sparked. Air bags exploded open around Fiona.

It was dark. Her ears rang. She couldn't move.

Sensation then returned and she found herself upside down.

Robert pulled her free and helped her stand. He looked into her eyes and spoke to her . . . but Fiona was unsure if it was English. Robert wiped the blood from his split lip and repeated, "Are you okay?"

"Yes," she answered slowly. "I think."

Next to her, Uncle Henry's race-car limousine was a wreck. The grille had crumpled up to the cabin. Engine and transmission parts were strewn all the way down the street. The rest of Midway Avenue was a war zone. Glass was everywhere. Buildings were on fire.

Fiona spied her brother lying in the gutter, struggling to get to his knees.

"Eliot!" She took an unsteady step toward him, but halted.

From the middle of the road, a pool of shadows rose. She blinked. No, it was a man in black. He managed get up on one knee, and that was enough for her to see that he was taller than the roof of the Pink Rabbit . . . and he had wings.

This giant turned and looked at her with eyes of blue fire. It spread its wings and bellowed at them, the sound of a hundred people screaming for mercy.

She felt the blood run out of her body. Fiona believed that she would never be afraid again—not after what she had been through the last few days.

But she was wrong. This thing scared her as nothing ever had.

"Stay here," Robert told her. "I have to finish him off before gets up." He made a fist and the brass knuckles on his hand thrummed with power.

He charged the half-standing beast. Robert's uppercut thudded into its gut. He hit with so much power that the blow lifted it off the ground. It fell over backward.

Robert closed and pulled back his brass knuckles for a crushing blow to its head.

The beast caught Robert's arm, however, and with a judo throw it whipped him into the air as if he weighed no more than a rag doll.

Robert wheeled past the Pink Rabbit and struck the steel pole of a streetlamp. He fell to the sidewalk in a heap and didn't move.

Fiona started for him. That blow could've snapped his spine.

The beast wheeled on her. "Even the Valley could not hold you? How delightful. This shall be a true test then."

She froze as she recognized a familiarity in those eyes of blue fire. This was no mere beast. It was family.

None of that mattered at the moment, though. She had only one thought left: to save Robert and her brother. To fight this thing.

All traces of fear evaporated as her blood heated to a boil.

"No more tests." She stretched her rubber band to a single taut line. "This is the real thing."

Fiona's heart hammered in her chest so hard, she thought it would explode. She didn't wait for the beast to attack. She moved first, sprinting toward it, cutting edge held before her.

The beast looked shocked, then amused. It rushed her, closing the distance in two steps.

A wing shot forward—much faster than Fiona had anticipated. She saw it had spurs for tearing flesh.

She moved her cutting edge perpendicular to the wing and let momentum do the rest.

Her line passed through. A wing tip landed wetly on asphalt, feathers fluttered in the air, and the scent of coppery blood was overwhelming.

Her adrenaline surged. Rather than being terrified or repulsed by the blood, seeing and smelling it made her crave more.

She turned, arms in a fighting stance and her cutting edge ready.

But the beast had more than wings. That had only been the first part of his attack.

It screamed in pain and anger.

Fiona only registered a blur as its left fist came up and hit her in the chest with a force of a pile driver.

Her world exploded into black stars. She flew into the air, landed head-first on the street, tumbling through broken glass, and slammed to a stop against the bumper of a VW bus.

Unlike her dreamy disorientation when the Maybach ran over the beast and flipped, Fiona remained acutely conscious for every bit of this. She felt each pebble of asphalt and bit of broken glass as she rolled over them. And she definitely felt the impact against the solid-metal bumper.

Every bone in her body should've been pulverized. All she felt, though, was her blood pump faster and hotter, carrying unquenchable anger to each cell.

She stood.

Only peripherally did it register that while her gray sweats were tattered and torn, she did not have a scratch on her body.

All she understood was that this fight was far from over.

She started toward the beast again.

It grinned fangs and chuckled.

Which just made her *more* mad.

It held both its wings high, poised for an attack, and it fixed her with its fiery gaze. "Feel how strong your blood is? You are one of us. Born to fight and cut and kill. I can indulge you as much as you like . . . or you can come with me, and I can teach you how to *always* feel this way."

Fiona halted.

She'd never felt so strong. And it *did* feel good. No one would be able to tell her what to do again. She would be in control of her destiny.

Then she remembered that she *had* felt this way before.

She lowered her arms.

The first time she'd eaten the chocolates from the heart-shaped box . . .

that had felt this good. So much pleasure, and so much power. She felt as if she could have done anything.

Just like now.

But if she felt like this all the time, what would happen? There would be no Robert, no Eliot, and no real family for her. She would be one among a pack of murderers and liars with only broken pieces surrounding her.

Eliot—she had entirely forgotten him.

She spotted him limping away. Not running from the beast, but moving toward his violin up the street.

Fiona maneuvered to the edge of Midway Avenue. The beast tracked her motion, but did not yet move toward her.

"What shall it be, child?" it whispered. "You will never best me."

Fiona kept moving, turning so she faced the beast as she backed toward her brother. She caught up to him and wrapped an arm around his waist to steady him.

"Thanks," Eliot whispered.

They moved together the last few steps to his violin.

"Maybe *I* can't win against you," Fiona said. "But *we* can."

The beast stared at them and shook his head. "So be it."

It beat its wings once, twice, three times, and the wind rushed around it and into a great spiral, sucking in paper and glass and smoldering ash. The roofs of the nearby stores disintegrated into clouds of debris that caught fire and made the air a pillar of flame.

Fiona's ears popped. The wind pulled at her and drew her a step closer to the vortex.

Eliot set his bow on his violin and played a long, scratchy note.

The air about them calmed a bit, enough so Fiona regained her footing.

The beast roared and its wings clapped together, aimed directly at them.

The airflow reversed—a hurricane-strength furnace blast that struck Eliot and Fiona.

Eliot covered his face as bits of glass pelted him.

Fiona tried to move in front of her brother to protect him, but the rush of air forced her back. She had to lean into the wind to stay standing . . . but even that wasn't enough, and it knocked her back onto the street.

The air screamed over her head. It got hotter and carried with it the laughter of the beast.

She clutched for purchase on the road. If that gale got ahold of her, it could carry her off.

The atmosphere near the ground was comparatively still . . . but so thin. It was getting harder to breathe.

She had to do something. The anger she had felt before was, however, draining.

She gasped. Her lungs burned. She couldn't think straight.

Was this how it was going to end? She struggled to raise her head. The air was a mix of tornado and fire and dust. Behind her, Eliot clutched the leg of a securely bolted mailbox. If she could only get to him. Cee had said they were stronger together. . . .

She lowered her head, unable to move. All the strength had been sucked from her.

The wind abruptly ceased.

Panting, she tried to get up and managed to rise to her knees.

A foot was planted squarely in the middle of her back, forcing her down.

"I don't think so," the beast whispered. He reached down with his black claws and slid up along her wrist.

Fiona tensed, expecting them to cut her flesh.

They pulled instead on her rubber band, snapping it, then plucked it from her grasp.

The beast hauled her up, feetfirst, and dragged her down the street to her brother.

It kicked away Eliot's violin, crouched, and ran a claw over its strings—severing them with explosive twangs.

Eliot still breathed, thank goodness, but he was out cold. The beast picked him up and threw him over his shoulder.

It then set Fiona down, yanking her to her feet. She had the strength to stand again, but barely.

She was shocked to see not a titanic winged beast before her, but a man. He was tall, bare-chested, and wore a cloak of feathers. About his neck was a leather thong and a hypnotically gleaming sapphire the size of her fist.

He shoved her ahead of him, keeping one hand on her arm and twisting it up past her shoulder blade. "Playtime is over," he told her. "Time to go home."

He marched her toward Ringo's . . . or what was left of Ringo's All American Pizza Palace. Two small sections of wall stood, charred and blasted. The rest of the building was a jumble of splinters and twisted pipe and chunks of plasterboard. It smelled of olive oil and roasted garlic.

In fact, it seemed as if every building on Midway Avenue was either destroyed, teetering, or on fire.

Far away, she heard sirens.

Was Oakwood Apartments still standing? Were Cee and Grandmother safe? If that place caught fire, it was so old and dry, so packed with books . . . no firemen in the world would be able to put it out.

She struggled to pull free of the man's grasp. He shoved her arm farther up, until the joint popped.

They halted in what had been the alley. The brick and cinder-block walls were partially intact, stacked precariously. Lines of chalk had been scribbled over them and glowed hot pink, lemon, and robin's-egg neon. Arcs and symbols blazed on the cratered asphalt as well. Static rolled up her leg as her feet crossed the lines.

The man set Eliot down next to her.

Eliot stood, shaking his head as if waking from a bad dream.

There was a metallic clink, and the man wrapped a large chain around both of them, three times, binding them together while he kept Fiona's arm immobilized behind her back.

Eliot wriggled next to her, but there was no play in the chain.

This only annoyed Fiona. He was touching her, jamming his elbow into her ribs.

"We have to get out of here," Eliot whispered. "Louis made this diagram. He said it transferred power, but I think—"

"Louis," Fiona spat back. "Like he knows anything. If you hadn't noticed, getting out of here doesn't exactly look like an option."

Eliot blinked, taking in the sight of the ruins and the man standing before them. "Beelzebub," he murmured. Surprisingly, no fear was in his voice.

The name sounded familiar to Fiona, as if she'd grown up knowing it all her life.

Fiona stared into Beelzebub's shockingly blue eyes. "What are you going to do with us now?"

He unsheathed a jagged obsidian knife. The glistening blade was as long as Fiona's forearm. "Now I shall sever any mortal flesh clinging to your souls. We shall finally see what you are made of . . . Immortal or Infernal."

Fiona struggled against the chains, but to no effect.

This seemed only to please Beelzebub. Smiling, he raised his knife over

his head, but then paused, considering Eliot and Fiona. He pointed a finger at each end and said, "Eeny meeny, miny, moe . . ."

Fiona, for once in her life, didn't mind Eliot's being so near.

There had to be a way to escape. Could she use the chains around her
as a cutting edge? No, even if she could, it might accidentally cut through
her or Eliot. Or maybe she could use the chain to cut itself?

She couldn't concentrate, though. Couldn't figure it out.

Her free hand found Eliot's and held it.

"It's okay," Eliot whispered to her. "We'll get through this somehow."

"Sure," she whispered back. "I know. Together, right?"

"And I pick you." Beelzebub's finger landed on Fiona. "Ladies first, apparently."

Fiona stood tall. She wished she could spit in Beelzebub's smiling face,
but her mouth was suddenly dust dry.

She held her breath. She wanted to close her eyes, but she forced them
to stay open.

There was a noise: the crackling of bone and splitting of sinew and skin.
Fiona inhaled, shocked . . . but didn't feel a thing.

Beelzebub stood before her, his obsidian blade *still* raised over his head.

A different blade had been plunged through Beelzebub's back, piercing
him through and through, protruding from his breastbone—the jagged tip
of a broken sword.

He looked down, his smile fading as a web of black poison spread across
his chest.

Someone had stabbed Beelzebub, someone standing *behind* him.

"Louis!" Eliot cried.

Louis Piper, Fiona's supposedly estranged father, emerged from the
shadow of Beelzebub.

"Traitor," Beelzebub whispered as blood bubbled from his mouth.

"Thank you, Cousin," Louis replied. "I accept your most gracious compliment in the spirit it was given."

Fiona didn't understand this. Louis was a mortal stripped of all his
power, a bum, someone who scavenged pizza from Dumpsters . . . not this
person standing before her looking powerful, clean, and just having saved
her and Eliot.

"Dad?" she whispered.

Louis turned his attention to them. His gaze softened for a fraction of an instant, then immediately hardened. "Ah, yes, children. I'll have you out in a moment. Just one or two things I must take care—"

Beelzebub gritted his teeth, and with his obsidian dagger he pushed the tip of the broken sword back through his chest.

Louis's eyes widened. "You cannot do that."

Beelzebub's smile returned. "You think I did not take precautions?"

The black lines of poison spread over his chest like a road map contracted to a point and faded.

"You think when Sealiah first appeared before the Board," Beelzebub continued, reaching back to remove the blade with a great wet sucking sound, "that I would not search for an antidote to its most infamous venom?"

Louis for the first time was without words.

Beelzebub considered the broken weapon in his hand, then tossed it aside. "Such toys belong in the days of old, dear Louis. Not in a world with biochemical laboratories at one's disposal."

He slapped Louis with the back of his hand.

Louis barely managed to raise the sleeve of his camel-hair coat to block the blow. It did little good. The force sent him flying into, and through, the remains of a cinder-block wall.

"No!" Eliot screamed.

Fiona's blood pumped hard and fast through her body again. She was mad. No one did that to *her* family—even if it was her weird father.

She had one hand free. She had to find something to cut this monster.

"I'm shocked by such sentimentality," Beelzebub said to the dust-smoldering hole that Louis had made. "You have been human too long. If only you could see yourself. When I kill you in a moment, it will be for your own good. You will thank me later."

Beelzebub turned back to Eliot and Fiona. "But first, more important matters."

The hole in his chest sealed. A tiny scar was all that remained of what should have been a mortal wound.

But that was the point, wasn't it? Beelzebub wasn't mortal.

And maybe she wasn't either.

Eliot elbowed her.

Fiona (irritated that her brother would pick this one, perhaps final, moment to distract her) tore her gaze from the blade poised to slash down and cleave her open and glanced at Eliot.

He was looking at something . . . not Beelzebub's blade, but rather the jewel dangling about his neck. Eliot shoved his elbow into her ribs again—hard—and nodded above the ornament for emphasis.

She looked. It was difficult to take her eyes off the magnificent sapphire, but she did, and then she understood what Eliot was trying to tell her.

It was staring her right in the face: the jewel was on a leather cord.

A cord looped around Beelzebub's neck.

Her free hand shot out and up, fingers twining about the leather thong.

Fiona would forever remember Beelzebub's smile. So charming. So evil. So confident that he was all-powerful and had them at his mercy.

No one would *ever* make that mistake again.

Her focus was laser sharp. The cutting edge materialized the instant she touched the cord.

Fiona pulled with all her might.

The loop around Beelzebub's neck became a circular guillotine blade as it sliced—smooth as glass—through skin, flesh, bone, and then whipped free through the air.

His smile faded and he almost looked peaceful standing before them, holding the means of her death in one hand . . . before the head of Beelzebub, the Lord of All That Flies, toppled free from his shoulders.

75

FAMILY REUNION

Beelzebub's head hit the asphalt and rolled to a stop, eyes staring up at the stars. His headless body crumpled like an empty coat.

Eliot braced himself, expecting a spray of blood, but only a trickle oozed from the severed stump. Bugs crawled out, however, and took wing: mosquitoes and gnats and flies all swirled about Beelzebub in a cloud . . . that then faded to wisps of smoke and blew away.

It all happened so fast. Another few seconds, and it would have been Eliot or Fiona on the ground dead.

Eliot tore his gaze away from the gruesome sight. "You okay?"

Fiona didn't answer him. Instead, she tightened her grip on the sapphire and leather thong and glared with a pained expression at the decapitated head.

"There was no other way. You had to do it. You saved us."

"Of course I had to do it," she snapped. She finally looked away. "I'm sorry. I just always seem to end up cutting and killing things. . . . Maybe it's what I was born to do."

An explosion lit the horizon. It came from what had been the gas station at the end of Vine Street.

Eliot coughed and smelled acrid smoke. He pulled against their chains. "You better get us out of these."

Fiona pulled on her twisted arm to no effect. "Give me a little room so I can get free."

Eliot exhaled to make himself smaller, but he stopped when he spied Louis crawling from the hole in the wall.

"Louis," he said. "Help us."

Louis didn't look at them. He strode directly to Beelzebub and spread his arms over the corpse.

Fiona tensed as if she were going to have to fight.

Louis, however, kept his distance. His lips moved, but Eliot didn't hear any words; rather, he *felt* them in the air. It was as if the entire world became still to listen to these inaudible sounds.

The lines of chalk on the walls and street glimmered and glowed. The arcs flexed, and the symbols pulsed with life.

Power transfer. That's what Louis had said the diagram was for.

The chalk flared and burned magnesium brilliant—sparks danced upon the lines.

Eliot felt power surge through him, too. It made his hair stand, tingled through every fiber, and filled him to the bursting point.

It felt as if he were drowning in the stuff.

Fiona gasped, feeling it as well.

But Eliot didn't think this power was meant for them. The lines seemed brightest near Louis. The air crackled about him. He was swathed in light.

Louis's body stretched, fingers elongating and nails pointing, and horns curled from his skull. Behind him, a barbed tail swished. Bat wings rose from his spine and spread across the night, blotting out the stars, cloaking the world in inky blackness.

The flow of energy abruptly ceased. The lines of chalk sizzled and disintegrated to dust.

Their father stood before them, as he had been before, immaculately groomed in his camel-hair coat. Only there was *one* difference: Louis looked as if he now owned the universe.

"At last," Louis breathed. "It is good to be back."

Fiona grunted and finally freed her other arm. She severed their binding chains with a single stroke.

Louis regarded her, his eyes lingering on the sapphire in her fist. "I see neither of you need my help."

"We don't need *anything* from *you*!" Fiona told him.

"That's not fair," Eliot said. "He stabbed Beelzebub, risked his life to save us."

"Sure he did," Fiona replied.

"No, no," Louis said to Eliot. "Your sister has every right to be angry, especially with me. I placed you both in great danger. I assure you, though, the only way you shall survive both families is with your father's protection—a father with his full Infernal status intact."

Eliot and his sister shared a look. What they had seen a moment ago . . . was that their father's true form? Like the woodcut in *Mythica Improbiba*?

There were so many things Eliot had to know. "Let's at least listen to him," he whispered to Fiona.

Fiona lowered her arms.

"Both families want to use you," Louis explained. "I may be the only one who wants what's best for you . . . because I love you."

Fiona scoffed.

None in the family, apart from Cee, had ever told Eliot or his sister that they loved them. When Louis said it, it sounded like a foreign language to Eliot's ears . . . something he could almost understand . . . but not quite.

"Come with me." Louis held out his hands. "There will be no rules. To-gether, we are stronger."

"Like a real family?" Fiona asked, half-disbelieving, but also half-intrigued.

"Yes," Louis replied emphatically.

Eliot saw a riot of emotions on his sister's face. In truth, he was con-fused, too. If he had learned one thing in the last few days about his fam-ily, though, it was that he had to think and be careful—because nothing was as it first appeared to be with these people.

But Louis was his father. This felt different. He trusted him . . . or, at least, he wanted to trust him.

"What do you think?" Eliot asked Fiona.

"I . . . I don't know."

Louis beckoned to them with open arms, and his smile filled the shadows.

But that smile abruptly vanished.

He looked past Fiona and Eliot, past the rubble and burning buildings, to Midway Avenue.

"Of course, *now* you show your face," Louis muttered. "How like a woman to have the most perfectly inconvenient timing."

Eliot and Fiona turned.

Robert limped out of the shadows, helped along . . . by Grandmother.

Fiona wanted to run to Robert; he was hurt. She only took a single step toward him, though, before she stopped—feeling a tidal pull between

Grandmother and Louis. They were like the north and south poles of the magnet, equal but opposite, and Fiona wasn't sure which way to go.

Eliot touched her arm. "Wait."

He must've felt it, too.

Despite the ruins and flames surrounding her, Grandmother looked as she always did. She wore her khaki silk top, faded jeans, and combat boots. Cee had told them Grandmother was sixty-two years old; tonight in the firelight, though, she looked timeless.

Grandmother gathered herself taller than Fiona had ever seen as her eyes shifted first to the remains of Beelzebub, then to Louis. Her cropped silver hair glowed like a halo. Her expression—one of placid hatred—could've been chiseled from alabaster.

"Find us transportation," Grandmother told Robert.

"Yes, ma'am." Robert limped off, holding his ribs. He gave Fiona a quick glance and a nod as if everything were going to be okay . . . but his eyes were full of unease.

"You are lovelier than I remembered," Louis said.

"Step away from the Abomination," Grandmother said to Eliot and Fiona, "before he does more harm."

Fiona looked back and forth between them. Grandmother and Louis recognized each other. Fiona had a sinking feeling, though, that this was much more than simple recognition. "You two *know* each other?"

"Know?" Louis's lips quirked into a devilish grin. "Of course. The question is, children, do *you* know who this woman is?"

"She's our grandmother," Eliot said, his words fading into uncertainty.

Fiona felt the wrongness of her brother's statement as well. Had *everything* they'd been told been part of some great deception?

"Who are you?" Fiona whispered to her grandmother.

Grandmother stood stoic and silent.

"Allow me then to make the necessary introductions," Louis said.

"You dare not," Grandmother breathed.

"Audrey Post," Louis continued, ignoring her threat. "She has been called the Pale Rider; She Who Cuts the Threads of Life; the eldest Fate, Atropos . . . and the woman I fell in love with almost sixteen years ago. Eliot, Fiona, allow me to introduce you to your mother."

The word rang like a cathedral bell in Fiona's ears.

Mother?

The way Grandmother—no, her mother—glared at Louis: the anger and betrayal etched on her face . . . yes, Louis had just revealed her greatest secret.

Their greatest secret.

Fiona loved her. Admired her. But this hurt more than the trials, the cutting, the poisoning from the chocolates, or anything she'd been through the last few days. Her mother—so long had she dreamed that against all odds she might be alive. How many nights had Fiona cried herself to sleep wanting her mother to hold and comfort her? She had grieved all her life . . . but for no reason. Her mother had always been by her side.

Lying.

Fiona had to know more, but something had just broken inside her and she couldn't make her mouth form the words.

Her brother, however, was stronger and voiced the one thought in their minds.

"Why?" Eliot whispered.

"I told you, children," Audrey said, her tone icy cold, "step away, so I may destroy this monster."

"No," Fiona said softly, and then louder, "we're not moving until you tell us why you lied. Didn't you love us?"

Audrey took a step backward, looking as if she'd been slapped. "That is not a question with a simple answer."

"Please, Audrey," Louis said, and crossed his arms. "Don't be shy. We are rapt to hear your explanation of this delectable deception."

Audrey regained her composure and narrowed her eyes at Louis. "It is true. I am your mother. What I've done, I had to. I would change nothing . . . save one mistake when I spared one who deserved neither my love nor my mercy."

"Mercy?!" Louis laughed. "I would've hated to see your undiluted wrath, m'lady."

"Come, children," Audrey said, her face flushing. "Now is not the proper time for this discussion."

Fiona felt the world spin around her. Her mother. Right in front of her. She wanted to run to her and scream that it had all been so unfair.

Fiona steadied herself against Eliot. She may have not liked her brother half the time; he constantly annoyed her and was forever getting into trouble, but at least she knew who he was. He hadn't lied to her his entire life.

Fiona looked at him and Eliot glanced up at her. He nodded, communicating that he felt the same way.

Fiona faced her mother. The world was burning around them, but they weren't leaving this spot until they got some answers.

"There *never* was a proper time to discuss this. So tell us. Now."

Audrey's slender eyebrows arched. "That, young lady, almost sounded like a threat."

"Almost?" Fiona whispered. "Let me be clear then: it was a threat. One more order from you, one more lie . . . and we go right now with our father. At least he's willing to talk."

Louis clapped his hands. "A fine ultimatum, my dear. Just a hint of irony to it, as well. Brilliant!"

Audrey stood motionless, considering a long moment, then said, "Very well, Fiona. The truth you shall have. All of it." Audrey's gaze fell; she could no longer meet Fiona's unwavering stare. "I severed my maternal ties," she whispered, "all those feelings . . . I had to. The imposition of our household rules, the discipline—no real mother could have inflicted those things upon her children. There was nothing I could have denied either of you, I once loved you so much."

Fiona could not count the times she had wanted her mother's love— instead she had rules, chores, or a history lesson. Tears blurred her vision and a dozen images of Audrey swam before her.

"Had I not fabricated the charade," Audrey continued, "had you learned who you were and discovered your talents sooner, they would've found you. You would have not been prepared for the families. Adopting the pretense of being your grandmother, allowing you to think your parents both dead— it was the only way to keep you isolated . . . and alive."

It made sense intellectually. Having an emotionally distant grand- mother instead of a mother—having to live like hermits—Fiona and Eliot had learned to depend upon each other instead of a loving parent. Maybe that all added up to their having a chance of surviving the Infernal and Im- mortal families.

Still, in her heart, Fiona could not find forgiveness.

"You must give her another chance," Louis whispered. "We have *all* done terrible things because we think them best." He looked to Audrey. "Even now, *I* shall not hate you, my dear."

Audrey's face quivered with barely restrained emotions.

"Another chance?" Fiona whispered. How could she forgive her mother when all that was left inside her was cold grief and boiling rage?

Eliot touched her arm. "It's over now. All their tests and the trials. The families"—he glanced at Louis—"both of them, have revealed themselves. We can make a fresh start."

Fiona remembered what Cee had told her that night in the hospital: that Audrey had cut herself as well and made great sacrifices for them. Severing her love for her children? What did that leave? Only maternal duty? Fiona couldn't imagine what that must have been like. Had it been an act of ultimate love? One of wretched weakness? Or both?

"Okay," Fiona whispered to Audrey, then turned to Louis. "We're done here. Eliot and I won't be fought over like prizes. We've survived the three trials, and whatever the other side of the family had planned. We've earned the right to be treated—if not like Immortals or Infernals—then at least like adults."

Eliot stood closer, united in this stance against their parents.

For a moment neither Audrey nor Louis spoke.

"Magnificent," Louis breathed. "Truly masterful rebelliousness. I am proud to call you my son and my daughter."

Fiona couldn't quite tell if he was mocking them or not. But it didn't matter what Louis thought. This is how she and Eliot felt. This is how it had to be.

"Of course," Audrey finally replied. "It shall be as you say."

"And the rules," Eliot said. "There's going to be changes to the List."

Audrey pursed her lips, not liking this pronouncement one bit, but nonetheless she nodded.

Fiona felt it was finally over. One life had ended and a new one was about to begin. She wasn't sure if it would be better, but it would at least be one on their own terms.

"Let's go," she told Eliot.

"Go, yes," Louis said. "But go where? My offer remains. You have an entire other family who would be delighted to meet you. Well . . ." He made a rude gesture at the deflated corpse of Beelzebub. "He hardly counts anymore."

"I don't think—" Fiona started.

"There are different worlds," Louis continued, "new lands you have never seen or imagined . . . to explore . . . or to conquer and make yours."

Fiona looked at her brother and slowly shook her head. He nodded in agreement.

"We're not saying no," Eliot told Louis. "But we're just not ready for you.

It's going to take us a while to figure out who we are and where we fit in *this* world before we deal with the other side of the family."

"I understand," Louis said with a sigh. "Very wise. I will always be here for you, though. Just call upon me and I shall come."

He took a step into the shadows of the sole remaining wall. He then bowed to Audrey. "My lady, deepest regrets that things have not worked out differently."

Audrey gritted her teeth. "If I see you again, if I even hear that you have been near Eliot or Fiona . . . I shall find you, Louis, and this time sever much more than your power."

Louis laughed. "I look forward to that encounter. Have I expressed how much I still admire and love you?"

He bowed and bowed and continued to step back into the shadow that was only a hand's-span deep . . . fading from view until their father, Louis Piper, Lucifer, the Prince of Darkness, was gone.

"Good-bye, Dad," Fiona whispered. She thought she might actually miss him.

After a moment, the Posts walked back to Midway Avenue.

Eliot ran to his violin, plucked it out of the gutter, and cradled it to his chest.

Audrey frowned at the thing with its tangle of broken strings, but said nothing.

Del Sombra was dying—every building demolished or on fire or both. At the edge of town were flashing lights and plumes of steam, but the center of Del Sombra . . . no one was even trying to save it.

A Humvee rolled down the street, nudging cars out of its path. It stopped. Robert got out and opened a door for Fiona.

"Now we go," Audrey said.

Fiona took one last look at the place she had spent her entire life. Ringo's, the Pink Rabbit . . . and farther down the street, Oakwood Apartments blazed—all three stories of it engulfed in flame and billowing smoke.

All her books. All her things. Everything that had been in her old life—gone.

"Go where?" Eliot asked.

"Away." Audrey set her hands consolingly upon Fiona's shoulders. "This place has served its purpose. We need it no more."

Fiona climbed into the Humvee.

She wasn't sure where they'd go or what fate had in store for them, but at least Eliot would be with her, and now her mother, and somewhere out there even Louis.

No matter how strange, no matter how dangerous or awkward or dysfunctional, they were . . . and always would be . . . her family.

SECTION

VIII

A NEW GAME

76

DECISIONS

Eliot and Fiona took shelter from the sun in a scalloped alcove. There was a marble bench, a view of the sparkling Aegean Sea, and a statue next to them of a man with an elephant's head.

Eliot smiled at it and gave it a little wave. It might be some distant relative for all he knew.

Uncle Henry had offered them opulent rooms in his estate to wait, but it felt better out here in the fresh air.

"How long do you think it will take?" Fiona asked.

Eliot shrugged. The League Council might never decide if they belonged with this side of the family. How could they when Louis, the Prince of Darkness, was their father? How could they when they shared genetics with a monster such as Beelzebub?

He told none of this to his sister, though, because the only thing he could predict about his family was . . . that they were unpredictable.

"It's not fair," Fiona muttered, "just leaving us here while they talk. We should be there."

"Like anyone on the Council is going to listen to us."

Fiona nodded and sighed.

Just around the corner was a tiny rock island. That's where the Council's amphitheater was—where they had first met Lucia and Aaron and all the others, and where they had started their heroic trials.

"Audrey" was there now, speaking on their behalf.

After a lifetime of thinking of her as "Grandmother," Eliot couldn't switch gears and start thinking of her as "Mom." He'd settled on calling her simply by her name until he sorted out his feelings.

Plus, what was all that talk about her "severing maternal ties"? Fiona seemed to understand that better than he did, but wouldn't talk about it.

In fact, he had never seen his sister so quiet.

He studied her. When they had arrived, Uncle Henry's staff had been waiting. They found a dress for Fiona, some silk thing that left her arms bare. One man had helped pin up her hair. She looked more like a girl than Eliot had ever realized she could . . . even, possibly, approaching pretty.

After what they'd been through, he knew they had both changed. He felt as if he sat next to a stranger.

Fiona caught him staring. "What?" she demanded.

When he didn't immediately answer, she fussed with her dress, suddenly looking like the old Fiona, uncomfortable and irritated in anything she wore.

"Can't speak?" Fiona asked him. "Case of pneumatolith? No surprise with all the stuff you put up your nasal passages."

Pneumatolith meant "rocks in the lungs." Not a bad insult, especially with the implied slur of nose picking. But all the Latin roots made her try at vocabulary insult way too easy.

"You need to brush up on your knowledge of taphonomic cranial processes," he told her. "Obviously, though, kind of hard to think with your condition."

Fiona's forehead crinkled as she started working *that* one out.

She'd get the word. *Taphonomic* came from *taphonomy*—the study of making fossils. Hence with "taphonomic cranial processes," he was basically calling her a "rock head." Added bonus points for the "hard to think" quip.

By his insulting his sister, life felt normal again, just for a moment. No gods. No fallen angels. Nothing stranger than his and Fiona's trying to get on each other's nerves.

"Good one." Fiona pursed her lips as she formulated her counterinsult.

But before she could say anything a shadow fell on them.

It was Audrey. She looked as commanding and detached as ever. Something was in her gaze, though. A bit of tenderness? Or just the wind in her eyes?

"It is time," she told them. "Come."

Eliot jumped to his feet. Butterflies rioted in his stomach, but he wanted this over—one way or the other.

Audrey reached down and straightened the collar of his polo shirt.

Uncle Henry had given Eliot clothes, too: a black shirt, navy blazer, and khaki slacks. All new and fitting perfectly. It was a completely alien experience after wearing Cee's homemade clothes all his life.

They walked along the covered path. On one side sprawled Uncle Henry's palatial estate with its Ionic columns and French windows, and on the other side the ocean churned and seagulls soared effortlessly.

"We have questions," Eliot told Audrey. "About the family, about you, and about us."

"We have all the time in the world for that now," Audrey replied.

Did that mean the Council had decided in their favor? Or was this just some new delaying tactic?

Audrey stopped. She examined their suspicious faces. "I'm sorry you had to go through this. The trials . . ." She looked away. "Everything."

Eliot had never heard her say she was sorry. He felt for her. Why, he wasn't sure, because they were the ones who had been lied to all their lives. But Audrey . . . his mother, must have suffered, too.

He took her hand and squeezed it.

His mother returned the gesture.

Fiona sighed, then also took Audrey's hand.

They walked together until they came to the span of stone that arched from Uncle Henry's estate to the island off the coast. The bridge was unmortared stones that curved up and over whitecaps and sharp rocks.

Unlike the first time he had crossed this perilous bridge, Eliot hardly gave it a thought as he walked over.

He stepped off the opposite side onto dark sands.

Fiona and Audrey followed right behind him.

Ahead, Eliot heard a great number of voices. As they mounted the hilltop, he halted at the sight of the amphitheater—filled with two hundred people . . . all of whom fell silent and turned to stare.

Now he was frightened.

It wasn't only the Council who were here to decide their fate. It looked as if the entire League of Immortals had come to watch them be judged.

Under the scrutiny of so many, he felt tiny, awkward, embarrassed, unsure, but then he stared back at them—just as boldly and standing as tall as he could. Let them judge him.

They were the strangest collection: every race was present, men and women, old and young, beautiful and ugly, the poor and the fabulously rich. There were farmers and kings, some completely nude, others wrapped in furs as if they were freezing. Most, however, looked like people he might meet anywhere. Normal. Almost. They still had that look—as if they stood over you, peering through a microscope at your every flaw.

Eliot took a deep breath. He glanced at Fiona. She looked scared but defiant, as well.

They strode down the stairs through the silent crowd. The temperature chilled with every step, until it felt as if it were freezing, and they stood in the center.

The Council sat on blocks of stone—Aunt Lucia in a flowing red dress; Uncle Aaron looking serious, arms crossed; Cornelius, who didn't look up from his notes and tablet computer; Gilbert, whose golden hair seemed to glow; Aunt Dallas smiled; and one dark, tall Council elder in a top hat who looked as if he had eaten a few lemons.

Uncle Henry was nowhere to be seen.

No one moved or spoke.

Eliot took a small step closer to his sister, and they stood together, shoulder to shoulder.

He swallowed and addressed the Council. "We've passed your three heroic trials." Eliot's voice was small, but amazingly steady. "Souhk has been vanquished."

"Amanda Lane has been rescued from Perry Millhouse," Fiona said.

"And we retrieved the Golden Apple," Eliot finished.

"We've waited long enough." Fiona nervously pulled at the rubber band on her wrist. "Fifteen years of not knowing who we were or where we belong."

Audrey set a hand on their shoulders. "On behalf of Eliot and Fiona Post, I hereby petition the Council to accept them into the League of Immortals."

Aunt Lucia gazed at Eliot and Fiona, then over the entire amphitheater. "Despite certain absences," Lucia replied, "we have a quorum, and we shall so consider this petition. Please join us sister and be witness to our judgments." She motioned to the stone block on her right.

Audrey gave Eliot and Fiona a quick, reassuring squeeze and joined the Council.

Uncle Henry appeared at the top of the stairs. "A thousand pardons," Henry said to the audience, ignoring several angry stares, and waving to those who smiled. "A few last-minute and completely unavoidable details to attend to." He bowed before Eliot and Fiona. "Hello, children." He settled onto the last stone block on Aunt Lucia's left and attempted to smooth his wrinkled tuxedo.

Aunt Lucia's glare was one of practiced annoyance—as if she had had to put up with this for thousands of years.

She plucked a tiny bell from the folds of her dress and rang it thrice. Sweet silver tones echoed throughout the theater. "I call this session of the League of Immortals Council of Elders to order. All come to heed, petition, and be judged. *Narro, audio, perceptum.*"

Eliot wondered if the Council accepted him and Fiona as their own, would life get easier? Or would there be new tests and adventures?

And if they didn't accept them?

Eliot's hand itched, the poison burning up the vein in his arm. He wished he had Lady Dawn.

Aunt Lucia turned to Fiona. "Miss Fiona Paige Post. You have shown yourself to be a fearless warrior, unyielding in the face of extreme adversity. For that, and for imbibing the Golden Apple, we pronounce you . . . goddess."

She presented Fiona with a silver rosebud.

The flower opened as Fiona took it. It perfumed the air with scents of lilac and honey and shimmered with diamond-dust pollen.

"I so invite you to join your cousins in the Order of the Celestial Rose," Lucia said.

"It's beautiful," Fiona whispered. "Thank you." She curtsied. "Yes, I definitely accept."

Eliot breathed again; he hadn't realized he'd stopped while Lucia declared his sister part of the League.

Dallas bounded to Fiona, hugged and kissed her, and escorted her back and made her sit with her. Aaron came to her side as well and clasped her hand.

Fiona looked flustered, delighted, and then her eyes found Eliot's and she was suddenly unsure of her new happiness.

He was alone now.

Lucia turned to him.

"Master Eliot Zachariah Post." Lucia's authoritative voice quieted all. "You have demonstrated cleverness and clear thought in the face of chaos and imminent death, as well as unflagging loyalty to your sister. For that, and all your other exalted deeds, we pronounce you . . . Immortal Hero."

Eliot smiled, but it froze on his face.

Hero? Not a god like his sister?

He had daydreamed about being a hero his entire life. Why then did this seem like a huge disappointment? As if it were something *in between* winning and losing?

Lucia took a step closer and held out an amulet on a chain. It was a gold-and-lapis eye that looked like an Egyptian hieroglyphic. "I present you with the Eye of Horus and invite you to join the Brotherhood of Immortal Heroes."

Eliot reached for it . . . but he hesitated.

This didn't feel right. It wasn't because they had proclaimed Fiona a goddess and him a mere hero (although that *did* annoy him). It was something else that whispered that he didn't belong with these people.

Yesterday they might have killed him had he failed their test. They might *still* kill him and his sister if half of what Audrey said about their politicking was true.

Lucia looked concerned as she continued to hold out the amulet. "Come, join the prestigious ranks of Gilgamesh, Hercules, Arthur, and Beowulf. Immortals all. You are their equal. Their kin."

Eliot felt hundreds of eyes upon him. His hand trembled. He should just take the thing.

No—that's what the old Eliot Post would have done. The scared-in-the-shadow-of-his-sister Eliot Post. The "good little boy" who always did as he was told.

He wasn't that person anymore.

And then Eliot finally understood what all the fighting and trials and lies were about. They were trying to influence him . . . but in the end this was *his* decision.

He got to choose whether he joined the League or sought his father and became part of his clan.

An Immortal or a fallen angel . . . both seemed dangerous . . . was there another option? A way to be independent of *both* families?

He looked about the amphitheater, into faces full of anticipation and cruelty, curiosity and hope.

His gaze fell on his sister. Fiona leaned forward, confused by his delay. She looked as if she wanted to come to him and help with whatever was wrong.

Aunt Dallas and Aaron, however, held her back.

That was the thing: if he didn't join the League, he might never see his sister again.

Life without Fiona? No more insults, no more racing, no more putting up with her relentless competitive drives? Maybe that wouldn't be such a bad thing, after all. But, Cecilia had said they were stronger together—and that had been proved true over and over these last few days. How many times would they have died without each other?

Eliot had a feeling they'd need that combined strength for whatever happened next . . . a small price to pay for her constant-annoying factor.

Besides, Fiona was his sister. He couldn't just leave her alone with these people.

"Okay," Eliot whispered, then louder said, "I accept. I'll join you."

Aunt Lucia started to loop the amulet over Eliot's head.

He reached up and took it from her. "Thanks."

She nodded, not understanding, but nonetheless releasing the Eye to his custody.

There was no way Eliot was ever wearing *anything* around his neck. Not after what he'd seen happen to Beelzebub in the alley.

He turned and held up the amulet for all to see.

A great cheer sounded through the amphitheater.

Fiona rushed to his side and they hugged.

It was over. Finally, they could rest, be happy, and have some semblance of a normal life . . . at least for a while, he hoped.

Others quickly surrounded them, Gilbert, Uncle Henry, Cornelius— others whom Eliot had never before seen, embracing him, shaking his hand, and all talking, so he couldn't understand what anyone was saying.

Lucia rang her silver bell. "Order. Order!" she cried.

The crowds quieted.

"Very well," Lucia said. "I see no further League business will be accomplished today."

"Only the business of celebration," Uncle Henry shouted. "I have prepared a feast and music at my most humble domicile. I invite all to partake of my hospitality."

A new cheer erupted, louder than the first.

Lucia rang her silver bell, but this time everyone ignored her, and Eliot barely heard as she yelled, "I hereby declare this session of the Council of Elders dismissed."

Gods and goddesses, heroes and Immortals of every shade, stood and clapped and hooted. Everyone mingled and pressed to the center to greet Eliot and Fiona.

"So many relations you will meet tonight," Uncle Henry said, draping his arms about them. "This is where the real tests and trials begin. Family politics."

Lucia maneuvered close to Henry. "And the matter of your escaped Driver? He must be punished."

"I have taken care of that," Uncle Henry assured her. "I promise you, Robert Farmington's penalty for his misdeeds will be unparalleled in the history of torture."

Eliot and Fiona locked eyes, horrified.

77

THE END OF SUMMER

Fiona eased back into Robert and his arms entwined about her.

They stood at the railing of the *Wayward Lost* and watched the Caribbean Sea roll past. The sun had yet to rise but she had already gone for a swim, played with the dolphins, and had breakfast. It was going to be another glorious day in the Bahamas playing on Uncle Henry's sailboat.

"Does it have to end?" she asked.

"No," Robert replied. "Just close your eyes. We'll always be here together."

Fiona was not one for daydreaming, but for this, she'd make an exception. She closed her eyes.

"Remember the beachcombing?" he whispered in her ear. "All the glass floats you found?"

"The midnight walk," she whispered back. "The turtles coming onshore."

"Snorkeling on the reef."

"That beach of red sand. I don't think anyone had ever been there before."

She'd done things she had only ever read about. It was the life she had always wanted: travel, adventure . . . and, of course, there had been Robert—strong, tanned, ruggedly handsome, and forever cool.

That's how she would remember this week.

There was only one thing she would've changed. She glanced at the aft deck. Uncle Aaron gently snored and rocked back and forth in a hammock strung between the mizzen- and mainmasts.

She was sure he watched them. He was always watching. Uncle Henry's idea of a chaperone.

Aaron hadn't said much the entire week. He seemed to sleep most of the time, yet he had the uncanny knack to be around every corner, just over the next sand dune, waiting, and making sure that she and Robert didn't get into any trouble.

After everything that had happened, Fiona realized that family trouble could be very real, especially for the people around them.

Del Sombra had burned to the ground. No one had died, but dozens of people were hurt, and many homes and businesses lost.

That, however, wasn't exactly the kind of trouble Uncle Aaron was here to stop.

She and Robert had taken moonlit swims in the bay, stolen kisses, walked hand in hand . . . but nothing more than that, although she desperately yearned for more.

On the other hand, maybe a protracted and protected romance wasn't such a bad idea. Things between her and Robert could get . . . complicated.

She took Robert's hand and drew him around so they both leaned over the railing. "Are you still going to drive for Uncle Henry?"

"I think so. If Mr. Mimes can finagle it past the Council." Robert gestured to the boat. "I'm supposed to be getting punished."

"Maybe you should stay away for a while."

Robert smiled. "What? Get fat here in paradise? I don't think so. There are no roads, and I was born to drive." He patted her hand. "Don't worry, Mr. Mimes won't let anything happen to me."

Fiona wasn't so sure about that, but she understood that Robert would never let anyone coop him up. No one told him how to run his life. That was one of the things she admired about him.

She absentmindedly touched the rose wrapped around the string of her bikini top. Fiona wasn't sure if it was a real plant or jewelry. It felt both like metallic silver and organic. It had gone everywhere with her, impervious to the sun and water and wind, and still as fragrant as when Aunt Lucia had presented it to her. Every time she inhaled its perfume, it made her smile, reminded her that she had accomplished something . . . and that she was in the League.

Her fingers interlaced with Robert's on the railing.

"There are rules about Drivers dating people in the League," she said.

"Some rules were meant to be broken." Robert gently stroked her fingers.

Fiona removed her hand from his and set it back on the railing—close, but no longer touching him.

"I don't know."

"What do you mean?" he asked, suddenly serious.

"I mean . . ."

Fiona couldn't make the words come. She had faced death, gods, and devils—this was harder. It had to be said, though, if not for her sake, then for Robert's.

"I mean, I'd love to spend every day with you like this, but that's not going to happen. The League is going to be there, watching, and drawing you into their politics because of me."

Robert turned to her, the hurt plain on his face.

She turned away. "I'm not saying this is the end. It *is* the start of something between you and me . . . I'm just not sure what. I need to take some time to figure out how it's all going to work."

Robert lifted her chin so she had to look him in the eyes. "I get it. You're afraid I'm in over my head. That I'll get hurt."

"You *are* in over your head," Fiona whispered.

A shadow crossed Robert's features as if he remembered something unpleasant—just for a moment—and then it was gone. He nodded and exhaled. "Maybe you're right."

They turned back to the ocean and watched the waves, neither saying anything.

What was there to say? She wanted Robert, but not if he was going to get hurt or killed because of her.

It was all so unfair.

It was like a big chess game with hundreds of pieces—aunts, uncles, cousins—and rules she was just starting to learn. It was exciting, yes, but confusing and dangerous as well. She couldn't drag Robert into that.

And what about Audrey? Where did she fit on the chessboard? Had she protected Fiona and Eliot only because it was her duty? Or was there *some* love left in her heart for them?

Is that what it meant to be a goddess? To be completely isolated? Cut off from your own emotions?

Fiona tried to feel something.

It had been hard ever since she severed her appetite; a little easier after she'd taken a bite of the Golden Apple—but still, she had to concentrate to feel the warmth she knew was there for Robert, and the loyalty toward her brother. And for Audrey? There was a sense of loss . . . and some hope that there might yet be something between her and her mother.

All these ambiguous feelings were for the "good" side of her family. What of her father, Louis, and all the other fallen angels?

Fiona knelt and rummaged through her book bag. Inside was her straw hat, swimsuits, a waterproof camera, the yo-yo Uncle Aaron had given her—and there: a leather pouch.

She pulled it out and removed Beelzebub's sapphire.

The jewel had shrunk to the size of an egg. Fiona let it hang on its leather thong, swaying over the water.

It was beautiful. Hypnotically so. She gazed into its depths. It had hundreds of facets, each one a precision cut, but without any pattern—a series of random planes and angles that all puzzled together upon the surface of the stone. It flashed with the blue of flickering flame, the wide-open sky, and endless ocean.

It was far more than just a priceless jewel. She carried it as a reminder that an entire side of her family was still out there complicating her life.

What would *they* do to Robert if they knew he and she were officially boyfriend and girlfriend? His life would be in constant danger.

"What are you going to do with that thing?" Robert asked.

She dropped the jewel to the end of the leather cord. "I could just toss it into the ocean. Let the fish take care of whatever evil is inside."

"Not a bad idea." Robert's eyes locked onto its sparkling facets.

It would be easy to let go . . . forget about Louis and the others.

But that would be like forgetting about a part of herself. Louis *was* her father. Half of his blood pulsed through her veins. The fallen angels *were* her family, too. She wasn't going to deny that . . . but she wasn't ready to embrace that unpleasant fact yet, either.

She popped the cord, caught the sapphire in one deft motion, and stowed it back in her bag.

"I'm not going to worry about it," she told Robert. "At least, not today."

Uncle Aaron rolled out of the hammock. He glanced at the horizon. "The plane will be here soon," he announced.

Fiona sighed. Her vacation was over. Uncle Henry's Learjet would land on the private airstrip in two hours and whisk her back to the real world.

She leaned against Robert.

Together they watched the horizon redden and turn brilliant with sunrise. Dolphins poked their noses out of the ocean and called to them.

"Time left for one more swim," she said.

Robert peeled off his shirt and jumped into the water. Fiona joined him, splashing and laughing, and gave him one long kiss.

Audrey, her brother, Immortals, and Infernal politics and schemes—all the realities of the outside world—they were going to have to wait.

Fiona had a feeling that trouble was on the horizon . . . and that she'd have to make this vacation last a long, long time.

78

LIVING WITH LIES

liot slid the box onto the stack of other book-filled boxes. He opened the flap and saw three volumes of *St. Hawthorn's Collected Reference of Horticulture*. Where had he put the other five in the series?

The motel room was crammed—wall-to-wall and overflowing on dresser, bed, and nightstands—with such boxes.

He pushed his new glasses up the ridge of his nose. He didn't think he'd ever get used to them, but he had to admit his vision had indeed been blurry.

Eliot blinked at himself in the mirror over the dresser and sighed. The wire rims made him look younger and dorkier than he could ever have imagined. His journey to nerd-dom was now complete.

Cee shuffled into the doorway. "I've finished cataloging room six," she said, her hands trembling as they held a clipboard.

Eliot closed the box. "That was the last one. I think we're done for the night."

"Night?" Cee glanced outside. "It's almost morning, sweetie."

Eliot joined her and looked outside. In the distance the buildings of downtown Alameda, California, stood silhouetted against the lightening eastern sky. He'd been so preoccupied he hadn't noticed they'd worked through the entire evening.

No one else had been here to distract him. Cee and Audrey had rented out every room in this little roadside motel. It was where they had decided to store all the things saved from the fire.

How Cee managed to box and move it all, Eliot hadn't figured out. It was as if they had planned the move ahead of time.

All their important books had been carefully cataloged, wrapped in paper, then set in color-coded boxes. It had taken him and Cee the better part of five days to get all unloaded, organized, and safely stored in two dozen rooms.

"I think we've earned a little rest." Cee patted his hand. "Why don't you get cleaned up and we'll have breakfast at the diner."

Eliot nodded. One advantage of having the old place burnt to the ground was that Cecilia wasn't cooking. The diner down the street served scrambled eggs, sides of crisp bacon, and gallons of fresh orange juice. It was heaven.

He started to his dingy room to wash off the dust and the book smell—then halted.

Eliot didn't like being ordered around, even if it was by Cecilia. Ever since he'd officially been welcomed in the League, he hadn't liked *anyone* telling him *anything*.

To be clear, though, he had never liked being ordered around . . . he'd just never questioned it as he had now.

Was that because he'd been declared an Immortal Hero, or was it just part of growing up?

He marched back to Cee. "Where's Audrey?"

Eliot had wanted to ask "Where's my mother?" but he couldn't quite say that. He had had a hard enough time not calling Audrey "Grandmother" anymore. That he had a living mother (let alone a father, too) was still taking some getting used to.

"I thought she was going to be around," he said. "That we were going to be more of a family."

"*More* of a family?" Cee looked puzzled. "We have always been family. It is not something you could have more or less of, my darling."

Eliot frowned at this obvious diversion. "Just where is she, Cee?"

"Come, walk me to my room." Cecilia slipped her arm through his, and Eliot helped her amble along the covered sidewalk. "Your mother is dealing with League matters."

This was news. When Eliot had asked Cee before, for all he had got was a vague "away" or "busy." Cecilia's guard was down . . . so he pressed for more.

"The Council is back in session?"

Cee nodded. "Your mother's sister Dallas has stepped down, and another had to fill her spot. No surprise with that one. I never understood how one with so much power could be so irresponsible." Cee touched her lips, appearing shocked at the boldness of her words.

Eliot tried to look Cecilia in the eyes, but she would not meet his gaze. "Does that mean Audrey's going to be away all the time? That there are going to be just as many secrets as there were before?"

Cee sighed. "There will always be secrets, my dearest Eliot. It is a constant of the world in which we live."

Wait. Eliot rewound their conversation. Cecilia had said "your mother's sister Dallas." If Cee was his great-grandmother, wouldn't Aunt Dallas and Aunt Lucia be *her* daughters along with Audrey? Wouldn't she have said just plain "Dallas" or "my Dallas"?

He had long suspected that Cecilia was not really his great-grandmother, but it wasn't something he wanted to dwell upon. She was the only one who had ever showed any real affection for him or Fiona.

Which was only more evidence that she wasn't related to the Post family.

She was bent with age, always trembling, her shawl wrapped tightly around her neck. She didn't look like Audrey or Uncle Henry or any of the others, her features more rounded, wrinkled . . . more human.

Why would Audrey let her pretend she was a relation?

"Who are you?" Eliot whispered.

Cecilia stopped trembling and smiled. "I am someone who will always be your Cecilia, my dove. I will love you more than any ever could."

"So you're not—"

Cecilia touched his lips with one finger, silencing him. "Do you *truly* wish to know?"

"The truth is always best, at least, that's what Louis said."

Cee laughed and it sounded like dry leaves. "The Infernals and their damned irony," she muttered. "Is truth *always* good for you? What if it brings pain and ruin? Have you never lied to protect someone's feelings?"

She leaned closer.

Eliot suddenly smelled the ocean and smoke. He felt wind on his skin. He imagined that he stood on the steps of an ancient temple and Cecilia stood before him, gazing into a pool of water, a burning bunch of sage in one hand, and a crooked twig in the other. She was younger, his age, with raven hair that fell to her waist.

He blinked and the image vanished. Old, trembling Cee stood before him, patting his arm, with her usual bleach-and-soap scent.

For once Eliot's curiosity wasn't in control of his thinking. He was tired of dealing with the truth. Maybe it was okay to just let a person love you, not ask questions, and accept his or her affection for the rare gift it was.

He and Fiona had lived with lies for fifteen years. It hadn't been such a bad thing; it had protected them from the families . . . maybe even saved their lives.

Lies obviously served *some* purpose other than evil.

It was a slippery concept. Eliot wasn't sure he understood all the ramifications of this "beneficial" lying, but he was sure that he loved Cecilia, and that he wanted to continue doing so.

"Okay," he whispered. "Great-Grandmother."

Cee gave him a shaking hug, and he hugged her back.

She then pushed him gently away and opened the door to her room. "Come for me in half an hour. We'll then have a nice breakfast together."

"Sure."

He gave her a wave and went back to his own motel room.

It was dingy and dusty, and he didn't feel like being cooped up, so he grabbed his backpack and went outside again.

The sun hadn't risen, and from the dull gray-pink tinge on the horizon, Eliot figured it wouldn't be full daylight for another twenty minutes.

He climbed a fire ladder to the gravel-strewn rooftop of the motel. The view was of a dozen billboards, the glowing signs of fast-food restaurants, and mist-shrouded hills. Eliot wanted to collect his thoughts and breathe air that didn't smell like rotting paper.

He missed his old life. Not the boredom, being kept in the dark, or the bullying parts, but the people. He'd likely never see his friend Johnny from Ringo's again. Robert was supposedly hiding somewhere. Fiona was on vacation at Uncle Henry's invitation. And Julie? She was probably in Los Angeles already settled into her new life—better off without him.

He sighed.

There was no going back. He couldn't pretend (even with his new glasses) that he was simple bookwormish Eliot Post anymore after surviving three life-or-death trials, defeating a fallen angel, and being proclaimed an Immortal Hero.

He pulled the Eye of Horus amulet from his pocket. The golden eye gleamed even in the twilight. It felt heavy and made him feel as if he'd really done something special. Still, he hadn't put it on yet . . . and he wasn't sure why.

He pocketed the thing and it clattered against the dice in his pocket. He'd kept the dice as a souvenir from the Last Sunset Tavern. He'd tossed them experimentally a few times. It was fun to rattle and throw them, but he'd stopped because they reminded him of the other side of his family.

Eliot wished he could just forget the families—both Immortal and Infernal. He was scared that he'd make a mistake with all the intricate politics and get more people killed.

He imagined that none of this had ever happened and he and Julie were together somewhere, maybe skiing the Swiss Alps, then relaxing in a secluded hot spring afterward, completely isolated from the world.

But he shouldn't do that kind of little-kid thing anymore. He couldn't afford slipping off into his fantasy worlds. If he didn't keep his mind on reality, keep focused on the dangers in orbit around him, he might get himself or Fiona into trouble.

He flash-backed to Beelzebub poised over them, his jagged obsidian knife glittering, ready to slash down and part flesh from his soul. He and Fiona had bested the fallen angel . . . in part because of Eliot and his music.

He pulled Lady Dawn from his pack. Cee had gotten him a violin case, battered and worn, but much better than the rubber boot he had been using.

Lady Dawn had never looked better, despite all her adventures. Perfect and polished, her strings taut and tuned. She was much more than mere wood and sinew, though. After her strings were snapped, they had regrown overnight by themselves.

He stroked the wood and flexed his hand. The poison still throbbed in his palm. He had wanted to tell someone in the League . . . but it felt like a secret. No—more than that: it felt as if they'd do something bad to him if they ever found out.

Besides, it didn't hurt that much and it got better when he played. It also reminded him there was a price to pay for his music, and limits to his control.

As he considered his music, he realized that part of his talent was due to his imagination: the choir of voices that accompanied the old songs, seeing children romp about a maypole as he played the "Mortal's Coil" nursery rhyme, envisioning the death of all in the *Symphony of Existence*.

So maybe daydreams weren't little-kid things, after all. They were the first step in transforming fantasy into reality.

He propped Lady Dawn on his shoulder and set bow to her strings.

Six crows circled overhead, cawed, and landed on the edge of the roof. They beat their wings as if applauding, then settled and stared at him with black, glittering eyes.

Eliot took a step back. He didn't know what these birds were (besides the obvious common raven species, *Corvus corax*). Were they messengers sent by someone in the families, or here just because they liked his music?

Whatever they represented, Eliot decided there was no need to be rude. He bowed to the birds with an extravagant flourish as he had seen Louis do, then he played.

He started with the simple "Mortal's Coil," then his thoughts drifted to Julie Marks and her song. As the music turned dark, clouds gathered, but Eliot quickly moved on to the hopeful part of her song—embellishing and improvising, expanding the good feelings, and wishing that her life was better, and that wherever she was, she was happy.

His heart broke and he poured its contents into the music, sweetening every note, making it so filled with longing that the air felt as if it could no longer hold the sound . . . as if it would burst.

The world hesitated. The universe paused.

The sunrise exploded over the horizon and filled the land with color and light.[70]

Eliot played and played.

The crows squawked and beat their wings.

Eliot played for Julie. He played for the entire world. He played like a madman. He played for the pure joy of making music.

70. The sunrise along the 121° longitudinal demarcation was six minutes twenty-three seconds *early* that day. Initially it was dismissed as light reflecting off clouds, but reports soon came in of the sun's early arrival where there was no cloud cover—from Seattle, Washington, to Lompoc, California. The phenomenon remains to this day utterly inexplicable and a cornerstone myth of the Post Family legend. It was the first time (although certainly not the last) when Eliot Post's power would be so publicly displayed. *Gods of the First and Twenty-first Century, Volume 11: The Post Family Mythology*, 8th ed. (Zypheron Press Ltd.).

79

Sealiah spurred her Andalusian mare, Incitata, and the beast trampled the servants opening the gate of her villa, Doze Torres. Sparks flew as steel-shod hooves shattered paving stones.

She raced at breakneck speed down the winding mountain road and entered the Valley of Fragrances. She pulled back the reins and paused to see for herself what her guards had reported. Incitata reared back and snorted, angry at being slowed, but nonetheless obeying her mistress.

There. Upon the horizon, the perpetual mists and gloom boiled, and gray glowed silver.

The sun was rising.

In almost any other place this would have been normal. In the Poppy Realms of Hell, however, the sun had been banished. For countless millennia Sealiah's land had lain submerged in twilight gloom. Mist shrouded and fog layered; greenhouse effects trapped the heat. Her orchids thrived in the sweltering humidity and shade. They could not withstand the direct rays of the sun.

She squinted and perceived the beginnings of the dawn—never closer to showing itself since she had taken this place for herself after the Great War.

What else could it be . . . but a prelude to invasion?

Let them try. They would find the Queen of the Poppies more than prepared.

She closed her eyes and felt the distant sun warm her face.

Deceptively comforting. And close. Just over the next hill.

Sealiah gestured at her jungle. Vine and creeper parted. Incitata trotted onto the newly made path through the thicket, and up the opposite hillside.

Sensing its mistress's excitement, the jungle opened fleshy blossoms to her, blanketed the atmosphere with toxic perfumes, and drizzled nectar and streamers of pollen.

As Sealiah crested the hilltop, she pulled Incitata's reins, halting before the brightest spot in the growing dawn. Nothing grew here save a single Hellspiral tree.

Sealiah bit her lip, surprised that the light sought this place. And yet, this made sense: another link to the Post twins, specifically Eliot.

The Hellspiral trees within her domain were a treat for those who had especially offended her. Planted as a tiny helix seedling, the tree quickly grew around its victims. It fed upon suffering, twisting about limbs, caressing, warping, pulling, and stretching, until the embraced was no longer recognizable . . . at least not as human. What remained after the tree had grown to its full height was a bag of flesh and torn sinew and pulverized bone.[71]

Upon this particular tree, so contorted she could barely breathe, were the remains of the mortal once called Julie Marks.

Surrounded by curling runners, a single blue eye upon the tree winked open. "All hail the Mistress of Pain," Julie said, and laughed.

It was defiant laughter, or the laughter of one gone completely mad.

Under normal circumstances, Sealiah would have burned the tree and its occupant for such insolence. She needed, however, much more than a momentary satisfaction.

Sealiah let her blood cool. In truth, there was something to be admired in the girl. Few had ever shown a fraction of this courage.

"Greetings to you, worm food," Sealiah said.

"What do you want?"

71. Devil's hazel (aka Hellspiral). Extinct species. Closest relative was the ornamental corkscrew hazel (*Corylus avellana* "*Contorta*"). According to oral history, the devil came to Ohio in the late eighteenth century to bargain for souls. So successful was his business that he fell into an exhausted sleep under a hazel tree. Old Scratch's evil perverted the tree's seeds, and they sprouted black-barked saplings that covered seven acres in a single night— trapping squirrel and deer and crushing them to death. John Chapman (aka Johnny Appleseed) oversaw the removal of this evil taint. After several failed efforts and two fatalities, he ordered the entire wood burned, and the earth salted and then dug up and cast into the Olentangy River. *St. Hawthorn's Collected Reference of Horticulture in the New World and Beyond*, 1897 (Taylor Institution Library Rare Book Collection, Oxford University).

"To ease your pain."

"Words I have heard before," Julie whispered. "The pain always returns. What's the point?"

"This is different. I offer a road to the source of your suffering, your young Master Eliot."

"Eliot?" All defiance left Julie's tone. She said nothing for a long time, then whispered, "I can hear him. Can you? He's calling me."

The light intensified about the Hellspiral tree and its leaves shuddered.

Sealiah heard the notes of a faraway violin. Straining and yearning, they called from an incalculable distance. It was the song Eliot had composed for the girl, so sad—but then bursting full of life, growing louder, and now filled with . . .

The sun rose.

. . . hope.

Clouds boiled away. The full strength of the sun poured upon the hilltop.

Not beheld in this land for thousands of years, every winged creature took to the air terrified; every crawling thing scurried for cover; tangling vines withered. The Hellspiral tree steamed and popped. It shook its leaves free with a long sigh and died.

The teeth of Julie Marks's mouth curled into a broken smile. Her twisted fingers reached toward the sunlight . . . reached toward her beloved and his music that sounded triumphant throughout the Valley of Fragrances.

Sealiah blinked at the alien sun, furious at this boy who had dared violate her realm, impressed as well that he had the power to do so.

Yes, Eliot Post had tremendous power, but he lacked experience. He had just tipped his hand with this display of sentimentality, a mistake even the most juvenile Infernal would have avoided at all cost.

The light intensified to noontime brilliance and the violin crescendoed, but then the notes trailed off, still playing, but sounding now distant as they Dopplered into silence.

Clouds covered the horizon.

The sun sank back behind the hills, and the light dimmed.

Julie sighed upon the now dead tree, her crooked smile still there, but fading as well.

"Was it everything you wanted it to be?" Sealiah asked.

The last of Julie's smile vanished. "Don't talk to me about him. I've made my choice: Eliot over you. He hasn't forgotten me. There's still hope."

Hope in hell. What an amazing and terrifying concept. Even Sealiah would not torture her minions by giving them hope. It was far too cruel.

"Indeed he has not forgotten."

Julie chuckled. "And that must drive you crazy. Him coming for me like that."

Sealiah could almost pity the girl had she not had a need for her. Blind faith was ever balanced on a razor's edge and so easily toppled by a few choice words.

"I heard his music, yes," Sealiah replied. "And I saw the sunshine. Briefly. But was there more? *Is* he coming? Was he even playing for you?"

"It *was* for me! One day he will come."

Doubt, though, tinged the girl's voice—proof that Julie Marks was not entirely a fool.

"Of course he will," Sealiah said. "As all men do: riding to the rescue of the women they love. Has not every man done thusly for you? Even after *you* left *them*?"

Julie was silent.

"I am sure he appreciates your nobility. I am sure he will serenade you every day. After all, what could distract the young man? Surely no other woman has found him."

Julie's lips quivered. "You lie."

"I only lie to you with the truth, child."

Julie Marks knew the nature of men. She understood that even gallant Eliot Post would not remain so forever. He would play now and then . . . but his passion would dim to memory . . . and he would eventually move on . . . as they all did.

And then Julie would be alone again, her hope-filled heart as broken as her physical form.

Tears corkscrewed down the black trunk of the Hellspiral tree.

Sealiah touched them with their fingertips and tasted the sorrow. "There may yet be a way for you."

Julie's eye blinked away the tears and narrowed suspiciously.

"As the attention span of a man is only as long as his arms, you must *be* with him."

Julie closed her eyes. "Go away," she whispered. "I . . . I can't take any more of this."

"You misunderstand. I came to offer you a new deal."

"Like you did before?" Julie asked indignantly.

"Before my terms were *too* generous. A mistake I never make twice. This time there will be no bargaining, no rolling for terms. You must become my creature, not only your soul, but your heart, your mind—all that you are."

Julie blinked quickly, thinking.

Sealiah admired this: still thinking even after she'd been wracked with pain upon the tree. Still thinking even though her heart had just been broken. It was promising.

"And I will leave hell? Go back to him?"

"This will forever be your home, and I will send you where I need you. But as your primary duties will involve Eliot Post, you will surely see him."

Julie struggled against the trunk of the tree, some instinct in her human body trying to escape the inevitable. The hope still poisoning her.

Eventually, though, she stilled.

And then, after a long time, Julie finally whispered, "I'll do it. Everything I have—just take it."

"Even your hope?" Sealiah whispered.

"It hurts so much." A ragged sigh shuddered out of the girl. "Yes."

"You must be my slave. My plaything, if that is what I desire. Or if need be, my instrument of destruction."

"Yes."

"The Pact of Indomitable Servitude is irrevocable. Once taken, you will be mine forever. But you will see Eliot again, that I promise."

"Yes," Julie whispered so softly that Sealiah barely heard.

"So be it then."

Sealiah touched the Hellspiral tree. The dead wood splintered and crumbled. A pile of skin and broken bones that was Julie Marks fell at her boots.

Incitata snorted and backed several paces away, her equine sense of smell offended.

Sealiah dismounted and knelt so her shadow fell over the child, blocking her even from the half-light, letting the darkness within deepen to utter black.

Sealiah removed her riding gloves and touched her. Julie recoiled and quavered, but it was too late for her now.

Sealiah whispered ancient words . . . words that she had not uttered since she had done this for her Urakabarameel so long ago . . . words she'd thought she would never have occasion to speak again.

Sealiah slit her own flesh with a fingernail, and a single drop of her precious blood pooled and clung to her—so filled with power and life that it refused to part.

She touched this to Julie's corrupted flesh and continued to chant the ritual words.

The green-black drop became a slick that spread over the girl's form, burning away the weakness, consuming all that was imperfect.

Julie Marks screamed.

It would be the last time she would ever do so.

Flesh and bone reformed. Shadows cloaked the shuddering figure.

Sealiah unbuttoned her shirt and removed the emerald nestled within her navel. Carved upon the gem were the runes of her clan. She cleaved a single plane from the stone the way one might deal a card off the top of a deck.

She reached down and pulled up the newly made hand, pressing the sliver of emerald deep into the palm.

Julie fought, clawed at Sealiah, but to no effect.

The emerald took root. It would be a mark upon her to show that she'd been adopted by the clan Sealiah. It was also a gift of power—deadly and fearsome. It would make her one of them.

"Arise," Sealiah commanded.

The lump of shadow at her feet obeyed and stood.

She wore a hooded cloak of the blackest velvet, twining vines and midnight orchids embroidered upon its edges. The creature within had skin flawless and snowy white, so untainted by the rays of the sun that blue-green veins could be seen pulsing underneath. She was muscular without its detracting from her ample femininity. Her nails were blood-red and pointed. Her hair shone platinum and curled in honor of the Hellspiral that had once held her captive. Her eyes were the color of jade and full of an intensity that could captivate the heart of any young man. She was beautiful beyond words.

A tinge of jealousy flickered within Sealiah before she remembered that this was entirely her creation.

"You are Julie Marks no longer," declared Sealiah. "You are reborn, an Infernal agent, and henceforth all shall know you as Jezebel."[72]

---

72. Like the title *Satan, Jezebel* (along with other names, e.g., Cain) serves as an honorific within the Infernal order, and only one being possesses one at any given time. The hierarchical arrangement of such titles, however, remains largely a mystery. *Gods of the First and Twenty-first Century, Volume 13: Infernal Forces*, 8th ed. (Zypheron Press Ltd.).

Jezebel groveled before Sealiah. "Command your most humble slave, mistress."

Sealiah set one hand upon Jezebel's head—to caress or dash upon the stones as she saw fit.

"Stand," Sealiah whispered. "We have a party to attend."

80

TRADE-OFFS

ouis stood on the fore observation deck of his eight-hundred-foot ultra-luxury ocean liner, *Vainglorious*. The sun had just set upon the Indian Ocean, and porpoises played in the bow wave of the vessel.[73]

He had started his welcome-back party a day earlier in Shanghai, and it showed no signs of dissipating; in fact, it had picked up steam and grown into a delicious floating festival of debauchery.

Louis had, however, just received word that the Board of Directors was going to appropriate his ship to convene an emergency meeting.

He nursed his Bloody Mary. He had been drunk, and then this "honor" by the Board had been heaped upon him. It had reminded him that within the family, diminished mental capacities usually preceded the end of one's existence.

So . . . sober from now on he must be.

He turned to the grand ballroom and watched his cousins and their respective entourages dance and drink his priceless champagne and cognac. New china had been flown in by helicopter as every plate had been smashed hours ago in a bout of Greek dancing.

---

73. The *Vainglorious* (if this is the vessel's true name) fails to appear on any nation's maritime registries. It confounds engineers as it appears to be assembled from state-of-the-art equipment (radar arrays and satellite dishes), but also bits that precisely match photographs of the USS *Cyclops* (lost without a trace in the Bermuda Triangle in 1918), the *Graf Zeppelin* (the only Nazi-produced World War II aircraft carrier), the *Andrea Doria* (sunk in 1956), as well as portions believed to be from oil-drilling rigs. The *Vainglorious* has often been described as "the most expensive and the ugliest thing afloat on the seven seas." *Gods of the First and Twenty-first Century, Volume 6: Modern Myths*, 8th ed. (Zypheron Press Ltd.).

Once upon a time, he would have joined them, but now it all seemed pointless. They were only interested in gloating over Beal's fall from power. And no one had so much as whispered congratulations upon *his* return.

Well, mistakes would be made by his happy and drunk cousins, and he would gladly take advantage.

Louis spotted Mulciber at the buffet table, poking the finger sandwiches, but not actually eating any.

He waved at the curmudgeon.

Mulciber surprised him and smiled back. In the old days, he would've attempted to plant a dagger in Louis's back before such an acknowledgment.

Beal's death apparently had everyone in a good mood. After all, what was more stimulating than fighting over the scraps of the former chairman of the Board's power?

Only, there was nothing to fight over.

Beal's power now thrummed through Louis's veins—the result of a masterful plan where Louis had used his children as bait. What would his cousins do if they knew? Tear him to pieces in a fit of jealousy? Or applaud his daring?

Louis curled his fist. Yes, Beal's power was there, although not all of it. Some had dissipated into the aether, the normal tiny losses from any transfer of power.

But Eliot and Fiona had been caught in the transfer pattern as well. They had to have tasted a portion of Beal's soul as well. That could complicate things in the future.

Oz staggered on deck and collapsed on the railing next to him, reeking of wine.

"Deep in thought, O glorious Morning Star?"

A lace bandage covered Oz's face. He wore a costume of a seventeenth-century French courtier with frilled collar, gold brocade vest, juxtaposed with silver spandex pants and the platform boots of a rock star.

He made Louis feel decidedly conservative in his diamond studs and Armani.

"How can anyone think with all of this?" Louis waved his hand at the party raging about them.

"There's more to celebrate than you know," Oz slurred. "This just got posted on our newsgroup."

He handed Louis a palm computer, sticky with caviar.

Stock prices and headlines streamed across the bottom. Plastered in the center of the screen, however, was:

FOR IMMEDIATE RELEASE. *All heed, petition, and be judged.* Narro, audio, perceptum. *This is a legal notice of status change. The League of Immortals Council of Elders rules that Miss Fiona Paige Post be inducted into the Order of the Celestial Rose. Master Eliot Zachariah Post has been transferred into the Brotherhood of Immortal Heroes. Said changes are immediate and irrevocable. Adulation and wonder at these glorious events! In accordance with the Pactum Pax Immortalis no external parties may interfere with the legal, social, or political affairs of the subjects, which now fall under the jurisdiction and protection of . . .*

"Bold of the League, no?" Oz said.

Louis didn't, in truth, know quite what to think, so he donned his armored smile. "Did you expect anything less?"

Oz frowned at this casual reply. He had obviously come to extract information from Louis, who had adopted the air of knowing all things related to his offspring.

"They say that the girl actually *fought* Beal hand to hand . . ." Oz's voice trailed off and his face slackened as something new caught his attention.

Louis followed his gaze and spotted Abigail striding purposefully toward them.

So the Board had finally gathered for business—which from the look on Abigail's face might include something particularly nasty for Oz. Would the first order of business be to remove Oz from the Board? So obviously weakened, Oz had been a fool to show himself. Perhaps his vacated seat would even be offered to Louis.

Oz dumped the contents of his wineglass overboard. "You must excuse me, Cousin. I appear to be dry." He scurried off.

"Abigail," Louis said, and threw open his arms, as much a gesture of greeting as an assurance that he had no desire to engage in combat.

She wore ropes of gold that wound about her slender albino form. The ropes seemed to twitch as if alive. Scarab beetles the size of baseballs nestled upon her shoulders and waved their antennae aggressively at Louis.

She presented a childlike smile, which he knew could mean anything from pleasure at seeing him . . . to the prelude of a vicious bite.

Much to Louis's relief, though, she offered him her hand to kiss.

With any other Infernal this would have been an invitation to take advantage. But one did not casually entice a Destroyer (there was so much blood involved), so Louis took her tiny hand and kissed it in the most gentlemanly manner.

"Rogue," she whispered, blushing slightly. "How I have missed you. We must make up for lost time."

"We must," Louis breathed, feeling his pulse race.

He stopped himself. Aligning with dear little Abby was dangerous under any circumstances, but doubly so now since he did not know the politics of the moment. Until he understood better, such pairings could be more perilous than usual.

He changed the subject. "Have you heard the news?"

Abigail's smile deflated slightly and she sighed. "Oh, yes . . . that. The entire Board is drunk with the irony of it."

"Indeed," Louis stated, now fishing for details himself. "The League declaring the twins as their own. Legally binding. As if that means anything."

The ship tilted and rolled upon a perfectly calm ocean.

Louis glanced about and spotted the source of the disturbance: lumbering toward them from the buffet tables was Lev.

Abigail scowled at him and made a little shooing-away motion, which Lev ignored.

"Louis!" Lev draped a massive arm around him. "It's good to see you again, buddy."

Louis did his best not to flinch. Lev wore none of the signature jewelry about his walruslike neck, although he did have on the same polyester jumpsuit that Louis had seen him in sixteen years ago. From the thickening atmosphere, it seemed that Lev had yet to wash the thing.

Lev carried a silver platter heaped with hors d'oeuvres and steaming meat. He stuffed his face with morsels from the tray, then remembered his manners and offered the tray to Abigail.

She took one fiber of meat, sniffed it, and tasted a tiny nibble. "A little gamy. What is it?"

Mouth full of food, and grinning, Lev replied, "Our former chairman of the Board."

He offered some to Louis.

Louis held up a hand. "Thank you, but no. I only eat the ones I love."

"Suit yourself," Lev said. "You talking about the League? Looks like they just helped us figure out what we wanted to know."

"I agree," Abigail said, lowering her voice. "Assassinating Beal and now legally declared Immortal? What more proof do we require that they can break the neutrality treaty?"

Dual lineage.

That's what they were talking about. How thick of Louis not to see this before. He now understood why all were so interested in his children. They were going to use Eliot and Fiona to attack the League—and possibly more than that.

Much more.

He had to carefully think through all the ramifications. And how to best use them to his advantage.

Ashmed joined them, curling one arm through Abby's.

Louis had been so deep in thought that he had not seen Ashmed approach. The Architect of Evil wore a charcoal gray suit and a sterling silver tie. Certainly underdressed for a party, but perfect for radiating the necessary authority at a Board meeting.

Ashmed's style was timeless, though, subtle and effective. He had been careful to remain one step away from the center of power and thus had few enemies. The time was right for him to become chairman of the Board, if that was what he desired.

"Louis," he said, clasping Louis's hand before he could retract it. The handshake was mechanical, and he released Louis—but not before he gave him a squeeze of power to demonstrate his superiority. Ashmed nodded to Lev.

Louis continued to smile, but his mind raced.

How friendly they all were. How wrong this all was. There should have been at least a brawl by now. Was it the allure of war and total destruction that had pulled the clans together?

Change was in the air: perhaps the end of the old world and the beginning of a new mortal realm dominated by them. For some reason this notion made Louis ill at ease.

"We are ready to convene the Board," Ashmed told them. "Louis, I would like you to join us."

"Of course."

Abigail and Lev exchanged a knowing glance.

"I better grab some food and a couple of drinks," Lev muttered. "A guy could starve while everyone talks." He left them.

Abigail smiled at Louis, graciously withdrew from Ashmed's arm, then also departed.

Louis started after her, but Ashmed touched his shoulder. "A moment, Cousin," he whispered. "Someone else wishes a word with you."

He pointed to a curtained gazebo set on the opposite side of the Olympic-size pool.

"Take care," Ashmed said, then walked away, leaving Louis to ponder his vague warning.

Louis was relieved. He had expected *some* confrontation. It was unnatural to be among his kin for so long without spilled blood. Still, such an obvious trap to walk into, and yet, he yearned to prove himself.

He had taken precautions for this eventuality. He was armed, armored, and was he not the Master Deceiver? Charlatan extraordinaire?

He strode over the teak deck to the gazebo, every step his confidence building.

Let this waiting aggressor *try* to lay a hand on him. He laughed, delighted with himself.

Louis slowed, however, three paces before the parted curtain of the gazebo. He smelled the overwhelming scent of vanilla and poppies.

The shapely silhouette of Sealiah appeared in the opening. "Come in. There is business to discuss." Her tone was chilled malevolence.

There was history between them: millennia of romance and blood and all-out war. Before Louis had found true love, he and Sealiah had danced in an eternal orbit of hatred and lust.

Sealiah was one of the few who could surprise him. Louis should have suspected this subterfuge was hers, though; she was the most obvious of his kin to have reason for a vendetta. Had he not killed her precious Uri?

At least this would not be boring.

He took a deep breath and stepped inside.

The green velvet curtain of the gazebo fell closed behind him. Upon a table covered with red linen, a candelabra with six silver candles shone.

Sealiah stood on the far side with a girl attendant. Sealiah wore lace finery that looked part wedding gown, part nightgown, and all allure. Her girl was cloaked in black, which contrasted with her platinum locks and pale skin.

Louis saw no runes upon the wooden floor or the curtains. He sensed nothing in the shadows. Still, what other purpose could Sealiah have for calling him other than a trap?

Her attendant was a lovely thing, though. Distractingly so. She was

more blond and beautiful than Sealiah preferred her servants, and too perfect to be entirely human. Perhaps *she* was the trap?

He had seen her before, but the specifics of when and where eluded him.
He tilted his signet ring and let the cabochon diamond scan her for later
study.

Louis gave the Queen of the Poppies the slightest of bows—not out of
disrespect, but rather because he had no intention of lowering his guard before her. The ultimate compliment.

"Destroy everything you touch," Louis said.

"Lies and salutations, Cousin," Sealiah offered.

Something rustled under the table.

Louis smiled, but tensed, and his left hand snaked to the sheath that
held Saliceran.

"Let us be quick with this." Sealiah narrowed her eyes. "My blood heats
at the mere sight of you, Louis."

What could Louis say that would *not* provoke her? He was not fool
enough to deny that he killed Uri, so instead he simply stated, "He died
well."

This was true enough.

Uri died trying to double-cross Louis on her behalf. What more could
the giant of a puppy desire?

Sealiah sighed and seemed to relax a tiny bit. She nodded to her assistant. "Jezebel, show our cousin what we have brought him."

The girl dragged from under the table a plastic animal carrier. Within
the darkness of the container, a pair of yellow-gold eyes blinked at Louis.

"You have something of mine," Sealiah said. "I want it back."

Of course, she meant Saliceran, a weapon that could kill Infernal and
Immortal alike. But no matter what horrors she had inside that cage, Louis
would never willingly part with the legendary blade. Did she think him a
fool?

Sealiah ran a fingernail over the carrier and made a hideous scratching
noise.

The thing inside whimpered.

"When you left us," Sealiah said, her face now a mask of disdain, "I took
the liberty of caring for your 'animal.'"

She turned the cage so the door faced him.

A mangy, black feline hissed and spat, puffing so one could not tell
where its midnight fur ended and the shadows began.

Amberflaxus . . . Louis's cat.

He smiled to hide his panic. Amberflaxus was the only thing in the universe Louis could even remotely have called a friend. He hadn't considered it a possibility the animal had survived his fall to mortal-dom.

"I thought about keeping it for myself," Sealiah cooed. "You know how I love cats."

The only way Sealiah loved cats was diced, stir-fried, and with wontons.

"Well," Louis tried to say nonchalantly, "you don't want *that* animal. It is impossible. Pees on everything. Scratches the furniture. Has to be let out at all hours of the evening."

"Just like its master. The blade, Louis. Set it on the table and let us trade."

She wanted to trade straight across?

So, the calculating Sealiah was not infallible, after all. She had no idea who the cat actually was . . . or what it could do.

Louis expelled a great pretended sigh.

He made a show of looking pained as he took the sheathed blade and set it next to the cage. One hand still on the hilt of Saliceran, he opened the door, reached inside, and withdrew squirming Amberflaxus.

The cat growled, clawed at his arms, and flattened its ears.

Louis stroked the creature, and it bit his hand for his trouble.

"Yeeeees," Louis roughly reassured the animal, "there, there."

Sealiah drew Saliceran, inspected the broken blade, then resheathed it and secreted the weapon.

"No threats?" Louis asked. "A warning to never cross paths? Not even a casual stab at my heart?"

"I did not know you had one left. No, no threats or violence. We have a Board meeting yet to attend, and a long, long dance together before our music ends."

Louis didn't like the sound of that. Sealiah had plans for him. She always did. He made a mental note to become celibate the first chance he had. Perhaps even a eunuch.

"I look forward to it." He bowed to her. This time, lower and more magnificently than before.

Amberflaxus tried to wriggle free of Louis, but he held tight.

Her attendant parted the rear curtain for her mistress. Sealiah and then the girl stepped through, leaving Louis alone with his pet.

He stroked the creature's head and it finally calmed . . . although still clawing at the sleeve of his tuxedo.

"Wretched animal," Louis said, and gave it a good shake. "Stop that. There's much to see to. Family business."

The cat stilled.

Why did Louis even care? Part of him wanted to follow the great Satan who had become disgusted and left the families long ago.

And yet, were there not a few things here that still compelled him? He had once loved, truly loved, a woman who had been his equal. She hated him now, but did that matter? He had proven love was possible for one such as himself. Perhaps lightning would strike twice.

And there were also his children to consider.

He stepped outside the gazebo. He ignored the festivities and watched the stars brighten in the night sky over the sea.

Did he love Fiona and Eliot? Already, he was beginning to forget how he had felt for them as his mortal self had watched them walk to work every day. Perhaps only as a urine-drenched waste of flesh could one appreciate such things.

Had he not gambled their lives to capture Beal's power? Even used his son as bait? Were those the acts of a "loving" father?

Or had it all been a desperate venture to stand united with his fledgling family against terrible odds . . . and save them all?

But did he *love* them? Did he even know what that word meant? Or was it just the power that Eliot and Fiona represented that attracted him so?

Could not both things, love *and* exploitation, exist side by side?

Louis frowned and ceased petting Amberflaxus.

The cat nudged his hand and purred.

He might have been the Great Deceiver to the rest of the world, but Louis could never lie to himself (perhaps his greatest failing). A choice was inevitable. One day he would *have to* decide between his love for Eliot and Fiona and his using them to rule the Infernal clans.

He did not have to decide, though, this very second.

Louis found a silver tray with bubbling champagne flutes. He raised a glass to toast and wished upon his star—Venus reigning over the darkening horizon—that his son and daughter would be happy, if for nothing else the time being.

Let them enjoy a moment of life . . . before all hell broke loose.

81

WARRANTS

Audrey sat in a folding chair, her family surrounding her. She had never felt more miserable.

Not even after parting with Louis when she had discovered he had tricked her and his love all those months was just a game—this was a thousand times that pain. He had been so obviously guilty. Today, though, she must condemn the innocent . . . her own.

"I have not taken this action lightly," she whispered.

She could not even look at them. This was so hard.

"As soon as they accepted their place among us," she told them, "Cornelius and I researched the ancient codes—from the Genesis Tablet to the Pactum Pax Immortalis. Our conclusion: we face annihilation."

Audrey hated herself for sounding so weak. It would not make her case more compelling. With so much at stake she could not afford the luxury of self-pity.

She finally looked up and straightened, feeling her strength return.

The Council had reconvened inside Henry's Gray Lotus Room.

The unadorned concrete walls, low ceiling, and bare lightbulbs hid the location's sophistication. Henry had renovated and made a personal meditation chamber out of what had once been a nuclear command center buried in the heartland of America. Beyond were layers of counterelectronics, anti-aetherics, and tons of rock that prevented any form of eavesdropping.

It was the perfect location for a secret meeting to determine the fate of the world.

The Council sat in folding chairs in the otherwise empty room. Henry,

Kino, Aaron, Cornelius, Gilbert, and her sisters, Lucia and Dallas, had come to listen and judge.

"'Annihilation,'" Henry said, exhaling a cloud of blue smoke. "Really, I thought *I* was overly dramatic at times." He sounded hollow, though, his denial a vain attempt to lighten the mood.

Henry did not look well. He wore the wrinkled, three-day-old remains of his tuxedo, and his nicotine-stained fingers trembled.

Dallas stood from her seat and marched to a corner, folding her long arms over her chest. "Don't try and change the subject," she demanded, stamping her foot. "I can't believe you're doing this, Audrey. I'm your own sister!"

Dallas looked ridiculous in her little mock-uniform minidress and green beret. Who was she trying to impress with such attire?

"No one thinks you're taking this seriously," Audrey coldly told her. "It's nothing personal."

"It's *all* personal," Dallas said, raising her voice. "I love them, and I'm going to do whatever it takes to protect them."

"Alas," Lucia whispered, "that is the trouble." She straightened the pleats of her business suit. "We need clear, unbiased thinking on this Council."

Lucia sat next to Audrey, and they presented a rare unified front. The two sisters never agreed on anything, but even Lucia understood the gravity of this situation . . . or perhaps it was Audrey who had finally understood.

"Let us proceed with the vote and get this over with," Lucia continued. "All in favor of keeping Dallas on the ruling Council, raise your hand."

Dallas raised her hand, as well as Aaron.

Aaron wore his fighting clothes: jeans, cowboy boots, and a T-shirt proclaiming VIVA LUCHA LIBRE.[74]

"Against?" Lucia asked.

Kino, Lucia, Gilbert—and surprisingly even Cornelius, who steadfastly remained neutral in all family matters—raised their hands.

"I abstain." Henry's gaze dropped to the floor.

Dallas held her head high. "This is a mistake."

"It has been decided," Lucia said. "Remain and listen if you must, but refrain from addressing the Council unless you are first recognized."

Dallas opened her mouth, then closed it and beamed pure hatred at her sisters.

---

74. *Lucha libre* means "free fighting" in Spanish and refers to professional wrestling (usually masked) within Spanish-speaking countries.—Editor.

Audrey felt sorry for her. It was not Dallas's fault that she felt too much. On this particular subject, how could anyone not? Her only flaw was that she was blinded by it.

So much for the easily removed opposition.

Audrey glanced at Aaron and he unflinchingly returned her gaze. The real question now was, could the Lord of War be convinced to see past his passions? This decision *had to be* unanimous.

Her gaze darted to Kino, and he nodded, understanding.

Kino stood, towering over all. The Keeper of the Doorways of Death inhaled deeply and faced Aaron. "We require a strategy for this. My friend, I like not the conclusion any more than you." Kino's mask of dispassion faltered. "The children have impressed me, as well, and softened a heart I thought long impervious to such things."

Gilbert set a hand on Aaron's shoulder. "But the facts cannot be ignored."

Aaron shrugged off Gilbert's hand. "Facts," he spat back. "Rules. You twist them into the things you want."

Cornelius also stood. Only half as tall as Kino, this display, however, was more dramatic. Cornelius was ever quiet, consulting his charts and timelines, almost invisible among such overwhelming personalities. He was, though, the oldest of them . . . and perhaps the Maker of Time was the most powerful as well.

"You are correct," Cornelius told Aaron. "They often do just as you say. It is logic, however, pure and mechanical, not politics, which brings me to the same conclusion."

Aaron closed his eyes and tilted back into his seat, his anger draining. "Very well, tell me again, Old One."

"The two subjects—" Cornelius said.

"Eliot and Fiona," Aaron interrupted. "They are not 'subjects.' They have names."

Cornelius looked embarrassed a moment, but recovered. "Of course, forgive my error. We extended to Fiona an invitation to join the impressive Order of the Celestial Rose and to Eliot the equally impressive Brotherhood of Immortal Heroes. When they accepted, it constituted a binding legal contract."

"Just words," Aaron murmured.

"No," Gilbert said. "Accepting the tokens of these offices is an act prescribed by ancient law. No mortal or Infernal can touch these items . . . only an Immortal."

"So they are Immortals." Aaron stared into the distance. There was understanding in his voice . . . but no joy.

Kino sat next to him, leaning forward. "But there is the matter of the Infernal lord Beelzebub."

"I witnessed them standing over his corpse," Audrey said. "Just slain, with Fiona holding the instrument of his death."

"They could not have done that if they were one of us," Lucia said. "The treaty encompasses *all* Immortals—in or out of the League. It is binding and absolute."

"So they could not have done both things," Henry said, looking hopeful.

"Unless," Aaron whispered, "they are Immortal *and* Infernal."

Cornelius sat.

A long stretch of silence unprecedented in the history of the League Council followed. Within the hermetically sealed room, the quiet was maddening, and Audrey wanted to scream. She imagined it was the pause before Armageddon.

Henry finally broke the stillness. "So they are something new. Like the gods were to Titans before them." He cast an apologetic glance at Cornelius. "I'm sorry to bring this up. I know how it pains you."

Cornelius held up his hands and looked away, but nodded, indicating that Henry should continue.

"The Titans had to be destroyed," Henry said. "It was kill or be killed—but those times were different."

"Different, yes," Kino said. "We are in more peril now. We have not only Infernals to contend with, but must stop a potential schism within our own family."

A war with the fallen angels could be cataclysmic. The League would only prevail if they worked together. But Audrey knew if they divided . . . even over such a noble cause . . . it meant their end.

Lucia removed two alabaster scroll cases from her jacket. She shook out the vellum sheets within and smoothed them.

Aaron glanced at the titles of the documents, and the color drained from his face.

Henry looked at the documents as well, closed his eyes, and sighed.

"Aaron, old comrade," Kino said, "you are right to be disdainful of our politics. It has ever been the League's greatest weakness. It makes us slow to act." Kino tapped on the two pages for emphasis. "This predecision circumvents all politics and gives us the decisiveness . . . if it becomes necessary."

"Or would you have us debate this all over again if and when the critical moment is upon us?" Lucia asked.

"You know the might of the Infernal armies better than any," Audrey whispered. "What chance do we stand divided?"

"You of all people," Aaron said. "How can *you* advocate this?"

Audrey felt as if she were being torn apart inside. "How can I stand by and not act?"

Lucia took a silver fountain pen from her pocket, hesitated only a moment, then signed both documents. "There. I've gone first. We must all sign, otherwise there will be dissent within the League."

"No," Dallas pleaded. "Please, Sister, don't."

"You were warned," Lucia said, leveling a lethal gaze at Dallas. "Breaking our rules of decorum—"

Henry intervened between the two women. "Let it pass, Lucia. We all feel for the children."

He turned and examined the parchments. Tears welled in Henry's eyes and fell freely. He worked his mouth, trying to saying something . . . but could not speak.

He took the pen and signed both documents.

Henry returned to his seat, set his face in his hands, and quietly wept.

Cornelius signed next, wordlessly.

Gilbert paused only to glance at Aaron, but then he, too, signed.

Kino made his mark. He handed the pages and pen to Aaron.

Aaron read every word, blinking furiously to keep his focus. He set the pages down.

"Audrey, if this is what you want, I will do it. I know the strategy is sound, but in my heart . . . I, too, have always sought to protect that which I love. But this . . . this . . . I cannot understand."

"Do it," Audrey gently told Aaron.

Pen clenched tightly in his hand, Aaron finally relented and signed.

He deflated and dropped the pages onto Audrey's lap. He staggered to Dallas and wrapped his arm about her to steady them both.

All eyes turned to Audrey.

Trembling, she took pen in hand.

Everything hung in balance now. Annihilation from their enemies. A civil war that could break the League.

It was her fault this had happened, and her responsibility to make this right. She had brought Eliot and Fiona into this world.

How odd, a week ago she had vowed to kill any who threatened her children. She had severed her ties of love, yes, but there remained maternal duty and vigilance, one of the most ancient of familial instincts.

What had so radically changed her perceptions?

Eliot and Fiona had. When she had seen them standing with their father—the most despicable and cowardly Louis Piper, the Great Deceiver—she had finally realized they were *his* children as well, part diabolical and, for all she knew, legitimate heirs to the Prince of Darkness's Infernal domains.

Or could they be more than mere god or angel? Could they be something different, the heralds of a new age? An Age of Enlightenment . . . or one that signaled the End of Days?

The League had to be prepared for *either* contingency.

So why could she not sign?

How she wished they were simply Eliot and Fiona Post, still living in the apartment where she could teach them and be near them, protect them, and watch them grow up like ordinary children.

That was a futile dream, though; it had always been.

If there was a way—any way—for them to survive, she would do everything in her power to give them that chance. She knew, however, they would have to balance upon a razor-edged path between the two families to accomplish this.

She could deny it no longer. She set the point of the pen on Fiona's contract. A dot of ink welled upon the vellum.

"Only if it becomes necessary," she whispered. "Only if *absolutely* necessary."

She made her mark, an infinity symbol and a line through it.

Then to the document with Eliot's name.

She heard his music somewhere, tremulous and pleading, but it faded. It must only have been her imagination . . . or perhaps her guilty conscience.

"I am so sorry."

She signed his contract as well.

All that remained was to fill in the date and the contracts would become legal and binding—an irrevocable declaration from the League of Immortals.

That time might never come, but if they needed this terrible power, it would be ready.

For the first time in millennia, tears blurred Audrey's vision and made the room swim before her. She held them back, though, blinked, and her gaze fell to the document's hideous title:

WARRANT OF DEATH

82

ONE LAST BIRTHDAY SURPRISE

Fiona hefted a cardboard box and slammed it onto the lift gate of the moving van.

"I hate this," she told her brother.

"Me, too." Eliot wiped the sweat from his face. "Cee said no movers, though. She doesn't trust them."

"Figures," Fiona muttered.

Eliot had greeted her the moment she stepped off the bus. He'd been moving boxes. Stacked in the parking lot of the motel were hundreds and hundreds of them. Six moving vans sat with open panels, waiting to be filled.

There was no one else here so, of course, Fiona had to help. She hadn't even had a chance to change out of her good vacation clothes.

She'd only been gone five days, but Eliot seemed like a stranger—and it wasn't just his new glasses (which made him look older and distinguished). He was quiet, as if he had a million new secrets to keep.

He still annoyed her, though. *That* hadn't changed. Just being near him, the heat from his body added to the sweltering last-day-of-summer temperature.

"Where're my clothes again?" She peeled the tape off a box.

"Not there," Eliot said, irritated. "Cee has every box coded. The stuff from your room is marked with green circles."

Green circles, red stars, black checks—why couldn't they just have written her name on them?

Eliot hopped off the lift gate. He held out a hand to help her down.

Fiona ignored it and jumped down on her own.

She brushed off her new dress, one Robert had bought for her, but only managed to smear dirt over the beautiful batik pattern. She sighed. Cee with her homemade soaps was sure to ruin the fabric.

Robert. She wished he were here.

He hadn't dropped her off. He said he had to "lay low" for a while. With the Council still mad at him, she didn't blame him.

He told her that he'd catch up with her in a few days . . . but Fiona wondered if she would *ever* see him again.

Eliot searched through the piles, found a box, and pulled it toward her.

How Cee had ever gotten most of the books out of Oakwood Apartments before the place had burned to the ground, Fiona couldn't figure.

"This one is yours." Eliot dragged the box next to her.

Fiona ripped it open. Sandwiched between several dusty books was her antique globe. She ran a hand over the world's wrinkled surface and smiled.

She was glad her globe had made it. She would've missed it. It had represented her desire to travel to new places. That wish had come true . . . with more unexpected consequences than she had ever dreamed possible.

"Here, look." Eliot pulled out *Marcellus Masters's Practical First Aid and Surgical Guide* from the box. "Cool, huh?"

He looked as if he had found buried pirate treasure.

Nothing about this was cool. Their old home destroyed. Now they were moving. How could her brother still be such a child?

"What's the matter," he asked, "dyseidetic?"

It was a subtle insult. Dyseidetic was the visual subform of dyslexia. In other words, Eliot had asked if she had a hard time reading due to brain impairment—as if she didn't read *twice* as fast as he did.

Fiona hands clenched and she ground her teeth.

Her anger crashed through her like a tidal wave. She let it swell . . . then fade. She had learned to wait. The red tide of primal blood that washed through her emotions came with increasing regularity since the night she'd fought Beelzebub.

She knew, though, that if she waited a few seconds, the rage would pass.

She wasn't angry at Eliot. He was just being her brother . . . although that in itself was still extremely annoying.

So what *had* made her so angry?

Maybe it had been *Marcellus Masters's Practical First Aid and Surgical*

Guide. Here they were moving a small library of books, still doing everything Audrey and Cee told them to do like good little boys and girls.

Hadn't *anything* changed?

She took the slender volume from her brother and ran her hands over its
worn leather cover. She'd read this at least three times. She had learned all
the emergency techniques that any good eighteenth-century battlefield
medic should know. A few weeks ago, she thought she would never need it.

"Hardly dyseidetic," she told Eliot. "Although I think I might have brain
damage from being so near you, 1,4-diaminobutane toxicosis."

Eliot tilted his head, thinking that one through.

This was familiar ground for Fiona. Trading insults was like visiting a
long-forgotten childhood (even though it had just been a few days since it
had all seemed normal). The verbal sparring broke the ice, though. Fiona
almost felt as if she'd come home.

She set the book inside the box and smoothed back the tape.

"Okay," Eliot said. "I give. What's 1,4-diaminobutane?"

"You'll need to reread *Marmat's Guide to Autopsy*. 1,4-diaminobutane is
also called putrescine. It's produced by decomposing flesh—it also con-
tributes to halitosis."

Eliot pursed his lips, frustrated at not knowing this.

"Halitosis . . . that's bad breath."

"I know what halitosis is," he muttered.

Vocabulary insult was a trivial, stupid, little kid's game . . . but it *still*
felt good to win.

Eliot nonchalantly picked up a clipboard with the moving van's mani-
fest, doing his best to look as if losing the first round didn't matter.

"This van's half-full," he said. "We'll need to leave some space. It's supposed to pick up some new furniture along the way."

"Along the way to where?" Fiona asked, leaning closer.

He pointed to the bottom of the sheet. "There's the address."

The street name didn't mean anything to Fiona, but the city was San
Francisco. "We're moving to the city?"

San Francisco wouldn't be like Del Sombra. There would be thousands,
hundreds of thousands, of people—exotic restaurants—libraries—museums!
Her enthusiasm, however, chilled. A hundred thousand people? All of them
strangers?

"Maybe we're not going there," Eliot said. "San Francisco is a port. Our
stuff could be getting shipped to anywhere in the world."

"I wish someone had asked us where *we* want to go."

Cee emerged from room number 4 of the motel. Blinking in the sunlight, she called, "Eliot . . . oh, Fiona—you're back!" She waved a lace handkerchief to make sure they saw her. "Come, children. It's all almost ready."

Cee looked the same in her homemade sepia dress from the turn of the century. Some things would never change, and Fiona took comfort in that.

She and her brother started to walk toward the room, until Eliot tried to edge ahead of her, then Fiona broke into a run—left him behind in her dust and thoroughly trounced him getting to the door first.

She paused, panting.

Inside it was dark and her eyes had yet to adjust. "What's almost ready?"

Cee moved into the bathroom, shutting the door behind her. Fiona got a glimpse inside of the good china plates and silverware on the counter.

"Oh, no," Eliot said behind her.

"She's not going to cook, is she?" Fiona whispered.

Cee left the bathroom, hiding whatever was in there with great care. She trundled to Fiona and hugged her with shaking arms. "Oh, my dove, how I've missed you. Five days seemed like forever. Why, you have a tan. It looks . . . wonderful. And a new dress?" She looked suspicious as she examined it. "Well, I can let it out a little here—and let down that scandalous hem."

Cee pulled Fiona into the room. "Come. Come. Sit."

Eliot opened the curtains to let in some light.

Fiona did a double take. The bed had been removed from the room. In its place were four chairs and a table with their old tablecloth and lace doilies. A dresser had been pushed by the window and piled high with books.

Cee had done an excellent job of re-creating the dining room of their old apartment.

"It's . . . it's perfect," Fiona breathed.

"I thought you might want to see the place one more time," Cee whispered. "To properly say good-bye."

Fiona hugged her. "Oh, thank you, Cee. Thank you!"

Fiona hadn't realized until now how much she was going to miss the old place and her old life. She had known nothing else. Moving forward into the unknown, she felt ungrounded—and although she hadn't realized it until just now, scared, too.

"This is great." Eliot ran his hand over the dresser and read the titles of the stacked books. "Hey, here are the books we got for our birthday!" He pulled out his H. G. Wells, *The Time Machine,* and then handed Fiona her Jules Verne.

Fiona held *From the Earth to the Moon* with great reverence. "I almost forgot."

"The best is yet to come," Cee told them.

"What do you mean?" Fiona turned just in time to see someone step into the room's open doorway. She didn't have to see her face to know who it was.

"Hello, Mother," Fiona said.

Audrey replied, "Happy birthday, children."

Eliot saw that Audrey wore a simple white cotton dress. He'd never seen her wear white before, and for some reason it gave him a chill. With her pale skin and silver hair backlit by the sun she looked as if she belonged in some ancient tapestry.

The only word he could think to describe her was *regal.* As if she were a goddess.

She stepped into the room and the illusion partially faded.

Audrey may have been all those things . . . but she was still his mother, wasn't she?

Yes.

He rushed to her with open arms . . . hesitated just before he made contact because she just stood there, looking confused at his display of affection.

Then she opened her arms and drew him to her.

It was *almost* a real hug. If he closed his eyes, he could imagine it was full of warmth and caring.

She rocked him back and forth, then gently pushed him back. She went to Fiona and embraced her as well.

The gesture was tender, but different from the way she had hugged Eliot. Some barrier was between Fiona and Audrey—nothing bad, just a layer of mutual respect that hadn't been there before.

"Where were you?" Eliot asked.

"Making travel arrangements," Audrey replied. "We can't live in a motel for the rest of our lives, can we? Thank you, and you, too, Cecilia, for getting everything arranged and into the vans."

"So where are we going?" Eliot asked.

Cee cleared her throat.

"Ah, yes," Audrey said, "I believe Cecilia has something for you two before we discuss that."

Cee beamed and went to the room's bathroom, returning with a cake box. "Happy birthday, my darlings!"

Fiona's face went slack seeing the box, but Cee quickly opened it and showed her what was inside: carrot cake.

"Don't worry," Cee whispered. "I know. No chocolate."

Fiona looked immensely relieved.

Cee set the cake on the table. From her pocket she produced thirty candles, which she then carefully screwed into the cream-cheese frosting.

"We never finished our party," Audrey told them. "I couldn't let your birthdays pass without a proper celebration."

Eliot couldn't believe they had remembered.

"Now for fire." Cee opened a book of matches, ripped one out, and struck it with a shaking hand. The flame reflected in her dark eyes.

Eliot said, "Maybe you better—"

"Let me do it." Audrey smiled, and added, "Please, if you would, Cecilia?"

Cee nodded and gave her the lit match.

Audrey quickly touched it to all the candles, lighting them. The match burned close to her fingers, until she squeezed the flame to a hissing ember.

"Now," Audrey said, turning to Eliot and Fiona, "time to make *new* birthday wishes."

Eliot and Fiona stepped forward. He looked at his sister. What was she going to wish for? More time with Robert? New clothes?

No, he had a feeling she wanted the same thing he did.

She gave him a knowing nod, and they leaned forward, inhaling.

Eliot wished for a mother that would adore him, a father who would be proud of him, a sister to tease and to share his adventures with, and a dozen score of aunts and uncles and cousins . . . a family, a real family.

Sure, it would never be perfect. But what family was?

They blew at the candles.

The flames guttered and went out—save for one that winked back to life. Fiona and Eliot quickly puffed again and extinguished it.

Close enough.

"Let's eat," Fiona said. "I'm hungry for the first time in weeks."

"Wonderful." Cee clapped her hands in delight. "I'll get the plates."

"Wait," Audrey said. "There's more."

"Oh, silly me," Cee said. "I'm so addled. How could I forget the most important part?" She opened a dresser drawer and withdrew two packages wrapped in brown paper.

"The rest of your presents," Audrey told them.

Cee set the packages on the table, one before Eliot, the other before Fiona. Cee's gift-wrapping skills left a little to be desired: they were full-size grocery bags stapled shut.

Excitement fluttered in Eliot's stomach. He hefted the parcel. It was light and soft. Clothes. Had to be. From the volume of the bag—almost full—there must be a full laundry load's worth of stuff inside.

With so much changing could these actually be store-bought clothes? Maybe even jeans so he could look normal . . . possibly even cool?

"Go on," urged Cee. "I can't wait to see your faces."

Eliot tried to carefully undo the staples and save the bag.

Fiona tore the top off hers. She brightened as she reached inside. "So soft," she murmured, but then confusion creased her face.

Eliot gave up and ripped open his bag, too.

Just as he thought: store-bought clothes.

There were neatly pressed and folded slacks, both pleated khaki and navy blue woolens. No jeans, though. Still, a million times better than what Cee had sewn for them over the years.

He felt a little guilty about that thought. Cee *did* try her best.

"I don't understand," Fiona said as she pulled out stockings, shoes, tartan skirts, and white dress shirts.

Eliot also had white dress shirts, long- and short-sleeved, as well as leather loafers, and even new socks. At the bottom of the bag was a navy blue blazer.

He pulled the blazer out. Embroidered upon the breast pocket was a heraldic device. Among frills and curlicues sat a shield, and balanced atop the shield were a helmet and sword. Below the shield was a dragon curled up asleep. The center part held a snarling wolf head, a winged chevron, and a golden scarab beetle.

Under all this were the words THE PAXINGTON INSTITUTE. EST. 1642.

It felt as if the bottom had dropped out of the room. While Eliot was delighted with the new clothes . . . something was very wrong about them.

Fiona held out a girl's jacket as well, examining an identical insignia. She glanced at him, worried.

"Uh . . . they're nice," he said. "Really nice. But what are they?"

"Uniforms," Audrey answered with a smile.

"Uniforms?" Fiona whispered.

Everything was changing again. Eliot had just gotten his bearings, and now what?

"I thought after all you've been through," Audrey explained, "after you had bested Infernal and Immortal alike, that now you two were ready for a *real* challenge."

Eliot and Fiona stood together and faced their mother.

Eliot had a feeling that something was coming that neither he nor Fiona could ever be prepared for—something that would stretch their abilities and their loyalties to the very breaking point.

And he would soon discover he was not wrong.

"The Paxington Institute is a school," Audrey explained. "A high school."

READER'S GUIDE

Eliot and Fiona Post live with their grandmother in a household dominated by rules, and have been told all their lives that their mother and father were dead. But their parents *are* alive. Their mother is an immortal and their father is Lucifer, the Prince of Darkness.

When the twins turn fifteen years old, both sides of their families claim them. No one knows which parent they will take after, however, so the immortals test their lineage with three heroic trials, and the fallen angels test them with three diabolical temptations. Depending on how Eliot and Fiona pass or fail these tests will determine if they get to live as diabolical or divine creatures . . . or if they get to live at all.

1. How are the twins, Eliot and Fiona Post, alike? How are they different?

2. Discuss how, at the beginning of the novel, the Post family seems like and unlike a normal family.

3. Most people struggle to find out who they are and where they fit in as they grow up, but for Eliot and Fiona this goes beyond a normal teenage "coming of age" experience. How do the adults in the story try to convince them (and each other) who and what the twins are? What conclusions do Eliot and Fiona reach for themselves about their identities?

4. The immortals are not technically the gods and goddesses of legends. They were mistaken for deities during their very long lives. What other

names has Henry Mimes (Uncle Henry) had? What other mistaken gods and goddesses can you link to the different immortals?

5. Some characters in *Mortal Coils* are, or become, addicted to various things. What's the difference between an intense desire for something and an addiction? Who eventually breaks free of their addictions? Who doesn't?

6. What are the differences between the Immortal and Infernal families? Do they have *any* similarities? Discuss the advantages and disadvantages of each.

7. Why did Audrey cut her maternal ties? What do you think would have happened to the twins growing up if she hadn't? Do you agree with her choice?

8. Why did Julie Marks choose *not* to betray Eliot? What would have happened if she had told him the truth?

9. What is the significance of the singing that Eliot hears when he plays the "Mortal's Coil" song and the "Symphony of Existence"?

10. Is what the Immortals and Infernals do to the Post twins fair? What's at stake for the families? Do different ethics apply to them?

11. Some footnotes in the novel indicate a rich future for the twins. What do you think happens to them next?

12. What would you do if your parents revealed they were Immortal/ Infernal? If you had to choose one family, which side would you pick?

For more information on Eric Nylund and *Mortal Coils* visit www .ericnylund.net, which includes a biography of the author and additional information about his novels.